AGAAT

Also by Marlene van Niekerk
Triomf

AGAAT

A NOVEL

MARLENE VAN NIEKERK

Translated by Michiel Heyns

Tin House Books

Library of Congress Cataloging-in-Publication Data

Van Niekerk, Marlene.

[Agaat. English]

Agaat / Marlene van Niekerk ; translated by Michiel Heyns. -- 1st U.S. ed.

  p. cm.

First published in English in South Africa by Jonathan Ball Publishers under the title The way of the women (2006). FICTION V217809 5.10

Translated from the Afrikaans.

ISBN 978-0-9825030-9-6

1. Women farmers--South Africa--Fiction. 2. Women domestics--South Africa--Fiction. 3. South Africa--Social life and customs--Fiction. I. Heyns, Michiel. II. Title.

PT6592.32.A545A6513 2010

839.3636--dc22

2009039476

For Lou-Marié

TRANSLATOR'S NOTE

Agaat is a highly allusive text, permeated, at times almost subliminally, with traces of Afrikaans cultural goods: songs, children's rhymes, children's games, hymns, idiomatic expressions, farming lore. I have as far as possible made my own translations of these, in an attempt to retain something of the sound, rhythm, register and cultural specificity of the original. Where, however, the author has quoted from mainstream Afrikaans poetry, I have tried to find equivalents from English poetry. I have also taken the liberty of extending the range of poetic allusion. Readers will thus find scraps of English poetry interspersed, generally without acknowledgement, in the text.

Certain Afrikaans words I have judged too culturally specific to be translated into English; indeed, almost all the Afrikaans words I have used in this translation occur either in the *Oxford English Dictionary* or the *Oxford Dictionary of South African English*, as having passed into South African English usage. For readers not having ready access to these sources, a glossary of Afrikaans words is appended.

I am grateful to Lynda Gilfillan for her meticulous editing of this translation, and to Riana Barnard for her efficient and cheerful administration.

—M.H.

'This new volume seeks to interpret the growth, passion and expansion of the soul of the nation. May the indefinable element—the force and flavour of this Southland—be found, felt and experienced, then the nation will press it to their hearts and adopt it as their own.'

> From the Introduction to the first edition of the *FAK-Volksangbundel* [National Anthology of Song of the Federation of Afrikaans Culture Organisations]. H. Gutsche, W.J. du P. Erlank, S.H. Eyssen (eds.). Firma J.H. De Bussy Pretoria, HAUM. V/H Jacques Dusseau & Co, Cape Town, 1937.

'That is the beauty, the value of this book: that it was born out of love and inspires to love, that nobody can doubt. And with that a great service is done to the nation, for who feels for beauty, on whatever terrain, has a contribution to make to the cultural development of the nation.

'The area this book makes its own, is a specifically feminine one and through that contributes to the refinement and beautification of the domestic atmosphere. Such an atmosphere distinguishes the culturally aware nation from the uncivilised.'

> From the Foreword by Mrs E. (Betsie) Verwoerd to *Borduur So* [Embroider Like This], Hetsie van Wyk, Afrikaanse Pers-boekhandel, Johannesburg, 1966.

'This Handbook . . . serves as a key to the unlocking of the treasure chambers of climate, soil, livestock and marketing potential on each of the 93,000 farms of our country.

'Just as the Bible points the way to spiritual perfection so will this Handbook also point to ways and means to more profitable farming and to greater prosperity for every farmer in every part of the country.

'I should dearly love to see this Handbook finding its way into every farm dwelling and coming into the hands of every person who farms or who is interested in agricultural matters, because it is a rich mine of useful information.'

From the Foreword by His Honour General J.G.C. Kemp, Minister of Agriculture, to the *Hulpboek vir Boere in Suid-Afrika* [Handbook for Farmers in South Africa]. Written by civil servants and other experts, Government Printing Works, Pretoria, 1929.

PROLOGUE

Matt-white winter. Stop-start traffic. Storm warning. And I. In two places at once, as always. Snow on my shoulder, but with the light of the Overberg haunting me, the wet black apparitions of winter, the mirages of summer. Tumbling lark above the rustling wheatfields. Twitter machine. A very heaven, the time of my childhood. How could I tell that to anybody in this city? Heaven is a curiosity here. Hereafter. Strange word in my head. My reaction to the telegram strange too. First numb, then anxious, tears later. An aperture in the skull. Now the memories are a stream, unquenchable.

For parting is no single act, it is like a trailing streamer.

That first descent here eleven years ago, stiff in all my joints. Didn't close an eye on the whole fourteen-hour flight. Fear, worry, feelings of guilt. What was I? Who was I? A ten-day beard, a vacation visa in a passport, a loose cannon without letters of accreditation. A farmer seeking asylum, as far as the Canadian bureaucracy was concerned. A deserting soldier with his training certificates, his pilot's licences, his oath of secrecy. What more could I give them? A confession?

Left home without greeting or explanation. That morning, still dark, the smell of wet soot, Gaat giving me the little key to the sideboard so that I could take out my papers. Her face grey and sad, her cap askew. Four o'clock in the morning, the only one who knew where I was headed and why. Will I ever be able to forgive myself? For saddling her with such a responsibility?

White drifts of snow banked on both sides of the road. Windscreen wipers at full speed. I can't wipe away the images. Banded watermelon under the Herrnhuter knife, Boer pumpkins nestled in hairy dark-green leaves, a brown-tipped fleece of merino wool breaking open, heavy with oil, on the sorting table. Blue lupins chest-high in flower, yellow cream of Jersey cows, the sound when you crack open a pomegranate, the white membranes gripping the clustered pips. Red and white, just like blood on freshly shorn sheep.

Lord, I sound like my mother. Melancholy over-sensitive Ma. Now dying. Will she recognise me? With the beard? Gaat will. Willy-nilly.

1

Have been having the same dream, over and over recently. Gaat calling me, us calling each other. Awake. Disturbance. An abyss where sleep should be. The calling with our hands cupped in front of our mouths, she in the yard down below in her white apron, visible to me where I'm hiding in the kloofs above the house. Later long whistlings that you could pick up on the dryland at the back if you were below the wind. Later still the blowing on Hubbly Bubbly bottles.

Slowly to the surface, awake to wind-borne whistlings. Sleepless in Toronto. Night music. Till I drift off again, dreaming that we signal to each other on the ram's horn, soft low notes. How careful we had to be when we were looking for the purple emperor in the woods. Grey-black, folded shut in the shadows till it opened its wings, blue on one side only, scintillating, vapoured with silver, blood shaking my heart.

Leaking heart.

On and on the blue flickering sliced by the sharp sweep of the wipers. Salt on the road, broth of snow-slush on the windscreen, on the rear window. Lapis lazuli, it flickers, the colour of the dream, a blue iridescing from moment to moment, between inhaling and exhaling, first on one wing, then on the other. Book of vespers. *Apatura iris*. The giant purple emperor butterfly.

Miracles. Catastrophes. Continent that tops up its water level with blood, and that fertilises with blood. Who wrote that?

Here the blood has long since been spilt. Cold. The massacres efficiently commemorated, functionally packaged, sanitised. Only I, more freshly cut by history, trying to find my own way in the cool archives. Cut grass lies frail. My smell attracts other vulnerabilities. Found the Sainte Marie files yesterday, Bleeding Heel, Broken Shoulder, Wounded Knee, for the new instrument studio in Toronto. A percussion theatre where the visitor will rattle seed pods, brush the tin cymbals with a handful of grass.

When I got home, there it was. On the doormat, in the snow. Post office envelope.

MÊME DYING STOP CONFIRM ARRIVAL STOP LOVE AGAAT.

Eleven, almost twelve years. Will I still recognise Ma? In the last photo Gaat sent, she was tiny amongst the panache plants in the front garden, eyes deep in their sockets. Almost completely grey. Had a book with her, index finger between the pages, *The World's Famous Piano Pieces*. Recognised it by the dusky pink cover. Always used to sit and sing to herself from the sheet. So as not to get rusty, she used to say.

Ma and her airs, Ma who dreamed: Little Jakkie de Wet, the lieder singer, famous from Hottentots-Holland to Vienna. *Lieder eines fahrenden Gesellen*. Indeed!

And Agaat, poker-faced, her pop-eyed glare with which she could flatten you without a single word, the glance which she could switch off for days to punish you. Wooden eye. How old was she when I left the place in '85? Thirty-seven?

Gaat, Ma's nurse. Lord, what a piece of theatre that must be. Mourning Becomes Kamilla. Or, better still, The Night of the Nurse.

Gaat with her starched cap, distant snowy peak which she sometimes inclined towards me so that I could look at it from close by, so that I—only I—might touch it, the fine handiwork, white on white, of which I never could have enough. The needle flashing in her hand in front of the fireplace, Gaat's left hand with which she fed logs into the Aga's maw, stoked it so that it roared, strong warm hand on which I explored the world—pure fennel! The little hand on the wrong-way-round arm hidden further than usual when she had to serve Ma's friends, or the dominee on his house call.

And I, having to sing to the guests, Ma accompanying. Good Lord. O bring me a buck in flight o'er the veld, *Heidenröslein*, depending on the audience.

What's it like, there where you grew up? Your country? The eternal question when I first arrived. Always had Larkin's reply ready: Having grown up in shade of Church and State . . . Took me years to fashion my own rhymes to bind the sweetness, the cruelty in a single memory. Later nobody asked any more. Only then could I fantasise about an alternative reply.

Pass under the boom, a red elbow. Parking disk in my hand, cold, smooth, obol with lead strip. Fare forward, traveller! Not escaping from the past. *International Departures*.

Was it on Ma's behalf, or secretly dedicated to her, the fantasy of a song, an alternative reply to my inquisitive interlocutors?

Look, Mother, I've forgotten nothing of it. I'll sing for you. Of the foothills fronting the homestead, one piled on the other, the varied yellows and greens of fynbos, pink and purple patches of vygie and heather. Or of the mountains I'll sing, but in a sparser register, a wider perspective, the powder-blue battlements furnishing a fastness to the eye of the traveller along the coastal route.

My fantasy. Always the exordium on the rivers, the vleis full of fragrant white flowers in spring. This music crept by me upon the waters. A cantata of the great brown river, the Breede River, its catchment deep in the Grootwinterhoek, the great lair of winter, fed by the run-off from fern-tips, from wind-cut grooves in stone, to a hand's-breadth rill, a leap-over-sluit amongst porcupine-rush, a misty waterfall where red disas sway in the wake of the water. Until all waterfalls flow together over a base of black rock, and the stream starts cutting into the dry land, finding a winding of its own making, at last becoming a water-way, wide enough for shipping, deep enough for bridges, for ferries, for landing-stages and commerce.

This stream, the first which a European would deign to give the name of river, according to Di Capelli. Afterwards Rio de Nazareth. Le Fleuve Large. Hottentot names, certainly, but what remains of those, and who still cares? The Sijnna River, possibly derived from the Nama, Quarrel River?

Who first told me that? Must have been Ma.

Quarrel country.

Cacophony.

Check-in counter. Window seat or aisle seat. Tweedledum and Twee-dledee. Boarding-pass. Charon behind computer screen.

Woods. Deep mysterious woods. Koloniesbos, Duiwelsbos, Groot-vadersbos, the woods of the colony, the devil, the grandfather. And mountains. Trappieshoogte, Tradouw, Twaalfuurkop, the height of steps, the way of the women, the peak of noon.

The rivers of my childhood! They were different, their names cannot tell how beautiful they were: Botrivier, Riviersonderend, Kleinkruis-rivier, Duivenhoks, Maandagsoutrivier, Slangrivier, Buffeljagsrivier, Karringmelksrivier, Korenlandrivier: rivers burgeoning, rivers without end, small rivers crossing; rivers redolent of dovecotes, of salt-on-Mondays, of snakes; rivers of the hunting of the buffalo, rivers like buttermilk, rivers running through fields of wheat. Winding, hopeful, stony rivers. What can have remained of them?

The rivers could not be blamed. Not of thy rivers, no.

My country 'tis of thy people you're dying. Where, from whom did I first hear that? Buffy Sainte-Marie with quaver-tremolo and mouth-bow, a musical weapon? That moment of enlightenment, the realisation! Twenty-five, not too old to start my studies afresh. Arts, music, history. Less ambitious than some of my contemporaries. The finely cultivated, the intellectuals, incredible how they elected to live after the foul-up in Angola. Attack and defence as always, one after the other self-exculpat-ing autobiographical writing, variants on the Hemingway option. How you get to an uncivilised place in a civilised way. And stay there. A grim tussle with mother nature. I was not in accord.

Took a sheet of paper and a pencil when people here questioned me. Drew a map, lifted out a little block from the map of Southern Africa, from the lower end, from the south-western Cape Province, enlarged it freehand onto a sheet of paper. On the dirt road between Skeiding and Suurbraak, parallel to the motorway of the Garden Route, parallel to the coastline from Waenhuiskrans to Witsand, between Swellendam and Heidelberg. There. Five little crosses. Five farms in a fertile basin, nestling against the foothills of the Langeberg, the range running all the way from Worcester to eternity where it turns into the Outeniqua. Grootmoedersdrift, the middle farm, between Frambooskop to the east and The Glen to the west. There. From the middlest, inbetweenest place. Ambivalently birthed, blow, blow—that story!—waterfalls in my ears. Perhaps that was what delivered me from completedness.

Translate Grootmoedersdrift. Try it. Granny's Ford? Granny's Passion? What does that say? Motor cars there weren't yet, when the farm, named after my dreaded great-great-granny Spies on Ma's side, was given its name. And after the shallow crossing near the homestead. Dangerous in the rainy season, the bridge flooded, slippery with silt, sometimes cut off from the main road for weeks. You have to go slow there. As we all know. As we all always warned one another.

Careful on the drift!

Now I have only myself to remind. Face scanned by the passport controller. Charon behind bullet-proof glass.

Only once in my life did I see the drift totally dry. Skull-like stones, the dusty wattle bushes. No water, only rock. Just stood and stared at it, flabbergasted by the silence of the frogs, the disappearance of the whirligigs.

Gyrinus natans. The question always bothered me: What happens to the whirligigs, the little writers on water, when there is no water?

Such matters would not interest them, Mother. I could see their attention straying from the details, the topography of my first world, the thin, unsteady lines leading there, to your yard, Grootmoedersdrift. A little further down next to the drift, on the road's side, the labourers' cottages.

Dawid, would he still be there? Next to the turn-off to the farm, in the first of the cottages on the bank of the furrow?

Black fireplace and tin guitar. Wire-car world. White bone-whistle in exchange for a Dinky Toy. Was I inside once, twice? Gaat and I? With medicine, a little bucket of cinnamon porridge? The smell of soot and human bodies, the half-light. Shame, Gaat, but they don't even have beds. Never mind, Boetie, let be, let's go now, if you help one of them, you get stuck with a whole history before you know it.

A hanging bridge from Dawid's front door into the black-wattle wilderness on the opposite bank. Rickety and full of holes. Forbidden ever to set foot on it.

Flight AC 52 to Cape Town now boarding. Voyager for the sake of the voyage. Nomad without a flock. Safer like that. A listener outside the tent, an ear, an eye, that's all, that's enough. But who can play the ethnographer at his mother's deathbed?

When the inquisitive insisted, I sometimes played the draughtsman, roughly sketched on a second sheet of paper the house in which I grew up.

The homestead of Grootmoedersdrift, half H-shaped, the left leg shorter than the right. The stoep in front and on the east, the backyard open to the south, with storerooms, a servant's room. Gaat's room. In front two jerkin-head gables with big windows, Ma's room on the right, Pa's room left. The weathered doves in low relief under the overhang. Thatch. In front of the house to the north, the strip of level river-grazing up to the river's edge. Planted pasture for cattle, a seam of indigenous trees next to the water, wild olive—blaze at the core—(*Olea africana*), true yellowwood (*Podocarpus latifolius*).

The song. The other answer for my questioners. Fantasy for a snowed-in farmer. For reed pipe, for Jew's harp, with sniffles, wordless. Lord, am I up to this? All these years. Please fasten your seatbelts.

Rapidly rising range of hills on the other side of the river. Deep kloofs overgrown with protected bush, the old avenue of wild figs next to the two-track road. Poplar grove—whispering poplars. Yard with sheds, stables, milking-stables and feeding-stables. Ma's garden that she used to live for. Used to live. To the left, the dam. At the back to the south, on the other side of the drift and the dirt road, the dryland, for wheat and sheep. Smallish round-backed hills, the upper stretches cultivated, in between steep patches of rough scrub. Hills with plots of grass and soft brushwood for the sheep to overnight, and bluegum plantings around their drinking troughs.

Swill-trough. God, the word. Pa's word if he didn't like somebody. Swill-trough, dung-hole, choke-weed. My pompous headstrong old man, drilled the shit out of me with running marathons on farm roads. Obstacle courses through dongas and drinking troughs. Spleen-stitch. Inguinal hernia. Up and down those mountains. It will make a man of you. What would he think of me now, a woollen cap with six summer shirts in a suitcase, butterfly in the heart? Open and shut, open and shut go the wings. Are there windscreen wipers for melancholy? No electronic equipment, please.

Translations for *wolfneusgewels*, *rûens*, *droëland*, *drif*: jerkin-head gables, ridges, dry farming-land, crossing. Prosaic. Devise something: wolfnosed gables, humpbacked hills, dryland, drift. Always the laughter at the office, good-natured, collegial, at my attempts: grove of whispering poplars. I romanticise, they say. Quite a fan of the homely hymn, that's true. Homesick for the melody and so on. But that's only the half of it. The rest is granular precision, unsingable intervals.

Charon with passenger list. Dr de Wet, are you comfortable? Do you need assistance with your coat?

Everybody wears a coat.

Do they see through me nowadays, the older students? Do they want to set me talking, get me going? Do they think I need bloodletting, like a feverish horse, moonstruck lovers, inconsolables? What would they know in any case of such old folk remedies, a bunch of contemporary musicologists, what as much as suspect? Of the compulsion to tell? Of the subcutaneous refrains?

The bottom of the bottle.

Now ready for take-off. Please check that your seatbelt is securely fastened, baggage safely stowed away, emergency procedures in the seat in front of you.

For the most part I keep to the climate when they question me.

Sometimes drop something by accident, an impression, of the Breede River, *De Breede Rivier* above Malgas.

Aeolian harp.

1

It'll be the end of me yet, getting communication going. That's how it's been from the beginning with her.

This morning I had to stare and stare at the black box where it's been lying for eleven months. Eventually I managed to catch her eye, and point my stare, there, where the shiny black varnish of the box showed, under the pile of reading matter. Under the growing pile of little blue notebooks, under the *Sarie*s, under the *Fair Lady*s, under the *Farmer's Weekly*s on the dressing table in front of the stoep door, there!

At first she thought I wanted her to read to me. She smirked. It wasn't reading-aloud time. It wasn't even breakfast time yet, before eight, right after she'd wound the grandfather clock in the front parlour, right after I'd heard the door of the sideboard go tchick and she came in here with her little book.

She'd already marked the bit she wants to read tonight, the corner of the page emphatically dog-eared.

The blue booklets on the pile all seem thicker than they are because of all the dog-ears. Sometimes she says I have to guess which bit it's going to be. Then she says she could never have guessed everything she was going to read there. But sometimes she opens the book on her lap and recites what's written there, long stretches. As if they were rhymes, or a lesson. Then she asks me if it was good like that, whether I can remember when it happened.

As if I can reply.

She always checks to see whether she's left anything out, marks it with her red pen.

How long ago would she have started learning it by heart? Or does she invent bits as she goes along?

As if I can remember everything exactly as I wrote it there. Thirty, thirty-six years ago!

She tore out my inscription in the front of the first booklet and fixed it on the reading stand right up against my nose. *As directed by the Almighty God*, it says there, next to the other text which she wants me not to lose sight of. The table of my sickness. The table of symptoms, medicines and therapies.

She never removes them from there, the two sheets.

As if the one should be a constant reminder to me of what I'm suffering from.

As if the other is proof that everything she reads to me from the little books was written by myself.

As if the two documents belong to the same order of truth.

I'm sick of staring at the two tattered pieces of paper every time she removes my book or magazine from the reading stand and packs it away. Sick of having to listen too, because she spells it out aloud for me, presses her finger on it, on the table, on the dedication.

Symptom: constipation.

Medicine: Pink Lady.

Therapy: Exercise, increased intake of fluids.

As if I can do Canadian Air Force exercises.

As if, in these barren regions, there is anything that can quench my thirst.

As if medicine can help. You take medicine to get better.

The writing on the torn-out page doesn't even look like my handwriting to me.

As directed by the Almighty God, Ruler of our joint Destinies and Keeper of the Book of Life . . .

I was young. And it was not the first entry. The real beginning of it all I never wrote down.

Never felt up to revisiting those depths.

Not after I'd found out what I'd brought upon myself.

Where, in any case, does something like that begin? Your destiny? Where does it begin?

The 'dedication' I thought up much later, when things were going well for a while, just after Jakkie's birth. Then I inscribed it in the front of the first booklet on the inside of the cover. Date and all, 14 September 1960.

Now she wants to come and force it down my gullet. My unconsidered writing, on an empty stomach in my sickbed, and to come and confront me with my constipation. What's the sense of that?

As if I can protest.

As if I can eat.

Breakfast.

Can one call it breakfast?

I have no choice but to swallow it.

I heard her talk in the kitchen. Dawid was there and Julies and Saar and Lietja. They were waiting for Agaat to come and issue the order of the day. At eight o'clock sharp they have to fall in. They were talking loudly. Agaat was in a hurry. She wanted to go and silence them. They fall silent when they hear her approach.

I pointed with my eyes, the box, the box.

Just wait a while now, she said, later. She didn't catch my drift.

Do as I say, I gestured.

Now who's carrying on agn so ths mrning, she said.

A new thing, the speaking without vowels. Mocking me. Nastier than Jak ever was about the diaries.

She moved the bridge closer over the bed, brought the reading stand and set it up.

Do you want to read your covenant once more? Just can't get enough of it, can one? Perhaps it will give you an appetite.

That was a good start. She thought I wanted to read myself.

No, I could signal, that's not what I want to read.

That's my technique nowadays. Progress through misunderstanding. I just had to get the misunderstandings going first. The first would lead on to another until I had reached my goal. It's a kind of retarded logic, a breaking down of each of my intentions into the smallest intermediate steps. Gone are the days of the shortest distance between A and B. Now we're doing the detours, Agaat and I. By rolling my eyes at a pile of reading matter I can see to it that she ends up at the black box. I always have to fix her attention on the surface first. It's a start. And then I have to get her delving. This morning she obliged me, she put the pile of blue booklets aside and started rummaging through the magazines.

What do you want to read, Ounooi? She paged rapidly though a *Sarie*.

Four ways of getting your husband on your side and keeping him there. No.

No, she said, I don't think so either.

I looked again at the pile on the dressing table.

She took a *Farmer's Weekly* and opened it.

New developments in the practice of crop and pasture rotation: The south-western districts after 1994? Nay what, you know all about that. What about: The future of small-grain cultivation in South Africa? That's just up your alley, Ounooi, the future.

Lietja laughed loudly in the kitchen. There was a jingling of milk cans.

They're getting out of hand there in the kitchen, I have to go and check, said Agaat.

She clamped the magazine to the reading stand, on top of the torn-out sheet, on top of my symptomatic-treatment list, set it up more upright so that I could see, put my glasses on for me.

The future. She placed her finger under the words.

No, I signalled with my eyes, no, no, don't come with your silly games now.

Again she turned to the pile and went through the magazines.

Now where are all the *Fair Lady*s then, they were here?

She started to unpack the whole pile, fixing my eyes in the mirror.

Ounooi, you're making me late now. I don't see the *Fair Lady*s, wait, there's one here. Fine Foods for Fine Occasions.

It was the last magazine down. I forced her eyes down, still further down. There was the shiny black box now, open to the eye. She couldn't follow my glance in the mirror, had to turn round to see better where I was looking.

Tsk, she said and shook her head, no.

Yes, I said with my eyes.

She took out the contraption. It was still assembled just as she'd packed it away. She straightened my fingers and fitted it over my hand. It wasn't necessary to unfasten the buckles. All the brown leather bands were tightened to the first hole and the chrome wing nut was screwed in as far as it could go. A long piece of wire stuck up above the head of the nut like an antenna. The thing looks like a glove for handling radioactive waste. Long since been too big for me. Long since too heavy. Like all Leroux's gadgets that he comes peddling here, it works for a while and then no longer.

I looked at my hand. I braced myself. I gestured, pen please. And paper. I can't write on air.

Agaat looked about her.

Now she knew what I wanted to do but she pretended she'd forgotten where to find writing materials. It's been a long time since I wrote myself. When I made the lists, when we cleared the house, a year, year-and-a-half ago. Eventually I dictated and she wrote. Or she wrote, and with my last strength I ticked off what had to be thrown away. The blue booklets. I said throw out. She read the instruction and ignored me.

Now she's acting stupid. As if she doesn't regularly get out the clip-board to press on when making her latest lists, take out her red pen from the top pocket of her apron. And there's the pencil, hanging from its string next to the calendar. She's always making notes. Writes them up everywhere. What do you want the people to eat at your funeral, Ounooi? Stewed tripe? So what do you want me to have inscribed on your headstone, Ounooi? *And then God saw that it was good*?

Yes or no I can signal. Or I can close my eyes.

She hauled out the clipboard from the lowest half-empty rack of the bookshelf.

Tsk.

The books fell over. She had to go on her knees to set them upright again. Shiny jackets and old canvas covers. Some of them were still my mother's. I threw out most of them in my great clearing-out. Agaat kept them. As she kept the diaries. She recited the titles as she put them back. With a straight voice, the whole list. *Late Harvest*, *The Mayor of Colesberg*, *Carnival of the Carnivores*, *Seven Days at the Silbersteins*. That was nothing. *Forty-three Years with the De Wets*, *Floodwaters in the Fall*, *On Veld and Ridge*, *Chronicle of Crow's Crag*, *Circles in a Forest*, *Straight Tracks in the Semi-desert*, *Turn-off*, *July's People*, *As I Lay Dying*, *The Downhill of the Day is Chill*, *She Who Writes Waits*, *The Long Journey of Poppie Nongena*, *Breeders Don't Faint*, tsk, try *The Midwife of Tradouw*, *This Life That Death*, *Miss Sophie Flees Forward*, *The Portrait of a Lady*, *The Story of an African Farm*, hmf, rather then *In the Heart of the Country*. That's what she read last, recently. Nay what, she said, she could farm up a piece of land better than the wretched old Johanna who lost her marbles for no reason at all, and she wouldn't let a bunch of forward kaffirs get her down. That was before she read *The Seed is Mine* which the woman from the library brought along last time. That shut her up. I know what was in her head. Fennel seed.

Like old acquaintances all the titles sounded as she put them back, like the names of family. She read them all to me in the last few months, or turned the pages on my stand so that I could read for myself. She'd read all the old ones herself long ago and first sampled all the new ones before reading them to me. She knew whole sections by heart. She said not one of them was as good a read as my diary, all you had to do was fill in the punctuation and write everything out in full, then you had a best-seller.

And then on top of that there are all Jakkie's books and magazines, sent on over the years, in which there are chapters and articles written by him. Agaat reads aloud from them regularly, very taken with her own importance, struggling over the long English words, but I've never really understood much of it. *Private Speech, Public Pain: The Power of Women's Laments in Ancient Greek Poetry and Tragedy, Mourning Songs of the Dirty Goddesses: Traces of the Lamia in Orthodox Baptismal Rites of the Levant, Echoes of the Troll Calls in Romantic Scandinavian Choir Music.* Terribly obscure, all of it. Another one about the polyphonic wailings of Australian aboriginal women when somebody dies off. The stuff he finds to waste his time with, the child, after all, he has a perfectly good engineering qualification in aeronautics. Chucked into the ocean. For ethnomusicology, whatever that may be.

There was something written on the front page of the clipboard. Agaat looked to see what it was. She looked at me. She wanted to say something, I could see. She thought better of it. Ten pages she had to turn over. On every page her eyes took in the contents. Funeral arrangements to date. She wants to create work for herself. And for me.

She opened the clip and pulled out a clean sheet from underneath and slid it in on top. She let the clip snap shut loudly, tsk-ed again with her tongue.

Then she made a great show of burrowing in the dresser drawer for a pen, every gesture exaggeratedly emphatic. In the mirror I could see her pushing up her sleeve and testing the pen on the back of the little feeble hand. Provoking me on purpose, where was the red pen all of a sudden with which every day she underlined in my diaries, and annotated and rewrote on the counter-page? As if she were a teacher correcting my composition. As if I had to pass a test.

It writes, she said with a long jaw.

She placed the pen between my thumb and index finger and pressed them together as far as she could reach amongst the buckles and the leather and the screws. She pushed the clipboard in under my hand. It was a laborious arrangement. She had to push and pull and balance the splint and the pen and the board and my hand. She made a ridge in the bedspread to support the whole lot. As you do with a rag doll when you want to make her sit up in a chair. Pummel her in the ribs. Punch her in the chest. Head up. Tail down. Sit, doll, sit. Filled with sawdust. Or lupin seeds. Or clean white river sand.

Then she put her hand over mine, the strong hand. The effect was comical.

Ai, Ounooi, you're making life so difficult for yourself. How on earth do you think?

I could see what she was thinking. Haven't you perpetrated enough writing in your life? That's what she thought.

Be quiet, I said with my eyes, you just be quiet and leave me in peace. Take away your hand.

She jutted out her chin and replaced the Foamalite packing and the plastic in the box and closed the lid.

Tripple-trot out of here. In passing she snatched up her embroidery from the chair. I know what that means. That's the other punishment. Today I'll be seeing her only at meal times and medicine times. Otherwise she sits here with me for hours embroidering, a big cloth, I don't know what it is, looks complicated. She counts and measures as if her life depended on it, the whole cloth marked out in pins and knots. It's been carrying on ever since I haven't been able to get around by myself. Otherwise I would have investigated long ago. She's mysterious about it. Taunting at times. Sometimes she looks at it as if she herself can't believe what she's embroidering there. Or like now when she flounced out of here, she grabs it as if it's a piece of dirty washing that she wants to go and throw into the laundry basket, glares at me, as if I was the one who dirtied it.

All that was quarter of an hour ago. The grandfather clock in the front room struck. Quarter past eight.

Now I must begin. Now I must write. Now I must make it worthwhile. What I unleashed.

I gather my resources. I try to find handholds inside myself. Rye grass, klaaslouw bush, wattle branches to anchor myself against the precipice. Diehard species. I feel around inside me. There's still vegetation, there's water, there's soil.

To start I need a preamble. The preamble is just as important as the action itself.

Everything on this farm must be properly prepared, everything foreseen and anticipated so that no chance occurrence can distract you from your ultimate objective. That was the first commandment, has always been. I instructed Agaat accordingly.

You don't just blunder into a thing, you examine it from all sides and then you make an informed decision and plan it properly in distinct phases, always in tune with the seasons. And then you round off the phases one by one, all the while keeping an eye on the whole, the rhythms, the movements, just like rehearsing a piece of music.

That's how you retain control, that's how you prevent irksome delays at a later stage.

That's the one principle of a self-respecting farmer, especially for mixed farming. That's how you get results. That's how you build up property. With built-in rewards in the long and the short term so that you can have the courage to carry on. A foothold.

But my preamble here is not mine. It's been marked out for me on the surfaces of the room as Agaat has arranged it. Nothing has been left to chance. Death is her objective. She has prepared it excellently. I couldn't have done it better myself.

First she emptied the room.

Everything redundant she carried out. To the cellar. I heard her bump and shift, here right under my bed, to make space for the stuff. The sofa and footstools, the doilies and cloths on the dressing table, the ornaments and wall hangings. The clothes horse, the hatstand, the walking stick stand, the walking frame, the wheelchair, the snows of yesteryear, the posies of dried everlastings.

So that she could move fast and clean easily, she said.

Because there shall be no dust or obstacle. It will be the best-managed death in history, you'll see, her eyes said. Her mouth was a thin line.

The carpet was taken out, the wardrobes with my coats and dresses, the chests of drawers with my jerseys and blouses.

I was the one who started it. I planted the idea of the great clearing-out in her head.

Only the bookshelf from Jakkie's room she carried in here to hold the extra reading matter. She selected all the books in it. And the television she brought in from the living room and took away again later because the contents would upset me, I ask you.

Perhaps she was the one who was upset.

There are already too many things happening in this room, she said, without our having to make space for *People of the South* and *The Bold and the Beautiful*.

Now she wheels it in only when she thinks I want to watch a video. But I no longer want to see Agaat's selections. *Ben Hur, Mary Poppins, My Fair Lady, A Day in the Death of Joe Egg*.

The radio was permitted to stay. For the idle hours, she said. Morning service. Praise the Lord. Listener's Choice. *Moto perpetuo*. In these sacred halls. Almost time for Christmas carols. They've been starting earlier every year. Then Agaat will walk through the house again singing high and low with her descants and her second voices.

You like your music, don't you, Ounooi.

She switches the radio on and off. She selects the station. She selects the tune. Sometimes she pushes a tape into the slot. Not always what I want to hear. Red Indian croakings from Jakkie if she wants to irritate me.

That she left the three-panel dressing table, that's a miracle. It hunkers there like a museum piece, its dark wood conspicuous against all the other stark objects in white and chrome. I can see myself in the central panel, the one that was put in later and reflects bluer than the others. She turned the dressing table exactly in that position for me.

So that you can keep yourself company when I'm not here, she said.

The drawers are empty now. But that wasn't my doing. I didn't have the heart to clear them. The trace of Chanel No. 5 and lipsticks which hovered in them, must have evaporated a long time ago. Sometimes I miss perfume. Would she have given it all to the servants?

It's the last time, Agaat said, on the morning of my birthday, go ahead and enjoy it. A woman has to look her best on her birthday, not so?

She marked the date on the calendar. 11 March 1996. Seventy years old.

Then she made me up for the guests. I could see them blanch when they came in here.

She never liked making me up. She had to do that from quite early on, when only my hands were paralysed, when we still went into town together.

But I know by now, birthdays always bring out the nastiness in her.

Then I looked like a blue-headed lizard, white spot between the eyes, the one I'm always given right there when she makes me up, to warn me against spying, to remind me of what I shouldn't have seen that time with my head against the whitewashed window sill of the outside room. Mascara. Blazing Bat on my drooling mouth. My neckbrace doused with six kinds of perfume and the powder-puff creating clouds around my head. And drowned the sense in odours. Just about choked in powder that day. So then she had an excuse. So then she tipped out the drawers of the dressing table into black plastic bags.

Claims she was acting on advice from Leroux, but she's always been one step ahead of him.

There must be nothing to irritate the nose, he's supposed to have said to her.

We've thought of that already, she said. No dogs, no plants, no dusty shoes or dirty things ever enter this room. And from now on no face powder, no perfume, no under-arm sprays that can make her sneeze or snort.

She had to stop herself. It was one of those days.

So now she'll just have to shine and stink, was on the tip of her tongue. But Mum and calamine it was to be.

Keep a good record of everything, Leroux said, and Agaat pointed out the farm calendar where she'd long been making notes in the empty columns. With her hands clasped in front of her she listened while he read out her list. Urine, bowel movements, eat, sleep, headaches, phlegm, temperature, breathing, state of mind, force of deglutition, medicine, exercise.

She'll want to judge me in as many categories as she can think up, that's certain. Sphincter pressure, melting-point, share suction, sowing density, rust resistance, siphon level, tailwind, drainage slope, crimp index, inverse proportion, *Sphaeropsis malorum*, core rot. O rose thou art sick.

I can see that you're a very good nurse, Agaat, said Leroux after studying the calendar. Excellent records. Keep up the good work.

And she did. Unstoppable she was. She unscrewed the inside door of my bedroom because my new bed wouldn't pass through.

Don't be stupid, I wanted to say, bring it along the stoep and through the swing-door. But by that time I couldn't really speak all that well any more.

Perhaps it's better like this. Now I can hear everything that goes on in the house. I can hear Agaat approaching. I can hear what her foot-steps sound like. I can adjust myself.

My bedroom door was the last door she unscrewed. The other doors in the house disappeared one by one.

So that Ounooi shouldn't have to turn doorknobs, so that Ounooi can get in and out easily with her walking sticks and her walking frame and her wheelchair, she said.

But that was just one half of the reason. The other half is her own problem, Agaat doesn't like closed doors. And she doesn't like cluttered surfaces.

She carried in a melamine surface on trestles and on that everything we need is arranged in rows and piles against the wall. Packs of swabs, neckbraces for every occasion, quick-drying sheets, mattress protectors, clean hospital gowns, bedpans. Under the trestle table are three enamel pails with lids.

There's a triple-level stainless hospital trolley with washbasin and clean cloths and towels and disinfectants and medicinal soap.

And a smaller trolley of hard plastic with removable baskets con-taining my medicines and pills in bottles and boxes. Fresh water in a carafe. Sponges, cotton wool, ear-buds, ointment for my lips that dry out, paper towels for accidents, tissues for drool, for tears. Things get disordered quickly in the trolley. Agaat tidies it every day, sees to it that all the bottles and tubes are tightly shut.

And then there's the bridge, a broad flat shoulder on one steel leg that fits over my bed, and on which my little bowls of food and my spout-jugs full of thickened tea can stand. And my reading stand.

Above my bed is a reading lamp, 100 watts with an adjustable head on a long arm, which can extend.

Enough light in the shearing shed, says Agaat, you don't dip a sheep in the dark.

But normally she doesn't switch it on at night. Only when absolutely necessary.

Next to my bed is a wooden stool on which she sits when she's feeding me. In front of the window is her upright chair on which she sits when she reads to me or when she embroiders. She brought it in from her outside room in the backyard. She never sits there anymore anyway she says, she only washes and changes there. It's now just her locker room, she says.

She sleeps in the passage. She needn't, she knows that. There are many rooms in the house.

All the rooms of my house, the progress to where I am now, the history leading to this last room, the domain remaining to me. Shrinking domain. I'm locked up in my own body, my limbs form a vague contour under the bedspread.

Now my preamble stretches over my feet. They're flat, they lie open. The bedspread subsides over my shins. My kneecaps form two bumps, the flesh has fallen from my thighs, between my hips there is a hollow. Further than that I cannot see myself. My neck is locked at the angle determined for me by Agaat. Her pillows are stacked like bunkers around me. In the mirror I can see something, a shadow of myself, my sloping shoulders, my face on which my features appear vague, as if an artist had rubbed his sleeve over a preparatory study, or flattened the modelling clay with his palm. Because the beginning failed, because the first attempt came out wrong. Because the underlying structures were not clear.

I resist. Give me a chance. Let me try myself, a self-portrait, an autobiography, life and times of Milla de Wet, her place of origin, her purlieu, on Grootmoedersdrift, her hereditary home. An honest likeness. From the mirror, over my feet, along the length of my paralysed body, all the way into my head. Between my temples, above my nose, behind the frontal bone, there.

In the marrowy pulp I feel for the beginning, for an inspissation, the graininess of a germ cell. I continue only until I can imagine fine threads in the uniform texture. I roll them between my fingers until they find a grip in my imagination. And then, carefully, so as not to disturb their vague beginnings, I start drawing them together in strings, until they're thick enough to plait, first three, then nine, then twenty-seven and so on. Three hundred and sixty-three. Until I'm ready to feed the whole coil securely into the hollow of the brainstem, into the hole of the first vertebra. I wait, I hold everything together well, before I pull it through and spread it open on the other side like a sheaf. Finer and finer I imagine the filiations, a mesh just below the surface, until I'm sure that all points are served by my will.

I want to write.

To the string running down my right arm I devote particular attention. I imagine that it's dark brown. I gather it into a thick smooth bundle, shiny as kelp in the swell, an elegant tassel at the far end, long sensitive strings of seaweed with fine ramifications in each of the first three fingers of my right hand.

I wait for the right moment. Nothing to lose. Breathe in, send the signal, breathe out for the leap.

Write!

With precise electrical flashes I mark each bight of the current, from high up in the brain pulp through all the plaitings of nerves I've laid down in their circuits. With extra momentum I force the command down into my hand to the furthest extremities.

Write!

I manage to draw one leg of the m before the pen slips from my fingers and rolls over the bedspread and falls from the bed.

My hand lies in the splint like a mole in a trap.

*

The first time you slept with Jak was the day after he came to declare his intentions to your parents. He was eager to get away that morning after the engagement, eager to get away from under your mother's eyes after the sermon he'd endured from her the night before, and especially eager to get his hands on you.

You knew it, Milla Redelinghuys, you played him.

How did you experience him then? Can you really remember it?

Don't forget the keys, Ma called. She jingled the great bunch of keys to the Grootmoedersdrift homestead behind you as you walked down the steps of the stoep to Jak's red Spider.

Catch! She called and threw the bunch at him.

You were watching him closely all the time, that much is certain. He snatched the bunch out of the air with a flourish. Ostentatiously, from a height, he dropped it in your lap, showing off to your parents, seeing you off on the steps. Frail they seemed against the house and the sky. But you didn't want to notice that, you looked down at the keys nestling between your thighs in the dip of your dress. You jingled with your fingers amongst them, you fondled the old worn key-heads. The front door, the kitchen, the loft, the outside rooms. You imagined how you were going to unlock all the doors.

Thanks for everything! Jak called and waved.

Old Sweet 'n Sour, he said under his breath.

Jak, please, she's my mother, show some respect, you said. But you laughed with him, because she'd been at her worst the night before. It started at dinner when Jak put the expensive engagement ring on your finger. Diamonds are forever, he said. Too expensive, you could see Ma thinking, too showy. It was a burl of a diamond set in gold. You could read her mind. That kind of money would have been better put to some practical use, something for the farm that had now become yours because you were getting married. But she said nothing. Because you who hitherto could never find favour in her eyes, would at last be complete. Somebody's wife. In the normal course of events, somebody's mother.

And then, money wasn't everything, work rather, toil and sweat and grit. There was a great deal to be done on Grootmoedersdrift before it could be called a model farm. That you never hid from Jak. And you didn't fool yourself either, from the start you expected him to get cold feet. He was no farm boy. His hands were soft, he was the only son of the GP in Caledon, schooled at Bishops to be a gentleman. He would have to learn everything from scratch. From you and your family he would have to get it, because both his parents had died young.

Ma was sceptical when you first told her about him. About how he accompanied you to music concerts and plays in Cape Town. Pure flimflammery, your mother said, show me the man who prefers music and drama to rugby. You wanted to ask, what about Pa, but Pa put his finger to his lips and you bit back your words. And it was true, Jak got bored after the second act. Your mother was adamant. After Jak had got his degree in law at Stellenbosch, she said, you had to see to it that he did a diploma at Elsenburg Agricultural College to prepare him for farming. Either that, or he doesn't set his foot on my land, she said.

You knew you had to manoeuvre things very carefully between your mother and Jak. And you had to make sure that neither felt they were drawing the short straw.

Did you think then of what you yourself could lose in the process? Can you remember it clearly now, after all that has happened? Then was different. Then you were a winner. Was there love? Enough for a start, you thought. Jak blossomed under your encouragement. You were in love with his pretty mouth, with his boyish way of doing things.

And he would grow with you. That was what you believed. You didn't doubt his desire, from the start of your courtship you'd really had to lock up your rubies.

I want to see your papers, young man, Ma said on the evening of the engagement, and I'll ask you a few questions myself so I can hear whether they taught you anything at that college. She glared at you both in turn.

I hope you're as sensible as you're attractive.

Jak was riled, even though you'd warned him beforehand, only one person had a voice in the house where you grew up, and that was your mother.

Your father got up and went and stared out of the window. You kicked off your shoes and under the table you rubbed your feet against Jak's ankles. After a while he took your hand under the table. You pressed your leg hard against his during the whole sermon on the correct way of working with sheep and wheat and cattle. You stared in front of you at the table, at the dark grain of the wood. You'd never been able to look her in the eye when she spoke like that. It was as if she were talking about more than just the demands of mixed farming.

You protested, laughingly, trying to lighten the atmosphere.

Ma, you'll scare Jak off, talking like that.

He's man enough, she said. I thought you said he was such a good talker himself? But I'm glad to see he can listen as well. The expression on her face said: He'd better, otherwise what do you want him for?

What did I want Jak for? Wasn't it clear to her? He was rich, he was well educated, he was attractive, witty and well-spoken, and well-liked by people. He was everything that you felt you were not.

But even though you felt insecure at times, and even though you weren't exactly the most beautiful of women, you knew you weren't stupid. You had a BA with languages behind your name, with your extra music and drama subjects completed almost to licentiate level. In addition you had plenty of practical experience of farming. The two of you would be an asset to the Overberg, not only as farmers but also for the cultural life in the region. And you knew that he also thought he was getting a good bargain in you. He said you suited him, short but sharp and could carry a tune on top of it.

Your father observed it all ruefully. The most important thing is for you to be happy and healthy, my child, he said, the rest is incidental, and don't neglect your music. Once you've moved in and settled over the mountain, you must come over every Friday evening, then we can listen to music. Remember, my whole collection will be yours one day.

Jak listened to your father with wary respect, they didn't really take to each other, you could see that. However fond you were of your father, you were irritated with him that weekend with his sentimentality and his reserve, there was a new kind of energy running now, and new priorities.

You're not scared of becoming my farmer boy, are you, Jak, I said as you drove away through the main street of Barrydale in the direction of the pass.

You were on your way to show him the farm over the mountain for the first time. You knew you'd have to open on a high bid.

Your 'farmer boy'! Jak snorted, but he looked down at the keys between your legs, and you knew he was snared, tail and trotters and all.

My Farmer then, with a big F, you said. You placed your hand high up on his thigh and leant over and kissed him in his ear.

You're a slypuss, he said. Move closer. I have my own schemes for you.

And you intend to tame me, if I understand rightly, you teased. You stroked his thigh.

So, Milla Redelinghuys, your story was launched. The situation provided you with an interesting kind of titillation. So here you have two fish hooked, you thought. A farm and a husband. But you didn't feel entirely at ease. Without the bait, would you have caught the fish?

So tell me again everything we're going to farm with, you and I? Jak asked.

You counted your words, you fed him a few trivial facts that wouldn't alarm him. You paddled your hand lightly, to the beat of the information you were feeding him.

Ma kept a couple of hundred merinos and a few Jersey cows on Grootmoedersdrift. There was a foreman on the farm, OuKarel Okkenel, of the Suurbraak Okkenels, and his half-grown son Dawid, who also lived on the farm. OuKarel was a widower, a respectable man, distant descendant of the Scottish mechanics who came out in 1817 under Benjamin Moodie. OuKarel sowed a few morgen of wheat for Ma every year for a share. She was worried that the farm was being neglected. After Pa inherited his land and they went to farm on Goedbegin, they used to go and check every week that everything was running smoothly on Grootmoedersdrift. Ever since you were small, she and Pa drove over the mountain at shearing time and lambing time and harvest time, and stayed on in the old homestead for weeks on end to keep an eye and to take things in hand. Often it was only you and Pa, those were your best times, he taught you opera arias and took you on expeditions in the veld. Your father with his long stride and his perfect hearing, you couldn't believe that he had turned into the lopsided old gent with the shuffling gait.

They're getting old, you said to Jak, they can no longer keep crossing the mountain and manage two farms. We're getting married at the right time. We have to take over the wheat farming from the Okkenels, the local market is famished for fine white flour now after the war, we have to extend the sheep and cattle herds, there's excellent grazing next to the river for a dairy herd, we must make of Grootmoedersdrift what it can be, a textbook example of mixed farming, we have to live up to the name.

You moved your hand and massaged the inside of his thigh.

You're driving me mad, Jak said. He squirmed in his seat and accelerated even more.

Don't get carried away, darling, stay on the road, you said.

He tried to keep himself in check. He shook his head, brought up last night's conversation.

Lynx-hide thongs! What kind of story was that last night, he asked, I hope you don't take after that mother of yours too much, you'll finish a man off.

You laughed, you pinched the soft flesh of his inner thigh.

Well, I don't know who you take after, you teased back. You took a deep breath and said it, you were shy, but you said it.

You're very close to finished before I've even started, was what you said. With your eyes you gestured towards his fly.

You knew what the effect would be. He was the kind who liked off-colour comments. At times he said things to you that made you blush, but you never went too far when you were petting. You were a virgin and that was your price.

Good heavens, Milla, Jak exclaimed, tell me more!

There's a sentinel before my mouth, you teased.

Just you wait, Jak said, you'll end up with the sentinel in your sweet-talking mouth.

You weren't altogether sure what he meant but you laughed along with him.

Jak was right about your mother. She had finished off your father. He'd become ever more silent with the years. Must have been ill already the evening of the engagement. You could tell from his reticence while your mother took out the maps and spread the papers of Grootmoedersdrift on the dining room table. It had been her ancestral land for generations back in her mother's line, from the Steyn and the Spies lines. They were the ones, according to her, who planted the wild fig avenue there and traced the foundations of the homestead with lynx-hide ropes.

You don't throw away your birthright, your mother said to Jak, that which your ancestors built up in the sweat of their brow, that you look after and that you live up to.

Yes, you said and winked at your father. You knew he knew, like you, what her next sentence would be.

Those were people who had to hack bushes and stack stones. There was no time for sweet talk and twaddle, you said, all three of you.

It was your mother's favourite expression.

You could see Jak glancing around, puzzled, not knowing what was happening.

It's in Kamilla's blood, you must realise, Jak, she steamed ahead. Her great-great-grandmother farmed there all alone for thirty years after her husband's death, way before the days of Hendrik Swellengrebel. There was a woman who could get a grip and hit home, blow for blow. She fixed Jak with a glare like a bayonet. If you can't do that, young man, then you'd better stand aside because then you won't do, then you're just a nuisance to others.

You were ashamed. You twined your fingers through Jak's and leant over him, so that your breasts rested on his shoulder while you were pretending to study the map. You knew the map by heart. Ever since you were a little girl your mother had slid it out of its long sheath to show you the farm that would be yours one day.

Jak heard her out meekly, his face expressionless. Now, as you entered the pass, he was openly mocking.

Once upon a time, long ago, when the world was young, in the time of the Lord Swellengrebel, he commenced, there was a great-great-grandmother Spies, a boer woman without equal . . .

He changed down to a lower gear on the uphill.

. . . And she called her farm Grootmoedersdrift after herself and laid out its boundaries with, can you guess with what? With lynx-hide thongs!

How does that sound for a beginning? He looked at you.

I particularly liked the bit about the woman who could get a grip and hit home, blow for blow. Tell me more about that.

You started rubbing his groin. The first time you'd ever done a thing like that. Jak lost his head completely, caught off guard, he took the pass as if were a race track. The car kicked up stones. It was still the old pass, in 1946, with narrow hairpins, nowhere a kerb. Every now and again Jak would glance at you and you glanced back. If you had so many things in your head, you wondered to yourself, what must he not make of it all?

Slow down, Jak, you said, it's a pass.

What will you give me?

Anything you ask.

Don't you know?

I can guess, you said. You tugged open the buckle of his belt.

He looked at you in surprise, groaned.

So, and what are you going to give me in exchange? You wanted to know.

Anything you ask.

And don't you know?

I'm not as clever as you.

Well, in the first place you must slow down.

But you're making me want to get somewhere very fast!

You removed your hand. He took it back and you resisted, but not too much, so that he could put it where he wanted it.

Right, I'll slow down, he said, and in any case, it looks as if you've got a watermelon lorry on your side.

Some way ahead on the pass, with a long line of cars following, a lorry filled with spanspek and watermelon was trundling along.

No, it's you who has the watermelon on your side, you said, and pulled open his fly and put your hand inside.

My God, woman, Jak said, and threw back his head and closed his eyes for a moment.

Keep your eyes on the road, De Wet, you said.

That's what you said, but you thought: I'm the one who directs everything, the roughly ranked rock faces, the dark waterway far below, the curves in the road, the clouds far above.

So what problems are these that your mother talks of, there on Grootmoedersdrift? Jak asked with a charged voice, and swallowed.

He shook his head as if he were seeing stars. You had a firm grip on him, long-term promises in your grasp.

Tulips, you said, and sat forward so that you could work your hand in under his testicles. After that you could never get enough of it. The contrast between the silky shifting balls and the immense length of the erect flesh above. You were fascinated by it, surprised that you knew what to do.

There are wild tulips next to the river, and if the cows eat them and they drink water afterwards, then they die as if you'd fed them arsenic.

They're little bulbs. You have to take them out by hand. If you plough them they just multiply.

Well then, said Jak, sounds easy enough. What else?

It's too wet down there next to the river.

Hmmm, rather wet than dry, he teased.

The cows get sores and fungi and things on their hooves from it. The horses get mud-fever.

Mud-fever? Never heard of it. So what can one do, my handy farm wench?

Drain, drain extensively. In any case, you can't plant grazing on waterlogged soil.

Still doesn't sound like a disaster to me.

Well, and then there are the slopes on the dryland. It's too steep to plough there. It washes away. We need contours there and terraces. And run-offs must be stabilised and grass courses laid on for the drainage.

You turned towards him and fumbled open his clothing and pulled down his underpants and added your other hand and made a quiver with your fingers.

Stabilised. Jak forced the word out.

It's a surveyor's job, you said, and it will take months.

You reckon, Jak said. God, I can't hold out any longer!

He sat forward and accelerated, and with one hand folded your hands tighter around his penis. Between your legs it felt warm, your head was ringing.

You were only half aware of the road, the few cars ahead of you, the lorry.

Hold on, said Jak and started overtaking.

Jak, careful! You shouted, but you were feeling reckless, floating, a regent of the whole Tradouw, the near side and the far side of the mountain, in the valleys next to the rivers and over the roundbacked hills from the Heidelberg plain as far as Witsand. It swam in front of your eyes. Everything your domain. You felt your mouth, your throat, there was a tang on your tongue as if you'd eaten radishes.

In a shower of stones Jak pulled off the road in a lay-by on the mountain's side and pressed you to him and kissed you and stroked your breasts. You thought of stopping him, the car's roof was open and you were visible from the road. But you didn't really care. You had a fantasy that your mother would see you. See with her own eyes how ownership and history and heritage all were finding their course, as it was predestined, with the brute energy of a good start. That was your movie. As you'd always wanted it, as you thought your mother had wanted it.

What other problems? Jak panted in your ear. He was wild, out of control, he tried to mount you and get inside you but the gear lever was in the way and the space too confined.

Lynxes in the kloofs, you said. You bit him in the neck.

More?

Bearded vultures. They peck out the eyes of the newborn lambs.

You took your breasts out of your bra and pressed his head against them. You immersed him in them. He had to surface for breath. Something about his neck and head seen from above looked like that of a little boy. His mouth, the irresistible mouth of Jak, now desperate and trembling, endeared him to you. His voice was hoarse.

I will do everything, he said. Plough and sow and shear and milk, I promise.

And help me make a garden?

And help you make a garden.

Like paradise?

Like paradise.

And never leave me?

And never leave you.

You pushed him away gently. You stroked his head to calm him. You wanted to drive and get to the other side. On the other side of the mountain you would lie down for him, on your property, as it had to be in your story-book.

You helped him to arrange his clothing. Breathe deeply, you told him.

I don't have to tell him everything now, you thought, he'll get the whole picture in time.

You were the only child and heir of your mother, and your farm was the most difficult one. Your land-hungry cousins would inherit your father's farms. They claimed they wanted no part of the farm beyond the Tradouw in The Spout, as the area was known among the farmers. They were small deciduous-fruit farmers in the Barrydale district. They were intent on helping to put bigger and bigger sections of Pa's farms under irrigation for peaches and vine.

No thank you, they said when your mother wasn't around, Grootmoedersdrift is a nightmare. You'll end up on the bones of your backside there with all the capital outlay you'll have to make, the money you'll have to borrow, the time it'll take you to get the farm arable, and all the hay you'll have to make to pay your debts on top of it all.

You were pleased that your father's family wasn't present the evening of the engagement. All three cousins coveted your farm above all else on earth. They could make life difficult for Jak. You'd told him that, too.

Now you want to feed me to those cousins of yours as well, Jak said when at last you got up from the table, your mother's bad enough. The house was quiet. Your mother's house was always filled with that dense, ominous silence. Jak stood in front of the mirror in the guest room and ran his hand over his face as if he wanted to make sure that everything was still in place after his confrontation with his new mother-in-law.

You stood behind him, flung your arms around his shoulders, you were just glad the evening was over.

I know everything about farming, you whispered in his ear, I grew up with it, I'll help you. I'll show you everything tomorrow. Now rest, you're tired.

You nestled up against him, but his body was tense. There was something in his voice, in what he said then, that you didn't want to hear, you thought you were imagining things.

Yes, he said, you'd better, I can't wait, tomorrow's the day, you'd better teach me and you'd better help me so that I can get the taste of it. And you'd better show me everything. I want to see where I'll be farming. I can't wait. Seeing that I've allowed myself to be set up in a golden frame here.

That was the day that you crossed the Tradouw pass for the first time with Jak de Wet, the great Tradouw, the deep Tradouw, the way of the women in the Hottentot language, as your father had explained to you when you were little.

You were a real woman now, a ring on your finger. Now the two of you just had to get to the other side. You were excited about it. So many times you had fantasised about how it would be to make love to him, to lie with him, to kiss him for endless hours, feel his back under your hands.

Oh lord, no, not again, Jak swore.

You were behind the watermelon lorry again.

That's what you get for canoodling in a lay-by, my dearest Jakobus, you said.

Now the blue fumes of the exhaust were in your face. It was a ramshackle affair, full of dents and scratches, painted over by hand, and patched.

Just signal that you want to pass, you said, then maybe he'll pull off at the next lay-by.

Jak hooted and gestured and flicked his lights, swore.

It happened very fast. The lorry swerved to the left. The load shifted.

Watermelons over the railing, bouncing all over the road, red flesh all over the windscreen of the Spider.

You were too close. You were going too fast. You grabbed the steering-wheel.

Don't brake, don't brake! you yelled, you'll skid, keep close to the mountain!

Old lessons from previous experiences, your mother's words.

The car jerked to a halt, cut out. Jak was stunned. You sat there for a while, watched the lorry driver trying to clear the road. Then Jak started the car again and you drove off slowly, stupefied with shock.

Fortunately, you said, you did the right thing.

You did, Jak said. He looked at you quickly and looked away.

Then he started.

I would have stepped on the brake and tried to pass on the right if you hadn't stopped me.

In his voice was the slightest undertone of a sulk.

You were wonderful, you consoled him, you drive well, I feel safe with you.

You shifted up your skirt and took his hand and pressed it between your legs so that he could feel how wet you were. All the way to Groot-moedersdrift he drove with one hand and touched you with the other. In your lap the homestead keys jingled as he moved his hand.

You closed your eyes, but you couldn't banish the image of the spilling spattering scattering melons from your eyes. The whole car smelt of it.

*

how does a sickness begin? botulism from eating skeletons but where do the skeletons come from? loco-disease nenta preacher-tick-affliction smut-ball bunt black-rust glume-blotch grubs beetles snails moths army caterpillars all invisible onsets soil is more long-suffering than wheat more long-suffering than sheep soil sickens slowly in hidden depths from tilling from flattening with the back of the spade from heavy grubbing in summer wind i am neither sheep nor wheat did i think then i was god that i had to lie and take it did i think then i was a mountain or a hill or a ridge and who told me that and who decided stones had no rights for stones can waste away from being denied from being abused and who decided who is the ploughed and who ploughs and why did i not get up and why not go away and what would have happened if i had resisted her my mother my instructress of amenability foot-rot will-wilt green-sick nasella-clump charlock disillusioned despot skeleton in the ground now it has struck will strike at me because i did not strike back i smother in words that nobody can hear i clamp myself gather my waters my water-retaining clods my loam my shale i am fallow field but not decided by me who will gently plough me on contour plough in my stubbles and my devil's-thorn fertilise me with green-manure and with straw to stiffen the wilt that this wilderness has brought on this bosom and brain? who blow into my nostrils with breath of dark humus? who sow in me the strains of wheat named for daybreak or for hope? how will my belated harvest reflect and in what water? who will harvest who shear who share my fell my fleece my sheaf my small white pips? who will chew me until i bind for i have done as was done unto me the sickness belongs to us two.

*

21 April 1960

Off to a good start today with the fixing up of the rooms the outside room and the nursery. Understand for the first time why everything had to happen the way it did God's great Providence. Had the nursery painted & the outside room whitewashed inside & out nice & tidy snow-white. Plascon for the one & whitewash for the other—economical—can always redo it. Washable Plascon for nursery busy little hands dirty little feet! A good opportunity while I'm about it to have all the outside rooms rewashed & for once to get everything in the backyard nice and tidy.

A. is getting the middle storeroom it has the largest window and a small one at the back as well.

Had carried out & sorted & thrown away & managed to squeeze everything into two other little rooms spades forks wheelbarrows small garden tools chicken-feed & pigs' supplementary feed & bone-meal & bags of compost for the garden had everything packed in the one and all the old furniture in the other. Had best bed & mattress & kitchen table & scrubbing-table and washstand (the one with the little tiles) carried into A's rm. All the necessary fortunately in stock. Considered a carpet but J. won't have any of it will make a plan left-over length of linoleum fitted loose for the time being easier to keep clean in any case.

Now everything is as it should be suppose it's the right thing to do for everyone's sake. It's not as if there was any other way out. Phoned

Beatrice to tell her of my decision & she's now considerably relieved & full of sweet talk & wants to propose me for chairlady of the WAU. Imagine! I could slap the woman, really.

Situation with J. God be thanked better now that I'm doing something about the matter. That it should cost so much but I'd rather not think about it. How long will he remain satisfied? He's threatening to burn my diaries. He says if he has to clear out his stuff all the time as if it's trash why can my books litter the place secret writing without full stops and commas perhaps I should go and read it out loud on radio so that he too can get to know the soul of woman and the distress of hr hand-maid.

Would in any case have to get in a nursemaid farmgirls too dirty & uneducated. J. thinks he's now shown what he can do with wheat & isn't all that interested in the farm any more & I ever more involved in the farming it can't be neglected with the arrival of the child. A. will have to be my eyes and ears here on Gdrift. Must be ever more vigilant & keep my hand on routines of shearing & sowing & slaughtering. Planning & management bore him. Soil & water are all my responsibility & I tell him that's the difference between a living and a dead farm. He says he's going to write a piece in the *Farmer's Weekly*: The options of a gentleman farmer, a living farm with a dead wife or a dead farm with a living wife now I'm giving up pleading.

J. at least looks after the purchases & that's where I let it be now. Just wish he'd do his own research about implements & stop messing around with agents. Have a way of disappearing off the face of the earth with their commission & only when you're stuck in the middle of the harvest with a broken-down combine do you hear about faulty parts that you should have had replaced before you even switched on the thing. A careless species. Cheap psychology & flashy talk. J. will just have to learn through his mistakes.

Will really not be able to manage without a good childminder. A. can write & read & cook well can trust her 100% very diligent very conscientious should really not be too much of a problem & she'll develop nicely in time to come.

Considering salary, savings account post office. Still have to convince J. of that he says she gets food & clothing & a roof over her head from beginning to end that's better than life assurance with Sanlam. For the time being he's satisfied with his stoep office.

Have to put on a brave face all the time. Feeling nauseous. Faint. See black & have to sit down. All these things that change so quickly. Must just keep going & think of nothing. Or listen to music. Bach. Bach always helps. Have to wait till J. is out otherwise I'll have to hear again put a sock in the holy barrel organ.

2

Half past nine on the alarm clock. Punctual to the second. From her footfall I can tell that I've gone and unleashed something again. Tchi, tchi, tchi, go her soles on the floor as she approaches down the passage, extra emphasis in the heels. Touchy when I want something out of the normal routine. Better not look her in the eye then. I keep my gaze on the white paper on which my hand lies in its splint.

She puts down the tray on the dressing table. She picks up the pen that has fallen from my hand. She grunts as she comes upright.

Ai, ai, she says, ai ai ai, what monkey business is this now?

She pulls out the clipboard from under my hand, turns it upside down, looks at it and tilts it back at me again. She holds out the paper with the wavering line and taps on it with the back of the pen.

L, she sounds, l, so that I can see her tongue in the front of her mouth.

L is for lie, she says. I know you're lying.

She adjusts three of the bed's back panels so that I tilt slightly, at a bit more of an angle, my head higher, but still on my back. That's my best position for breathing.

Lie lady lie, Agaat singspeaks through her teeth on the inhalation, lie lady lie, while she pushes in the pegs and retightens the screws.

A change, she says, is as good as a holiday. Are you lying more comfortably now, Ounooi?

I blink my eyes once very slowly. That means I'm lying more comfortably now, thank you, but you're missing the point, use your intelligence, say all the letters of the alphabet containing a downstroke, say them: p, h, f, m, n, l, t, i, j, k.

Our telepathy isn't operating today. I blink once more, a whit faster. That means, let me be then, take it away.

33

She pulls the splint from my hand. She doesn't have to loosen it, it's wide, the whole sleeve and hand, like the arm-guard of a falconer it looks. If only my word would come and perch on it, tame and obedient, if I could pull a hood with little bells over its head. A lesser kestrel with the speckled chest, with the wimpled wingtips, that glides over the land, that hangs in the currents of air, tilting between the horizons, Potberg in the south and Twaalfuurkop in the north, here on the back of my hand, a witness.

It will take time to make clear that the downstroke is the beginning of an m and that m stands for map, that I want to see the maps of Grootmoedersdrift, the maps of my region, of my place. Fixed points, veritable places, the co-ordinates of my land between the Korenland-rivier and the Buffeljagsrivier, a last survey as the crow flies, on dotted lines, on the axes between longitude and latitude. I want to see the distances recorded and certified, between the main road and the foot-hills, from the stables to the old orchard, I want to hook my eye to the little blue vein with the red bracket that marks the crossing, the bridge over the drift, the little arrow where the water of the drift wells up, the branchings of the river. A plan of the layout of the yard, the plans of the outbuildings, the walls, the roof trusses, the fall of the gutters, the fig-ures and words in clear print. I shall walk along a boundary fence and count the little carcases strung up by the butcher-bird, I shall find an island in the river, overgrown with bramble bushes, I shall duck under the beams of a loft and settle myself on a hessian bag and revel in know-ing that nobody knows where I am. Places to clamp myself to, a space outside these chambered systems of retribution, something on which to graft my imagination, my memories, an incision, a notch, an oculation leading away from these sterile planes.

Agaat moves the bridge closer to the bed and places the tray on it.

She puts on the neckbrace.

Headlock, she says, otherwise the old beast will waggle.

She takes the bowl of porridge in the good hand, the teaspoon in the tiny fingertips of the other hand protruding from her sleeve. She spoons the porridge to cool it, blows on it.

Not what goeth into the mouth defileth, she says.

She brings the first spoonful, holds it close, waits until she can see the rhythm of my breathing and puts it into my mouth between the inhal-ing and the exhaling. I keep the little bit of lukewarm porridge on my tongue until I can swallow it. I can feel that it won't be long now before I have to start using the swallowing apparatus.

But I postpone. It's a risk, apparently. What can I lose? This forced feeding? This forced life? This crush pen to eternity?

And then, when the gullet gives in, says Leroux, he will do a tracheotomy and insert a feeding-tube under the epiglottis. The next step is the ventilator plus another pipe in my stomach. With that I'll then have to go and lie in the hospital in town.

But I don't want to. I want to stay here, with Agaat, in my place that I know. I have signed, she has signed. Nobody can force us. It's the two of us who risk each other.

I feel the porridge ooze down both sides of my tongue before I'm ready for it. I close my eyes and picture the sluice in the irrigation furrow, the water damming up, a hand pulling out the locking-peg and lifting the plate in its grooves, letting through the water, and lowering it again, so that it bumps shut in the track of the sluice frame below. That's how I try to activate my swallowing.

Every time a risk, the chance of an enfeebled reflex of imagination.

That's how Leroux put it to us. Every mouthful a leap in the dark.

On that score, according to him, there should be no misunderstanding between us.

Misunderstanding.

He doesn't know what he's saying, the man.

I swallow once more.

That's it, says Agaat, who dares wins. Concentrate, Ounooi, there's another one coming. Third time lucky.

The third swallow exhausts me. I close my eyes, bit by bit I manage to filter it through. When at last it's down, I open my eyes, I open my mouth and I try to say m. I know very well how it's done. I must close my mouth, take my tongue out of the way, press my lips together and breathe out quickly, abruptly, through my nose, and open my mouth a soft nasal plop. A short, humming sound it must be, unvoiced, a vibration as brief as a second, a whimper of pain, a murmur of assent. M for map.

Gaat rushes to my aid.

Are you choking, Ounooi? Wait, wait, I'll help you. Calmly now. Just a small breath now and then swallow and breathe out. Swallow, Ounooi, swallow, I'll rub, come now, swallow just once.

I feel her fingertips on my throat. Lightly she massages, as Leroux demonstrated, only better because she's fed countless little dying animals in her life.

Fledglings. Nobody who could raise them like Agaat. With bread, with raw wheat-pulp from her mouth, chewed with her spit. From pigeon to bearded vulture. All of them she brought through. Always.

And let fly eventually. Out of her hand, into the open skies. Sometimes the more dependent kind kept returning for a while. She'd be flattered, would still put out food for the first few days, every day a little less, to wean them. Later she chased them from the enamel plates that she no longer filled with bread and seed.

Fly! Grow wild again! Look after yourselves now! she called and waved her arms in the air, the powerful left chasing away sternly, the puny little flutter-arm following.

Remove the food bowls, I used to say, otherwise they keep hoping.

Lightly, on the in-breath, all the way up my gullet she rubs in small circular movements, and with the exhaling she rubs down, down, trying to strengthen the last little bit of my swallowing reflex. To swallow, to cross a mountain, up on the one side, with effort, and down on the other, downhill but no easier. How false are the promises of the poets.

Über allen Gipfeln
Ist Ruh',
In allen Wipfeln
Spürest du
Kaum einen Hauch;
Die Vögelein schweigen im Walde.
Warte nur, balde
Ruhest du auch.

Why am I thinking of this now? The little old poem learnt by heart with Herr Doktor Blumer when I was still a student?

It's not my time yet, far yet from fledgling-death.

I open my eyes wide, quickly. I'm not a shitling! I want to see a map of my farm! This domain enclosed in chrome railings, this sterile room where you've got me by the gullet, I'm more than that! I'm more than a rabbit in a cage!

Agaat takes away her hand quickly.

What now? Is there something in your mouth that bothers you? Let me have a look.

It's a logical second, a familiar problem, food that can't be swallowed and gets stuck to the roof of the mouth. That's the drill.

Agaat presses my tongue flat with an ice-cream stick, she peers into my mouth. I try once again to get out my m, perhaps it's easier now that the front part of my tongue isn't clinging to the roof of my mouth.

If you want a nice surprise, open your mouth and shut your eyes, says Agaat.

I keep my eyes wide open to keep her attention. She looks. Like one standing in bright sunshine at the mouth of a cave, she peers into me.

I blink my eyes slowly, regularly, as encouragement.

Find it, Agaat, find the word in my mouth, find the impulse from which it must sprout, fish it out as intention, as yearning. The outlines of Grootmoedersdrift, its beacons, its heights, its valleys. You cannot deny me that.

M, I try again. Agaat's mouth opens. I flicker rapidly. Now you're warm, it says, now you're on the right track. She flickers back. My heart beats faster. Now there's understanding. Peering into each other's throats is the name of the game, two throats in search of a word.

Good, good, Agaat, watch my lips shut and open, then you imitate it, then you sound it for me, then you say 'm', then you say 'map', then you bring the sheaths out from the sideboard there, and then you take out the rolls and unfold them for me so that I can see where I am between heaven and earth, because my bed here is too small for me. My mouth is open, her mouth is open. Try once more. I can see your lips, Agaat, and I will signal when you move them correctly.

Suddenly I smell Agaat's breath. Of sweet rooibos tea it savours, of an hour ago, of the enamel jug.

Agaat closes her mouth. Her hands press on mine.

Don't go exciting yourself unnecessarily now, she says. She stands back. Cautiously.

Let's go through our list, she says, then we see what it is that you want.

*

12 December 1947. The day before your wedding, that was when it happened the first time. Afterwards, the days after, the first weeks, you listened to music to calm yourself. You told yourself that Jak had just been panicky about the wedding, nervous about all the new responsibilities, scared of his mother-in-law.

And then you were nagging away at him as well. That's how you tried to rationalise it to yourself. The thought of telling Beatrice you banished from your mind. Your father was the other possibility. The evening before your wedding he'd come to stand next to you and put his hand on your shoulder. I'm fretting for you, my child, he said, is something wrong? You looked into his face, grooved and emaciated with his disease. What would happen if you told him? He would do something about it immediately. He would tell Jak a few things straight out. And you couldn't afford to lose Jak.

You so badly wanted the house quite ready before the great day, because the reception would be on Grootmoedersdrift. The garden was another matter. It was untidy and overgrown. For that you had great dreams, but they'd have to wait. There were more pressing matters. And in any case, you were sentimental about the old-fashioned plants growing there. You'd always want them there. The March lilies and the morning glory and the nasturtiums round the foot of the water tank, the unruly jasmine hedge that had climbed into the old guava trees and the black-eyed Susan, the old-fashioned purple bougainvillea that had colonised the side stoep, the stocks and the fragrant dwarf carnations, the tuberose. Looked at rightly, it was a paradise already.

Pa's wedding present to the two of you was generous, a brand-new thatch roof for the old homestead, thatched by the foremost thatchers of Suurbraak, and a new floor with a spacious underfloor area with proper air vents broken into the foundations. For the sitting room Pa managed, on his last legs, to get hold of some yellow-wood beams from an old house being restored in Swellendam. The old-fashioned narrow knotty-pine slats he'd collected over the years so that there were enough when the floors had to be laid in the rest of the house. Ma got a whole team of Malays from the Hermityk to do the work. It was in their blood, she said, bricklaying and carpentry. A section of the stoep staircase that had crumbled away they built up neatly and fashioned air vents in the jerkin-head gables so that the new roof could air properly. The two little doves under the overhang of each gable, the secret adornment of which you'd been so fond ever since childhood, were touched up, so that if the afternoon sun was at the right angle, you could see them there, heads towards each other, cooing in white plaster. The front door they sanded down and painted green, and fitted an old copper doorknob and lynx-head knocker from Ma's heirloom-trunk. They carted out all the rubbish from the cellars and dug the spaces deeper for storage. You can never have enough storage on a farm, said Ma. And Jak will probably want to keep his wine somewhere. She came herself to supervise the work on the cellars and sorted the stuff to be got rid of from that to be put in the storerooms behind the house. There was lots of furniture that you wanted to have fixed in time, she pointed out the most valuable pieces to you and tied labels to the legs. The books she and Jak wanted to get rid of, all of them, but you stopped them. Don't think that just because Pa is ill you can do as you like with his things, you said. Many of the old books were beautifully bound in leather jackets; encyclopaedias and reference works on insects and animal behaviour and rocks; also dated popular-science works that had belonged to your father. They'll look good in the sitting room, you said, and you never know when you may need information on unlikely subjects. You packed them in the shelves next to the poetry collections, the novels and dramas you'd read at university, next to T.S. Eliot and Donne and Hopkins and the Complete Shakespeare and the *Oxford Collected Poems* and *Wuthering Heights* and *Northanger Abbey* and *Belydenis in die Skemer* and *The Cherry Orchard* and *Die Heks* by Leipoldt and *Kringloop van die Winde* and *The Soul of the White Ant*. The old reference works with which you'd grown up, you would study them too and make them your own. Your father used to read to you from them when you were small, about the soil-flea *Collembolla* with the spring under its tail that could destroy a lucerne field overnight. It was part of your farming equipment, you said, while carrying in piles of the old volumes.

In addition you had the inside and the outside painted and all the woodwork sanded and varnished. You had a few small cracked panes replaced and assigned carpets and spreads and curtains to their proper places. Everything crucial was done before the wedding date. Your nest was feathered.

It was more than good enough for a start, but you couldn't leave it at that. You nagged at Jak to help you at the last minute to paint the kitchen cabinets.

It looks bad, you said, what will the other women think of you with such kitchen cabinets? They look dirty. What will your mother think of the two of you that you can't even do a little thing like that for your-selves? That was what he couldn't stand. That you were threatening him with the opinions of other people. Not what you thought of him, but how others would judge him. Because that mattered greatly to him.

Then it happened. The day before the wedding. Dragged you by the hair across the back stoep of the homestead of Grootmoedersdrift. Pushed and shoved you in the chest so that you fell on the cement. Left you lying just there and walked away.

That evening you examined yourself naked in the mirror in the room of your mother's town house in Barrydale where you were staying over before the wedding. You pulled your hair back with your hands so that the shape of your head showed. You examined your body, your fea-tures. You were not a pretty woman in the ordinary sense of the word. Your mouth was crooked, your eyes out of line, your body did not have the regularity and proportions that the magazines held up as models. Your hair was inclined to fly out in points, bat-like. It formed crowns in the wrong places.

You felt the scrapes and bruises. There was a large bump on your head. You had trouble bending one knee. You sat on your bed and cried. Stopped later. You wouldn't appear in front of the pulpit with swollen eyes, not you.

You washed your face and put Pa's old 78 rpm with *Frauenliebe und -leben* on the turntable in your room. When lovely woman stoops to folly. Kathleen Ferrier could cry on your behalf. You sewed long voile sleeves and a stand-up collar of stiff lace to your wedding dress so that nobody would notice a thing. The wedding dress was made of the finest damask from your mother's trousseau, originally meant as a bedspread, too good for a bedspread. Between stitches you looked up into the mirror. Battered bride, you thought. Nun hast du mir den ersten Schmerz getan.

You were spoiling your wedding dress, it was starting to look like a fancy nightgown. You told your mother that the dress was too revealing. She narrowed her eyes to slits, she didn't believe you. She knew how you dressed, revealing had never been a problem for you. Perhaps, she said, you're not too taken with the idea of getting married in a bedspread, but as far as that's concerned you'll just have to get rid of your finickiness, because from now on you're the bed.

The properly made-up wife, you thought, the squared-off, the folded-back, the freshly covered wife. A wife with inner springs and a solid headboard, a wife with copper mounting.

You worked the fine stitches, carefully pulled the thread through, stitch for stitch you sewed yourself in, into the concealing sleeves, into the collar that had to cover the bruises on your neck.

And as you worked, you sat and thought of the first time. The first time was before your wedding, that day when you almost had the accident with the watermelon lorry.

You neither of you wanted to wait, you were just as passionate, as reckless as Jak. But there where you sat sewing camouflage onto your wedding dress, you gained another perspective on that afternoon.

He carried you over the threshold and threw you onto the old bed in Ma and Pa's sleeping-over room and had his way with you. Without ceremony or softness, nothing.

Wait, you still asked, wait a bit Jakop, slowly at first, but he couldn't hear you.

The mites drifted from the broken ceiling and the floorboards creaked under the squeaking bedstead. You were dismayed. You thought, no, not like this, but you gathered yourself into yourself. From inside you protected yourself while he drove home his will. It will come right, you thought. You would get to know each other in time.

You were taken aback at the quantity of blood on the spread afterwards, but he shrugged it off.

It's natural, he said with his back to you, you're a boer woman, aren't you? Now you're well broken-in. A little crash course. Don't be so namby-pamby. What did your mother say? An Afrikaner woman makes her way in silence and forbearance.

When you'd done finishing-off your dress, you were a different person. You thought you understood what you'd let yourself in for. You thought: It's better that I should understand it now rather than later. You experimented in front of the mirror with your hairstyle so as to hide the damage. You could not share your new insight even with your mother.

Your cousins were all there, but you trusted nobody there enough to tell them. Beatrice, your friend from schooldays, looked at you enquiringly a few times. But you gave no quarter. You smiled and did everything right for the whole day of the wedding. It would not happen again. It was nobody else's business. And you did love Jak and you were sorry for him amongst all your people, your father shaking his hand all too solemnly and your cousins slapping him on the back too hard.

Pretty Jak, they called him, Jak with the woman's face.

They admired him for his way with words. Because he made a thunderous bridegroom's speech, your Jak, as you'd known he would. You'd got to know his style. His toastmaster club at Stellenbosch to which he dragged you as student. You didn't enjoy it much, but it was in exchange for the lieder evenings he in turn had to sit through in the little Conservatorium Hall. He always had the people at his feet, liked you to hear it. Just as with the wedding speech.

Once upon a time there was a most beautiful little farm, he started, and winked at you.

At the foot of a mountain, close to a stream, with a thatched house between the trees. But the yard was silent and deserted. In the evenings the trees sighed and the house creaked and the mountain whispered to the river: Now when are we getting an owner, a man and his wife who will bring life and laughter to the yard and will love each other above all?

Were you the only one who heard an undertone of mockery? You caught your father's eye. He didn't like it, that you could see, but he composed his face and smiled.

Perhaps Jak intercepted the glance. The mockery disappeared from his voice. He charmed himself and all the others, roused them even. In the end he had all two hundred wedding guests singing. O farm of my blood, o soil of my birth, it thundered over the yard of Grootmoedersdrift, yours I will be till the end of the earth.

When he had done, everybody believed fairy tales could come true.

Only after midnight, when the guests were starting to take their leave, you withdrew into your own space, but you did not cry, you pondered and planned and mustered your wits. Jak came to look for you. He was tipsy, full of talk, and amorousness itself after the commotion of the marriage feast.

He came and stood behind you in front of the mirror where you were sitting in your petticoat, caressed your neck.

Sweetheart sweetheart sweetheart, he sang to you, will you love me ever.

You hummed along for the occasion.

I could never marry a beautiful woman, he said, it would cost me too many a sleepless night.

You smiled. My dear husband, you said, what more could a boer woman ever wish for than a husband who leaps out of bed in the morning fresh and rested for his day's duties.

*

how long do wild peas lie before they mould? how long does a sheep suffer a sick tongue before it turns blue? how long in my symphyses did the midges multiply? in what creases or folds of the collar and the crotch the invisible mite of the mange? how many years the incubation of terror? in what subterranean seams does history precipitate? a catchment of rain does not elect itself the mountains choose and a mouth for the stream is gifted by the sea how was I then reservoired so wrongly such a still mephitic pool?

*

Wednesday 12 May 1960

Everything is starting to seem more real now that I'm making the lists. Two processes (three!) they keep each other on track but there are many things to think of at the same time. As long as I think of the things and not of the reasons. Heaven help me sometimes it feels too much.

Kriel & Co. list 1

Baby (a little girl or a little boy?!)
Nappies & pins
Blankets (holding and covering, woolsey) (5)
Vests (long-sleeved it will be winter) (7) Ma says you can never have enough of them.

Crawlers (button-front)
Nappy covers (waterproof)
Cradle (perhaps after all get my old white cot from Ma? Or is it still down in the cellar here?)
Push-chair (Dunlop adjustable)
Pillows & covers

2 baths (thick plastic)
Towels (4 large & 4 small)
Baby shampoo & soap
Bath oil
Baby powder
Cotton wool
Earbuds

Small scissors
2 x 4 bottles + rings + teats
Bottle-brushes 2 (Saw a little frame with coloured balls that rattle & twirly things full of angels & birds to hang over the cradle)

Kriel & Co. list 2

7 Long-sleeved uniform dresses (black—could probably make them myself but don't have time now)
7 Aprons (high bib backstraps crossed cf. Royal Hotel)
7 White caps with elastic bands (try Good Hope Café if Kriel & Co don't have the coloured girls wear them there ask Georgie's wife)
Hairpins (2 x 24 large)
Bloomers (strong black woolsey school section)
Scholl shoes (rubber soles)
White socks (dozen)
Flannel nightgowns (2)
Nylon nightgowns (2)
4 bras 32 A (will just have to grow into them I see the titties are pushing fast)
Towels & washcloths (curtains?) I can make up from the odds drawer of the linen cupboard. Bedding & pillows enough. Off-cuts!—phone Needle's Eye—will have to run up a Sunday dress or two for her quickly needlework she can enough already she'll just have

to jump in herself & muck on I won't have time can really not buy everything new
Dr White's 4 dozen (Facts-of-life talk! When will the right time be?)
Elastic with loops
Mum (rub-on kind)
Lacto Calamine Lotion
Lifebuoy soap x 6
Johnson's baby powder (will have to teach her how to keep lace-up shoes fresh!)
Pepsodent x 6
Black polish (& brush & buffing cloths)
Three small black irons & iron-ing board (she mustn't use those in the house in the mornings must emerge fresh as a daisy from the outside rm finished & ready for the day)
Vim
Scoop & brush
Omo
Washboard
Starch (write down recipe for her: cold water and ordinary)
Reckitt's Blue
2 Tin buckets

Sunlight soap (X4)
Zinc bath
No water as yet in outside rm
electricity one point?
(Two-plate stove?)
Tin kettle
Big pot for heating washing
water
Jug
Rooibos tea
Frisco
Powdered milk
Sugar (tin)
(NB for her needlework basket:
extra buttons for the uniform &
darning mushroom needles pins
scissors crochet hook crochet
yarn oddments of wool for more

of the jerseys she wears she
will start knitting them herself
now)
Bible
FAK (old one)
Cook & Enjoy?
Farmer's Handbook (Pa's old
copy, A. must learn the principles
old & new methods you never
know & it's good discipline)
Embroidery book

Optional:
Tin of ginger biscuits
Tin of rusks
Marie biscuits
Acid drops
Peppermint humbugs

Just a little something to suck on & something to enjoy with hr tea in the evening before going to bed. So much to do still. Quite ill with thinking of it. I ask J. doesn't he feel anything about everything happening now he says it's not necessary for him to feel anything I've got enough feelings for two. Next thing I see he's gone & bought himself a whole box of new clothes. A new noise on Gdrift he says & after all he can't appear without costume for the next act. I say why don't you rather go & read something to improve yourself your whiplash repartee no longer impresses me. Since I've been pregnant, he's at least more careful. Doesn't seem as if he wants to as much as touch me, never mind beat me. But the language he utters. Comes along just now & grabs the diary from under me. Blessed is the maker of lists creator of heaven and earth he exclaims. Blessed are the poor in spirit I snap back. What must become of us?

13 May 1960
Everything goes as if preordained. Three rooms furnished at the same time nursery & A.'s room & the gable room of the left wing for J's office. He's sleeping there most of the time now anyway & with the baby it will definitely be better he says so himself.

Now quite exhausted after the whole day's organising. Scared all the time that I'm forgetting something important. Anxious. What a disruption it is! I know it's right but I nevertheless hold my heart about it all.

Had cradle & chest of drawers put into the nursery with hole in top in which the washbasins fit & enough space next to it to attend to the child. Under the bath space for nappies & bath things. Had single bed carried in there & an easy chair so that I can lie there if necessary & a place to sit for feedings & chest of drawers with enough drawers so that at one glance I can put my hand on everything.

Bought curtaining with half-moons & stars the windows open into the backyard so that A. can help listen at night.

Had linoleum nailed to the scrubbing table for hr kettle to stand on. OuKarel has fixed cross-planks between the legs of the table for hr tin bath & hr suitcase. Had a plank screwed down on iron brackets over the table on which she can keep hr coffee & tea & mugs & soap & cleaning material & hammered a nail into the wall for mirror one corner cracked but perfectly usable. Had a copper pipe inserted in the wall between the two partitions where shelves of the storeroom were to hang hr uniforms & dresses (look for old wire hangers NB) devised a two-strip curtain on a cord so that hr stuff needn't be so exposed to view next to the bed a crate with a cloth over it for hr Bible & hr glass of water for the night & hr candle almost forgot about the candle add to list 2 (Inside crate she can keep hr other reading matter.) Got Dawid to nail 4 apple boxes together & painted two coats of white & screwed in two hooks & and made a curtain for that as well for hr shoes & shoe polish below & hr wool & cloths & her needlework basket.

Little old yellow vase for a bit of homeliness with nasturtiums inside should look pretty there. Walls still bare & light-bulb without shade but there's no point in having her think this is a hotel old bathmat in front of the bed so that she won't stand on cold linoleum with the getting-up & hung old kitchen curtains a bit skimpy had to undo the pleats but still quite serviceable.

What can she think of it all? Will just have to be good enough. Fortunately nice & sensible.

J.'s office now in stoep room. Desk & filing cabinet & farm papers that used to be in second pantry carried over & his exercise apparatus out of the bedroom thank Heaven. Photos & trophies & things that stood

& hung all over the place. Ma'am's on the rampage baas on the stoep maid's in her hovel & all's right with the world sings Jak. Lord the man. At least he'll be able to face people again now he says. And at a glance see what's happening in the yard. As if the yard mattered a whit to him. Just as long as he's satisfied now don't have time for his nonsense too on top of everything. Expect Beatrice Pulpit-Polish will also want to come & do inspection some time. Missing a brain-bobbin, as Pa would say.

3

The morning sun lights up Agaat's cap from the back. Full of embroidery holes it is, densely edged with shiny white thread. The points of light in the weft flicker as she approaches. She hesitates over my bed, inclines her head, feels along the high peak with both hands, touches the base on both sides, whether it's well pinned, whether it's properly seated. If the cap is on as it should be, she'll be empowered to walk through fire. Her crown of glorified cotton, her mitre, her fire-barrel specked with light, that gives her dominion over the underworld. She deliberately touches it in such a way that there should be no doubt in my mind regarding her intention. She is mustered, she is prepared, I mustn't give any more trouble, she'll sort me out here, she's the commander of my possibilities.

She's going to list them for me, the options remaining to me, without skipping anything. As the Spirit moves her, with allusions to my incapacity.

The list gets shorter all the time.

She revises it ever more frequently.

At night on her camp stretcher she ponders what she should delete.

Three years ago the list was full of interesting variations.

Shall we ride to the lands with Dawid?

Would you like a picnic in your wheelchair next to the dam?

Must I take you rowing on the drift? Joke.

Do you want to walk up and down on the stoep in your walking frame?

Do you want to write with the splint on your hand?

Do you want to do exercises?

Do you want to sit on your own in the garden, next to the lavender hedge, next to the rambling rose, under the honey-bread tree?

47

Do you want to read notes and hum?

Do you want to go for a swim in the reservoir?

Shall I make you some custard with apricot jam and bananas?

But that's all in the past now.

I close my eyes.

I have a life beyond your lists, is what it wants to say. I have needs that you cannot imagine, even if you were to cast your cap in bronze.

It maddens her. That she can't meet my every need, that she doesn't know everything I think, that frustrates her beyond all measure.

To peer into my head at what is playing there, that's what she desires. There's protest in her voice when she speaks, but I know that's only the upper layer, that's what she can afford to have me hear.

Shall I draw the curtain a bit?

Do you want to listen to the morning service?

A tape?

Wine women and song?

The pan for number one?

The pan for number two?

Too cold?

Too hot?

Sit up straighter?

Lie down flatter?

Eat a bit more porridge?

Fruit pulp? There is cold melon? With a bit of salt?

Water?

Tea with honey and lemon?

After every question she waits for me to reply, but I keep my eyes shut. That means you're cold, you're far out, you don't have a clue, my need is a subtle one.

I open my eyes. I seek her gaze. I widen my eyes.

No! No! and again no!

Everything is swimming before my eyes, but she carries on. She coerces me, I must comprehend the extent of her goodwill. Nothing she wouldn't do for me. Anything within the bounds of justice and reason.

I close my eyes again.

Her voice rises by a whole tone. Slightly faster it comes now.

Read? Must I set up the reading stand and page for you?

Must I read to you?

Genesis?

Job?

A psalm of David?

Revelations?

The Bible according to Agaat. God's delirium and man's tremble-ment.

I open my eyes but I give no sign, I fix my gaze straight ahead of me. That means: Go away, you're irritating me.

From the corner of my eye I see her hitch up her shoulder. She rustles a finger through the pile of little blue books on the chair.

Or something from your own pen? That always interests you doesn't it? The good old days, 'Agaat and the garden of Grootmoedersdrift 1980'? But this one is empty. It says 'paradise' at the top and then it's just a list of plants.

She runs her finger down the page. Moonflower, flowering quince, silver birch, she reads. She slaps shut the book.

Pity it's not the whole story, she says, her mouth pleated, it's just a skeleton. And the gardening was quite pleasant. She taps the front of the book.

Perhaps I should write it up in here myself. But perhaps we should finish furnishing my paradise first before we start on yours, don't you think? We're right in the middle of it now. Hr little rm that you fixed up so nicely for hr in the back here, remember? How did the baas always say? Something for the *Guinness Book of Records*. First time in his-tory. Interior decoration for an outside room. Thought you could hide it from me. Then the ounooi came to do inspection and left the door open. Then Saar saw. But by then I'd known for a long time.

Agaat is trying to provoke me. I give no quarter. I keep my eyes neu-tral.

Ad nauseam I've heard it in a variety of performances. Perhaps she's going to sing it again this evening. Seven aprons, seven caps, one dozen white socks and a little vase for homeliness.

Perhaps she'll beat time with her shoe in her hand on the armrest of the chair. That would be better. Anything would be better than her sitting still and reading and glaring at me every now and again as if I'd done her some wrong.

Let her leap, let her dance, let her grab one little book after the other and put it down and spin around in the middle of the room, a starched-aproned dervish without the blessing of release.

As long as she understands I also have my rights.

I want to see my ground, I want to see my land, even if only in out-line, place names on a level surface. I want to send my eyes voyaging.

Perhaps you feel like a video?

She's not looking at me, she's looking at the books on the little pile.

I saw her counting them the other evening. There are sixty-three. I thought there were more.

The one about the snow wolves? Or the black-and-white killer whales? Or the giant bats of the Amazon?

A grimace on her mouth. As if she can see me hooking tiny damp claws into the mane of a horse, how I attach myself to the jugular vein, as if there's a close-up of my ingurgitating mouth-parts.

Anything rather than having to confess that I'm locked up here as if behind thick one-way glass and she's out there and doesn't know what on earth it is that I want.

Or a story movie? Before I go to exchange them tomorrow?

A Passage to India?

Where Angels Fear to Tread?

On Golden Pond?

How many syllables can you speak without saying an 'm'? Utter how many sentences without using the word 'map'? Think how many thoughts before you stumble upon the idea of a schematic representation of the world?

You'd think it would be indispensable, like the air that you breathe.

My cheeks are wet.

I close my eyes. I keep them shut. I give up. I flicker my eyelids without opening them. Cheeky, that's supposed to mean, surely you can see it's something completely different, get the hell out of my room with your damned lists.

I hear her turn on her heel. Rapid steps down the passage to the bathroom. She returns with a warm cloth. She wipes my face in two swipes.

Stop blubbering, you'll choke, say her eyes.

It's tooth-polishing time, says her mouth.

I flicker through my tears, polish yourself.

Aitsa! says Agaat, how-now.

She pushes the plug of the electric toothbrush into the socket. She holds the green toothbrush with the rotary head in the air to test it. Tsiiimmm, it goes, tsiiimmm-tsoommm. She unscrews the lid of the powder-stuff. She presses the head of the toothbrush in it. It's a dry polish. It tastes of lime, of dust, of blackboard chalk. Against the light I can see the dust particles eddying around her hands.

Right, says Agaat, the full piano, tooth by tooth, from the middle down the front to the back, first cheek-side then tongue-side, we start at the top.

She puts down the toothbrush in a bowl on the trolley. She puts on a pair of latex gloves. The rubber clicks and snaps. The small hand looks like a mole. It burrows blindly into the glove. The other hand looks like pliers.

The monkey mourns the monkey's mate, she sings on a held-in breath.

She takes the mouth-clamp out of the sterile water. She lets it drip. Then she spins the screw closed. Wrrrr, it turns back on its thread. The drops spatter my face.

I flicker with my eyes, please watch what you're doing!

Ag so sorry, she says. She swabs my cheek with a piece of cotton wool. Swab, swab, swab. Left right left.

And monkey tears are cold and wet, she carries on singing.

Lord, I say with my eyes, Lord you.

I beg yours? asks Agaat.

She compresses the spring of the screw and manoeuvres it into my mouth. The flat cold foot of stainless steel rests on my tongue, the curved upper part fits into the hollow of my palate. She releases the spring. My mouth starts to open.

Jacked up, says Agaat.

She looks out of the door while she winds open the screw in my mouth. She knows the procedure. She likes Leroux's gadgets. The dry-polish toothbrush was a real winner. It gives her an opportunity to get into my mouth, under my tongue, behind my teeth.

Dry polish spares you, she said that day when she unpacked the toothbrush, we must use that mouth of yours for nothing but swallowing.

Now, she says, concentrate, breathe.

My jaws creak.

A bit more, says Agaat, she turns the screw, so that we can reach everywhere nicely, she says.

With the last few turns she looks at what she's doing. She avoids my eyes. Her gaze is fixed on my mouth cavity. There's a flickering on her face.

In the road is a hole, she says.

I know the rest. In the hole is a stone, in the stone is a sound. Riddle me ree, perhaps you can tell what this riddle may be.

Now she's looking into my eyes.

We do it in one go, she says. That's better than stopping half-way. Otherwise you taste the nasty stuff, right? And then you want to swallow, but we're saving your swallowing for food, right?

Tsiiiimmm, goes the brush, tsiiimmm-tsoommm in the air.

I close my eyes. I feel Agaat pulling away my upper lip from my front teeth. It can take half an hour or five minutes. It depends. If she sees tears, I'm punished. The toothbrush is on its slowest setting. It makes a low drilling sound when it touches my teeth. My whole head vibrates with it. The powder drifts up my nose. I concentrate. I breathe. I mustn't choke.

And day and night in sun and moon, she takes up the song, as if nothing has intervened. She works her way through the teeth in my upper jaw. She lifts up my lip like the edge of a carpet.

The monkey sings the same old tune.

She peels away my lower lip from my guns. For my lower jaw she has a hymn.

Delay not, delay not, o sinner, draw near, she sings, the waters of life are now flowing for thee. She switches off the toothbrush.

Keep still, she says, I hear a dog barking. She pulls off one glove, shrrrts.

I lie with my mouth prised open. The air is cold in my mouth, the chrome plate presses against my palate. On my tongue seeps the chalky taste of the powder.

I hear no dog barking. Turtledoves are what I hear.

The doves of my yard.

Everything carries on as always, everything will be as it was, the shadows of the bluegums, the doves of morning. The next morning even, when I am gone, will be filled with the usual sounds, as if nothing had happened. The bail will jingle against the bucket, the storeroom door will scuff the threshold, the laughter of the farm boys down by the drift playing with their wire cars on the little bridge, you'll hear it all the way from the yard, as now, the screen door will bang with the morning's in-and-out around the kitchen.

Agaat scrapes her shoes on the front-door mat. She comes down the passage. I heard the bakkie come back. Perhaps Dawid had gone to fetch post from town. Perhaps there was a letter from Jakkie. Or a tape with some kind of pigmy music.

But when she comes in, her gaze betrays nothing of the kind.

Where were we? she says.

Every surface is attended to. She says nothing further about the dogs. I know her by now. She goes away and leaves me like this just so that she can come in at the door again. So that she can have a fresh view of her patient. Of the progress of the operation.

In the stone there is no sound.

Gone is the sun and gone is the moon.

The monkey's mouth's in a metal mount.

She undoes the screw, whirrrrs it in my mouth, pulls it out, plops it back into the water.

There's a mite too much attitude to the wrist. As if she's arranging flowers before an audience.

Right, she says, now for the dusting. She dips a swab in water. She wipes my gums, my palate, the corners of my mouth. There's a special sponge to remove scurf from my tongue.

Say 'ah' for doctor, says Agaat.

I close my eyes. What have I done wrong?

The little mole-hand nuzzles out my tongue. The screw has squashed it in my mouth. My shrunken tongue, fallen in, deformed by the paralysis. There was a time when I could put it out and look at it in the mirror, read the signs myself. Your tongue betrays everything about your intestines.

I feel a tugging at my tongue. The grip tremors with a faint temptation: Where is it fixed? how firmly? with what strings? how long is it?

My tongue is being staked out for its turn at ablution.

The sponge is rough. With vigorous strokes my tongue is scrubbed down. It tastes powerfully of peppermint. Three times the sponge is recharged before Agaat is satisfied. My tongue feels eradicated.

There, she says, pulling away my lips from my teeth to inspect her handiwork.

Ounooi, she says, full piano.

She lets my lips slump back, arranges them decorously over my teeth so that I don't smirk, and regards me hand on hip.

The only other option is simply to pull all your teeth. All in one go. Then the tooth fairy will put money in your shoe. The question is, she says, a glint in her eye, how much does one pump into you so that you feel absolutely nothing?

She turns away for the punchline, pronounces it as if it's the most normal of sentences.

It's not as if you can squirm or scream.

She rinses her strong hand in the bowl of water.

Only the gums and palate to go. That you like, don't you?

She dips her fingers in the peppermint mouthwash. She puts her thumb and forefinger on either side of my mouth. She massages my gums, first the lower and then the upper. She looks out of the stoep door while she does it. The rhythm of the massaging action calms her. She becomes more tranquil. Her fingers move more gently, more kindly on my gums. Then it becomes caressing. Forgive me, ask the fingers, I also have a hard time with you, you know.

Now she's not looking at me. You can't talk, say the fingers. How in God's name must I know what you want? For days now you've been nagging at me about something you want. I don't know what it is! I can't hear what you're thinking!

More passionate the movement becomes. Agaat curses me in the mouth with her thumb and index finger. Bugger you! I feel against my palate, bugger you and your mother. I didn't ask to be here!

I read her sign language with the membranes of my mouth, eyes closed.

If I could rub some speech into your mouth, then I'd do it, you hear! You'd better watch your step with me! You'd conk out without me! You're conking out as it is, I can't help it. And it's I who conk out, I'm actually the one who suffers here.

She takes her hand from my mouth. Long strings of drool she draws out. She takes off the gloves. Slap, slap, they fall into the bin. She wipes my face, the tears from my cheeks.

Thank you, I signal briefly.

You're welcome, says Agaat.

She turns her back on me. She tidies the things on the trolley. She looks at her watch. Suddenly she's in a hurry. She draws the curtain with quick little plucks, arranges the covers over me.

I lie with my eyes shut. My mouth feels numb. Better that she should not see my eyes. Better that she should not think now that I'm asking her something. I'm waiting for her hand on my shoulder. That would mean: We do what we can, as well as we can, you and I, and: I'm not going far.

I wait for her voice, for her to say something like: I will think what it can be, I will find it out, just give me a chance, in the end I always riddle it out.

But she says nothing, slides something cold under my hand.

Joke.

The finishing touch to the scene.

It's the hand-bell.

You ring your little bell, and I'll ring mine.

Relentless, her memory.

Perhaps I can let the bell roll away over the bedspread, make it fall off the bed.

Now you just stop your snivelling, says the glance she flings at me. She draws the curtains completely, all but a chink, walks out with brisk steps.

In the front room the grandfather clock chimes eight o'clock. I hear Agaat opening the glass door of the clock and winding it. From the tempo of the winding I can tell she knows I'm listening. She turns slowly, so that I can hear the cogs clearly, the spring, how it coils in on itself.

Time flies, that's what the shutting of the clock's glass door means.

Clink, she puts the winding-key down behind the pediment of the clock.

Tchick, is her next sound.

It's the sideboard's dark little door. You can weep yourself blue, but your time you've had, is what it says.

Consider it well, says the shutting. Tchick.

Elegant symmetry, Agaat, that opening and shutting of yours in the front room. You can't resist it. The emptying and the filling.

Time that streams away backwards, time that ticks on ahead, time being wound up for the running down.

There, behind the little blue books, lie the maps that I want to see.

And you may have dominion over my hours that you count off there and apportion with your devious little snake-hand and your white casque in front of the clock face, Agaat. But there is also space, carto-graphed, stippled, inalienable, the mountains, the valleys, the distance from A to B, laid down in place names for a century or two or three, Susverlore or Sogevonden, farms Foundlikethis or Lostlikethat.

Would she be able to see the sheaths, there where she's bending over now? How many books would there still be blocking her view? There was a third pile. Of that we've read nothing yet. Would that be what's blinding her?

With a mouth full of peppermint I lie here.

What am I supposed to do if I'm not allowed to cry? Crying is a last capacity in my depleted demesne. It's something that can still come forth from me, something other than pee or poo or condensation. These three. She would want to measure and weigh them, absorb my sweat in a vapour-cloth, and store it in the cool-room. I can see it on her face when she removes my excretions. That I exude something tangible, has great persuasive force. Why then is she so indifferent to my tears? For them she would be able to develop a unique index. Salinity, sob-factor, specific gravity of grief. She would be able to taste, connoisseur that she is: The taste of guilt, the essence of almonds in my tears, and craving and confusion, tincture of eucalyptus, trace of fennel. Now is the time when she should be improvising with me, instead of nursing me single-mindedly, but she can't grasp it. Once upon a time she could, but she taught herself not to. I taught her not to.

I listen to Agaat setting the rest of the day's duties in train. She hands out orders in the kitchen. Her tone is authoritative, she speaks slowly and with emphasis. When she's finished, there's an immediate accelera-tion of activity. The screen door bangs. That would be Lietja going to fetch the cream and the milk for the house from the dairy, and the milk for Dawid's clan, to put it in bottles in the big refrigerator till this evening. There, that's the door of the small storeroom scraping open.

Do I remember the smell of fine chicken-meal? Can I count the steps from the backyard to the chicken run?

Agaat will go and feed the chicks, and then she'll return and fill a few bottles from the milk left over in the buckets. She'll feed the hanslammers, give them all a turn at the teat, for the smallest the longest, while she softly tells him or her everything.

Behind the drawn curtains I can hear the stoep furniture being moved. That is Saar. Tock, goes her broom, tock, tock, as she sweeps the corners of the stoep. Tock, tock, tock. There's her face now in front of the chink, an oblique section of Saar, headscarf, many-coloured apron. Of the chink in the curtain, if she spots it, she takes no notice. Her gaze terminates against the little glass panes of the swing-door. I might as well not have been here.

*

Soil is everything, you said to Jak, healthy soil yields healthy animals and healthy people.

You were on the fallow land where OuKarel Okkenel and his son had harvested the previous November. It was your first March together on Grootmoedersdrift, 1948. You stepped on the spade, a chunk of the crust broke loose, you picked up a handful of soil, rubbed it, let it sift through your fingers. The fine grains that become slightly clayey in rainy weather, you'd known it from childhood, knew what it smelt like when it got wet.

It was ten o'clock in the morning. The sun was blazing down on your head. You'd with difficulty got Jak to accompany you. The previous day you'd had to negotiate with OuKarel.

You and your clan stay on on the farm, Karel, you said, I'll pay you a wage, but we're now going to sow ourselves.

Ai, Kleinnooi, OuKarel said. You saw how wrinkled he was. He stood there crumpling up his hat in front of him. I thought my Dawidboy . . .

You interrupted him. Dawid can stay on if he wants to work, oldster, you said, but I'm saying the sharing is over, we're going to farm professionally here now, you plough in the wrong way, the soil washes away, we're going to start ploughing with rippers on the contour.

You tried to explain the idea of the soil blanket to him, but he just stood there gaping at you.

You'll get your rations same as always, end of the month, you said. He just nodded, put his hat back on.

Jak was the next one who had to be instructed in how things were going to be run.

I want to go and show you something, you said.

It had better be something big, he said from behind his motoring magazine.

It is, you said. It's the beginning and the end of everything.

You loaded a spade and a pickaxe and a sieve into the bakkie. You wanted to teach him about soil, but he just stood there next to you on the land kicking at clods. You thought: How must I move you? Must I first till you here amongst the stubble? Will that make you listen to me?

That was what you thought, but what you said was: You really must help me to think here, my husband. Without you I can't tackle this thing.

Don't think you can bribe me with sweet talk, Jak muttered.

You kissed him on the mouth. He drew away slightly. He didn't like kissing.

Look, you said, this is now the one type of dryland that you find here, shallow soil on shale. Tends towards acidic. Poor in phosphorus.

Jak shrugged. And?

And so lime supplements and superphosphate. And salt lick for the animals.

You'd brought along the ground-plan with illustrations. You'd made a thorough study, you thought he had to get on top of things. He wouldn't touch the new publications on the agricultural development of the district, never mind listening to the extension officer. There on the land under the bright March sun you tried again. You stood close to him. You made sure that your hip was pressing against the small of his back. You showed him the photographs of the vertical sections.

Nine inches deep on the hills and then rock, you explained, it's a pretty slender resource.

You'd noticed how meagre his knowledge was. His so-called diploma, he'd just seen to it that he enrolled, attended one or two classes, never even did the practicals. You had to teach him to sit on a tractor. A cow's udder gave him the creeps.

You get yellowish and reddish shallow soil along the hills, you tried. Mispah and Glenrosa. Sometimes it stretches down a bit deeper. Down below on the slopes in the untilled veld it's different, Hutton and Clovelly soils, medium-depth red and yellow solids that drain well. But up here where you can plough, it erodes easily, here we have to make good contours and run-offs.

You rocked lightly against his body, adjusted the rhythm to the pace of your instruction.

Jak stood behind you. He pressed his body against you.

He pointed over your shoulder at the grazing below in the direction of the river.

So here it's dry and down there it's wet, he said with a snigger.

Just so, Jakop, you said. You laughed at his innuendo while in truth you were irritated, you pressed back against him with your buttocks.

Along the river the water table is high in winter and there you find that the soil puddles and becomes waterlogged, there we have to dig drainage troughs.

Really? Now tell me Mrs Soil Expert, what do you call the resource down below? Crumpet catch, hmmm? Banana bower? He placed his hands on your hips and drew you tightly against him.

Estcourt, Westleigh, Oakleaf, you rattled off the names, Longlands, Dundee, Avalon. You showed him the pictures in the book.

Some are shallow wet duplex soils and others are wet saline alluvial sand-loam or clay-loam. Also on the poor side.

So how are we going to get rich on poor soil, tell me that? His mouth was in your neck, you had goose pimples all over. He knew the sign.

Slowly, you said, very slowly and gradually.

He misunderstood you, had only one thing on his mind, took off his belt, said he was a hasty hound, wanted you to service him right there on the open land. But you thought the lesson would take more readily in a cool room at home.

That's the way it is with most things when you're dealing with men, your mother had taught you, you have to dip your demands in a dab of sugar. Remember, the truth is nothing in itself. Package it prettily.

You unbuttoned the top of your blouse and said that to get rich on Grootmoedersdrift would take years, a decade or more. You took his hand and held it against your breast and told him stories about farmers who grew too rapidly and went bankrupt just as rapidly. You took off your dress while you instructed him in the principles of crop rotation, you opened his fly slowly. Button by button you tried to get his mind round the subsurface method of cultivation. You slid your hands under his shirt and rubbed his nipples and explained to him why soil had to lie undisturbed for long periods and that rest was the best way of getting the soil structure rich and crumbly. You bowed your head over his abdomen and pleasured him and swallowed it all, because spitting out you knew he took as an insult.

Well, said Jak that morning in bed, his criterion for good healthy soil is a good healthy yield.

Regular activity, my wife, that's all that's necessary, on the home front as on the farming front. What goes around, comes around, or as the farmers say, eating is easy, threshing is labour.

And you lay back and for a second time let him have his way. Strike, you thought, strike your sword on the water, you think you possess me, but you don't know me. Penetrate, you thought, invade me. What are you without my surfaces for you to break? My surfaces are merely my surfaces. Underneath I am unfathomable and you are a splinter in the void. When he rolled off you, he sighed and took your hand, squeezed it.

Just think, my little Milla, in a few years' time there'll be a whole string of little de Wets who can help sow and harvest one day. So we'd better make enough profit to buy some more land for them.

That was the beginning of the differences. Jakop and little Milla's differences. He wanted to plough under the large stretches of natural veld on Grootmoedersdrift immediately for small-grain. You said it was of incalculable value, you should divide it up in camps and use it just like that, unspoilt, for rotation pasture. He wanted to plough the fallow lands five discs deep and clear them and level them with a section of rail track as he'd seen other farmers do. You said no, we break up the soil just enough to sow, with a ripper so that it doesn't get too much air and we anchor the stubble only lightly in the topsoil. He said it looked like hotnot farming. You said it was a blanket, it preserved the moisture, it preserved the nitrogen. He wanted to sow all the fields at the same time every year with wheat. You maintained a four-stage cycle was best: Wheat, fallow, old land, wheat, with a green compost like lupins ploughed in every other cycle and dryland lucerne sown under the wheat for grazing when the harvest was in. All he wanted to concede was two-stage. Wheat, fallow, wheat, fallow. He wanted to plough straight down with the fall of the land on the steep slopes as the Okkenels had done all the years. Over your dead body, you said, there had to be contours because the soil had already eroded badly in places.

The outcome could probably have been foreseen.

He said, well, then you farm on your own.

You said, but you're my husband, the land belongs to both of us, you promised to farm it with me.

Next thing you knew, he'd taken a loan from the Land Bank with Grootmoedersdrift entered as security and bought a large tract of adjacent hilly land to the south.

Let's see, he said, you do as you see fit on your precious little farm and I farm the new land.

Fortune favoured him. After he had applied new fertilisers on a massive scale, he sowed double-density, new varieties of short-stem wheat on the ploughed land. He must beware of rust on the delicately bred strain of wheat, you warned. Oh my dear little prophetess of doom, he laughed. And indeed. Only goodness and mercy followed him. No summer rain to speak of, the air dry and clean, no sign of fungus. That October you saw farmers pulling off the road and clambering through the fences to walk in Jak's lands and to feel the long fat ears and the short thick pipe of the wheat. Never again Klipkous, they said to one another. It was the last mature land in which you saw your father standing, hand on the hip, with a faraway look in his eyes.

Congratulations, my boy, he said to Jak, you're sounding a new note here on the farm. But you could hear his heart was not in it. '48 that was, the year before his death.

Jak imported a big New Holland grain drier from America and made doubly sure that the wheat did not rot in the bag. He brought in five bumper crops in consecutive years, bought vehicles and implements, demolished all the old sheds from your mother's time and built big new structures with sliding doors and shiny steel roofs, and bought new stud animals to improve the cattle and sheep herds.

So what do you say now, Milla my wife? he asked. Now it's only you who must show that you can increase abundantly.

He tapped against your stomach as one would tap against the glass of a silent clock to see if the hands won't move.

*

was that the beginning? the first tangible beginning of it? good friday nineteen ninety-three the ewes of easter in the green on mountains and in dales waiting for the dropping of the lambs the distant singing of sheep in the night while the flock increases silently and in the mornings the first twins of april are standing knee-deep in the pasture in the beneficent oats stand on first legs in the underground clover stand on tiny amber paws under a mizzle under a general muzzle of blessing muzzle of bounty huddled against the slopes of hills stand tottering along with the cranes in the vleis and what is it that pricks in my fingers? i stammer i think with being undone in the lambing time it is autumn the leaves are falling but this time it is different as if i am big with something or sick with that melancholy that sickness insinuates before it like a foot my foot is heavy i falter my hand is heavy all of my right side with my lips i want to say easter agaat it's easter the year of our lord ninety-three let us bake a cake an easter cake in honour of the lambing time yolk and white I separate

the eggs and seven fall seven eggs on the ground a general egg-fall I am
unhandy senile a sign of the times a melancholy of the eastertide you
break the eggs gaat let me sit at the edge of the table so that i can slice
jewels for the king's crown the pineapple the cherries and the figs red
and green and yellow the jewels and shards of angelica.

*

4 July 1960 ten o'clock morning
Specially went into town heavy of body as I am to go & arrange A.'s
savings book at the post office spotted my chance when the coast was
clear & put hr baptism certificate & hr inoculation records polio &
diphtheria & pox in a velvet drawstring-bag & went & tucked it in
under hr underclothes in the top shelf of hr wardrobe.

Checked everything once again more nobody could do & more would
be wrong. J. perhaps right on this how would I know. A. mustn't at this
stage get accustomed to more he says then you just get trouble later A.
will never make trouble I say J. says it's not she it's the other workers
who'll make the trouble because she has privileges that they don't have.
I ask how? you never know the country is restless the kffrs are already
growing very brazen in the North & he doesn't want to see a bunch
of brazen htnts in the South it will be a horse of a different colour we
don't want to prepare a Sharpeville for ourselves here in the Overberg
he says. I say the undrprvlgd we will always have with us. It's no use our
blinding ourselves to their need.

Beatrice is coming over to tea. Time rests too heavily on her hands the
woman. Can't she understand I'm busy? Truly don't feel like sanctimonious prattle.

After lunch
This morning a long time in the outside room. Checked everything
again if I hadn't forgotten something.

Seven bloomers maybe two more? in case of accident & then had a
thought spread undersheet & remade the bed remember how copiously
one can bleed when you're young.

Curtain in front of the clothes rail doesn't pull nice & smoothly over the
steel wire rubbed with candlewax so that rings don't make the scraping

sound put the candlewax on shelf above wash-table so that A. can re-do it will wear off quickly curtain will just have to be closed always. I had to stop Jak he actually wanted to nail shut the window says he doesn't want to be confronted with a servant-girl's bed every time he comes out of the kitchen door it's not a good idea either that the other workers see how luxuriously A. has it here with the whitefolk.

Rather said nothing about its being my plan for a long time to build new houses for the workers. First for Dawid & them the hovel in which they live is still from Ma's time & the walls crumbling badly roof leaks & and there's a whole string of little ones as well from Dawid's cousins who materialised suddenly. Everything gradually D. will just have to make a plan himself in the meantime will give a few sheets of corrugated iron frm the shearers' cooking huts. Don't know what when they come again next season sufficient unto the day.

Now everybody must first just get used to the situation with A. in the backyard.

Before supper
Strange feeling can't stop writing about the outside room I keep on thinking of something else to add. This mrning I opened the Zion bible on the crate next to the bed & then had another thought & went & fetched the crocheted bookmark from Ma from my Bible placed it in Psm 23 the Lord is my shepherd I shall not want.

Can't stop scrabbling around there just like a broody hen really. Put a twig of fennel in the little vase then the smell suddenly made me cry must be the hormones that are mixed up. Tears idle tears I know not what they mean.

Rinsed the kettle & boiled a bit of water on the two-plate stove. Suddenly felt I wanted to have a cup of tea there. Wanted to test A.'s mug & taste the rusks I baked I made the rooibos sweet as she would like it & dunked the rusk good batch nice rich buttermilk. Tin mug too hot to hold burnt my fingers waited for it to cool & took all A.'s other reading matter out of the crate where I had put it away & so read the introduction by Her Honour Mrs Dr Verwoerd in the embroidery book & must say was really quite inspiring: The book conceived in love for the development of the nation & the homely atmosphere that embroidery creates because it's the mark of a culturally conscious nation underlined the words & wrote in the front: May this book provide you with much pleasure yet in the empty hours on Gdrift. It looks so dry but what else could I say? Then had another idea. Went inside & got a pencil & knife to sharpen it & empty notebook from J.'s office wrote in capitals on the cover: My own Patterns and Designs had to press hard because the cover was of glossy paper & the pencil wouldn't bite properly & then put away the embroidery book again in the crate with the notebook on top.

The old FAK Songbook cheered me up a bit. Softly so that nobody could hear me I sat there in the back & sang songs to myself. The bridge on our farm. On the death of an owl. On my old tin guitar. By the old millstream. Will it give her comfort too? The idea that she will sit on her own in the back & sing. So then I put the songbook away again because then I just wanted to cry again.

So then I drank the sweet tea & read the chapter on hides in the old Handbook for farmers the removal of hair in bran & in manure & braying of the thongs till dressed & the cawr snow-white ('core'? old book = full of funny words & spelling mistakes must point them out to A.) & tanning of small & large hides with vitriol & barkbush. Methods that few people know about nowadays.

Pa taught me the importance of this old knowledge he said the wheel always turns my child there will be a time again of poverty & need & the farmer who doesn't know about the old ways then will be gone to glory & then there I sat crying over Pa's underlinings in the parts about the deterioration of the veld in our country & the exhaustion & ill-treatment of the soil. That is what A. must also learn the old ways & the care of the defenceless earth, the little pans & the vleis & the 'tor-tisses' & how we must protect it all against the onslaughts of so-called civilisation because how many centuries does it not take for mother-rock to crumble & disintegrate to soil & then humans come along & destroy it through avarice & carelessness.

J. is actually the one who should be reading it all but it's not as if he takes any notice of me also laughed that time when I said I wasn't selling the donkeys that mother kept what is a farm without a donkey. If the plough broke or the tractor wouldn't go in those first years & the parts couldn't arrive immediately from town then one could carry on with the animals & hand-plough so that one didn't fall behindhand too much with the work. Then one regained some respect for the blood-sweat with which Gdrift was carved out of the earth.

Underlined in pencil for A. the sentence in the Foreword that says that the Handbook will help the farmer in his material growth just as the Bible helps him in his spiritual growth & then I lay down on her bed because I was suddenly very tired & closed my eyes & prayed for my child who has to be born into this world. Must have dropped off for a while because next thing I saw a broad strip of sunlight was slanting over the linoleum. Inside the lunch was already being brought to the table J. was at the table & he frowned when he saw me & pointed at my forehead with his fork if it wasn't one of A.'s caps that I'd tried on there in her room in front of her mirror so light it is you don't even know you're wearing it. What is that? asked J. is that your mothering-bonnet? Fortunately I could take it off before Somebody Else saw it.

4

Agaat stirs on her bed in the passage. I see the first glimmering through a chink in the curtain. It's five o'clock on the phosphorescent hands of the alarm clock on the night-table.

Agaat doesn't need an alarm. Every morning just before the grandfather clock chimes the hour, she awakens. By then I have been lying awake for a long time. Sometimes I pretend to be sleeping so that she can sing. Gaat sings me awake.

There's only one creak as she sits up on the camp stretcher. While the chimes echo in the front room, she doesn't budge. What could she be thinking of in between the five strokes? Would she be steeling herself there on her bed, looking down the dark passage with the first light falling from the rooms, from door frame to door frame? Would she be swiftly running through her schedule for the day? Praying perhaps? No, Agaat doesn't pray, she only prays on my behalf, she says, that will have to suffice.

At the beginning of winter she carried in the stretcher for the first time from the storeroom. Too flimsy for her to my mind, she's filled out these last few years. Since she's been looking after me she no longer works so much around the house and in the garden. Dig here, scrub there, I hear her handing out orders.

At night I don't hear her stir. She sleeps like a ramrod on that bier. I can see it before me. On her back with the hands on the chest. The sleep of the vigilant. Twice a night, once before midnight and once after, she comes and stands by my bed in the dark on bare feet. She is not officially awake. Nor am I, I pretend to be asleep. Sometimes of late she then goes out at the back and stays away for an hour or longer.

I don't hear her go into the back room. Where on earth would she roam?

There's the first stirring now. The stretcher creaks as she stretches to reach the switch of the passage light. She takes one gulp of water from her mug. The enamel krrts on the floor as she sets it down. Another creak as she swings her legs off the little bed. A swish as she puts on her housecoat over her nightdress. A squeak and a bang as she folds the stretcher, a shuffling as she slides it into the second broom-cupboard next to the bathroom.

She walks down the passage. Thud, thud, thud, go her bare feet on the boards. She unlocks the kitchen door, talks to the dogs, closes the lower door behind her again. The screen door squeaks, the screen door slams, seven paces, the outside room's door is opened, the lock, the bolt, the lower door that scuffs on the linoleum. Washing and dressing is what she's going to do. Use the bathroom in the house, I try to get through to her, but she pretends not to understand me.

Koffie and Boela make whimpering sounds. I hear them paw the lower door of the kitchen. She no longer allows them in my room. On Leroux's advice, she says.

I don't believe her. From the day that she started to read from the booklets, she forbade them here. As if she wanted to be the dog herself.

She cannot abide to see other life in my room.

Just as little as she can abide the idea of moving into the guest bedroom and to stay in the house decently with me. Why not? There's more than enough space here, I gesture, but there's no getting her to understand.

I miss the dogs. Always when they came galloping in here, I felt as if I was still somebody's owner. First with the front paws on the bed's edge, wet muzzles pressed in under my hands, smell of dog bodies in my nose, laughing mouths and panting breaths, a whole warm brown fur-covered life here over my white covers. With their wag-tails they whisked the air into life here in the room in the mornings. After a while they would calm down and settle on the little mat by the glass door next to Agaat's chair, and I would look at how their eyebrows twitched as they watched me for a while and how they at length would sigh and go to sleep. I could watch them like that until they started dreaming, till the hind legs started kick-kicking, and the little muscle started twitching in the forepaw and the lip started quivering with a muted growl. Chasing rabbits.

Now it's only Agaat's chair there in front of the glass door. There she sits and embroiders during the day if she has time, if she feels well-disposed towards me, and in the evenings until I fall asleep.

It's a big cloth. She's been working at it ever since I've not been able to move, all of eleven months. Started it a long time ago, it seems, because one side had already been thoroughly worked when she brought it in here the first time. I often signal with my eyes, let's have a look, but she pretends not to see. Now the first light darts through the chink in the curtain onto the embroidered cloth where she put it down on her chair. The decoration is dense and thick in white satin thread, an intricate combination of drawn stitch and shadow stitch. If I focus in a certain way, the strip on which the light falls looks like a band of white marble with convoluted detail sculpted in low relief.

She's made great strides with the embroidery, Agaat, she'd by now be able to add a few chapters to the embroidery book.

Quarter past five, it chimes. She's back in the kitchen where she put the kettle on on her way out, so that now she only has to add boiling water to the bag and the thickening agent. Here she is coming down the passage. First tray, set out last night, second quarter-hour of the day. Tea. Morning medicine.

With her smell of Lifebuoy and Mum and calamine she enters the room.

Praise the Lord, rise up rejoicing, she sings. She stops when she sees I'm already awake.

Her uniform crackles. Her cap shines like a beacon. She is wearing a clean white housecoat with short sleeves, over that a white crocheted jersey. I can smell the cold-water Omo. The apron is stiff with starch. Her rubber soles sough as she tacks about my bed.

She cranks me up, she pummels my pillows, she hoists my neck out of my body, she props up my head, she arrays me.

Wake and shake, make and take, she says.

She comes with a wet lukewarm sponge and wipes out my mouth.

Mole from the mouth, she says.

She unfastens the nappy between my legs, puts it aside in a bundle and slides the number one pan in under me.

She puts on my bib.

She clamps the jug with the long spout and the little tube to the railing of the bed. She bends the drip-stem with the mouthpiece so that it's suspended above my lips. She adjusts the drip-hole. She puts the mouthpiece into my mouth.

Ten counts between each swallow, she says. Ready steady go!

She eases open the valve. The first drop of warm thickened liquid spreads over my tongue. Rooibos. One mouthful tea and one mouthful breath and count to ten, says Agaat, think of the undrprvlgd.

A mouthful of consonants. Lest I forget what I wrote.

I do my best. Half runs down my chin.

She watches me closely while she prepares everything. She tucks the bib in further under my chin. She wipes my chin. I get hold of the rhythm. I am thirsty. I count to ten. I swallow. I count ten tens and ingest ten mouthfuls, a quarter-mouth at a time. This cup.

Agaat fills the plastic basin with hot water from the kettle that she's brought with her from the kitchen. She arranges the towels, the wash-cloths, the soap and the sponges, everything neatly on the large hospital trolley that Leroux carted in here.

I drink three more tens.

Drinking merrily she is this morning, says Agaat. Have you peed yet, Ounooi?

I signal, no, you can see for yourself the nappy is dry. She doesn't look.

I'm asking, have you peed yet?

Now she looks. I signal again no, I have not and don't be so crude so early in the morning.

Well go on pee, Ounooi, I haven't got all day.

Don't look at me, I gesture, look in the other direction.

Agaat makes little whistling sounds between her teeth to encourage me.

It won't come.

I hear nothing, she says. She puts her hand behind her ear.

Is the little tap stuck this morning, hmmm? Well, perhaps you can't drink and pee at the same time. Let's close the tap up here, then maybe the one down there will open.

She keeps her face straight. She closes the tea drip and takes the spout out of my mouth. Her rubber soles suck noisily at the floor, it sounds as if there's extra torque, extra weight in her tread. I recognise it. That's what she does when she discovers she can't make me. She turns her back on me. I know what she's going to do. She swirls the water around in the washbasin. She wrings out the cloth to make it drip in the water. Still nothing. I know she's listening. Her ears point backwards. She takes a glass, she pours the water, over and over, from a height.

I try to think of something else. My bladder is full. I want to. I didn't want to in the nappy, else there would have been all manner of com-mentary. And I don't want to make extra problems, I don't want to distract her.

Pee and tea is not the problem. Agaat is the problem. She acts stupid. It's been five days now that I've been gesturing there is something, there in the front of the house, in the sideboard, in the front room, with the photo albums.

She doesn't like the idea that I want to take leave. Perhaps I can kill two birds with one stone. Perhaps telepathy works better through piss in the pan than transmitted in waves through the air into the rock-hard skull of Agaat.

Streams of grace abounding, Agaat sings, flow from God above, sacred source of freshness, that was pledged by His love.

I think of the water map. I think of the underground water-chambers in the mountain, of the veins branching from them, of the springs in the kloofs, of the fountains of Grootmoedersdrift, the waterfalls in the crevices. I think of the drift when it's in flood, the foaming mass of water, the drift in the rain, when the drops drip silver ringlets on the dark water. And just after it's cleared, when the black-wattle branches sag heavy and sodden over the ditch and the frogs clamour in the drenched grass-thickets on the bank. Memories in me and I awash between heaven and earth. What is fixed and where? What real? If only I could once again see the places marked on the map, the red brackets denoting gates, cattle-grids, sluices, the red is-equal-to sign of the bridge over the drift, first and last gateway over which the livestock of Grootmoedersdrift move and will continue moving when I am gone. Sheep, cattle, cars, lorries, wire cars, mud and time. Slippery, supple, subtle, silvery time.

Maps attend lifetimes. What is an age without maps? I see it, chambers full of idle melancholy cartographers in the timeless hereafter. Hills there surely will have to be in heaven, but eternal, Eternal Humpbacked Hills, and Eternal Fairweather. Idle melancholy meteorologists. What is a real human being? A run-off. A chute of minutes for God the sluicer. He who paves his guttering with people.

Perhaps I've been infected by Agaat. She's blasphemed for a long time.

It's coming. Here it comes, through my blessed piss-sphincter, first passing of the day.

Good girl, says Agaat. You don't perhaps want the number two pan as well, seeing that you're in the swing of things now? Lesson six, remember? You don't want dung and piss all over everything if you can help it.

Quite right, I flicker, but I'm not a slaughter animal.

She flickers back.

Otherwise we'll have no choice but to dose you with a Pink Lady again, she says, a Pink Lady for the lady of Gdrift, it's five days now that her guts have been stuck. Perhaps that's what's making her so restless. What goes in must come out, after all, good heavens!

Take away the pan, I gesture.

No, you first drip-dry nicely now. Then we fix up your uppers first.

It's a quarter-body wash this morning. Half-wash is every second day and full wash every fourth day. A lick and a promise, Agaat calls the quarter-wash.

She wipes my neck and face with a lukewarm cloth. Then my chest. She works in the cloth under my hospital gown, over my shoulders. She brushes my hair with a dry shampoo. She supports my head with the little hand, so that it doesn't loll or roll. She rubs cream on my face and ointment in the corners of my mouth. Now the neckbrace. Krrts, karrrts, she rips loose and refastens the Velcro until it's seated properly. It expands all the time. My neck feels loose.

She brings the hand mirror closer. I close my eyes. Take away your mirror. We haven't looked in the mirror for a long time. I recognise the mood. She wants to torment me. She's quite capable of digging up the lipstick and mascara from somewhere again.

Mirror, mirror, on the wall, says Agaat, who's the fairest of them all?

I keep my eyes shut. My face flushes hot with defying her. I refuse to look, I wait until she moves away. I hear her adding water to the wash-basin. She pulls out the pan from under me. I hear her walk away with it. I peep from the corner of my eye to see what she's doing. She puts on her glasses, examines the contents in front of the window. She puts it down on the trestle table, covers it with a cloth. She writes on the calendar with the pencil suspended there on a string, Leroux's urine record that he wants to see every time he visits me. My logbook. The motions of my entrances and my exits. Today Agaat looks into the pan again and again as if it contained a message. She takes her magnifying glass out of the dressing table drawer. She peers through it and she writes and she looks again. Augur of my elements, who will prevent her from prognosticating my piss? Perhaps it contains tadpoles.

Quite satisfactory under the circumstances, says Agaat, a slight little cloudiness, but nothing to fret about.

She pages the calendar back, taps on it once before she replaces it in the hole for November. She replaces the magnifying glass in the drawer. Ting, go the dressing table's swing-handles as she slams shut the drawer with her thigh. She knows I'm peeping at her.

She throws off my covers. She wrings out the washcloth, gives me one quick wipe between the legs. It's too hot. She knows very well it's too hot.

I keep my eyes shut.

Pees like a mare, says Agaat, nothing wrong with the pee.

I wait for her to cover me again, I'm cold.

She waits for me to take the bait.

A pretty light yellow. Clear except for the little trail. And not at all over-sharp on the nose, she says, just about perfect pee.

What can I reply to that? What acrobatics of eyelids to convey: Your sarcasm is wasted on me. If I could die to deliver you, I would do so, today. Go and find somebody else to pee perfection for you on command. You're the one who wants to be perfect. You want me to be perfect. We must not be lacking in any respect. If you can do without, I must be able to do without, that's what you think.

A perfect nurse. A perfect patient.

As I taught you.

According to the book.

What more can anybody expect? you think. And what sticks in your gullet is my surplus neediness, and that you no longer know who I am, and that I've changed, that I'm still, every day that I lie here, changing. And that I require something specific from you.

I open my eyes. She's standing next to my bed with one hand folded into the other.

Everything's fine, Agaat, I signal, don't get so het up about nothing, I'm as contented as a little snail in a salad.

But that's too easy. She's not looking for an easy victory. She wants to see me angry. She wants to see insurrection. She wants to see what insurrection looks like in the spine of a paraplegic. In my chest I feel a sigh. I have too little breath to sigh. A groan escapes me. I feel tears. I hold them back, but it's too late, she's already caught me at it.

Time for your exercises, she says, the chin jutting out. Nothing like movement to lift the spirits, she says, and to get those old guts of yours going.

Your arse, I signal.

Seize the day, says Agaat. She opens the curtains, light streams into the room.

The bedclothes are all pulled off the bed, yanked out at the foot-end, the mattress quakes under me, the bedsocks are stripped off my feet.

No, I gesture, please not now, I'm tired. I close my eyes again, slowly. Last defence, play dead, play at aestivation. Wild pea.

Tired, what's with tired! Doctor's orders are doctor's orders! says Agaat.

Cunt.

Hey! says Agaat, such language! Come now, pat-a-cake, pat-a-cake.

She bends over me and picks my arms up by the wrists and moves my hands in a slow applauding motion.

One, two, three, one, two, three, we greet, we greet, the mighty sun! Nice deep breaths, she says.

She brings my wrists next to my sides, suddenly drops them.

Oops, she says.

She's at the foot of the bed. Fast. This is still just warming-up. She presses her fists against the undersides of my feet in a kneading motion, a mimic of pedals under my soles. One pedal is weaker than the other.

Busy little feet, she says.

Stop it, stop it, stop it!

Any complaints so far, Mrs de Wet? She doesn't look up from my feet.

She moves around quickly to the side of the bed, faces me head-on. Her voice a parody of gentle persuasion.

You get sore, you get stiff, your blood doesn't flow properly, you get cold, your feet get blue, look how blue they are already, you get constipated, your general condition deteriorates if you won't allow me to exercise you.

Allow, I say with my eyes, allow!

She grabs one arm by the wrist, straightens the elbow with the little hand. Wide circular movements she makes, first one way round and then the other way round.

Windmill in the south-east, she says, windmill in the north-west. Ickshee, ickshee, ickshee. Water in the dam, mud in the ditch, step on her head, dirty rotten bitch.

My arm terminating in its stiff claw swings through the air. Agaat is breathing faster, her eyes are shining.

Now bend, she says. She works the elbow joint.

Knick knack knick, she says, bend the tree, snap the stick.

My other arm is a lighthouse tower. It sweeps over wild waves. Agaat blows the horn. Two bass notes.

What do you say, Missis? We're having fun, aren't we? Now we're giving this old body of yours a run for its money.

My bonnie lies over the ocean, she sings, my bonnie lies over the sea.

Agaat's colour is high. Her breath comes panting. I catch her eye.

Agaat, you're hurting me!

Just don't be touchy, she says.

Slowly, I flicker, slowly with what's left of me.

Shuddup, now the legs, says Agaat, but no sound comes from her, only her lips move.

Giddy-up, Shanks' pony, she says aloud, and with my legs she forms an angle of ninety degrees above my torso. She bends my dangling feet up and down.

Her feet are going east, she sings, but she is going west.

Agaat plants corner posts. She puts them into holes. She hammers them in with a ten-pound mallet. She anchors them with braces, she paints them silver, she hangs the droppers. I smell tar. She sets up the drawbar. She tightens the wire till it sings. My ankles, my toes.

We have take-off, she says as she propellers them in her hands.

And now, she says, now to rise above this earthly vale of tears. Nourish also our souls with the bread of life, oh Lord.

She gathers me, the little arm under the backs of my legs, the strong arm under my arms.

Dough, dough, she says, rise for us. Hup! she says and lifts me, almost lifts me up, off the bed.

Kneaded well, waited long, she says, hup once more.

Shake out the raisins, she says, shake them out, God-hup helpyou!

I bounce slightly on the bed as she lets go of me.

She stands back. Arms akimbo. Her chest rises and falls.

Lighter by the day, she says.

She extends the little hand to me. With her strong hand she extracts the stunted little finger from the bundle of fingers of her crippled hand. She keeps the little finger apart between thumb and index finger, in the air before my nose.

Soon, she says, soon I'll lift you with my little finger.

*

The first seven years on Grootmoedersdrift. Every day of the month you adjusted yourself again. Took iron pills and ate radishes. Prayed and spread your legs for Jak.

During the day you worked yourself silly on the farm. Tennis elbow from cutting silage, wrist infections from helping with the milking, cramps in your calves from walking the contours on the steep slopes with the surveyor day after day. In the evenings you had to lie in the bath for hours on end with the mustard extracts that Ma had given you.

Why do you drudge yourself like that? Jak asked, you're not a bloody slave!

He was furious when you were ill. You could feel it in the body that he rammed into you.

Modern appliances are the answer, Milla, he said, these aren't the Middle Ages any more. Why churn on with lucerne and lupins and compost when there's fertiliser?

It's all about synergies, Jak, you tried to staunch the flow, a game one has to play. With nature. It's subtle. Nature is subtle and complex.

Everything is important. To the smallest insect, even the mouldering tree, the deepest stone in the drift.

The deepest stone in the drift. That made you cry.

You're a fine one to talk! Jak scolded. Subtle! Bah! Nature! And you can't get pregnant!

I'll go for tests, you sniffed, for treatment, there are modern aids. For men too.

Was that when Jak conceived his strange theories about you?

Over my dead body, he said, there's nothing wrong with me. Nor with you. It's in your head something is wrong. It's because you wear yourself out like that, he said, just stop bawling, then things will come right, it's because you complain about everything, because you flap about here on the farm with a long face. Where is the loving gentle Milla that I married? Look at you, pale as pale, as if you're anaemic.

He thought you were putting it on when you said you were tired. Invited Beatrice and Thys in the evenings on purpose so that you should have to go and get dressed and made up.

Just see how much life there still is in her after a day's toil, a real never-say-die, my little Kamilla.

And then he winked at you, and rubbed it in even further.

Just a short while ago she was hanging from a branch, furled like a bat, dead-tired, now she's chattering like a finch. Goes to show what good friends mean to you here in the Overberg.

You saw Beatrice looking from him to you and back again. I'm here if you need me, she'd already whispered to you a few times, but you resisted her. She was more inquisitive than anything else. And greedy. For power, for status. Constantly comparing her husband's position in the community with Jak's. And the gossip over who was, was going to be or wanted to be chairman of this or treasurer of that. Mud-slinging. Jealousy. The secession of the Swellendam members of the National Party from the Bredasdorp branch was the latest, and how she'd had tea with the wife of Van Eeden, the new chairman. You in your own terms were not an item. Barren. Dry ewe. You felt that everybody was against you. Jak was starting to sound like your mother when he provoked you. And the gossips were agog for news from Grootmoedersdrift, for reasons, for scandal.

Ma was concerned on the one hand, but also critical of your childless condition. You could hear it in her voice on the telephone, sometimes sneering, you thought. Even so you phoned her every evening. With who else could you talk about it? She recommended traditional remedies. Like standing on your head afterwards, like drinking an infusion of stinging nettle.

Some evenings you couldn't stop crying after putting down the phone. This infuriated Jak.

That mother of yours, he said, a violent tea cosy if ever there was one, cosy on top and down below she latches her claws into you.

Then you really cried. Jak was right. It wasn't about what you could or couldn't do. It was yourself, something in you that offended her. Your character.

I am who I am, how can I help it? you sobbed.

Jak slammed doors and stormed out of the house and drove off when you were like that.

Just don't leave me alone, you pleaded.

You tried everything to prevent him from going. Played on his feelings, flattered him, nestled up against him.

Get out, out of my guts! he pushed you away, for heaven's sake go and blow your nose!

But you knew that if he got rough enough with you, you could keep him with you. Then at least he was involved. You learnt to use his anger, the energy of it. It was less than nothing.

A smack in the face, a blow on the back.

Billing and cooing on Grootmoedersdrift.

You couldn't stop crying about it all. Am I then never allowed to feel weak? you asked, but that only infuriated him further.

It went quickly. Two, three years. You no longer guided his hand over your body to teach him how to touch you. You were after something else. You bent your head and sucked him off and caught his semen in your hand and tried to inseminate yourself.

His preference in any case. I don't want to see your face when you're so miserable, he said. Often he didn't even notice that you were crying.

You prayed every time that you would take, made pictures in your head of cells simultaneously shooting, a comet shower, a cataclysm, a fusion.

Why can the animals manage it so easily? Am I of the wrong nature, then? Comfort me then, just hold me, you pleaded at times.

But if he didn't put a cushion over his head and turn his back on you, he took his blanket and went to sleep in the stoep room.

Weekends and holidays were worst, and the quiet times on the farm between seasons. Because then he wanted to go mountain-climbing or running or rowing, or to read his books by Ian Fleming and Louis L'Amour, always as far away as possible from you. You had to think up things to keep him on the farm. Painting, a new silage tower, large-scale yard clearance, the big compost project with the adjacent farms.

You saw to it that other people came to inspect the work at the most dramatic moment. When a project had just been completed, you arranged parties, lunches for the neighbours, agriculture days with information sessions for the members of the farmers' associations.

Then Jak beamed in the glow of all the attention, his best foot well forward.

Let's redesign the garden, you said, there's nothing that makes a homestead look as attractive as a garden. You haven't forgotten, have you, that you promised it to me, my paradise?

Don't think I can't see through you, he said, you're more wily than the snake. That's the only bit of paradise that there'll ever be on this farm.

You thought, if we can't be lovers, let us then at least be friends. Friends can learn to differ, even over paradise. But he was forever wanting away, to other people.

You tried to console yourself with work. When there was plenty of pressure on the farm, things that had to be done urgently and accurately, you were at your happiest. You liked working with people in a team, according to a fixed plan, with a predictable outcome, with a view to the long term. That's the only way a farm can work, you'd learnt from your mother.

We can buy you an American saddle horse if the wool price is good, you said to Jak, or a new car if we sell the new Jersey heifers.

If you rewarded him, he helped you well at times. But simply to ask him for something, that wouldn't do.

Why must I always hold your little hand in everything that you want done? After all, you're the real farmer here, or so you'd have me believe.

It took you a long time to accept that if you wanted things done on the farm, you would have to think it all up yourself. And that you should turn to OuKarel and his son to help you take things in hand and make a start. They looked at each other and OuKarel wordlessly signalled to Dawid: Do as you're asked to do. That Jak did not like. If he saw that they were helping you, he would make a show of lending a hand for a while. They soon discovered what was going on, pressed him for more pay.

They'd lost their sharecrop, was OuKarel's argument, how was he supposed to support his dependants? Not that you knew who exactly he meant, he'd been a widower for most of his life, and Dawid was to all appearances a loner, but as Jak with time succumbed to the pressure and restored half of the Okkenels' status by making them foremen on Grootmoedersdrift, the dependants came and presented themselves: OuKarel's second cousins and their wives and children who couldn't all live off the carpentry business that his brothers ran in Suurbraak. A never-ending influx it was. The houses were over-full, but Jak refused to build on and forbade them to construct shacks.

Do you want the whole mongrel rabble with their so-called Scottish surnames and mission-station affectations here on your front stoep, Milla? Over my dead body, he said, enough is enough.

You tried to keep the peace by seeing to it that enough bags of flour and pails of milk found their way over the drift to the labourers' cottages. And you tried to establish goodwill by regularly going to buy a chair or a little table from the family business in Suurbraak. The five Okkenel brothers, all of them like OuKarel with the high brow and the green eyes and the sharp nose, looked at you with shrewd understanding and knew just how to fix a price that accorded with your feelings of guilt. With the passing of time you realised that it had been a mistake to abolish the sharecropping. It was their only source of capital for buying good timber for furniture and there was enough wheat left after they'd sold the surplus to supply the whole clan with bread flour.

Jak would not hear of reinstating a sharing. He dreamed of a completely mechanised farm that would require only one or two pairs of hands.

There was never a contract, he said, your mother kept the people here for her own convenience, we are under no obligation. The fewer of them the better.

You were ashamed of the attitude. Where were the people to go? It was their land as well, after all, their place, and they also had to work and eat.

Why did you keep your mouth shut, Milla? What were you scared of? Why could you never think that there were other possibilities? And Jak, why did you tolerate his bluntness and his selfishness and his vanity? You were bemused at the time by the short stories you read in the magazines. The heroine who exclaims with flushed cheeks: Now I've had enough, now I'm leaving you! Otherwise not a single magazine would sell hereabouts, you thought. But you thought no further.

You tried to assess other wives' husbands dispassionately and you couldn't really see that you were in a worse position. Jak was still the most attractive and the most intelligent of the lot. Not one of the women you knew was 'fulfilled', as they said. You could see that in their faces. But they were unshakeably loyal. It was Basie this and Fanie that and Thys came first clap your hands. Especially those in your circle of friends. And yet everyone was always starved for company. Always somebody who wanted to listen. Not one of the women you knew of who didn't get lonely on a hill-farm. Not that the exchange of commonplaces could keep you going.

For a few months at a time you could keep a reading group going, or a music-appreciation group, but the women sat taciturn in your sitting room. As if the music of Schubert and Brahms and Mahler embarrassed them. Bach was acceptable. Sounded sufficiently like church. The books that you lent them they returned unread to the half-moon table in the hall and for the rest spoke of patchwork and complained about their servants who stole soap.

What failed most miserably was the walking club for amateur botanists that you tried to get going. You didn't know all that much yourself, but you'd inherited your father's books on trees and fynbos and as child had learnt the first principles of plant identification at his knee. But after you'd invaded the foothills a few times with the little ladies, stumbling along in their Sunday-best shoes, and their dresses that snagged on everything, and the anxious out-of-breath countenances solely concerned about what they had to serve their husbands for supper, you gave it up. You were not like them, you thought, you'd been born to more adventurous ways.

But you lost the way the first seven years on Grootmoedersdrift, and the loneliness started getting you down.

Your mother was a last resort when you were too lonely.

Then take me to Barrydale, you said when Jak wanted to go away on his expeditions on public holidays or for long weekends after lambing time or sowing-time.

Not that you really wanted to be with her all that badly, because her you could never satisfy. She was even worse after Pa's death. She set snares for you, to test you, you felt. The quarrels were even more intense than at home with Jak. Against your mother you had no defence.

That was the summer of '53. Ma had problems with her workers on the farm. She made you feel you had to find a solution. You accepted the challenge, wanted for a change to show her one needn't be a victim of circumstance, needn't allow other people to become victims.

You're making a bed for yourself, is what she said, when she heard what you wanted to do. You're meddling with things you'll never hear the end of.

You were standing in the pantry, 16 December 1953, you wanted to take food to the workers' huts. You were standing with a cooked leg of lamb in your hand which you wanted to pack to take to the people.

What on God's earth are you doing now? she inveighed. Are you trying to bribe them? and then I'll be left with the mess when you've left.

That was the last straw. You started shouting at her.

So what will ever be right and good for you, Ma? I thought you wanted me to help you, I thought I had to help your people here, on your behalf? What do you want me to do then? I want to give you the best I have, my faith, my ingenuity, my love, my courage, the best years of my life, and you're still not satisfied? Why can I never be good enough for you?

You were so beside yourself, you could have sunk your teeth into the meat and torn it apart, but you only lifted it up in your hands. This is my body, you thought. You dropped it at her feet. She folded her arms and looked at the meat on the ground.

Or do you want to take me apart and reshape me over and over again until I am to your satisfaction, to a T? Will I be right then?

You're wasting food, she said.

She turned her back on you. You were incensed. You took a step backwards.

Then it rose up in you. You started saying it. You could not stop. She turned round when she heard the new tone. You spoke quietly, to her face.

Or is your problem that you don't know exactly how you want me, Ma? Is that your real problem? Because there is no image on which you can base me? Because there is only a hole there where you are, a silent hole in the ground? Well, I am something, Ma, you hissed, I am not nothing, I am somebody and I know what I want from life and I know what to do to get it. I will provide for myself.

That was the only time in your life you'd ever seen her scared. Her pupils dilated and her mouth gaped, but she said nothing. You pushed past her. It was she who was left on her own in the pantry.

That was the first and the only time. After that she was different with you until her death.

I wash my hands of you, she came to tell you later that evening at your bedroom door. Just that, and closed her bedroom door.

You were alone with the plan which would change your life.

The whole story of how it all started, nobody knew except you and Ma. Not even you yourself understood it very well. All your life you've wanted to record it, just for yourself, to try to gain some clarity. But you never got round to it. It was a skipped chapter. You couldn't bring yourself to do it.

*

threshold kerbstone step do they brood over these barricades dally dawdle halt camouflage the tread the stumble-step nightly from window to bed the foot that falters on the fringes of carpets the bump in the garden path how did it begin? was it all the comings and goings

of my years right over the pebble in the shoe right over the heel-wart
regardless of the toenail growing in was it the hot sand? that running
with one sandal? that lunging-after and catching by the neck of the
white-foot hare? was that where the germ entered my heel the iron
around my ankle the black pound-weight swinging from the bridge
of my foot? foot that drags foot that hangs foot that sleeps and every-
where that milla went the lamb was sure to go.

*

12 July 1960 8 o'clock (after supper)

What a day! Half restless. I have a sense that I'm forgetting something,
but what? Have just gone and peeked if the light in the outside room
is off yet, but it's still burning. Jak says it's the first time he's heard of
a skivvy's room with electricity is this my interpretation of the Light
we're supposed bring to the Southern Tip of Africa. Simply put my foot
down. She has to be able to see to read & to embroider how else is she
supposed to occupy hrself in the back there in the evenings? J. looks at
me as if I'm off my trolley.

The door is still open a crack as I left it behind me I suppose she's drinking hr tea I suppose it's all very new for her perhaps she's washing hr
clothes. Don't know how she'll get the blood out of the white jersey.

Honestly thought it would be good if she could work herself to a standstill before moving into hr room. Went this morning & put the brown
suitcase with hr possessions on the half-shelf under her little table. Was
at first tempted to surprise her & to unpack everything for hr like fairy
godmother but had second thoughts. She has to be independent. In any
case you have to find your own bearings in a new place perhaps she'll see
for herself now that hr old things don't go with hr new things & perhaps
she won't even unpack them & forget all about them that will be best.

And I must also forget. Otherwise I'll go mad. Or get sick. Can't afford
it now with the child in me.

Took the precaution yesterday of devising a whole list of things to be
done today so that she can stay busy one shouldn't have too much
time to think on a day like this. First little routine chores with which to
warm hr up sweeping the stoep washing dishes doing laundry & ironing & folding & packing away then the sheep-slaughtering.

I imagine that with the child I won't have time to supervise personally. A. must become the slaughter-hand on Gdrift. Sent message to the cottages last night Dawid must teach her the basics & I'll stand by so that he can behave himself. Ten o'clock this morning he's standing in the kitchen door, no the slaughter animal has already been picked do I want to see it first he asks no I say tether the sheep in the shade & give water because I didn't want to go too far away from A. she was still ironing shirts & sheets in the spare room & I had to show her how you get the collar smooth without wrinkles & how you fold the sheets.

Everything went reasonably smoothly with the slaughtering except for myself who felt unwell later on at the slaughter-drain. D. & two helpers brought the sheep closer a well-set little wether still half lamb from the little camp of hanslammers that we had to cull. Take it by the ear I said to A. don't be timid she goes & takes the ear with the little hand & the wether stands & looks at her use your strong hand I say he'll jerk loose & right then the wether steps back violently I give A. the knife in hr good hand & I say hold her hand show the way next thing D. is all giggly from being so close to the girl's body & takes the wrong hand so the wether jerks its head & bleats & steps back & squitters a green splodge over D.'s shoes & against A.'s dress & her leg & the farmworkers roll around laughing & next thing the whole yard's littl'uns are there heyno shouts Dawid he doesn't know about this if it's going to work Mies.

A. is still too small for sheep-slaughtering. He must keep his mouth shut & she must learn everything I say she's clever.

First lesson of sheep-slaughtering I teach her the animal must eat nothing for 3 days so that the gut can be nice & clean & the last day you give bran that absorbs everything that could still be in the stomach & it washes out easily now with all the talking the little sheep was all wild but make it lie down hold it down I say. So D. ups & says usually I get hold of a little sheep like this from behind in the camp before he knows what's happening to him his throat is cut while he's still standing & thinking it's Christmas in the lucerne flowers then when you eat him his meat is sweet because he was never scared.

That's the second lesson I teach hr: sheep that get panicked before they're killed have bitter meat they secrete something from the adrenal with the fear so never dawdle with the killing so then they cast the sheep & held its neck over the edge of the cement furrow & the little wether struggled something terrible it can't carry on like this I thought now I count to three I said to A. her eyes bulging in the sockets come nearer says D. Oh come nearer oh all ye children of the Lord the kitchen-girls sing bend says D. to A. he grasps her hand in his & quickly they draw the blade over the wether's throat the blood spurts everywhere. A. stands back & the knife falls from her hand & rolls down the incline of the slaughtering-floor no-no-no I say you don't throw away your knife like that climb in there & take it out the workers kill themselves laughing there you are Arsgaat check that farmgirl they shout. Be quiet I say the dogs lick the blood from A.'s shoes she stands stock-still D. goes to pick up her knife & presses it into her hand. Saar comes with the white enamel basin the workers yell catch the blood eat the meat the wool is white the meat is sweet give over I scold it's hr first slaughtering-turn & then the little wether's eyes roll back in its head & its upper lip retracts & the ridges on the nose smooth out & the ears lie flat I show A. all the signs & right there the wether's body contracts into a lump & he gives an almighty kick against her shins all the hands let go & he lets fly another splodge all over her feet.

Take note of lesson 3: You don't let go of the feet too soon it's a convulsion kick it's a death-throe & the animal is half-dead but that hurts the most.

And there I see Jak standing hand in the side & watching the whole business. Now that looks prosperous to me Milla, he says: Butcher baker butler then you can make her head-girl over a hundred. If only he'd rather attend to his own business it's after all entirely at his insistence.

Have just gone to peek again if the outside room's light is switched off yet do hope everything works out right with hr there in the back I feel all the time as if I've forgotten something.

10 o'clock
Everything quiet windows shut tight back there must be sleeping I can't get the slaughtering out of my head after all it's just ordinary sheep-slaughtering. Why do I want to write up everything? Did I leave something undone? Didn't I teach her everything, step by step? Not easy but everybody must go through it the first time.

Lesson 4: Bleed well till empty otherwise the meat is spongy.

Lesson 5: hygiene. Provide a cloth & water you can't slaughter if you're covered in sheep manure look how the flies swarm. Bent down there heavy of body as I am & washed the sheep manure from her legs & shoes & next thing her knees start jerking fits fits yell the littl'uns be quiet I say no more from you or you don't get any lung.

I took her hand with the knife & I bent behind her & I started cutting open from the gash in the throat. Had some trouble with the sternum now you & D. carry on alone I say to A., & press the knife in her hand sing I say to D. so that she can take some strength sikketir sikketir sikketeat sings D. the lamb comes to the block with its wool & its meat sing along A. I say so that you can get some life but her mouth is a straight line & then suddenly she gets some life & she looks me a very straight look & she takes the knife.

Not to cut too deep I say here is lesson 6: We don't want dung & piss on everything & she cuts shallow & clean all along the belly-line really quite to my surprise.

Then D. took her two hands in his & he pulled the entrails loose & the whole heap of guts fell out & I felt sick & went into the house but I vomited & had done because we were right in the middle & I couldn't leave A. there alone, then they sorted the intestines so that she could see the dirty & the clean the pizzle & the bladder & the gall-bladder & the small intestine & the large intestine on one side & heartlungskidneysliver on the other. A.'s right sleeve by that time full of blood as if she'd been injured & I nauseous all the time & irritated with the circumstances & the spectators.

Lesson 7: The one place where you can soon find out whether a sheep is healthy is in the intestines. Look for worms in the gut & parasites in the lungs they must be nice & spongy & red & the liver soft & dark the right size like the fist of your right hand. Small & hard or waterlogged means there's something wrong with the heart quite probably with the whole sheep the heart is the blood's windmill I teach her if it doesn't cast the whole animal dries out.

Made A. touch everything & identify everything. Just after a while couldn't take the bloody sleeve dragging through everything any longer either you take off that jersey I say or we push that sleeve up but A. latches onto the bloody sleeve with her thumb. Dawid hangs the sheep under the bluegums from wire hooks in the heels so then A. can't reach. He brings an apple box no I say it's not strong enough cut longer hooks so then the kitchen-girls start singing oi oi oi five pigs in a heap, raise the girl or lower the sheep.

Shut your traps I say but they dance buttocks in the air all around A. her lip trembles & I say it's just kitchen-skivvies don't take any notice of them they're getting only head & guts & tonight you're having chops.

There the sheep is hanging cut off the head I say it's dripping on her feet. So then I see D. first cuts off the ear & pushes it into A.'s pocket without notches not marked yet for slaughter as we do with the hanslammers. Saw him say something to A. which I couldn't hear & I didn't want to ask in front of everybody (must beware of intimate contact between A. & the men-workers).

Then D. shows A. how she should loosen the skin & push away the meat from the membrane & I hold it & at first it's a struggle she cuts now too deep now too shallow. I say take your fist knead the skin loose from the membrane while you feed the blade & only then it improved a little the right fist in the white crocheted jersey a bloody stump looked as if it had been amputated but she persevered well even though it took three times longer than usual but then she knew all the cuts also from the neck to the loin & the groin & what one can best use it for, for braai, for roasting, for baking in the oven or for stewing.

Well done my little girl now you know meat. Next time we slaughter an ox you'll get to be the prime butcher here on Grootmoedersdrift I said we'll just have to think of something for that little arm of yours a butcher's sleeve.

5

Noon silence. The floorboards in the passage creak. Is it somebody standing by the telephone table, shifting weight from one leg to the other? Or studying a photograph on the wall, or hesitating, overtaken by a thought, an afterthought? To-ing and fro-ing? Pro-ing and conning? The floorboards creak of their own accord.

There is nobody there. These are the sounds of an old house.

My house can make more sounds than I.

Sometimes I imagine that I can hear footsteps, swiftly from the front to the back all the way through the house, a hurried, peremptory tread in the mornings. At night, in the afternoon hours between two and three, a laboured pace, a shuffling gait, a walking stick.

As if somewhere a recording has been made of all the times that I've walked in the passages and rooms of my house, as if it were now being played back to me on a worn audiotape, a record without clear information.

What must I make of it? What is the message? I was intended to be an upright animal? Intended to stretch my limbs, delimit four quarters in the air, a golden section, my reach the compass of my intentions? Created to swim, to walk, to climb, sufficiently sanguine to attempt flight?

Here I lie. Drawn and quartered would be preferable.

Sometimes there's a knocking on the rooftop, once, twice, thrice, four times, loudly as the roof beams contract in the night. Then I wake up and wonder who has arrived.

Who wants to come in? I want to cry out, who is there?

But there's nobody there. When Agaat leaves me alone, like today, I am nobody. Between me and me no fissure of differentiation.

In the mornings when the roof beams heat up, there's a tick-ticking above my head for an hour. As if there's a pacemaker wanting to help me think, an apprehension that on my own I cannot shape into thought.

I am less than a roof.

I am a gutter.

I hear, sometimes, a rustling in the door frames. Woodborer it must be, mice perhaps, or cockroaches. Gnawings sifting down between the wood and the wall, mice probably, insects.

I should be able to impress upon Agaat to bring me a cockroach in a bottle so that I can see it scampering with its grey flat body, scrabbling with its feet against the glass. She'd find mirth in my envy of a cockroach.

My bed in which I'm tilted, makes my weight palpable to myself. My loose weight inside my fixed weight. Each time I can feel my intestines welter inside me. My heart in a basket, my guts a roll of chewing-tobacco tumbling about inside a crate. That's all she's done for me today. Came here to tilt me. Without a word.

My meat is unfairly distributed over my bones. The weight of my skeleton is my only honesty. My meat makes me cry.

I see the contours of my feet under the cover. My feet are logs. The tension has deserted my toes. My feet look like knees, my knees look like wodges, like half-loaves, my hip-bones form ridges and in-between is a basin. My chest inclines towards me, on either side of my breastbone there's been nothing but folds of skin for a long time now. I remember the weight of my breasts, the shadow of my breasts.

Now light plays around me, a clod in a field, a shallow contour. It gradates itself over my heights and depressions, a crafty modeller. The cover is white, the shadows blue. The light sketches the railings of my bed around me like a barred cage. I am a skeleton within a skeleton, a crate in a truck, but I still have time, in me is my time, my wasting flesh preserves my time within me.

One should consist entirely of bone when the dying starts. But an animated skeleton. A skull full of flashes, a hand that hinges like a railway signal. One gesture must be granted you over the creatures that are permitted to die in innocence. And then you have to step back into line.

Darknesses slip along the skirting boards, light rings out over the floorboards, over the chrome, over the piles of white linen, over the jars and tubes and cloths. Stipples and stripes and spots. What is the time? I don't want to know. In the front room the grandfather clock ticks.

My room limns itself from hour to hour, completes itself every day. My room is a perverse painter. I am the still-life. The fold in the cloth, the turned-open book.

I page myself to the outside. The sounds of the last harvest come to inscribe themselves in me.

It must be just before afternoon, time to unload the morning's harvest and to make repairs and to draw breath, to rinse the itchy chaff and the straw from the eyes. The combine harvester that went out this morning comes droning back up the yard. The driver calls: Open up! The door slides open scuffing on its rollers, on its track of steel set into the threshold, the engine echoes darker with the rolling-in under the roof. Here comes the first tractor now, I can hear it's pulling a wagon full of bales. The second tractor is hauling a wagon full of sacks, it's labouring harder. To judge by listening, it sounds like a year of hefty weights.

They're shouting in the yard. They call: Carry in, carry in! Grab hold! It's Dawid and Kadys and the new man, Kitaartjie. I hear a bakkie. That must be Thys coming to cast an eye. Towards the back in the caverns of the shed there's a ting-tinging of ball-peen hammers. I know the sound. They're clinking new blades onto the red harvester's cutting-rod. The hay must be strong because the blades hop, the blades wear out.

Perhaps they can carry me out into the yard one more time, on a stretcher. They can fit my neckbrace and strap me in and stand me up under the wild fig-tree. So that I can see. So that I can smell the dust, so that I can see the black plume of diesel fume spurting from the tractor, so that I can assess the swing of the wagon on the drawbar, and count the bales as they are carried into the shed, and count the stalks on the back of the bearer, praise the one who will break open a bale before my feet so that I can see the density, the power, and the glory, the one who shall know to gather me a handful from the centre and press it against my cheek.

Somebody must bring the small scale before me and hold it up in the air until the hand stops quivering.

A bushel of Daeraad I want to see weighed, a bushel of Kleintrou, a bushel of Sterling.

And somebody must stand in front of me and take a mouthful of Vondeling and chew it for me and look into my eyes and I want to see the pupils contract as the grains crack open, and hear soft singing while the molars grind, hey ho, hey ho, yoke the oxen now. And as the cud starts to bind, I want to see the eye start to shine.

And somebody must bring a coop of chicks and enfold my hands in their hands and put chicks in my hands and feed them with the wild pulp in which spit and bran are stippled. I want to feel once more in my palms the chirp and throb of the body of a chick.

And somebody must wipe my tears and somebody must see to it that I don't choke.

Because the map I must still see.

They must unroll it in the dust and place stones on its corners so that it doesn't roll shut. Four red-blue shards of shale.

They must remove the brace so that my neck can bend.

They must take my head in their hands so that it doesn't become too heavy, and lift it up and lower it as the rod points on the map and the hand points over my world, so that I can see the map of Grootmoedersdrift and its boundlessness. The blue waverings on paper of the Korenland River to the west, from the Duivenhoks and the Buffelsjag on the east, the dense contours, fingerprint-like, of the Langeberg in the north and the Potberg in the south. The square dots of the encircling places: Suurbraak, Heidelberg, Witsand, Infanta, Struisbaai, Port Beaufort, Skipskop, Malgas, Swellendam, Stormsvlei, Riviersonderend, Caledon, Bredasdorp, and Barrydale just over the Tradouw and Montagu and Robertson and Worcester.

And amongst the mountains and towns and rivers, with the straight red line of the bypass traversing its body, the extent of my farm. The dotted lines of the boundaries, the white dots of the beacons, the green of bushes and orchards and the gardens in its domain, the silver dams, the number of watering-places and stored waters on the dryland, the stables and the sheds and the kraals. The grass pasture next to the Klip River and the lands, the camps for the lambing and the summering, the plots of fallow land, the shallow basins where the sheep sleep, and the black shadow of bluegums.

Between the land and the map I must look, up and down, far and near until I've had enough, until I'm satiated with what I have occupied here.

And then they must roll it up in a tube and put on my neckbrace again like the mouth of a quiver. And I will close my eyes and prepare myself so that they can unscrew my head and allow the map to slip into my lacunae.

So that I can be filled and braced from the inside and fortified for the voyage.

Because without my world inside me I will contract and congeal, more even than I am now, without speech and without actions and without any purchase upon time.

I pile up three breaths. With my chest I create an incline. The hand-bell that Agaat put under my hand rolls from under my palm with a tinkling. First it falls against the iron railing and then further, onto the floor.

The farmers in the vicinity liked inviting you and Jak to their parties, the glamorous, chic, childless couple of Grootmoedersdrift. And if you invited them back they were all too eager to accept. There were harvest festivals, wool festivals, water festivals on Grootmoedersdrift, a festival of triplets in the lambing time, a festival for the new tower silo with automated mowing-trunk and conveyor belt. And your parties were always the swankiest in the region.

Jak was urbane and talkative at these gatherings, as always appreciative of you in front of guests. The festival fairy he called you. Not that he ever lifted a finger to help you. As a matter of fact, nobody knew how much the success of those dinner parties in the late '50s on Grootmoedersdrift owed to somebody that you could count on at all times. Everybody assumed that it was Jak who was supporting you. Nobody could have guessed that the farming didn't interest him much. And nobody knew that it was to the back room that you went for comfort when he left you on your own.

You saw how they fell for him, the flocks of twittering wives and the freshly scrubbed young farmers. He was the *pièce de résistance* at every occasion. You recognised yourself in them, in the way they couldn't get enough of him. You could see what they were thinking. How did she contrive it? How can a woman be so lucky?

Their eyelids fluttered at the sight of Jak's new cars and lorries and implements and innovations, his imported stud bulls and rams. They ogled his fine Italian shoes and the cut of his trousers, and blushed at the casual way in which he turned back his shirtsleeves once over his tanned wrists. All this while you were lightly conversing about books and music, just enough to bind the company around the dinner table while yet leaving everybody free to indulge their flights of fantasy around Pretty Jak de Wet.

That suited you fine. You didn't want to draw attention to Jak's weaknesses. You wanted to show to advantage yourself. Your job was to camouflage him. Because apart from his toastmaster's jokes he didn't have much in the way of conversation. Boast, that he could do, and wittily comment on what he'd read in the papers, the plans of the Party he could explicate, and the mechanisms of his implements, but he was too light-weight for you. Often in that sitting room resounding with laughter, you bit your lip. You wanted him stronger, more independent, less transparent, you wanted him to possess more of himself, of his own substance.

What did you want him to be? An anchor post? A trailblazer? A source of insight? How could you expect him to understand that?

You didn't understand it yourself. You could only hint and squirm. You were in the shade. That was what angered him without his knowing what was bothering him, this: That you replaced his guts with your own projects.

But when did you start to see it in this light? Not with so much clarity in those first twelve years.

You wanted a child.

And for that he was good enough.

Because that was something you didn't have. It was in him. His seed.

1 January 1960. The day that you heard that you were pregnant you'd been invited to a New Year's party on the neighbouring farm Frambooskop for the welcoming of one of the Scott brothers who'd returned from Rhodesia to take over his father's farm.

You didn't want to tell Jak immediately. You were all a-flutter. You put on your prettiest dress, a black one with a low neckline and bare shoulders, with sleeves that fell open when you lifted your arms. You'd last worn it on the evening of your engagement. It still fitted you perfectly. It made you blush.

You felt eyes on you, eyes that interrogated you, a face that was unsure of this new mood of yours. But you kept the secret.

Who laid a hand against your arm as if your temperature would warm her? Who touched the hem of your dress? Who twirled over and over again in her hands the tubes and jars and lipsticks that you'd taken out to beautify yourself? Was there somebody who could guess something and wanted to share in your excitement?

No, you were alone. You wanted to be alone. You became a different person. Everything altered in interest and in scale.

Twelve years you had waited, twelve times three hundred and sixty-five days. So you made the sum for yourself over and over again while you were getting dressed. Why should it have happened now suddenly?

The doctor had phoned an hour earlier with the news.

Good news for the new year, he'd said, I had to go and collect something from the consulting room and then there was the result from Cape Town. Just be careful now, my little woman, he said, you're a few weeks gone already, remember no emotional upsets, not too much movement in the first few months, no lifting heavy objects, not too much alcohol, not too much rich food, pregnant women are inclined to heartburn.

You took your time over your make-up and you couldn't stop repeating it to yourself: After all the years, after everything that you'd had to endure, after everything that you'd undertaken, however good or bad, long after you'd given up all hope, the reward.

You smiled at yourself with red lips in the mirror. It had been worth the trouble keeping everything together against all the odds. You caressed your neck. You lifted up your arms and spun around to feel the fall of the sleeves, the swishing of the cloth. You couldn't remember when last you'd done something so indulgent. It felt as if your limbs, the hair on your head, the nails on your fingers were inspired, as if your body vibrated, your body, always inadequate, always inferior, but now too much, too full. You were filled full with something that for once in your life you had not planned or calculated and of which the execution and the rounding off was not a laboriously artificial and forced affair, but an entirely natural process.

Good heavens, but you're tarted up tonight, what's got into you, Jak said when you came out onto the stoep where he was waiting.

You smiled.

My dear husband, you said, you look so good yourself in that tuxedo of yours and just look at the new bow tie!

You felt it coming out of your mouth. Like a noose it fell around his neck. You drew him nearer, pulled up his cummerbund slightly, adjusted one cuff link, dusted the shoulders of his jacket.

You started laughing. You couldn't believe it. You no longer needed him so badly. You needed nothing and nobody as badly as before.

What are you laughing at? Jak asked.

Because you look like a model, you said, because I can't believe it.

So, you think I look good? He inspected himself from all angles in the mirror in the entrance hall while you were grooming him.

Fantastic, you said, absolutely fantastic, you belong in a fashion magazine, in Paris.

Clay in your hands. And you could flatter him from pure generosity.

Pregnant.

He could not know it. He had caused it, but he could not know it with his body. It was your knowing alone. In you it was attached, a glomerule of cells that for three weeks already had been sprouting and dividing at its own tempo and with its own plan while you had been eating and sleeping and working.

You noticed that evening how other men looked at you. You looked back, nodded, smiled, felt that you had the right to enjoy yourself.

You look breathtaking, Beatrice came and whispered in your ear, is there something I don't know?

And you look stunning, you said, how are your suckling pigs?

Jak darted you a look.

Over coffee the people at your table bickered over agricultural matters. The new owner of Frambooskop excused himself, clearly didn't want to get involved in an argument at his own party. It was about profits and costs and optimal utilisation of soil.

Two-stage! Two-stage! everybody shouted and Beatrice's Thys beat out the syllables on the table with his hand. Wheat, fallow, wheat, fallow, or, better still, wheat on wheat. With the new fertilisers one couldn't go wrong, was the consensus, bumper crops every year, it was an Overberg miracle. They looked at Jak, who was living proof of the miracle, even though after five years he'd sold the land that had treated him so well to start farming beef cattle.

Jak hit the right notes. The soil analysis laboratory of FOSFANITRA had impressed him from the start, he said.

Modest enough he could be.

With his gentleman's hands he demonstrated. They could scientifically determine exactly how much phosphate, how much nitrogen, how much potassium one needed per morgen for a good yield.

Scientific or not, I don't agree, you said.

Jak looked at you, taken aback. You felt yourself blushing, took another sip of wine, but you could also see the people waiting to hear.

That's a mistake farmers can always make, you said, that they prepare a rod for themselves and their dependants with which everybody will be beaten one day when the wheel turns.

Ag, Milla, what rod and what wheel are you talking of now, my dear wife?

You laughed. He was so hypocritical. 'My dear wife' before the guests, my dear tarted-up wife who looks like nothing unless something gets into her.

You were angry, twelve years' worth of anger. You intercepted quite a few covert glances. People didn't want to say it out loud, but everybody knew that Dirk du Toit, to whom Jak had sold the land on which he had made his profits, was as good as bankrupt. You knew why.

I'm speaking of the wheel of Lady Fortune, you said, and I'm speaking of her assistants the moneylenders, my dear husband, they who make themselves indispensable by offering certain essential services and goods on credit, and I'm speaking of monopolies.

They waited for you to continue, the guests, they couldn't believe their ears.

For farming that's always a dangerous thing, you said. Here in the Overberg we've known it since the days of the Barrys. The lessons of history are there for those who want to take the trouble to study them.

You're telling me, said one, I'm still farming today on a little triangular slice of the original round family farm. Staked out way back by my great-grandfather on horseback, a beautiful round farm. He was mortgaged up to his ears to the Barrys' firm and when they went bankrupt, he lost all his land. From one day to the next he lost everything, he kept just a little sliver like that.

It was a freckly chap from Bredasdorp, a Van Zyl. His jacket sleeves were too short. His thick wrists covered in dense red hair protruded as he described a triangle with his hands to indicate the portion.

Oh my goodness, somebody exclaimed, a slice of pie, but that should be quite enough for you, Flippie!

People laughed at the naughty innuendo, but it didn't help. There was muted grumbling. The director of the fertiliser business was within earshot and quite a few officials of Agricultural Technical Services gathered around when they heard the subject being broached. You thought, good, let them hear for once by all means.

My point exactly, you said. My mother still has an old five-pound note of theirs. A kind of bank they were, you remember. 'Here for you, Barry and Co.' is written on it. So much so that when the whole lot went under just about everything ground to a halt from Port Beaufort, the whole Heidelberg plain, the whole Overberg from Caledon to Riversdal and over the mountain all the way to Worcester.

Well yes, in these days I suppose one has to say Fertilise or button your flies. That was the contribution of one of the sallow Dieners of Vreugdevol.

The roar that arose drew more people to the table.

What's going on here? We also want to hear! What's the joke?

Jak was uncomfortable. He tried, but he couldn't get up because people were crowding around the table. He fumbled with his bow tie, took large gulps from his glass.

Ask Milla de Wet! one called out, she started it. Ask Jak, looks like she's got him under her thumb!

You were angry, but your secret of the day made you impetuous. Jak would just have to look after himself for once, you thought.

Look at the condition of the soil, you said. Thinner and poorer by the year. Just look at the dust when the wind blows before sowing-time, look how it erodes in winter. From sowing wheat all the time. From greed. And from worry. Because the bought-on-credit fertiliser still has to be paid off. And the Land Bank is squeezing.

That's right! Round and round on the merry-go-round all the way into the ground!

That was Dirk du Toit, who'd bought Jak's land.

Tell them, Dirk, I called, tell them what happened to you, you see they don't want to believe me.

Dirk made a cutting motion across his throat.

Yes, I owed them. Then they forced me to sell all my wheat to them, at cost. Their idea is, it's our fertiliser, so it's our wheat. Then they sell it again, then they keep the profit.

Everybody started talking at the same time. Out of the corner of your eye you saw Adriaan, one of the Meyers brothers, owners of the fertiliser company, surveying the palaver, a parsimonious little smile round the corners of his mouth.

You tapped on your glass with your knife.

Listen, you said, that's not all, the real point is this . . .

Aitsa! the little four-share plough of Grootmoedersdrift! Now she's going for the middle furrow!

It was Gawie Tredoux of Vleitjies. He was United Party by birth and a Freemason and he liked you. He passed along a glass of dessert wine to you. You lifted it in his direction and took a sip, put your finger in front of your lips, indicated that you couldn't drink too much. Oh come on, he gesticulated back and took a big gulp from his own glass. You put your hand on your stomach. So? he signalled with his eyebrows. Really? You nodded. He raised his glass high: Congratulations! Jak intercepted the exchange. You smiled sweetly at him before speaking again.

The real point is: The Overberg is the bread basket of the whole country. Remember: Good wheat and good bread, and the nation's well fed.

She's a poet and she doesn't know it! somebody shouted and rapped on the table.

Jak looked away.

You knew of one more supporter at the table, the new young extension officer, Kosie Greeff. The little chap glanced around somewhat anxiously when he saw that you wanted to say something. His wife looked at the glass in your hand. Beatrice as well, all the women at the table thought that when a woman opened her mouth like that in male company it had to be because she was tipsy. You're welcome to look as much as you like, you thought to yourself and smiled at Beatrice.

It was young Greeff who'd convinced you of the new rotational system. He was having an uphill battle in the region. Now he was red in the face because it was his area of expertise that had cropped up in discussion.

Mrs de Wet is right, he said, and what's more, gentlemen, the soil problem in the hill country is a bigger problem than the so-called colour problem.

I agree, you exclaimed. You were in full flow now, you could hear you were preaching, but you kept at it.

You can't take more out of the soil than you put into it, you said. And here we are now, a little group of people at the southern tip of Africa in the process of totally destroying this national asset within the space of a few decades. All the fertiliser crops may make you rich, but it's not a long-term investment in the soil. Fallow is the answer. It's a tradition born of respect for nature. In a state of pseudo-death you restore your substance. Even a frog knows that.

Hear hear! the people shouted.

Froggy went a-courting and he did ride, red-faced Flippie sang with a suggestive fillip to his voice.

A commotion erupted.

Beatrice looked at you dumbfounded.

Milla, please, stop, you're making a fool of yourself, Jak said under his breath, his voice hoarse with irritation.

Give her a chance, chaps, Gawie shouted, such an opportunity you won't get again soon!

You fixed their eyes as you spoke.

It's the rhythms of nature that you have to respect as the Creator determined them. That's what agriculture should be based on. This new greed is barbaric, it's a form of sacrilege.

And then a thought came up in you and you said it before you thought about it. Perhaps the sips of wine together with your exhilaration had gone to your head.

If a farmer clears and levels his land year after year it's as good as beating his wife every night. In a manner of speaking, you added, but the words were out and they had been spoken.

You saw Beatrice gasping for breath and putting her hand in front of her mouth.

A heavy silence descended.

Gawie came to your rescue.

Food for thought, chaps, definitely food for thought, let's hear what Thys wants to say, he looks as if he's going to burst a blood vessel if he's not given a turn.

Now it's enough, Jak hissed, now we're leaving, you and I.

At the door Gawie greeted the two of you. You he kissed on the cheek and pressed your shoulder.

Congratulations, Jak old friend, you married a first-rate wife, look after her well.

He shook Jak's hand emphatically, but Jak didn't know what it was all about. He released his hand quickly.

He got into the car and slammed his door without opening the door for you. Of that he normally made a big show in front of other people.

It was rally-driving all the way home.

Good God, you, Jak swore, think you know everything!

At home he staggered out of the car and urinated against the first tree. He swayed on his legs, he was so drunk.

Your mouth is too big! he shouted as he entered the front door.

You went to your room, heard him pour himself a whisky from the carafe in the sitting room. He came to look for you in the bedroom, came to stand in the doorway, and glared at you.

Jak, I have something to tell you, you said.

So, and what could that be? That you have something on the go with Tredoux?

Jak, he's our friend, he was just congratulating you.

And on what, may I ask? On your speech? What gives you the idea that you can sit and preach to farmers on how to cultivate their lands?

What must they think of me? You and your mother, you're tarts of one crust, you think you know it all. How am I supposed to show my face ever again at the fertiliser company?

Jak, I said, I can't help your feeling like that.

Come here, you said to soothe him.

He stood in the middle of the room plucking at his clothes.

And that soil is like a woman whose husband beats her! What kind of crap is that, I ask you? You're looking for it, you know it, you're looking for me and you'll look for me till you find me!

Yes baas, you said to him.

He wasn't used to that. You stared into the slap without ducking, straight into his eyes.

Jak, you can't do that to me any more, you said.

He shoved you back onto the bed.

If you want to be my soil, I'll do on it as I want to. Slapping is nothing! Shoving is child's play! Now tell me, pray, what kind of soil are you? Clay, perhaps? Dirt? Shale? A bloody rock-ridge? Come on, you're supposed to be the expert here! Grade yourself for us, perhaps it will be of use to the man who has to plough you!

You got up from the bed. He knocked you flat again.

What does one do with soil, eh? What does one do with it?

You drive a post into it, you grub it, you quarry out a dam! Or you dig a hole for yourself and fall your arse off into it. That's what happened to me!

He approached threateningly. You held your arms around your stomach. You saw him noticing it. You altered your gesture, you stroked your abdomen.

Jak, you said and put your foot on the arm of a chair, you pulled your dress up into your groin and started undoing your suspender, won't you please undo my zip?

Do it yourself, he mumbled.

But from his tone you could tell that you had him where you wanted him. You didn't even have to look in his direction. He stood rocking on his legs, glared at you with bleary eyes.

You undid the zip and stepped out of the dress, unfastened your other stocking and slowly rolled it down your thigh while you looked at him. You slid the straps of your black petticoat over your shoulders and went and lay down on the bed.

What does one call that? So spread open? You wanted to feel it, his powerlessness. It excited you to wait for it. You felt you had the advantage, for the first time.

He was very rough. He just unzipped his trousers and half pulled you off the bed. On your knees against the bed he forced you. He tore your petticoat and gripped your wrists. You turned your head to see it.

Look in front of you! Look in front of you! he yelled and slapped you against the head.

Jak, you should be ashamed of yourself, you said. But you heard your voice. There was a kink in the words. You were in it together, in the shame.

Whore! Jak shouted, whore!

You laughed, that was what you did. You thought you saw a movement in the mirror but there was nothing. There were only the two of you. You and your shadows, it was the red cummerbund, it was the rags of black petticoat over your white shoulders.

What are you looking at? he shouted.

He grabbed a footstool with one hand and threw it at the mirror and shattered it.

He rammed himself into you.

You fastened your hands around the back of his hips and pulled him deeper into you. You dictated a rhythm. For yourself.

Come now, you whispered, you're still the best, come now. We're made for each other!

That was what you heard yourself say. You wanted to feel it. Dry. Sore. Good. You had him where you wanted him, you were done with him, he was good only for decoration. To know that, was the reward.

I have something to tell you, you said when he was done.

He leant against you in a daze.

I am pregnant, Jak, you said, and if you ever lift your hand against me again, I will sell the farm and leave you and take your child with me and you will never see him again.

He was too numb to answer back. He half-crawled over you onto the bed and drifted into sleep. His penis dangled out. It looked like a piece of intestine.

A son, he mumbled.

He flung his arm across the pillow and straightened his legs, foot on your face where you were lying at the end of the bed.

You pushed his feet out of your face. You looked at yourself in the shattered mirror until he started snoring. Then you went and ran a bath and lay in it for hours adding hot water. You listened to the sounds of the house.

Before going to sleep, you picked up the shards of mirror and gathered your torn clothes in a bundle and threw them away in the bin in the backyard. The side panels of the mirror were undamaged. You turned the panels towards each other and inspected yourself from one side and the other. You couldn't get enough. After twelve years of despoilment you, Milla de Wet née Redelinghuys, were going to be a mother.

You folded the wings of the mirror so that in the morning the damage to the central panel would not be visible.

The bigger you grew with child the more time Jak spent on his appearance. He became fastidious about what he ate, combinations of certain foods at certain times, power supplements that stood around in tins in the kitchen. You couldn't keep up with cooking what he wanted and the servants understood nothing of it.

Then cook your own food, you said, and so he ate nothing but raw grated vegetables and macaroni. Every night before coming to bed he trained with his weights in the stoep room. Every morning and every evening he went for long runs in the mountains and almost every weekend since you fell pregnant he went off to take part in tennis tournaments or races. He became the Overberg long-distance champion and the Tradouw's prime mountaineer. His only responsibility towards the world, he seemed to think, was that he shouldn't get fat, that he shouldn't with time come to seem coarse and heavy like most other farmers. His only bailiff was his stop-watch, his only judge the bathroom scale.

His achievements he displayed all around him. He kept the maps of Grootmoedersdrift in his new stoep room. If he could have lifted his leg like a fox terrier, he might have had his way with them. There they hung surrounded by his shelves full of trophies and mounted medals with ribbons in display cases, amongst his photos of himself.

The photos in themselves constituted a whole history of one man's vanity.

Jak on graduation day in his gown, Jak at Elsenburg with the agriculture students' athletics team. Jak with his first sheaf of short-stem wheat, Jak with the agent next to the new combine, with a glass of wine in his hand at the regional caucus of the NP, Jak on his Arab mare, booted and spurred for a horserace, Jak at a farmer's day in his white clothes, leaning against his first red open sports car, Jak in close-up, in a studio portrait, brilliantined hair, smoothed back, charming Jak de Wet, the gentleman farmer. A dead ringer for Gregory Peck, as your mother used to say.

In the time of the fixing up of the new rooms you got into the habit of going into Jak's office when he wasn't there. Who is this beautiful man? you wondered. What has he got in him? Nobody can be so beautiful from the outside and so hollow from inside. Not even in a third-rate novel. When is he going to reveal himself? When is he going to show who he really is? You could tell that he was brooding on something, but what?

Over and over again you looked at the display, picked up all the trophies and read the inscriptions, removed the medals with their satin ribbons from the glass cabinets and weighed them in your hand, examined the photos from up close, touched all his strange hard apparatus and reins and harnesses, fastened and unfastened the buckles and belts, tried to budge the weights, smelt and tested the powders and oils between your fingers.

Perhaps there were other reasons for these sessions. If Jak, indeed if anybody, had had to see you in his room, they would have imagined that you were feasting on his fame.

That may be what Beatrice thought when she found you there one day. You hadn't heard her approach. Then she saw you there in front of the photos, came and stood next to you, and produced a sigh, cunningly, now you think back on it.

Ai, Milla, what a wonderful man you married, if only Thys were like him.

You played along for a while.

What's wrong with Thys? you asked, he looks like a real pillar of strength to me.

Thys, he, he is . . . hard.

But with you? you asked, with you he is surely soft?

Beatrice looked away.

What got into you? Did you want to shock her? Perhaps you thought your pregnancy gave you licence, gave you power, liberty to be open-hearted.

Pretty Jak de Wet is a dog, Beatrice, you said. A Doberman if you like, fine of build with a beautiful muzzle, but a dog nevertheless.

Then you told her about Jak, about how he treated you. She listened. You told her everything about the painting of the cabinets and the dragging across the cement and the scratches and the bruises and how it had gone on over the years, and how he had withdrawn into himself, a time-bomb waiting to explode. She'd always thought there was something wrong, she said. The more you told, the less she wanted to hear, but you kept her there.

Why did I marry him, Beatrice? you asked, who is this man? The more I stare at these photos to try and understand, the more the mystery deepens.

Perhaps, Beatrice began, you could see she was hesitant, perhaps you wanted to share in his . . . in his . . .

Beatrice looked away. You waited for her to continue.

Perhaps you're dependent on his . . .

She took her handbag, left her sentence hanging in the air. You changed the subject.

No, you said, don't go yet, it's your turn now, you talk to me now, I also guess my guesses about you, you know.

And then you saw it, how she clammed shut, how the defensiveness came over her, over her mouth and into her eyes. More than defensiveness, disgust, judgement. Of you, not of Jak.

I shall never talk out of the house, Milla. Marriage is holy and it's private. Everything depends on that. Thys has his faults but he's a good human being, a good man, and I stand by him through thick and thin, as I promised before the holy Lord.

On her heel she turned and walked out. You went and sat on a chair there in Jak's room, in his display case, as if his displayed wares had to forgive you for what you'd let out of the bag. What dark mood was it that drove you out of there? You took his camera that was lying on his desk, and went looking for him.

You found him in the implement shed with the new ripper. You walked across the yard slowly, your body was big, it was a month before Jakkie's arrival. The plough had been delivered that very morning by the agent of International Harvester. You had a good reason to go and look for him because lunch was on the table. The shed was dark, you stood still for your eyes to adjust. Jak was standing caressing the seed hopper of the new plough. His lips were moving.

Soilmaster, you heard him say. The word sounded clearly in the shed. He squatted into the backside of the plough, his eyes closed while he played his hands up and down over the teeth.

You wanted to turn away and leave, you held the camera behind your back, but he'd already seen you.

Milla, he called after you.

Come and eat, you wanted to say, but then you said something else.

Then you said to him, move the plough out under the wild fig, I want to take photos. And you walked back to the house with your heart filled with dark feelings and you paged through his wardrobe until you found an olive-green shirt.

This will show off the red of the plough more clearly, you said, they're complementary colours, red and green.

And then you posed him, like this and like that, and you aimed from below and from above, from near and from far, full and half and quarter profiles.

Smile, you said. Pensive. Say cheese, sing, happy days are here again, sing, I talk to the trees.

The farm kids also wanted to be in the photos. They swarmed all over the plough like bats and fiddled and fidgeted everywhere as if they might find something edible there. And then Jak said abruptly, that's enough, he was tired now. Certainly the first time that you'd heard him say that of a photo session.

When at last you were seated at table, he looked at you, pale-faced, said he felt terribly exhausted, he hoped it wasn't his heart, and then went to lie down without eating.

You sat there for a long time over the cold food, a taste of iron in your mouth.

*

easter it is easter I want to say let us bake a cake for the twins for the triplets and for the quadruplets of the four we shall gather the tiniest the little one who was last the one lying with her muzzle just above the clover her we shall gather in our arms I want to say a name we shall give her of clouds a name of rain a name of autumn that drifts in quince trees she who is one of a quatrain of heaven earth god and mortal sweet we shall call her sweetling sweet-flour spit of mercy I want to say but I get mired my tongue up against my teeth eggs on the ground quips I say and queep and speet in stead of sweet and eater instead of easter and instead of honey money how did it come about? so it came in my mouth like the next minute like a thief in the night like the slow inclination of the underground clover-flower to place her seed next to her foot in the ground like the nocturnal rising of dough in my body it came like yeast the sleeping seed the dodder plant the white lamb that pushes out of me and disempowers me.

*

12 July 1960 11 o'clock at night

The more I think back on the day the more I feel I should perhaps have done the whole thing differently first talked & explained everything but how does one ever explain everything to a child?

She wasn't at all at ease after the sheep-slaughtering this morning just stood there in the kitchen door right sleeve stretched smeared with blood & looked straight at me. Arrange your face I said we still have lots to do I thought take no notice take no nonsense but she stayed there chin on chest & and put one foot on top of the other & fist in the mouth. There, go & wash yourself I said see what you look like & stand up straight & take your hand out of your mouth & go and take off that jersey one doesn't walk around like that. Next thing she throws her arms around her body the one arm over the other & I grab her by the shoulders Saar shakes her head & sucks her teeth as if I've now done something wrong don't you meddle here I say & go & fetch my old red jersey in the bedroom she can't walk around any longer in that blood-stained thing. And then A. doesn't want to take it off in front of me so much for gratitude! So I gave her a piece of sunlight soap & said go & take it off yourself outside at the tap & soap it in so that it can soak & I gave her a bucket because I didn't want her to go into the house then but she mustn't go into hr outside room either. That would spoil all my plans right there & there she stands & she refuses flatly. I have another jersey like this one she says where's my jersey I want my own jersey it has the right sleeve.

Simply had to talk over her objections because hr case with hr clothes was already in the outside room. So I had to think quickly to put hr in hr place & I quickly pushed my hand into the pocket of hr dress in front & this sheep's ear? what's it doing here? I don't want to see any superstitions in you & then I threw the ear into the bin & then she looked so sad so then I said when you're clean come & have tea there are ginger biscuits you were very good about learning to slaughter we all have to do things in this life that we don't like & then I gave her my red jersey to take with her and to go and put on behind the house in privacy.

After lunch she polished the stoep & I instructed Saar to help hr next thing there they are singing together. Good sign after the business of the morning.

> If I have a whip I must have a yoke
> Hard at work's the name of my yoke
> Don't let slip's the name of my whip
> Looksmart's the name of my cart
> Pair-of-socks is the name of my ox
> Spick-and-span's the name of my man
> Meek and mild's the name of my child
> Love of my life's the name of my wife

Next thing I hear A. teaching Saar a new line: Stand in the shade's the name of the maid & All in a whirl's the name of the girl piece of liver piece of lung food to keep the old man young. Heaven knows what's going on in that head of hrs but she made good progress through the list looks as if she picked up some spirit in the course of the day. Praised her wherever I could.

> Plaited onions
> Took out potatoes
> Weeded the vegetable garden
> Took pumpkins down from stable-roof
> Loaded cabbage & pumpkin in the trailer for market

At 5 o'clock she told me her hand was tired. Had seen it coming but I was ready for her: Nay what I said lots of work will make that hand of yours strong soon you won't even know about it. Got a cup of coffee into her & pushed through till 6 o'clock & then said go and make a fire now we're going to have a nice braai you can clean yourself afterwards you're just going to be standing around in the smoke now anyway.

12 o'clock
Over-tired. Over-exerted myself can't get myself to bed. Still nauseous shouldn't have eaten that meat must be more careful. Hope A. has gone

to rest she'll just have to get accustomed in hr own time. Was fed at the kitchen table everything that we had for supper she'll never have to fret about that fresh sheep's liver in caul fat & chops & bread & baked beans & tomatoes. Didn't want to put her mouth to the food do you think I want to poison you? I asked but the chin stayed on the chest.

Waited till she'd finished washing dishes then I said come see here in the back is a surprise for you.

Pity about the hinge not fixed yet so there the lower door scuffed garrrr over the linoleum. Showed hr nicely you just pick it up slightly & I switched on the light in there & the room looked a bit barer than I'd thought the bulb cast a dark spot on the linoleum & the bed looked too high (remember to find another apple box tomorrow to put in front of the bed).

So this is now your room A. I said, yours alone for your convenience it's for your own good you're a big girl now, aren't you. And I opened the little curtain taterata-a-a! and showed the black uniform dresses. That's all you'll wear six days a week then you can save your house clothes I said & I showed they all had nice extra long right sleeves as she likes it & I showed I had specially sewn on broad white cuffs for her.

Explained about the aprons one for every day of the week. See that they're always clean & stiffly starched & ironed. Showed hr where all the cleaning materials & ironing board & the irons are & the borax & the turpentine for the starch & the blue for the whitening. Underlined I don't ever want to see stains & creases on hr uniform when she's work-ing in the house & demonstrated how she must take turns heating the little irons on the electric plate but not red-hot so that they scorch the ironing & how she should iron the aprons under a damp ironing-cloth. The caps were the most difficult. I said I know you don't like things on your head but you'll just have to like it or lump it. Asked her nicely she must put on a clean one every day & pin it up nicely. Do you under-stand? I asked because she was just standing there & staring in front of her. I thought I'd show her how to put on the cap & I said I don't want to see a strand of hair.

It's nothing to be ashamed of or scared. It's as it should be. You'll be my special help here on Grootmoedersdrift I said. My right hand in your case my left hand & I pinned the cap in place & she held her neck stock-still. The little face actually looked quite small under the white band. I wanted hr to look in the mirror but the mirror was too high & and I was afraid it would crack further if I took it down so I said look into my eyes how do you look to yourself?—like a smart Dutch house but she looked right through me and didn't look for her reflection.

Close your eyes I said because then I really felt quite queasy but she kept on looking at me like that so then I pressed 5 pounds into her hand. It's more than the other servants together earn in a month I said & that will be your daily wage & if all goes well I'll increase it every six months a penny saved is a penny earned. Showed hr the savings book. Will teach hr how to work with it hrself I said but nothing made her excited or glad. Stored her first note in it. Put it away again in its proper place I said but she didn't move. Cat got your tongue? I asked & put the kettle on the stove & I showed the rusks and everything.

Don't be ungrateful I said & if you have something to say say it now don't nurse grievances but the mouth is set in a thin line. Have a nice cup of tea before you go to bed I said & you can let me know if there's anything more you want. Don't you say thank you, then? What kind of manners is this? Didn't feel like hassling further so I issued the orders instead. 6 o'clock in the morning she must be at her post in the kitchen & make me a nice cup of coffee in the blue coffee pot with the proud-pourspout and for the baas in his room on the stoep & milk & sugar & rusks on the tray and I don't want to see a long face.

Suddenly out of the blue she asked where are my things what happened to my things? I showed hr the suitcase under the washstand. Do you think I want to steal your stuff? I asked. But by then I was feeling really sick couldn't get to the house in time vomited copiously in the drain there next to the kitchen my stomach in revolt I took a bucket from the kitchen and said at her door throw water in the drain and wash away the puke because the dogs will come and sniff at it there & when I left I said lock your door at night remember you're a big girl now there are no-goods about.

Well then, more I can't do for her salvation & my pen is almost dry. Must remember to buy a new bottle of Quink.

Half-past twelve
Did after all just go & peek through the nursery window into the yard

& her light is still on at least the door is closed now but the bucket is still just where I left it & there's a smell of puke in the air in the yard. It will have to be as it wants to be. Too tired to talk once again. Must get to bed now otherwise tomorrow will be too difficult. The child feels as if it's pressing down in me.

6

Agaat comes in with my midday meal. She speaks with cinnamon. It floats behind her, a pennant of persuasion.

She allows me my nose today.

I must rejoice in my privileges.

I must grit my teeth and put behind me the tooth-polishing and the post-planting, the windmill and the borehole, I must remember she's also only human and she has her limitations.

As if that convinces me!

I must simply reconcile myself to the fact that she's left me alone for hours on end the last few days.

I mustn't hold it against her that she did no more than her duty, thoroughly and at the right time, but without blandishments, without words.

I must know I was asking for it.

I mustn't be difficult.

I mustn't go around signalling something that nobody on God's earth can guess at. I must keep it simple please she has her hands full as it is thank you.

I mustn't accuse her.

She does everything as well as she can.

She does her very best for me.

That's the argumentation, the sophistry of spices as she's sprinkled them for me and mashed in with a fork: the cinnamon, the cardamom, with the butter, the sugar, to a perfect pumpkin puree.

I smell for all I'm worth to get all the messages. If I could, I would have sniffed loudly to say: I understand, Agaat, your meaning is crystal clear to me. Mashed potatoes with meat sauce, sweet pumpkin with cinnamon, red jelly with custard. What more could one want? It's a whole story on its own, Sunday food on Grootmoedersdrift.

But it's not Sunday.

What day is it? I ask with my eyes on the calendar, I can't see that far any more.

Agaat puts the tray down on the trolley. She picks up the hand-bell from the floor where it's been lying for three days now, it looks strange in her little hand, the gesture with which she puts it into her apron pocket contains an element of self-chastisement.

Monday eleven November, the year of our Lord nineteen ninety-six, she says, the fields are white with wheat.

What would she want me to say if I could talk? Would she ever have said something like that to me when I could still talk? She sometimes says such things with a straight face and uninflected voice as if it's the most ordinary thing, as if she's talking to herself. The fields are white with wheat. Must I become something that I am not yet?

Dawid got hurt, she says, she doesn't look at me, she sterilises my teaspoon in a glass of boiling water.

Got a cut on his hand from a combine blade that broke and I had to bandage it first, that's why I'm late today. You must be hungry by now.

Clink, she puts down the teaspoon in the saucer, tests the temperature of the potato with the back of the little finger of her left hand. Still too hot.

She talks with her back to me while opening the curtains and the lace linings wider. Her movements are less curt, she trains her voice to moderation. The purple glow of the bougainvillea rushes into the room.

Hay is strong this year, she says.

There is an unevenness in her voice, she clears her throat.

Grains are swollen out, we're winning more than five bags of Sterling per morgen. I made Dawid grind a sample and I baked a small loaf and it, it, rose right out of the . . . tin.

Her voice fades away towards the end.

Did you smell it? she still manages to add.

I see her vividly, standing over the mixing of the sponge at first light, over the dredging of the table with white flour, sprinkle-sprinkle with the little finch of the right hand that knows to snatch dab-dab with gathered fingertips in the flour bag, I see her mix and knead, knead and knock back with the palm of the strong hand, fold over with the small hand, knead and knead till the dough springs back, then the covering in a cool quiet place for the first rising, the knocking-back, the proving and the kneading-through, I see her at the shaping in the tins, at the putting into the hot oven and an hour later bending for the testing with the steel knitting needle, the tapping on the back of the small brown rabbit, the turning-out on the old bent wire rack. How many loaves, how many cakes, have been turned out on that little frame? That she would not have thrown away, absolutely not.

And the eating, Agaat? The slicing and the buttering and the apricot jam and the tasting all alone at your set place when you've done with me here in the front of the right wing?

Of bread I am told.

Hunger is imagined for me.

Light is granted me.

Time.

Colour.

Life flows through me as if through a transfusion rigged up between her and me. She monitors the rate of flow.

The bougainvillea scorches my eyes. Agaat stands in front of the door and looks out, she hangs there, she hooks herself in place there for strength.

It's flowering as if it's being paid, she says, took a long time, but now it's found its feet at last.

I look at her back with the cross of the apron bands.

Turn round, I want to say, look at me, forget about it, it's over now. You do everything you can. I want for nothing. It's not your fault. You are the best nurse one could wish for. We'll try a different route. How, after all, can you be expected to guess what I want? The day will come when you will think of it yourself, of your own accord. Then you'll come in here with the maps under your arms and with triumph on your face.

And I know what that mug of yours will look like then, your jaw-bone will be all the way out there, you'll suppress your smile but the mole on your cheek will be an exclamation point. So you can come away from the door now, it's not all that bad.

Sometimes when I stare at her back hard enough, she feels it, then she turns around. Brave, as open as possible to receiving everything transmitted to her.

Today I can tell from the shoulder perched at a slight angle that she's not ready yet. But it's lower than it was yesterday, than it was this morning. And she's talking about bread.

I mustn't stare, I must let her be.

Agaat's talking shoulder.

I wait, I look in the mirror. The green of scraps of tree, the varied greens of the ornamental cypresses and the water-berry and the honey-bread tree, red flecks in between from the weeping bottlebrush that has sprouted again after she had it pruned at the end of winter. A shiny shard of the roof of the shed, a haze of hills further along, everything framed by the dark purple of the bougainvillea clambering over the trellis on the stoep. And in one corner, one could easily miss it, Agaat's profile. She doesn't know I can see her front, from the side only, but enough to read it. There's a frown on her face, as if she cannot comprehend the bougainvillea, as if she's trying to fathom the bread.

Like Christmas, it's flowering, says Agaat again.

She lifts her hands, pat-pats at her cap.

Right out of the tin . . .

I make room, I give her a chance. I look at the reflection in the mirror, look with Agaat who doesn't know that I'm looking with her. She will see the whole garden, framed in the purple. For me it's carved up and jumbled together in fragments in the three panels, bits of the flowerbeds. The central panel is brighter than the other two. The one that broke long ago. For eleven months now the mirror has been standing in the same position with its panels at the same angle. I know the content of the reflections, I try to imagine the bits left out, the avenues of agapanthus that must by now be in full bloom, the borders of gillyflowers and wild pinks and snapdragons and purple and white petunias that Agaat sowed and had planted in the late spring, in the early summer, so that I might still experience it, and the people who will come for my funeral.

She came in September and held in front of me the packets of summer bulbs and seeds.

Choose, she said, I've bought ten packets of everything and ordered 500 bulbs from Starke Ayres.

Everything, sow everything, I gestured, sow everything, it's my last garden.

There I was right, I could see, she wanted to sow everything, her eyes shone. She blinked quickly and turned round and for three days on end sowed seeds and planted bulbs and walked singing and whistling round the house so that I could hear where she was working, and at mealtimes came and told me three beds of white gladiolus at the back and purple dahlias in the middle and right in front purple and white sweet alison. And in-between fennel for fragrance and for the fine feathers of foliage and for the yellow flower-heads that will mitigate the strictness of dahlias and gladioli and break the purple and white.

Tobacco flower, Californian poppies, and common poppies, and Queen Anne's lace for delicacy, and in the dry beds sunflowers and zinnias and painted ladies high and low. Would she not have drawn a plan? Would she have done it free-hand this time? Somewhat more carelessly, extravagantly, more higgledy-piggledy than usual? For the music? For the departed?

There must be a show garden in flower out there.

A bower of beauty.

She's watered it every day. From early every morning I can hear the sprinklers go tchip-tchip-tirrr over the lawns. Until the sun heats up at nine o'clock and then again in the evenings when the plants have regained their composure after the scorching of the day.

Agaat knows how to make a garden grow.

This evening if there's no wind, if I'm lucky, if her mood continues to soften, she'll open the stoep doors. For me to smell everything that's in bloom. Perhaps by following her movements, by concentrating on her intentions, I'll have my way. Perhaps I'll manage to usurp her will on the sly, and keep it warm in me, without her even noticing that I have it, meld it with mine so that we can have one will for these last days.

Smell the world! Take the scent, all along the flowerbeds and further along the boundary fences! Show me the outlines! Fetch the maps from the sideboard!

She catches my gaze in the mirror, catches me out in a calculation, in a fantasy. I see the indignation leap in her face, her eyes narrowing. I should have kept my eyes shut. When she turns round her mien is neutral, but the battle continues, I can hear it in her heels.

I didn't mean it like that! Please!

She adjusts the bed so that I sit up straight, she fits the neckbrace. Her hands are cold and swift. She puts the tray down hard on the bridge.

I blink my eyes to say: You're too touchy! One can't do anything without your taking offence! I don't want to eat! I'm not ready for your fragrant favours!

She ignores me. I blink my eyes.

I say again: I don't want to! I'm not ready!

She pretends not to see. She puts the bib on my chest, she pulls and plucks at it. She bends her head.

Bless us oh Lord and these thy gifts, she prays.

She scoops the first teaspoon half-full of pumpkin.

Now she'll watch my breathing, bring the spoon into my mouth, tilt it towards the back where she can get hold of my swallowing reflex. I look at her, I look at the spoon, I look at the mirror.

For what are you looking like that, Ounooi?

Ounooi. For the sake of bread and bougainvillea!

She looks where I'm looking in the mirror, its edges brimming with bougainvillea, suspended in a tree-lined landscape. There's a flash.

Birds, tiny birds, white-eyes that fly away from the fig tree I can't see, that grows just around the corner. That I, Lord, can't see. The early figs at the top ripe bells. The first light-green figs on a plate arranged with a flare of purple bougainvillea, that was how I served them, for the season, to mark it, to celebrate it, midsummer on Grootmoedersdrift. My figs.

Hmm, says Agaat, we must see if there are any figs yet, the tree around the corner here is dragging its branches on the ground this year.

She suspects something, she swivels her neck, she keeps on looking with me in the mirror. Determined to twist my arm to eat. The windmill must turn, the thresher must churn. The pumpkin must in.

And the bougainvillea, it's flowering as if it's never going to stop.

Is she taunting me? Does she think I must take my cue from it, from the flowers, from the wheat, from the bread?

I have ears to hear, I flicker, how many more times are you going to say it today? Since when do you expect me to compete with bougainvilleas? But she doesn't look at me.

She keeps on looking away at the stoep door. I see her neck, the neck of Agaat from the side with the constellation of dark moles, and the row of hairpins securing the white cap.

Slowly she turns her head back, careful on her perch to get the best from the moment, focused on putting me in a place where I'll submit and blink my eyes to say, yes I will eat, you may approach with your teaspoon, Agaat, depress it slowly on the tip of my tongue and slide it firmly upwards all along the middle to halfway, so that I have less work to do, and I will swallow what you have prepared for me. So nourish also our souls.

But I don't do it. The fragments of green in the mirror are a reproduction, a repetition of another plan, in another format. As a map is of a place. If I can get her to grasp the analogy. Mirror, map, reproduction, repetition.

I press my gaze against the front of Agaat's white cap. As if it's a sail and my will a wind.

I look past her at the mirror and then quickly at the wall next to my bed. At the mirror, at the wall. From the fragmented garden to the off-white surface of the wall. From what is lacking in the reflected summer to what is lacking on the despoiled wall, an image, a hill farm on a flat plan, suspended by its loop from the picture rail. To and fro I look, to and fro, with the white-eyes that flash in the mirror, around the invisible corner, to the invisible fig tree. Agaat, don't you see then, the unseeable, this goodly frame the earth, don't you see it, quartered by the compass, east west south north! The yard, the dam, the mountain, the drift!

Slowly she retreats from me. She places the teaspoon on the saucer's edge. She slides off her high perch next to my bed.

Lower the girl, she says softly on a held-in breath through her teeth.

To and fro she looks, as I looked, I flicker my eyes all the time. She looks at me, she looks where I'm looking, she nods slowly.

Mirror, mirror, she says, is it bothering you? Seen too much? On the wall? Seen it all?

That's a start! I signal. You're warm! That's excellent progress! Yes, I signal, yes Agaat, you're on the right track! Now just think further! Now just think: map on the wall, think flat earth, think pictured palm of hand, think life-line, think fingerprint!

Agaat gives me her eyes. I look deep into them, I take hold of her eyes with mine, I bend them to the door, down the passage, all the way to the front room, to the sideboard next to the wall, to the quivers lying there, behind the photo albums. I close my eyes slowly and keep them closed. I gather a sheaf, from behind her apron, from out of her chest. I see a great sailing ship tacking against the wind with billowing sails. Keel-deep in the waving wheat she comes towards me, hill crest after hill crest, disappearing in the troughs, every time bigger as she reappears till I can hear her apron creaking in the swells and can make out her figurehead, the profile of a Fate, the jaw set to brave without retort the storms that she has predestined.

*

Only when it really dawned on him that he was going to be a father, did Jak start treating you slightly better. You didn't altogether trust it. It was the eighth month of your pregnancy and all of a sudden you were being showered with all kinds of gifts, an LP with saxophone music which, it must be said, didn't do much for you, *Wonderland by Night*, perfume by Elizabeth Arden, a new tea set. He even took you into Swellendam for *Die Heks* by Leipoldt which an amateur dramatic company was staging. Not that he'd given it much thought, but you appreciated the effort.

You had to listen to his fantasies of how the child would look just like him, what sterling blood flowed in the de Wet veins and how he was going to bring him up to be strong and fit just like his father, a gentleman farmer. In the evenings he drew plans of toys that he wanted to build for the child. Kites from which one could hang, aeroplanes, rockets that could really take off.

You asked, what if it's a little girl? In his family, Jak said, the first-born was always a boy.

You watched this husband of yours in the evenings as he washed his face and brushed his teeth, standing stooped over in his underclothes. Sometimes as he removed the towel from his face, it seemed to you as if he was going to cry. Sometimes you found him paging through one of your books on the night-table and shutting it quickly when he saw you looking. At night he left the stoep room and came and lay behind your back like a little boy. In the mornings when you woke up he was gone.

As meek as he was with you, so volatile was he with the labourers. He would berate them for the slightest infraction. You'd always chosen to overlook those things, the sugar and the coffee disappearing from the house, the dogs' bones vanishing from the meat cooler outside, but Jak took up arms against them. He lay in wait for the kids who stole pumpkins from the roof of the shed at night, and shot at them with the air gun. You knew about it because their mothers brought them to you mewling with the pellets that had become infected in their buttocks. You had to remove them with needles burnt clean and provide ointment and plasters until the wound had cleared up. They never said what had happened, and some of them didn't even know, because Jak of course didn't let himself be seen. When you dug out the pellet with the mother holding down the screaming child on the kitchen table, you said, don't look, and spirited away the evidence between your breasts.

One evening you put the pellets in Jak's plate. There were five of them.

Jake, these are children, you said, they can take as many pumpkins as they like, it's not as if you eat them. And you don't plant them either and you don't water them and you don't stack them on the roof, they're my pumpkins with which I earn a little extra at the market to pay the servants, I might as well just regard it as part of their wages.

He said nothing, put the pellets in his shirt pocket.

The children grow up here on the farm, you said, when they're grown men they'll remember it, aren't you ashamed of yourself?

The creatures just breed here, Jak said, I've a good mind to fire the whole lot, they can't do as they like on my yard, they're just loafing about and getting up to mischief.

You can't do as you like on the yard either, you said. They're human beings, remember, not cattle.

You stopped talking when the food was brought in. You put your finger on your lips to warn Jak not to talk further.

But he'd already said it.

You get the creatures accustomed to everything, Milla, he said, you're the one who creates expectations, not me. Remember, give them the little finger and they'll take the whole hand, don't come and complain to me one day if they come to confront you with all kinds of demands. Mark my words, the Romans knew it long before us, give a hotnot a hard master and he'll long for a soft master, give him a soft master and he'll start dreaming of being his own master. Is that what you want? And then where do you think we'll bloody well end up in this country?

It was the old pattern. The political justification of downright meanness.

Shooting at children as if they were baboons, you said, has nothing to do with politics, Jak.

And you teaching them the alphabet as if they were parrots? What does that have to do with? And then you think you can contain it afterwards? You may think you know all about farming, Milla, but you mustn't come and tell me about politics.

What could you do? You couldn't even stop him ranting for all the world to hear.

Let them hear who have ears to hear, Milla, he said when you tried to silence him, I won't be shunted around in my own home. Not by a long shot.

That last while before Jakkie's birth you couldn't inform yourself at first hand, your legs were swollen and you no longer went out into the yard so often. But you knew in a matter of minutes if anything happened.

Who came to tell you about the fighting? That Jak first shoved Koos Makkelwyn because he gave him lip?

Initially it wasn't clear to you what had happened. And you could get nothing from Jak himself. Bedraggled, his riding clothes full of dust and horse manure and his riding-helmet dented, he arrived at home in the middle of the afternoon to take a bath and then he left again in the bakkie without a word.

Makkelwyn was a sturdy, neat man in his fifties whom Jak had hired specially to look after his stable horses. He was a farrier and breaker-in of wild horses and in the mornings arrived, quite the dandy, on a dapple-grey ambler from The Glen, where he was stable-master. His people, the McCalvins, had since time immemorial been the farriers in the region.

You had Dawid called in when Jak had left. So then he brought along his father.

You can still see them standing there in the kitchen, the old man in his seventies, and his son, both with the Okkenel crooked mouths and light-green eyes, and with their oily khaki hats in their hands. In

Dawid's other hand the gleaming riding crop, incongruous against the dirty pants, the scuffed shoes.

What happened in the stable, Dawid? Spit it out!

You were irritated. Why had the old man come along? When OuKarel put in an appearance in the kitchen, you knew from childhood, then there was trouble. You were tired. You weren't in a mood for trouble.

Dawid looked at his father.

Talk, the old man said to him, I'm here as your witness.

Dawid looked you straight in the eye. You didn't like it.

Mister Makkelwyn ticked off the baas. He rubbed against the leg of his pants with the crop.

Over what?

Because the baas rides the horses through the piss and then Mister Makkelwyn has to struggle with foundered horses for days.

And then?

Then the baas shoved him in the chest and told him to shut his bloody trap.

And then?

Then Mister Makkelwyn said he wouldn't shut his trap and he wouldn't be sworn at and shoved around by a pipsqueak who had no respect for a noble animal.

Dawid shifted his weight.

Carry on, OuKarel said.

Then the baas whipped him across the face with the crop and then Mister Makkelwyn grabbed the tip of the crop and then the baas pulled Mister Makkelwyn down on the ground and wanted to kick him and then Mister Makkelwyn grabbed the baas by the leg and then he fell and by this time they're both flat on the ground rolling in the straw and horse-shit and the baas can't get the better of Mister Makkelwyn, because Mister Makkelwyn holds him down so that he can't do a thing.

And then?

And then the baas shouts at me and says why am I just standing there can't I see the bloody Spout-mongrel has him by the throat I must help I must take the hay fork.

The Aga's door slammed and the fire leapt out of the plate-holes as the evening meal was being warmed.

Dawid looked away.

Nooi, he said, I'm sorry . . .

For what, Dawid?

Again Dawid looked at his father.

The old man was to the point, but you could see he had something else on his mind, there was an expression on his face as if he was rehearsing to look pathetic.

My hip is sore, my boy, have your say and have done, Karel said, the people want to cook their evening food here.

You saw how OuKarel was looking at the saucepans as the lids were lifted and the food was stirred with the pot-spoons. Meat with dumplings and sweet potatoes and fennel bulbs with white sauce it was. The beetroot salad was being grated together with onion. There was a bacon and spinach soup. A lot of food for three people. The old man's eyes were starting to water from it all.

And then, Dawid?

Then I said, Baas, the way I see it the hay-fork is meant for shovelling hay and I'm not being paid to do the baas's dirty work, I'm the foreman, and all I did then was to close the stable door so that nobody could see further what was happening in there because then they were rolling this way and that way there and Mister Makkelwyn pinned the baas's arms down so that he couldn't use his fists.

Two new loaves were being turned out of the tins, a pound of butter was being taken out. The sounds in the kitchen were loud in your ears.

And then?

So then I stood there because then I wanted to see that Mister Makkelwyn came out of it okay. But I needn't have worried because the baas was completely winded by then and then Mister Makkelwyn got up and dusted his arse and put out his hand to help the baas up and then the baas slapped away the hand and then Mister Makkelwyn said well then the baas would have to manage on his own with his fancy horses and the baas must please take the money he still owes him to his brother's house in Suurbraak this very evening he'll spare him the embarrassment of arriving at The Glen to apologise to the stable-master, and it will be so much and so much and if the baas doesn't do it he'll go and charge him with assault even if it's just for a case number in the book and even if it's just to warn the sergeant about what's happening here on Grootmoedersdrift.

There was a silence in which only the swishing of the riding crop against the pants was audible. You were weighing up what to say next.

OuKarel took the gap.

Grootmoedersdrift, ai, ai, a . . . I've now been coming along for ever . . . He shook his head.

Here, you knew, the real story was coming out.

I'm tired of working, Kleinnooi, I'm asking for a little pension, Kleinnooi, I must buy medicine for my rheumatism and I now want to rest at home and now and again at least eat a bit of meat and buy a tin of peaches.

You were amazed. As if it was nothing, not one word of commentary about the happenings in the stable, a stone in the stream, to step over on.

I'll see what I can do, Karel, you said.

You knew better than to ask: But what does this have to do with anything and why now?

It was a time-honoured negotiation and it was as effective as it was subtle.

Dawid was not behindhand either.

We're hungry, Nooi, our children follow the baas and pick up the guinea-fowl that he shoots to glory but then he chases them away, we can't live on milk and askoek alone, Nooi . . .

There was a pause. He put the crop down on the kitchen table.

On milk and askoek and . . . pumpkin, Nooi, can the nooi not top up our rations with a bit of pork and fat and beans?

I'll see what I can do, Dawid, you said.

Pumpkin. The word was flagged for you like a red pennant, a red pinhead with which one marks a critical point on a map.

You had two big enamel bowls of food dished up, and a little pail of soup and both the loaves and the pound of butter and had a bottle of preserved peaches brought from the pantry.

Jak, you knew, wouldn't be returning for supper, and you weren't really hungry.

Ai Nooi, I didn't really mean . . . OuKarel said, and you believed his self-exoneration, but Dawid's face, it was a whole little drama when he took the baskets of food from you, emboldened with his own words about what had happened over in the stables, backed up by his father's request. Even though the request had come from loyalties of a former time and even though it was grafted onto old understandings.

Ai, but this is now going to taste like something, he said, and thank you very much, Nooi, I'm glad we understand each other here.

Come Dawid, OuKarel said and put on his hat. You could see from the old man's back that he thought his son was going too far.

What you had to understand, what had been implied as understood, was more than you could write down in a day.

In the doorway Karel turned round.

I'm also not altogether useless, Kleinnooi, I can show the young men how it's done, I can still lend a hand with the little soft jobs, just let me know if the kleinnooi needs me. And send regards when the kleinnooi talks to the ounooi, when the ounooi comes here, tell her to have me called there at the drift, I want to see how the ounooi is getting on.

That was another clear message.

You knew better than to confront Jak, he the fit muscled master of Grootmoedersdrift wrestled to the ground on a stable floor and pinned down by a coloured man twenty years his senior.

You saw to it that his riding clothes were washed and ironed and his leggings polished and his riding helmet dusted the dents beaten out and the plush of green velvet brushed up. You collected it all neatly in a little pile for him on the sofa in his stoep office with the leather crop that Dawid had brought along, buffed to a shine and leant at an angle against the curve of the helmet.

In the end it was the dogs. You were always furious when you caught him at it.

But he turned his hand into a caress, redirected his foot at a ball or a stick. He said you were mad, he was just playing with the dogs.

Ma did not seem surprised when she discovered it one day. It was the first weekend of July. She had come over to help with the final preparations, did at least say that the new rooms were a good idea. At you she looked with a mixture of disapprobation and fascination and pity. You were heavy and slow, your knees and ankles thick and red.

Jak was volatile. You were scared on the Saturday afternoon that he would unleash something when he got home, worked up after his sports meeting. That was why you had summoned your mother.

You were in the nursery putting up a gauze curtain. You'd opened the window to get rid of the smell of paint. Ma was in the kitchen making coffee after her afternoon nap. The kitchen door was open. Across the yard you could hear the rattling of cups. The bakkie drove in and the dogs barked. Jak was back from the rugby match, back from the bar where he'd socialised afterwards, you could tell from the way he drove into the yard, the slam of the bakkie door. He would come in by the back way. A movement drew your attention. The door of the outside room was still open from Ma's inspection earlier in the afternoon. Was it your imagination, or had something moved behind the curtain? The cups stopped rattling.

Then Jak came round the corner and swore and looked under his soles. He'd stepped in dogshit, and was instantly furious. His new calf-leather boots. Salomo the ridgeback and Sofie the half-bred Scottish terrier were grovelling towards him on their sides. They knew better by this time than to jump up and to lick. Hand on the hip he stood and watched them. Under Sofie the cement grew dark with pee. Salomo's ears were back and his lip was pulled up. His whole body was quivering.

Jak grinned, coaxed the dogs nearer. Behind the screen door you could see the white blotch of your mother's face. You stood back behind the gauze curtain.

You could have stopped him, you could have opened the window, you could have said Jak, the coffee's ready in the kitchen, how was the rugby? But you said nothing. You knew that your mother would not betray her presence either. Witness, was what you two wanted to do, witness, and be each other's witnesses. Again a stirring in the outside room. How many pairs of eyes were there that afternoon?

Jak had his back to you, right in front of the kitchen door. You could hear everything.

You think you can growl at me, you think you can bark me off my own backyard, you think you can crap all over the place here!

Then three kicks. One at Sofie before she could get away, and two into Salomo's body where he was lying on the ground.

So get away! he hissed at Salomo through his teeth, sag-balls! Should wear underpants, you, he snarled. Powder-prick! No-good, you'll let them rob us blind here!

The dog struggled up, limped away glancing back nervously. Jak scraped his soles clean with a twig, washed his hands at the tap in the backyard and dried them on his pants, looked at his watch.

Then you pushed open the window of the nursery.

Jak, you said, the coffee is ready in the kitchen, Ma made it.

He looked at you, then darted a glance at the screen door. He walked away quickly, in the direction of the sheds.

You sat down on the chair in the nursery and waited. You unfolded the toy lampshade that you still had to put up. A yellow face with a wide laughing mouth. Open and shut, open and shut you folded it, the sun a fan in your hand.

Your mother came in with a tray and three cups. She put the tray on the washstand, closed the open window, drew the curtains.

She said nothing, waited for you to speak.

Jak is frustrated, you said.

You kept your voice light. It felt as if it was you who'd kicked the dogs. You got up and started fiddling with the baby things on the washstand.

He's not really a farmer, Ma, you know it yourself.

She said nothing. She waited. You stole a glance at her. She already knew every word that you would say.

He feels worthless, then he takes it out on the dogs.

She made a sound.

He feels I've got him under my thumb. And now I'm pregnant, at last after all the years, the centre of attention. I suppose he feels neglected.

Your voice dried up. You were starting to get angry. Old bat preying on me, you thought, first he wasn't good enough to farm on your land, then he's the golden boy for twelve years while he's mistreating me, and you shrug it off as if it's nothing, and now that I'm pregnant, he's suddenly a villain if he kicks a few dogs. Keep your nose out of my affairs, you thought. Your cheeks were burning.

You opened the curtains again. The door of the outside room was now wide open. Somewhere in the house you heard a door slam. Something fell onto the floor in the back room. You felt dirty. Your house felt dirty.

Your mother's voice was like a dipping-rod in your neck, down you had to go, down into the white milky poison.

Milla, look at me, she said, sit down on that chair so that I can talk to you. I'm old, I know more, and I understand more than you think. My life is almost over, I'm free to talk now, I must talk, so that you can't say one day your mother kept up a front to the day of her death.

Ma, just let it be! You waved your hands around your head.

You will listen, Kamilla. And the walls will listen.

The floorboards in the passage creaked. You signalled with your finger in front of your lips.

But she only talked louder.

Too much understanding of the evil-doer and too little indignation with the evil, she said, that's how women make a virtue of their own suffering and how men get away with murder. You needn't keep spinning me pretty tales. Nor he. And don't try and absolve yourself of all blame in this. Jak de Wet kicks his dogs for two reasons: Because they can't flatter him in full sentences and because they can't tell anybody what a two-faced churl he is.

You protested, she held her hands up in the air to stop you.

Let me finish, she said.

Do you want to carry on being his dog? You know that you're now the mother of his child. You know that you can keep him at bay with the same arts with which you caught him. Don't think I didn't notice how you worked him. But you can do more. You're now a fully fledged woman. People will listen to you now. You can tell people what's happening, your woman friends, your mother. We women may be the weaker sex, but we're actually in charge, you know that as well as I. We just work in different ways. We needn't be scared. We've got hold of them where it hurts most.

She stretched out her hand. The elbow was stiff. It was only half bent, slightly extended in front of her. You wanted to look away, but you couldn't. The hand cupped itself around something imaginary, from below, caressed it, the fingers writhed, grabbed, twisted. At last she dropped her hand. There it lay, in her lap, large, weathered, with gnarled joints.

A story, she said, is an easy thing to spread.

You couldn't look away from the hand. You thought, let go of me, I'm infected already, you can't make me any sicker than I am. You don't know why you thought that. All the time in that little room you felt undermined and underpinned at the same time. Fed and fed-upon at the same time. You rolled your shoulders and blinked your eyes to get rid of the feeling, you tried to see her as she was, tried to hear what she was saying, because for the first time in a very long while she was actually trying to talk to you.

If the story hasn't spread already, she continued. There's nothing, is there, like a good housemaid to send the truth into the world. You need only speak the word. They're women. They know about things. They live for their mistress, what else have they got to live for? Their husbands? You need only encourage one of those a bit, and there it runs, a veld fire. Kitchen, co-op, consistory. You have quite a few here, don't you, that you can recruit. The little young one strikes me as particularly suited to the purpose. A rumour in these regions, I'm telling you today, is the best way of keeping a man in his place. If the people know, they'll look at him askance, pass him by, push him out of places where it matters to be seen, to belong to. Then he'll come and cry on your shoulder. He'll come and ask you to help him. Then you can set your terms. He'll do everything and anything to get back in favour. He'll stop, I know the kind, then he'll stop.

Ma, stop, you said, it's not your business.

I know the kind of man he is, Milla, take my word for it. I'm your mother, and I know you too. They find strong clever women attractive, men like Jak, they can't exist without approval. They live on reinforcement and affirmation as if on air. They're like children. As scared as children are of the dark, so scared are they of not being liked.

The corners of her mouth pulled down, she pushed her lips forward as if she was gulping something down.

So, you decide what he's worth to you from now on and use him accordingly.

You wanted to scream, I know it! I've known it for a long time! But that you didn't want to concede to her. It was a snare. She was provoking you, she was jealous, she wanted to run down your dead father to you, your father who had loved you just as you were, unconditionally, she wanted to find out how far things had gone with you and Jak. She would use your reaction, whatever it was, against you. She spoke loudly on purpose. She looked at you meaningfully, with every word she rolled her eyes in the direction of the yard and the doors and the passage. There were soft footsteps in the passage.

What old wives' tales are you spinning here?

Jak appeared in the doorway, leant against the door frame, hand in the pocket to strike an attitude. He was in his socks.

You were sorry for him. He looked small. His face was confused. Your mother got up and brushed past him. In the passage she turned back and looked at you from behind his back.

The SPCA, Milla, do they have a number in the book?

The phone book is there in the passage, Ma, see for yourself, you said.

Jak looked at you, helpless.

You got up and walked to him and rubbed your hand through his hair. Never mind, you said, she's old. Her bark is worse than her bite.

You whispered so that she shouldn't hear. But you couldn't speak softly enough. Without looking up the number in the book she strode away with loud footsteps from the little table in the passage where the telephone was. She had an excuse not to phone. You had provided it.

*

descended to hell my right hand a fall of stars it is raining the bleating in the fields all night long I lie awake spasms knock at my rings thumb and index pressed against each other form the eye of a rabbit there leaps wrong shadow my thumb buckles pen paper slips out of my hand a rustling in shrubs a lizard a mouse an emperor butterfly under a roof of leaves how does one hold an egg the stem of a rose a doorknob a window-catch everything I leave open were you born in a church? made like that and left like that? button and button-hole remain apart to what end the display of your glory? that is the question agaat

*

12/13 July 1960 after midnight
Have just now come to sit here in the sitting room shawl over my nightdress. Woke up from the creeper an eerie little shadow-hand against the window & couldn't go to sleep again.

Bright full moon outside. Quite cold. Feel like something but I don't know what. Tea & ginger biscuits? A glass of warm wine would help but it's out of the question now it's just as if I'm waiting for something just as if I'm missing something. It's the child probably I can feel him kicking usually he stirs in the early evening & then he calms down at night.

Labourers' dogs would have barked ducks would have made a racket at the dam if there'd been anything amiss but it's quiet. Crickets. Frogs. Perhaps I should go for a walk in the yard for fresh air. Half-nauseous feeling won't go away.

1 o'clock

Yard quiet but something's not right. Don't want to wake J. he'll say it's my imagination he'll say I'm sleep-walking again but I'm awake & I was awake just now even though I feel all the time as if I'm walking just above the ground on somebody else's farm in a dream in somebody else's head. But it's my farm. It's Grootmoedersdrift. Pinched myself even.

There was nothing outside that I didn't recognise & didn't expect the yard in the moonlight & everything taken care of everything the image of order & tranquillity. White gables of the shed's gateposts at the entrance to the river-grazing black & upright sentinels the black shadows of the lean-tos under which I know the wood & bales & rolls of fencing & droppers are piled neatly in the sweat-sweet smell of plaited onions from the onion store. A trace of that yesterday-today-and-tomorrow that always flowers out of season? Can one dream such a smell? Would one smell trouble better by moonlight?

Made absolutely sure went & tried all the locks checked the gates on the yard & checked that the sluice of the irrigation furrow was closed if the hanslammers were lying against one another in the little sleeping-shed behind the vegetable garden. They're always a bit restless after one of them has been slaughtered & checked the railing of the trailer full of pumpkins saw that all the pipes were fitted securely into the holes so that they can't come unstuck if the load were to shift on the pass.

Not a single thing out of place. Even pushed open the gate of the feed-store & felt the bales of lucerne lukewarm as they should be wouldn't get any warmer.

Went in at the side entrance of the implement shed & stood there in the dark until I could see the outlines of the machinery in the dark I could distinguish the nose of the Massey Ferguson the relief of the chrome lettering. Unreal feeling. But who would dream of reading by touch in the dark?

In the chicken run sleeping sounds of hens on their perches & the smell of manure & feathers. Walked along the blind side of the house to see if the outside cooler where the fresh meat is hung to cure was latched against the foxes. The little foxes from across the drift. They would you believe it have now taken to standing on each other's shoulders to get to a leg of lamb or the dogs' shinbones. Am I imagining things or have they become more audacious since the day I started fixing up the outside room heaven knows how they found out so quickly must have been Saar who tattled perhaps they think they now have an advanced forward position in A. Perhaps A.'s been in cahoots with them for a long time. Ai shame on you Milla that's surely totally & completely improbable.

Twenty to two

Was just going to crawl back into bed when suddenly I knew what's wrong it's Agaat! That door of the outside room was still open when I went by there on my way from the meat cooler. Just ajar! Knocked at the window. Could she really be gone? Must go & look again!

Two o'clock

A. is gone! Please God she hasn't slept in her bed the suitcase is gone two Sunday dresses missing lots of clothes gone counted even 8 hairpins & a cap Lord help us! one pair of shoes & one pair of socks also missing & the pack of Dr White's was open & one pad was taken out & brown suitcase with all hr own belongings GONE! Looked everywhere but didn't want to call & wake everybody up I told dogs search I'll warm her bottom for her if I find hr ungrateful little scrap where could she be? My red jersey that I lent her hung by your leave on the hook by the kitchen door cheek! she knows where the dirty clothes should go I'll sort hr out in a wink haven't got time for impertinent creatures here on Grootmoedersdrift what must I do?

Switched on all the yard lights & the house lights so that she can know there where she's hiding that I've discovered that she's gone. J. must in God's name just not wake up then all hell will break loose he'll fire her.

Ten past two

Went to switch off all the lights again wouldn't want her to think I'm eaten up with worry!

Half past two

Now did you ever! A. is on the mountain in her new uniform! I was standing on the stoep just now first I thought I heard singing then I thought I saw something white stirring on the little foothill thought at first it was the guano bags I tied there to show where the wattles must be hacked out then it turned out it was A. all the time. Could make hr out clearly with J.'s binoculars. Can't see what she's getting up to there odd steps & gestures against the slope.

Nine o'clock morning 13 July

Lay awake all night & couldn't get warm again after all the roaming around outside then I heard six o'clock a stirring in the kitchen I thought now I'm pretending not to have an inkling & next thing she comes down the passage tchi-tchi in her new soles not a crinkly curl in sight neatly dressed in hr uniform cap pinned just right & proper coffee on a tray slight smell of grass & shrubs but beyond that without a trace dogs following her & pushing their snouts into her. Know what that means or perhaps it's just the uniform that smells of shop.

The running off in the night. Feels as if I could have dreamed it all. What a fright she gave me, heavens! But I don't let on. Perhaps she'll tell me one day what exactly she went to do there what in God's name got into her & what became of the suitcase & hr house clothes the two pretty dresses made for hr & the dirty clothes from the sheep-slaughtering. Not that it would be a great loss if they're gone was a lot of old stuff anyway & would be too small for her. My red jersey on the hook. Pennant & signal I know hr.

That to-do on the hill I can't figure out. Sideways & backwards knees bent foot-stamping jumping on one leg jump-jump-jump & point-point with one arm at the ground. Then the arms rigid next to the sides. Then she folded them & then she stretched them. Looked as if she was keeping the one arm in the air with the other arm & waving. Thought at first oh so I'm late I suppose it's been carrying on for a long time the nocturnal meetings but I didn't see anybody coming no whistling or calling just the thrumming two three notes over & over.

How strange all the same. Hr head in the air, looking up at hr little arm as if it's a stick. Walking stick? Fencing-foil? Then again held still in front of hr, palm turned down palm turned up. Judgement? Blessing? Over the hills over the valley along the river? A farewell ritual? Where would she get it from? So weird it all is I can't put the images out of my head I think of it all the time. Why up there? What could she have wanted to see? Can imagine well what it would have looked like in the moonlight the river between the trees the grazing on the valley-side the moon-grey hills on the south-eastern side & here & there a clearing so that one can see the great plain stretched out behind. Nothing that she hasn't seen many a time before.

Could the binoculars have been playing tricks upon me? Hr arm a pointer? Pointing-out pointing-to what is what & who is who? An oar? A blade? Hr fist pressing apart the membrane & the meat as if she's dressing a slaughter animal? But not a sheep, as if she's separating the divisions of the night. Or dividing something within herself. Root cluster.

Far-fetched, Milla! Your imagination is too fertile for your own good. But surely one couldn't think it up. A. in hr working clothes in the moonlight in the middle of the night doing a St Vitus's dance. I could surely not have dreamt that. There must be a simple explanation. Perhaps she's working herself up to running away. I suppose I'll get to the truth of the matter one day. Must go & see perhaps the suitcase is back.

7

A broad sheaf of light spills into the room, light that I know well, the yellow light of late afternoon. Ten to five? It's somewhere between the quarters, stray time. The alarm clock is hidden behind a box of tissues titled Inspirations.

But something is different. The opening is not in the middle of the swing doors as always aligned with the door knobs, the curtains have been drawn so that the opening is slightly to one side of the glass doors. And the gauze lining hasn't been drawn as usual, it's been swept back over the white cord that runs above the door frame, it's been pushed away behind the curtain. I can make out the garden through the slight distortion of the little old glass panels in the stoep doors.

But it's not only the gibbous glass. It's the light itself inside the room that quivers. It's filled with something, a restorative rippling, pellucid, watery, beckoning.

From where this light? What can lend such a quality to this chamber of death that I know in every last detail? Over which my eyes wander daily, filled as it is with the signs of my end, the nursing-aids that promise no recovery, that are applied to the polite dismantling of my body, to the daily cleansing of my limbs, four, my three axils of armpit and pudendum, the clefts of finger toe and buttock, the crannies behind my ears, the hollow of my navel, the subsidences above my collarbones, my head with its seven holes, the little bottles of pills for the relief of my spit, my tears, for the singing in my ears, for my wasting spasmodic muscles, the instruments for the measurement of my remaining reflexes, for the notation of the statistics of my going hence.

What an ado about nothing every day!

What a farce!

Pastime, Agaat calls it sometimes. Respite. Of late she's taken to reading me poems from the collections circulated by the South African ALS support group. Who will get them after me? Such recyclable frail-care books, it's as good as bequeathing your coffin to the next candidate for one day's lying-in-state.

And now in the midst of so much attrition, the light comes and announces itself in my room like an unfamiliar word. Like a word that you recognise as a word but of which the meaning just evades you. Sculp. Scullogue. Scuggery. Scuffle-hunter. Agaat's and my dictionary games. What will she play with me now, now that words fall ever more into disuse in this room? Light-and-shadow chess? *Trompe l'oeil*?

Now I know what it is! It's the dressing table!

It's turned differently, at an angle towards the stoep side. The two side panels have been adjusted. Like the wings of a thing flying forward, and stumbling the last stretch, yearning to catch up with something, to capture.

There's a view of the garden in the mirror, but sharper, clearer than a garden can be. My garden I see there, cut out on three levels, abounding with detail, the most alluring prospects.

It's cornflowers I see, deep blue cornflowers in the one wing and in the other wing a cascade of long bent stems of light-blue agapanthus. And crepusculating on the central panel, in a pool of jacaranda shade, the voluptuous powder-blue heads of hydrangeas in full flower.

Cautiously I sip at it, choking with emotion would spell the premature end of this story. Could Agaat have started understanding me, at last! If it wasn't coincidence, if she could get that far merely on the basis of eye signals, endless possibilities remain ahead, then I mustn't spoil it now with an attack of sentimentality.

The mirror reveals a perfect result. The best I've ever experienced the garden. This is how I had always imagined the north-east side could look. I planned it in terms of all the different shades of blue in the catalogues. This is how I imagined it. Blue perennials, iris, agapanthus, hydrangea, bushes of kingfisher daisies, annuals sowed in the low borders every year, first for the winter plain blue pansies and forget-me-nots that started coming up by themselves in tract upon tract and then ageratum for spring, and after that for summer, cornflower, cornflower, and again cornflower. Because of blue one can never have enough in the barren yellow and brown of summer and also not in winter when it must help the rains to fall as the old people believed.

Now Agaat has arranged it for me in mirrors, a vision. How shall I know whether she reacted to my request or if it was mere chance?

Or could she have been planning it for a long time? First the emptying out of my room, the drawn curtains and now the light, the restoration of colour and objects? So that I, as I am drained of myself, can fill up with what is outside myself, as the poet says? So that something can start floundering upstream in the run-off? You never know with Agaat. She is witched. Sometimes I think she's playing games with herself, and I'm a mere excuse for her inventions.

In the beginning she arranged fresh flowers in the vases every day, as she knew I liked it, but then Leroux apparently said we should beware of dust and pollen and insects.

That was Agaat's story.

Perhaps she's sorry now, wants to make up for it now.

As always at this time of the day shadows are playing on the wall next to my bed, but now there are lively stipples of light, points of blue, a general tint of agapanthus cast on it by the mirror.

A multiplied garden.

One visible through the window, one in the mirror, one on the wall.

How long could it have taken her? How many times of walking to and fro, softly so as not to wake me?

Perhaps she flew, changed herself into a dragonfly. Or a wasp. Landed on my pillow, her head in line with mine, to see through my eyes, and then back to adjust the angle, the angle of the dressing table, the angle of the three panels in relation to me, to one another, to the cornflowers, to fit everything together. One degree to this side or that side could lose the hydrangeas, could include a chunk of brown stoep wall instead of a bed full of blue flowers.

And then there are still the maps, Agaat, what must I do to get them? Heaven and earth it would seem you would move in order to have me buried in a cheerful and contented state. You'll see to it that I'm not left here impaled like a grasshopper on a thorn.

Poor Jak. What makes me think of him now?

Perhaps he's wandering around restlessly. Perhaps he's approaching now through the wattles to see what's become of me. For him it was all so sudden. One two three, I'm coming! Premature! No time for second thoughts. His mouth was gaping with it, his eyes as big as saucers. Good Lord, now I have an urge to laugh! Our father who art in heaven, that I want for breath to laugh! Earlier Leroux thought it was one of the symptoms of my bulbar paralysis, these uncontrolled fits of laughter of mine, but they were always about Jak. It was always about that trajectory. What goes up must come down, there's no escaping that. But the curve of the arc differs from case to case. As I got progressively sicker, I started wondering more and more whether it would be better to go like him, and then I always started laughing.

Wretched Jak, Hollywood to the last gasp, or perhaps not Hollywood, at most a Leon Schuster farce.

Two days after his death I said to Agaat: Clear out, pack all the papers in boxes so that the executors can come and collect them, carry everything else out into the back here, everything so that we can sort it. I didn't want to see anything more of him. The car I had towed away immediately without further ado, I didn't want to have to stare at it every time I drove out.

Ai, the baas, the baas, Agaat said with a straight face when she came in with the piles of photos and asked what she should do with them all.

Throw away, I said, take them all to be burnt, everything, out, away, I have no use for them. Just roll up the maps nicely for me.

About the racquets and the training-bench and the weights and the abdomen-strengthener and the mountaineering ropes and the crash-helmets and the knee-guards and the calf-vibrator and the lumbar-massage wheels and the electrical foot-palpitator I wondered, a sale I thought, an auction, but I didn't feel up to the faces of the people. I had it all carried to the scrap-iron heap behind the implements shed. From there, I knew, it would in time be drawn, with the rusted ploughshares and old pieces of corrugated iron, into the recycling vortices of the farm.

That was in 1985. For years after that I would see the children on the farm walking around with the medals around their necks or playing in the dust with the silver trophies. That's all they retained of Jak, his toys. And the adults who experienced it, to this day I sometimes hear them talk amongst themselves about the spectacle. The master of Grootmoedersdrift, shrike-spiked like a beetle.

Jak's law books and action novels, his piles of magazines and photobooks full of sports heroes, catalogues of sports cars and expedition diaries of mountaineers and sunglassed adventurers in the Alps and the Sahara and the Amazon and the South Pole I donated to the town library. I immediately regretted doing it. The little librarians gazed wide-eyed at the material, as if they wanted to ask how I'd handled all that virile energy. As if they wondered how a mouse-face like me could have kept up with all the grandiose flights of fancy of my Camel Man.

But that one could never try to explain to the Swellendam town librarian. And also not to the chairlady of the Women's Agricultural Union. Her I didn't even warn that a mirror was imminent, a wall-sized mirror that had covered one whole side of Jak's office. I had its panels unscrewed and packed and delivered to Dot Stander's house with the message that it might be just the thing for fitting out the hall where the annual flower show was held. Forget-me-not, I thought, I'd often gone myself to clean the mirror there, the sweat-spatterings and the other splotches, I didn't want the servants to see them.

Only the maps I kept, the old map of conveyance, the one that I'd found amongst my heirlooms after Ma's death, with the little painted pictures of all the special places on the farm. That map was the most original of the collection. Then there was the old transfer-duty map with the boundaries and beacons. And the water map on which the rivers and the underground veins of water, the boreholes and watering places and the fountains were shown, and later the surveyor's map when the irrigation scheme from the Theewaterskloof and the Duivenhoks was laid on. And the topographical map with the fall of all the slopes marked on it, the contour lines, the heights above sea level written on every numbered hill and mountain slope. Jak later had the rest requisitioned and ordered from the divisional council, district maps with all the other farms in the vicinity. On these you could see that Grootmoedersdrift was the biggest farm in the area and had the best soil and commanded the best grootbos, fynbos and the best water catchment area. The big soil composition map I'd had compiled by Agricultural Technical Services with, incorporated on it, the photos of the vertical sections showing all the soil types of Grootmoedersdrift, the red sand and the yellow sand on brittle stone, the clay loam and the sandy loam and the riverine turf. Then there was also the whole of South Africa, and a world map, Jakkie's school maps on which he and his father drew with compasses and calculations the exact proportions and location of Grootmoedersdrift darted with dovetailed arrows.

Roll them all up together, tie them with string, I said to Agaat, and put them in the sideboard with the photo albums. They belong with our records.

It can't be long now before she remembers it.

The garden hangs suspended, shimmering, in the mirror, a blue cradle, a nest dandled in the afternoon light. I hear a rustling. In the mirror I see a veil of mist irrigation slowly precipitating over the flowerbeds. The leaves scintillate, the stems start bending as the flower-heads grow heavier, my garden in all its glory.

The back door opens. Quarter past five. Agaat has been to collect the eggs before the skunks can carry them off. I can hear from her footsteps that she's carrying a precious cargo, the round-bellied basket with straw in the bottom. I can imagine how it was. Grope-grope under the puffed up bibs of the lay-away chickens. Softly clucking the tip of the tongue against the roof of the mouth, so that they shouldn't take fright, the close watching of the hen, her austere yellow-rimmed bead-eye, because she can be vicious and peck the hand that's pilfering her eggs. Amongst the prickly-pear trees Agaat would have gone to look, behind the chicken run, under the pomegranate bushes, in the quince avenue, next to the old orchard. All the lay-away places she would have traced.

She carries the basket to the pantry, she takes the egg cartons off the shelf to fill them. How the good hand takes the red-brown eggs, the dunnish dust-brown ones, the small-yolked ones one-by-one out of the basket and assesses them, the largest apart, for selling in town, how she eases them into the little hollows, large ends downwards, half-dozens full. A quarter-hour chimes. From the time it takes, I guess that there are more than a dozen eggs today. Now she will write the date on the box, as we always did. What day would it be today?

A map of days, a calendar, that I have and that she writes on every day. But I can't see that far any more. And what do I care for time? One day is like another in this decoction she has devised for me. Purgatory according to Agaat.

There was peace and tranquillity after Jakkie's departure, after Jak's death, for the first time in a long while on Grootmoedersdrift. Not an obdurate eye, not a hunched shoulder, and the mouth gentled for a change, the lips often livened up with a smile. How long was it, the truce? Five, six, seven years? Until I got sick, but the first year, year-and-a-half, while I could still move myself, with my walking sticks, with the walking frame, in the wheelchair, then still it was all love and harmony. I could hardly believe it, sheer bliss, I thought, Freuden sonder Zahl, to enjoy my old age with her. When did it change? When I could no longer speak, when I could no longer write, when I became completely helpless and had to come and lie here? Was it that that released the poison? That I was more dependent on her than I'd ever been? I've always been that, from the beginning. But with every step of my retrogression it felt to me she was becoming more rancorous, more furious. Had she pent it up all those years?

I hear her going back to the kitchen, I hear the water from the tap, that's for filling the kettle for coffee. Her late-afternoon coffee so that she can remain awake for the evening shift. The silence while she drinks it. I can feel her thinking something, considering something. Then she comes down the passage, more slowly, stands still and turns back to the pantry.

It's very quiet.

Agaat has a plan. The one sprouts forth from the other. The drill has struck water.

I pretend to be asleep when she comes into the room. I spy on her through my eye-lashes. She regards the wall next to my bed where the blue specks of light play. Didn't think it would work so well, did you? I wish I could say that to her. I see a little incipient smile. She comes closer, even closer, she comes and stands by my bed, bends, until her head is at my height. There's a wisp of straw in her hair behind the gable of her cap. Lay-away chicken nest! She comes upright, looks down at me. I open my eyes and find hers.

I've seen it! I blink.

I flash my eyes at the wall, at the mirror, to and fro, try to move my eyebrows. Thank you very much! It's wonderful, Agaat, my garden.

Mirror, mirror, on the wall, who has the loveliest garden of them all? she asks.

Satisfaction on her face.

She puts her hand into her apron pocket.

Close your eyes.

She places something in my hand, something cool and smooth it is, she holds her hand under my hand.

Open your eyes.

It's a big brown egg.

A double-yolk, I bet, she says. Tonight I'm making you scrambled egg, Ounooi, you've been eating far too little of late. Not a lot into you, not a poop out of you. And I haven't embroidered a stitch. We must eat early tonight. I want to get working.

Work, for the night is coming, that's what I think, but what I signal is: that will be nice, I've been wanting an egg for a long time.

Then that's fine, says Agaat, a good appetite is not to be sneezed at and a wink is as good as a nod to a blind horse.

I close my eyes. I can't trust my gaze. Better not take any chances. Give no cause for misunderstanding. Rejoice in the success of the first round.

I hear her clatter in the kitchen. It sounds extremely lively in there tonight. Renewed effort? At what? Courage for what lies ahead? How long? The yolk and the white are whisked together. From cradle to grave. The screen door slams. She goes in and out at the kitchen door. Scrambled eggs. What an ado simply to scramble an egg? Sounds like a five-course. I can feel her excitement. Positive energy. The Cape is Dutch again, how long can it last?

She brings my tray. A candle? A vase? And, for the first time again in how many months—a twig of the rambling rose! Crepuscule! Floppy copper-coloured petals, the inside darker, a lively rust colour, a Cape robin's bib. The evening has been brought indoors for me.

The eye is the window of the soul, but a mirror helps, says Agaat. A picture of primness, but I can see she's very pleased with her handiwork.

She cranks down my bed.

Lower the sheep, she says through her breathing.

She pulls herself up on her stool.

Raise the girl, she says. Her voice is soft, palliative.

The egg goes down well. She has brought it to the exact degree of just-done, but still good and moist, and, if I must judge, strained it twice through a tea-strainer so that the texture is uniformly smooth.

Without hurry she spoons up the egg pulp in small spoonfuls, and brings it inside, sees to it that I swallow, once, twice, everything without emphasis.

Her little hand is resting on my waist, in its white crocheted sleeve. With that she gauges my breathing so that she can bring in the tea-spoonfuls at the right rhythm and tempo. Her starched clothes make a sound every time she leans forward, the shoulder bands of the apron as they tense and relax, her arms as they rub against the turn-ups of her sleeves. The stool creaks rhythmically as she shifts her weight.

I am hungry. There is something beneficent about the taste of the egg. It tastes of butter and cream. Agaat wants to pamper me, and herself, for the breakthrough, for my gratitude.

I understand the bustle back there. I can see her, spatula in the little hand, the bowl with the whisked-up egg in the strong hand, standing by the frying-pan in which the butter is already foaming, and then suddenly having an idea, putting everything down, removing the pan from the heat, and in the falling dusk going to the dairy to ladle a little jug of fresh cream from the pail. For scrambled egg de luxe. And how the one inspiration inspires another. In and out at the screen door as it occurs to her. She went and picked a twig of parsley, from the pot next to the back door, and put it on the side of the plate, too dangerous even to sprinkle finely-chopped on the egg, but for the look, and for the smell. She crushes the leaves between the fingers of her right hand, she holds it under my nose. Her lips come forward, her eyes glisten.

I smell it, Agaat.

Ai, Ounooi Ounooi, say Agaat's eyes. She looks away. My face is too much for her. She divides it up into manageable fragments. Under my nose she mops up a drop, from my forehead she whisks away something that's not there. She puts another teaspoonful of egg into my mouth.

I eat a highway through the double-yolk.

It's a wind-still evening. Agaat has opened the swing doors so that I can hear the yard-noise of milk cans and the returning tractors and the closing of shed doors.

Now it has gone quiet. Now I hear only the sprinklers and the pump down by the old dam, that Dawid will go to switch off at ten o'clock. Closer by is the twilight song of thrushes and Cape robins, a light rustling every now and again in the bougainvillea on the stoep, a few slight sleeping sounds of the small birds, sparrows, white-eyes, that settle there for the night in the centre of the bush.

On the mirror an abstract painting is limned, midnight-blue like the inside of an iris, with the last dusk-pale planes and dark stains from which one can surmise that the garden is deep and wide, full of concealed nooks, full of the silence of ponds, full of small stipples of reflected stars on the wet leaves, full of the deep incisions of furrows. Green, wet fragrances of the night pour into the room, from water on lawns and on hot-baked soil and dusty greenery.

I smell it, Agaat. Everything that you have prepared before me.

She removes the spray of roses in the little crystal vase from the tray and places it next to my bed on the night-table with the candle.

Had enough? Was it good? Are you feeling better now? No way you could have gone to sleep on such a hungry stomach.

She clears away the tray, switches off the main lights.

Now how about warm milk, with sugar and a drop of vanilla?

That's good, later, I gesture.

On her way out she takes her embroidery out of the basket. She looks in the little blue book lying on the chair. She reads the last page and sighs. She searches through the pile, pulls out another. She puts it down on the embroidery. I can always tell when she wants to give up the reading, when she becomes disheartened with it. But these are her two projects. She doesn't leave a thing half-done. Especially when she doesn't yet know how it is to end.

The candle casts a glow on the wall next to my bed. In it stirs the shadow of the crepuscule in the glass vase. Longer and shorter stretch and shrink the buds. The air freshens from the window. It billows the gauze lining at the open doors outwards and inwards. The flame stirs, casts a silhouette of stems on the wall, crystal and water and tiny air bubbles trouble the light. Doubly magnified in the shadow on the wall where he perches in the rose twigs, front feet clasped together, I see the praying mantis.

She wouldn't bring a thing like that in here without intention. The most exemplary motionless creature she could think of. Little hands folded in prayer. The green membranous wings like coat-tails draped over the abdomen, the triangular head with the bulbous eyes.

I look at the mirror. I see the candle flame and its yellow glow, the shadows, the coruscation of the water, the vase, the rose, the spriggy limbs of the praying mantis. These then are the things reflecting in the three panels where the garden has now darkened. When the flame stirs, the shadows dance, the reflections of the shadows dance, the supplicant raises its front legs in the rose.

Does a mirror sometimes preserve everything that has been reflected in it? Is there a record of light, thin membranes compressed layer upon layer that one has to ease apart with the finger-tips so that the colours don't dissipate, so that the moments don't blot and the hours don't run together into inconsequential splotches? So that a song of preserved years lies in your palm, a miniature of your life and times, with every detail meticulous in clear, chanting angel-fine enamel, as on the old manuscripts, at which you can peer through a magnifying glass and marvel at so much effort? So many tears for nothing? For light? For bygone moments?

A floating feeling takes possession of me, to and fro I look between the shadow picture on the wall and the reflection in the mirror. A story in a mirror, second-hand. About what was and what is to be. About what I have to come to in these last days and nights. About how I must get there over the fragments I am trying to shore. I step on them, step, as on stones in a stream. Agaat and I and Jak and Jakkie. Four stepping-stones, every time four and their combinations of two, of three, their powers to infinity and their square roots. Their sequences in time, their causes and effects. How to join and to fit, how to step and to say: That is how I crossed the river, there I walked, that was the way to here. How to remember, without speech, without writing, without map, an exile within myself. Motionless. Solid. In my bed. In my body. Shrunken away from the world that I created. With images that surface and flow away, flakes of light that float away from me so that I cannot remember what I have already remembered and what I have yet to remember. Am I the stream or am I the stone and who steps on me, who wades through me, to whom do I drift down like pollen, like nectar, like a fragrance, always there are more contents to be ordered into coherence.

Through the open doors I smell the night ever more intensely. It permeates my nose like a complex snuff. Can one smell sounds? I hear the dikkops, from a northerly direction. Christmas, christmas, christmas, they cry in descending tones, christmas comes. The yard plovers cry as they fly up, a disturbance at the nest? The frogs strike up, white bibs bulging in the reeds. Under the stoep a cricket starts filing away at its leg-irons. Here next to my head something prays in the void. That I may be permitted to make the journey one more time, on stippled tracks for my eyes, pursuing place names that are dictated to me, the last circuit, a secret, a treasure that neither moth nor rust can destroy, a relation, a sentence hidden amongst words.

Suddenly I see Agaat. In the dark door-cavity with the tray in her hands. She's watching me from the shadows, I can't make out her face, just the cap, a small white tomb in the air.

Would she sometimes simply be curious, an onlooker at a fainting incident in the street, a visitor to a cage in which a snake is shedding its skin? How would I ever know? How could I hold it against her? How would I want her to look at me here where I am lying?

I close my eyes. I thought she'd already left for the kitchen. I wouldn't, after all that, have dared look around again. Not if I had known she was still there. I hear her walk down the passage, turn round, walk back slowly. She's in the spare room. She stands still.

I count to twelve before she moves again. I hear her put down the tray in the kitchen but then none of the usual, the sounds of clearing the tray on the work surface, of scraping leftovers into the bin, filling the wash-basin with water, washing and drying and packing away dishes, taking her own plate out of the warming oven, the sound of the kettle being filled for her tea, pulling out and pulling up the kitchen chair and then, as always, the silence as she eats her evening meal. None of this I hear.

She walks around the house, every now and again she stops, a few paces to this side, a few paces to that, and then stops again. In the dining room, in the living room, in the sitting room, in the entrance hall I hear the floorboards creak and then again down the passage on her rubber soles she walks, tchi-tchi-tchi past my door, a glance at my bed, further along to Jakkie's room, to the spare room, a hesitation before the walk to the back room, and back again down the passage and back and stop and carry on. I can hear her thinking. I can feel her looking for empty spaces. The already-cleared house that echoes lightly. Out at the back door now. Keys. It's the big bunch. First the storage rooms in the back, then round the front.

What is she whistling for me to hear there where she is in the dark?

Oh ye'll tak' the high road and I'll tak' the low road . . .

What is that rattling under my bed? The cellar door? Here right beneath me in the right wing? What would she be looking for there?

Muffled from below the floorboards, under the concrete floor layer, the whistling sounds just loud enough so that I can make out the tune.

An' I'll be in Scotland before ye' . . .

The extra mile, Leroux said, that woman walks the extra mile for you.

*

night of resurrection sunday night one foot before the other slowly in front of my mirror it is I here I stand four limbs nothing that is wanting here roll away the stone before my foot I ask slowly until I stand in front of the pantry shelf flour bag in the palms sugar bag in the palms mixing-bowl in the palms milk jug in two hands god in heaven restore to me in your name the grip in my fingers six eggs one by one in each palm a cake is a manual exercise forgive me my trespasses sieve spoon pan oven I will I want I can the cock of monday morning crows a dent in the flour separate the whites from the yolks the first egg breaks wrong the second remains closed hopefully whole the third also falls and so the fourth to the fifth and the sixth there are seven shells in the flour.

*

12 August 1960 ten past eight

A. is going to give me grey hairs yet, I can see it coming. This morning when she brought in the coffee the dog prodded his nose into her again.

Smelt nothing just Mum & starch & a tiny line of mud on the seam of hr apron from hr nocturnal escapades but for the rest spotlessly clean everything.

Have just been to do inspection in her room. Old black umbrella standing in the corner & a paint tin on a sack tip-tip, it drips in the tin. There's a patch of mould on the ceiling suppose roof must be rusted through will have to take it in hand. For the rest everything clean & tidy. Looked in hr cupboard she's wearing the bras I see even though they are too big & the pack of Dr White's has not been used further I suppose she doesn't know how but I seem to remember one of the elastics to which it's fixed was missing the evening when she disappeared with hr suitcase. I know that dog it does that with women who are bleeding. Had half hoped she would pick up the Facts of Life from the other servants but no help from that source. Leave hr alone she's white I heard Saar say to Lietja. Had hoped that with the move to the outside room she would throw in her lot with the others—not altogether of course but just so that she can learn to know her place.

So I had hr called & went & spoke the necessary there in the back don't know if it was enough you can't be strict enough with them at that age. If you start bleeding between your legs every month I said to hr you're a risk here on Gdrift you can bring to nought everything that we've done for you overnight & I know you wander about after dark & if I ever catch you in the labourers' houses or discover you've been to D. & his crowd at night I'll give you the boot in the blink of an eye where will you go then? Your place is here on Gdrift I said so see to it that you toe the line. She just stared at me. Don't act stupid I said. You know what the bull does to the cow & what comes of it? just pain & suffering & you're not quite right you're deformed & they did bad things to you when you were small so you can't have children in any case even if you want to & maybe it's hereditary & you know what happens to the late lamb whose mother casts him off? We can't go around raising them all as hanslammers it takes too much time & trouble.

Count yourself lucky I said that you were chosen & kept on & that you got to where you are today where there are people who look after you it's sheer mercy & if you bleed I said you put on the pads. Demonstrated with the elastic & the loops 5 times a day the first 3 days & you wash yourself every time you put on a new one with hot water & soap & rub Mum in your groin when you put on a new one & if I ever pick up a whiff on you there's trouble & the dirty ones you put together in a paper bag & you push it deep into the bin where the dogs can't get to it. If the bleeding ever stays away don't even come & tell me, just take your things & go because then I never want to set eyes on you again.

12 August 1960 10 past 10

Don't feel well since I've been there in the outside room must get more rest I suppose at this stage. Week 34. Dr. did say I would tire easily but I must make time for myself. Would be good to have more time to write up everything that happens here. Might just skip things that could be important. Saar says A. isn't all there she looks as if she walks in hr sleep. See A.'s light's on late at night I suppose she's reading because I forbade hr to read in the day it sets a bad example to the other servants & she has more than enough work to do & I'm scared J. will catch hr reading he's totally opposed to the idea teach a baboon to read tonight & tomorrow he'll be dictating to you he says perhaps I can teach her the basics of embroidery it's a better pastime at least then she'll be producing something.

12 August after lunch

Slept this afternoon. Feel it's close now. Two weeks too early? Every-body says the firstborn is late mostly. Worried about A. I think she's scared of me of what is to happen to me & she tries to hide it behind affectations this morning again when the rain stopped at last. Bring along your embroidery book & come & sit here with me on the stoep I said because I wanted to comfort hr a bit too after the whole sermon on the monthlies & I might as well use my rest break usefully & give hr something of value. Did after all envision it like that from the start just didn't get around to it. Bring your needlework basket I said.

And right there it begins. She turns around as if a snake has bitten her & looks me straight in the eye rude! All I'm saying is you must bring along your needlework basket but then & there I lose my temper com-pletely because I'm made to feel I must justify myself. Who does she think she is the little scallywag full of airs & adopts a pose standing half to attention the feet together the back rigid the arms bent at the elbows the right hand in the left hand held under the chest & the chin stuck out all the way to wherever.

What do you want me to say? I thought. So I said what I wanted to say in any case: your embroidery book & your needlework basket bring them but she just stood there as if she were on stage. So that will be all thank you was all I said as if I were also on stage & only then she looked satisfied. Nods the head as if she's a doll & off she goes with little measured steps the legs hinging only from the knee down as if she's scared that something will drop out from under her. Where would she get that from? Had to shut up the other servants because there they go laughing like drains about the little airs. Ignore I said it passes by itself.

Went to look for an off-cut of coarse-woven material in the ragbag. Halfway through I had another idea. In the bottom drawer of the linen cupboard I remembered there were still precious lengths of material from my mother's trousseau that she'd never used & so I chose the biggest most beautiful piece 2 cloths 6 x 3 yards Glenshee linen still wrapped in the white tissue paper just as Ma must have got it. I thought let me reward her & give her something to show I understand it's not all such plain sailing for hr.

Here next to me on the bench I showed her she must sit when she came out on the stoep but she didn't want to. Brings the stoep chair closer by your leave & puts it next to the bench. So there I had to move closer myself to be near enough to page through the book with hr. You're provoking me I thought but rather said nothing. Sheep-slaughtering I said is not the beginning & the end of the world or stoep-polishing or onion-plaiting or pumpkin-stacking. Farming is only one half of a housekeeper's work. Thought I had to put the point strongly because I've been driving her a bit hard this last month.

Embroidery I said is the other half & fine decorative needlework & knitting & crocheting. They belong to the finer things in life they are age-old arts & rich traditions from the domain of woman. Look at me I said because she was staring in front of her & pretended to be struck deaf. I want you to be knowledgeable & I want you to teach yourself & make it your own that will be proof that I haven't wasted my time with you I said to her.

So I opened the book at my inscription in front & made her read out aloud what I had underlined in the Introduction. Embroidery creates an atmosphere of true values in a house & speaks of the personality of its creator it demonstrates the difference between a developed & an uncivilised nation.

Showed hr all the prettiest examples of drawn-fabric work & white-work & black-work & shadow-work & ravel-work & showed pictures how an embroidered table cloth makes all the difference to a full tea-table setting & how embroidered napkins can make any meal look like that of a king. Told her about the wall hangings of the tab-ernacle as described in Exod. richly embroidered by hand & about the first piece of embroidery from the 4th century B.C. & about the embroidered cloths in which the mummies of Egypt were wrapped for the long journey to the realm of the dead & of the pelicans & the jackals & all the figures of the gods & of how everything was embroi-dered with the greatest of care on fine woven cloth so that the deceased should not feel alone & would arrive in the kingdom of heaven com-pletely wrapped up in his culture & history & faith. Also explained about the church embroidery at which thousands of nuns sat labour-ing day after day in poor light in their cells to the glory of God of the Opus Anglicanum & the great French tapestry of the walled garden in which a snow-white unicorn comes to rest with its head on the lap of the Virgin Mary.

The picture of the strange horse with the bump on the head where the single whorled horn emerges of course interested her mightily. Saw her sta-a-a-ring at this lot & wanting to ask something but the mouth remained drawn in a thin line. So I just said the horse is a symbol of the wander-weary soul & the Catholics believe that the Mother of God is also a mediator but it's a superstition J C is the only way to the Father & the mother is secondary.

Did my best to impress upon A. all the possibilities & showed her examples of our embroidered National art & the representations of our History the ships of Van Riebeeck & the distribution of the first farms on the Liesbeeck & the fat-tailed sheep that the Free Burghers exchanged with the Hottentots for beads & cloths & the Voortrekkers & the Oxwagons & the Boer War & the History of Gold & Diamonds. She doesn't yet realise how advanced such embroidery is but one day when she has learnt for herself how she will understand I said. It's like that with every art form I explained. You start with the simple & then you practise faithfully every day until you're ready one day to tackle the scenes from Hist. & then Heaven.

On the off-cut cloth I showed her the first drawn stitches with which the hems of embroidered cloths are finished. Punching hemstitching double hemstitching & Italian hemstitching & then the first basic stitches in the book dice-stitch & step-stitch & Algerian-eye wave-stitch & satin-stitch blanket-stitch & diagonal ripple-stitch prepared everything for her in practice strips on the length of off-cut cloth so that she could practise further on her own.

Explained nicely what a good discipline it is how it calms one after a day's hard work. It keeps you humble & it keeps you out of idleness it focuses the attention on something useful & distracts from negative thoughts & feelings it calms other people around you & creates a homely atmosphere & it makes time fly & it's better than sitting in your room in the evening counting your toes practise I said & you'll never be sorry you learnt it & at the end of the week I want to see the first three practice strips completed.

To encourage her I promised that if in a few months' time she feels secure with the principles of drawn fabric-work then we can start on her first adult effort on a prettier cloth & then I said to show what I expected of her one day when she's grown-up—here are the very prettiest cloths that I have enough for a tablecloth for a large table when all its leaves are opened out & then I took the lengths of Glenshee out of the paper & I opened them out on my & her laps. Feel such cloth I said you won't get your hands on that nowadays but I know with you it will find a good home.

She didn't touch it just sat there with her hands folded in her lap a little mound under the cloth & hr eyes on the ground as if she wanted to stare a hole into it.

Took no notice & folded the cloth again & wrapped it in the tissue paper & held it out to her. Bless me if she didn't get up from her chair so ramrod-formal I thought my girl do just what you want you're not getting me down but she just carried on standing there & damned if she didn't force me to say what I didn't want to say & then I said it. Thank you that will be all you may leave. So then she packed everything together in her needlework basket click-clack she snapped it shut & walked off with hr new short-step.

How on earth must I now bring A. round? Won't have so much time in the next months to devote to hr. Remained sitting there on the stoep for a long time with my hands on my stomach felt the child kicking under my heart. Tried to imagine him in there with his little star-fish hands his progress through blood & water but all that I saw was the parcel of white tissue paper being borne off through the front room out by the kitchen door across the backyard white with new lime the white cloth in its folds in the tissue paper & its being carried into the outside room across the loose linoleum that creaks on the cement & I heard hr think where shall I put it? a clean safe place? The deepest one that she could find in the cupboards & drawers that I'd had nailed together for her. Knew that was what she wondered because I taught her myself precious objects you hide far away where nobody can get to them & you take them out only when you have a very clear idea of what you want to do with them.

I was still sitting like that when next moment there she was in front of me the hands together on the stomach heaven knows where she acquired that affectation. Mothballs! she says to me. Might as well have been a curse so abrupt. Good idea I say. Was really not going to let myself be upset by a little snot-skivvy & I walked to the cupboard in the passage to find it aware all the time of hr eyes on me & how she's looking at my highly pregnant body as if she wants to burn a hole through me but I just kept myself aloof. Now I think of it that's what I did right from

144

the start consistently with her: kept my cool & kept my head & swallowed my words. A. has this way of creating dramas where there are no dramas. So I pretended not to see anything & opened the packet of mothballs a gust of moth-killer took my breath away. There she stood with hr hand extended & I was quite startled at the face the eyes wide open as if she's going to have a fit from what? from tissue paper? From light-and-shadow work? from lengths of cloth that will take a lifetime to embroider? from the biggest midnight-eye mother-moth that heaves her powder-heavy wings before an onslaught of moth-killer? Heaven knows what goes on in the creature's head.

Two balls are enough & don't look at me like that I'm not a ghost. Two she said in a hoarse voice the good hand extended as if she's waiting for punishment. So made sure I didn't touch the hand & rolled the balls into her palm & quickly she closes her fist zip-zap gone but no running it's just the new clockwork-step enough to make the apron creak. Remember to wash your hands! I called but my voice wouldn't come out & I was angry something terrible with her & with myself for reacting like that to hr tricks. Must be the hormones. Dr. said people do have trouble with them during pregnancy.

But I have the feeling deep in my bones & I'm writing it down here now for the record: From the moment that precious cloth left my two hands I've felt there is a snake in the grass as sure as my name is Milla de Wet. Must remember to store the mothballs in a different place.

*

Jak was repelled by your pregnant body. He couldn't stand being close to you, he couldn't even hide it any more. Gone he was suddenly on that morning of the twelfth of August with the bakkie to an obstacle race with rowing and swimming and cycling at Witsand. He took Dawid along to transport his bicycle and his canoe for him to the various starting-points. You would have to look after yourself. You'd been booked months in advance into Barrydale's clinic to be close to your mother. Your suitcase was packed weeks before. You weren't going to be caught unprepared.

Then the first contractions came right there in the passage after the to-do with the mothballs.

You had to sit down on the telephone stool in the passage. You'd thought another two weeks. The first convulsion had made you feel faint. You phoned, who else, the omniscient.

Look at your watch, your mother said. Note how far apart the contractions are and plan your movements accordingly.

Her voice was hard, business-like, reproving.

You can get here taking your time, even after your waters have broken. The first one usually takes a long time, she said, I had a terrible struggle with you, nine hours on end. Sheer hell it was, so you might as well prepare yourself.

Ma, you said, please. She cut you short. There's no time for chit-chat now, Milla, steel yourself and get on the road. I'll phone the maternity sister so that they can prepare for you. And bring Agaat along so that we can teach her with the child, I have a sore hip, I can't be running after you any more.

You called Agaat. You were scared, you could hear your own voice coming from afar.

You have ten minutes, you said, pack for a week, take your embroidery stuff along, we're going to the Ounooi, the child is coming, he's early, you'll have to help . . . if necessary.

Her eyes were big. Her hands that she was holding in front of her, fell open, the little arm hanging like something that had been loose all the time, something that had broken off that she was hiding. You thought, God help me, you need two hands for a delivery. But you didn't really think it would be necessary. Ma would know, after all.

Pull yourself together, Agaat, you said, we don't have time to waste. Pack your suitcase.

Suitcase, she said, what suitcase, I don't have a suitcase.

I shouted at her.

Where's your brown suitcase that I gave you? If you can't look after the small things, how can I ever count on you in important matters? Take pillow slips, take an onion-pocket in the store, take an apple box, take anything, just hurry up!

You started writing a letter to Jak.

Dear Jak

You tore it up. You started again.

Jakobus Christiaan de Wet, your child is being born, you know where you can look for the mother.

You crumpled it up.

Let the baas know where I am, you said to Saar, phone the hotel in Port Beaufort. Go and open the motorcar shed. Go and tell them to open the gate to the main road. If the drift is still under water, tell two boys to stand on either side on the kerb so that I can see where I'm going.

You called out orders. Agaat ran to and fro with wild gangling legs, the stiff little steps quite forgotten. Her mouth was open. You ordered her around. You remained sitting in the passage on the stool, your legs were lame. She was quick, she did what you told her to. Now it's you and me, you thought, it's always been just you and me. That you realised then, for the first time so clearly.

Sharp scissors, you said, sharpen a meat knife, singe the blades in a candle-flame, wrap them in clean cloths, the big enamel basin, the one with the three roses in the base, Dettol, take the half-full bottle and the new one. And cloths and sheets and packs of newspaper and blankets and matches and rolls of cotton wool and gauze.

She knew where everything was. She kept the whole list in her head as you dictated it. Her lips moved as she repeated it after you. She took hold, sure-handed as you'd taught her. Saar got a trunk off the shelf, put it down at your feet.

Must I come along, Mies? Saar asked. You just gave her a look, made her pack the things as Agaat brought them.

Don't worry, you said to calm them as well as yourself, it's just in case, we have enough time, we'll be there in time.

You remembered the smelling salts, flasks of hot water, a roll of dental floss and string for the tying-off, a box of paper towels. One bottle of sweet tea.

You wrote your mother's address and telephone number on a slip of paper. You put it in your purse. You see, Agaat, here I'm putting it, in case, remember it. You explained how it would work. You had to get to the pass in twenty minutes and then you would stop for a while for the next contractions and then in another twenty minutes you would be on the other side. Jak always used to do it in quarter of an hour. Further than that you couldn't think.

You would take the Mercedes, you decided, that would be safest. You had to slide the seat back to fit behind the steering wheel. You put newspapers and a blanket on the seat under you.

Agaat was trembling. You had to reassure her, now she had to feel sure of herself, as sure as she could. Never mind, you said, we've caught lots of calves, you and I, haven't we? Everything works in exactly the same way, you know it by heart. But it won't be necessary, it's like with the first calf, it comes slowly.

The drift was still flooded after the rains. Two of Dawid's brother's children stood on either side on the edges of the bridge, with the water washing around their ankles. They started laughing, high, long, merry yells when they saw how fast you were approaching. You put the car in a low gear and charged through at full revolutions. You could feel the silt under the wheels, you skidded slightly when you got out on the other side and took the curve. To and fro you corrected in the slippery road. The wipers left long muddy streaks on the windscreen. In the rear-view mirror you saw the children sopping with brown muddy water looking after you open-mouthed.

On the Suurbraak road the next set of contractions arrived. You pulled off the road. Looked at your watch. Twenty, twenty-five after the first? Suddenly you weren't sure. When you could drive again, you started explaining to Agaat what she had to do if it came to the push. You had to concentrate hard on the road because it was wet, again and again you skidded.

Don't be so pale, you said to Agaat, and don't even think of puking. Your car-sickness you can keep for another day. You just pray that there isn't something slow in front of us in the road. Now listen carefully. It's for in case, it's not to say . . .

Her face was tight. She looked straight in front of her in the road. You talked fast, emphasised the main points. Water. Breath. Push. Head. Out. Blood. Slippery. Careful. Slap. Yowl. Bind. Cut. Wrap. Bring to. Wash. Hitch-hike.

That was the easy scenario.

If the little head can't get out, she has to take the scissors and cut, you said, to the back, do you understand? towards the shitter, she had to cut through the meat of your arse, so that he can get out. Saw if necessary, she mustn't spare you. If he's blue, she has to clean his nose and wipe out his drool, out from the back of his throat and from his tongue and blow breath into him over his nose and mouth until he makes a sound. As we do with the calves when they're struggling. She can leave you, you said, even if you're bleeding something terrible, it doesn't matter. And that again is different from the cows, you said.

You can still hear your voice.

We'd rather lose a calf than a cow. But a child, a human child, was something else, a human child comes first.

Ashen, Agaat was. She swayed from side to side in her seat as you took the first bends of the pass. You couldn't go too fast, the road wasn't tarred yet in those days.

The next contractions were too quick. You pulled off in a small parking area on the left side of the road. You tilted the seat as far back as possible so that you could half lie, but it didn't help. The pain was in you like a lip of lava thrusting, thrusting slowly into a street.

The first thing I'll teach you if we get through this is how to drive, you groaned. Do you hear me? You'll learn to drive even if it's the only ride you ever get.

You took off your watch.

Here, put this on your arm. Time how long it goes on for.

The contractions lasted for seven minutes. When they abated, Agaat filled the lid of the flask with tea. She held the flask in her strong hand to pour. Her weak hand trembled as she tried to pass the lid to you clasped in the puny little fingertips.

God in heaven, you thought, just grant that we get across the pass in time, because there really are not enough hands here. For the first time you realised it. You closed your eyes, tried to get in the sweet tea in little gulps.

Is it very sore? you heard a whisper to one side of you, as soft as if somebody was twirling the tip of a feather in your inner ear.

You couldn't stop the tears.

Never mind, you heard, or thought you heard, deep in you, a sound that stirred lightly in your navel.

There is nothing, the voice said, nothing to about cry.

There is nothing.

The sound of feathers being settled in place before nightfall.

Never mind.

The sound of a rivulet trickling from a slope after it's rained high up in the rock faces.

Nothing to cry about. Agaat's first grammar.

You drew courage from that. You started the car and looked at Agaat. Her face was neutral, you must have imagined things.

It was almost twelve o'clock. Fortunately the road was drying out. You drove hard. The rock faces loomed up, closer all the time, rougher, greyer, swallowing you. Deeper and deeper, it felt, you were sinking into the body of the mountain, deeper into the black shadows, with every corner that you took.

What does the river look like? you asked Agaat to divert her attention.

Full, she said.

What else?

Shiny.

Is it far down?

Far. And near.

She whispered. There was a white ring around her mouth.

Suddenly it was lukewarm between your legs. Inside you something dropped and heaved and pushed. It was your time. It wasn't going to take nine hours, Ma was wrong. It would be Agaat's baby, you knew, but you didn't say it out loud.

You were in the middle of the pass. The lay-bys were on your right. After fifteen minutes you had to pull in at the first one that appeared. This time the pains lasted longer. You breathed deeply. One more shift, you thought, another fifteen minute's driving, perhaps we'll make it after all. Suddenly you were angry with your mother. Furious that you'd listened to her hard voice and her harsh advice. You could have simply stayed at home. Saar was there, you could have summoned Beatrice. The one stank of body odour and the other of sanctity, but at least they had experience. You could have had the doctor called from Swellendam. There were hundreds of things that you could have thought of yourself instead of asking her. As if she had a monopoly on wisdom, she had after all only had you, the wisdom of a single child. Your resentful thoughts inclined you to brutality towards Agaat. You couldn't stop yourself. Now you sounded just like your mother.

Yes, Agaat, you said, that's the way of the world, you see what life's like. So it has been written. Come, you know your Bible, don't you. What does it say in Genesis about having children?

Agaat got out two words.

In sorrow, she said.

From the corner of your eye you saw her tighten her mouth, look at the watch. Seven minutes, she said.

My mamma has a goat, you started reciting, because you hadn't meant to sound that fierce, my mamma has a goat, she wants to have him shod. Come Agaat, what's next?

One two three four five six seven, said Agaat, her voice was quavering, but mamma doesn't know how many nails she's got.

You watched the lay-bys as you passed them. You had to fight against the illusion that it was the car that was stationary and that it was the mountain that had wrenched loose out of its grooves and was gnashing past you, a merry-go-round of grey rock faces, rocky inlets. You knew them all, the stopping-places. You were aiming for the one by the waterfall. There was most space there, there were a few bushes to park behind.

Tradouw, you thought, a child of the Tradouw. Gantouw, the way of the eland, Tradouw, the way of the women.

You brought the car to a standstill in a shower of stones.

Agaat did as you said, placed newspapers and blankets on the back seat, with two doubled-over clean sheets on top. You had to lie down. It felt as if you were tearing apart, as if your spine was splitting.

Sing, you said, sing me something.

Breathe, said Agaat, you said I had to tell you to breathe, breathe, and blow. Blow! Blow!

She waited till you started breathing and blowing. Then she herself took a breath so deep it lifted her shoulders and struck up. Oh moon, Agaat sang for you, you drift so slow on your bright throne.

Her voice emerged too high, out of tune. She cleared her throat, started again. Firm this time, and low, nicely on pitch. The moon, kept on a short tow-rope, tight and low along the horizon. She pulled off your wet underclothing over your legs and covered your upper body with a blanket as you did with the cows in winter. She put a blanket roll under your head.

So calm so clear, she sang, and I so sad and lone.

Now wash your hands, you said. Pour the water into the basin, add two caps of Dettol, wash your hands again, wash me from below, take a cloth, take the red soap, wash well. Have ready the scissors, the knife, the floss, the string, the cloths, the sheets, the smelling salts, line everything up where you can reach easily. There'll be a lot of blood, don't get a fright, just do everything you'd do with a cow. And sing, carry on singing here for me, so that I can get hold of a rhythm. Sing something fast.

The boys are cutting the corn tonight, corn tonight, Agaat sang.

Her voice rose, you blew.

My love's hanging in the berry-bush, berry-bush.

You felt pressure in you, downwards, outwards pressure like a tree-trunk.

Now push, she said, my love is hanging in the bitter-berry-bush.

Breathe! Push! Blow!

You bellowed.

Breathe, breathe, breathe, push Agaat said.

You felt her weak hand low on your belly, there it was feeling, this side and that side of the bulge it pressed, like a spatula against a ball of dough, and gathered you lightly from below your navel and stroked down over your lower belly, one two three times. As you had taught her to feel over animals, whether the lamb was lying transverse or the calf was breeched.

Push, said Agaat, he's lying right, his head's in the hole, I can feel him.

Look who's coming in from outside out, she sang, on the intake of breath.

Breathe in, push, blow, blow, blow!

The other hand was inside you, you felt, the strong one, it reamed you as one reams a gutter.

Breathe in and blow, now you must push, Agaat said, he's coming, I feel him, he's hanging in the bush, he's hanging nicely, he's hanging like a berry, head first.

Now you must, now you must, Agaat coaxed. Softly, rapidly, urgently, the language that you spoke to the Simmentals that had such trouble calving. You heard yourself, your voice was in her. You heard your father with animals, when you were small, when you stood next to him in the old stable on Grootmoedersdrift, the language of women that he could speak better than your mother.

> Now take a breath now, a gasp, a groan
> get yourself up now little tradouw
> little buttermilk stand ready
> now I'm pulling your même her ears to the front
> mother macree little mother cow
> point that cunt of yours
> nowwe'regettingthere!
> now now now push the womb
> blow on the bellows
> throw this wombbeast of yours out of the crate
> throw over the rowers of dattem
> throw out the iron
> push him
> give him
> give him littlecalf to me
> give the bluegumbloom
> give him in the nest the shitling
> ai!

You couldn't any more. You were depleted.

He's stuck he's stuck his head is stuck in the hole.

Agaat was in panic, you could hear.

Take the scissors! you screamed. You felt it, the cold steel against you, it felt too slow, she was hesitating.

Cut, God! you screamed, cut open all the way to the hole!

You felt the sharp incision, one blow, another blow. There was a spurt of blood out of you all the way up to the upholstery, it dripped back onto you.

You felt a slipping, you tore, you were open, you screamed, you called, bitterly, you listened to, held your ears like. Like tarns, like eddies, like echo-bearing chasms, like wind-winnowed waterfall, you held them till you heard what was neither of you nor of Agaat.

The sound.

You strained upright, heard the scissors clatter to the ground, saw the strings dangling, slime and threads of blood out of you.

A bundle was put down on you, a bawl swaddled in cloths, your arms were gathered together from where they were dispersed, the arm from the river first and then from the mountain, from left and from right your arms were placed around the bundle, a tiny white cocoon with red palm-prints, a big one on one side, an unfurled fan, and on the other side the bloody forepaw of an otter. Agaat's mismatched hands that had performed the deed for you.

Blood drenched it, Agaat's apron was red all the way to the bib, Agaat's cap a cockscomb, there was a plashing in your ears, a poppling, your heart was open. Full and shiny, far and near. A waterfall. From the highest cliff a down-feather twirling on the foam, a little lily bobbing after the haze of your body, a patch of scarlet in black moss, a throat, a tongue, a gong in the dripping sparkling jet.

There was a ride on an open vehicle, the wind was cold on you. You bled on cabbage leaves. You came to every now and again and sank away into a faint again. The mountains fell on you. Agaat was in front with the driver. That you still knew, that she came and told you, close to your ear.

Everything is fine, she said, my même, she said, I've got him with me, he's safe, I'm holding him for you, we'll be there now-now!

We drive like the wind with you and your child, we ride, we ride, round curves wild and wide, snip-snip went the scissors, snip-snip, and my cap, my cap, how red is its tip.

You came to in the hospital and cried. Where is Jak, you cried, where is Agaat?

Jak's in his canoe on the Breede River. Agaat's sitting in the fireplace, she won't come out.

It was your mother. You did not want to see your mother.

It's a boy, she said, a fast boy. A real De Wet. All its toes and fingers and a handy spanner. His father's pretty mouth. You tore badly, along the cut to the top.

She indicated with her thumb and forefinger.

That servant-girl of yours got hold of you a bit roughly. They still have to sew you up.

Your mother's smile was strange. Was it fright? Shock? Schadenfreude? Judgement? You didn't understand it. You cried. They brought the bundle, you didn't want it, you cried.

Bring me Agaat, bring her here, go fetch her, bring her to me, you cried, bring Agaat, I want Agaat.

Blew snot, your hands over your mouth, your hands on your collarbones. You wanted to choke, you wanted to die, you wanted to get back in under the mountain, trail your heart behind you, drag it in, a bloody trail, a fist on bloody cords.

They dosed you with medicine. They said you were suffering from shock. They sewed you up. They brought the bundle and took it away, brought and took away. Your milk wouldn't come. You were taken to your mother's house.

Agaat was there in her white apron and her white cap, at the garden gate.

She'd come out of the fireplace.

Not a stipple of soot, not a spot of blood, you heard yourself say, from the water, from the fire, from the hollow under your lip.

She held out her arms.

Give, she said softly, give him to me, I'll watch.

8

On the trolley next to my bed the hot water is steaming in the wash-basin. It smells of Milton. Over the fume of disinfectant I detect the fragrance of lavender. Agaat knows Milton sets my teeth on edge. But she persists with it. She says she prefers it to Dettol. Dettol is for hospitals and for childbirth.

Sometimes she adds lavender to the Milton water, or fennel, to make it more pleasant for me, at other times mint, or lemon verbena. She's read up in our gardening books, she says, herbs are good for the blood, for the concentration, for the nerves. I get the message. I must concentrate, I must have nerves of steel. And about my blood, I know, I mustn't worry overmuch, she'll pep that up for me with mint.

Agaat lifts one side of me. She manoeuvres a triple-folded bath towel in under me. Then she walks to the other side and tilts me and straightens the towels under me. All this she does with the strong left hand. With the right hand she steers and pulls and slips and folds. Like a conductor, with the one hand she beats time, with the other she signals the major entries, for percussion, for the trombone, and with that she gives the feeling, passionato, grazioso, every wash-time a concert.

The little right hand feels different to the left when it brushes against my skin, cooler and smoother. It's as if recently she's been touching me more often with the weak hand, a sweep of the knuckles, or a fluttering of the four gathered fingers, a weightless shell-shaped palm resting on my stomach for a moment.

It's as if she's less concerned about my seeing that hand of hers. Now and again I catch a glimpse in the folds of the facecloth when she puts it in the washbasin, in the pleat of a curtain as she opens it. Then it steals away before I've had a good view of it. It hasn't changed. A little frizzled paw with a folded-in thumb such as one sees in verrucose chickens.

155

Every day she wears one of the light crocheted jerseys that she's made part of her uniform, the right sleeve lengthened so that it covers the hand all the way to the knuckles. But I've caught her a few times now stripping back the longer sleeve when she washes me. She knows I see.

Butcher's sleeve, she says then.

She folds back the bedding all the way and drapes it over the railing at the foot of the bed. She adjusts the bed so that my upper body is marginally more upright. She fits the rigid support so that my head is stable. Head Lock by LimberUp & Co.

We're doing a full-body tonight, Ounooi, it's midweek. Then you'll feel a whole lot better.

She spreads a bathsheet over my body from my feet up to my waist.

And seems to me we'll have to massage the feet, they feel a bit cold to me.

I feel her hand on the bridge of my foot. It's the left hand, it feels warm. She does a little rub there, as if my foot needs cheering up. Hang-foot. Sometimes, to prevent my muscles from shrivelling as happened to my hands, she fits the foot-support. Foothold by Feet & All. The stirrups, Agaat calls it. But mainly I ride bareback. Lord, imagine, me in my present state on horseback, hairy death, the ceaseless whinnying, because he'll know what's mounted him.

She unties the ribbons of the bed-jacket behind my neck, she pulls it down over my arms until she can take it off over my hands.

It's thin sleeveless hospital-wear that Leroux brought, for easy effective handling of your patient, I heard him say to Agaat.

But she'll feel the cold, because the muscles are dead, so always keep her covered under several layers of light covers, even though it's summer now.

Leroux speaks to Agaat in the passage outside my door. He thinks he's in a hospital where voices can't be heard over the rumbling of trolleys and clattering of crockery and buckets and nurses rushing around. He tells her everything about his latest conclusions and proposals and he issues his latest directives. I hear him clearly. It's only the floorboards that creak as he stands and rocks on his toes, and the ticking of the grandfather clock in the front room. Agaat never says anything in reply and she never asks any questions. She knows I hear it all. And she doesn't want to tell me herself. About my lungs that are getting weaker all the time. And about my swallowing. She wants me to hear for myself and decide for myself about the appliances and the hospital.

She's simplified everything to a single question: Do you want another nurse?

To that my answer is no.

Agaat covers me with a large towel before she pulls the tunic, under the towel, from my body. She lifts the washbasin from the trolley onto the serving-top and draws it nearer across the bed, over my body.

First the left, she says, and takes my arm from under the towel and lays it down on the bed close to my body. She handles it like a fragment, something that belongs to me only by loose association. A dead arm, but a life-like replica. Like an artificial arm. But an artificial arm needn't be washed like this.

Breathe calmly, Ounooi, says Agaat, and tests the water with her left elbow, as I taught her with Jakkie long ago.

Her grip is gentle but firm. She anticipates on my behalf the impact of the wet warm cloth by keeping constant contact with my body, a hand on my shoulder, a hand on my hand. She hasn't forgotten a single one of her lessons.

Now wash me and I shall be whiter than snow, she sings on the in-breath.

She soaps the cloth, wrings it half dry and washes the arm with firm soapy strokes up to the armpit. She swivels the wrist, the wrist can still swivel. She washes it as if it could still be stained from the silver bangles that I used to wear, and my palm that she folds open, that she washes as if I'd just deboned a chicken. And between my fingers, which she straightens, and up against the cuticles she washes as if I'd been working in black garden soil.

She washes with conviction, just as if I'd lived a full day as of old and were good and dirty, and she talks of lavender.

She says the bushes are flowering this year as if they're paid to do it and the bees are buzzing about like mad there amongst the purple florets and she thinks they've nested in the hollow of the burnt-out bluegum she'll have Dawid take a look and how would I like a little taste of honey, lavender-flower honey fresh from the comb? There's nothing, she says, to touch comb honey, and she must remember to get a jar ready for Jakkie when he comes, as he likes it. Illuminated campaniles, it seems, remind him of honey in the comb. That's what he wrote to her once from Canada.

Agaat wipes the soapiness from the arm with another cloth, a soap-wiping cloth. She dries the arm, puts it back next to the body and drapes the towel over it.

Now the leg on the same side. The leg looks blue towards the foot. She washes vigorously between the toes so that I can feel how much life there is in my foot.

You know, Ounooi, she says, it took me a long time to figure out why you're forever looking at the wall, at the mirror, to and fro like a lizard taking its bearings on a rock, but now I understand. This wall next to your bed is too bare. You want something else to look at here by your bed than this old calendar, perhaps it only irritates you. The mirror in the corner over there, I reckon, is not enough by a long shot, even though you can see the bits of garden that I chose for you.

As she works, Agaat covers the clean leg and arm with the towel as if nothing's the matter. Straight face. Butter wouldn't melt. As if I'd imagined it all about the quarrels. As if it had been a squabble with the nightingales.

Was I too slow? Are you cold yet? she asks.

That's her camouflage enabling her to look me in the eye, to catch a response from me without her having to ask anything directly. Catch a fly from the old mare's back, ha.

I play dumb. No, I flutter with my eyebrows, I'm not the least bit cold and what are you talking about now?

She folds away the large towel from my trunk, so that the washed arm and leg and my abdomen remain covered. She sets her gaze to neutral. That's her way with my nakedness. Well heavens, she says teasingly, you'd really like to know that, wouldn't you, what I'm talking about, as if you haven't for days on end been leading me a dance with your blinking and fluttering, so, you can forget about it then, all I'm pleased about, madam, is that you're not cold!

She soaps my trunk from the base of my throat to the navel. She lifts my breasts and washes under them. One for you, she says, and one for me. She wipes away the soap under them. She swabs me dry, but under the breasts she dries twice with a fresh towel.

The animals went in two by two, she says as she dries them.

I note the inspection. There fungus threatens, there she keeps a sharp eye. Sometimes she checks there with her magnifying glass, mould is like a thief in the night, she says, a lurking menace.

Agaat covers my trunk again. She moves around the bed to the other side. As she moves past the foot of the bed, I manage to catch her eye.

Come on, you can tell me, I flicker with my eyes at the wall and back. You win, I admit, you've guessed right, of course, you always guess right, and good for you, you're wonderful, you're fantastic, as ever, standing ovation!

Hmmm? she says with a straight face, hmmm? Just in passing, she pretends. She juts out her chin just a touch.

I know what she's doing. She's making the washing easier for both of us with a gripping story and she'll postpone the denouement until we've

finished. As reward she'll present it. Triumphantly. As consolation. For
the exposure. For the shame. For the blue feet. For the tremendous art
that it is to treat a half-dead relic like a whole human being.

Right, says Agaat before she bares the other arm, we're on the home
stretch. She's cheering herself up. There's still all of the back.

Are you still holding out, Ounooi? She leans over me and looks into
my eyes while she begins to wash my arm.

And so I thought to myself, she says, and looks away again, let me
collect everything that I can think of that can hang or be pasted that
you want on your wall, everything that you said I should throw away in
your great clear-out, everything that I kept and stored in the cellar, and
everything that's still here in the house to be inherited or given away, as
you directed, and hang them one by one on your wall here next to your
bed until you're satisfied!

As an afterthought it comes, love will find a way to get the camel
through the needle's eye.

She covers the arm and takes out the leg, peeps at me for the effect,
but the effect has been spoilt.

I protest. I am not a camel! And I'm not yet ready for the needle's
eye! Please watch your language! And don't sound so smug, it's not
appropriate!

Sorry, Ounooi, don't take exception now, it's just a proverb, says
Agaat, but she's put off her stride immediately. She drops the cloth into
the washbasin.

Early to bed and early to rise makes a man healthy wealthy and wise,
she says, a penny saved is a penny earned.

Every time the stress on the last word. As if she's defending herself with prefabricated sentences that she appropriates to her purpose
through tone and emphasis. Old trick. She has no respect for what the
proverbs really mean, she invents her own language as she goes. That's
her way when she's discombobulated. The old parrot ways. Double-
barrelled mimicry.

Oh come now Agaat, in God's name, don't be so touchy, I'm the one
who's dying here, look at me dammit, I flicker, but she doesn't look.

Speech is silver twixt the cup and the lip, when the cat's away we
throw out the baby with the bathwater.

She pushes the bridge with the bowl of water across my body to the
foot of the bed.

Almost, she says.

She pushes her chin far out, moves my legs apart and washes my
abdomen with quick soapy strokes.

But don't count your chickens yet.

Once more she rinses the cloth and once more she wipes.

Where there's smoke there's fire, she says.

She dries my loins. The towel feels hard.

I'm sorry I protested. Don't step on the toes of the living dead. Feeling starts at the feet.

I wish I could talk back, counter with my own idioms.

Men must endure their going hence, even as their coming hither.

Ripeness is all.

I plead with my eyes.

She doesn't want to look at me. She's looking at her towels.

Let's turn you on your side then we thump out the phlegm before I wash the back.

Businesslike she is all of a sudden.

She rolls three towels into sturdy bolsters to support me from the front. Firmly she wiggles them in next to my side. A self-conceived plan. Leroux said she couldn't do it alone, especially not with one hand, she needs help, she will need help in future, he'll send a nurse, don't I want a live-in nurse.

I signalled such a one would never in a month of Sundays survive with the two of us.

Agaat translated it for him as: Mrs de Wet says no thank you all the same, she's too particular.

Bolster me with rolled-up towels because I'm over the hill, Agaat, translate me, I'm sick with remorse.

She rolls up another few towels to support me from behind as well.

How many towels does Agaat have? How many does she have washed every day? How does she keep tally of all the linen that passes through here? How does she keep sane?

She covers my body completely with an extra towel, large enough for a king.

I hear her scrubbing her hands, is it possible to get any cleaner?

She returns with white sterile cloths over her shoulder. She places them under my cheek so that I can spit on them.

She turns her back and puts on two new gloves of white-powdered latex.

She unscrews the caps of three jars, her hands are pale, the right glove fits like loose skin.

She mixes two ointments and a liquid in a saucer with a rod of stainless steel. She rubs it on the base of my neck and under my nose. It smells of eucalyptus and friar's balsam. It's to help the mucus rise, to help dissolve it.

She pours warm water into the hollow of a silver kidney.

She places mouth sponges at the ready in a row.

She screws in the mouthpiece of the phlegm-pump.

How much slime does she expect to get out of me anyway? My cough reflex is almost completely gone.

She extends the arm of the bedside lamp as far as it will go.

She turns the head so that it shines full on my back, I feel the glow. It's to keep me warm, I know, she could knock my phlegm loose with her eyes shut.

Ounooi, open your eyes and listen well now.

Her eyes are soft again. Her voice is soft. Close to my face she talks. Through the eye of the needle she'd want to help me. That's really all, I can see it now. And bring me back.

All the way to the cow-shed.

Iron on the hoof.

Pumpkin on the roof.

As it was, always, as it was in the old song.

But was she happy with how it was?

You remember how we do it? asks Agaat. You take a breath, I turn you on your side, you hold your breath until I've propped you up nicely, three rolls behind the back and three rolls in front, then you exhale, then you rest first, then you take another little breath. Just as long as you need. There's no hurry. We just work at our ease until we've finished. You warn me with your eyes, you blink them slowly if that's enough for now, then we take a pause, then I suck out what there is, then I make us some tea. Then we do the other side. Or we do the other half tomorrow. It doesn't matter. Have you understood well, Ounooi? Get ready for the first breath. On your marks, get set, go!

Lord, Agaat, what race? And how many rounds before the knock-out? And what bell? And what white tape against my chest? And the one who sets the pace, will she drop out before the end? Head between the knees in the slow track, too exhausted even to watch how the record is broken?

Record in long-distance dying, best time in cross-country with obstacles. All the way to where the strokes fall one-by-one from the white tower in the throbbing heat of afternoon with cicadas in the pepper trees and a procession escorting me. Or no, it will be different, everything here on the farm, Agaat will carve my headstone.

Don't perform like that, says Agaat when she catches my eye, into every life a little rain must fall, just co-operate, I'm asking pretty please. Come now, ready?

With a firm yank of the towel under me she gets me toppled onto my side. She keeps me in position with her strong forearm pressed length-wise behind my back. I feel her inserting the rolled-up towels behind me, the back of the weak hand nudge-nudging against me, like a muzzle.

She works fast. No sound issues from her. She holds her breath with me. She begins the auscultation. Down below on the short-rib she cups the little hand. She knocks on it with the other hand. Up, up, up come the knocks, to under my shoulder-blade and then again from below. After every third sequence she vibrates over the ribs with the strong hand. She's firm. It's not unambiguously pleasant what she's doing. I can feel something coming loose in my lees. It feels like old solid pieces of me. This is the critical stage. Now she'll stop and with the Heimlich manoeuvre help me try to cough. And then she'll suck the product out of me with the phlegm-pump.

I feel faint. Stones and grass glide below me, as if I'm approaching a landing strip, one foot without a sandal. My tongue sticks to the roof of my mouth.

Agaat exhales. Right we are, she says, she joggles the towel out and makes me roll back slowly. You're hanging on nicely, Ounooi. Come let's sit you up straight first so that I can help you cough.

I can feel her seeking out my face.

Look at me Ounooi, so that I can see what's going on.

I try to open my mouth. I want to say, a piece, you are a piece of me, how am I to quit you? The landing strip is approaching how am I to land? The urge to cough stirs in me, but it's vague, un-urgent, a phantom cough, like an amputated hand with which in an unguarded moment you think you can still lift something.

I feel pressure in front against my teeth, on both sides I feel pres-sure on my jaws under the ear, my mouth is being opened for me, a flat stick inserted between my front teeth to separate them, I feel fingers on my tongue, pulling threads out of me, I feel the suction of the phlegm-pump, the sound of my fluids, and then a damp sponge that wipes out, my cheeks, under my tongue, inside between my lips and my gums, and then a new sponge, drool runs out of me, another sponge, cool, damp on my tongue, and a strong arm that lifts my head and a voice that says:

You can breathe now, the slime is out, get ready to swallow, you're thirsty.

And a spout of small finger-tips between my lips that squeeze out the drops for me. One, two, three on the back of my tongue.

I can't swallow it, I can't.

Jak was angry with embarrassment at his absence from the birth of his son.

An apology he couldn't get past his lips.

He'd won the race, yes. He'd been first in the senior class out of forty-six contestants who were all younger than he. The tide had come in. The wind had come up on the river-mouth. Twice he had capsized and got stuck under his canoe. Exceedingly tough had been the inclines on the cycle routes. He'd grazed and bruised himself falling. His knees, his elbows. Look. Raw. He'd had to change a wheel all on his own in the gale-force wind. He'd been just about knackered. And on top of that, yomping across the loose sand of the dunes, for seven miles.

Ad nauseam you had to listen to it. But when you started recounting how Agaat had kept her wits about her, how brave she'd been, how she'd cut you with the strong hand and delivered the child with the other, how she'd done everything right from beginning to end and stopped a vegetable lorry to take you to hospital and how with hands and apron red with blood she'd helped stack cabbages to make space for you to lie, and how you'd bled on the cabbage leaves, and how she'd got into the front with a complete stranger with the baby, he interrupted you.

He's just glad that you're safe and sound, he said, and he's so proud of his son.

It was the same lay-by, you said.

What lay-by?

Where we the first time, where we almost that time, when we were on our way together, the first time, do you remember, the day after my mother had harangued you so, when we almost in broad daylight in the open sports car, do you remember, when you pressed your head between my breasts, the waterfall was in flood from an unseasonable shower, just like the other day, as if there'd been no time in between.

You tried, you didn't know how to say it, you so badly wanted to recover something of that youthful beginning with him, now that you at last had a child.

Jak looked at you, and looked away. Could not, would not remember it. He was nervous, didn't want to be alone with you, phoned all the world and brought them into the room where you were lying and kept company with them. Ma was the one who put a stop to that. Milla is tired, she said, respect that.

He returned to the farm after two days, only phoned now and again. He kept himself apart from then on. He knew everybody was angry with him.

The Mercedes was sold without his trying to clean it. The upholstery was permeated, he said, with blood and stuff. The first night after you returned to the farm he got hold of you briefly. Half-angrily and deliberately. You were still sore, even though it was three weeks after the birth, but you let him have his way. Where pain was concerned your standards had shifted. He wouldn't get the better of you any more.

For weeks you were tired and weak. You had problems with your milk. The little one was fretful and that got on his nerves.

In the first weeks he tried to build a toy aeroplane in the backyard. It wouldn't come together. A few times he kicked it to pieces in frustration. You tried to bring him to his senses.

Jak, you said, surely you know by this time you have two left hands, just don't get yourself so worked up about it, in any case it'll be years before the child is big enough for a toy like that.

He wouldn't give up. The whole backyard was eventually cluttered with pieces of plank and nails and open paint tins and clamps and glue-pots.

You had to keep shushing him with his electric planes and drills there under the nursery window.

Be quiet! you screamed at him, day-in, day-out you kick up a racket, don't you have any consideration?

Then he took umbrage and went running in the mountains, only to return with a red face to start chopping and hammering where he'd left off.

You said, forget about the propeller, but he had to install a dashboard with flashing lights and build a propeller into the nose that could turn with electricity.

One day when he was out, you had the mess cleared up and sorted and carried under the lean-to next to the stables.

You're in our way here, you said, go and play over there.

He looked at you, opened his mouth and closed it again, and walked away stiffly. Give me a break, his back said, give me a break, I'm also here. But you didn't want to see it, your heart was cold.

Once you went to him under the lean-to, with a mug of coffee. Flat on his back under the fuselage he was trying to jiggle the electric leads for the dashboard lights through holes that had been drilled too small for them and trying to tinker the wires into place behind the propeller-head. The blades that he'd taken out of an old lawnmower and filed down to make an airscrew were too heavy for the little plane, they looked completely out of proportion. You pointed at it. He looked at you. You lowered your hand.

164

One evening he called you and Agaat from the bedroom where you were attending to Jakkie.

Come and see, he said, his voice exaggeratedly jaunty, bring that lad of mine along, we're ready for our maiden voyage.

For the demonstration he'd dragged the little plane from under the lean-to to the middle of the backyard. There it stood under a piece of black plastic, ready for the unveiling. From under the plastic a thick white extension cord snaked out. It was supposed to be connected to the electric cord with the plug that was dangling out of the window of the nursery.

You stand over there now, he instructed you and Agaat, who was holding the child. You had to stand in front of the bathroom window on the closed-in side of the backyard for the best view.

All the doors and windows of the rooms facing onto the backyard were open. He switched on all the lights that could switch on, from the kitchen all the way to Agaat's room, the storeroom and the nursery, all the main lights, and left the doors wide open so that light could shine on his handiwork.

With a grandiose gesture he removed the plastic cover. Beneath the bravado, you could see, he was tense.

It's turned out well, you said. From a distance, under all the lights, the toy did in fact look impressive.

It was painted silver with orange and blue stencilled on the fuselage and on the wings. Jakobus de Wet, Jr., was written on the one side and a black outline represented the five points of the castle. On the wings were rings and dots and crosses.

It's a Spitfire, said Jak, and now we're going to get it going.

Will it make a noise? you asked, because the child had just calmed down after a long struggle with feeding.

Not too much, Jak said, otherwise you just cover his ears.

Agaat looked at you. She stepped back. You put your arm around her shoulders.

Are you ready? Jak asked, it may move a short distance but it's not working all that well yet, I must still adjust the propeller's angle. You felt half sorry for him, so clumsy, and you didn't want him to make a fool of himself in front of the farm children, because by now there was a whole cluster of them who'd come to see, trampling one another at the open end of the backyard.

He pushed in the plug. The propeller creaked, turned once, twice. Jak twirled it by hand. Then the propeller took suddenly with a high keening sound so that he had to jerk back his hand and jump back.

Jak called something and gesticulated with his hands behind the grey haze of the propeller. You couldn't hear. The little plane moved forward fitfully, then it looked as if something got stuck in its throat. It dipped forward, heaved backward, and exploded.

A grey object flying loose, whirring blades.

You saw slow wavelike movements. First you saw Agaat turning round and growing. Her back ballooned out backwards and grew up into the air lengthwise, a mast. The cross of her apron bands white over her shoulder blades. She bent her head low over the child. Her white cap descended over his little pink face like a keel. Pieces of wood flew around. The propeller came straight at her. It struck her a glancing blow on the back of the head and bounced up into the air and broke the window of the nursery and was left dangling in the steel frame of the panes.

Agaat slowly sank down with the shards of glass shattering around her head. Her arms were locked around the little bundle. Her shoulders were hunched forward like shelters. At the nape of her neck a stream of blood coiled out from under her cap. Everywhere on the ground wrenched-loose wires smoking. The dashboard on which two little red lights were blinking, lay at your feet. Then there was another explosion, three, four more in short succession and more glass tinkling. Short circuits in all the rooms around the backyard where lights were on. The whole house blacked out from front to back. The backyard was pitch-dark. You couldn't utter a word. Your knees collapsed under you. You sat down on the ground. It was dead quiet.

He isn't hurt, Agaat said after a while out of the darkness. He doesn't have a scratch.

Her voice was matter-of-fact.

You saw the white cap coming upright slowly.

The child started crying frantically.

Jakkie! Jak called, his voice high with anxiety. Give him to me!

You crawled over the splinters of plank and glass to Agaat.

You're not laying a hand on my child, Jak de Wet, you said. You're not getting anywhere near him.

I'll put in new fuses quickly, he said, his voice rising higher all the time, I bought new ones.

You're not touching anything further around here, Jak. You keep your hands to yourself, and you go and sleep in your canoe in the shed, you said. You were quite calm and collected. You were furious. Your words issued from your mouth dispassionately.

I'll have in an electrician tomorrow, we should have had new fuses installed a long time ago. And don't worry about us, there are lamps and candles and the Aga. Agaat is here, she'll help me. And tomorrow morning when I get up, the last shred of trash here will be cleared up, I don't want to see one shard or splinter, not one, do you hear? And you take your car and you drive to town as soon as the shops are open and you have glass cut for the broken panes and you get putty and you put out all the tools here in a row. I'll ask Dawid to put in the panes. Is everything quite clear to you now?

Jak stood there for a while yet before he turned around and crunched away over the glass.

Against the light of the stars you saw him clench his hands behind his head and cast them down by his sides, and he cursed three times in himself, the same curse, and shook his shoulders downwards as if he wanted to wriggle himself out of his clothes into the ground.

*

something's wrong
you're just getting old
I'm sick
not sick senile maybe who would want to bake a sponge cake in the middle of the night
look the spasms they come from nowhere
donkey twitching under the yoke have a mustard bath
can't get the button through the button-hole
let me help you
my shoulder aches
it's from putting it to the wheel all your life rest for a change
that's not funny it's stiff
cold shoulder I know it well frozen shoulder it's the chill of may that gets into your bones
something's wrong
you're just old
I'm sick
stop complaining
my fingers prick
prick back
my rings won't come off
use soap
it doesn't work
shall I phone the goldsmith for you?
what can it be?
seasonal indisposition silver-leaf sickness

I'm falling
the leaves are falling soon the rain will be falling then we can plough
then you'll see it's all over
but I fall all the time
a falling fashion trying to attract attention that's all
I'm sick
hypochondria
really sick
affectation
anxiety's palsy
it's the inbetween-time's sickness the fallow land must come to rest
the oats has been raked in everything is holding its breath for rain.

*

3 September 1960 after lunch
Starting to feel halfway human again & feel like writing again even though I still cry a lot. Just after the birth I felt I should keep my diary up to date but the first weeks lame & no strength & the nightmares still carrying on. Post-natal depression says Beatrice. Comes & sits here with me sometimes when I'm playing Pa's old records but I don't want her here she gloats over my situation & she gets bored when I try to tell her about Brahms & his eternally unrequited love for Clara Schumann. She says no wonder I'm depressed it's the dismal Brahms that I listen to der Tod, das ist die kühle Nacht, das Leben ist der schwüle Tag & that was apparently also my father's problem. Then I think nothing of saying I want to lie down so that she can be on her way & A. is not behindhand & fetches her coat.

The brave little servant! how will I ever be able to repay hr? Oh moon you drift so low with constricted throat shame & Ma slipped her 20 pounds when Jak came to fetch us & an old church hat as well you can't be confirmed without a hat she says I ask you. A. says thank you nicely & just gives the hat a long look & later on the way home she says: I've got seven caps what do I want with a hat as well? I see the silly little green hat is hanging there in her room from a nail in the wall with turkey feathers in the band. What would Pa not have thought up to thank her. He would have written a limerick.

A. was off to town at the first opportunity with D. to buy embroidery thread & cloth & buttons with the money from Ma & wouldn't that woman from Eye of the Needle see fit to phone. Whether I'm aware of the two dozen imported porcelain buttons & goods to the value of altogether over sixty pounds cash that A. bought from her. Apparently she first selected everything & then went & drew some more of her own money at the post office. Had to bite my tongue not to say listen here madam thread-pedlar aware or not that little girl was my midwife & my refuge in my hour of need & no cloth of purple or thread of silk or ivory of Sheba can be too good for hr hands but then I thought better of it & said nothing otherwise the whole district would have feasted on the story again. Don't I know how they batten upon death & birth & servants' bugger-ups not that A. is a servant or buggers up but they draw no distinction. Seems in any case as if A. is making excellent progress with the embroidery I see washcloths & tea cloths & some of my handkerchiefs have acquired edges & roses too pretty for words. I show them to Jak but he just goes hmf. Just keep my shirts out of her hands I don't want to look like a bloody Turk with a tulip on my shirt pocket says Jak. Don't know what she's got up her sleeve with the bought stuff there in hr room but I no longer go in there to check.

6 September 1960

I was reading back tonight everything that I've written so far in these booklets it's quite a little pile by now & wouldn't make much sense to an outsider who doesn't know the circumstances. It comforts me to write up everything about home & hearth whatever Jak says. His latest is that I must sell it to Femina but he first wants to insert punctuation everywhere otherwise they'll think his wife with her Brahms & her French can't write properly & it's also much too long-winded according to him I must remember he says the housewife market wants things out of the oven in a jiffy & they want joy & sorrow with capital letters & enough commas so that in-between they can have a cry & a cup of tea. Can't understand why it irritates him so. It's not as if I'm trying to write a history book for high schools, is it?

On the other hand when I page through the booklets like this then I wonder what's become of me. Of my interests & my talents. Always in a hurry or sleepy or tired when I write. Just trying to keep up with myself on this farm every day. Husband child & servant over & over & that's where it gets stuck. What on earth would Dr Blumer have made of such subjects? Perhaps I should try to write in English. Perhaps domesticities will sound better to me in a world language. Can just imagine what Friedman the little whipper-snapper of a professor in the English Department in those days would have said. Always filled the margins of my essays in his myopic little hand. You have come seriously unstuck here, Milla, what has become of your style, your wit, your vocabulary? According to the experts even psychology has to read like a thriller. Pace, remember, pace, texture & wry moments, only wry moments will satisfy my appetite. Of wry moments he would have had enough here if only he'd put on his glasses. More at any rate than in his great hero Charles Lamb. On Saying Grace. Where are the days. So vain the idea I had of myself then.

Odd how much one forgets even though it's only about pots & pans. Had to add or correct things everywhere. Then I had a sudden inspiration to write the dedication that had been in my heart all the time but the time was not yet ripe for it but now it seems as if all my trouble with A. has after all been rewarded. So sweet-tempered nowadays. Three attempts before I was satisfied. Difficult to sound heartfelt on paper but that's how I feel. Must still copy it neatly into the front of the first book.

10 September 1960

Can place my trust 100% in A. She has a remarkable way with Jakkie that much is definite. The first weeks she sat up by his cradle hour after hour & even now still every day. Is patient helpful quick to learn knows her place. Has undergone a major change of attitude it seems. Honestly didn't think I was going to stick it out with hr. Before Aug. still thought I'd be forced to find some other refuge for her because I could see nothing but hardship ahead. But what on earth would I have done without hr now? She picks him up when he wakes up & changes him when he's wet & cleans him when he's dirty & bathes him & dresses him as if it's the child of her own blood day & night immediately she's on the spot when he cries & she sleeps with hr window open to hear him at night. Says she's awake even before he can as much as squawk & then she comes in at the back door & soothes him & sings to him that always calms him down. I've told her she can sleep on the camp sretcher with him in the nursery while he's so small it would be more convenient she pretends not to hear me suppose she doesn't feel comfortable with the idea & so I just dropped the matter because I suppose Jak would also have something to say about it. The Hottentot Madonna of the Langeberg he says St Agaat of South Africa the halo is in place when can we expect the canonisation. If only A. hadn't gone & overheard him.

It's not an easy child. Ma says firstborns just are like that. Beatrice has all sorts of theories. He's scared of my hands scared of my face & I have trouble suckling & as it is I have so little milk. A spring lamb says A. always has more whims than autumn lambs but with her she says he behaves himself as if it were April all the way.

She's always cheerful & tireless. Often watch her when she doesn't know I'm looking so tender & hr mouth so soft & hr body even though she's no more than a child herself (have now written her name on the birthday calendar 12 July exactly one month before Jakkie. Won't forget it again!) so protective of the helpless little creature. Feel myself in her shade her inferior by far in terms of patience & ingenuity. Feel weak in the face of the task. Still often weepy but at least somewhat less than at first. Often sit in my chair in front of the glass door feeble & listless then A. comes & lays the baby fragrant in his little white blankets & soft clothes gurgling in my arms. As if she wants me to share in the well-being she awakens in him or if she wants me to be kindled by the first little smile she gets out of him. But his little face clouds over immediately when he notices me & he frowns as if he's seeing a dreadful problem on my face & he grimaces & he cries fit to break my heart so then I return him to A. she always has a plan. Let's push him in his pram to the dam let's sit there for a while in the shade of the willows let's sing to him so he can grow human let's go for a drive with him over the ridges so that he can feel the lie of the land up & down over the hills sikketir sikketir over drift & fields all the way to the old bridge of Vaandrigsdrift let's take him over the plain to Malgas & sail with him over the river on the ferry so that he can get used to crossing the deep & dark places.

14 September 1960 afternoon

Allowed myself to be carried along with A.'s proposals this last week & every day today again we packed the baby-case & packed a picnic for ourselves & got into the car & followed our noses. A. doesn't want to sit in front wants to sit in the back with the child in his crib. Watched hr in the rear-view mirror how she looks at him every now & again & rearranges a little blanket or covers a kicked-open little hand or foot & then gazes out again this side & that side over the land in its light-green spring attire the lambs playful on the dam walls the crops hand-height the fennel—her fennel!—in flower next to the road (once she opened the window to smell it & smiled with me in the mirror) the tops of the bluegums sprouted shiny-red what is she thinking? but I'd rather not ask. She rocks & she soothes the child.

I drive & show hr the world. Over the ridges over the plains over the rivers. Storms River, Breede River, Korenland, Buffelsjag, Karnemelks, Duivenhoks. We have picnics with hr favourite food cold sausage & bread with apricot jam & red cooldrink & sago pudding on dam walls & banks in the shade. Even dug up my Oxford Collected Poems & read to her & taught her a few new English words. It's all really to console hr & to mollify hr to remind hr of the good things which should not come to nought. I look at hr & I cry secretly because I know it's my little child in hr arms there that makes her now at times totally forget the quick steps & the stiff formal air that she affected & in unguarded moments become again as she was.

14 September evening

Reread the little books from the beginning. What is it with me this need to go over everything again now as if I'm searching for something that I lost? Tell myself I've lost nothing. I have what I've always wanted. And I've also got A. back & it's all good it has all come to good as the Lord wanted it. So then I wrote the inscription that I composed the other evening in block letters in the front of the first booklet with today's date so that I can remember one thing: That I owe it all to the coming of little Jakkie.

17 September

It's been 3 days now & I still don't know how to write it up & if I should write about it at all if writing can countenance it. J. would murder her if he were to know. Can't tell it to anybody.

Have been seeing wet patches on the uniform for a while now & when I ask she says he must have drooled on me or he most have burped a wet wind will go & change. Without twitching a muscle. After the first few times she must have taken precautions. She knows the rule child-minding or not the uniform must be spotlessly white every moment of the day. So then last Wednesday one of those little spring mizzles & I had a nap in the afternoon & I wake up there's a silence in the house heavy & deep & I stay lying on my bed listening to the dripping & looking over the stoep scattered with flowers from the wisteria like little blue butterflies in the wet & the gutters are dripping softly a turtle dove calls it's almost done raining & I feel happy & grateful that I've always in spite of everything been able to keep everybody on track on Gdrift & when at last I get up & go to have a look there I find the cradle empty. Feel the covers still lukewarm from his little body & I press my nose into the blankets they're so sweet & I know A. has come to fetch him to give him the bottle everything is so quiet.

Didn't want to call or make it known that I was awake wanted to shelter in the hushed sleeping afternoon as in a nest in the rain. Softly to the kitchen on bare feet there the back door is wide open & smell of wet is so sweet & everywhere it's dripping with rain. The water on the stove in which we always heat the bottles of milk was still warm I felt & 3 clean bottles were standing upright on the tea cloth A. somewhere feeding him with the fourth one I knew. But then she wasn't in the sitting room either there on the green sofa & not on the stoep either & not in the spare room either.

So then I saw from the nursery window that the outside room's door was closed but the outside latch was off & then I knew immediately that's where they were & then I wasn't easy the servant's quarters is not a place for my child but I thought perhaps A. had just gone there to put on a clean apron & had taken him along. Put on slippers & went out into the backyard & A.'s curtains were tightly drawn but I didn't want to knock & then I was ashamed of myself because Jakkie was nowhere safer than with A. Walk around the back because then I remember there's a small window at the back & it's muddy & I clamber onto a paint tin & the window's open a chink & I cling to the window sill to peer into the room.

There is A. with her back to me on the apple box in front of her bed. Hr one shoulder bare the crooked bones of the deformed side wide open to view & I look & I see & I can't believe what I see perhaps I dreamed it the apron's shoulder band is off & the sleeve of the dress hangs empty & her head is bent to the child on her lap. Could just see his little feet sticking out on the one side. Perfectly contented. There I see on her bed on a white towel untouched lies the fourth bottle full of milk. There I stand in the drizzle on the paint tin that's sinking away in the mud with my forehead pressed against the window sill & I listen to the little sounds it sucks & sighs it's a whole language out there in the outside room I can almost not bring myself to write it.

Went & put on my raincoat & wellingtons. 'Have gone for a walk' I wrote on a piece of paper for A. & the exact time half past three so that she could see I was awake. Walked along next to the drift & stood by the deep places & looked at the drops falling on the water in ringlets

& the eels coming to see if it was food dropping. Saw to it that I stayed away for an hour.

A. busy bathing the little one when I returned her strong arm under his little back supporting him hr little hand soaping him as I taught her there he lies gurgling in the water & smiles at me. I stand in the door of the nursery & I just look & I find nothing to say.

Look who's here Jakkie, your même she's been for a walk but I wonder where she was she's got a white spot on her forehead like a blazed mare!

I look in the mirror & there it is, the lime of the little window through which I was peeping.

9

My tongue is being wiped. It's not Agaat's hand. Not the little hand that ventures beyond my uvula. The fingers are thicker, more innocent. Something is pressed on my face, over my mouth. A thing is placed in my mouth, a mouthpiece, plates between my teeth that pull my lips apart, flatten them. Cool air is blown into me.

Behind my back there's a whispering. Two voices. Agaat's and somebody else's. I am lying on my side. There are four hands working on me. The starling, the crow and two other, cooler hands. I'm being rubbed with something.

Shadows in the mirror. A glow on my ribs. I eavesdrop. Can one eavesdrop if one is mute?

Everything's fine, you're managing pretty well here, there's nothing that could have been prevented, Agaat. And they say it's going to get cooler, perhaps a little summer shower, that will also help. Then you can open the doors for a while, it's stuffy with the room closed up like this.

It's Leroux. He clears his throat. I smell his aftershave lotion. Cloves.

But why did she . . . ? She's never just passed out like that while I was knocking out her phlegm.

I'm sure she has. You just haven't noticed. It's a lack of oxygen. That's what's lacking here, oxygen. Beyond that we can't do anything.

She's been different of late.

How do you mean?

Restless, sort of. To and fro with the eyes, like that, to and fro all the time like a thing looking for escape. I thought I knew what it was.

What?

I thought she felt trapped in here, she wanted out, outside, so I turned the mirror so that she could see the reflection of the garden. It's better than nothing. But it's something else. She wants to see something, something that's outside and inside. Outside and inside at the same time.

You must expect that, the boundaries will start to fade now.

How do you mean, doctor?

Between waking and unconscious. She'll start going into coma, remain in a state of half-sleep, be unconscious for long periods, be confused when she wakes up, mix things up, like who you are, and where she is. You must try to imagine it. It's someone who can't communicate, somebody who perhaps more often than you think is delirious, an endless tunnel you must imagine full of shreds of yesterday and today and earlier times. And then when she comes to, she can't talk and she can't move, and then she gets into a panic.

I can imagine Agaat's face behind me. Set to neutral. She is representing me there behind my back. She knows I can hear everything.

It's not that, doctor, I know, she was quite lucid, she knows very well who I am, she knows what she wants, she wants something from me, she wants to see something, she asks, with her eyes, continuously, if she gets the opportunity. But I've made a plan now. I've selected a few things, I'll hang them here, by her bed, until I see that's the right one, that's what she wants to look at.

Agaat, you must do as you must do. You two chose it yourselves and had it set down before the law, it's in the will, you may decide everything, she gave you the right, so I can't force you. Don't over-exert yourself, see to it that you get rest, you can phone me at any time if you want an assistant. I can send you a sleep-in nurse, two even. To relieve you, twice, three times a week.

That's not necessary, we're still managing. She won't tolerate anyone else now.

That's meant for my ears. Tolerate.

Well, just remember that it's also a matter of how much you can tolerate. Give the oxygen as I showed you when you think it's necessary, when you do the auscultation. Beforehand and afterwards as well. It could have been a fright too, shock, remember she feels everything, it's possible that in her condition she's more sensitive, registers pain more quickly than is normal. To faint would then be a kind of flight reaction.

Faint, yes doctor, she's fainted easily, all along, when she was having a hard time, but not . . . not flight.

Can tolerate her, only her, with no possibility of flight. Hand over hand Agaat casts her lines in my direction. The doctor has long since become merely an excuse to get it all said. She got a fright, now she's aggressive. Push and shove at a dead thing to get some life into it.

Would Leroux suspect any of this? His voice is soft and businesslike. You can take off the mask in an hour or so, he says.

The towel is taken out from under me. Two pairs of hands turn me on my back. Under my knees I feel Agaat's arms, the lever and the little auxiliary brace. Leroux takes uncertain hold of me by the upper body. Stupid is his grip, stupid and bereft of messages, such hands, enough to make you feel you're dead already.

Look, says Agaat, the eyes are opening.

The eyes. As if I'm a perverse child.

Mrs de Wet, can you hear me? This is Leroux.

Fingertips snap before me.

She doesn't like things in front of her face, says Agaat.

Again the snapping of the fingers.

She's completely conscious, I can see, doctor.

Mrs de Wet, it's Doctor Leroux, everything's under control again now, the phlegm has been knocked out, we cleared your air passages. You fainted, we gave you a bit of oxygen, now you're as right as rain again.

Leroux's face looms above mine. He looks at my eyes as if they were the eyes of an octopus, as if he's not quite sure where an octopus's eyes are located, as if he doesn't know what an octopus sees. He shines a little light into my face, he swings it from side to side. I look at him hard, but seeing, he cannot see.

Agaat catches my eye. Wait, let me see, she says.

Leroux stands aside. He shakes his head.

Agaat's face is above me, her cap shines white, she looks into my eyes. I blink them for her so that she can see what I think. The effrontery! They think that if you don't stride around on your two legs and make small talk about the weather, then you're a muscle mass with reflexes and they come and flash lights in your face. Tell the man he must clear out.

A small flicker ripples across Agaat's face. Ho now hopalong! it means. Her apron creaks as she straightens up. Her translation is impeccable.

She says thank you doctor. She says doctor is welcome to leave now, she's feeling better. She says thank you for the help, thank you for the oxygen, we can carry on here by ourselves again now.

I close my eyes. He must think she's crazy.

Again the fingers snapping in front of my face.

She's conscious, really, doctor, you can leave her alone now, she's just tired, when she shuts her eyes like that then I know. Everything's in order, she says, she just wants to sleep now. I know, I know her ways.

Agaat, I don't know about that, aren't you imagining things? How can you know it all with such certainty? You can't get into the ounooi's head, no matter how much you want to. You know this kind of illness that locks people up like this in themselves, they get a bit dement . . . senile from it. It's the loneliness, it's the isolation. You can't trust that you're reading them correctly. It's better to attune yourself to literal meanings, to their essential needs, without subtle intentions, without complicated messages. Otherwise you confuse them, or put all sorts of unnecessary stories in their heads. And as it is they have a hard enough time of it. Don't you want me to stay over tonight? Do you think . . .?

No thank you doctor, I'm not imagining anything, I know her, she's far from senile. Perfectly sound of mind still.

Agaat looks at me.

I signal to Agaat yes, and you're also quite sound of mind. Tell the man our imagination is a shared one, tell him we thought each other up and he's early, it's not my time yet, tell him a lot of water must pass under the bridge here, tell him I want only you here. And he must stop snapping his fingers in my face as if I'm a poodle. That I find a wee bit too literal, thank you.

Agaat widens her eyes. Ho now! it means, behave yourself. But glad to see you've still got some kick left nevertheless.

Leroux steams ahead. It would be no problem at all, I brought an overnight bag, I can sleep on the sofa in the sitting room . . .

Perhaps the language of women is impenetrable to men anyway. Even when the women can say everything out loud. Or perhaps it's the language of the nurse and the patient of which the highly-educated physician has no inkling.

It's not her time yet, doctor, Agaat parries, I'll know, she'll let me know.

As you see fit, Agaat, then I might as well go now, just come and collect the other oxygen tank from the car, the extra mask.

I'll be back in a moment, she signals to me behind the doctor's back. She makes a sign to show she's working him out, she's getting rid of the intruder, him with his little light and his case and his sign language for dogs. He mustn't come and interfere here. We're man enough.

Suddenly I feel weak. It's their backs, first Leroux's, his back in a grey suit with the double vent at the back and then Agaat's with the stiff white bow of her apron. For my sake she tried to walk backwards, so as not to leave me alone too abruptly, to reassure me. But now she's turned around. And here I lie, here I'm left behind. Perhaps we're not up to it, perhaps he's right, the doctor, perhaps we are jointly out of our minds to think we can complete this project in the allotted time. All the parts of it. The remembering, the reading, the dying, the song.

She pretended not to see my second thought. Leroux's footsteps stop in the passage. Agaat walks on.

And all these things lying here? I hear him ask.

Agaat doesn't reply, she has passed him, she opens the front door for him.

I'm asking, what are all those things piled up there in the passage?

Just some old stuff. She wanted to throw it away a long time ago, when we cleared out the house. Then I didn't believe it. So I kept it all in the cellar. Now she's asking to look at it all again, her little things from long ago.

I see, says Leroux. There's suspicion in his voice.

That's what I think she wants to see, says Agaat.

Well, you know she must remain calm. She mustn't upset herself unnecessarily. The slightest thing that makes the breathing irregular, anything that brings too much spit to the mouth, grief, consternation . . .

I can just see him, how he bobs with his head. Then she's had it, he wants to say.

The man is a bit unpolished. I've known it for a long time. He's improper. He does rounds in the zoo, where the creatures are caged in and he has to feed them, give them oxygen, mumble little anodyne platitudes. The only diversions, he thinks, are his visits. An outsider representing the real world and the wisdom of the wise.

I don't upset her, says Agaat. If she wants to see things, she'll see them, she still has quite enough of a will of her own. Agaat sounds determined, as if she would sponsor my will of my own to the end of all time.

Leroux's footsteps resound loudly. Well then, go ahead and bugger up, his tread says, past cure is past care. You complicate the course of events with your little games.

His parting words I half catch.

It's of no use to anybody, he says, if you drive yourself to the brink . . .

I can't hear any more of this. What could he have said? It's of no use to anybody if you drive yourself to the brink . . . of death, of somebody else's death? . . . to the brink of insanity, somebody else's insanity?

The brink of the abyss. The last frontier. Before the hinterland. Before the Hottentots-Holland. Before the Overberg. No-man's-land.

No, the man is too obtuse to think up something like that, the wind blows his words back into the sitting room. The front door bumps against the doorstop. They are standing on the stoep. Under the front-door light.

Where the geckoes sit with their mouths full of moth. The message is clear. Agaat, will she hold back the door with her little hand, keep it open so that I must hear?

It's of no use to anybody if you drive yourself to the brink of exhaustion, Agaat. Remember, you're the only care-giver here. If you also collapse, we have an even bigger crisis on our hands. Do the necessary. Spare yourself, cut out the frills. See to it that you eat regularly, get enough sleep, go for a walk in the veld, in the mountains. You can't hold her. She's withering away, every day a little more. You must accept. You must resign yourself. It's time. Nobody can battle against death.

They're out on the stoep, down the steps, the boot clicks open, slams shut again. The engine idles. Last instructions, inaudible directions, a car door slams, lights swivel across the yard.

Then Agaat calls the dogs back into the yard, she removes the door-stop, closes the front door. She puts something down on the floor. It sounds like deep-sea diving equipment. She rustles something in the passage.

She comes into the room with a rolled-up length of cloth, tied with bows in three places.

Ai mercy, the doctor, she says, he's a meddler.

She looks at the wall.

Ounooi, it's only your breath.

She brings a chair.

You have a lack of breath.

The cloth has a piped seam that is threaded onto a bamboo rod. One of those that we used to train tomatoes. Tomato-rod. There's a string attached with a loop and a picture hook. She smoothes the seam with one hand, so that the cloth is in the centre of the rod.

Shall I take off the mask now?

The simplest question on earth. From the start. So shall I break the eggs for you? Shall I fasten your dress? Wipe your bottom? Hand you the walking sticks? Bring the walking frame? Push the wheelchair?

Crank up the bed? Farming as usual. Milking, slaughtering, shearing, harvesting.

She climbs onto the chair. Measures the length of the string. Fits the hook to the picture rail.

You don't like things near your face, do you, Ounooi.

She picks loose the first bow, bethinks herself, looks at me.

And you look like something from Mars with that thing on your face.

Mars. On the brink of Mars. Don't waste your breath, I flicker at Agaat. One with too little breath in this room is enough.

Wait, she says. She gets off the chair. First things first. Then the surprise.

Agaat has a sequence. There is nothing, she believes, that so reassures and motivates for the execution of a difficult task as the knowledge that you will be rewarded for it. She smiles at me. The you'll-never-guess smile.

Poor Agaat. What has my life been? What has her life been? How can I ever reward her for daring to come this far with me here on Grootmoedersdrift? How does one compensate somebody for the fact that she allowed herself to be taken away and taken in and then cast out again? And to be made and unmade and remade? Not that she had a choice. I even gave her another name.

First the mask, says Agaat. When it comes off, I'm going to press you lightly on the chest, Ounooi, don't get a fright. Gently up and down. You blink with you eyes, I follow you. I learnt it from the doctor just now, it's to assist your muscles. So that you can breathe. Come, let's first sit you up a bit more.

Agaat aims to adjust the bed so as to get me more upright. She doesn't want to take her eyes off my face. Her foot searches for the pedal, her hands grope for the screws.

Oh, oh, she starts singing, softly, on an intake of breath. But the white-throat crow doesn't follow, plummets into emptiness, Agaat's face crumples, her cap wilts, her mouth gapes, wounded.

A little bundle of bones and feathers she drops, down through the blue and the white of the skies, the brown horizon a whirling haze, down, down, black-and-white, a rushing, before she comes to herself and opens her wings and the air buoys her up and she can fly again.

Agaat's foot finds the pedal, her hand finds the wing nut. The bed erects itself with a hissing sound and a light shock.

She puts my arms next to my sides. Wings that can no longer fly.

Go from here to great Tradouw, she resumes on the right note, the crow taken for granted, skipped, omitted from the text, but without loss, because a song that we both know can tolerate that all too well.

Flying high and turning low.

What kind of cloth could it be that's hanging there rolled up? Agaat's décor for the great breathing-scene? It would be the first handmade decoration to hang in my room again after she carried everything out of here.

Went there fast and came back slow.

She unclasps the buckle of the mask behind my head. And the elastic over my nose. One hand is on my chest pressing lightly and rhythmically and letting go. It's the weak hand. It feels like a bird perching on me, smaller than a crow, bigger than a finch, a starling perhaps. The starling helps me breathe.

There we are, in for a penny, in for a pound. Blink at me, Ounooi, blink with your eyes whether you're managing.

She fixes my eyes while the strong hand puts aside the mask. The strong hand replaces the weak one on my chest. Bigger than a finch. Strong shiny wing-beat.

White-throat crow.

From here. To the wall, to what is hanging there.

Now, says Agaat, now I reckon we've got you going full-steam ahead again.

The hand pumps lighter and lighter all the time, until it gives only the smallest pulse. Then I'm on my own.

Agaat contemplates my solo flight.

You can be satisfied, Agaat. Visibility poor, plenty of tailwind, but I log them, one by one, the turbulent nocturnal hours, the hours of stormy flight, I know, the landing lights are on, I blip clearly on and off on the radar screen.

She ignores me. How are the slimes feeling? she asks.

Clear, open, thank you.

Did I knock you too hard?

Her voice is low.

My back feels like tenderised steak, the skin of my ribs as if I'd leant for hours on end against a running baling-press.

Don't exaggerate, says Agaat. She smiles on my behalf.

Now I'm going to clear up here and then you can see what I've hung up for you.

Agaat puts on the soft neckbrace. EasyHead. She swivels my head into position for a good view. She supports it on both sides with pillows. She turns the bedside light to the wall. She pulls it out to its full extent and tilts it so that the shade looks like the head of an eager spectator. She gets onto the chair again. A horizon arises. Black seam of the house coat, white seam of the apron, folded-over white socks, brown calves of Agaat, crêpe-soled shoes of which both heels are slightly worn down at the back. Dig-in and hang-in hocks, tug-of-war heels.

Doctor says I must be careful not to upset the ounooi, so that the ounooi can carry on breathing nice and evenly.

From up there on top of the chair comes Agaat's voice, slightly strained as she stretches to arrange the cloth, but with the mockery directed at the doctor, at how he thinks our relationship is, at how he thinks she addresses me.

Now I've chosen something to send you to sleep restfully. Now you look at it till your eyes fall shut.

She unties the other two ribbons.

The cloth unrolls with a shuurrr. It radiates down on me.

The great rainbow.

An embroidery experiment, from the time Jakkie went to high school in Heidelberg, when Agaat had to conjure away the empty time.

Everybody thinks they know what a rainbow looks like, she said, but when it's from close by like this, they'll wonder what they're seeing.

I remember the start of it, impossible, I'd said, a waste of time, why don't you rather make something one can use, but she'd just looked at me.

She anaesthetised herself with the work, for hours on end, in the mornings on the front stoep, before the arrival of the moment that she lived for, three o'clock, when she heard the chug and the squealing brakes of the school bus and she could run to go and fetch Jakkie at the drift, sometimes on the other side of the drift at the road, the time that she could sit with him while he ate, the hours that she could bend over his homework with him, and could learn with him about the French Revolution and the World Wars and the Boer War and he taught her everything that they sang at school, *Ne'er your children need ask who are true, O God of Jacob.*

Folded on a chair it lay aside then, the great rainbow.

And here it hangs now.

A straight inside section of the body of the rainbow. All over the cloth. The yellow of the spectrum runs off into creamy white, then pure white. The veld gradated so subtly that my eye reels, that I seek for a stay inside of me, for the blue-green of the Waenhuiskrans horizon, for yellow-green shoots of self-sown oats, water-green pineapple drink, lime peel, sunflowers, orange cannas, a dust-dimmed sun over stubble field, a harvest moon blood-red, a watermelon's flesh. And Geissorhiza radians, Babiana purpurea, amongst dark bracken the seven other purples of September. Swift effulgences, pleats of light.

But here is neither place nor time. It's an embroidery of nothing and nowhere. What Agaat must have imagined to lie behind the tender despair of defenceless creatures, behind the firefly, the evening star, the poppy, the blond lad in his corduroy pants. Everything that slipped out of her grasp, Jakkie's whole childhood, replaced with this embroidered emptiness.

Around me Agaat is clearing up the battlefield. She thinks she's distracting my attention with her rainbow. The buckets with the swabs full of phlegm she bustles away first, the kidney-shaped dish with the gouts of wet cotton wool, the sponges, the cloths, the water that smells of Milton and lavender. Swiftly she works, before her work of art's effect on me evaporates.

But I hear the screwing of the lids of the jars and tubes, see the sure-handed strokes with which the trolley is wiped, the quick snatch with which the slimy sponge on the bridge is grabbed away, the jingling assurance with which the brand-new rigging of oxygen tubes and snorkels and mouthpieces is rolled up. That, all the movements conspire to assert, now belongs to the past. Now we are in another safer place. The rainbow has been brought in for you. A complete colour chart. The origin, the fullness, the foundation of all.

What am I supposed to do with it all? It's the wrong medicine. Completeness. The death of the song, of the small dusty tale.

Rainbow of death.

Is it meant to hypnotise me?

Perfection, purity, order. Adversaries are they all, the devil's own little helpers.

How my heart burns to tell her this! Now that I can see it. Now that it's too late.

*

Friday 23 September 1960 nine o'clock in the evening.
A. is terribly excited about Jakkie's christening in a week's time. Have just gone out at the front door & surreptitiously walked round the back of the house & peeped into the kitchen window to see what she's getting up to there. Wouldn't she close the kitchen door after supper & tell me I'm not allowed in now she'll come & call me when she's done. Looks like at least two cakes & a savoury tart that are under construction there as far as I can see. The whole table is packed with stuff & there's a hectic beating & a mixing & a singing at the top of her voice all my recipe books open in a line bowls full of batter & icing-sugar & grated orange peel & plates full of chopped bacon & onion & parsley. Everything for the dominee & his elder who are coming tomorrow morning to discuss the arrangements for the christening.

Saturday 24 September quarter past eight morning
Have just had to go & do inspection. A. came to call me to come & see if everything's right. Fresh flowers arranged in the sitting room (she's been up since crack of dawn) & her cakes have risen beautifully orange

184

& chocolate covered under netting on tea table & the best cups put out & cake plates & forks the savoury tart is all ready to be baked everything is ship-shape. I did think this was all rather a to-do, & the eyes shine & the chin juts all the way out & then it came out: Seems she wants to carry Jakkie into the church. I ask you! Won't I big-please get the dominee's permission.

Now obviously this is totally out of the question! Couldn't bring myself to tell her this on the spot, what with all the trouble she's gone to with the baking & all. Oh good heavens.

To crown it all she's embroidered a christening robe for Jakkie. Here & there a bit of a tangle but it's something quite exceptional. Morning glories & bunches of grapes round the seams & the collar everything white on white & the most delicate little white buttons & ribbons & belts of soft brushed silk cloth with a slight sheen—good enough for a little prince. Must have taken hours & hours of work. But it's obviously unheard of, a coloured girl in church & everything has already been arranged in any case, & Jak's niece will bring him in in their old family christening robe.

A. says she wants to hold him for the sprinkling isn't she a baptised child of the Lord as well she says & he won't cry if she holds him. There she does have a point.

Saturday afternoon 5 o'clock 24 September
Too upset really to write but dear Lord in heaven how on earth could I have proposed it to Ds van der Lught? Perhaps I should really have done it & then she could rather have had it from his own mouth she was in any case listening behind the kitchen door all the time.

So there is the christening robe on the sideboard neatly wrapped in white tissue paper & A. serves the cake all prim & properly with little serviettes & Dominee praises her extravagantly but he doesn't eat any cake only the elder nibble-nibbles a bit because of course by that time they'd been on house visits all morning & already full of cake & there she had to recite Psalm 23 & Dominee asks her everything about sin & redemption & she knows it all & he praises her to high heaven isn't she so tidy & in her place & so clean & he can see her heart is as white as driven snow. All I could see was that Jak was going to lose his temper.

All the time she's signalling to me with her eyes so that only I can see: Show him my christening robe with the result that I ate far too much cake just to show her it's good thank you you're my right hand & later she brought Jakkie in & then Jak sent hr out because then we had to kneel & pray & I looked at the chintz on the chair & when it was my turn to pray I couldn't get out a word & Jakkie started screaming & A. comes & picks him up & soothes him there so that he can have the pre-baptismal blessing pronounced upon him & Dominee prays & the elder prays & they just can't seem to stop & under the prayer I look at A. & she's standing there with open eyes big-please asks her mouth but I couldn't ask & then we still had to sing as well The Lord Bless thee out of Zion & A. joins in with the second voice & Dominee & the elder look at each other & they say let's sing another verse but I feel ashamed because coloureds don't sing with white people in the sitting room J. almost has a fit on the spot but he has to behave in front of Dominee & I see he's threatening A. she must stop but sing she does.

When at last they left I rushed out of there & I walked off in some direction with Jakkie in his pram sick of all the cake & when I got to the dam at the ducks' landing place there was would you believe it the white parcel; with the christening robe. The same that had just recently been on the sideboard! I thought at first I was seeing things.

Come out! I shouted Come out! because then I knew A. was hiding there somewhere amongst the reeds to torment me. Lord knows how she got there so soon must have taken a short-cut through the little vlei but she wasn't coming out & then I took the parcel & chucked it far into the dam. Then it took a long time to sink & all the time I knew she was watching. Threw a few clods of earth in there to chase her out but it didn't work. What a spectacle, good Lord.

So now we're going to have a whole drama about it again.

Better go & have a look at what's happening it's been dead quiet all afternoon. A. nowhere to be seen. Jak had to see to his own lunch. Six o'clock now. Still don't hear anything stirring in the kitchen. Perhaps she'll come back when it's Jakkie's bath-time. How are we to look each other in the eye?

Last Sunday of September 1960
A. in a mighty huff. As good as her baking was for Dominee's visit so

disastrous was everything for the christening tea. Deliberately upset a jug of milk on the tray & the guests' shoes were full of dogshit because she hadn't swept the garden path. Remained sitting in the car during the christening service even though Dominee had said she could sit in the side-room & listen to the service. Didn't even want to pose in the little church park with the blue cranes for a photo with Jakkie in his christening robe.

Will bloody-well not let myself be buggered around by her. Will make her work until she is tractable so that she can see what it cost. Faith & sweat & blood of generations just so that she who's Agaat can live off the fat of the land on Gdrift & pluck the fruits through no effort of her own.

Must I skin her alive? I asked & then I had an idea. Tanned & brayed you must be that's punishment number one & if that doesn't cure you then I have a few others.

3 October 1960

Have been watching her though the binoculars where she's sitting & braying the thongs in the back under the bluegum trees. Had D. provide her with a bray-stone & handle. She'd better sing I told her so that I can hear where she's working. As long as you keep jibbing you'll bray hides I said. Will teach her to pull up her shoulder at me. I see J. has gone & added three more lynx hides to the heap it sickens me how he decimates the small game. New sporting rifles with sights they can't miss take a trap I say then at least the poor things also have a chance.

5 October 1960

It's my will against hers & she knows it. The chin is stuck out there & she carries on with the one arm. Up & up she winds the thong till it drips & plucks the stick out of the handle & down & down winds the thing & then up again on the other side. Has broken two bray-poles already. A mob of farmboys mocking her. That's how the first rod broke says Lietja one got a blow against the head that had the blood flowing so now they're more careful stand there at a safe distance.

6 October

I cut off a piece of thong with the knife & press it under hr nose. See the hide is tanned & the core is white. I take a raw thong & I cut it & show her look the core is black. Just like that it will be with you. I'll wind you up until all your black sins drip out of you & wind you down & wind you up again in the other direction till you're a decent servant-girl who doesn't leave one in the lurch when you need her most. She gives me that wooden eye I could slap her.

7 October 1960

Four days of curing thongs & A. just gets worse all the time. Breaks things in the kitchen when she has to help cook in the evenings. Mixing bowl glass jug in shards two saucepans so burnt had to throw them away milk sour from bottles not washed properly clothes get stained in the washing whole baskets of eggs get broken hens have stopped laying & Jakkie constantly fretful. Must look after him myself all the time now can't lie there in the open under the bluegums with A.

I ask hr: But don't you miss Jakkie then during the day? Don't you just want to leave off your quirks now & become good again? Conceived & born in sin she says. I scold her about the thistles in the flower garden & charlock in the vegetable garden & the hornet's nest on the stoep they fly in at the front door & go up & down with their abdomens against the curtains. Take down the hornet's nest I say just now one will sting Jakkie. Can't reach she says. Very well then I say then you'll plough an acre with a handplough & a mule.

J. says you & that coffee-toffee of yours can't you just fire her next thing she'll drop dead with exhaustion & what will you do then? Just remember I'm not erecting the monument.

Don't have an answer for him. Feel guilty. But the guiltier I feel the angrier I get.

9 October 1960

On purpose at first gave her an old plough with a rusty share with the wrong blunt point & a bent beam & saw to it that the hauling-chain was first hanging too high & then too low & watched her struggling with the share that wouldn't grip & kept on sticking & somersaulting head-over-arse or climbing point first out of the furrow & the mule eventually getting all confused & headstrong.

Waited for her to get good & tired & then I said now you go & read your Handbook well where they explain the art of ploughing by hand & then you come & say your lesson to me & when you know it & explain to me why you're struggling like that then we make a plan but plough you will the field one arm or not. D. says Ai Mies. I tell him to keep his trap shut if she wants to be otherwise she'll find out at first hand what that means. A good servant is like a shiny share that shears with ease.

11 October 1960

A is walking with an even tread on one side of the plough with the strong hand on the handle & hr shoulder pulled up high & talks to the mule & sings to awake the echoes: Big baboon climbs the hill farmer's wife takes a pill. Knew everything when I tested hr this morning. The whole logic of the plough-bottom. Share-point inclined to the unploughed ground. Hollow under hoof. Mould-board. Tow-line on the centre of the share. On the tips of her fingers.

Took her to the co-op & said now you choose yourself a plough here & shares that look right to you for that damp river-soil. So then she knew exactly what is what & as cheeky as you please asked me right in front of the salesman: Do we have a wire brush & grease & graphite & fine oil to soak the bolts after I've finished ploughing & do we have paint otherwise this plough will lie & rust just like the old one. Punish me as much as you like said her crooked back as I walked behind her.

Must think up something else. Feel terrible. But can't stop.

13 October 1960

J. says he feels like going to live in a flat in town & becoming a lawyer he's had a bellyful of being an extra in my concentration-camp movie. Says he's had enough of the mess in the house & what's happened to my wonderful house-slave she can't even iron a shirt properly & why must she struggle with a handplough or is this now my latest design for a hotnot hobby first the flat seam now the plough furrow. Had to throw away three shirts this week with scorch marks on the collar. Made her waterproof a large tarpaulin with fat & linseed oil over & over again on both sides.

If I can't break her with sweating blood I'll get into her mind then we can see at the same time if she's really as clever as she thinks.

I'm humiliating myself. God in heaven.

14 October

Instructed D. to move the McCormick seeder onto the tarpaulin in the shed & to jack up one wheel & to loosen all the gears & to put out a few bags of wheat seed. 150 pounds is what we must sow per morgen I said to A. Now you calculate how we must set this machine's gears so that it's going to sow the right density & how much seed we need to sow 16 morgen & while you're about it teach D. as well & you needn't come home & you needn't be given food before you've done the sum go & read your Handbook & help yourself to pen & paper in the baas's office. Since you tell me you know how to multiply & divide. Bless me if she doesn't talk back & tell me it's not sowing-time it's almost harvest-time don't I rather have a sum for harvest-time. I restrain myself. The labourers are watching me with eagle eyes. Tsk I hear behind my back. They look at me as if they don't know me.

Do I know myself?

14 October 1960 1 o'clock.
A.'s light is still burning & there's been a droning on three notes all evening. I know what she's struggling with. They don't say how many square yards in a morgen & how many feet to a yard. If she's clever she'll look on the farmer's almanac tables behind the kitchen door.

Have dried up completely now. Jakkie full of colic from drinking cow's milk.

16 October 1960
Heard a to-do in the shed early this morning & D. is in & out of the door. So there was the seeder sowing on the tarpaulin & A. is turning the jacked-up wheel with a piece of rope tied to one of the spokes so that she can count the revolutions & there is the Handbook & the almanac with tables & I see hr papers with the sums. By then they were setting the seeder's gears for the third time already to try & arrive at exactly 150 pounds a morgen. So then I relented & gave back the rowel that I'd removed & then the machine worked properly & the sum worked out & A. all but put out her tongue at me. D. gives me a straight look & says lord Mies but nothing further & next thing I see Lietja is giving A. a plate of rice & mince with vegetables in the kitchen & I happen to hear her say never mind it's over now you're terribly clever. Like a serpent as clever as a cat as sharp as needles but now just must start eating slowly otherwise your stomach will get a fright & then you must go to bed in your room you look like a ghost shame.

Made myself scarce because next thing I heard sniffling there in the kitchen & I don't know whether it's Lietja or A. that's bawling but A. doesn't cry of course. Then I heard J. there in the kitchen egging A. on: Go & sing your white stepmother a little song, go on: Anything you can do I can do better.

A. in the outside room all afternoon. Very quiet.

There's not a single farmer of my acquaintance who could do that sum. How can I do it to her?

That October after Jakkie's birth, after the battle with Agaat over the christening robe, five things happened that changed everything on Grootmoedersdrift. First Jak had the cattle-troughs with licks & the salt blocks removed from the lands. And then you noticed one day that the farm boys' wire cars were no longer built from wire but from bones. White vertebrae, white ribs, white collarbones, little white carts of death rattling over the yard. Without your putting two and two together. The third thing was Jak's new hunting rifles. What was he on his way to do when he left the house with the long leather bags? You didn't want to know. And then there were your diaries. Somebody was reading your diaries. Or that's what you thought. But most important of all was the change that came over Agaat. You saw her looking with new eyes at the two of you. But mainly at Jak, as if she was noticing him for the first time.

Five things that preceded that first catastrophe. Five things that helped shape all future catastrophes.

In the evenings there were the squabbles over the farm as usual, over your compost heaps, over your pumpkins amongst the pear trees.

It's not a laboratory, Jak, you said, it's mixed farming, the surfaces can't be bare and sterile without a sign of the processes that keep a farm healthy.

There he sat, pushed away his plate of food, taking apart his rifles and putting them together again, firing silent shots at the ornaments in the sitting room. Through the sights. Click. Click. You thought it would drive you mad. It fascinated Agaat. Not the rifles. Jak's face, his hands.

Then she brought home the story one evening. End of October 1960 it was.

The cows are eating tins.

Just as Jak was taking his first mouthful.

What tins now?

You had Jakkie in your lap, were trying to get him to take to his bottle.

Paraffin tins, car-oil tins, turpentine tins, sheep-dip tins, molasses tins, she said.

That they pick up where, Agaat? you asked.

You were incredulous. Why would cows eat tins? You thought she was inventing it to pay you back for the punishments she'd suffered.

Agaat was silent.

Ag, the stupid cows of yours, said Jak, probably calving again, you know they're always full of shit then, if it's not the trembles, then it's something else.

I'm just asking, where do they find that particular collection of tins to eat? Do they select them in the supply shed?

You looked at Agaat.

The tins are lying in the little grazing at the back next to the river amongst the stones, Agaat said.

Full sentence with prepositions. From a grammar book for second-language speakers.

She jutted out her chin.

Jak pointed his fork at Agaat. They're my tins, leave them just there where they are, or you'll be given another field to plough!

You handed Jakkie to her. He wouldn't drink so well with you. She just stood there with the child in her arms.

It's my shooting range, dammit, I do target-shooting at the bloody tins! Jak exploded. And that'll be the day that I let myself be put off by a bunch of silly cows from enjoying the little bit of healthy recreation that I'm allowed in this internment camp.

You gestured to Agaat that she could leave. At her leisure she walked out, her ears flapping backward under her cap.

She must keep her nose out of my business, I'm telling you here and now, she's carrying on as if the farm belonged to her. And . . . and . . .

Jak was red in the face. With an oil cloth he polished furiously at the barrel of his rifle.

Yes, Jak, and what else?

You were used to it. Always in such situations he brought it up. Agaat was the cause of everything that went wrong, and you were the cause of Agaat. With your finger to your lips you signalled he should lower his voice.

And, he said, if I ever have to hear again that my child, my little Jak-kie . . . I'll cut off her two tits for her one by one and throw them to the pigs! What must the people think? Jak de Wet's child is being . . . suckled by a . . . by a cast-off kitchen-goffel!

You were startled. Who had read, who had seen, who had told whom? You kept your cool. Where do you find such rubbish? you asked.

Jak was on his feet, he knocked his chair over backwards.

I hear it from the labourers! I hear them talk! They know everything that happens in this house, you say so yourself! Dawid's cousin says Saar saw it. They piss themselves laughing, the hotnots. Where do you think this must end? What must they think of me? So-called lord of the manor?

You don't know how much Agaat is worth to me, you said. You would probably never even have had a son if it hadn't been for her. And perhaps not even a wife.

Bluff back. But your heart was beating in your throat. Could Agaat have planted the story herself?

Dammit, Milla, once again that pretty-pious little story of yours, how long do you think you're still going to entertain me with it, your stupid serial? Go and write it up for Springbok Radio, go on, you've hardly put that skivvy of yours in her place than you start praising her to the skies all over again. Agaat of Grootmoedersdrift, Littletit of the Overberg! Then they can listen to it on the wireless every day from Caledon to Swellendam.

Jak slammed doors in his storming out.

A mite vehement about cows eating tins, you thought. A mite fierce over a mere rumour amongst the labourers. But it was only the following day that you realised why Jak had been on the defensive.

You were numbering the diaries that were full. From '53 onwards. In the correct sequence, with the periods that they covered written clearly on the cover. So that you could keep exact tally of how many there were. High up in the bedroom wardrobe you were putting them away. Under the eiderdowns.

Then Agaat came to call you.

Come and have a look, she said, the boys say it's not just tins that the cows are eating.

You followed her to the grazing next to the river. There against the wilderness of brambles the pregnant cows were standing and eating white ribs, the carcase of a cow that had been lying there for a long time. The white shards were sticking out of their mouths as they were chewing. You gazed at the drooling and the crunching, too shocked to put one foot in front of the other. To one side the cows' off-colour calves were standing neglected, watching.

Dawid says he shot Blommetjie and Gesina yesterday, Agaat said, they must also have eaten funny stuff.

She went to show you, two cows on the other side of the river.

Blommetjie had already burst open. You could see the dead foetus of her calf. Blommetjie, a great-granddaughter of Grootblom, another one of the Grootblom clan from your mother's old herd.

All that you could get out of Jak was that the cows wouldn't get up and that they were lying in the grass drooling with their heads in their flanks and that he'd wanted to put them out of their misery.

You phoned the vet in town. He would come and see what he could do but he didn't have serums, he would order them immediately from Onderstepoort. If the sickness was what he thought it was. It could take a week to arrive.

You grabbed Agaat by the apron and shook her.

Why didn't I hear the shots more often? Why don't we ever hear anything? Why do I only learn about this now? Why did nobody come and tell me that the cows didn't seem right? Why don't you notice things, I know you know what a healthy cow looks like!

She looked you straight in the eye, her body ramrod-stiff. You could see the hurt settling in her gaze. On top of the poker face, a film of aggrievedness. More than that.

He screws a pipe into the front of the rifle's barrel, she said, her voice neutral.

You let her go, she retreated. When she spoke it was soft, but clear and controlled.

I saw it yesterday for the first time. All you hear is thud like a bag of salt falling off a wagon. But I know what it sounds like now. From now on I'll know to listen for it.

Don't let him see you, Agaat.

You are my eyes and my ears, you wanted to say, he knows in the long run I find out everything, but just don't let him discover that you're spying on him.

You were silent, blew your nose. Her gaze forbade you to say anything further.

You should have said you were sorry you scolded so viciously. You should have said you would be more alert yourself. Never mind, it's not your fault, Agaat, you should have said, you're with Jakkie all day, how could you know what was happening in the fields? But you didn't. You stepped past her, your hands to your face. Shattered because of the cows. Over those injured eyes of Agaat's you stepped. Right over the insinuation flickering in that eye.

Must I see the germs even before they hatch? Must I keep death itself from your body? There was reproach on her face.

Sobering it was.

You gathered yourself. Saw to it that the old bones and tins and car-tridge-shells and rusted wires and everything on the old grazings next to the river were cleared up. Jak trembled with dismay when he heard the name of the sickness. He buckled down and helped. You controlled your-self, said if it was really necessary, then he should go and lay out a proper shooting-range with real targets at the back of the fallow land in a special camp where he would be out of the way of man and beast. There would never again be a single thing shot and left lying in the veld, you said.

You immediately started administering bonemeal with the salt, for the sheep as well, and gave instructions for the making of new little troughs that would ensure that each head of cattle would get its eight ounces.

You got in a team of convicts and had the whole farm, next to the rivers and on the side of the drift, scoured for bones. More than a hun-dred bags full were collected.

You wouldn't forget that, the shaven heads of the men as they moved stooped down in a slow phalanx before Agaat's white apron over the lands. The old hymns there on the fallow, carried by the wind, you could hear them as far as the yard, Agaat's descant high and bright above the deep voices of the men.

> From depth of dark'st disgrace
> of deliverance bereft
> where hope's forlorn last trace
> in despair my heart has left;
> from depths of desolation
> oh Lord, I b'seech thee, hear,
> and let my lamentation
> ascend, Lord, in thine ear!

Everybody was flabbergasted. Cows that eat skeletons. As if death itself had nutritional value. Even Saar and Lietja who could produce a ribald laugh on any occasion, stood there in the kitchen singing, dragging it out with that lugubrious bending of the notes that the brown people could give to a song. A weeping and wailing it was in those days on Grootmoedersdrift, as the wagons full of white bones arrived in the yard. And as the digging of the trenches began and the skeletons of skunks and meerkat and guineafowl, and the carcasses of cattle, were cast into them, Agaat led the workers in the singing of another verse.

> Hope, Israel in your sorrow,
> trust, o nation that grieves;

His favour light'ns the morrow,
His grace your grief reprieves.
Then shines a sweet salvation:
all Israel is free
of trial and tribulation.
Do like, Lord, unto me!

It set you crying all over again. For more than the cows. For Agaat's eye that was dry and sharp with supervising. In her mouth it was a battle hymn, that you could hear, and it was directed at you and you felt how she was piling up her case against you. It was a case for which she could locate her injustice in the very hymns of your own church, in the very mouths of the prophets of the Old Testament.

Did she have everybody on her side even then?

Jak could in any case not endure it too long under Agaat and her convicts. He left his bag of bones and tried to assist the vet. You yourself tried to hurry along the bone-collecting. If the singing were to carry on any longer, you felt, the walls of the homestead would tumble down like those of Jericho.

The bonemeal feeds that you administered helped to get the oxen, the bulls and the cows that had not given birth that year back into condition. But the best dairy cows, all of those that would have calved that season and that had been put to graze in the little back camp next to the river, were lost.

Three days long the deaths continued. Over and over the process repeated itself, the staggering gait with which it started, the glassy stare, the puzzled gaze, the drooping ears, the tangled coat, and the dried-up nostrils. One after the other they lay down. One by one the heads became too heavy there where they were lying in the grass. They turned their noses into their flanks trying to support their heads. The flanks collapsed. The jaws were paralysed, the tips of the tongues lolled on the teeth in front, drool and foam glistened around the mouths, heavily the great brown gullets moved up and down. One after the other soft, pining death you accompanied, your hand on the flank, your hand on the little crown between the ears. You wept by your cows. The best of them were descendants of the animals you had known as a child. Aandster's great-great-grandchild, Pieternella's distant cousins, all the meek caramel-coloured mothers.

When the convicts had gone and all the cows were buried, Agaat came to you. She came to sit by you in your room with Jakkie drinking his bottle in her arms. She put the old green Handbook on your lap.

Her voice was neutral. Her eyes shone.

Open on page 221, she said, open, and ask me anything, I am fully learned now, about anything that can possibly happen to a cow.

*

the countenance of doctors is the seat of dissimulation the whispered consultation behind the screens i don't add up on any side am wrong geometry am failed electricity am vapour before the sun am nothing more than particles and waves my irradiated skeleton a room-divider my head in a tunnel my neck in a hole my leg in a bath my arms weightless groping for nothing in sleeves of lead in cylinders full of pink water wild and waste is death before death in a solution of salts i am dipped painted with mediums contending for dominance water earth fire and air a quadruple judgement hangs over my neck invisible eels prick the skin of the fingertips skin that provisionally enshrouds my failure a fascicle of breath engirdled by fate against him the intact the voluble the preserved in his coat of whitewash i fear mrs de wet the worst oh my soul you are audited by a battery of stethoscopes gallery of savants who are gauging the woman who cannot break an egg the woman who cannot sweep with a broom the one in hundredthousand mrs de wet oh genuflecting deeply edified congregation of god in swellendam all in the twinkling of an eye compassionate in tones of gloating resounds the intercession she must fall safely as rain in winter o Lord must descend soughing like a manna of edible butterflies while silent assistants connect me to electrodes transilluminate me weigh me the specific gravity of my spirit which i must surrender if i correctly understand the explanation of gradual enfeeblement on the dials of the control panels of the angels with flaming swords the electromyographers their needles in my flesh they whisper in unison the sickness of charcot the sickness of lou gehrig now the sickness of grootmoedersdrift the mother of all sicknesses you are besieged in your head a tongueless bunker with loopholes

10

In the grey light of morning the rainbow looks different. Darker than last night by lamplight. Then it looked like an empty bright stage-set where actors were due to appear, singers, to bring life to it. Now it looks like a hole in the plastering, a dark plane against the white wall. Dark rainbow.

Agaat is tired this morning. Her face is withdrawn. She appears by my bedside less frequently than usual. She avoids my eyes. Her embroidery lies folded on the chair. On top of it lies the little blue book open at where she was last reading before I fainted. The building of the fireplace.

Sometimes I think it's no longer I who am the target of the reading. She does it for herself, to generate energy. To squeeze anew from history a last pressing of indignation, but not so as to destroy me with it the more easily, but as a shot in the arm, as fuel for herself to carry on nursing me every day.

Because her arms are tired. I can feel how she struggles when she has to turn me, lift my legs, my hands.

Her feet are sore, I can hear she walks with difficulty. She's burnt out.

How valiant was she not at the start, in those early days when we had just heard what was wrong with me. Fired with enthusiasm even. She thought she would handle it, as she had handled all illness and death in her life.

She was upset that I wouldn't take her with me to Cape Town, alarmed when I came back after a week.

Leroux came to fetch me and brought me back again. I pretended to be sleeping in the car. I didn't want to listen to his chatter. I thought of Agaat, how I was to convey it to her. A few times I felt the wind buffet the car, heard him swear, felt the car swerve as he corrected. It was a

198

wild wind typical of the change of season and it raged all the way from Groote Schuur to The Spout. When we got out in the yard I could see the willows by the dam being blown to one side. I could smell the fennel, sharp as always when the wind blew just before the rains.

12 May 1993 it was. A Wednesday afternoon. Agaat served tea and rusks in the sitting room.

In her eyes the full orchestra was playing.

So here you are again! Alive and kicking! Pure affectation! Didn't I tell you! Or what am I saying? Let's have it! If there's more to know, I want to know it! Now! This minute! Winter pains? Frozen shoulder?

I shuttered my regard, answered cautiously, later-later-clear-out-now.

It was what he'd suspected all along, said Leroux and added milk to his tea.

Not hypochondria. Not this time.

Small smile, quickly wiped away. In front of him lay the papers with the results of the tests.

I must plan, he said.

One and a bit of sugar.

I must make provision.

Doctor Stir-well.

I must start formulating a living will.

Doctor Dunk-a-rusk.

You're never done with such a testament. You can always change it again. In the end it really only has to state in black and white what must happen one day when you can no longer change anything yourself.

Tchirr-tchirr, the creeper against the pane.

Who must do it then . . .

Picks a crumb out of the tea.

Who may change something then . . .

I heard a dog's bark downwind blow away right out of its mouth.

Who may change something on your behalf . . . take decisions on your behalf . . . now do I understand what he means?

Ticks, with the teaspoon in the saucer.

I must consider it well, I have enough time, he said. Three years, maybe five in my case. I must realise he himself does after all think very progressively about these matters, he always wants only to alleviate all and any suffering as much as possible and he is at my service I need only speak the word, do I understand?

As far as possible. Alleviate he wants to.

Up-and-down with his eyebrows. Read-me-I'm-an-open-book-my-name-is-Euthanasia-Leroux-MB Ch.B.

Well, in my book there's little scope for speculation, Doc. I was born Redelinghuys, house of reason.

I beg your pardon?

I said, time will tell.

I wanted him to leave. Agaat was listening from behind the kitchen door. I could hear the floorboards creak. She had taken a dislike to the man from early on, could imitate his would-be fatherly blanditudes to a nicety.

At the front door he pressed a transparent blue plastic case full of blue and red pamphlets and brochures into my hands, also a book on all kinds of atrophies and publicity magazines on appliances, and folded my thumbs around the handle for me.

Do take well-informed decisions now, Mrs de Wet, he said, fortunately I know you are of a practical bent, somebody who wants to be in control at all times. And you are a farmer. Illnesses and suffering are a farmer's daily bread. And fortunately you have no dependants at this stage who could hamper you . . . er . . . whom you have to concern yourself about.

The self-correction was half lost in the thunderous bang of the back door.

Grootmoedersdrift is situated in a draught. That was what we always said to one another at that time of year.

And wait, he said, it almost slipped my mind.

Three paces and he was next to his car. A big white plastic bag appeared.

On appro, he said, the newest appliances on the market, I thought I would do some shopping for you in the meantime while I was in town. Try them out, see what works, we can settle later.

He pressed the bag into my arms on top of the case.

A sheet of paper fluttered to the ground, he snatched it up and stuck it on my chest on top of everything else.

Oh, and then there's this table, the whole profile at a glance, he said, symptoms, medicine, therapy.

Bedside manner in the Overberg, I thought, physician heal thyself.

And as he drove out at the gate, I thought: Milla has all of it.

Only now do I realise what I was trying to think that day. Because now I almost have it all behind me.

To make of nothing an all.

That was what Agaat made of me. The lamer, the more nothing I became, the more she put into me. I never had any defence. It was her initiative. To make me a lucky packet of myself. The person who has to wither so that the book of her life can be filled. As in like manner the great God had to shrink to make room for his creation. Or something to that effect. Even now I still can't quite get a clean grip on the idea. It's a sort of sum with varying balances but with retention of all the contents, only distributed in very specific packagings.

I went to lie down on my bed until Agaat rang the bell for supper. She had cooked specially to celebrate my return: Lamb pie, green beans with onion and bacon, stewed peaches, potatoes, boiled, floury as I like them, a ripe red tomato salad with onions. Damask. Candles. Flowers.

Welcome home.

Even a bottle of wine from the cellar.

Eat, she said, it will give you strength.

She served me, poured wine for me. The meat in the pie was finer than usual, so that I didn't have to cut it. I was hungry. I was melancholy with feeling what hunger felt like. I wiped my eyes with my napkin. She pretended not to see it. While I was eating, she talked softly, gave me an edited-for-the-sickbed version of what had been happening on the farm in the meantime. She made me at home in my room afterwards. Hot-water bottle, new bedsocks, softest wool, look, I knitted them for you while you were away. Waited for me to speak, pleaded with the eyes, please, I'm Agaat, I'm here, with you, speak to me, tell me what is happening.

Another time, I indicated with my hand.

She switched off the light.

Sleep, she said in the dark in my direction, then you'll feel better.

Later I became aware of a murmuring and got up to go and see. I listened in the passage. It was her voice.

Dys-pha-gia, can't swallow, dys-ar-thria, can't talk, sia-lor-rhoea, incessant drooling.

She was sounding the words. I peeped through the chink of the kitchen door. The plastic case and the white bag had been unpacked. Papers and brochures were spread out on the kitchen table. Agaat was studying my illness over her supper. On her hands were two grey palm socks to which a clumsy knife and a fork with three prongs had been fixed.

Spas-ti-ci-ty, she read on the table next to her plate, wrist pains, cramps, spasms, as-piration, depression.

Slowly she spelled out the big words: Movement spec-trum exercise. Mo-di-fied food con-sis-ten-cy.

And in the same breath she said, I've finished eating, you can come out now from behind the door, we might as well get to work on this, you and I.

You and I. Indeed. We're still getting to work, if work is what one can call what has been happening in this room the past few months.

One could have decided not even to get started on it.

Because it would be too much.

I would have had to settle it on my own while I could still move, that's what. Short and sweet. But I procrastinated every time. Just this first, just that first, must first clear up, first get my life in order before I put an end to it one day neatly tied up with a string. But I couldn't.

I left the decision to her.

Euthanasia isn't something that she can even consult me on any more. Such a possibility doesn't appear on her list.

How would she in any case have to formulate it?

Must I put an end to you?

Are you ready?

How do you want me to prepare you?

Or must I overpower you unexpectedly?

Do you want to know how I'm going to do it?

Do you want to choose the method yourself?

A pillow over your head? A drink? A pill? A crowbar? A knife?

She'll never be able to say it. She chose the strait and narrow. Simply doing from hour to hour what was given to her hand to do. First things first, one thing at a time, according to a plan. As if it made sense, as if it held promise.

Why does she ignite the little bit of hope in me every day? Hope of a turn, a way out, a satisfactory conclusion, of which you could say with certainty that it was good?

I find that on some days I long for it more than on other days.

I heard the phone ringing early this morning. It was Leroux.

She was short with him.

Perhaps he had been hopeful. Because, no, she said, she's still with us, and well. Well, well, well. I understand. I'll do that. Right. Goodbye doctor. Yes, doctor. No, doctor. Goodbye.

And now she thinks I'm sleeping again after drinking my thick sweet tea with the bit of chilli powder that she believes is good for me. I heard her send the servants home. She wiped my face quickly this morning and beyond that did not touch me, as if she were suddenly scared that I might fall apart. I tried to reassure her.

Thank you, I feel better after the phlegm is out, lighter, I breathe more easily.

But she avoided my eyes, didn't want to help me speak, knew it was just to comfort her.

I can't help her.

Twice already I've heard her pick up the receiver and put it down again. She wants to phone. I wait. What does Agaat want to say? Whom does she want to phone?

She phones often, the chemist, the co-op, the shop. Orders things, organises things. And people phone here and she speaks to them and tells them, according to who is phoning, more or less. Rather less, more less, less and less. Platitudes. Truisms. The chickens are laying well, the harvest is almost in, her feet are cold sometimes. When she says that, they ring off quickly. People don't want to hear about my ever more chilly feet.

If it's Jakkie, she speaks loudly on purpose, repeats everything he says. About his research amongst primitive tribes, his travels. He gets to all of Africa, it seems, just not South Africa. Here he apparently only wants fieldworkers. Agents it sounds like, who listen to songs and send them on to him. To then be preserved in the Canadian Centre for Ethnomusicology. It seems to her Americans have money to waste, says Agaat.

Jakkie.

Sometimes I think she makes it up, that he rings, that he asks after me, that he says he will come.

But how would I know?

My child the great absence.

What he inherited from me and Jak is definitely recognisable. Slightly melancholy, sometimes quite sharp with his tongue. Agaat one hears most clearly in him. The sayings, the songs, the rhymes, in which he has an obsessive interest. Sometimes she sings something on the phone for him if he can't remember the words any more.

The bottom of the bottle.

The Sunday morning.

Ai, the ordinary little old songs, and then he did have such a beautiful voice, the child. Would it be him that she wants to ring? A last chance to come?

When he wrote to say he was starting to study all over again, I wrote back saying but surely there's a department of Afrikaans cultural history at Stellenbosch, isn't there? And then in his next letter he delivered himself of a whole lot of stuff about how he wasn't a Patriomanic Oxwagonologist, but an anthropologist, and that meant that it was the rubbish bins of the worthy professorial Brethren of Stellenbosch, not their ideas, that he had to scrutinise under a magnifying glass. The ideas, he wrote, spoke for themselves, they flared to high heaven like pillars of fire in the desert, they couldn't be missed by a deaf-and-dumb dog with a blocked nose.

It upset me, that the child could now turn so sharply against his own people. Being radical surely didn't oblige you to become disrespectful. It wouldn't have been wise of me to react at that stage. Those were his refractory years. Not that he ever fitted in altogether. Even as a child always half-apart, never really interested in his peers, tied to Agaat's apron strings here on the farm. Later, too, not much time or taste for the antics of his fellow-students or for the other officers in the Defence Force. Herd animals, he said, always had to have a bell-wether and a scapegoat, without those they couldn't function.

Nowadays he sounds more concerned. Not about the headline news, he writes, but about 'the little grey bushes', whatever that's supposed to mean. Surely one can't live with so little faith in the world?

He writes but rarely. When he writes to Agaat, she no longer shows it to me. Not that she ever really showed his letters, she just read out from them, quoted what she wanted to.

There was just the one letter, the one that she had to show us, Jak and me, the first one after he vanished. Of that I saw only the first line. And when I saw it again, it was so besmeared with blood that the pages were stuck together.

She would supposedly still read it to me. Nothing came of that. More than a year later only did Jakkie report on everything. Rather synoptically. No reference to that first confession and plea.

Did we bring him up wrongly?

Can't have been too wrongly, for he has a job and a house and a will of his own.

It's Agaat who's been most badly hurt. She pines for him, I can see it, when she gazes out of the door in a certain way and closes her eyes for a moment, or, sometimes at night, when the doors here are thrown open and she lowers her embroidery and turns her head askance to listen, her cap tilted at an angle like a radar dish.

Does she want to phone him this morning? Perhaps she's struggling with the dialling codes for overseas. Perhaps she wants to pretend to be phoning him, for my sake. Perhaps she's trying to think what she'd better say then, how she should say it, for the benefit of my listening ears.

But I know what her face looks like when she thinks she's going to be talking to Jakkie.

Perhaps it's the undertaker, rather, that she wants to phone. For a preview. Perhaps she hopes that it will encourage me, such a quantity surveyor's assessment. Just as well that I've been deprived of speech.

Of the friends it's only Beatrice that Agaat still allows to see me, if she should want to, that is. After that conversation in Jak's office she's rather withdrawn herself from me. Scared of her own emotions. Only now do I realise how widespread it must be. Blunted men, suck-weary women. Only death can still whet their appetites.

Agaat keeps their visits brief since she's realised it. Gives them tea in the sitting room, lets them greet in the doorway, not a step closer, takes them out again. Closes the front door on their backs. Sometimes they slip through, down the passage. The inquisitive mainly, the spiteful attracted to the bed of affliction.

Such vanity, it all seems from here. The endless stream of visitors that I had here at one stage. Until Agaat decided that was enough now. Now it's her turn and her turn alone.

Now that I have only my thoughts that I may think, without ever having to express them, the last scrapings of my senses. Light, dark, heat, voices, open doors, wind. The ruin that Agaat helps me to inhabit. A squatter in my own body. Wind-blown settlement. A perilous freedom.

So she would be able to spend the rest of her earthly days writing down what she went through with me. If I provisionally have the advantage, that's only because I won't live for long enough to read her writings one day.

She'd be capable of putting my head in a clamp to force me. Specially intended for my eyes. Niche market.

There she is dialling the number in the passage now, she sits down for the conversation. She'll dissemble more if she thinks I'm sleeping.

This is Agaat, she says. Her voice comes out low.

She clears her throat. Lower the girl.

This is Grootmoedersdrift, Nooi Beatrice, Agaat speaking.

That's better. In her place. Sharp and clear. The soul of innocence. The brownest servant in the land.

Morning, Nooi, how are you, Nooi?

No, so-so, Nooi. Nooi, I want to ask if you can help me, Nooi. I must get to town tomorrow, Nooi, with Dawid. I want to ask if you could come and watch over Ounooi here for a few hours, please Nooi.

Watch over. Masterly choice of words, Agaat.

What was that, Nooi? No, I must buy all sorts of things, at the chemist and from the shop. And I must arrange things with the printer, for the cards and the programme as the ounooi wants them all for the funeral.

Yes, there'll be many people, Nooi. If everybody comes it will be close to a hundred people, we'll have to stir our stumps, Nooi.

Stir our stumps. Lord. Is she making it up, perhaps? Perhaps she wants the farm exchange to hear. Perhaps she's talking straight into the monotone of the dialling tone.

No, Saar and Lietja wouldn't know, Nooi, they're farm people, they're unwashed.

You're right in there, my old body-servant, all the way to my neighbour's wife's tonsils you're in.

Yes, everything in order here, Nooi, just last night we almost had a mishap. No, the slimes, the slimes, you know, go and settle under in the lungs, as you know she can't cough for herself any more.

No, I knock it to the top as doctor taught me, then I remove it with a little suction pump, I know how to by now. Doctor was here, yes, he gave oxygen. We have oxygen here now.

Yes, he showed me how.

Not much, about two hours at a time, but then I get up, then I look.

How do you mean now, Nooi?

No, Nooi, the ounooi plays along very well, she knows I must do it all, she understands.

Yes, Agaat, she lies here and she understands. And she listens to the price you have to pay there on the telephone for a simple neighbourly favour. Old vulture's beak smacks as she devours the line. Feed her, Agaat. Feed her till she's gorged.

Agaat lowers her voice. She coughs.

No, quite clear. Completely conscious still.

No, doctor says you can't do more at home than I'm doing. He says otherwise she must go off to hospital.

That really wouldn't work, Nooi.

No, I just know, she doesn't want to. She signed the papers.

She doesn't want the machines on her. She thinks doctor wants to prescribe to her how. How she must, you know Nooi, how she must . . . go before . . .

Agaat shifts her weight on the stool. The boards creak in the passage. She is quiet for a long time. Would she be patting her cap to make sure that it's seated properly? Would she be concentrating on the floorboards?

No, says Agaat, she would never, she's too obstinate, she wants to do it herself.

I'll watch well, Nooi Beatrice, you know don't you, we know each other, the ounooi and me, we've come a long way together. She only wants me here.

No, I understand her, Nooi, she still wants to see everything, she wants to hear, I know, she still wants to taste and everything.

No, I just know. No, she can't, not a word, but I look at her then I know.

Yes, Nooi, please, Nooi. As early as you can, yes, Nooi. Eight o'clock, half past eight. There'll be breakfast here for you, Nooi.

Yes, by twelve we'll be back.

First to the co-op, yes, Dawid must get things, parts for the combine harvester that he has to keep in order, yes, and sacks.

Baling wire, yes, there's enough, the railway bus delivered.

A bit of a squeeze everything, yes, and the harvest is late this year, but I knew it would be around Christmas sometime, so my side is ready.

Yes, so now we can only wait . . .

Agaat's voice sounds tired.

Yes, yes, only to town, as I say, Nooi. We have to deliver things. No, the eggs and the milk. Pumpkins. Onions too. And I must exchange the videos. But the story films upset her, now I keep to nature films. *National Geographic*, yes.

That's right, Agaat, butterflies, bats, killer whales. Juicy bribes for the neighbour's wife.

Agaat rubs out an insect on the passage floor with the point of her shoe.

Yes, Human and Pitt, she says.

Quickly she speaks now.

Yes, that's here already, it's standing in the shed. They want to come and do it here. Yes, they say it's better at home when somebody has been lying for such a long time already.

Dominee, yes, he phones regularly and asks, yes, Mrs Dominee as well, but Ounooi doesn't want them here, nor the elder.

I do the service.

I do it, yes. I pray and I read when she feels the need, and I sing.

Yes. It will be here on the farm. In the graveyard here.

Yes, it's been dug for a long time. Next to her mother's. Wire netting over it so that things can't nest in it.

Weeded, yes. Whitewashed, too, the wall. Everything tidy. I sowed a few painted ladies seeds there, they're nicely in flower now.

Who? Jakkie? Last time he still said he was coming. It's snowing there, he says it's lying thick. Tomorrow I'm sending him a telegram so that he has it, black on white.

He's working, yes till just before Christmas, they don't have a holiday now.

No, it's arranged. Everything's arranged. So will you please come tomorrow, Nooi? Thank you very much, Nooi. Till tomorrow then, Nooi. Thank you, Nooi. The same to you, Nooi.

I beg your pardon, Nooi?

No, doctor says he thinks less than a month, Nooi, perhaps a month.

No, Nooi, yes, Nooi, we can only hope for the best, Nooi. Well, that's fine then, Nooi. Till tomorrow, Nooi. Goodbye, Nooi.

Tsk, Agaat sucks her teeth.

I don't hear her replace the receiver.

The board next to the telephone stool creaks as she comes upright and then it creaks again as she sits down again. Then it creaks again. Then she replaces the receiver with a soft click. Then it clicks again as she lifts it.

Is everything in order, Agaat?

She slams the phone down hard on the cradle. The receiver falls off, I can hear it banging against the wall as it swings from its cord.

Tring, goes the telephone. Again the receiver is slammed down.

She walks down the passage with loud confused steps. She walks past the kitchen door, she walks blindly into the sitting room. She kicks over something there. She sets it upright. It falls over again, metal on wood. Other things fall. Thud, it goes, thud, thud, thud. She's back in the passage. She wants to come to me, but she can't. She's dragging something, wires across the floor.

What do I hear? A groan, a curse, a sob?

Two doors slam. The kitchen door, the screen door. And then another one, the outside room's.

A dog barks.

What else do I hear? Windows are slammed shut, stiff copper catches violently pulled over the lip of the window frame, and then opened again.

Curtains are yanked shut, too far so that half of the window is exposed again. Plucked to and fro, two rings come undone.

I understand, Agaat. It was too much. Your voice, your words, your news, your request, it was too much for you to hear.

I see you. You're standing in your room, you're standing and you can't stand any longer. You bend at the middle and you bend at the backs of your legs, your back hunches, you crawl forward over the linoleum. You take the poker, you pull out the grate. You crawl into your hearth, white cap first. You go and lie with your knees pulled up in the old black soot. You make yourself heavy and you make yourself dense and you sink away under the concrete with your fist in your mouth.

How can I blame you for wanting to vanish, Agaat? That you want to get away from me, away from the tyranny of me? More inescapable than ever, now that I can say or do nothing, now that I myself am floundered, and am immoveable as the stones. I would want to open myself to you and take you up into myself and comfort you. But I cannot, because I am your adversary exactly because I am as I am, mute and dense, and you are looking for a safe refuge from me. Under your own stones.

How can I accompany you to where you are now? At the heart of the hearth, under the soot, where you want to conceal yourself, under the foundations, under the stone strata, where they are blue, where you find a crevice into which to disappear, and haul in the block of stone on top of you, so that you can be occluded, with your arm over your head, with your fist in your mouth? Until nobody searches for you any more, to draw you out, to split you into parts and stretch you over spars and to infuse you and to chafe you and to rap you till you scream, till you sing, till you dance to their tune? Till you feel time click shut behind you and everything else falls silent, in your mouth no taste any more save the clean chalky tang of lime and scale?

So that I can come to be there with you, with my hand on your hip bone, with my hand on your shoulder tip to wait with you in the dark. For them to be rendered white and tidy, your bones, one by one, your clavicle, like a rudder, like an ensign, your shoulder blades like fans, your ribs shiny spokes, inside them a cleared hold, with every mast and beam caulked and planished in the dense rock face, the rock that retreats before your entry, a small fanfare. So that you can come to rest with all that is yours fixed and impermeable like pitch, your sails furled.

How can I be with you while you become a fern, a jaw of something inchoate, a keel, a beckoning nodule that flows in the grain of stone?

I shall go and lie with my head in that corner, with my ear on the place where the last trace of you lingered. I shall draw the suppurate stain of you into my nose, careful that you should not mark me, so that you shall be free of me, and free of yourself, a fume, a dark blemish that mists over the stone on which I am lying with my cheek.

*

Open at page 221, Agaat said. Her voice was clear. She put the old Farmer's Handbook on your lap. End of October it was, 1960, the year of the botulism.

Ask me from the beginning, she said, ask me all the symptoms, and all the cures, ask me trick questions, I've learnt it all, I know everything now, I'll never make a mistake again.

Never mind Agaat, you wanted to say, but your voice wouldn't come. You sat there crying but she struck up and launched into her lesson. She wanted to force you upright. In spite of the battle between you, or for its sake, because how was she to fight you if you were weak? How was she to hate you?

You couldn't come to terms with the loss of your Jersey cows, and her voice trying to create order and call things by their name, made you cry more. It was the third day that you had stayed in your room after the catastrophe with the botulism. Jakkie was with you most of the time in his cradle. Even his rosebud mouth, his little hand around your finger, couldn't console you.

First bone-hunger, then general dirt-craving, she started. First os-teo-pha-gia, then allo-tri-opha-gia.

She sounded out the big Latin words.

Degenerated appetite it was. That's how the vet had explained it to her, she said. Then she went and read up all the rest in her book.

Agaat looked at Jak who had come to listen in the doorway. He nodded at her to carry on. You felt how the accident had brought you closer to each other, closer, but in complex self-conscious ways. Jakkie woke up later in his cradle, he was the only one who reminded you all of your capacity for innocence.

When you could no longer contemplate the deaths and the putting-down, you took the child and left Agaat there with the autopsy. You saw how she came forward to lend a hand, her white apron like a standard in the midst of the carnage. And there she stood, three days later, grey with exhaustion, but with all the pieces of wire and cartridge cases and tin and horn and bone that had come out of the stomachs, scrubbed clean in a bucket to come and show you.

An unnatural craving, she said, her recitation-voice wilted with exhaustion, that's what causes cows to eat carrion. Sheep can also get it. Then they eat the wrong things, then they get sick. Of germs in carcases. Bo-tu-li-nus germs. But it's the soil that lacks something first. Phosphorus. And then the grazing. The problem is in the soil. It works through the grass into the blood. That's what causes the wrong hunger in the first place, the lack in the soil.

It's the first time the vet has seen it in The Spout, Agaat explained. Mostly it occurs in the north-west, it's a poverty disease.

She indicated with the little hand an approximate direction supposed to represent the north-west.

We are rich, she said, but you have to know well on what soil you're farming. It's not just botulism they can get, but stiffsickness as well, cro-ta-lism, then the back hunches and the limbs thicken and the mouse swells up.

On her strong arm, on the knob of the joint she showed where the mouse was situated, behind the front foot of the cow, just above the hoof.

Jak was standing in the doorway listening. You smiled at each other at Agaat's book-learning, a small smile. He was flabbergasted. It was the first time that you'd seen him of his own volition deliver a pocket of onions and a pocket of potatoes and a leg of lamb to the vet to thank him, over and above his fee, for his support. And it was also the first time that you saw him give Agaat a present—a little bag of liquorice and a *See* magazine when he came back from town.

Even picked Jakkie up in his lap. As long as you just stay good and healthy, Pappa's little bull, he said and stroked the child's head.

That was not the only disaster with cows during Jakkie's infancy.

Was it August of the following year? No, September '61 it was, a month after Jakkie's first birthday that Jak decided to add some more new Simmentals from South West Africa to his herd. New stud material needed to be added, he said, to the first herd of the German cattle that he'd started to build up in '55 when he tired of his wheat experiment. You were reluctant. Jerseys were what you knew, delicate of hip and legs, finely-moulded of head. A Simmental, a dual-purpose animal with a blunt head and full shoulders and heavy legs, was to you an alien concept. To milk cows, help them calve and then after a few years to sell them for slaughter, felt to you like treason.

The calving was another story. That you knew well enough from the first group of Simmentals. They were small-hipped and calved with difficulty. Nights long you and Dawid had to struggle in those first years to turn breached calves. Jak assisted clumsily, walked off after a while in impatience and from squeamishness at the blood. And then you remained behind alone, with over your shoulder the pair of eyes there on the stable's partition wall, under the lanterns, murmuring after you the little words which you prattled at the cows. Six or seven she must have been then.

If you put new animals from a different environment with old herds that had multiplied for generations on a farm, it always caused problems. You didn't fancy more problems. The problems in the backyard were already simmering again. And now, a year after the botulism disaster, another seventy of the Simmentals arrived. You insisted that they should be kept in a separate herd and that most of them be utilised singly for slaughtering while you would continue the dairy farming with which you were familiar, with the Jerseys.

How exactly did it come about on that spring day that the new herd of Simmentals were grazing with the Jerseys next to the river amongst the blue and yellow flowers? A gate left gaping? The new stable boy,

Dawid's town cousin Kadys, who didn't know any better?

The guilty one would never be found. It was a Saturday afternoon, not a good afternoon for searching for culpable parties. And Jak wouldn't listen to you about the glass flagon that he gave each worker on weekends with their rations. Otherwise I have to take them to town and then they drink in any case and I don't drive with drunken hotnots on my lorry. And I don't milk with drunken people over weekends, you said, but it fell on deaf ears. And now here was the trouble.

And if it hadn't been for Agaat. She'd gone for a walk with Jakkie in his pram.

We're going to the river, she said as she packed the bottle and his hat.

You knew why there specifically. It was sorrel time. It was the time for stringing garlands of pink sorrel and yellow sorrel on the long thin leaves of the wild tulips, an old game of Agaat's, you had originally shown her how. You pull the sorrel flower off the germen so that the flower has a little hole at its point underneath and then you string them one by one tightly packed against one another on the tulip string until it's full and then you tie the two ends together in a knot. Then you hang it around your neck. The garland of flowers, once in spring around her neck, around your neck. Such a garland took two hours to string and served as a necklace for a quarter of an hour. Then it was wilted. You knew that on that afternoon she would sit Jakkie down on his little blanket in the grass and plait him a garland and sing to him. In veld and vlei the spring's at play. There was a hare, a fox and a bear, and birds in the willow tree. All the old spring songs.

Agaat came into your room, ten minutes after she'd left, without knocking and gave the child back to you in your arms.

And now? Are you back already? you asked.

And then you noticed her cap that was crooked.

They've been to the water already, they're shitting slime, Agaat said.

She gulped to recover her breath. She push-pushed at her cap with the one hand.

You knew at once that it was the Simmentals she was talking about. They'd been to the poison plants. Cows that have grown up on a farm with wild tulips, don't eat them. They learn from an early age that they're more bitter than grass. So the old herd of Jerseys were safe even though the tulip bulbs were juicily in flower. It would be the new cattle, South West African cattle with a mindless hunger for greenery. After their arrival they'd been herded into a bare south-facing camp with hay and dry powerfeed and radishes to get them back into condition after their long journey in trains and lorries. Let loose in a green camp they would eat as if they were being paid for it, the young tulips first. And that would make them thirsty. And then they would drink. And water on tulips, that everyone knew, was as good as arsenic.

Agaat couldn't talk fast enough.

Chased them out of the grazing shut the gate so that they can't get to the river but there's a small drinking trough in that dosing-camp where they are now it's probably also been drunk dry they're thirsty they're shitting green strings their eyes are watering they're going to die off Hamburg's in the holding pen in front of the crush pen but he won't take one pace farther will have to get him in the headclamp quickly!

She was right. A bull like that, even when he's ill, couldn't just be doctored in the open. One swing of his head and you'd all be sent sprawling in the mud.

You wanted to know where Dawid was, where Kadys and Julies were.

I had them called down there by the cottages, they don't come out.

How did she get the bull into the holding pen single-handedly?

Agaat was trotting down the passage to the pantry. Jakkie put up a bawl. Jak was gone, would only be back from tennis by milking-time. Saar and Lietja arrived heavy with sleep at the kitchen door with a cluster of littl'uns. Big and small stretched their necks to see into the kitchen if under the licence of irregularity there was something to loot.

Hey you, back! Agaat scolded them.

You had your hands in your hair. That sort of time on Grootmoedersdrift. Agaat gave you a look of pull-yourself-together-on-the-spot.

So listen well now, she said to Saar and Lietja, the new cattle have eaten tulips. Do just what I say and do it quickly! Coffee first, four cans full, double-strength, with sugar!

She looked at you. It could mean only one thing. Hamburg was critical. Sweet strong coffee was all that could save the most valuable animals.

Agaat issued orders non-stop while she worked. The little canister of raw linseed oil she'd already had rolled out of the pantry and the bag of linseed had also been dragged out. In the big white basin with the red roses on the bottom she measured out three measuring jugs of linseed oil and added hot water and stirred with a spatula as she talked. In another gallon-drum she ordered ten measuring jugs of barley and water.

You just stood there, your legs paralysed.

Brandy! she shouted at you! Quicklime! Five double handfuls!

You managed to secure the child in his pram. He would just have to scream now.

Four dozen eggs, whites and yolks separated! she ordered Saar.

Four cups of brandy with the whites! Stir! In the hanslammers' bottles! Screw shut! When the coffee's brewed, get it cooled down! Pour it into cooldrink bottles! Be quick quick quick! Bring the roll of rubber piping with the elastic ring around the end behind the pantry door! And a knife! Have it ready! Get a move on!

Now you felt the adrenaline, quickened your pace, grabbed Jak's ten-year-old brandy out of the cabinet, went and dragged the bag of lime out of the storeroom. You understood everything that Agaat commanded. You just couldn't have remembered it all yourself so exactly. You knew what was at stake. The new bull was a champion and had cost tens of thousands of rand. You threw a few handfuls of lime into a canister. How much water? you called.

Fifteen jugs! Mix well!

Agaat was already measuring off the raw linseed oil in the big glass rusk canister.

Together you added the lime-water to the oil and shook it up in the bottle, you with your hands above and below, Agaat with her unbalanced grip round the sides.

First to and fro! Agaat directed. Up and down!

Now it's right, leave it, put down! she called when it had formed a thick cream.

The vet! she called after you. Ring him, give him a list of our medicines, ask him if it's right, tell him to come, quickly!

In the topsy-turvy you hadn't even thought of that. But she was right. There had to be a control. So that nobody could say that you'd made mistakes.

Doctor is playing golf, said Mrs Vet.

Take a pen, sweetheart, you heard yourself say, and write! Raw linseed, lime, barley, tannic acid, coffee, brandy, Hamburg tulip poisoning, crisis Gdrift, 13 September, 5 p.m., have you got it? You rang off before she could reply.

You went and fetched the bakkie and parked it in the backyard. Agaat had the bakkie loaded with bottles of sugared coffee and the bottles of egg-whites with brandy, the big rusk bottle full of lime-and-oil cream, the drum of barley water and the drum of slimy raw linseed on water, all sorted into boxes. And the thin rubber tubes, the Coopers dosing-syringes from the shed, a bottle with tannic acid, a measuring spoon, the thicker rubber tubes and cans for the enemas, plastic funnels, tins full of boiled water and bottles with screw-tops and extra bottles and containers.

The whole rescue mission was ready to roll within an hour.

Everybody wanted to bundle into the back of the bakkie. Agaat looked at you, now you had to speak. She tried to calm Jakkie. He was bawling his head off with the hubbub.

That they had to be very calm not to frighten the animals, you said, that they had to work slowly and with a plan to your and Agaat's orders nothing more and nothing less, that they must not talk loudly, and make no restless movements, that everybody first had to go and scrub their hands and rinse them every time between every animal. And that Saar and two big boys and one littl'un were in your team. And Lietja and two striplings and the other three littl'uns in Agaat's team. And that they should remain behind you when you arrived in the camp because you first had to get to the bull in the holding pen to doctor him.

O-alla-got, Saar said and tied her headscarf tighter.

Don't come and o-alla here now, where are your menfolk? you scolded. Why can't you keep them on track?

Saar looked away. But was there also something else in her attitude? Because she'd seen Agaat ordering you about and you doing everything exactly as she said, a little servant-girl of hardly thirteen? Her face was cunning. There wasn't time to say arrange your face. In any case you thought twice before saying that to the kitchen-maids.

You sent one of the boys to go and commandeer OuKarel. You knew Agaat had everything right about the medicine and you had learnt from your mother about the procedures with tulip poisoning, but experience was what was lacking. You needed OuKarel's eye there, you felt. You remembered your mother's belief that a bull, not to mention a new one, wouldn't co-operate if there wasn't a man in the company.

In the camp the animals were huddled around the drinking trough as Agaat had predicted.

And there was Hamburg, his hump seven hands high above the rails of the holding pen. He'd be able to flatten it like nothing. His head was hanging, strings of drool from his mouth, and the piss and the thin slimy dung ran out of him. He pressed himself against the back of the partition.

How had Agaat got him in there? How would you move him to the threshold of the crush pen? Would the headclamp be in working order?

Wide-eyed the maids stood staring. Agaat trotted off to test the lever of the clamp. Up and down she pressed it so that the flat shaft first bent at the hinge in the middle and then lifted up. Open and shut she operated it, the steel arms of the clamp flashing in the sunlight over there at the far end of the crush pen.

How are we going to get him in there? you asked her.

He's already half dead, Agaat said, look how deep his eyes are, he's wonky in the front legs, he won't give us grief.

How? you asked with the eyes.

Agaat hooked the index finger of her strong hand in front of her nose.

With the bare hand on his nose-ring?

That's how I got him there in the pen, Agaat said.

You didn't believe her. The holding pen's gate was wide open. You were sure she'd prodded him in there from behind.

The holding pen was one thing, one would still be able to roll free under the lowest bar of the pen. But the crush pen was a narrow gully with high cement walls. There was one escape route, that was to the back. But how would you worm past the bull if you were in front of him and he gored you? He would fill the gully from wall to wall.

At the front end, in front of the headclamp, there was a shutter of steel that could be lifted if he should decide to rush forward.

But what if everything happened very quickly? You'd be paralysed with shock, you'd slip, the one who had to lift the shutter could lose his nerve, you'd be trampled.

Who should take the bull in there?

You hesitated.

I'll take him, said Agaat, her mouth set in a straight line. He knows me. He's soft in the nose. He won't bugger around for no reason.

Ho my mother, said Saar.

You go and sit in the bakkie with Jakkie, Agaat said, and wash your hands before you touch him.

Push the other cattle away from the drinking trough, she ordered Lietja, count them, there should be seventy.

And for you she tallied on the fingers of her strong hand. One bottle of egg and brandy, one bottle of coffee, two pints of the rusk bottle's lime-and-linseed water mixed with two tablespoons of tannic acid to the pint, decanted into two Coopers canisters.

She would lead the bull as far as the clamp, you had to secure his head. Then somebody had to open the shutter so that she could get out in front.

Agaat ordered two boys to go and fetch planks and to build a scaffolding on little drums outside the crush pen on both sides so that you could reach across to dose the bull.

What if he gores you? one whispered to her. What if he tramples you?

They retreated stepping on one another's feet. Mush! they giggled. Arsgaat!

Dry up, said Agaat, a bag of acid drops for everybody, if you help nicely here. Stand ready, hand us what we tell you and keep your big traps shut or I'll make dog-mince of you.

You'd never forget it, the sudden subservience of everybody, big and small. Something changed gear that afternoon on Grootmoedersdrift.

Agaat put the medicine containers precisely in sequence on the wall on either side of the headclamp. She blew into the rubber tubes to check that they were clear. She squeezed the triggers of the dosing-canisters and squirted medicine on the ground until she was satisfied that they were working correctly and without air bubbles. Her mouth was set in a line, her chin jutting far forward.

Bring a rope, you called to the boys, bring a stick.

For what? Agaat asked.

So that I can have something with which to pull you out if he runs amuck, you said, then you grab the rope or the stick.

She looked at you. Agaat Lourier can't pull herself out of the gully with one arm, her face said.

Or I push the stick under your apron's shoulder-straps and lever you out, you said. You couldn't look her straight in the eye.

The gully is too deep. The stick is too short. You're too weak. It wasn't even necessary for her to say it.

Perhaps we should rather wait for the vet, you got out. Your voice was low.

Wait till I'm in, she said to you, climb on the wall and walk behind me. Don't put things in his head. Think one thing and think it straight.

First try to prod him from behind, you said.

You try, Agaat said, he doesn't want to, he's too buggered.

You went around the back of the holding pen. You prodded the shit-ting bull in the flanks with a stick. He didn't budge.

Agaat straightened her cap with both hands. There at the gate of the holding pen you saw it. The one shoulder pulled up, the pace forward, the pace back, the genuflection. Then she opened the gate and went in and closed the gate behind her. Plumb towards the dead strip between the bull's eyes Agaat advanced, bold and high her mien.

Water came into your mouth, of iron it tasted, of blood.

She hooked her finger into the nose-ring, turned her back, took a pace forward. Through the bars of the holding pen you saw the bull bend its knee, dragging his hind leg, starting to move forward. Six, seven, eight paces and Agaat was in the crush pen with him.

You climbed onto the wall, the stick and rope in your hand. The bull lowered its head. On both sides of his muzzle gobbets of drool were hurled against the cement walls. His small sunken eyes were on the cross of Agaat's shoulder-straps. Soon she was invisible. You could only deduce, from the steady pace at which the bull moved forward, that she was there walking ahead of him, and that she was exerting a constant force of traction on him.

The blood in your temples! The whole twenty, twenty-five, thirty yards of the crush pen! Triumph when the bull pushed his huge muzzle over the crossbar, when you pressed down the lever, and wedged in his head, and Agaat escaped through the shutter. A yelling from the littl'uns, cries of admiration as she emerged there.

She was opposite you on her scaffolding on the other side of the gully. She wiped her hands on the bib of her apron. She pushed at her cap. On her shoulders something glistened in the sun. It was wet where the big bull had drooled on her.

Agaat held out her little hand, the back, so that the bull could feel the warmth on his nose. He tried take a step back, felt his head was fast. It would be a business if he lay down in the gully. You had to work quickly. Agaat looked at you across the hump.

You wanted to praise her because she was so brave, but the expression on her face prevented you.

First the coffee, then brandy, he needs a kick-start, she said.

The main thing was that the liquid should not end up in the lungs. Agaat passed you the bottle with coffee.

Press on his cheeks, she said, you have two hands.

You pressed on the release knobs, the sensitive salivary glands. The jaws parted slightly, you pressed down the lever a notch to pick up the head another few degrees and lifted the lip and inserted the thin tube along the gum behind the back molar on the tongue.

Swallow! Gaat said.

The coffee went down without any problems. But then the egg mixture wouldn't pour smoothly down the tube. Agaat took it mouthful by mouthful out of the bottle and blew it into him through the tube.

After that it was the raw linseed-and-lime cream. The full two pre-scribed pints.

Then the two of you unlocked the clamp. Enlivened by the stimulants, the bull allowed himself to be prodded out of the crush pen. You drove him slowly to the clean straw that you'd had brought in and covered him in sacks where he stood, because then he had the shivers.

When did OuKarel appear on the scene? Next thing you noticed, there he was crushing his hat, a vaaljapie breath issuing from his mouth.

You had to flash a warning look otherwise Agaat would have scolded the old man. He was just sober enough to help. You rounded up the cows three at a time and dosed them with the boys holding their heads up. The cows shat and pissed and tried to step back and coughed. Then everybody had to let go to let them finish coughing. Raw linseed oil down the wrong gullet was the greatest risk. Terrible pneumonia could be the result.

Twice you and Agaat rushed back to the house to mix more medicine.

By six o'clock you trained the bakkie's headlights on the scene and sent home for lanterns. Agaat and yourself you fitted out with head-lamps from Jak's mountaineering equipment. Like a cyclopic eye Gaat's headlamp shone in the dark.

One cow looked as if she was going to succumb and had to be given a stomach-pump.

Jakkie was cold and hungry and cried.

Take him, Agaat, you said, go and bathe him and give him food, he's upset, I'll take charge here now. Wait until he's asleep then you come and call me.

At half past six Jak returned from tennis. Flabbergasted. In white clothes and all he plunged into the ooze of manure and mud to help. Anew you doctored the bull with coffee and brandy to stimulate his heart. At seven o'clock the vet turned up from the clubhouse, even more sozzled than Karel. Jak went and dragged Dawid and his cousin out of the huts to come and help. Agaat returned with Jakkie tied to her back in a blanket. She went and stood in front of Dawid and Kadys. With-out a word she made them both drink half a bottle of sweet coffee and three gulps of laced egg-white to fix the hangover. The bakkie lights were on them. Everybody was watching. They did as they were told. The women and the boys whispered. Dawid's face was squint. The vet stood back as if he was scared he would also be accosted.

Now you two go and milk the Jerseys, they must be sore by this time, she said. You sent Saar along to keep an eye because they were stepping very high indeed.

Men! you and Agaat signalled to each other with the eyes. But your part of the message was vitiated by her look. Some women! it said.

By four o'clock that morning the tulip poison had been counteracted. You administered barley-water and linseed-lime because the animals couldn't drink ordinary water. But the new herd had been saved. Ham-burg was starting to see better out of his eyes. He stopped peeing and started shitting less and less. Just the one cow that had been given the enema was looking weakish.

Everybody who had helped was ready to drop from hunger and fatigue. Agaat went home and for the second time that day washed and dressed in clean clothes.

The kitchen was a chaos, lime and oil on the floor and all the separated yolks standing around everywhere in dishes and bowls. All the egg, Agaat said, overwhelmed for the first time that day, you could see.

Never mind, we can use it, you said, let's make food for the people, they must be starving. You mixed the batter and Agaat started baking vetkoek and bacon and fried onion and pans full of scrambled eggs. Along with big jugs of sweet rooibos tea with milk you helped her to serve it in the backyard.

Aitsa, such a whitecap cattle-quack, the servants teased Agaat, how she blows a bull full of brandy!

There was new respect in the teasing and in the attitude, even of the big men when they brought back their plates and came to hand back the mugs into her hands.

You served Jak and the vet indoors. They were quiet.

That little coloured girl of yours deserves a medal, Thom Smuts said after a while to Jak with his mouth full of egg.

That's Milla's department, Jak replied, and gestured with his head in your direction where you were pouring coffee. It's she who should get the compliment.

*

my nurse takes me under my own law she counts my blessings for me minces my meals flushes my guts wipes my arse twists my buttons into their holes coat-buttons blouse-buttons jersey-buttons knots my shoelaces girds my buckles zips up my side-zips back-zips breast-zips my hooks my eyes shrouds my body closes off my openings she cleanses me combs me powders me paints me I am a well-rounded woman an effigy of a woman a scarecrow on a broomstick

doll and gaat go to town they pretend nothing is wrong gaat starched mrs de wet packaged they step with tiny tiny steps four legs and a walking stick they nod tiny tiny nods good morning good morning good day they invite the world to tea and cake mrs de wet is sixty-seven her hands they lie in her lap she drinks through a straw her vitamins for who would ever drink tea through a straw?

next to her waits her walking stick the finches twitter in the rushes who's afraid of a broomstick who's afraid of a walking stick?

o who's afraid of a walking stick

the first one was a knob-stick but soon the knob was too knobbly the second had a crook-neck but soon the neck was too crooked the third had a finger-grip but soon the grip started to slip the fourth was of light metal with rubber on the tip and rubber on the grip and a silver hoop to support the wrist

and then there were two of the same

one for each elbow

hopalong down the passage a clumsy camel on the stoep calump calump here comes kamilla a bat on crutches a gothic letter who said we do not hear the coming of death?

the fifth had four legs and a name in chrome on the shaft

viking strider

the strider itself had a calf-foot rest she walks like a sentinel in athens her head on her neck a pitch-black tassel her heart waggles like a gyroscope

*

3 October 1961

What more must I think up to get hr down? Braying hides ploughing waterproofing tarpaulins seeder-sums! All in vain! It's a year later & again it's exactly the same damn nonsense as last year. Seems seasonal. Don't want to end up in those maelstroms with her again.

So tonight the macaroni comes to the table again burnt to a cinder & Jak takes one look & gets up & drives away at speed. Waited till Jakkie was away & took a mouthful of J.'s brandy to calm myself & then went & knocked at A's door. Said she had to come to the kitchen immediately. At first she won't utter yea or nay & stares at the ground.

Now you're going to look at me my girl I say look me in the eyes & tell me what in heaven's name is wrong this time? A small flickering on her face but I keep my cool—would it do now to give hr the idea that she's won here & I ask: What on God's earth must I do with you to get you good again? & then of course I said the wrong thing: I can't live any longer with such a person in my house. But wouldn't she give me a quick look. I'm not in your house she says I'm in the outside room right there I almost explode with anger but I restrain myself & ask again: What must I do to get you good?

I want a fireplace, she says. I ask you!

Full of specifications on top of that: a grid & fire-irons & a mantel-piece. In my room. It's damp. Its walls are mouldering. I'm cold.

Just like that full in my face.

It's October I say. It'll be winter again she says. It's winter when I have my birthday.

Oh Lord is that what's been going on all the time! With Jakkie's birthday being in August A.'s in July of course went by disregarded again. How can she expect of me to remember that as well? But then for the sake of sweet peace I said I'm sorry & I said: A fireplace—what do you think of yourself! She gave me that look of hers & showed with her fingers & she said: I took your bull for you by the nose so that he could be dosed.

What could I raise against that? Her list could have been much longer.

9 October 1961 half past seven

From early this morning there's been a breaking & hammering in the backyard & A.'s stuff has been carried out in a pile. Decided after all to have a fireplace installed in her room. It gets cold back there in the winter & Jakkie is now spending all his time with hr. Will have to teach hr to drive as well. Don't want another crisis when Jak or Dawid isn't here.

Where have you ever in your life heard of slave quarters with a built-in fireplace says J., does she think she's a royal skivvy with a pedigree in Scotland? If I were him I say I'd keep my mouth shut she led his holy Hamburg by the nose for him & blew wine spirits into him while he the so-called master was prancing about volleying on the tennis court.

Had the dish & grid welded last week & had the lime mixed for the whitewashing on the outside & the black chimney pot is standing ready & the iron cross-beam to go above the grate so that the whole operation can be completed in a few days. See to it that it draws properly I said to D. there's no point in going to all the trouble & then we're stuck with smother & smoke inside the room. It must be got ready & right before we start the harvest there's no time for toiling & moiling.

Quarter past nine

Have just been to have a peep in the backyard. Hearth-hole has been broken through. It's going to be a half-outside roundbelly fireplace otherwise it will take up too much space inside. A. is standing in the middle of the floor with hr hands in front of hr & looks at the foundation of the hearth being laid. The labourers yell so can we come & fry our scratchings by your fire? our sheep's tails our sheep's heads? can we stew our porcupine over your coals or are you going to be otherwise with your fire? She doesn't twitch a muscle but I know her she's very taken with it. More than that. She looks inspired. Lord in heaven help us the girl.

Second day of hearth-building 12 o'clock
D. had me called to the kitchen they've finished plastering & white-washing on the outside he says but inside's a problem. Apparently A. is particular about the plastering around the hearth-hole. They must do what she says I command. He feels queasy says D. the builders are teasing A. between the legs. Send them home I say he'll just have to help her on his own with the finishing-off inside just as long as it gets finished.

She doesn't want to be helped says D. she wants to do it herself on her own it's her altar. Heaven help. Altar. For what sacrifice?

After lunch
Strangely quiet in the backyard all afternoon. Went & looked out of the nursery window & lo & behold there are Saar & Lietja peering into A.'s window they're pushing & shoving each other. Had better go & investigate.

5 o'clock
A. had gone to dig potatoes in the field for supper so then I went & peeped through the window. A cloth draped in front of the fireplace a bucket of plastering-cement & a pointed trowel & a bucket of water & a snow-white block-brush & a few shoe boxes all with lids on. Typical. Grabbed my opportunity & went to have a peek. Quartz pebbles & skulls & shells & baby's toes & sea urchins from Witsand. Couldn't look any further.

13 October
Instructed D. to teach A. to drive the bakkie. She refuses point-blank. Will just have to teach her the ropes myself. In a week we're mowing.

15 October
Waited till J. was out this afternoon before taking the old Chevvy down to the fields with A. & Jakkie. Coaxed & wheedled there you have your fireplace now I said exactly as you wanted it now it's my turn. She looks

at me askance won't give me the child to hold won't get in behind the wheel. Perhaps I should just let it be. The fireplace seems in any case to have the desired effect. Everything is running smoothly again. Bread is rising chickens are laying flower garden spick & span big fires every evening. Hear her singing & telling stories to Jakkie there in the back. Every morning the white cloth is draped over the opening. Can't see anything of what she's been getting up to there only the heaps of ash & the half-burnt logs on the ash heap next to the compost heap. She cleans it up every morning early. Tends her fireplace like a verger.

20 October after eight

Went to peep what they're doing there in the back. Sparks from the chimney fireworks on the outside room's roof it hisses & sputters as the hot ash is blown into the rain (October rain! Two fields harvested already. Does though seem as if it will clear tomorrow. Can't abide a hassle with wet wheat).

Peered through the chink in the curtains could only make out the silhouette A. on an apple box in front of the fireplace with Jakkie on her lap. No other light a tremendous fire. Pressed my ear against the pane couldn't hear anything. Jakkie in his crawler his hair a halo around his head A.'s cap illuminated with the glow of the fire looks as if it could burst into flame at any moment. All the strange things plastered into the fireplace not exactly what one would call a work of art. Mouldings half Romish & creepy where does she get it from?

Jakkie pushes his little fingers into the black nostrils of the lynx skull A. strokes over the imprint of hare's-foot fern he points at the horse-shoe in the middle above she counts the abalone shells set around the edge one two three four five she holds him so that he can touch the marbles quick with the fire the taws with the green & yellow bande-roles inside the small milky marbles bluish & reddish she shows the hollows of the dassie-foot he stirs the spoor of the steenbok she shows the tears of the snow he laughs at the shiny puddles of water she tickles the pistil of the arum the vaulting of the lily's lip the ravel on the tip with which the lily's body was bound before it opened in the vlei. From her mouth I can see she's singing to him. Her foot is marking time her knee is hopping. Wide-eyed he listens. Points at the black mole on her cheek she opens her eyes wide he presses on it with his tiny pink finger she pretends it's a switch a magic spot she moves her scalp to wiggle her ears & the point of her cap he laughs he roars.

11

Milla, can you hear me? This is me, Beatrice.

Her voice is loud. As if she's trying to penetrate a wall.

Beatrice of Friswind, you know me, don't you!

What further aspect of herself would she select to remind me who she is? How much does she think my memory has shrivelled from lying still?

She opts for the more recent past.

I was at the signing of the will not so long ago, do you remember?

Hatted and gloved, I remember. I too was powdered and lipsticked for the occasion. Agaat's great pleasure in life. With a white spot on the forehead, to remind me that I am a snooper at freshly-whitewashed window sills. But how does Beatrice expect me to show that I recognise her? Smite my hands together and jubilate? Long-time-no-see-how-is-your-suckling-pig-farming?

I don't even want to open my eyes.

It's me, Thys's wife, can you hear me? Now her voice is lower, with feigned sympathy, as if she wants to say: Me, you nearest neighbour to whom you told everything about your life.

Why did I ever tell her anything? Now she's lusting after more. She's here for the scrapings from the pot, for the last meat on the bones.

She hangs over me, her face inches from me. She smells of sweat and powder. She comes even closer. Her breath smells of frikkadel. Her sympathy smacks of frikkadel.

She knows nothing about me, can now no longer know anything about me. What I told her at that time about Jak wasn't news to her. I could see on her face that I was just a mirror for her, the darting glance, the shame, the repressed rage. Confession in the kitchen, we know, is treason against the sitting room. And it's the sitting room that must be

225

defended, at all costs. That I now understand. And that's where Jak was right, I suppose. All hands on deck, I remember, he used to call on reporting for duty in the sitting room when people came to visit.

If I could suddenly find my tongue, I'd be able to tell it to you in so many words: All that we could think up to do, you and I, all our lives, was to unbosom ourselves in our inner chamber before the Lord. Oh hearken to me, your little girl-child meek and mild, oh preserve me, your bleeding virgin, bless me, woman of your nation, but what did that make Him? An insurance agent placating his policy-holders? A panjandrum of the harem? I don't know about you, friend, but in my married life God was not on the side of the unmaskers. He was the great Mask himself. Our polygamous Heavenly Spouse. Do you remember Mrs Missionary van der Lught's recommendation? That we should pray to Him in our Overberg Version of Psalm 119, Turn away mine eyes from beholding vanity and quicken thou me in thy way. Indeed. Here I lie now, biered for the fatherland.

Would you understand that, Beatrice? In your book, I imagine, the dying may not mock?

Nevertheless, dear neighbour, note, my mask nowadays is made of hard green plastic. My life has changed. I am harmless to you, impervious to that God of mutually humbugging neighbourliness and pretentious poets. I am delivered to the mercy of my diary of former days. And it runs deeper than little kitchen secrets, I can tell you. And at present God is vengeful as in his youth, and it feels a whole lot more honest. Indeed, He has become a woman. He is now named Agaat, not that I think you can understand Greek. 'Agaat', do you know what else it also means apart from the name for a semi-precious stone?

I can feel Beatrice shying away from me. Unsatisfied. What did she expect? The Ave Maria in sign language?

How would she have got in here? What's happened to Agaat?

Through half-closed eyelids I can make out that the curtains are drawn. But it's not the morning light shining through, it's not morning.

It's afternoon, late afternoon. What's Beatrice doing here? She was supposed to come in the morning, tomorrow morning. Then Agaat would be away in town.

But Agaat didn't come to say goodbye, didn't say she was leaving now. She put on the oxygen mask for me. That was the last time I saw her.

She said, rest a while, breathe easily.

She said, just don't faint again, please not.

That was after lunch. It was today after all. Could the days be starting to play tricks on me? First spoon of jelly then I almost choked. So then she had to thump me again to get it out, first come and sit behind me to do the Heimlich, several times in succession. The first time that Agaat has entered my bed in broad daylight.

Today it was, I'm not confused.

Her heart thumping against my back. Her legs on either side of my body. Her arms around my stomach. A trace of anxiety mingled with her starched medicinal smells. After she'd got me calmed down, she was pale, didn't want to look me in the eye.

She put on the mask, her hand on my chest, regulated the oxygen, drew the curtains.

Rest a while.

Let me die, I asked with my eyes.

No, Agaat said with her eyes, don't be otherwise.

The elastic of the oxygen mask pulls my hair at the back painfully. No way that I could convey this to Beatrice. And what could she do about it? She'd sooner touch the tail of a crocodile than me. And I have one Tamer. She who can open the doors of my face.

I hear the chirping of sparrows. Late afternoon. Exuberant sparrows that can breathe again after the scorching day. Thirty-eight degrees, Agaat said. Oh, for the breath of the tiniest sparrow! If I could inhale it into me. I would live the better for it. I'd be able to spit in the face of the inquisitive wife of my neighbour. By her sneezings a light doth shine.

Could we open the curtains just a bit?

We. Overberg plural. The fact that Beatrice can consult the realm of death on domestic matters makes her light-headed. Light streams into the room. I can feel her watching my face.

I'm sorry if I gave you a fright. I thought I might as well come this afternoon. I'll stay over if you like. I spoke to Agaat on the phone this morning. She wants to go to town tomorrow, she asked if I would stay with you in the morning. But then she didn't sound altogether together to me. So I came over quickly to see if you're managing here. You never know what the creatures will get up to if you don't keep an eye on them. And with you so helpless here, for all you know they're robbing you blind, I don't mean Agaat of course, I mean the others. It's not as if she can be everywhere all the time. I wonder where she is. Somewhere in the back I suppose. I knocked but nobody came. And the front door was wide open. And there's a whole pile of loose stuff in the sitting room, looks as if it's been put out to be carried off. I'll tell her she should really lock the doors, my goodness, you two women so alone here in the place, nowadays you can't be sure of your own life. I must say, Milla, I've often wondered whether she's really competent enough to look after you here on her own, but I hear from Mrs le Roux that Doctor is very satisfied. She's better than a nurse apparently, knows every need of yours, and is very meticulous with everything. Ai, one can just be grateful that some of them are still like that.

Beatrice opens the curtains further.

Is it too light?

I open my eyes as wide as I can.

Lord woman! Can you see me then?

She comes nearer. Looks me in the eyes. I can see the plan forming in her head. She holds a finger in front of my nose, moves it from left to right. I follow my neighbour's wife's finger with my eyes.

Heavens, she says, so you can really still see . . . and . . . everything.

Yes, see and everything, hello Beatrice, I blink. She wants to giggle, swallows it quickly.

She closes the curtain slightly again. Nervous, uncomfortable with me, can't face it. I can't face her either. So much embarrassment on the face, so much fear and aversion, all at the same time. She'd look at me much more readily if I were a stuffed pig with an apple in my mouth. She did look at me more readily when I was stuffed. Mrs de Wet with a sentinel in her mouth. Would Beatrice ever have given Thys a blow job? She certainly always could open her mouth wider than anybody else on the church-choir gallery. To articulate with emphasis. Thy praise shall linger on my lips.

Shall I open the doors a bit, it's a bit close in here.

Beatrice tripples to the stoep doors, opens them.

Here comes a play for voices. And for smells. For neighbour's wife, sparrow-fart and the intimations of mortality.

A-g-a-a-a-t! she calls in a little high-pitched voice. A-g-a-a-a-t! first to this side and then that side of the stoep.

A swarm of sparrows takes off from the bougainvillea. Beatrice's dress is the wrong shade of blue next to the purple.

I wish she would leave. I wish Agaat would come and take her to the sitting room and say she'll manage thank you and give her tea so she can get herself gone. I'll signal off, off here with the Neighbour's Wife in search of a Drama, she can keep her heartfeltness for when I'm cold and coffined, thank you. I'll blink my eyes until Agaat understands: I'll be content with Saar, Saar can sit with me tomorrow when she goes to town, I'll go mad with such sanctimonious blethering in my ears all morning, stark staring mad. All that Saar ever says is 'oumies'. When she sweeps the passage, she stops for a moment, straightens up, and looks in here. 'Oumies,' she says then, an acknowledgement of my existence, on the same small scale, the single word, as the scale on which I now live. She looks at me as one looks at a sheep that has long since lain down with bluetongue. 'Oumies'. Ounooi. Indeed. What more is there to say? It's honest at least.

Sickbed comforters generally don't talk to you but to themselves, especially if you're in the process of dying. You're a trial run for their excuses.

I wonder where Agaat can be, says Beatrice. I hope she doesn't often leave you on your own like this now, after all, you can at any moment . . . you can at any moment need her. Ai Milla that you should lie here so at the mercy.

Beatrice clicks her tongue. She looks round the room. Her eyes dart swiftly, scrutinisingly over everything. She thinks I'm not all there. She thinks I can't really see, I'm just a reflex of pupils. She thinks I can't see how she slides open the drawer of the dressing table and peeks into it while she's talking, how she picks up the folded towels from the two bedpans and looks into them, how she picks up the medicines from the trolley and screws up her eyes to read the names on the little bottles, how she runs her finger along the bedpost, how she glances askance at the camp sretcher against the wall.

Must say everything looks nice and tidy here, she says, clean and all. I suppose it's better than the hospital, familiar isn't it, I suppose one would rather just be at home.

The volubility of the living. Her cup runneth over. Bountiful she wants the harvest to be from death's dominion, from death's ante-chamber. She wouldn't have wanted to come for nothing, that's clear. I can just hear her account: Nothing in the bedpans, doesn't look as if they've ever been used. I suppose everything has just about ground to a halt in that department. The woman eats almost nothing. The maid says just little-little bits of thin gruel.

What the one madam wishes the other: thin gruel and a seized-up internal mechanism. I can see it, the smugness of the impeccable messenger, the primly-pleated pout, it would take more than a bedpan under her backside to conquer her conceit.

Shall I go and see if I can find Agaat?

Beatrice comes to loom over me. She looks as if she wants a twig to prod me. She should just open her eyes, there are sticks on the trolley, flat ice-cream sticks and ear-buds, she can choose. I want to say boo! I want to put out my tongue. I open my eyes, wide, suddenly, and then I peel them back for her, and I flicker for my neighbour's wife by my bier of death, the flicker of death, sustained and unmistakable, the vibrating blackwhite eyelash butterfly. *Leminitis camilla*. Map butterfly. Liberated in the occluded valley. Haven't felt so lively in a long time. The effect is all one could desire. It is sung. Mezzo-soprano in The Spout.

O Lorrrd Mil-la, Oh Go-o-od he-e-l-ep! Steps back, back, her eyes glued to my face. Boer diva in stage shock, Jak would have said.

Yes, don't look away, Beatie, look, that's what you get for coming to stand by my bed with a fastidious smirk on your face. Look how my eyeballs quake! It's my last little bit of muscle power! With that I can move worlds!

She runs down the passage. Gaat! she screams. Her voice is shrill.

Gaat, come quickly, Gaat! Help! The oumies!

Out at the back door. Cat-twah! the screen door slams. I hear her hammer on the outside room's door, a window is pushed open. A scream. I count the seconds. Then the screen door slams again. Another scream.

Lorrd Jesus please, help! Beatrice exclaims. She's by the telephone in the passage. I hear the back door open again. I know who it is. I know who's waiting surreptitiously in the kitchen to hear what's going on, I know who's standing behind the door and listening attentively. I want to laugh. I wish I could laugh. Water comes to my eyes. Beatrice the emphatic, Beatrice whom Agaat could imitate so well since childhood. We eavesdrop on her together, Agaat and I. We wait behind the curtains.

Thys, Thys is that you Thys? Thys, yes listen Thys I'm here with Milla de Wet and I think she's on her deathbed the woman, and I think that maid of hers is dead already.

Agaat, yes.

No, I told you don't you remember, she phoned this morning and asked I should come tomorrow she has to go to town for all sort of business and funeral arrangements.

Thys, no, listen to me now!

No, I thought I'd rather come and have a look this afternoon already, the maid sounds half odd to me.

No, towards five o'clock. Didn't you get my note that I left you on the sideboard?

No, when I got here everything was wide open and the yard deserted and Milla was lying all on her own in a pitch-dark shut-tight room with a green thing over her face.

Over her mouth and nose, yes.

In any case so then her eyes peeled back and her eyelids started fluttering, something terrible.

No, Thys, I didn't touch her.

No, that's what I'm telling you, she was nowhere to be found, so I went to see where the creature could be when you needed her and then I found her in the outside room lying with exactly the same green thing on her face!

No, through the window, the door was locked, but I could see, the girl's bed is next to the window.

No, I don't know, I was out of there so fast.

A tube? No, I don't know about tubes, Thys.

What?

Poison? No, Lord, Thys, I don't know, but now is not the time.

Yes, I hear you. Just come. No, Thys, gas or poison, it doesn't matter.

No, the point is that I've now arrived here unexpectedly, don't you see? Perhaps I've just come upon it too soon, if you understand what I mean.

No, Lord, Thys, why must I always have such a time getting something into your head, my dear husband. Suicide! Suicide! That's what I say yes. Perhaps they both, you know, how do they say? a joint, a shared, how does one say? a linked, perhaps they decided it's the only way out of the misery, a team effort, ai, what is the word again? Because I tell you it's crawling with pills and pans in there and it smells of dead!

No, Thys, I'm not going into that room again!

No, Thys, please. I'm not going to revive Agaat, I don't doctor coons!

No, I want to leave now I feel too weird here. It's a . . . a . . . double-decker! How does one say it?

Well then just come immediately please!

No fine, fine, I'll wait till you come, I'll wait outside. And Thys, ring the doctor and ring the police and ring Dominee van der Lught. I'm going to ring off now Thys, I have to get out of this house, it gives me the creeps, I'm waiting for you in front, just come, bring Magda along, she lays out bodies doesn't she, tell her it's a twin, bye Thys bye!

Beatrice picks up speed down the passage. Trot-trot slip-slide into the sitting room as she cuts the corner. Clicks-clicks go the heels. Rattles the front door. Must have locked behind her when she came in. Neighbour's wife incarcerated with cadavers. My cadaver, your cadaver, us together in our palaver.

Here comes Agaat now. Heard the whole phone conversation, that I can tell from the footsteps. From the kitchen she comes, from behind the door where she's been eavesdropping, down the passage, quickly. She looks agitated when she comes into my room, cap at a crazy angle. She comes and stands close to me, looks into my eyes.

What do I hear you've been flickering here? What kind of flickering with the eyes and what kind of peeling back? Are you feeling faint?

No, Agaat, it's a joke.

She's too alarmed to read me correctly.

Sorry, Ounooi, I overslept, completely, I'm sorry. Ai.

She takes off the mask, wipes away my drool, smoothes cream on my face where the edge of the mask has pressed against my cheeks.

I flicker with my eyes, everything's fine Agaat, I could die laughing, I laugh.

She doesn't see it.

Nooi Beatrice, she must have got a fright, I was lying there in my room with the oxygen mask, with the extra one, I wanted to see how it works, whether it works well, whether you can breathe from it. If I get extra breath from it, how it feels to get extra breath. Then I went to sleep, must have been from too much breath, then I went into such a deep, deep sleep, I'm sorry. Then I woke up from the window. Then nooi Beatrice pushed open the window from the outside.

Agaat fiddles with my eyelids, she draws the upper lid over the lower, presses on the soft spots under my eyes, as if she wants to arrange them properly, living eyes, that don't just peel back for nothing.

So what kind of flickering is nooi Beatrice talking about?

Relax, Agaat, it's funny, can't you see? Come on, laugh a bit! Laugh so that I can hear it. I want to hear laughter. Laugh Agaat, I want to see what you look like when you laugh, when last did we have a really good joke here? The laughing corpses. The one with peeled-back eyes, the other one drunk on air. The one old ghost was lean and the other old ghost was fat, do you remember, Agaat, the song? We used to sing it to Jakkie when he was small, when we were bathing him. Then I blew out my cheeks and you sucked in your cheeks and I sang high and you sang low and then he crowed with laughter.

Agaat pulls here and pushes there in the room. She's too much off her stride to interpret me. What matters now is what it looks like to outsiders.

Tsk, she says, here the stretcher still is, clean forgot!

She slams shut the camp stretcher, goes to stow it in the passage cupboard, prepares for inspection. Then she looks in the mirror. Just look at me now, she says. She pins her cap on straight. I catch her eye in the mirror. She's standing with a mouth full of hairpins. I've never seen Agaat pinning her cap in place.

Sorry, Ounooi, she mumbles through the pins, just let me pull myself together here.

Agaat, I flicker, please, can't you see how funny it is?

I'm coming Ounooi, I'm coming, I must explain nicely to baas Thys, I must go and see where nooi Beatrice is now.

Let the woman be, let her be, didn't you hear what she said? She doesn't doctor coons.

Agaat comes closer.

What are you saying, Ounooi? I'm causing scandal here? No, that's not what you're saying.

I roll my eyes back to the garden where Beatrice is now wringing her tiny hands, I show how I peeled back my eyes for her. I peel my eyes back and back, I flicker them, I look straight at her, I laugh. Over and over in the same sequence I explain. I make my eyes shine, I make my eyes sparkle.

Agaat, but look, look, I have only my eyes to tell a joke, my dear Agaat who wants to breathe on my behalf and falls asleep wearing an oxygen mask, laugh then, laugh with me!

A smile steals across Agaat's mouth.

Ho Ounooi, you didn't really pretend? Act?

She can't say it.

Yes, you've got it, you've got it, I Milla de Wet, née Redelinghuys, who has been lying here for months now on my back wasting away, I today pretended, yes, feigned, yes acted out the dance of death, so do your bit. If I can mock, how much more can't you? It's the last joke, can't you see?

Right, says Agaat, very funny. But this is not the time for games. You heard who all was being informed.

Exactly, Agaat, the whole titocracy wants to see the double-decker suicide!

Cars arrive in the yard, the dogs bark.

All the stuff in the sitting room, says Agaat. They must just not think I'm trying to rob you.

She's left before I can stop her. She's going to establish a firebreak at the front door. Agaat, but here you are alive and kicking! Questions, exclamations. She tries to explain. Thys and the dominee and Magda the cadaver connoisseur. Agaat does not invite them in. But they want to see, see with their own eyes. They press past her. But she gets to the front, I hear her soles in the passage, backwards, backwards. She precedes them into the room, her arms wide as if she wants to dam them up behind her apron. She signals at me with the eyes, I'm sorry I couldn't stop them. She comes to stand by my bed. Puts her hand on my shoulder.

I am framed, I am pre-eminent, my moment of glory. I turn my eyes slowly from her to the company clustering in the doorway craning their necks. I look at my neighbours, the keepers of law and order, the purveyors of benevolence, the profferers of prayers, the conjurers of contumely and catastrophe. One by one I cull their stares, until I have collected them all in mine, the stupefaction and the shame, and the fear.

We are prepared for the season, the ounooi and I, says Agaat. We have fruitcake and tea for you all, don't we Ounooi?

I blink my eyes slowly in affirmation. And I point them with an extended wink in the direction of the sitting room.

Go forth. Eat cake.

But now they're in a hurry. No, they don't want to sit down.

I listen to Agaat taking leave of the guests at the door.

He is so grateful for the good hands in which her ounooi finds herself, says the dominee.

We do our best, says Agaat.

I'll settle the hash of the sheep-stealers, says the sergeant.

Rather bring the troops, says Agaat, the robbers work in teams.

Twock-twock-twock Thys descends the stoep staircase in his big shoes.

Have a nice day, Agaat, bye-bye, Magda calls gaily.

Not a sound from Beatrice.

The doors slam. The cars pull off. The dogs bark.

The joke of the afternoon seems small. A small forlorn joke. I can feel it seeping out of me. I feel heavy. I feel dense. I don't feel sad. I feel tired. Agaat is sad. I know, I can feel it.

She remains standing on the stoep. She calls the dogs back. I hear them panting. I close my eyes. I can picture their tails wagging, their open-mouthed laughing with her. They come to have their heads stroked.

Look at you Boela, where have you been again?

Her voice comes with an effort. She tries to bend it into shape by talking to the dogs, appropriating the liveliness of dogs. Dogs that can come and go and wallow in the dust, in dead things, to appropriate the smell for themselves, to get up and to scrabble with the back feet.

Come here, Koffie, but my goodness, you too. Where do you find mud to roll in now? Oh sis, but you stink!

Agaat doesn't come in. I can see her standing there. She watches the gate being opened and closed. She remains there longer than usual. She watches the cars turning off into the main road, the billows of dust getting smaller and disappearing over the hill. She feels the weight of the evening waiting, she smells the last still black water of the drift, she sees the dark mountain rearing up and the black tree-tops of Grootmoed-ersdrift.

But that's better than nothing, it's better than me in my white bed in here.

She does not want to come in.

She does not want to enter the house. But there is nowhere else. Nothing else. Not as long as I'm here. This is the cup. This is the book. Drink it, turn its pages.

Ai, I hear, look at how dry you are.

I hear her go down the stoep steps. Water on the cement. It's the garden hose. The water splat-splats in a feeble stream. Agaat is watering the pot plants. She talks to them. She wants me to hear. That is how I taught her. Plants flourish when you talk to them, especially in pots. They grow shiny leaves. That's their reply.

Virgin's tears, she says, hen-and-chickens, hoya, Mackaya bella, delicious monster, peace in the home.

Tonight she gets no further than a roll-call.

The hose drags around to the other side of the stoep. One thing leads to another. Now it's the bed right under the stoep that the irrigation doesn't always reach.

Agaat is buying time. She considers what next. She makes plans. How to proceed. How to keep things well-aired and well-lit. Coping with the evening, coping with the morning.

One pot, another pot is dragged across the stoep. Wet terracotta gritty on the cement. The early December move. Then the late-afternoon sun shines in under the veranda and dries everything out.

There, now you're out of the heat, says Agaat.

She grunts as she comes upright.

Everything is wet. The tap has been closed. The pots have been moved. Now she must in. Now she can't do anything else. But it's grown dark. She has somewhere to start. The curtains to draw, the table lamps to switch on. A sign of life she can give. This is a farm. People are living here. Sweetenough's the name of the wife, Goodenough's the name of the maid.

I hear her at the front door. She wipes her feet on the cane mat. Once, twice, checks under the soles, once more. A sigh. Then she's in. She closes the door, locks, latches from the inside. She looks at the latch. She turns round. She looks at the sitting room. She takes one step in, another, she's on the carpet. Now she's ready. Now the hand does what it finds to do, the left hand in front, the right hand behind.

I hear a curtain, another, I hear a note, a phrase. Then she finds the tune. Then I find it. It's for me, Agaat, I know, sing for me there in the sitting room. *Blow the wind southerly*, she hums. She knows it from the old record of Kathleen Ferrier. Did we throw it away with the clearing-out? Her voice is weak. She clears her throat, starts again.

Sing, Agaat. You sing the old-old tunes. Sing the songs of yester-year. The music of the front room. Sing of the wind round the corners of the house, the south-easter, the north-wester. The song of the window frames, of the door frames and the curtains, of the standard lamps and the carpet with the red flowers and the sideboard of dark imbuia that has surrendered its secrets. And the riempie chairs and the riempie bench and the round table in the corner. The mute words of people, the still dense things, the old ornaments from which at the beginning you couldn't keep your eyes. Are you touching, now, Diana and her tame wolves in old brown porcelain? Do you pick up the little copper Indian shoe, the shoe in which you always in spring put the kukumakranka for me? And the swans of white blown glass, do you touch their necks and do you see the green vase for freesias, the blue one full of daffodils, the big grey vase that you stuck together, the one for the wild flowers of September, for the first blue lupins, for the blue-purple hydrangeas?

Sing softly of the evening's coming and of the evening meal, the sausage and eggs and the red tomatoes and the fresh loaf with the crackled brown crust, the milk in the jug that was a wedding gift, the square of butter under glass. The white tablecloth, the oven glove around the ears of the black iron saucepan, the sitting-down, the hands under low light, around the knives, around the forks, the spoons with the ivory handles, the people who look at each other, or do not look, speak to each other, or do not speak, or speak without words. Sing, that you may be consoled. Because that you now have to do for yourself, as you've always had to do.

Oh sing, sing, Agaat, of the wind that blows from the south and the ship in the offing, because it is in the offing. I see it in the distance. White is its bow and its splines are white and it's coming over the hump-backed hills, closer I see it coming, ever closer.

I understand. You don't think my joke this afternoon was funny. It's a sad song, that's all.

I open my eyes. The lights are suddenly on in the room.

Look, says Agaat, with all the hubbub you haven't even seen yet.

She points next to my bed.

The rainbow is gone. Now there is a mountain with a vlei in front of it. It is full of white water-hawthorn. The mountains reflect a darkness amongst the flowers. An early-morning scene, a painting from the sitting room. I thought we had thrown it away.

The blue blue hills of home, says Agaat, I went and fetched it from the cellar.

And look here, the portrait of the grandmother. I thought you might want to see it once more.

It's the portrait in front of which my mother used to make me stand when I was small. Her hand heavy on my shoulder. Look, Milla, it's she who farmed into being this little plot of earth. One day it will be yours.

A matriarch in the making, her mouth young, her plump white fingers folded round a rolled-up document, her hair pulled back tightly in a bun, her cheeks two touched-up red stains, the collar around her neck of fine white lace, the one eye small and fierce, the other one larger, clear-sighted, the eye over which something reflects distractingly on the gibbous glass of the oval frame, a rectangle of white, my bed, a smudge of grey, my head, my grey hair on the pillow.

*

Clear out clear out my iniquitous life! screams the bob-head-doll she strikes her stick on the floor give away! bequeath! burn! the wise hoard no button the prudent begin discarding at fifty a lifetime's gleaned-together rags tassels and tatters those condemned to death would have to clear out all save the rope of the gallows enviable the chaste suicide's furious meticulousness museums are in cahoots with the negligence of the dying a comb a necklace a shoe-horn writers hook after the last hung-up coat a hat behind the door rummage in bottom drawers they the custodians should rather have to sing inflammatory songs in the archives should with the last cadences have to dig holes in the cellars raise demolition-axes light purifying fires come beloveds let us expedite the onslaught of moth and rust! and let us inspire the breath of the blowing dust! start with the linen cupboard! start with the veil-netting of the third dress of a woman start with the redundant winding-cloths the cosy coverings with which one tries to charm death give away! bequeath! burn! I make the list and you make three piles for giving away burning and bequeathing and today you will be in paradise with me even before the cocks have crowed.

*

It was the day of the pork measles, the evening after the accident with the tractor winch, December '61, after supper. Agaat brought Jakkie in with 'great news' on her face, 'good news'.

237

She could hear you and Jak were having words again. She could hear it was going to go awry again.

She put the child down on the mat and brought in the coffee after supper and said 'something' had happened.

Jak was too annoyed to notice. A deputation of workers had come at knocking-off time that afternoon to tell him that they wanted new pit lavatories at their homes, the old ones were dilapidated. You heard it all, you were in your room, exhausted after the day. You'd often spoken to Jak about sanitation for the workers, he simply didn't want to do anything about it.

They were in front of his office door on the front stoep and you heard their complaints clearly.

Yes, Agaat doesn't do the right thing by them and Agaat says it's because of people's shit lying around that the pigs get measles and their slaughter-pig for the month was spoiled and they don't believe her they thought pork just had spots like that and why can't they get a sheep then to slaughter and the mies had said the privies would come and when are they coming then and Agaat had threatened the baas was going to shoot their dogs and is the baas going to do it and where are they supposed to find food for their dogs when they don't have any themselves and Agaat had said their wives can't work for the mies in the kitchen with germs.

You looked out of the open door of the room onto the stoep. There they stood. Lietja's husband, Kitaartjie, and Saar's husband, Piet Skilletjies. You saw them from the back, the ragged seats of pants, the bare patches in the hair from stab wounds, the sloping shoulders. You could smell them, the sharp sweat, the old dirt.

Our children have worms, we want pits with corrugated-iron huts over them and wooden seats, they said.

Jak knew nothing of the morning's doings, nothing of the medicine-dosing and the grumbling at the labourers' houses. He didn't understand what the slaughter-pig had to do with measles and latrines. He told them to get away from his office door, he was busy. You withdrew your head quickly from the window.

It was Dawid there in the office. He had come to speak about his cousin who had been caught in the winch-axle earlier that afternoon with the hay-baling.

Julies is lying in front of the fire and he's talking confused and the doctor said he has concussion, and his foot, his foot isn't so good.

Dawid's voice was calm and serious. He demanded nothing explicitly, just spelt out the details.

It was too much for Jak, all the accidents. You could see it on his face as he sat there twirling his fork that evening after supper. He didn't want to listen when you tried to tell him what had happened that day, of Agaat's doings. Agaat got on his nerves, he said. And there she was again now with Jakkie and 'something' that had happened.

He put his fork down and leant back in his chair.

What could it be this time? Has the dam burst? Has the horse drowned? How come, Gaat, that you're always the first on the scene? One would swear that there where your eye falls, there trouble erupts. What is it this time?

Later, you signalled to Agaat, tomorrow, now's not the time, make yourself scarce here. But you could see that she was excited.

I want to help you, she signalled with the eyes, I want to provide diversion here at the table. 'Something' has happened! Just give me a chance! She had Jakkie on her arm. He pointed a tiny finger at her cap.

Go and put him to bed, you said, it's bed-time.

You knew the expression on her face very well. It spoke of wanting to compensate, of wanting to make good all the bad things of the day, wanting reassurance, wanting to be set at ease. It was she who had had to put a stop to the slaughtering of the pig that morning and who had come to call you.

She was right, there was no doubt about that. The meat was permeated all the way into the muscles with little red globules. You had all the pigs caught and one by one you had the bit put into their mouths and you pulled out the tongues yourself with pliers to have a look. They were all infested.

Then you just couldn't any more. Then you made her the messenger.

It was she who had to tell the workers that there wouldn't be any pork this month, she who had to lock the smoking-cabin again where the fire had already been lit to smoke the bacon and had to send them all home empty-handed.

And then it was she again who had to go to the labourers' houses with the medicine and the acid drops in her apron pocket and had to doctor the whole lot against worms as you had instructed her.

When she stayed away for too long, you went to have a look, but you walked around the back so that nobody should see you. You didn't want to interfere. But you felt all of a sudden that it wasn't right that Agaat should be there all on her own.

There she was commandeering the mothers of the children left and right to catch them and bring them nearer because when they saw the medicine bottle they took flight into the wattle-wilderness. Agaat was pushing and pulling them to stand in line, the big ones full of scratches from the branches and snivelling tearfully, the littl'uns bawling in the dust.

You heard her scolding before you even saw her. You peered round the corner. You saw how she grabbed the children by the hair and pulled their heads back and clamped their noses until they opened their mouths. With every spoonful she scolded.

This is what you get for shitting in the bushes like wild things! Open your porridge-hole! This is what you get for wiping your arses with your hands!

Swallow! swallow! If you spit it out you'll get a swipe through your mug!

And then you guzzle vetkoek again with the same hands, what kind of black muck-mongering is this?

Swallow! swallow! dammit, swallow! and don't leak snot all over my clothes!

You're worse than pigs! They can't help it that they didn't get any brains. They eat your runny shit that lies around here stinking in the sun. That's why they're full of measles. If I come again, then I'll dip the whole lot of you wholesale with a forked stick behind the neck in the sheep-dip, the Lord knows what kind of pestilences are hatching here!

Just look at that child's scabies! When last did she smell a piece of soap? Godalmighty!

Just think what your guts look like! Pauperworms, they crawl up into your heads and gnaw out your brains till you're dancing around with the horrors. And what about those mangy curs? On this farm we shoot everything that has worms quick-quick right between the eyes.

Will you pee on my shoes, you little hotnot! Stand that way, shut your trap and swallow or I'll wind up your little prick for you like fly-paper. Where're your pants?

Agaat made her way through her line and stood back, wiped her hands on her apron. With the spoon in the air she stood and explained.

Now you listen well to me on this day today, you take a spade, you throw all your shit on one pile every day and you make a fire on top, lot of clump-arses that you are. And then you throw soil on top. Even a cat knows to cover up. If I catch one of you dropping your pants in the veld then I'll string barbed wire through his arse!

You stood back against the dirty wall. Your heart was beating fast. You had never seen Agaat like this, had never heard her talk like this. You saw the adults standing laughing at the performance, but not full-out, little half-mast laughs and looking covertly at one another. Then one of the striplings grabbed the bag of acid drops from her apron pocket and the children descended upon it like ravens.

Rubbish! she screeched and she up and kicked, one, two kicks into the bundle with her black school shoes so that they dispersed chow-chow.

You stood back and pretended to be coming round the corner of the house at speed.

What on earth! What's going on here! you exclaimed.

You looked at her sternly. You picked up the bag of sweets and shared them out in the little dirty hands. You went and stood in front of her. You wanted to cover her.

You explained the cycle of the tapeworm and its stages and its contagiousness. The people looked at you in solemn resignation. You promised there would be proper toilets. You passed the medicine to the women so that they could drink themselves and dose the men. You said there would be water and a washroom. You said you would find a clean pig for the slaughter. As you were saying it, a great murmuring arose and you could see from the faces what was coming. A list without end. Water, bread, meat, milk, roofs, shoes, clothes, soap, candles, sugar, coffee.

Come, Agaat, you said, come, you must go and scrub yourself from head to toe and put on clean clothes, I don't want Jakkie exposed to germs.

The child was on your hip. He felt heavy all of a sudden but you didn't want to hand him over. Agaat's apron was full of spittle and stains from the medicine and dust marks and her cap was at an angle.

Straighten your cap, you signalled with you eyes.

You felt the people looking at you, at you and your child and Agaat. She jutted out her chin and returned their stares and you wanted to say, Agaat no, one doesn't glare like that, but you didn't know how. You smiled ingratiatingly at the people. You wanted to apologise for her, she doesn't know any better, you wanted to say, she's still a child herself, you wanted to say, but they didn't return your look and you didn't know how you could appease them.

You thought you'd have a talk to her after lunch. You couldn't tolerate it, the irate eyes that refused to return to normal, the footsteps that sounded too loud, the outside room whose door was slammed too loudly after she'd been to clean herself there, the new apron that was too white and starched, the cap that perched too upright on her head.

You could have asked, what's the matter, Gaat?

She grated the carrots, garr-garr-garr, in the kitchen where the preparation of the midday meal had in the meantime fallen behind schedule.

She peeled the potatoes with long strokes and vigorously turned the meat over in the pot. She served the meal quickly and without a word and excused herself to go and wash her clothes.

One-fist Punch, Jak said.

You keep out of this, you said.

You heard the zinc bath and the washboard being dragged out into the yard. You could just see how fiercely she was rubbing the apron against the corrugations. After lunch she put Jakkie in his pram as you'd asked her to do to walk him to sleep so that you could go and have a rest.

You used the child. Only through him would she become good again.

You lay open-eyed in your dark room and tried to think about the morning's events.

Where did the words come from? You hadn't taught her like that. Clump-arse. Pauperworms. You had heard them with your own ears. The cruel hand, the hard foot, you had seen them. You turned on your bed, you wanted to turn away from the thoughts, the images of the morning, but they wound around your head like cloths flapping loosely in the wind, obstructing your view.

Then you heard the screen door slam, the wheels of the pram over the linoleum, the frame knocking against the door-jambs, her footsteps.

She spoke rapidly. Down the passage to the bathroom with a quick rap of the knuckles on your half-open door. You heard her yank the first-aid chest from under in the first linen cupboard.

Man in the axle! In the lucerne field! Dawid has switched off the engine. Head against the rocks. They had to cut him loose! He's bleeding, he's hardly breathing. Come! Quickly!

That was the message, but the timbre of the voice said even more.

Get up! it said. This eternal lying down of yours! I can't do everything on my own. It's your farm's botch-up. The whole botch-up of your life. It's your life that I'm stuck with.

You felt numb. The shock seeped into you on top of the consternation of the morning that hadn't yet subsided.

An accident, another accident!

Times without number you'd told Jak to see to it that the labourers did not bale or thresh without the tin sleeve of the axle and that they wore buttoned overalls at all times.

You hadn't seen the axle-guard for a long time. It was extra trouble to cart it along to the fields. Must be lying forgotten somewhere in a shed.

Take a rug, you said, and water. Bring the stretcher from the store-room.

He tried to hold onto the wheel of the trailer, his pants were winched off him, Agaat said.

You ignored the contemptuous tone, grabbed an old pair of pyjamas of Jak's from the linen cupboard. You'd heard of this kind of accident but this was the first time on Grootmoedersdrift. A sleeve or the tail of a shirt or a loose belt is caught in the open axle and you're flung arse over heels, round and round, limbs shimmying, head against the ground. It could be fatal if somebody didn't press the button in time to turn off the engine.

Go and fetch the baas in the office, you said, he must phone the doctor, tell the baas to ask him what we must do here, perhaps he'd better come out himself to have a look, or send a nurse from the clinic.

She stiffened her body, jerked her head around, her mouth trembled with the effort of containing herself. She looked you straight in the eyes.

She had often had to fetch him for you, but that day something struck bedrock. It was the language. The words. She had had to speak too many languages in one day, hear too many kinds.

Baas! she wanted to say, since when suddenly? Whose 'baas'? Yours maybe, but not mine. You, you are my baas!

Never mind, I'll do it myself, you said and walked to Jak's office. She followed you, came to stand behind you in the office door with Jakkie in her arms.

Julies got caught in the winch-axle, you said to Jak, he got hurt.

Says who? Says Agaat? Jak asked without looking up from under his newspaper.

It's because the sleeve was once again not fitted, you said to Jak, it's because they have to work with the machines in their tattered clothes, it's because they don't have overalls, Jak.

Jak jerked away the newspaper from his face.

The same old lamentation. Can't you have done with it?

His back could be broken, you said.

He's bleeding from his head, Agaat said.

The duet once again, Jak said, how about a cat's chorus?

Jakkie started to cry. You put your arm around Agaat and the child and prodded her out of the room.

Phone the doctor, you called to Jak over your shoulder.

Agaat's mood had still not lifted when the two of you arrived in the bakkie where Julies was lying in the lucerne field. She flung the rug over his exposed lower body.

Move your neck, move your neck, so's we can see if it's off! she said. You could see how Dawid looked at her. He had Julies's clothes in his hands.

You pushed her away. The man was broken. His shirt was in tatters. The torque of the axle had stripped his pants off his legs. His shins were grazed, everywhere he was full of green stains from having been keel-hauled through the lucerne.

He groaned when you touched him.

He grabbed your hand.

I'm dying off, Nooi, he moaned.

You held the hand. You dripped water into his mouth with a piece of cotton wool.

He fainted.

You held smelling salts under his nose.

It looked as if one shoulder had been dislocated but you didn't want to try to push it back into the socket.

You started cleaning the head wounds. There were ugly deep cuts that were bleeding freely. Soil and grit clung to them. Agaat calmed down as she passed you the cotton wool, as she dipped the wads in gentian violet and cut the lengths of bandage for you and prepared the plaster.

You talked softly to Julies while you were working. Jakkie was sitting wide-eyed in the grass to one side. Dawid went off somewhere.

Everything will be okay, Julius, you said, I'll take you home, the doctor's coming, I'll see to everything, don't worry. You'll have all the time you need to get better and you'll be paid through and all the doctor's expenses we'll carry.

It was intended for Agaat as well, the timbre you gave to your voice, the reassuring sentences, the holding of the man's rough hand.

Perhaps it was for yourself as well. You missed music, suddenly, which could always console you, bring you closer to yourself, make you feel closer to everything and everybody, but what had remained of your music in the midst of all the sickness and catastrophe?

Down there in the heat of the midday sun where the two of you were sitting on your knees by the groaning man with the thorns under your knees, and your and Agaat's hands that touched each other as you passed on and received the scissors and bandages to and from each other, there everything suddenly felt too much for you.

The ambiguity of the place, your farm, where you were passing your days, the destitution of the people around you, your inability to act rightly and justly, the catastrophes that beset you day after day, the eternal squabbles with Jak, your child who with the new fine grip of his little fingers was picking lucerne stems, and around whose head all these things raged without his understanding any of it yet. He'd start crying in a certain manner when the voices were raised, got a fright when the doors slammed, his little face was concerned when tension or crises brewed. How could you protect him against it all?

Your tears dripped on the man's face.

Agaat wiped them.

You tied the tarpaulin between the tractor and the baler to cast some shade over him. He had to lie right there until the doctor arrived, you agreed. You wouldn't pick him up or turn him in case he had a serious back injury. His foot you wanted nothing to do with. It didn't look like a foot any longer.

How did that day ever come to an end? How in heaven's name did you manage after all that to sit down together at one table and eat?

You looked at Jak's face as he sat there glaring at you. You remember the feeling, a sort of sickly equanimity took possession of you. His face was that of a stranger. How had you not at the beginning yearned to share something of your sensations and your intimate perceptions, something of the difficulty of the decisions and concerns of the farm with him? But never could you penetrate his resistance.

Jak, you said, let's give it up and go to bed, everything's in any case under control again, as well and as badly as possible.

That was when Gaat came in again. She had awaited her opportunity. You could always hear her calculating her entrance. Her footsteps were soft, for the first time that day.

Is the child still not in bed? you asked when she stood there again with Jakkie on her arm, in the heavy silence that hung suspended between you and Jak.

She put the child down next to the sideboard whose drawers he opened every day, the one with his favourite handles. He pulled himself up by it immediately.

She went and crouched a few paces further diagonally behind him. Jakkie swivelled back his neck. First to one side and then the other, his mouth a rosebud as Agaat had taught him.

Come, she said, come to Gaat. She held out her arms.

Terrifyingly, he turned around. The little hand let go of the handle, the first wobbling solo stance it was.

Come, said Agaat, show your father-him how well you can walk already.

His little face broke into one radiant laugh.

'Alk, he said.

Yes, walk, Agaat said, walk walk walk!

And there it was, the unmistakable independent sequential first steps.

With the last steps he let himself fall, crowing with laughter, into his nêne's arms. She got up with him, shook him up onto her hip, laughing into his eyes.

Pa's little bull, Jak said, and opened his arms to receive him from her.

*

1 October 1964

They disappear like mice nowadays. Only have to take turn away once & to call when I miss them & then I know it's too late for searching they want to be GONE. Wind & cloud they are together fern & water. Long hours together & full of secrets. Something about it makes me anxious. They're chronically there around the drift & the dam or they hide in the forest. A. can't swim & there are still baboons & leopards in the kloofs & A. with only one good hand & Jakkie not yet five & so attached to her one would swear she was his actual mother. Perhaps she is. I know she would protect him with her own life & yet.

Jak has plenty to say about it says I'm abandoning my child to wrong influences. He's just jealous. I'm the one & only influence even if it is indirect. But now I've stipulated that she may not disappear anywhere without telling me where to exactly & at what time they'll be back. After all, she has hr own watch that I gave hr for hr last birthday. She says she'd rather read the time from the sun but I tell hr put on your watch so that you can be back at the prescribed time I don't want hassles.

In fact it's not a hassle at all. Probably just needlessly concerned. After all she just takes him to all the little old places that I showed hr myself that were my places when I was small here on the farm & that pa had shown me. The tortoise cemetery the workshop of the elves the approach of the waterbuck the island with the blackest brambles where the dragonfly comes to nest on your shoulder a brooch of sapphire if it's blue of rubies if it's red but in reality the embodied breathing out & in of Him who dreams Holy dreams. I know in my heart that that is really all that Agaat tells him.

5 October 1964

Light-years says Jakkie. Prospect he says year-rings & krakadouw. He asks: Do eels also feel sad why do they stand up straight like that in the stream & what do whispering poplars whisper about & where's the brack in the brackbush what do the whirligigs write in the water & why do they wear boots? I know where he gets it from. What can I say? My father taught me & I taught A.

At full moon as a child I used to be able to see two bay horses in front of a buck-wagon with a wedding couple on their way to a place called Eendekuil. I suppose it's all really quite harmless. But there's something dogged about Agaat's way with Jakkie. Something about her energy that scares me.

Dreamt that she suffocates him & bashes his head to pulp with a brick. Not something I can tell Jak. Even less Agaat. Lord help me. I must attune myself to the beautiful & the good. Must pray that everything will conspire towards good here.

23 October 1965

A. is sixteen & I want her to be confirmed. So took hr last Sunday to the mission church in Suurbraak when we ourselves were on our way to church in Swellendam. Could see when we picked her up again that it hadn't been a good idea. Had warned her that she couldn't go to church in her cap & apron now she says she's not going again the people laugh at her. Spoke to Dominee van der Lught. Now she goes to church with us in town. Sits in the mothers' room with Jakkie. At least she now hears the sermon.

10 November 1965

Now I must feign blissful ignorance. Followed them all morning & ran home when they began to prepare to leave the forest. Must quickly get the afternoon meal ready otherwise A. will smell a rat but I can hardly contain myself. Am I jealous or angry or glad about what they saw?

10 November after supper

Great mysteriousness all day all parties under the cloak of secrecy. Why would they not want to tell me they'd seen it?

Agaat has been singing her own compositions all the time since they've been back & Jakkie is just about ready to explode with the secret but he's under strict oath.

This morning just after ten I caught A. taking two bananas from the fruit bowl but I pretended not to see because then I knew immediately what she was planning & then I looked in the liquor cabinet & then I saw the rum that I use for caramel sauce already a tot down. She could at least have asked me. Probably shy that I'll laugh at her how long did the two of us not sit & wait way back there in the forest with the stinking bait without seeing anything? & I really didn't want to spoil the whole adventure for the little one.

We're going to the Keurtjiekloof A. tells me with a straight face to look at the waterfall & we'll be back just before lunch. My washing & ironing have been done & the vegetables peeled & the beetroot is cooked & the meat is in the pot just add water at eleven everything in one breath to prevent me from raising an objection but I say nothing & don't bat an eyelid & I await my opportunity until they're well & gone. Put on my walking shoes & take the high road through the Boesmanskloof to the forest because I knew then she would take the easy road lower down with Jakkie even though it's longer. Estimated their pace accurately & lay in wait for them & when they had passed followed them to where A. decided to wait. A little clearing not far from where she & I that time sat for a whole week's mornings & then I had to creep up very slowly to get a good view but without their noticing me. A. I know can hear a ghost walking.

So there she takes out the bananas from her apron pocket & a small bottle full of rum probably about five tablespoons & two paint-tin lids & a fork. Mash, she says to Jakkie. He likes little goblins like you to mix his food & Jakkie presses with the fork & she holds his hand so that he can get it fine enough. Then a few drops of rum with it on each lid. Here taste she says to Jakkie he spits sis yuck. I'm glad says A. he's not here yet to hear you spitting because for him it's food for a king the more stinky the better & he's the emperor & she puts the lids in spots of sun so that the bananas can ferment.

Could get the smell from where I was sitting behind the trunk next to the rock fig. Then they waited & I waited. Half an hour later an hour so that my legs started cramping but I couldn't budge so dead quiet was it only a kokkewiet calling.

But when is he coming? asked Jakkie. Be quiet you'll hear him approaching up high there in the leaves said A. I could see Jakkie was getting restless. What do you think we're waiting for? asked A. For the emperor of course said Jakkie what does he look like? Black like the dark moon from outside said A. but all blue November-sky from the inside no not powder-blue rather wet-blue silvery & when he unfolds himself you look into the eye. What eye? Jakkie asked & he blink-blinked his eyes at A. No, it doesn't work like that she said. He folds open his wings & it's the Eye of Everything. But when they're closed, there's nothing. Like hip up hop down? asked Jakkie. Yes, just like a fire like great love it's all & it's nothing & your soul perishes in the flames but the story is told from generation to generation. Shhht I can hear him! He's coming!

Had heard the fluttering earlier. Always thought it was the forest thrush.

Close your eyes said A. to Jakkie. Bring him nearer with your will.

So there we sit the three of us with closed eyes & I add my will to theirs to make a miracle happen & there it happens!

The first thing I see when I open my eyes is Jakkie's face with a shiny spot reflecting from the lid onto him. But it's not only shiny it's blue as if a little window has opened on his forehead. There the butterfly is poised on the shiny lid & eats banana with its wings spread wide so that the one side shows blue. Apatura iris the giant purple emperor butterfly. There the two of them sit with the sun on their heads & the blue reflection leaps from Jakkie's forehead to A.'s cap & the butterfly opens & closes its wings & it flies away a hip hop jewel & then it descends again for more. Between the lids he to-&-fros. The span of its wings greater than you can imagine. As large as two open hands with crossed thumbs. Nymphalidae the family of the carrion eaters.

11 November 1965

They still haven't told me. Jak asks at breakfast this morning so what secret have the three of you got now do tell me too? Then I see A. looking at me from where she is bringing Jakkie his porridge but I pretended not to know anything & I ask: What did you see yesterday in the Keurtjiekloof? He puts his finger in front of his mouth & gives A. a secret look & says riddle me ree the night is black & the day is blue & the soul is closed at first & then folded open what is it? Eat your porridge says A. with a straight face & I see she hu-uhs at him with her eyes not to let out anything. It's time that you went to school said Jak you're becoming far too smart here under Gaat. But he's so inquisitive he comes & grabs my diary here from under me to see what I'm writing but he can't make out my writing just as well I'm always in such a rush.

Let go I say it's private. Then you should rather not sit & write it up in public he says, it's like lifting your skirts & peeing in the main street.

September 1966

What can it all mean? Sometimes so overwhelmed by what I experience every day I'm crying as I sit here & write. Don't know exactly what it is. Not sadness rather gladness & fear. Envy perhaps? but why? & of what?

Have just been to look for Jakkie & A. then I saw them playing in the orchard by the pear trees—snow-white in blossom—their latest game. Jakkie has discovered the airplane that Jak built for him way back under the lean-to only a skeleton & the paint is all peeled off but it still has wings & wheels. He made A. drag it out all the way down to the irrigation furrow. She fixed the head of an old fan to the front for a propeller. He sits in the seat & she sits in the grass with her back against the fuselage & looks in front of her. They pretend he takes off & flies away. Went & sat on the edge of the irrigation furrow behind the pomegranate orchard to hear.

How high are you now? asks Agaat.
As high as the mountains! says Jakkie.
Do tell me everything that you see.
I see a bird!
What kind of a bird is it?
I don't know!
Well then, ask him what kind of bird he is!
I can't!
Put your hand out & catch him & bring him home, then I'll ask him what kind of bird he is.
There he flies away!
Fly after him!
I can't he's gone!
Then I know what his name is!
What?
I'm not allowed to say it out loud, I must whisper it in your ear.
But I'm up here!
Well then come down again!
I'm coming! Here I come!
Come down, I can see you already! Here you come! Look out for the tower silo!
I come! I see you, here I am!

Then Jakkie jumps from the little plane into A.'s arms & she rolls in the grass with him & laughs they sit up & he holds his hand behind his ear & she whispers a whole long story into it & his eyes widen in surprise & she pulls her head away & he shakes his head for no & she nods her head for yes & he wants to ask something & she lays her finger on her lips & he lays his finger on his.

12

I'm itching.

Possibly because I couldn't laugh. The theatrics with the neighbour's wife yesterday, perhaps that was too macabre. Milla, the drama queen. Jak's name for me. What in heaven's name would he have said if he'd seen me here like this? Or done?

Closing scene. She-devil with shingles. Perhaps he would have emptied a bucket of water on me and lowered the curtain.

Thursday 3 December 1996. Twelve o'clock.

Itch.

Nobody who knows it or to whom I can say it. Possibly not a drama. Something for the stage, though, Jak. Art in miniature. The Scourge of the Seven-Year Itch.

This bed. A chrome railing. Covers up to my chin. Under that my skin heaving with the itch.

Where is Agaat? When is she coming?

Itch.

Not a word that one could sing, except in a hotnot song perhaps, words for Agaat's St Vitus's dance with which she keeps the demons at bay. I hear the servants talk of it, the to-and-fro-ing over the yard at night.

The Sunday morning
The Sunday morning
I didn't care
My mommy's words keep
Fresh in Tupperware.

I can scratch myself—that would have to be the message of the Gospel.

Where is Agaat?

Job itched.

But he wasn't paralysed, and he had a potsherd.

Could it have been itching that caused the creation? They say the stress of isolation causes people to scratch their heads.

Why is Agaat not coming?

Who led the Bear out into the firmament? Who swathed the sea in a mantle of mist? All too pretty. Who clothed man in skin, made him susceptible to itching?

I can see myself in the mirror. As far as I can make out there is nothing swarming over my face, no nest of spiders erupted on the bedspread.

In a life-skills booklet, a Do It Yourself, I read that when you become aware of an unpleasant sensation in your body, you must concentrate on it. With a quiet mind. Deathward set. First you will become curious. And after that you will see it as an opportunity. Apparently you will discover that the sensation doesn't remain the same. What you had assumed to be one sense impression with one name, is in fact a sequence of different impressions, nameless and unnameable. Like clouds they will drift past and disappear. Temporary. Unimportant. Like everything. Like breakfast cereal.

Definitely a less far-fetched doctrine of salvation than the Resurrection after three days. Short Form. Doesn't need volumes.

In the beginning was the Skin and the Skin was God and the Skin itched in the outer darkness. No name needed, you need indeed then only say: I am who I am.

Where is the wretched Van der Lught with his chubby cheeks so that I can see his face when he hears it?

The world as the impotence of an itching God, and the sons of men, they scratch Him.

Milla, calm down.

Left side, front quadrant, twenty to seven if my head were a clock face.

That's where it started.

A prick, like that of a mosquito bite.

I said to myself, nothing can bite you here, no flea could survive here.

But one thing leads to another. A second prick right next to the first, twenty-three minutes to seven, as if from a mosquito grazing in a circle. Zimmmm-zoommm. Oh mosquito, where is thy sting? I would be able to extract it with my imagination.

But it was not a mosquito.

It was legion. Snap, Crackle and Pop. All over my scalp. But not Rice Crispies.

Harpies, swarming like seconds, like fractions of fugitive seconds, minuscule little black monsters, scourging the dome of my skull.

And if I'm not permitted to scratch, give me the Book then, I'll rewrite it, from front to back, with my hand set in a cast of iron. The waste and wild and the streets of jasper. With itching I shall replace them. It's momentous enough.

And after that the hordes migrated over my neck and they gathered their forces in pools of itch in the hollows of my collarbone. And their numbers were vast and they migrated along my backbone, in columns, in a multitude of battle arrays. And in the fullness of time they returned by the front route, with intensified force, all along my ribs. They excavated me under my breasts, arrow-headed letters strayed from a text. And they marched across my belly, an inflamed track of itching all the way to the pit of my navel, amen.

Preacher-tick.

Ringworm.

Rubella.

Shingles.

Scab.

So many mansions in my Father's house.

On my flank, on my shin, against my inner arm, squamous.

I wait, my hands inert hooks next to my sides, my mouth bitter.

Drool.

Squirm.

Tears.

Sweat.

Do it yourself.

My cheeks itch, my forehead, my gums underneath my lips. It itches all along the cleft of my buttocks, all the way into the inside of my hole, all along the white ridge running there, where Agaat cut me at the birth, and further, in every grey membranous fold of my posterior does it itch. Can I say it? All the way into my cunt. Cunt. Milla Redelinghuys's cunt itches. Who would ever have suspected she had such a foul mouth? Not if it is gagged. Cunt. What is deeper than cunt? All the way into the depth of my black irrational womb it itches me.

Here she comes!

Lord, Ounooi, what's the matter now?

She's next to my bed, she searches in my eyes. She swabs my face with a tissue. Gary Player.

Drenched with sweat!

She throws off the covers.

Now I mustn't mislead her.

Are you so hot then?

No, but carry on with your list, the list you made for me!

Is it the shivers?

No!

Can't you breathe?

No!

Are you in pain?

Is itching pain? How must I reply? No, itching is not pain. It's suffering, yes, but it's like somebody who suffers an urgent call of nature. Relief is what one wants. Not comfort. Not nursing. People with an itch and people with an urgent call of nature, they belong in a farce. In a Greek comedy, perhaps? A philosopher shitting in the shadow of national monuments, a guffawing catharsis. The yearning for inconsolability is something else. That's for tragedies. But nobody itches in tragedies.

So blink, Ounooi, blink your eyes, I can see you're in a terrible state here, I'm asking, is it sore somewhere?

Perhaps 'somewhere' is a start.

Yes, somewhere!

Your head? Is your head sore again?

Yes, my head!

Headache?

No!

But your head all the same?

Yes!

Headache syrup?

No!

Neck stiff!

No, no, stay with the head!

Head? Is it lying uncomfortably?

Uncomfortable yes!

If only she would touch my head, that could be a start. It's not the first time.

She rearranges the pillow. My head keels over on the pillow. Prickly pear full of Christmas lights.

Better like that?

No!

Well what then? With the head? Nightmares? Nasty thoughts?

No! Yes! Yes!

What, Ounooi? Be clear! You're giving double messages! No! or Yes!

That time again on Grootmoedersdrift! Yes-and-no time! say her eyes.

I must prevent her from getting angry. Nightmares, nasty thoughts, those she can't tolerate from me. I must just be good and stay good.

She holds out her little hand and then the strong hand. In, out, like switches. In, out.

Give with the one hand and take with the other it means. Yes or no. Be clear.

No! No! No! Agaat, my head! Put your hand on my head!

I flicker upwards with my eyes.

She places her hand on my forehead. Under her hands is an infestation of fine mites, under the palm it tingles, it squirms, it wells up out of the deep, it's not mites, it's maggots.

You don't have a fever, Ounooi, what is it then?

Don't take your hand away, keep it right there! I move my eyes to and fro, up and down.

Agaat strokes from my forehead, backwards over my hair. Backwards. Once. Once more.

My whole scalp erupts in one blaze, from the front, worse than ever.

I close my eyes, open them quickly, I to-and-fro them, turned up in their sockets.

Scratch my head! Scratch my head! My goddamned, scabby skull! Scratch it!

I see the light come on in Agaat's eyes. I see the smile. She wants to suppress it but she can't.

Stutterers, deaf-mutes, idiots, cripples, the lame, the itchers? Why does one want to laugh at them? I don't know, Agaat. And bugger you too, Agaat!

She postpones. Her eyebrows deliberate question marks. Then she scrabbles a quick scratching motion with her fingers, just a little one, an appetiser. She doesn't speak, she only shapes the word 'itch' with her mouth.

Silent movie. The Itcher and the Scratcher. How many acts tonight?

Need a scratch? ask her lips.

I close my eyes. It means you are an angel of deliverance. It means surrender. She must not remark any further urgency on my part.

The head, asks Agaat, and where else?

She puts her hand under my shoulder.

Here?

Tiny scorpions under a stone.

She pulls out the hand again, rests it on the point of my shoulder.

Three nymphae of the blue tick, their mandibles firmly affixed to my skin.

She puts her hand in the hollow between my breasts.

Small scaly adders in a nest.

Now she touches me with both hands. Lightly, here and there over my strings, over my stops, over my keys. Over my ribs, my belly, my thighs, my ankles, my toes. As if I were a harp. A harp of grass, of chaff and sand fleas and whirling itchy dust.

Everywhere? Is it everywhere?

She puts her hands in her sides. Looks me up and down.

An itch-storm? Ai me. Tsk.

Here comes a hand. It comes towards my head. It scratches, but in an unfocused way.

Harder?

Harder! Everywhere!

Now before we damage something here, Ounooi, let me first see whether you don't have a rash or something.

Agaat opens the curtains. She tarries by the window. How would I know if it's deliberate? Or resigned? Or tired? Or not capable of imagining for one moment longer my need? The spring unsprung at last? She spies on my eyes every day. My need her reins. The steerer and the steered and the bit. In whose mouth is it? It must be like sleeping in someone else's dream. Your own journey abandoned, your own repose an iron in the mouth. You just bite on it. You bite it fast. How she must curse me at times. Cunt. Bugger. But the word in the mouth, a stopper. Under the white standard of the cap a mouth full of bitter teeth.

Where she's standing in front of the window Agaat's strong hand creeps over her shoulder. Just above the white apron band on the right, on the thick flesh of the shoulder blade she scratches herself.

She sighs.

The Great Itch, she says, you and I, each other's itch.

I keep my eyes shut. Is she going to start scratching her own head to provoke me? Is she going to try and talk me out of it? Is she going to ignore it? How beneficent is her mood? Will she ever start a sentence with 'I feel' or 'I wish' or 'I hope'? Is it her itch that is erupting on me? Because she can't speak?

She switches on the lamp next to the bed. She unbuttons the bed-jacket. She eases it down over my abdomen. She takes out the reading glasses from the breast pocket of her apron. Onto her nose she presses them. Shirrt-shurrt she pulls on the latex gloves.

Let's see what's happening here, she says, nobody can just itch like that for no reason.

She looks on both sides of my neck, on my chest. Her eyes are large behind the lenses. She reads my grain. My knots and my flaws. Between the lines.

Excuse me, but I have to inspect all around here a bit now, she says. She avoids my eyes. She takes the magnifying glass out of the dressing table drawer.

She lifts my breasts. She looks under them. She looks in the wrinkles of the skin of my belly. She pulls open my navel and shines the head of the bedside lamp into it. I feel the hook-and-claw feet of a beetle scrabbling in there. Can one go mad from itching? The rose beetle has twenty-five legs and seven antennae.

Permission? Agaat asks with her eyes?

Granted!

The itch blazes on me like a coat of many colours.

She pulls the tunic off my lower body. She scrutinises my loins through her lenses. She folds open my labia.

From where I'm lying, I see her mouth move through the magnifying glass, a vague fleshy hole.

Pure as morning dew, she says.

She comes slightly upright over my lower body, blows on the magnifying glass, polishes it with the tip of her apron.

Impossible are your texts, Agaat. How are you going to explicate me one day? How are you going to explain everything to yourself? Collarbone, knuckle bone, jaw? Will you have a motto for every part of me? Perhaps that's what you're practising for? Perhaps you are now already calling me up. Poltergeist. But ghosts don't itch. That's all that still stands in your way. This last proof of external sensation.

Now she's inspecting my thighs, inside and out, the birthmark in the bend of my knee, the shadows under my knees. Under her magnifying glass the itch fumes a salty mist, like drifts of sand across a dune, my shins, my ankles, two rusty wrecks.

She stacks her towel rolls on either side of me, she tilts me on my side, each touch produces a fresh flush of itchy patches. She is behind me, she examines the rough ridges, the giant sungazer lizard with its spiny girdle sun-gazing on the Trappieshoogte, the aloes, the bitter juice, the rustling mirage.

She tilts me back.

I don't see anything. No redness, no dandruff, no rash, no scaliness, no bumps, no pimples. Not a bedbug in sight, mite-free definitely. Now tell me, are you still itching?

Agaat, I'm talking to you, look at me, the stars are old. Shall I give you a stone when you ask for bread? Just scratch me a bit for the sake of all the gods!

Very well, but just gently, I think you're imagining things. That's what I think she wants to say, because now her lips have stopped moving.

She goes and puts the magnifying glass back in the drawer, takes off her glasses and replaces them in the top pocket. Shirrrt-shurrrt, she pulls off the gloves. She washes her hands in the washbasin. I smell disinfectant. She dries them. She inspects her nails.

Her eyes look slightly unsure. What proof does she have that I'm not losing my mind? Her mouth is unfathomable.

She pulls the sheet back over my body. She wants to spare me that, spare herself that, the sight of her hands, the big one and the small, scratch-scratching over my naked emaciated body. Perhaps she wants to prevent herself from starting to laugh. Perhaps she wants to prevent herself from starting to tickle me. Perhaps she will all of a sudden want to tickle me. If I can itch I'm still ticklish. Perhaps she's feeling a bit hysterical. Perhaps it hasn't ebbed away yet after the great joke with the neighbour's wife.

I inspect the stirrings under the sheet. I cast the harness of my eyes over the ill-matched pair. The fingers are cautious. She follows the movements of my eyes on her hands. My eyes are her score. She does sight-reading. She plays the keyboard. By touch. Trills. Scales. A chord. The note-perfect rehearsed death I shall be, the virtuoso performed.

Left, right, no, a bit to the top, more, no down more, down, this side, no that side. There! Just there! More! Don't stop. Now up here. No, just next to it. Up! Down!

The clock strikes in the passage. That was a quarter of an hour's scratching. From head to toe and in all the little crannies, in front, behind and along the sides. A partita. Improper tempo. Fantastic execution. Complete relief. Applause! Flowers!

Agaat doesn't want me to thank her. She averts her eyes. She brings ice-cold wet cloths and wipes me with them, she takes a small, rough towel that she's warmed in the oven and rubs my whole body warm with it, she rubs cold handfuls of Lacto Calamine Lotion all over my skin. She waves it dry with an open diary. The pages flutter. A bat, a butterfly, a blue gryphon. She puts on my tunic, fastens it behind my neck. She covers me. She walks out of the room with a straight back.

Itch-free I remain behind.

*

14 December 1966

At long last a bit of a holiday. Really and truly feel I need rest after this year of calamities. J. constantly agitated & full of conspiracy theories about the assassination of Verwoerd. Mother hardly cold in her grave then that on top of it. Haven't really had time to be quiet & also not had much time to write how life does pass & Jakkie's growing up & the old people precede us & you forget the moments that were precious to you.

Just yesterday before we left Agaat & I went by Ma's grave to take some flowers & I realised then I didn't really cry all that much in July but if I were to mourn what exactly would it be for? Perhaps that in spite of everything I did after all yearn for her approval? For one spontaneous embrace? Her body forgivingly pressed to mine? So much that now cannot be set straight or talked about. Yes at last liberated from her. But what will I measure myself against now? Now that her judgemental eye no longer falls on everything I do? It's terrifying in a way.

Perhaps I wanted to cry because she died before I could tell her the whole truth about J. But in any case the whole funeral & the gossip that made its way back to me just made me realise anew that honesty & intimacy are not things that are easy to afford. But how do you defend yourself against your own mother? Her directions regarding the funeral felt like a last trial.

Fortunately I could count on A. Didn't have to spell out anything for hr. She was a real live wire with the funeral & supervised the cooking for more than a hundred people who had to eat. It was a palaver with seating on the stoep because then it rained a deluge. A whole saga at the drift of course. The coffin duly arrived all the way from Barrydale by horse-drawn cart as Ma had stipulated in her will—in her way also bent on her little portion of drama. So different to Pa who wanted nothing but for his ashes to be scattered on the Tradouw. So there the drift was flooded & the horses balked I suppose also because of the crape funeral coats wet and heavy on them & they refused to cross. So A. left everything just like that in the kitchen & went and helped D. and his team. Unload the coffin and carry it we don't want the ounooi to get washed away in the drift & bring the lip halters she says. They unload the coffin & then the horses rear up & the water splashes & they snort but she keeps hr side short & Dawid keeps the other side & they all keep their funeral faces solemnly composed & walk shoes & all ever so dignified through the water with Kadys and Julies with his floppy foot shlip-shlop bringing up the rear. So then they loaded the coffin back onto the cart for the last stretch up to the graveyard here next to the old orchard where it then was so wet & muddy that they had to put down planks & sacks for the people to stand on & had to pump the water out of the hole.

Heaven knows why one had to take so much trouble over something that in any case is going to waste away to dust in this case to mud because it rained incessantly all year from before June and thereafter. Ma's headstone collapsed twice & as far as we drove yesterday all the way from Skeiding to Port Beaufort the wild fennel was standing hip height on both sides of the road. A. says it's hr trademark. If I were she I'd keep my mouth shut about that I warn her. It's not everybody who likes a taint of liquorice in their cow's milk. She asks for who is the place in the graveyard between the ounooi & the great-great-grandmother?

Witsand 16 December 1966

Flag-raising & Day of the Covenant on the beach today quite moving such a bright blue windless day at the sea. There is no strand so wild or far away but there is found thy name in majesty. The minister prayed for the new leaders who must lead the nation after Dr Verwoerd was so brutally taken from us by the powers of darkness. Jak says Tsafendas is a communist. I say the poor man is mad who in his senses would dream of stabbing the Prime Minister of South Africa to death with a knife in parliament we're not that kind of country. Jak says don't have any illusions this is just the beginning.

A. stands firm as a rock next to Jakkie where he's frolicking in the little breakers. Three other nursemaids in the shallows this morning where the toddlers are playing. They tuck their gaudy frocks into the elastic of their bloomers so that they won't get wet—jump and scream when the waves come. They don't talk to hr. She keeps to one side & and she puts on airs with hr black & white clothes the whole holidays so far there've been many opportunities for striking up friendships. Shame A. is alone I say to J. Shouldn't have said it because that caused another spat. He says she's got everything a woolly could wish for & it's better that she keeps herself apart he really doesn't want hassles with a hob-nobbing then next thing you have young goffels climbing in & then she gets that way & then she's lost to us. I tell him that's not the point what worries me is that she's too old & too cold & too high & mighty even to think of young goffels but it's holiday after all & what does she have of her life as a young girl? Have! Have! J. shouts don't even start with have she has everything a coon-girl's heart could desire and furthermore she has Jakkie more than you or I have him or had him or ever will have. Why do you worry about her? Look at him. He doesn't make any friends either he just tags along with Agaat all the time it's not normal.

Haven't really thought about it like that but I suppose J. has a point. Notice that Jakkie gets bored quickly with other children. Even when he's alone with me. Perfectly subdued but if it carries on for too long he gets the fidgets. The moment Agaat is around he livens up. She always has a joke or a new game. Not that J. ever takes any trouble to help bring up Jakkie but that will probably start now. See he feel-feels him & says where're your muscles my boy.

17 December '66 morning
Is J. right? Does A. really 'have' Jakkie? I keep an eye where possible but the two of them are sometimes highly mysterious. Always try to listen when she tells him stories. She always begins with the 'first story' the 2nd and the 3rd etc. up to the 'last story'. They say fairy tales can have a strong influence on a child's mind. There's the one story that he always wants to hear last of all & of which he never tires & when she changes one word of it he shouts no! no! that's not how it goes even if he's already almost asleep. The no-shouting is all I hear of it except for a few times just the beginning which I eavesdropped on from around the corner: once upon a time there was a woman who was terribly unhappy & who lived like this & that & was she unhappy because she was ugly? & was she unhappy because she was poor? & was she unhappy because she had no friends? etc. & to everything the answer is no but then I can never hear the right answer. On Gdrift it's always the fire crackling in A.'s room which prevents me from hearing the 'last story' properly & now it's the rushing of the sea. A. deliberately opens the window on the beach side & talks softer & softer at the bed's head. Eventually he always goes to sleep from it however active and excited he's been in the course of the day & she Lord how it goes to my heart! she smiles complacent as a sphinx when she gets up there & rearranges her cap.

17 December '66 evening
Tonight after Agaat left I went and asked Jakkie what the 'last story'

is he says it's his & Agaat's secret he's not allowed to tell it. Agaat will bewitch him if he does. Bewitch how bewitch? I ask. White and black into a flycatcher says Jakkie ask Pappa. How does Pappa know? I ask. He also knows all the stories that begin with once upon a time doesn't he says Jakkie. Heaven knows what J. puts into the child's head but if I as much as write a little play for Jakkie he says I teach him attitudes. Jakkie has attitudes enough of his own. A. and I split our sides laughing at how precocious he is with his cloak and his sword as the prince in The Magic Flute. Wrote a simple version with songs for the children's concert. Also to help get him to play with other children. Jakkie says he'd rather be Papageno alone in the forest because the prince & all the other children are too wimpish. Jak walks out in the third act in front of all the people when they put it on in the little hall last night. That husband of mine does have the knack of embarrassing me.

Witsand 18 December '66

Here in a drawer dug up an old black bathing costume old-fashioned with the little frill round the edge & wire in the bust must still be Ma's. It's much too big but I thought I'd give it to A. perhaps she wants to swim. Please just at a time and place where she won't offend because the beach is for whites only. Not that I needed to say it. She knows hr place. She will most probably never even dare it but then I've at least given her the opportunity to enjoy herself I feel. She flattens her gaze and takes it without thank you.

Witsand 20 December 1966

Woke up early this morning not even light yet just a little moon then the gate squeaked and it was A. barefoot with her embroidery basket & with a purpose in mind I could see from her bearing. So waited for a while first before following in hr tracks. Far away on the beach she was walking a little black dot with white braces & then I followed hr duck-ducking behind the first row of dunes for almost an hour then it was quarter to 5 & day breaking & windless but the sea roaring so that if I were to call she wouldn't hear me. So there she went & stood with hr face to the water upright on parade & she makes the same odd gestures as that evening on the mountain with hr arms extended in front of hr as if she's indicating points of the compass or explicating the horizon. The sea was high with the springtide & a rank of black musselcrackers was also in attendance peering oceanwards & I smell kelp & clamour their legs are so red the creatures. Next thing there she is taking off hr apron and hr black dress & they fly te-whee-te-whee, off, off with their red beaks over the black water & she folds her clothes slowly neatly item by item I thought if there'd been a hanger she'd have hung them from the break of day but not the cap that's pulled extra firmly over the forehead & there all the time I couldn't believe my eyes she's wearing Ma's old bathing costume under hr clothes it hangs on her like the skin of a bat & she takes the white crocheted jersey out of the basket & she puts it on over the rest. Who is she scared will see hr kettle-spout arm hr legs hr shins the nail-clipping of a moon? & she walks over the sand deep washed-out pools of water straight into the sea straight ahead into the waves without hesitation or turning back or lifting of arms a prow. The possibility that something could happen to her. That she wants something to happen. My heart that starts beating & the taste of blood in my mouth. More than halfway in before she stopped. The waves bow down high before her & break & bubble white foam walls & the cap is only just visible & the crooked brown shoulder is high & she leans back slightly against the backwash & she stands firm & the bathing costume balloons black bulges around her body first to this side then to that & she settles her cap & she stands so rock-solid in the midst of the wild waves probably ten minutes. How high, how strong would the wave have to be that could flatten hr? Then she came out. Backwards-backwards she didn't take hr eyes off from where it was coming from & I thought who does she think she's preserving herself for? & then I was ashamed of myself & I sank down behind the dune & I cried I don't know why & before I'd finished I had to leave & I step on sticks & sharp shells because I can't see through my tears but I know I'd better be home before hr & in my bed when she brings the coffee. Then I must pretend to wake up & say hmmm I smell the sea & ask have you been outside yet what does the weather look like today?

21 December '66
Oh dear heaven must really be more careful. Was too sleepy again last night to put away the diary so then J. this morning saw the bit about A. who'd gone for a swim. He's bored at home because the wind blows too much to go out. Lord he said if you could only write something that made sense but it's just one long string of ramble as if you're bloody mixed-up in your head what's the matter with you? It's just getting worse all the time the yammering over bugger-all do you think you can make time stand still when you write such strung-together sentences? And then wouldn't he take it to the kitchen & read it out loud to A. fast in one breath. She ignored him but I'm sure she heard it all. Then I grabbed the booklet from his hands. Kettle-spout arm! Break of day!

Bat-skin! Nail-clipping moon! Wild waves! Jak exclaimed. Forty-five rotations per minute! For those who have ears to hear! Then in comes Jakkie and asks what's happening. In her deepest being my son your mother is a great poetess. What's a poetess? It's somebody with a pain in the otherplace & there's no medicine for it says J. What about Brook-lax? Jakkie asks in all innocence & fortunately that saved the situation because then everybody laughed uproariously & couldn't stop. A. has been walking around all day with such a little smile an odd expression in the eyes. Better left right there. After all didn't libel her or anything.

24 December 1966

Seems to me Jakkie has perfect pitch. He's been singing since infancy all the songs that he hears from A. and then tonight at the children's Christmas tree in the little hall he sang all alone and without accompaniment O Star of Bethlehem o wondrous light while they pulled the star jerkily through the air on a wire. Oh my heart! What would his grandfather not have said! To the very highest notes of the chorus O Star of Bethle-h-em, Wondrous st-a-ar Thou lead'st to Jesus the little soprano voice clear & pure. A. listened at the door we can't believe he sings so beautifully & then he can sometimes be so shy in front of people. Must get him to singing lessons. I believe there's a Mrs Naude in Swellendam who has a way with musical children.

1 January 1967 Witsand

New Year's message from the new Prime Minister on the radio SA the polecat of the world is performing excellently economically the powerhouse of Africa with mineral wealth we'll make it to the top. Bought A. a new blue bathing costume for this year's holiday with firm sponge cups because she's pushing a stout pair of cans there. I listen but I haven't heard hr go out in the early morning again. The bathing costume is still lying there in its box as I gave it to her & the old black bathing costume is nowhere to be seen doesn't matter old anyway & out of fashion.

A. stands in her uniform halfway in the water on one side & I on the other side & then we teach Jakkie to swim. He's managing very nicely indeed. J. wants to teach him but he's far too rough with the child & then he arrives home crying and choked with salt water. That's just going to make him scared of water I say. J. says he must toughen up the child there are hard bones ahead I ask what bones he says the bones of our fathers their battle which we must fight further our enemies are legion. He sits here every evening with his holiday pals & drinks red wine on the stoep and hatches plans for the party branch in Swellendam in the new year. Very worked up he gets could rather concern himself with the draining of the river-lands. We can't carry on like this it was the second wet year in succession & the cows develop fungus on their hooves.

Witsand 23 December '67

Every time I open this special Witsand booklet that's left to lie here in a drawer all year long I page back to the entries for previous holidays & I can't believe how time passes and how big Jakkie is already. Second year in school already! Eight in August next year! Invited a few people over for a Christmas concert. He hears a tune only once then he remembers it words and all. So then I taught him Ave Maria & Little Drummer Boy & Jerusalem & then he sang in the sitting room for the people & and a lot of other songs that he'd learnt from his teacher. Good intonation attractive colour in the voice good rhythmic sense but it's been like that from when he was small still he's developed very nicely since he's been having lessons.

Witsand 5 January 1968

A. back had gone with J. to Heidelberg after New Year to buy provisions we'll be here 10 days more then wouldn't she go and buy herself a fishing rod with her Christmas money. She's been watching other fishermen she says. J. laughs where on earth have you ever seen a fuzzy fishing but he has no problem eating the fish she catches. She now goes out in the morning while it's still dark takes Jakkie along then she comes back at seven with a silvery cob & now this last time a fat galjoen. A. is always soaked to the bands of her apron.

How does she do it I ask Jakkie. He says first she preaches to the fish to lure them & when the first crabs crawl out to hear the sermon then she knows the fish are there as well. Then she juts out hr jaw & walks into the sea fully dressed she casts only once zirrrr! and then it bites hu! & then she jerks ha! & then the rod bends but just for a while then the fish is tired out with struggling then she winds in the reel with the little hand whirrywhirrywhirry & presses the rod in her loins with the strong hand then the fish comes hop-hopping through the little waves and then she gaffs him schmak! through the thick meat with the two-pronged fork then she takes him by the tail & smacks his head shplat! one blow against the rocks because she says she gets queasy to the stomach at a thing lying there & dying without breath & when it's dead she says amen.

Baked fish steamed fish fishcakes pickled fish pink fish-moulds fish soup & salads & fish pies with fennel I must say we're feasting this year on A.'s catches. She really is becoming such a dab hand in the kitchen & thinks up all sorts of new fish recipes I say yikes Agaat take a short cut with the food & rest a bit you work so hard all year & she says it's hr holiday to catch fish & to clean it & to make nice food from it because at home it's always only mutton & slaughtering makes her queasy & she gives away fish to all and sundry when we have visitors. Rather sell it for extra pocket money for yourself I say. She says it comes out of the sea for nothing & catching them's a fluke it's not work but it's not swimming either because that she says she really can't see the point of.

Witsand 10 January 1968

Home tomorrow. Actually slightly relieved then everybody can get back into their routines again. Jak has had enough of his canoe & when the wind blows he can't go out on the river mouth then he sits here & ignores me if he doesn't provoke me & then we squabble. Last night again a domestic rumpus. There's a lot of bloedsappe here who rub Jak up the wrong way then he drinks too much.

Fortunately fine weather today. Think A. must get her monthlies then she gets out of sorts sits and sulks on the beach says she's hot. Take off your apron I say take off your jersey but she just looks at me and folds her arms. J. rows with Jakkie deep in the sea with a lot of other fathers and their sons I tell hr have a look with the binoculars the yellow canoe look at Jakkie in his red life-jacket but she doesn't want to. There's a playing & a laughing around us the colourful umbrellas & balls on the last day of the holidays. Have packed cold red cooldrink & some of the nice custard biscuits but no laughing too much of an effort the mouth remains set on sour. Jakkie full of chat when they come out because he was so deep into the sea & that he was allowed to hold the oar & row with his father. Let you & me he says to A. let's build such a big castle again with towers & dig a moat around it with a bridge of stones & snoek jawbones & coral but she refuses flat. Pure jealousy because he's growing up now.

This evening after supper I see she's embroidering a red & black cushion & she's ostensibly telling Jakkie his bedtime stories and there she deviates from Hansel and Gretel & makes the witch say to the boy: Look so you think don't you the sea is a friendly place where you play with coloured balls & chew sugarsticks & row in a yellow canoe there are black slimes below on the bottom there lurks an animal in the depths it blows through its nostrils filthy foams & it bites its own tail & it curls around the world like a clamp & it cramps in its guts with fury & then the water churns & that's where waves come from & you think you row & you think you swim & you think it's holidays with the colourful sun umbrellas but it's not. How dare she? So I fly up on the spot & I scold my goodness but don't be so malicious & I grab the cushion. A dragon it is with spiky wings scale by scale embroidered & above in death's-head letters WITSAND. I show it to Jak & he says don't come and moan to me now you filled that creature's mind with all sorts of things when she was small I told you to watch out you never can tell how it's going to hatch one day in a fuzzy-head.

Must get Jakkie under my hand a bit more. Spend more time music-making. That's all he enjoys doing with me. If I can just get him going first. Singing & recorder-playing.

Witsand 11 January 1968
All packed and ready to go this morning then Jak wouldn't leave because he's heard at the café that there's to be a beach race this afternoon for Father & Son in which he wants to take part with Jakkie. He's creating massive trouble for me. The fridge had been cleaned & the freezer defrosted & all the frozen fish & tupperware filled with bouillons that A. had packed neatly to take along in boxes. So then we had to unpack everything again & switch on the freezer & A. grumbles nonstop throughout. She'd heard what Jak said last night & she's good & fuming today. He has to watch his step she says the jaw stuck out all the way—I'll make him a nice puffer-fish soup I have the recipe of a widow from Port Beaufort. God defend us.

The lamb, Jakkie's hanslam. Was that the moment you felt something turning? Or before that already? You had hold of it in front by the neck-wool and Agaat was standing at the back with Jakkie in front of her.

You were under the eyes of Jak and under the eyes of Agaat. Between the two of them they had stared you into a corner. The lamb started bleating. Initially it had come running of its own accord. Agaat had called it.

Pietertjie. With its little fat tail. It thought it was going to be given the teat. But now it was scared. Now it started shying away with the head. You had to hold it tightly. It was actually too big already to be a hanslam but Jakkie was besotted with it. Every morning before school he went with Agaat to give it milk, a great greeting it was through the fence, a bleating. Every afternoon he went to fetch it out of the little camp. Then it came into the kitchen and stood head-butting while Jakkie was having his afternoon meal that Agaat had kept warm for him. Then they did homework, heads together at the kitchen table with the lamb that came and pressed against their knees.

It was Jakkie's eighth birthday. Agaat gave him a knife as a present. On special order. A real Rodgers penknife from England, Sheffield, with two blades, bought from the Malay in Suurbraak. You baked cakes, Agaat and you, cupcakes, sponge cake cut in cubes for the party. People had been invited, lots of children. He was shy but you made him sing for the guests and accompanied him on the piano. *Heimwee*, by S. le Roux Marais. The adults were amazed. Beatrice listened wide-eyed. The children stood giggling, with glasses of cooldrink in their hands and cheeks bulging with cake. Jak was embarrassed.

A boy who wants a knife, he said, when Jakkie had finished singing and he was given his presents, must be able to dock a sheep's tail. Then we can also see at the same time if that so-called English coolie knife is worth anything. Then Jakkie ran away.

Agaat, go and look for your little baas and bring him here, on the spot, Jak ordered.

You signalled at her with your eyes, look for him but don't find him. She looked back at you with blunt eyes. It didn't take her very long. Then you heard the crying. Across the yard she was dragging him by the ear with the little hand, by the arm with the strong hand, Jakkie straining back.

My goodness, but will you walk up straight and behave yourself on your birthday, Agaat scolded.

Where was the little blighter? Jak asked.

In the lucerne shed, right on top of all the bales. I had to drag him down there. Then he bit me, look.

Agaat held out her arm to Jak. Self-righteous. An open bite it was. Swollen, the tooth-marks still visible.

Well I never! Jak exclaimed, the choirboy, if he can bite a coon, he can dock a sheep as well! Bring the little bugger round the back, not through the sitting room, look how dirty he is. Where's his knife? Bring his knife!

You can still see it in front of you. There Jakkie is standing in the backyard with the knife shut in his fist. There you are standing, bent over with the lamb's head clamped between your legs. There is Agaat. She is pushing Jakkie forward by the neck.

Open, come on, open the blade, the big one, have you got porridge in your little hands then, my lad? Jak pretending it's the most usual thing on earth.

The children came closer. Great louts some of them, with voices like geese.

Glass-head, they shout. Sissy! Sing high false notes to mock him.

Why did you not stop it then? You could have stopped it. But you helped with it. You wanted to get it over and done with. You didn't know how else.

Jak's eyes were on you. Agaat's eyes were on you. Did they recognise each other's reasons? You did. You recognised everybody's reasons.

Jak had bought Jakkie a little motorbike to go for rides with him and you'd said over your dead body, he's too small, he'll get hurt. You'd quarrelled about it at table after dinner the night before.

He's a child, you'd said. Let him be, he's still collecting birds' eggs, he's still shooting his bow and arrow, he swims in the river, he plays hide-and-seek with Agaat, it's his life, now you want to come and spoil him with dangerous things that make a noise and smoke up a stink here in the yard.

You and your skivvy, you mollycoddle him, you talk your women's twaddle into his head, I can't get close to him or you surround him.

Agaat had come in with the coffee.

He's a child, you'd said, he's still only eight little years old. You can't expect from him now already . . .

Agaat had plonked the coffee pot down hard in front of your nose.

Not too much, she'd said to you, it's strong.

Her voice was direct. You were silent. She had silenced you. You knew the tone, for your own good you'd better not say another word, the message was clear.

Has the cake been iced? you'd asked.

Done, she'd said. Pink and green. Children's cake.

You two and your everlasting cake! Jak had said and got up and walked out.

And so then the crisis the following day, the lamb, the knife, was the beginning of a new alliance. If not the beginning, then a discovery of the possibilities.

You played along willy-nilly. You didn't know how else. You could find nothing to say.

Jakkie was white-faced, his head hunched between his shoulders.

Agaat pinched him in the shoulder until he bent his back. She put the knife in his left hand and held it there with her strong hand. So that she could help him, she said. Was it help? Jakkie's kneecaps were trembling.

Mamma, no, he whined, please, Gaat, please, I can't.

You can, Boetie, Agaat said, she looked at you, she was speaking for both of you, pretending to be speaking for both of you, and there wasn't a splinter's worth of space between her words.

You're Gaat's big boy aren't you! Your même is here, she's holding him nicely, and I'm here, a sheep can't walk around with such a long tail, it gets worms. Shut your eyes tight and make limp your elbow, then I'll help you.

The last she said softly, quickly, next to his ear.

But it was you she was looking at. Full in the eyes. Hold tight, here it is, the look said. One hanslam for you. And one for me.

Agaat cut, one quick stroke. The tail was in her hand. Jak led the applause. The blood spurted on Jakkie's legs. The lamb jerked loose, ran head-first straight into the wall of the backyard.

Take your bloody knife! take it, I don't want it! Jakkie cried. He threw the knife as far as he could. With long strides he ran out of the backyard.

Girlie! they shouted after him, girlie! Little hanslam! Pietertjie!

Rinse the blood from the cement, but this instant, you said to Agaat. And see to it that that sheep is given wound ointment.

This instant, she mocked. She went and picked up the knife where it had fallen, wiped the knife on her apron where you were standing by, the one side and the other side, two red gashes over the white cotton, and folded the blade back into the knife.

You know it stains, you said.

There is nothing, said Agaat, that you can't get out with cold water and Sunlight soap and a bit of Jik.

You woke up later that night. A floorboard had creaked in the passage. Jak had sent the child to bed without supper for bad behaviour and now he'd come out. To the bathroom you heard him pad on bare feet. You heard the lid of the toilet, thought you heard the door of the bathroom cabinet. Then a window opening, a soft thud in the backyard. The grandfather clock struck quarter past one. You'd known for a long time that they spoke through his bedroom window at night, he on his elbows at the window, she on the butcher's block against the wall. You knew that he sometimes climbed through the window and went and crawled into bed with her. From when he was very small you'd found him sleeping with her.

They both knew that it was against the rules, Jak would have a fit. Comfort is what he went to seek after his terrible birthday.

You lay listening with open eyes. You were sad. Who was there to comfort you? You'd had to eat Jakkie's birthday food alone with Jak at table that night.

Don't you think that was enough for one day? you'd asked. Can't he just come and have his food?

He must learn he doesn't disgrace his father in front of guests, Jak had said.

Agaat had served you silently. Her roast chicken and browned oven-potatoes and pumpkin fritters, Jakkie's favourites. You saw her afterwards dishing up her food in the kitchen. But she didn't eat. She washed the dishes and went straight to her room and left the two of you there without serving the dessert. When you took the trifle out of the fridge there was a big hole on the one side. You dished up in the kitchen so Jak shouldn't see it.

You couldn't sleep. You heard the outside room's door open and close again, more softly. It still scuffed, ghrrrr over the cement floor. It had subsided further over the years. Why had you never had it fixed? Possibly because you preferred to hear all the ins and outs? For a long time you lay like that, but you heard nothing more. Later barefoot to the kitchen without switching on the lights. There was a glow in Agaat's room, sparks above the chimney. The door was closed.

You opened the kitchen door quietly, held the screen door so that it shouldn't slam behind you. Peered through an opening in the outside room's curtain. There was Jakkie in front of the fire in his pyjamas. Agaat in her nightdress busy in front of her two-plate stove. Water on the boil in the big pot, the lid turned upside-down, a plate covered with another inside the lid. She was wearing her cap for the operation. The glow of the fire shone through it as she passed to and fro in front of the fireplace. It threw a long pointed shadow on the walls, the shadow shrank and twisted in the corners as she moved. Then she brought a white cloth and unfolded it on the floor in front of Jakkie, a glass of water on it. A plate. A spoon. In the air in front of his nose. Wiggle waggle. Sorry it's the only cutlery I have. Off with the covering plate. Steam. Agaat's supper. Jakkie's wing, the pope's nose, the back portion that had lain longest in the gravy.

Softly they spoke while he was eating. You couldn't hear. You could only see the faces, the cautious opening-up after the terrors of the day. When he'd finished she handed back the pocket-knife. In his palm she put it and enfolded his hand with hers. Jakkie pointed at her forearm. She rolled back the sleeve of her nightdress. Together they bent over the bite wound. He took a roll of plaster out of the top pocket of his pyjamas. No, it must remain open, Agaat explained. She bethought herself, took a pair of scissors out of her needlework basket, cut off a length and allowed him to stick it on.

Suddenly Jakkie pressed his head against her body. His face distorted. Agaat pressed him close to her with both arms. For a long time they sat like that. She rocked forward and backward gently with him. After a while she whispered something in his ear, got up, took the spoon to wash it, came back, set an enamel milk-bowl full of trifle in front of him.

You turned round. You couldn't look any longer. The faces in the soft light of the fire. The confidence. The ease. The forgiveness, asked, given, sealed. The soft bodies in the night-clothes. You didn't recognise your child, nor Agaat's body, the curves you could see silhouetted against the fire in the nylon nightdress. You saw her folding open her bedclothes for him. You turned back from the window, pushed your fist into your mouth so that they shouldn't hear you groan.

*

clear out! clear out! throw away! bequeath! burn! sheets and pil-lowslips how many guests are expected for the funeral? mattress protectors the ruttish bleeding sweating sleepers don't they long for rest? antimacassars where are the greasy heads of conniving patriotic sitting room-sitters? behind what ant-hill will they regroup? kitchen curtains checked floral striped prissy fashions of yesteryear why should kitchens have curtains? steam and splattering fat and dishes full let the hungry see them by all means curtains delay the course of his-tory teacloths dishcloths oven gloves dishing-up is historical drying is scorch-marks are and plate-washing but who writes it up? traycloths tablecloths serviettes the wine the salt the remorse everything is now reckitt's blue and white sobs of damask bath towels face towels guest towels facecloths the filthy living body its steaming dripping folds its unreflective splashing its lack of respect for decay nappies christen-ing robe babyclothes why does one keep them? mommy's child wring his neck tie a millstone round at the bottom of the dam ungrateful creature the son of mine don't you think? embroidery-linen that you may keep that I leave to you to fill your days when I am gone hoarded trousseau whereto crocheted doilies with beads? what faith in the mothball! what idle fear of flies they live for a day and a night without fanfare do not begrudge them a jug of perishable milk muslin velours felt cotton satin silk ribbon mattress-ticking chintz kaffirsheeting flan-nel towelling canvas sisal seersucker brushed nylon suiting tweed flax down sixteen plastic bags of wool what on earth did I ever want to do with it all?

13

Agaat flings a sheet over me. It balloons and flaps over my head.

If Jakkie comes, you have to look your best, she says.

The sheet settles over the bedspreads. She ties the two upper corners with a double knot behind my neck. She pulls it tight from my neck and tucks it in around the mattress. She places the round hand mirror on its stand on the bridge.

He mustn't think that I've just let you lie here and waste away, she says.

The sheet looks like a lampshade, a circus tent.

Plant a pennant in my skull and I'm the main tent, I flicker at Agaat. She flickers back without looking at me, to indicate she sees, but it's sheer bullshit that I'm flickering if even she can't understand it.

My head is the stopper in the hole in the roof-top, I persist, my neck the central pole. In the dome of my forehead glows forty watts. A circus tent full of sawdust, a lantern, a paper bag around a candle, shadows of trapeze artists glide to earth in the spotlight, inside resounds the applause of the crowd.

He must know his little old mother has been in the very best of hands, says Agaat.

She ignores my flickering, not inclined to risk a translation, doesn't even want to start guessing, practical matters first, the hour of the manicure has struck.

She places another towel round my neck, tucks the edges into the top of the neckbrace.

Right, she says, now you're nice and stubble-proof.

Doesn't feel up to another itching episode, that's clear. She slots a tape into the player. *Noonday Witch*, symphonic tone poem by Dvořák. A gift from Jakkie on her last birthday. Not exactly a lullaby, he wrote, but to remind her how she had 'snatched him from oblivion' on the Tradouw.

274

Who does she think she's spiting? What's driving her? The end, I imagine. It's the end that's hoving in sight for her. Then people tend to lose their wits. You can afford to fiddle while the drift burns. You start squandering the rations. During the day you ride your horses recklessly through the piss. Because you're almost there. There's a light at the end of the road. It's worse than the Great Trek, this stretch.

Now which hairstyle will it be this time? Agaat asks. Daisy de Melcker? Or Margaret Thatcher?

Very funny, I signal. Circus!

It's curiosity that's driving her. I can see straight through her. Feigned dressage of the half-dead! What's the use? She lies! She's standing outside the tent again peeping through the chinks to steal a glimpse. Of the ringmaster, of the elephant on all fours on a little drum, of the lion lying down before the whip. Of the strong woman lifting a horse. The clown tripping over the bucket. The only difference is that Agaat is no longer the child that she was.

When you can no longer laugh, she says, you might as well give up.

Does she know what she's saying? Give up! As if the logic of struggle and discouragement applied here! It's much simpler. All that needs to happen, is that I must die. And it seems the show must go on till then.

What will be the final number? The tattoo announces it, the spotlight is on the slit. But what emerges from it? Only a procession, everything we've seen before, the lion tamers and the gymnasts and the rubber man and the twins in the barrel, round and round the ring until they vanish through the folded-back flap. Until only the ringmaster remains behind. He lifts his top hat. Farewell. Auf Wiedersehen. Perhaps the clown will trip over his feet one last time. But then it's over. For me at least, not for Agaat.

I smelt it last night, the smoke, apparently the wattle forest caught fire there next to the labourers' cottages, everything is black with soot down there and one house was lost, and the roof of another caved in, she says. Apparently from a spark of their cooking-fire that leapt across, because the drift is dry, everything paper-dry there on the banks.

This morning I heard Dawid talking in the kitchen. Demolish, I heard and build and three extra houses please in the place of the corrugated-iron hovels that have been put up there for the children of Julies, of Kadys.

There was a long silence. It was only Agaat and Dawid there, she'd sent out the other two. At last she spoke, loud and clear so that I could also hear.

One thing at a time, Dawid, she said, you must just make do until after the funeral. Till after the New Year, I'd say. Draw up your plans so long, work out how many bricks and bags of cement it's going to take, corrugated iron, doors, windows, everything, I'll check it and then I'll see what I can do, but I'm telling you now there are too many of you, I'm not building more than two new houses, in the place of the old ones that are falling to pieces and exactly the same size, but I'm not building extra houses, you can decide amongst yourselves which three of the six and their families will go, we're never going to need all of them and I can in any case not carry on paying them all and I don't like unpaid hungry labourers sitting around here getting up to no good and stealing my sheep. And those who stay on, they must stop breeding or I'll have the women fixed, sooner rather than later. Everything is going to get smaller here now, that you've known for more than a year now, if I need people for big jobs, I'll hire kaffirs on contract, as at shearing time, it's much simpler and cheaper too, all the farmers are doing it like that now. They come, they work, they eat, they sleep on sacks in the shed and I pay them and their boss comes and fetches them. No drunken brawls, no stabbings, no loafing around and no babies that I have to catch and that get ill and that I have to doctor and keep healthy all their lives.

Dawid didn't talk back. There was a silence and then the slamming of the screen door.

Is that what's bringing out her nastiness? The new order?

Snip, Agaat cuts with the sharp-pointed scissors in the air, snip, snip, while she regards me from all sides. She pretends to restrict her gaze to my surface, to the wet strands of hair plastered straight against my scalp, up against the tent around my neck. She pretends that everything about me is purely a matter of layout and systematic attack.

But actually she's looking for a peephole. She wants to see what I think of her latest installations here in the room. Straight into me she wants to peer, direct, as if there were a silver screen behind my eyelids full of moving images that could provide her with a truer, more intimate version of my reaction. As if I could contain any secrets that she doesn't know.

She has carried everything she could think of into my room and covered the walls with it.

Only not the maps.

Why should she at this stage want to disregard the maps? From the day that I've been lying here and can no longer move around in a wheelchair, I've been hearing the door of the sideboard open. Tchick, open, tchick, closed. One of the imbuia pieces from my mother still, just like the dressing table here in the bedroom. With the powerful little magnets and the copper lips on the inside of the catches. Tchick. A seamlessly solid and impenetrable object, with its heavy undulating edge on top and scalloped fringe below. Congealed on ball-and-claw feet. Squatting. Full of dangling little copper handles and festoons. Like an old-fashioned American negress in the *National Geographic*. With many gold rings, earrings and nose-rings. Hunkering. Tchick, open, and after a while, tchick, closed. Then I knew Agaat had selected herself another blue booklet, to come and deposit here with me for the time being. With an announcement of the title that she had thought up herself, a foretaste of the evening's reading. Not backward at all in getting good mileage out of it. Now the books from two little parcels are lying here with dog-eared pages and I hear the same old stories ad nauseam. Where are the rest? Surely there was a third parcel?

Other than that there are only the photo albums in the sideboard, the title deeds of the farm, my marriage certificate. What else? In a little suitcase, all Jakkie's school reports and cuttings of his school concerts. His degree certificates and medals he removed and took away with him when he left that morning in '85. And then a few pieces of silver and old porcelain from my mother's house. A little set of Woodstock glasses. The coffee set with the desert scenes. Agaat knows it will be hers one day. Soon. In a few days. And the napkins that she embroidered with white gardenias for my fiftieth birthday meal. Too pretty to use. The golden year. 1976. Cape gardenias while the country was going up in flames. In two years' time she will be fifty herself. Perhaps she'll start using them then. With whom would she ever in any case sit down to such an elegant table?

Perhaps with Jakkie if he comes. Perhaps she will herself, of her own accord, set a place for herself at the table with him. Perhaps not, perhaps that's my dream for her, more probably he will have to make her sit with him, a meal for two when everything is over, before he returns. And she will sit down and pretend to eat.

Would it really be for Jakkie that she now all of a sudden wants to tidy me up? Or does she want to take it out on me that he still hasn't let her know when he'll be coming? Or has he? Tomorrow perhaps? Eye-wash! This hair-cutting has nothing to do with anybody else. It's just she who wants to get at me.

First she washed my hair. She dropped the back railing of the bed, released the brake and rolled it away from the wall. She brought up the small trolley. I could lie back with my head in the washbasin with the neck-support. She massaged my scalp, shampooed with anti-dandruff tar shampoo, rubbed in conditioner, rinsed three times, rubbed dry.

Special treatment. An ultra-thorough itch-repellent delivery. Energetic too. Where she gets it from.

It can't be from absent-mindedness that she doesn't want to fetch the maps. She will remember them, she had to unpack the whole sideboard that day to fit in the fat roll of maps from Jak's office in the back. I remember I found her there on her knees in the sitting room surrounded by all the stuff with the blue booklets tied with string on her lap. So what is this then? she asked. As if she wouldn't have remembered.

Just old stuff, I said. Throw it out, it just takes up space.

I could see she had other ideas. Her jaw betrayed her. But she said nothing.

With the last clearing-out, when I was half paralysed already, the diaries put in another appearance. The string on two of the packets had fallen off. I was sitting in the Redman Chief next to her with the Royal Reacher. I could still pick up or move the odd thing here and there. I manoeuvred the blue booklets aside, the third pile that was still tied up.

Onto the bonfire with that, I said. Take a little suitcase from the top of the cupboard in the passage and pack all Jakkie's things neatly in that, he'll want them one day. One day he'll want to see again what his teachers wrote there, his first composition book, his first swimming and rowing diplomas.

Suddenly I remember the whole hullabaloo. She made everything tumble down from the passage cupboard in searching for the right size of suitcase, small enough to fit into the sideboard, large enough for Jakkie's things. It sounded as if she was kicking around the suitcases there in the passage.

The house has always spoken up when Agaat has taken a vow of silence. When could she have gone to replace the blue booklets in the sideboard? And how long ago did she start reading the first two packets? Just wasn't up to the first little lot? 1953 to 1960, it's written on the cover, the dates. That was how I divided them up when I tied them that time.

I could hear from the way in which she pulled up the railing of the bed's head again that I was going to be subjected to more than hair-washing. That it was only the start.

Now she wants to manicure the whole imminent carcase. The full treatment. Everything has been set out neatly in a line. Pumice stone, nail scissors, files coarse and fine, razor, magnifying glass, tweezers. As if the cutting and plucking and shaving and filing will reveal something of my inner being. As if relieved of unwanted hair and nails and calluses, my shell will become transparent so that she can see my inner workings.

What does she think it will consist of? Gears, ratchets, cogs? A central axle driving everything? A little black humming box in which the motor is housed? A film on a reel, conducted through all the channels and grooves and spools? That's where she wants to end up, at the still frames, to see what I think of her resistance, to find out what more I want, to see why on earth I carry on whingeing like that. Preferably she would want to dismantle me, unscrew all my components.

Why does she think they lie so deep?

They lie around ready to be salvaged, compared with everything else she has carried in here from the cellar. Everything that I said we should throw away and burn and give away. Everything that we set aside for her to keep.

Like a stage-prop store it looks in here. Beach hat, fish gaff, old black bathing costume from the year yon. From day to day the exhibition is changed. She makes me smell everything, presses it under my hand to feel.

How does she think she's going to get everything out of here before Jakkie comes? Or is he not coming? Or is it all meant expressly for his eyes?

She's well-practised in the art of leaving tracks. It was one of their regular games. Follow me if you can. Broken twigs she taught him to read, spitballs in the dust, scratch marks on bark, turned-over stones. As I had taught her.

She jerked up the railing, rammed extra cushions behind my back, far enough from the bed-head so that she could reach easily behind my head, pushed the bed still further from the wall so that she could move around me freely. The black comb half protrudes from the top pocket of the apron, the curlers are clasped on both sides of the bib of the apron. A bottle of water with a spray head stands ready in the trolley. She comes and stands behind me. Ceremoniously. After the fashion of a salon. Chez Agaat. My stylist and I.

So, she says, today exactly a month ago we last cut and look, it's grown a whole inch.

With the comb she pulls a strand of hair away from my head so that I can see. A mouse tail, thin and grey. She looks at me in the hand mirror.

Just see how much vigour there still is in you, she wants to say. She bethinks herself. But the thought is a snare. She's already caught in it. In her own snare. I know it. The teeth are bared, the nails come out. It's a reflex. She combs hard, straight partings in my hair. She plucks up tufts of hair, she pinions them in stiff crests with curlers. Now I am also in battle array. Sound the horn! Charge!

Grow forth! would be the wrong battle cry. She wouldn't dare shout it out loud. But it's a snake from which a string of white eggs slip. I see them rise up behind her cap like thought balloons in a comic strip.

A whole inch of hair! Without sun? Without bread? What are these strings that can grow from nothing? How many metres in a lifetime? And whom would you want to appoint to measure it for you? Because there are still the few inches that have to grow out in the coffin. Threads of a worm that grazed in poplars. Spun of last thoughts. At last all bright and clear. Silver-white hair. Pitch-black blood.

Is that what she thinks? I no longer know.

Ounooi, she says, don't perform like that. I know you don't like it, but when it's all over you always feel miles better.

She drags the comb through a few times, walks to the calendar, marks off the date with the pencil suspended there from a string. 11 December 1996. She taps the back of the pencil on the dates of the past days. Has now pasted the old paper on the reading stand. Middle column, last row. Agaat's periodic table. Bisacodyl suppository. Tap. Lactulose. Tap. Know it by heart already. But it's one thing she won't scrap from her battery. She's besotted with the bizarre names of the medicines, the sadistic language of the recommended treatments. Symptom: large bowel stoppage. Therapy: Exercise. Tap, tap, tap.

Not difficult to decipher, the tapping. It's Morse code for The Pan. It says: More hairs come forth from your head, Mrs de Wet, than dung from your belly. The Skull Pan is replete but the Other Pan is empty. Almost seven days nothing but winds in it.

Shit and hair. The last secretions of the almost-dead. Shit and hair.

Like old oil still leaking from an engine on the scrap-heap. And piss and nails. That's why they stopper you with a plug or two. So that you don't start oozing and spoil your coffin, or interrupt the sermon. That's why they draw a little net over your hair. So that your skull doesn't start rustling. And that's why they bind up your jaw. So that the tongue doesn't erupt in post-mortem gabbling.

Beloved, go forth in peace and pinch your noses. In the name of the Lord who created heaven and earth because He also designed the fragrant death. The jaw drops open with a snap. Bluetongue put out at the pulpit cloth. Lisping among the lilies.

That's the kind of disgrace that must be guarded against.

I look at myself in the mirror. Wordlessly my eyes blaspheme. How many watts worth of sacrilege? Blasphemy without the use of the orbicularis oris muscles. That's what she wants from me. She wants to see how far she can push me. Drained to the last of the lees. On my knees in the sawdust. In the dry course of the drift. In the place where the last footlight fades to black.

Agaat puts the mirror down flat. She wipes my eyes, she wipes away the spit dribbling from my mouth.

Who needs the old mirror anyway, she says, rather look at what I've displayed for you, the whole of Grootmoedersdrift, Ounooi, from front to back. Better than the movies.

I hear another language in the clacking of the scissors.

What more can you want? Speaking of hair, it gets into my hair, I can tell you, it gets into my hair looking after you like this!

Tchip. A big shiny swallow with two sharp wings, a flying dive narrowly missing my eyebrows.

A dirty-grey skein of hair falls on the sheet. More than an inch I'd say, more than two even.

Agaat likes an open face.

It carried on for three days, the carrying-in. Where she had stored it all, everything that had been on the discard heap, I don't know. In the cellar? Sometimes I heard a bumping and bustling here under me. Other items emerged from the storeroom, from the outside room. Everything that she'd removed from the room here has been restored. The built-in cupboards are filled with my clothes again. She brought in armloads at a time with hangers and all and piled them up on my bed, spread out shawls and skirts before me, pressed the jerseys against my cheek. The soft red mohair, the little maroon one that smells of Chanel No. 5 that she was so mad about when she was small. The dances, the mountains, the snow, the sea. Everything back into the drawers.

The hat-stand, the walking stick stand with all the umbrellas, the walking frame, the trolley. She came wheeling in here at speed, in one or other of my wheelchairs, first with the Spyder as if she were taking part in a paraplegic race and then all whooshing with the Redman and then standing in the IBot with the knee-support flapped up. Like the Popemobile it looked. All that was missing was for her to wave blessings. The head-dress everybody would have recognised.

I went to sleep intermittently with all the activity. Sometimes I thought I was dreaming. When I woke up there was a clattering in the passage and then yet another object was dragged in from the shed. A bag of guano, a bag of chicken feed, a can of dipping fluid, a can of vaccine, the ploughshare from under the wild fig tree and the pipe for striking it, a silver corner post, three droppers, freshly-tarred, feathers of the red rooster, feathers of the white rooster, a sheaf of wheat, a bag of compost, a ram's horn, a horseshoe, a skein of the finest wool. Held in front of my nose for me to smell, all of it. Rustling, the grasses, the pods. Struck, the gong, shaken out, the coir sacks, just about the whole farm carted in at the back door on a wheelbarrow from sheep-shears to rake. I heard her give the labourers three days' leave so that she could complete it all in peace. Because whom would they suspect of being crazy? They know I just lie here. They know it's been a year since I said anything.

The trocar and cannula.

The lip-halter.

The mowing-snaffle.

A bray-pole.

A tine of the shallow-toothed harrow.

A rowel from the seed-hopper.

The tool with which the fencing-wire is twisted.

One by one she came and held the things in front of me. Until I signalled no, that's not what I want to see. Sometimes I thought she wanted to put the snaffle under my tongue, fit the halter to my upper lip, punch a hole in me with the trocar between my short-rib and my hipbone in hopes of deflating me, so that the sound from my hip would sound the word for her, the name of the thing that I'm dying to see, the old maps that for her own murky reasons she cannot find in her heart to go and dig up in the sitting room. As if she's scared that something might bite her there in the sideboard.

Tchip, tchip, tchip, go the scissors, faster and faster. I feel the blades against my ear. Hair goes flying. The whole awning is full of snippings. I see them dry, the little wet tails becoming fluff, puffing up, starting to roll around and disintegrate, thousands of crescents stirring in the slipstream of my stylist as she moves around the bed. Here comes the spray bottle. Zirrrts, zoorrrts, from all sides. As if I were a rose-tree full of lice. Rosecare. What's in a rose. Young Miss Redelinghuys. The rose of Tradouw.

She starts a second round of snipping.

I want to see the mirror, I signal. Now!

Wait, she says, I haven't nearly done. All the old fluff in the neck, she says.

Grrr, grrr, grrr, she saws at it with the serrated blade. My head is cold.

Almost done. Here's another loose strand. Here's another tuft. Oh well, that will have to do, Ounooi, it's not as if your hair is what it used to be.

She brings the drier. The little hand twists and tosses my hair under the stream of hot air.

It's too hot, I say.

Too this too that, says Agaat. She switches the drier to cold.

Don't come and complain to me if your nose runs, she says.

She brings the mirror closer again. Last time I looked like Liza Minnelli. Before that like Mary Quant.

It's the magnifying face of the mirror that she holds in front of me. My chin and cheeks bulge and distort, my haircut falls beyond the frame.

And then God saw that it was good, says Agaat, are you also satisfied?

Thank you.

Rather stingy with compliments tonight, aren't we, says Agaat, use your imagination. You look exactly like Julie Andrews.

The hills are alive with the sound of music, Agaat hums. One phrase, then she changes her tune.

My grandma's mangy hen.

Clack, she pulls the tape from the player. Too many tunes for one throat.

Now the ears, she says.

Well and good, my ears are exposed to view now.

The top comes off the little bottle of Johnson's ear buds. Plop. Agaat shakes the bottle so that it looks like a porcupine full of quills.

First wet, she says, then dry.

She dips the end of the ear bud in a bowl of water.

The deaf adder that stoppeth her ear, she says, full of old wax. Say if it's too deep.

She looks into my eyes while she pushes the lukewarm bud into my ear.

Just let me be please, I signal, it's been too deep for a while now, you don't need clean ears to die.

Oh yes, says Agaat, you do, St Peter sticks in his key to check.

She twists and twirls the stick. Liquid gushes in my left ear. It blocks up. One half of the world mutes.

Still waters, says Agaat.

The stick emerges with a dark-brown lump on its point. She holds it in front of my nose.

Well-greased, she says. Very healthy still. Pure turf.

She examines it minutely before she wipes it on the sheet and pushes the other end into my ear vigorously.

Please, don't you have any respect? I ask.

It could have been worse, says Agaat as she takes possession of the other ear. Her voice cracks, she swallows the rest. But I inspect her jaw. It's pushed far out and it's agitated with subterranean rumbling.

At least you still have ears to hear! If your gut looks like the inside of your ears we don't have a problem! Pure sweet-potato peat! All the way to the portals! Don't keep looking at me like that! What more can I do? Everything is here now. Must I then divert the water from the godgiven drift itself through this room for you? Install a pump down there and lay a pipe to the room and flood everything like a deluge? Well, let me tell you, it's dry! The drift is dry! There's nothing left in it.

Forgive me.

How's that?

Forgive me!

I didn't say anything!

Or do you think perhaps that you're in the ark here? That I have to cart in two of everything? You and I! That's the two! That's Two enough!

Forgive me!

Give you what? Arsenic or arsenite or arsenate? Don't be silly. We'll start with the usual medicine, otherwise it will just have to be an enema again. You can't lie here like this. You'll poison yourself.

She thinks she can scare me with her talk. I don't scare any more. I'm tired. She tires me. I tire her. There are dark circles under her eyes. Her ankles seem swollen. When she sits on the chair, I see her knees, bloated like those of a pregnant woman. We wear each other out. How is this to end if she doesn't want to make an end of it with me?

She puts on her glasses for the next task. Now the nails, she says, you know you dig holes into yourself. Just see what it looks like here, ai!

She straightens the fingers of my right hand. I've been feeling it for a while now. The cutting into my palms. But it wasn't on the list. When I looked at my hands to try and draw her attention to them, she briefly rubbed them or tucked them away under the sheets. She shies away from the shrivelled little claws of mine, I can see it in her face. But tonight they're on her list. Now that the room is full again, I'm the one who must be pruned back, scraped out all the way to my cuticles. So the wheel turns. Hip up, hop down.

In my right palm the nail of my middle finger has cut through the skin. The other nails have curled upwards where they've been pressed against the inside of my hand. Two are ingrown. That shuts Agaat up. Neglected area. Nothing that can inflame her more. She works away at every problem systematically. Little crescents of nail-clippings fall on the sheet amongst the hair. Into the quick the ingrown nails are filed away. The cuticles are pushed back. The cuts in my palms are disinfected, are given fresh plasters.

Now the feet. The dog's-nails are filed down. I smell horn. The calluses on my feet are anointed with emollient. The minutes are counted while they dry. Then the filings are rubbed off.

A quarter strikes in the sitting room, how many does that make? I've lost count. What could the time be? It feels like deep, deep in the night. No other sounds except those of these foolish ministrations, the click of the tweezers, the rasping of the files, the tchi, tchi, tchi of the rubber soles around the bed, the white cap that ascends and descends over parts of my body. Is she establishing a firebreak? Is it to save time when I have to be coffined? Her lips now and again relax out of the straight line, they gape, as if she's gasping for extra breath, now and again she compresses them completely, keeps them tightly pursed. A notch between her eyebrows. I can't see her eyes.

Agaat recovers the faculty of speech when she beholds my hairy shins.

Orang-utan, she says. She clears her throat.

I don't want to know what your armpits look like by this time. Stubble-field! Don't let us forget about them!

She takes her magnifying glass, inspects my face.

And the stubble on your chin. And just look at how your eyebrows curl up. Little brushes in the nostrils. Heavens, seems to me there are two evenings' work here.

Her voice is thick. She stands back. She takes off her glasses. She rubs her eyes.

Let's just shave the old legs and then go to bed, she says, tomorrow is another day.

My left leg is soaped. The first stroke draws blood.

Thin, she gets out, too thin.

Razor in the air she stands and looks at the blood trickling a crooked little line through the lather, blotting the soapiness pink before the rivulet divides and drips onto the sheet on either side of my calf.

Yes, look, Agaat. Now you'll just have to look well. Because there you have what you've been looking for. It's only blood that's inside me. Replete I still am with it. Heavy and dense I am with blood. And that is all that will flow from me if you make a hole in me. Blood! No ready-made pictures to make your skin crawl, nor a tent full of entertainment, that thing on my shin is no peep-hole of a kaleidoscope in which you can make glass fragments tinkle in pretty patterns. The costumes are your brainwave. The orchestra. The stage set you carted in here. It's behind your curtains that the play is waiting to commence. You will have to produce the lines. Because the void is in you.

The darkened coulisses.

Like gills they drape layer upon layer.

I hear the effort of your breathing.

Rippling.

*

Was it after that night, the night that everything changed between you? Was it two days after that that Jak broke down?

That night, the night that elicited it all, that was in the time when you started fighting anew for your marriage, when Jakkie was starting to grow up and a playmate appeared at table from time to time. With all your might you tried to cultivate a more loving manner, for a year or more you'd consciously tried to look more kindly on Jak, also for Jakkie's sake. He was quick to pick up tension between the two of you and then he would withdraw himself from everybody and everything except Agaat. Sensitive, just like you, was the child, even though in appearance he was Jak's child in every respect. To and fro you could gaze at that time, at your husband at your child and back again. With Agaat following every movement of your eyes.

There is something to you, there must be something in there, you thought when you looked at Jak's face. You refused afresh to accept that he was just a pretty shell. Late at night when you were on your own, you tried to get yourself in the mood with wine, with your old pieces of sheet music, accompaniments, almost forgotten, that you dug up out of the piano stool and played to yourself haltingly and sang to, after the example of the great singers on Pa's old records, Ferrier, Flagstadt, Schwarzkopf. So, somewhat mellowed, you managed to go to Jak in his stoep room more regularly. You switched on his bedside lamp because you wanted him to look at you, at the new black nightgowns that you had ordered by post to save yourself embarrassment in the shops in town. Every time he had swept the switch back with the flat of his hand. And every time it had been a few minutes' scuffle in the dark, without a word or a caress.

But you didn't want to give up. You were alone, it felt worse in your forties than ever before. Not that Jak ever had a wandering eye as far as you were aware. But nor did he have an eye for you any more.

What year was it that night? Sixty-nine? Or was it nineteen seventy already, seventy-one?

It was an evening in early summer, October, you could hear the rushing of the drift, full after a good winter. You were standing on the stoep after everybody had gone to bed and you thought, Milla, is this what your life has come to? Your only child in a conspiracy of games and secret language with his nursemaid, your husband estranged from you in his own wing on the stoep. What have you retained of it all? Of your education, your music, your books? Only Grootmoedersdrift? And what good did it do you? All the struggling to get the farming going smoothly, only then to be left feeling so loveless and forlorn?

Just like your father, you thought. And just like your mother.

You caressed your own body. What a waste, you thought, what a pity.

You wouldn't give in. You were different from her, different from them. You would make an extra effort.

That night it was.

You went and picked a bunch of blue larkspur and yellow fennel branches in the garden and arranged them in a vase, opened all the doors and windows of the house so that the sultry evening air could move freely through it, switched off all the lights and lit candles, opened a bottle of wine, took out the crystal glasses and went to have a bath, massaged your body with fragrant cream, brushed your hair in your new Liza Minnelli style that could best camouflage the shocks of hair and misplaced crowns on your head. You remember it, a touch of make-up around the eyes, the full-length satin petticoat. You looked at yourself in the bathroom mirror. The damage of years of demolition work was visible already, but like this, in a sentimental mood with a few glasses of wine in you, excited by the music, your face was soft, your lips relaxed, your eyelids seductive. You did not want to look at yourself for too long. You did not want to see what lay right under that voluptuous radiance. You were amazed that you could produce such an image at all.

The music you selected to suit your mood. Jak usually rolled his eyes at your music. A Strauss waltz he could just about tolerate. But this was not a night for Viennese waltzes, it was a night for violas, for mezzo-sopranos, for dark, melancholy sex.

What did you play that night on the old turntable? A cello sonata by Rachmaninoff? Lieder by Brahms? *O komme, holde Sommernacht?* *Meine Liebe ist grün?* And lieder by Schubert and Schumann? *Der Hirt auf dem Felsen? Widmung?*

Let me satiate myself with it, you thought, let me charge myself with all these subtle European yearnings. Let me ignite his blood with these melodies in my body, through osmosis.

What a massive over-estimation of yourself. To expect that you could attract him again after all the hard words, the slaps and the jibes and the grudge he bore you. To dream that surely there could someday be something more somewhere.

There was more to him. Much more than you could imagine at that stage.

That was your problem, Milla, a lack of imagination. You read him wrongly, looked past what was in him, you could assess him only in your terms, couldn't imagine that anybody, even Jak, shouldn't be able sometimes to yearn exactly like you—for tenderness, for excitement, for eyes mutually intoxicated.

How in God's name did you conceive this notion?

Romantic German Lieder! That had much to do with it.

Sehnsucht. Lust. Wonne. Duft. The words alone had enchanted you as a student, the impossibly beautiful melodies. You would never recover from it. But wasn't it a bit much to expect that you would, on wings of that kind of song, consent to being a muse for life in the Overberg the other side of Swellendam, to somebody, the son of a provincial doctor?

You were forty. You knew enough at that stage to be able to live with irony. You need only look around you and there were other realities, perhaps other songs that would be better suited to your world, other words to rhyme with and to sing.

Ewe, ram, kloof, buttermilk, barley, pizzle, ruttish, bluegum, wattle, lucerne flower, lark.

But that night irony was not in your repertoire. To you Grootmoedersdrift was all 'rieselnder Quell', all 'flispernde Pappeln', and in your slippery black satin garb you wandered through the sitting room to the left wing and pushed open Jak's door and went to lie on top of him and kissed him in the neck gently.

He mumbled impatiently but it was clear that your advance had an effect on him. You unbuttoned his pyjamas and stroked his chest, you put your hand into his fly. You took his hand and pressed it between your legs so that he could feel your moist pubic hair.

Not that such doings had anything remotely to do with 'Frauenliebe und –leben' or a 'girrendes Taubenpaar', but you thought you knew how you had to handle him. You thought so.

Come to me, you whispered in his ear, come, I'm in the sitting room, I'm waiting for you.

You put on a new record, a selection of Schumann songs, and went to lie on the sofa with a glass of wine in your hand.

Maja of The Spout! If you think back on it now! What third-rate play-acting!

Jak appeared in the door sleepily. His hair was rumpled, his pyjamas unbuttoned, the state of his excitement evident.

Come here, you said, come taste this wine.

It's the middle of the night, Jak said, you'll wake up everybody.

You opened your arms to him.

Good Lord, Milla, why here? What's got into you? Jak asked.

It was your reply that was wrong, your reply to the question of what had got into you.

Love, you said, love and longing for you.

You're sozzled, that's what, Jak said and gathered his pyjamas in front. He looked aside to where you'd placed the wine and the flowers on the table next to the silver candlesticks and shook his head.

You got up and pressed yourself against his back and moved your hands along his flanks.

What's with you? Are you randy all of a sudden because you're in love with somebody else? Jak asked. What would make me good enough all of a sudden, it's not as if I can do anything right in your eyes, is it?

Don't talk like that, you pleaded, you know there's always been only one man in my life.

Jak snorted, took the wine out of the ice bucket, looked at the label, took a long draught from the bottle and put it back.

Do you really not love me at all any more then, Jakop, you asked in his ear, just say that you love me, just hold me.

Why did that infuriate him so?

He turned round and grabbed you by the shoulders.

You, he said, you with your needle-sharp intellect and tongue to match, you've always been too simple-minded to understand that it doesn't work like that. Love is not something one asks for.

But you never give it to me, I do so long for it, I'm alone, Jak, I need you.

He let go of you and waved his hands about his head.

Jak, you said, smell the night, and went and stood in front of him and moved your pelvis against his.

We've made everything on the farm as we want it, can't we also try to make each other happy?

You took his hard penis in your hand. He pushed you away.

Leave me alone dammit, he swore, I'm not your toolbox!

You let the straps of your petticoat slip down your shoulders and pressed your breasts against him.

No! he said, no, Milla! and pushed you away, stood away from you, glared at you until you covered yourself with your hands. At last you could no longer bear his stare. You lowered your face into your hands. You collapsed onto the sofa.

Just tell me what I do wrong, you sobbed, I no longer know . . .

What you do wrong?! No, my dear Milla, you do everything perfectly right, all the way to the stage swoon, let there be no mistake about that. Right, I'll tell you what I think. You think I'm stupid. You think you can play with me. Who do you want to look like in all your silly get-ups? Elisabeth Schwarzkopf in *Some Like it Hot*? It doesn't work, you know. A bloody scrap of black lace, after all the years of breaking me down and disparaging me. I'd rather go and pull my own wire, thank you!

No names, no roll-call, he said, and turned round.

Jak, wait, you said, but he wouldn't hear you.

Jak, wait! he mimicked you in a whingeing voice, and gave the dining-room table a shove. You nauseate me, that's what, I puke from your affectations.

With a hiccup the table rolled off the edge of the carpet, the bottle of Nederburg Rhine Riesling chinking in the wine holder, the larkspur trembling in the vase, the candle flame juddering in the candlesticks. Jak gave it another hard shove. As far as the furthest wall of the sitting room it rolled, past the half-moon table with the white swans of blown glass, and stopped next to the gramophone under the portrait of your great-great-grandmother.

Poor Jak de Wet, look at him, see what his wife has made of him, Jak said, as if addressing the portrait. First the stud bull. Then the obelisk. What dost thou say, O Great-great-grandmother? You are after all the origin of the world around here!

Jak kicked against the table-leg. The table bumped against the wall. The ice bucket fell down and the bottle broke. The record got stuck. You saw the needle in the pick-up head slide and bounce over the grooves. Will you ever forget the disfigured song, the treacherous smell of fennel?

Du meine Seele, du mein Herz Herz Herz Herz,

Du meine Wonn', o du mein mein mein Schmerz,

Du meine Welt, in der in der in der in der ich lebe,

Mein Hi Hi Hi Himmel du, darein ich schwebe be be . . .

Was that when you saw Agaat standing in the door? Could you read her face? She was half in the shadows. You saw her eyes shine.

Go away! you signalled with your eyes, what are you doing here? Vanish!

She resisted you. There she was, in the middle of the night, perfectly pleated, cap and apron and all, reporting from the backyard. She was barefoot. With an unfathomable countenance she stood there, broom and scoop ready in hand, and listened out the last phrases of the song.

Du hebst mich liebend über mich,

Mein guter Geist, mein bess'res Ich!

Soundlessly she approached and lifted the needle off the record, replaced it on its cradle.

How much had she heard? Had Jak heard her come in by the back door before you saw her?

Aha, the stage hand, Jak said, like a moth to the flame. He took one pace, stepped on a shard and swore, lifted his foot over his knee and removed a piece of glass.

On his way out he rolled the wine cooler towards Agaat.

Let the one foot not know what's befallen the other, he said, please do see to it that she cleans it all up nicely for you here, Mrs de Wet, and kindly make sure that she puts on shoes, otherwise she's liable also to tread on a splinter.

You remained sitting on the sofa with your head in your hands, listened to Agaat sweeping up the glass, packing away the records in the shelf and the music books in the lid of the piano stool, leaving by the back door, without a word.

That was the last time, you decided, that German music would land you in a farce in your own sitting room.

That was how you dismissed it. A farce.

What Jak said, all the terrible words, and what Agaat could have heard, that you banished from your thoughts.

But that was not the end of the German problems. The Simmentals were next and they came up for discussion two evenings later.

You could see all the time that Jak was upset about the night of the music, but it was too difficult to talk about it. And there was Agaat's presence, whiter than snow spotlessly whitewashed and mockingly correct and attentive. You certainly didn't want to add fuel to her flame.

How did it begin? It was before supper even, when you remarked in the bathroom that you were tired. All day long you'd helped with the spraying against fruit-fly in the old orchard and afterwards saw to it that the anchor-poles were treated properly with rust-repellent undercoat and silver paint and that the young ewes were dipped against blowfly, all the absolutely essential maintenance on the farm of which Jak took very little notice.

Tired! he shouted from under the shower, it's more than tiredness that's wrong with you, you're not all there, that's what, it's work, work, work as if you're being driven by the devil and it must be this and not that, all the time with your melancholy mug and the whingeing and the whining, help me here, help me there, I can't do everything on my own. And when midnight strikes, then you're trans-figured into the great seductress, half-naked tarted up with your wine and your candles and your stupid music, and keep me from sleep, what's the matter with you? Do you think you're Marilyn Monroe on a Texas ranch?

You looked at the sinewy muscles of his arms as he dried himself. Something about his hard body, something about the emaciated appear-ance of his ankles and wrists disturbed you, as if his joints were under extreme pressure.

It's because there's always too much happening on the farm, he said, this is not a damned experimental farm.

You knew where this was heading. That was always his defence when you pointed out on your statements how much money was being wasted on Grootmoedersdrift, through sheer neglect, through the wrong purchases, through cattle diseases that could have been prevented with the right care. He got angry when you brought it to his attention, the proof of squandering. The seeder with the disks instead of teeth that he'd bought, when you'd told him all the time, disks don't work on shale, the stones get stuck in them and then the disks drag, wear away on one side and then the whole thing's gone to glory, the rowels that he never remembered to remove from the hoppers after sowing-time, so that they were rusted through from the guano remains when sowing-time came round again. And if only it had stopped there, with neglected machinery, but then there was the mastitis problem with the Jersey cows. Isolate the sick animals, Jak, remember the walk-through foot-bath at the entrance to the stables, strain the first milk from every cow every day, you had to insist time and time again without his ever paying any attention to your words.

Every time his story was that dairy cows were just a nuisance, the slaughter-cattle were far less trouble and maintenance. But with his Sim-mentals that he acquired time after time things didn't really go much better. They got eye cancer and every year there were deaths amongst the heifers calving for the first time. The vet's bills for Grootmoeders-drift were astronomical. Jak's solution was: Sell all the cattle.

Was that how it began? Jak's proposal later at table? Sell the cattle herds, before they put us even more out of pocket. The market is good now, we'll concentrate more on sheep and wheat, it's lunacy to want this farm to look like a picture in a children's book.

You made the mistake of protesting.

I'm not the one with the expensive hobbies, I'm not the one who's forever experimenting with this that and the next thing, Jak. Nor am I the one who walks around with my head in a dream about how easy it is to grow rich from farming. It's because you don't inform yourself of all the factors, it's because you don't study all sides of a matter before you make an investment. That's where the trouble starts.

You saw his face set in a grimace, but you couldn't stop yourself.

If you want to buy Simmentals, then you select them by hand, Jak, and you see to it that each and every one has a decent pair of spectacles. Everybody knows that white faces are prone to growths. They're spotted cattle and the spots must be on the nose and ears and around the eyes as well otherwise you sure as sure will have problems with growths. Don't sit there looking at me as if I'm talking Greek, this isn't Germany, the sun scorches the poor animals to a frazzle, seven, eight months of the year. But no, Jak de Wet of course thinks all he need do is take out the cheque book and phone the importer in South West Africa: Hello Mr Liebknecht, and I'm looking for seventy cows and the biggest champion bull south of the equator to service them, thank you very much, goodbye. And that then is supposed to guarantee success.

Come, Jakkie, Agaat said, I'll clear later, let's take a lantern, then we go and see next to the dam if the skunk that's been eating the ducks' eggs has stepped into the snare yet.

Jakkie looked at you.

Go ahead, you two, you indicated to him.

Jak clenched his teeth. He wanted to keep the child there to support his arguments. You knew about the promises when one day the cows fetched a good price, of the hang-glider and the microlight with which the two of them would inspect Grootmoedersdrift from the air and float over the kloofs like cranes.

How was a child to resist that? And how must you then present your case so as not to look like a spoilsport?

Sell the bull then if you must sell something, you said while Jakkie was still within earshot. After all we now have excellent offspring from him, younger bulls that would work just as well as him with the cows.

He glared at you. You could feel it was heading for a collision. You couldn't stop yourself.

Was that perhaps what you wanted, Milla? a collision, after your humiliation two evenings earlier? A collision if a reconciliation wasn't possible.

You pushed the point.

Year after year, Jak, you put the almighty Hamburg with the young heifers, year after year the calves are too big to be born independently, year after year I ask nicely: Please, get rid of the bull. It's never you who has to deal with the consequences, you lie snoring and I'm the one who has to play midwife right though the night.

Are you stark staring mad! Jak exclaimed. That bull is worth its weight in gold to me, all the farmers of The Spout phone me to get Hamburg to cover their cows, I'm thinking of fitting out a sperm installation, then I spare the bull and make a profit out of him at the same time.

Jak, you don't know what you're doing, you said. Do you want to increase the misery artificially now as well? It's very hard for the cows, they suffer unnecessarily, but what do you do? You always just walk away when it becomes too hard to behold, so you don't see what it looks like, you don't see how we have to damage the cows to deliver the almighty calves, one should have respect for the animals, one should assist them as much as one can . . .

For God's sake just don't start that again, Jak said.

You looked at his mouth, his lips distorting with exasperation, the ridges on his jaws as he clenched his teeth. Something in that excited you. What was it? You could never place it. You felt it in your own mouth, extra spit, and in your gullet, a kind of widening, in your gums, an itchiness. You waited for his delivery. You closed your eyes, so strongly did you feel it coming. His voice was high and hard, his speech-rhythm emphatic. You sat back, you knew how it was going to be, how it was going to enter you, the deluge of solid, heated sentences.

You're imagining things, Jak, you said. I'm not starting anything.

Jak slammed his hand on the table.

No, of course not, Milla, nothing said, nothing meant, I'm imagining things again, the old story, but I know what you think, you always want to get back to that. That I left you in the lurch with Jakkie's birth. That I deliberately kept myself out of the way because I supposedly didn't want to behold your travails. That you were unnecessarily damaged in the process. Those are always your exact words when you talk about it, so don't think I don't know what you're insinuating.

Jak got up, went and stood behind his chair, clutched the backrest so that his knuckles showed white.

He was too early, the child, that's all! A whole ten days! How was I supposed to guess it? I wanted to help you with it, and I wanted to be present, of course, it's my son after all! But you, you think the worst of me, always have, you don't want to think otherwise of me, you decided long ago, in the very distant past, that Jak de Wet is the villain of this story and he'll remain the villain. All written up and bound, what everybody most wants to read.

But do you know, Milla, what it's like to spend your days next to a woman who always knows better? In whose eyes you can't do anything right? For whom everything that you tackle is doomed in advance? What it's like to live with someone who's forever hinting that you don't love her enough? Who only cherishes her own little needs, no matter who you are, what you are, the whole you, that feels and thinks . . .

Jak had never expressed himself like that. His voice was strained and his mouth trembled, but he held your eyes and pushed through with what he wanted to say.

. . . the whole you, he said, with his own thoughts and dreams, not only yours, Milla.

His eyes were fierce and gleaming. You wanted to get up and go and put your arms around him on the other side of the table, but he retreated. That was when you recognised it for what it was, exactly what the strange expression was. It was fear, more even, hysteria it was. He tugged at his collar as if he needed air.

Just you don't come near me, woman, he said, you keep your hands off me! His voice was hoarse.

Jak, you said, don't, please, don't you see then? That's what I've always wanted, that you should talk to me like that, so that I could know what you're about.

You moved around the table to him. He groped behind him, knocked over an earthenware jug, he was almost against the curtains of the sitting room trying to escape.

Leave me alone, just leave me alone, I know you, I know who you . . . are!

Jak, calm down, you said, you're overwrought, it's not as bad as you're making out, you're imagining things. Come now, it's only me, Milla, you look as if you're seeing a ghost!

You! he screamed, short of breath, and extended his arm, pointed his finger at you. His hand was trembling. His chest was heaving.

He put his hand in front of his face, one hand around his throat. You were afraid he might have a fit. He plucked at his clothes as if there was something crawling on him.

You, you suck me dry, you worm my guts out of me, that's what you do, a leech, that's what you are! Nobody knows it, nobody can guess it, nobody can read between the lines, but don't think I don't see through you. Even if I'm the only one who sees, even if you fool everybody else around you. I hear how you talk to the neighbour's wife, I hear it all. I don't buy your story. I don't buy it any longer, do you hear! I don't buy it! Your tale that you spin everyone! The fine, intelligent Milla de Wet! How sensitive! How hard-working! Lonely! Long-suffering! It's a lie, an infamous lie! You don't suffer, you flourish, that's what! You're in your element here! A sow is what you are, an eternally ravenous sow with teeth like that! With wings! In Jerusalem! You're in the trough! In the trough with your snout in the swill! That's where you are! You batten on me!

Jak's voice broke with the force of his shouting. He sank to his knees. His shoulders were hunched. The bones of his skull showed through the stubble. You poured a glass of water from the carafe on the table and held it out to him. He didn't want to take it. He struggled to his feet. He stood in the corner of the sitting room pressed against the curtains, trembling, ashen-faced. You placed the glass of water on the coffee table, your hands in front of you to show that you weren't coming closer.

I'll go, you said, I'll leave the room, just calm yourself. Rather go and lie down. Should I phone a doctor? you asked.

He averted his face. His Adam's apple went up and down as he swallowed. The front of his shirt was stained with dark patches of sweat.

You went out onto the front stoep. You thought, what now? how to carry on? You looked back through the window at the uncleared supper table. The wine bottle was still more than half full. So Jak wasn't drunk. You looked out over the yard to see whether you could see Agaat and Jakkie's lantern. You could go to them.

They know that I'm good, mostly good, they know how gentle I can be. You remembered when you were small, how your father sometimes after he'd quarrelled with your mother, came and sat on the edge of your bed, and stroked his hand over your forehead, how your mother would later join him, and how they would try to effect peace between themselves by telling you bedtime stories.

You heard from the dogs in the backyard and the slamming of the screen door that they were back from the dam. Agaat would see to it that Jakkie had a bath and got to bed. You would go to them, to the steam and the aromatic soap and the white towels. You could get them to hurry up so that the table could be cleared, you could help Agaat with it, pack the leftovers in the fridge, and carry on with the normal things, with your life.

But you remained standing there on the stoep listening to Jak pouring himself a glass of wine. He came out and stood next to you.

There's another story here, Milla, he said, you don't want to hear it because you can't manage anger and disillusionment and breakdowns. It's doubly difficult for you because at the same time it's energy that you can't do without. But we know that you have your nose in the storybooks all the time. Perhaps you'll understand it better in the form of a fairy tale. Perhaps you'll get the point then. I can come and tell it to your whole cake-and-tea club one day, because you are of the same species.

You didn't look at each other. You gazed into the dark garden. You wrapped your arms around yourself.

Once upon a time there was a man who looked at himself in the mirror and thought that he was good enough, said Jak. He took a draught from his glass.

He was word-perfect as if he'd rehearsed it many times in his head. But he was silent for a long time before continuing.

I don't know if I want to listen to this, you said.

You turned around and went inside, but he followed you. Agaat came in by the inside door and started clearing the table. Her face was set straight, but you could see she knew exactly what was happening.

Jak started again, more emphatically. Did he want Agaat to hear? You knew that he liked playing to an audience, but here it was as if he was calling a witness.

Once upon a time there was a man who looked at himself in the mirror and thought that he was good enough, he said again, emphasis on every word.

He started stacking the plates himself, something he never did. Agaat kept her eyes averted, but you could see her listening.

To and fro between the kitchen and the dining room the three of you moved as you cleared the table. Jak saw to it that nobody missed a thing. His voice was still hoarse with shouting, full of bitter and sarcastic intonations. It was not the first time that you'd heard something in this mockingly bombastic strain from him, there had been previous times, bits and pieces of it, but now it was a complete tale, causes and effects and details.

Agaat, you said, get going to the outside room.

She ignored you. Her eyes were fixed on Jak.

No problem, Agaat is welcome to stay, Jak said, she'll be able to use it someday, let her hear by all means, it's good general background for any domestic drudge. I can do with a bit of credibility in her eyes. She'll know what I'm talking about.

The man, Jak continued his story, was a farmer, he was rich, he was clever, he was strong. So then he married a woman who admired his talents.

How good-looking you are, how good you are, how wonderful!

But it was all just lip-service.

It was because she thought herself weaker and more stupid than she really was. Ugly duckling, no swan in sight. Sob.

She thought, well then, I'll just find myself an attractive husband, then it reflects on me as well.

But she felt no better even though he shone fit to burst. She was always worried about everything and always complained about everything. She complained about the earth and complained about the water and complained about the air and complained about the fire. Nothing was ever to her taste. She wanted her husband to right everything that she found wrong on their estate. The ploughshare and the sheep-shear and the stable and the table and the roof and the floor and the mincers and the pincers and the pens and the hens. She wanted him to be the master and control everything as she would do it herself if she herself could be good-looking and strong and clever and rich and be the master. Follow my drift?

Help me with this and help me with that, she whinged and carried on as if she had no hands. Even though she knew everything about farming she fancied that she could initiate nothing without him. She wept when he had to go on a journey and when he was with her, it had to be in such otherwise ways which he didn't understand, that he got quite discouraged. Stuff me a teddy bear, whistle like a mackerel for me.

You don't love me enough, you don't care enough for me, she went around all day sighing and doctored herself with a glass of wine, with a sleeping pill, with cookies, with chocolate, with talking on the telephone.

And she was always full of complaints. My legs are heavy, my arms feel tired. And at night she sleep-walked through the house in her black shawls and with her fluttering eyelashes.

What strange behaviour, the man thought as he led her back to her bed. I give her everything, what else could she want from me? How can I ever make her happy? he wondered as he lay behind her in the dark until she calmed down. And thus he became a hero of introspection, without anybody's suspecting it, a silent ponderer of his fate, but that's best left there, dear members of the audience.

So what do you think happened?

Jak had found his stride. He looked at you and Agaat in turn. He opened the curtains and took a deep breath.

Wonderful, wonderful aromas of Grootmoedersdrift, he said, fennel and coriander, six of one and half a dozen of the other.

When he turned round, his voice was hoarse.

The man, he said, started thinking that he was not at all good enough. Not clever enough, not strong enough, not handsome enough, not rich enough. He thought he might just be the very worst farmer on earth.

And he was unhappy. But in truth he was angry. His heart was bitter.

And he, yes, sin of sins, he started manhandling his wife when she nagged. Slap, kick, shove, these three.

Jak held three fingers in the air, showed them in turn to you and Agaat.

He pushed her away when she begged that he should hold her. He scolded her, and despised himself that he could be so cruel with somebody that he loved. Ai, ai, tsk.

And guess what this man did then?

Jak, that's enough, you said.

He ignored you, closed the passage door so that Agaat couldn't get out there.

Guess what the wretched man did then? Here, Milla, have a little glass, don't think I don't know who drinks my brandy late at night.

The man trained to become stronger and farmed to become richer. The fool. He read to become wiser and bought the best clothes to look better in the mirror.

But all of this was of no use.

His heart was sore. And his wife just badgered him the more.

You're going to leave me, she mewled, tomorrow you're going to pack your bags and abandon me, I know it. When men turn forty, then they start cheating on their wives, all the psychologists say so.

What could he do? What does a man do with such erudite aspersions? The man protested for all he was worth.

Jak put his hand on his heart and looked at the ceiling. I shall never abandon you, what did I do to be distrusted like this? Woe is me!

And then his wife showed him her titties anew and lifted her little dress and pouted her little lips and praised him in front of the guests.

Behold, my husband, he is the best that there is and my husband says this and my husband says that and you should be glad that I'm sharing his wisdom with you.

His jacket that was hanging from a chair, Jak hooked over his shoulder, with his free hand he brushed a few crumbs from the table.

But flattery means nothing, that we all know, don't we Agaat, your missis here also has nothing but good words, not so, about your service, and how she can depend on you, she tells it to all the neighbours' wives, to her book club, no matter what she's done to you in your life and how she treats you behind the scenes and all the things she suspects you of, hmmm? And you do your very best every day, don't you, to show her how good you actually are, hmmm? Do you think you can convince her, my girl?

Jak, leave Agaat out of this, it has nothing to do with her, you said.

Jak struck himself against the forehead.

Oh dear, how could I ever make such a mistake?

When he resumed, it was softer, his eyes flickered to and fro between you and Agaat. He spoke rapidly.

But with the years the man ceased to trust his wife's attentions. She started setting his teeth on edge. Teeth on edge, yes, finger in the sea anemone. Schlupp! Brrr! He knew that all her compliments were merely a plot to keep him with her, to get the spanner round the nut, as we say in the Overberg. And oh, the poor man, as luck would have it, he had been blessed by the good Lord with such a handy monkey-wrench. How does that poet of yours put it again, Milla? Why were we crucified into car mechanics? But that's not the point. The point is: who else could siphon off his oil so expertly? But he knew that the siphoning was nothing other than hunger, and it froze him to the bone.

Pretty story, don't you think? Aren't you applauding yet? Anybody for film rights? Or an option on the material? For a learned case study? Jak made his voice deep and theatrical for the conclusion.

And so they lived. What could satisfy her hunger and thirst? His blood, his marrow, his soul? Was that what he had to give in exchange for her compliments? Compliments, yes, you heard aright. Not love? you ask, isn't that what he wanted from her? Her love? Where then can the love be in this tale?

Jak cleared his throat, spoke in a sing-song voice, his hand to his side as if he were doing a folk dance, Oh no, no, no my Milla, no, self-love, I tell you, self-love, the malignant, the contagious kind, that unfortunately is what this tale is all about.

So I am sorry to disappoint you, my dear ladies. All that I know further is, the farmer got thin and his wife got sickly but they couldn't do without each other.

Who would deliver them from their misery?

Their cattle?

Their stranger within their gates?

Their only-begotten son?

Their faithful maidservant, who worked for them?

To be continued, Jak said, and turned away to the front door.

Jak, wait, please, stay with me, let's talk, it's not true, you said, you can't do this to me, Jak, don't go. Jak, what's to become of us?

His face was white and his eyes gleamed. You felt you as if you were going to faint. You clung to the edge of the table. You felt Agaat looking at you. Was there a trace of a smile on her mouth?

What's to become of us? Jak echoed, he looked from side to side at you and Agaat. Is that what the two of you want to know? Well, all I can say is: Please be patient, your curiosity will be rewarrded. Otherwise, do use your imagination in the meantime, between the two of you you can calculate the precise degree of heat at which the earth will perish.

He went out and drove the bakkie out of the garage, drove into the night.

You stood on the stoep and watched him open the gate and close it again, first the white beam of the headlights and then the red glow of the brake-lights on his trouser legs. Would he have had it in his head by then already? He obviously had more in his head than you'd thought. You felt that he had plans. You felt that he was in resistance, you could see his desperation, from his body, from his eyes. You were shaky. Your heart was beating wildly. You told Agaat to mix you a sleeping-draught.

*

clear out! clear out! the whole caboodle is up for auction then you who remain behind can start afresh from scratch throw out the silver hand-bells for the table-summons for whom would you want to ring it anyway? the red copper and the brass the ornaments without reason throw them out! porcelain dogs! dark-brown diana with the wolves at her hem! reading nursery couple on the half-moon table, what a misplaced idyll! the silver coasters engraved with canadian swamp cypresses where in god's name does it all come from? the drift the vlei the mountain pictured oval mirrors stuck-together vases woven hangings birth-plate of delft blue take it give it to him when he comes or wrap it in foam and bubble-wrap and post it to the north gathered lamp-shades blown-glass necks of preening swans framed portraits the talcumed bloom of my great-grandmother my great-grandfather's waxed moustache mustard-yellow curtain tassels pewter ashtrays copper indian shoes cast-iron doorstops compotiers on precarious stems behold all this work of their hands cast cavities forged fillings riffled textures ornate weights leather upholstery chintz velvet macramé nests where spider and mite and self-satisfaction breed dense banal things that give a name to nothingness clear out the wardrobes! court shoes shift dresses wrapover skirts culotte pants double-breasted jackets bat-sleeve coats cable-pattern jerseys button-front cardigans raincoats windbreakers church hats beach hats pantyhose maidenform cross-your-heart bras step-ins panties don't give it to the servants they'll just fight about it select for the kitchen the essentials do away with the multitude of mixing-bowls the meat-mincer the dough-paddles endless breadboards sharpening-rods redundant knives wooden spoons plates from broken sets with autumn leaves empty bottles under the sink old pyrex dishes blackened pots the thick-lipped lieberstein cups the cracked römertopf the stained porcelain the worn gilt edges the faded glazing the lidless soup tureen the stopperless carafe the old enamel jugs the buckets and the cans and the zinc tubs with the slow leaks the sixty labelless frisco tins the brasso and the silvo with nothing as last dregs throw away the plastic bands and pieces of string and used sheets of silver foil the bags full of bags full of bags plastic paper string I must die in a year

*

16 May 1968

A. now measures Jakkie every week—Friday evenings much ado about his supposedly growing so fast. Have just again observed the operation there in the passage she calls it keeping up-to-date the 'growth rate'. He has to take off his shoes & exhale & open his ribcage & stand with his heels against the skirting board & his back up straight & his head to attention against the ascending ladder of pencil marks from each preceding birthday.

Suspect it's just an excuse that A. thinks up to touch him because of course he's starting to get shy nowadays. She presses & pushes his shoulders & neck & knees as if she's trying to stop him from changing sometimes I'm scared she's doing him some harm & then she brings the ruler & places it square & level over his crown & makes a small pencil line. Have just seen her holding him round the throat with hr strong hand while he's standing bolt upright against the wall with eyes shut tight. But you're growing way past me now you're going to get an Adam's apple just like your father just feel this almighty thick gullet.

What are these other lines? I hear Jakkie ask there at the end of the passage. Reply: low-tide mark depth of the drift height of the time length of the shadows who can tell? it's an old house maybe it's your mother who was measured there or perhaps your grandmother.

Who posted letters here? asks Jakkie & he clappers the copper flap of the post-slit. Internal correspondence says Agaat perhaps there was somebody in quarantine she says. What is quarantine? asks Jakkie. That's when you don't know what disease someone's suffering from then you isolate them otherwise they infect the healthy people then they communicate only in writing because talking is too dangerous because the germs live in the breath.

In passing I got an almighty look from A. What does she want me to say? What would Jakkie make of it if he knew? Does she want to protect him from the knowledge? Or does she want to protect me? Or herself? Suspect in any case J. has already told him everything. Although perhaps he'd rather hush up the past from his son.

Concerning Jakkie's birth there are several stories. One story is that A. changed into the noonday witch & caught him on the pass & stuck his tail into a pillowslip & chopped it off with an axe before de-hairing him further. But there are also always new stories & there is the last bedtime story that must always remain the same & of which I never can make out the ending.

I suppose it's time for the facts of life. Wonder if I should leave that to J. Perhaps A. has also in that left us far behind. Saw her the other day standing there on the front stoep with him hr little hand on his shoulder & pointing with the other hand down there by the river the stallion pawing his front legs in the air trying to get on top of the mare.

15 July 1968
A. & Jakkie's games—something about them I find disquieting nowadays. Do so badly want him to mix with children of his own age. Time that he went to school again.

They call each other from long distances. The game is apparently to see who has the finest hearing & turns up within a reasonable time. Sometimes it's a terrifying hissing deafening between-teeth-whistling & hammering on the yard gong in season & out of season & a sounding of the lorry's hooter fit to wake the dead. Put a stop to that the shouting with the hands in front of the mouth is bad enough. What on earth could fascinate them so about it? The one or the other vanishes into thin air & then the agreement is apparently to leave something behind in the vanishing-place like a handkerchief or a bottle-top (as proof of how far you could hear). The latest variation is the ram's horn. The notes don't really vary much. Sometimes though the duration of the notes & the intervals sometimes longer sometimes shorter. Just now again I was standing on the front stoep & heard one of them sounding up from somewhere in the mountain. Lugubrious it sounds plaintive it must have been A. she has a tremendous lung capacity from blowing fires into life in her fireplace & then very faintly from somewhere behind the ridges Jakkie answered. To & fro went the calling on the horn a code if I had to guess. What could the message be? Without content it would have to bore them very quickly but apparently they can carry on with it into all eternity.

12 September 1971

A. learns everything with Jakkie from his schoolbooks, asks him his idiomatic expressions & his multiplication tables. He teaches hr what they sing at school. Land of our fathers. She knows more verses of The Call of South Africa than he. You're making it up! he says & she shows him in black and white in the old FAK. You sound just like a donkey when you sing she says stay in tune now! Do hope he retains his love of singing after his voice has broken. A lyrical tenor I would guess.

16 September 1971

Am all of a sudden not allowed in the bathroom when Jakkie is having a bath. Not J. either. No, he's too big now says Jakkie but not for A. no she's allowed. In & out with pyjamas and clean towels all bustle and display for my benefit. Sits with him on an apple box while he baths & chatters (have already removed the chair from there to discourage hr but she takes no notice). Had to go and fetch a bag of down in the little store for two new pillows and stuff them there in the backyard otherwise J. will complain of the mess & then I saw through the steam the movements. A. adding water or getting up to wash his back. Then I heard him ask her: Where do you come from? what does your name mean? Long stories she spins him. Couldn't make out everything. She teases him he laughs and giggles he persists with his questions. A. says: I crawled out of the fire. Isn't true says Jakkie you're lying he says. Is true she says I was dug out of the ash stolen out of the hearth fell out of a cloud came up with the fennel washed down in the flood was mowed with the sickle threshed with the wheat baked in the bread. No seriously asks Jakkie what kind of a name is that? nobody else has a name like that. Baptised like that left like that. But it's actually A-g-g-g-g-gaat that goes g-g-g-g like a house snake behind the skirting board. Gaat Gaat Gaat says Jakkie, sounding the g in his throat as if he's gargling, it's a name of nothing. That's right says A. it's a name of everything that's good. It's everything and nothing six of one and half a dozen of the other.

So there she was singing him an odd little song with Scripture thrown in an odd tune I'm writing it up here what I remember of it. Perhaps J. is right A. not a good influence on Jakkie. Can't put my finger on it. After all she got it all from me but what she makes of it is the Lord knows a veritable Babel. Doleful in a way that makes me want to hide my head somewhere. This person!—how in God's name did she get like that?

> I'm the ear of the owl
> I'm the eye of the ant
> I'm the right of the rain

The song started off quite low & went higher & higher & faster & faster. Made me think of a choral piece. Which composer? Can't think that I would ever have told her about it can hardly remember it myself it was so long ago at university. I write your name on the sand & the snow on the white loaf of my days. Everywhere on everything that is dear to me, I write your name. And by the power of this word I shall start my life anew. I was born to call you by your name: Freedom. Something like that. But A.'s song was about something else. Couldn't make head or tail of it.

> I stand sentry at the meal of the mealy-mouthed jackals (here she sings in high head-tones)
> I'm the meal of the first milling
> Rejoice oh young man your joy is short-lived
> I'm the rising of the dough
> The lump in the throat
> I'm the mouth of the mother
> I'm the faith of the father
> And the babble of the baby in the bath
> Come come bath in my hands
> my hands my song of deformity (could that be? perhaps I misheard here? & it just went on and on)

I'm the riches of the ridges
The palms of palmyra are mine
Where's the what of the wattle?
Where the fen of the fennel?
With me!
I'm the end of the river-bend
And the breadth of the Breede
I'm the why of the whynot
I'm the where of the nowhere
I'm the blood of the bluegum.

Stop stop! Jakkie shouted please stop that's enough! No that's what
you wanted isn't it! A. said now you must listen! & she teases him
because he doesn't want to get out of the bath naked in front of her
& he can't run away & he just has to stay and listen there until she's
finished singing & then she sang even louder to irritate him & then
she patched together a little tune with talking in-between a whole
performance there in the steam condensing ever more densely on the
windows.

I'm my brother's keeper
His white apron strings
And the ash that turns to ashes
I have the tongues of fire of men and of angels
The riddle of riddle-bread I know
But my tongue is a stake in my mouth
Coals of fire I heap upon my head
Yes, less than lesser
The least amongst you
Bushwillow cedar and wild olive
The turn of the wheel is
the curl
of the tip
of the maidenhair fern
am I

On and on it went in that vein. Jesuschrist Agaat says Jakkie but you
really can sit and sing a lot of shit on a box get going I want to get out
now! but I heard him just now mutter-muttering in his voice that's starting to break—my child!—growing up so fast!—there in his room heard
him singing over & over on A.'s contrived tune her heathenish song that
carries on to all sides.

the why of the whynot
the where of the nowhere
the mouth of the mother
the faith of the father & the blood
the blood of the bitter bluegum.

14

A church hat, a stuffed lynx head, a ram's horn, a silver sugar-bowl, a braying-stone, a mouldboard. What a mess here in my room. I no longer want to look at anything, no longer want to be distracted by the light of day, the things of the light. They press on my eyeballs when I open my eyes. From now on I'm keeping my eyes shut, from now on I am gazing at the inside of my eyelids.

Unseeing in a more silent silence, in the black-red of shut eyes I want to lie, a cello in its case, in this made-to-measure niche that my body has become for me, here I want to dream my way to that whiter light of which the book of death speaks. Here I want only just to hear the last hurried footsteps in the passages, and there far away in the front of the hall, behind the last door swinging shut, the sounds of tuning, the concert, that without me may at last commence. I want to drift away from it all, replaced by a substitute who is following the conductor's baton out there with shining eyes.

This savage parade, the last illuminations.

I have seen enough, heard enough of this procession. What must I still know or try to understand here? What is the message of the moribund air in this vault? Or is this how the sheet of a last summer rests on one, a white drift blown backward from the comb of the wave? As if it wants to tie the wave back into the body of the sea, so that its breaking is aborted, begrudging the final spuming, rushing foam?

Unfathomable that which still weighs on me here. A warmth on my cheek at times, on my forehead, on my stomach, on my ankles, a hand that hovers above me with the weight of a longing, longing to pluck a string, to touch the shady side of a stone. As a stone would feel it, I imagine I feel it, the subtle longings, longings of a mountain wind, or a wind-blown seed, of a stray drop or a tiny lizard, of a blade of grass leaning against me. To what do they seek to edify me, these delicate bodies that waver around me? To what do they seek to move me when they measure their insignificance against mine, sink their all-but-insensible weight into my weight?

At times it is something that vibrates on my breastbone as if the stick of a toy fan has been planted there. At times, late at night, it becomes a flagstaff in a high wind, and I hear a rope knocking against the pole.

When I feel something pressing on me, so, then I know I'm still alive.

My skin presses on me, an underfelt, a rain-wet canvas. My skin torments me. My skin wants to fashion from my flesh another layer, a last pressing of itself. For what purpose? Why does my body begrudge itself its own closure?

What more do I have to learn about all my redundant parts? What am I to understand from my skin that rejects me? My skin is shedding me instead of the other way round. My skin is one jump ahead of me.

What lesson is contained in this reluctant diminution?

As if the helplessness on its own were not instructive enough.

I've had enough. I want to become light now, harmless, manifold like seeds of the thistle, I want to drift from myself, blown away from the stalk, floating.

Dust. Wind. Ash. Why is it denied me for so long? Desiccation should run a swifter course. Dishevelment should be more untrammelled. For whose sake must I endure it, this last coherence? The trivial weight, the barren bits of friction, of sheet on body, of head on pillow, of upper lid against lower, of eyeball in socket?

As if it's conceivable that of a whole concert only this would remain to listen to: The siffling of the sleeves encircling the wrists of the musicians, the creaking of the chairs on which they sit, the heaving of their breathing with the up and the down stroke of the bow, the riffling of the pages of the score. Only that, without the music. Harmless negative music, the soil without the cultivation.

A suite of last breaths I am. Solo breath with a dying fall. My breath weighs on me. Expelled it comes to rest on my chest and my chest refuses to rise again. My breath is lead, the opposite of what breath should be. I shed my lead from me, layer by layer.

If it is an art, then, of surrendering myself to weight, let it be heavy enough, dead weight, under which I am planished. Why still this margin of tolerance? Why this subtle pressure and chafing and surging about which I have to wonder, in which there is still warmth and something, a shadow of music, a light pulse billowing in my feet?

Can feet breathe? What then do I feel like a lung there under the arch of my foot? Is that how it begins when it begins? An inspiration from below? Something that lightens the heels?

Who will soothe my feet for me? Who could think up something like that on this rounded earth? Such a light nuzzling nudging together my ankles? Such a sweet weight breathing up against me? A cat, perhaps? A puppy, a hedgehog that Agaat has brought here to lie on my bed with me?

I open my eyes. It is she herself, it is Agaat sleeping at my feet.

She is lying with her head turned aside on her strong arm, the little thin arm is drooped over my ankles, the hand inside the sleeve all the way to the fingertips. My feet are lying against her chest, as if she'd gathered them there to hold them, like a child going to bed with a teddy-bear. To one side on the bed one of the Croxley booklets is lying open. I can make out the black ink, blots still from my old fountain pen. How many more? This is the last of the second packet if I remember rightly, and was there another packet? Were there three?

Why would Agaat have come to read her daily ration at my bed's foot today? Generally it is declaimed from the wheelchair, or from behind the walking frame. Not in the least a bedtime story. Rather to keep me awake. Now we have both slept. Now I have caught her out. In all the months that I've been lying here, this is the very first time.

Agaat's glasses are perched at an angle on her nose. Her mouth is slightly open. Her lower lip gleams. Her breath comes thick from her throat. The sleep of a person who is tired unto death. The late afternoon sun slants a band of light through the curtains. There are shadows in the corners of the room. The coats and hats on the hatstand, the pictures and cloths against the wall, an agricultural show before the opening prayer.

I hear sparrows. It must be evening already. A busy time of day.

Milk. Cream. Eggs.

Irrigation, dogfood, chickenfeed.

The opening of the doors, the pushing up of the sashes to air the house in the cool of evening.

Supper.

But it's a lapsed agenda.

Vaguely I can hear the clanking of cans, voices, a honking of geese coming to the dam, the door of the store being rolled open, the bakkie being pulled in.

Could I be dreaming it all? Is this thin distillation of yard noises the soundtrack of a dream? This golden radiance in the room, is it already

the light of another order? My sleeping nurse, could her slumbering be
a sign that I'm trapped with her in a bell-jar of oblivion?

The strips of sunlight shrink back from the walls, crawl down over
the foot of the bed. They catch Agaat's cap from the side, from behind
and from the front. I can make out the embroidery distinctly. From the
back it is darkly lit in silhouette, and from the front etched in relief.
Negative and positive simultaneously.

The cap's starched point casts a long rippling shadow on the pleats
of the bedspread. Like a horn it looks. Or like the shadow of an old
stringy snakeskin, semi-transparent in spots with the elongated shadow-
patterns of the weft visible here and there.

White on white the cap is embroidered, in places studded with
densely worked stitches. Only when the light falls on it as now, can you
see the almost jewel-like contrivance. Now in this late-afternoon light
it appears as if inscribed with a confusion of shadow-loops and lines.

Nobody, nobody except Jakkie when he was small, was allowed to
look at it straight on. Over the years ever more forbidden, that zone
above Agaat's forehead. When she caught me out staring, she made me
feel as if I were peeking through a transparent blouse.

But now she is asleep and I can stare to my heart's content. The light
plays over the riffles and stipples and eyelets and crenellations of the
embroidery. The edges of the cap are bordered above and below with
a satin fillet and finished with crocheted lacework. Are my eyes playing me tricks here? A design of musical notation I see, notes and keys
and staves. As the light quickens and dims through the trellis on the
stoep, through the panels of the glass door, through the gauze lining
of the curtain, I can make out what is embroidered there. Am I seeing
straight? A harp it seems to be, a syrinx, a tambourine, a trumpet, the
neck of a lute. And hands I see, all the wrists bent, all fingers on strings
and valves and stops.

Agaat stirs. She closes her mouth, she swallows. She feels my gaze. I
must close my eyes before she wakes up. I can't stand it any longer, the
fencing with the eyes.

But I can't stop looking. It's like looking into clouds. Everything is
possible. Wings it looks like, angels' wings. They arch out gracefully
from the backs of the musicians. But the trumpet-player has a pig's
snout. And the beak of the harpist is that of a bat. A wolf, grinning,
beats the tambourine. A baboon with balloon-cheeks blows the syrinx,
a rat with tiny teeth hangs drooling over the lute.

Agaat opens her eyes. Sleepily. She doesn't know where she is. She
blinks. Embarrassment steals over her face. The embarrassment is shed.

Defensiveness takes its place. Confusion over her arm around my feet.

Never mind. You were tired. Good thing that you could rest. Never mind, it's not serious. Calmly now. Give yourself time to wake up properly. There's nothing to rush us.

But she's angry. With herself. Angry that I saw her like that, angry that she's late with everything. That evening arrived without her. She sits up straight, adjusts her glasses, adjusts her cap.

Don't be angry. I saw nothing, I've also slept, I woke with you. We dreamt. All that I saw was a dream. See, I'm closing my eyes.

I can feel her distrust. Beneath the distrust, something else. Can it be true? I feel her withdraw. My feet miss the warmth. I hear the chair creak as she gets up. I open my eyes. She walks to the door. But she doesn't open it, she just stands there. Her hands are at her sides, the little one and the big one. Her little shoulder sags. She turns round, I close my eyes. She comes back to the bed. I can hear her letting herself down on the chair. Her arms come around my feet, she presses them against her breast, tight, still tighter, she bends her neck, she presses her forehead against the arches of my feet, hard. The wolf and the rat and the pig, the syrinx and the tambourine, the whole merciless music she crumples up with one stroke against my ankles.

*

Was it the day after Jak's breakdown that everything changed once more? Was it the morning after?

You didn't want to remember all the things he'd said the night before. A pig with wings. Was he out of his mind? And the so-called fairytale that he contrived for himself out of it all? How could he distort your lives together like that?

In spite of the sleeping draught you couldn't sleep. You were too scared to go and see whether Jak was back. At five o'clock you were up. Put on milk for coffee, went out into the backyard to throw away the shards of the earthenware jug that Jak had broken the night before. What goes up must come down, you said to yourself as you dumped the shards in the bin, your father's words for the aftermath of family clashes.

The upper door of the outside room was open. You heard Agaat mumbling to herself over her ironing, the creaking of the ironing-board, smelt the steam and the starch, the thud-thud of the little iron with which she always ironed, a glimpse of the white apron in the dark little room. She was already dressed in her black dress and cap and shoes. Was ironing the apron, for the second time apparently, the seam, the bands, the pockets on the bib and the stomach.

312

She was frowning, shaking her head, as if trying to understand something, lost in a world of her own. You put your hands over your ears and fled back to the kitchen. You wanted to hear nothing more, could tolerate nothing more after the night before, suddenly fearful for all of you so constantly getting in each other's way, trespassing on each other's private space, beset by each other's catastrophes. But there the milk was boiling over on the stove and you had to rescue it, clean the hob before it scalded. Then you heard the litany.

Help me with this and help me with that, and then a silence. And after a few thud-thuds of the iron on the board: She wanted him to be the master, she thought badly of herself, thought she was stupid, thought she was weak, she didn't want to be her own master.

The irons were vigorously changed around on the hotplate.

But this is bad and that is wrong and gibe, gibe, gibe, constantly, whatever you do.

There was a hissing sound as Agaat sprinkled water on the ironing-cloth.

It was Jak's emphatic strain of the night before.

God, must I listen to this for a second time, you thought, with the cloth drenched with burnt milk in your hands.

And what did he do, the poor man? He just tried harder to be good enough!

And then suddenly there was a another voice, higher, lighter, your voice.

What does that have to do with Agaat? She's the best in the land, the best governess one could wish for!

You unlatched the screen door from its hook to make it slam.

At the top of her voice it resounded there out of the dark door-hole of the outside room:

Praise the Lord with joy resounding, oh my soul how rich the gift!

An exercise in prayerful attendance indeed. Thunder in the outside room when there's lightning in the sitting room.

You went out onto the front stoep, the red bakkie was parked outside under the fig tree, its front wheels turned at an angle over the roots. So you must after all have dozed off, you thought, because you didn't hear Jak come in during the night.

You went to have a peek at Jakkie, snapped on the light for a moment.

Fast asleep with his cheek on Agaat's embroidered pillow slip, his room full of boy's smells, his mouth with the slight down on the upper lip slightly skew against the pillow.

Jak was at the breakfast table at the usual time. He was pale. You could see he was winding himself up for something. You said nothing. You hoped it would blow over as it did generally tend to do. But you felt that this time it was different. When he'd finished eating, he folded his napkin and cleared his throat.

Phone, he said, phone now on the spot where I can hear you. Arrange with Jakkie's school. Tell them Jakkie is going for a week-long scouting and survival trial in the mountains of the Tradouw with the Voortrekkers of the Montagu mountain club. That should satisfy them, or you can think up something better yourself, tell them he has mumps.

He smiled a tight little smile in Jakkie's direction.

You got up from your chair. Jak did not look at you.

But in fact he's only going with his father so we can get to know each other a bit better, not so? And so that he can taste a bit of what life's actually all about. What do you say to that, old man? Go ahead and tell your mother of our plans.

Jakkie was excited. It was obvious that they'd been planning it for a long time.

Agaat came in with the dish of oats. With your eyes you asked: So what do you know about this? She pretended not to see you.

Jakkie started chattering about the route.

From Twaalfuurkop they would climb over the intermediate ranges of the Piekeniers above Swellendam and through the Bergkwagga Cracks and along the bushman caves at the Four Sluices. He carried on about the compass and the ropes and the maps and the leopards in the kloofs, and about the descent into the pass by the red krantzes with the body halters and the bolts and anchors after hiking all along the horizon from the bridge so that you and Agaat would be able to watch their progress over the last stretch through binoculars, and could accompany them along the pass, all the way to where you had to pick them up at the deepest point of the road on the bank of the Huis River.

You looked at Agaat again. Her face betrayed nothing. She cleared the porridge plates and pushed a platter of eggs to the middle of the table. She passed the spatula to Jak and he served Jakkie.

Eat, little man, so that you can build strength, said Jak, you'll need it. We're taking only peanuts and water and for the rest we'll have to hunt dassies.

I won't allow that, you said.

Come, Jakkie, Agaat said, let's go and brush your pony, he's mouldering in the stable by now.

Jak put his hand on Jakkie's shoulder.

Jakkie's staying right here, Agaat, he wants to eat his eggs. You go and brush his pony for him and while you're about it see to the other horses as well, clean their stalls, take the muckrake and a spade and after that you might as well put out new straw in the stables, have the bales ready, just remember to take along the wire-cutter.

Jakkie looked at Agaat with wide eyes. She gave him a wooden eye. She wasn't perturbed in the least.

Gmf! she said. And Jak grinned.

What were they scheming?

Your eyes she resolutely avoided. What did you want her to do? Jak held Jakkie in front of him like a shield. You went and made the call to the school. You heard them giggling over the lie while you were spinning your tale to the principal. You knew that Agaat was listening in to every word.

There was something different about Jak. You could tell from the grim resoluteness with which the preparations were made.

Jakkie was given a pair of real mountaineering boots with blood-red laces and a compass. He couldn't sleep with excitement. In the evenings he and Jak calculated their hiking stages with compasses and pencil. Their halters and buckles and belts and slipknots and pulleys and hooks lay in the sitting room where they checked them for three days.

You did as Jak told you. You packed his rucksack and Jakkie's smaller one. 18 kilograms and 8 kilograms exactly, the underpants and T-shirts and socks, light windcheaters, plastic raincoats with hoods, long johns, cloth hats and golfing-caps, the billycan and matches, a little bottle of methylated spirits for sore feet, the sleeping bags, the peanuts, the salt, the glucose sweets. The catapults, the little rolls of smooth wire and string for snares, knives, a torch, a packet of birdseed, water bottles. Within the weight allowance you managed to fit a slab of chocolate, a few guava rolls and a packet of rusks into Jakkie's rucksack, but Jak threw them out when he checked the contents. Agaat stood in the doorway and watched it all.

Nay what, Jak said, this is not a picnic, we're going to match our strength against nature. You just see to it that we build up our stamina beforehand, and have the food ready when we return.

Was it all as unexpected as it felt that morning? Not really. The signs had been there had you but wanted to notice them. Perhaps even then Agaat had a much better overview. She was always the one to draw your attention to Jakkie's growing up, to his first steps, his first daring leaps, first circuit alone on the bicycle, first swim across the river. She was the one who always summoned you: Come and see, just come and see what he can do. Also when Jak taught him the abseiling technique down the tower silo. Your appeal: Just listen to what he can sing, made a feeble show against these achievements. You were tied to him only by this one thin thread of music, and you weren't sure whether he just played along to humour you.

When Jak heard you making music, he would lure him away. Musical morbs again, he would say, and took him along to go running or rowing. They achieved the best times for father-and-son teams in the holiday races at Witsand, came home with glittering trophies and gilt canoes mounted on wooden blocks. They had ventured into the mountains for a day on occasion. But this project was too large. The scratches and the bruises and the gashed heads that you would have to doctor again. But that would be the least. Now there was a risk of exposure, of getting lost, in the wilderness, in the cold.

But was even that your real concern? My child, you thought, I'm losing my child, first to Agaat and now to Jak, the child of whom I'd dreamt. You put your hand on Jakkie's curly head, felt him strain away.

I'm going along, said Agaat, she was behind Jakkie's chair, her hands on the backrest.

So am I, you said.

Jakkie looked from one to the other, his eyes uncertain.

We're going alone, said Jak. What do we want in the mountains with a wonky-legged woman and a one-armed golliwog? You could never leave your silly little farm all on its own? What would happen then?

He winked at Jakkie.

The cows would get scarlet fever, the wethers would drown themselves one by one in the drinking trough, go on, Jakkie, what else would happen?

The chickens would lay chocolates, the chimneys would start whistling, Jakkie laughed, relieved to be joking. He was in his father's team now.

Yes, you see, he knows it already, Jak said, the windows would bulge out, the windmills would run off, the goffels would cut out each other's goolies, the rams would cover the women. These two bat pilots don't dare look away for a moment. Just look at their control panel!

Jak was on a roll, with hands and feet he demonstrated.

Air pressure, altitude, tail-wind, cruising speed, wheels, wings, long-drop, snot-smear, squitter straight into the drift!

Jakkie roared with laughter.

Or is it a stupid old ship they're steering, Jakkie, port, starboard, goose-turd, sink!

There was nothing you could do about it.

Nothing Agaat could or would do about it.

But in whose team was she? you wondered. Perhaps 'team' was the wrong word, she wasn't in a team, a pivot she was, a kingpin, you'd felt for a while now how the parts gyrated around her, faster and faster, even though she was the least.

We're going along, you said again.

You two, said Jak, you stay exactly where you are and see to it that the bluegums don't contract typhus, and that Grootmoedersdrift doesn't disappear down a sinkhole, not so, Jakkie? And on Saturday 18 September you see to it that you're waiting for us in the pass with food and coffee and clothes. Come in the red bakkie so that we can see you clearly from up there.

It rained on the Saturday when you and Agaat had to go and fetch them. The whole week that they were gone you'd smelt it coming on, heard the susurration before the first drops fell. A countrywide rain it would become, as one could expect at that season in the south-western districts. Slippery the rock faces would be, the peaks covered in mist, the kloofs full of waterfalls. Agaat embroidered day and night, the big abstract rainbow cloth on which she'd worked over the years when she was troubled. The work was completed the day before you were due to depart. She came and draped it in front of you like an omen. But it was only an empty cloth.

You'd phoned rescue teams earlier in the week already and explained Jak and Jakkie's route to them. You'd found out about helicopters at Swellengrebel aerodrome. The more you thought about it the more you reproached yourself for not objecting more vehemently. It was ill-considered, altogether 80 kilometres over mountaintops and kloofs and through rivers. You couldn't believe that you'd permitted it.

Take more people along, take a radio, you had pleaded two days before their departure. At the last moment, when you went to drop them off, you put a little mirror in Jak's hand, offered to go and make appointments with farmers at the foot of the mountain to look for signals at a certain hour so that you would at least know where they were.

You want to be in a play, Milla, Jak had said, willy-nilly you must have a drama where there's none, with yourself in the lead. Plus a banner headline: 'Woman loses husband and only son in mountaineering tragedy'. The world as it is, is not enough for you, my wife. That's your problem. You're like the hungry cow in that children's book of Jakkie's. You bring misfortune down upon yourself, and upon me, upon us all here, it's you who needs the mirror, not me.

He pressed it back into your hands. His eyes flickered. In the back seat Agaat and Jakkie sat and took it all in.

The Saturday, a week later, the dark morning of rain. You didn't dare go look for Agaat in her room once again. All week while you were waiting, she was stony and taciturn, came and showed you the rainbow cloth once more, with an odd sentence added to it.

Break and be broken, she said, that is the law of life.

You knew better than to ask her what she meant.

Her other intentions were crystal-clear. She ordered you around with a list in her hand. You did what she said, you were too numbed with nerves to think straight. Blankets and towels and warm clothes she packed and thermos flasks of sweet black coffee. Barley water with sugar and salt such as she always gave to the diarrhoea babies down in the cottages. The first-aid chest. Extra bandages. Brandy. She made sandwiches, frikkadels, hard-boiled eggs, a bottle of preserved quinces, cookies, rice pudding, cinnamon sugar, sago pudding, custard.

They'll be as hungry as wolves she said and then they must start with mushy foods first.

You regarded her actions. The mugs, the plates, the spoons that she packed in the basket. Three of each and her own enamel plate and mug.

What if they don't come? you asked, what if you wait there all day till evening and they don't turn up?

Oh God our help in ages past, Agaat said.

The tone of her voice had little to do with God, and her 'our' didn't invite company.

She got Dawid to put the canopy on the bakkie and laid a single mattress in the back. You'd spend the night there if they didn't turn up, she decided, you in the back and she in front. You'd have to wait there until they arrived. She had a bag of wood dragged up for a fire in case it should be necessary. You started trembling as you were loading the stuff in the half-light of dawn. You realised you were furious, more furious than you'd ever been in your life, at what Jak had done to you. But your fury was without expression, like a thin cord inside you it was. You couldn't utter it, you would have screamed if you could, you would have cursed, but nothing issued from you. Agaat came and stood by you with one of your green pills in her palm and a glass of water.

Drink that, she said, you've got the proper heebie-jeebies.

What if . . . you began.

If me no ifs, Agaat said.

She was curt. You knew how she felt. You thought you knew. It would break her heart if anything were to happen to Jakkie.

But there was something else as well. Contempt. For what you'd permitted Jak to do to you. Rebellion because her hands were tied.

It was still twilight when you stopped to wait just beyond the bridge in the first lay-by. The idea was that they would appear there on the other side, on the skyline, and attract your attention and then move on along the horizon all the way to the descent.

As the light grew, Agaat started thinking you might have just missed them. You drove on to a place on the pass where you estimated that they'd have a better chance of seeing you, right opposite a kloof that they would have to cross on the horizon if they'd kept to the plan. The weather was blue with wind and water. A drifting mist covered the top of the lip of the cliff. A white streak of water was rushing down the seam. Lower down it dispersed, a fine spray down in the undergrowth, on either side the claws of a lion, as you as a child had learnt the formation of the foothills from your father, the roundings of the paws yellow with bitou-bush and then the toes, the shiny black rock-nails in the black water.

Now and again a glimmering flushed behind the clouds intensifying the colours of the rock faces. It felt as if you were peering though thick glass. No doubt because of the tranquilliser you'd swallowed, but also from the tension of having to wait there. The landscape was shallow and empty, the smell you got was of cold sheets, of black water and granite.

To and fro you and Agaat passed the binoculars between you. You had to adjust them constantly because your vision was weak in different ways, you near-sighted and Agaat far-sighted.

You couldn't find anything with the binoculars in the descending mist, tumbling down and down in the black undergrowth of the kloof. Once you saw in the grooves of the rocks your father's face, the sharp nose, the notch between the eyes, the sad expression around the mouth. Time and again you had to take the binoculars away from your face to try and see where you were. Later you gave up completely, just kept looking purposelessly until Agaat pulled at the cords to claim her turn. Without a word she buffed the lenses dry every time with the long sleeve of her jersey.

You thought of Jak who'd appeared in the door of your bedroom the night before their departure. He was quiet, his footsteps so light that at first you supposed it was Jakkie. He didn't say a word. Just came and lay next to you and placed his head on your breast. You didn't move, you heard him swallow, after a while you put your hand on his neck, startled at how sinewy he felt, how bony his back, his vertebrae, his protruding shoulder blades. You hoped that he'd tell you that he knew the route like the back of his hand, that he would protect the child with his life, but he didn't. He went away, as silently as he had come. Against the backlight you saw his silhouette, his skull with the shorn hair, his neck tensed.

You sat there in the bakkie for hours, you and Agaat. Sometimes an exclamation broke the silence when one or the other of you thought that you saw something, an arm waving, two figures standing next to each other on a misty skyline, a cloth hat amongst the silver bushes, a white collar disappearing into a crack. But it was always just the shifting of the mist, of the sun that from time to time glowed more strongly through the clouds and made colours flare up amongst the black rock faces.

Let's drive to the place where they'll come down, Agaat said after a while, perhaps they're waiting there already.

You drove slowly to give them time to arrive, then again faster to be in time in case they'd already arrived. As you drove further into the pass, in amongst the rugged rock faces, the black river far below, you remembered the trip twelve years earlier. Agaat was inspecting the horizon, the binoculars pressed tightly to her eyes. You could see from her mouth that she was thinking the same thing. You heard her mumble.

I'll climb up right here, I'll drag you out of the holes, I'm coming to fetch you down, I'll fill the pass with my barking from one end to the other, rousing all the baboons all the way to Swellendam so that you can hear with your own ears I'm looking for you.

Was it an hour, another two hours that you waited there in the deepest part of the pass next to the red rock faces? You had to switch on the engine every now and again to activate the windshield wipers. In between short bursts of sunshine the rain sifted down in blue sheets. You constantly looked at your watches, but it wasn't at the position of the hands that you looked, it wasn't ten o'clock or then eleven o'clock and then half past eleven, there were other distances, other circuits, revolutions between you and Agaat.

Just tell me that they'll come, you said to her.

She darted you a swift look. Me, the look said, you want me to reassure you, me, after you caused this trouble, you and your baas!

After a while she did after all mumble, looking straight ahead: They'll come.

It was Agaat who first spotted them, in the rain, two small dark bundles crawling slowly down the rock faces.

There, there! she shouted.

You both grabbed for the binoculars, her hand was on yours.

Give it to me, she said, give it to me, I'll look. She pulled the binoculars out of your grip. You let go. You pleaded with your eyes: Let it be true! She returned your look with the usual message: Don't make such a fuss, either it's them or it's not them, I'm not the Lord God on high.

You regarded Agaat as she adjusted the lenses. Her mouth was moving, mimicking what moved up there on the rock face. Or didn't move. What could she be seeing? Mountain-goats, lumps of sliding turf, sodden bushes worked loose and rolling down? The mountain had been playing you tricks all morning.

It's them, she managed to say.

You grabbed the binoculars. You couldn't find them, a swirl of surfaces and ridges and grooves of stone.

Where, where? you screamed. Agaat directed you. Pushed, pulled at the binoculars. A notch at the top. A little way down, to the left. There where the rock is a deeper red above the ledge.

There they were in their green windbreakers. Pressed flat against the rock face, motionless before both of them simultaneously switched a handhold, exchanged one foothold for another cranny. Jakkie was tied to Jak with a rope. But that, you could see, was useless. They weren't anchored to anything above them. They were carrying their rucksacks. Any disturbance of balance and they would fall down from there, the face was too shallow, handholds and footholds few.

You couldn't watch. You pressed the binoculars into Agaat's hand, lowered your head on the steering wheel.

She tried to tell you what was happening. Your ears were humming. You felt as if you were going to faint. What was that suddenly on your back? Agaat's little hand? What was it that she was tracing for you there? Jak and Jakkie's movements on the rock face, along the ridge of your spine, next to the knobs and depressions of your vertebrae, Tradouw, the way down. 'They've seen us! They're waving at us! Show your lights!'

You didn't want to look and you didn't want to wave and you didn't want to show your lights. Agaat reported step by step. How Jak hoisted down the rucksacks, how he hammered in the pegs, made the ropes longer, how he hammered in the anchor for securing the main rope deeper than all the others, how he checked Jakkie's halters, the pulleys, the clips, the nooses. How he slid down first.

Still you wouldn't look. When Agaat spoke again, her voice was altered.

A scraping and clicking, a clucking, a hissing, murmurings, mutterings, issued from her. You shut your eyes tighter. You could feel her stirring next to you on the seat. Her apron rustled, like a turkey drumming. Then she swore. Got! Got! Got! In a frenzy she got out, left the door open, a sharp herby smell suddenly in your nose, you lifted up your head, opened your eyes.

There she was in front of the red nose of the bakkie, right in front of you so that you couldn't see anything of what was happening down there in the kloof. You could see it coming, as if she were swearing with her whole body. She acted it out with her arms, with her feet, the hanging, the sliding, the kicking out. The point of her cap rose and fell like a thing, white and black, that scoops, that arches its neck, that pitches. She bent her knees, got on to her toes, swayed sideways, stepped forward and stepped back.

Then you could no longer stay in the bakkie. Then you had to get out.

There Jakkie was hanging, thirty metres from the ground, far away from the rock face, his legs too short to gain purchase, he hooked at the face with his claw-hammer, but he couldn't reach.

Swing yourself, Jak tried to instruct him from below, swing yourself forward, towards the mountain! Jak signalled with both his arms, forward, forward.

You could see Jakkie trying to impel himself with his legs. He couldn't generate enough momentum. His legs dangled. He looked up. Something wasn't right. It was the anchor on the ridge, it was working itself loose up there. He plucked at it, showed Jak: There's a problem.

Then part of the rope jerked loose and Jakkie's head's snapped back as the rope tightened again.

Jump! Jak shouted, untie yourself! Or so it sounded, you couldn't hear very well from up there. From Jak's gestures you could make out what the instructions were. Cut loose your halter! Hang! Hang by your arms until you're hanging still, dead still, keep yourself up straight, keep your legs together, cut loose. Let go! I'll catch you, I'm here! He struck his breast with the flat of his hand, I'm here, I'm here, I won't let you get hurt, I stand fast for you, here!

He turned round to you to show you, he's there, his hand on his chest.

And then suddenly it went dark in front of your eyes. Agaat put her small hand behind your head and clapped her big hand in front of your eyes.

When she removed it, Jak was lying on his back on the stones with Jakkie on top of him. You couldn't make out where the one stopped and where the other started.

Agaat threw her apron over her head and crouched forward.

Did you hear right?

Même, she groaned, ai Même, tell me they're moving, tell me, please!

It took a while for life to return to them. They slowly disentangled themselves from each other, their green clothes clearly delineated there on the white river boulders. And then they moved together again, Jakkie in under Jak's arm, his legs over Jak's legs. Jak rubbed his free hand all over Jakkie, put his hand in under the green windcheater. To count the ribs, to feel if they were all whole, the bones of your child.

*

what remains of the mending and the making and the joining and the fixing pass here under my unprehensile hands hundreds of reels of cotton and thirteen packets of singer needles singer bobbins an extra singer foot two silver thimbles varnished darning-shell darkbrown with serrated lip worn tape-measure knitting needles of steel of plastic in all sizes crochet-hooks for doilies for tablemats pin-cushions button-boxes for coats dresses blouses brandnew zips all colours of the rainbow buckles awls prickers flax-thread for leatherwork a roll of the thinnest thongs a ball of darning-wool for black socks eyelets bronze and black of steel stiffening for belts for dresses press-studs sequins felt loops gold and silver thread a length of hatband with three feathers packets of bloomer elastic narrow and wide sponge for shoulder-padding satin belt brocade cuff shoelaces white and shoelaces black shoelaces brown and red hatpins tiepins cuff links tassels for a beret pearls fresh and salt earrings brooches ma's ring with six garnets signet ring of my father's engagement ring wedding ring that my fingers cannot bear a tin of mica chips feldspar agate quartz a jacaranda pod an acorn cap both with their dates on from stellenbosch love three pulleys and buckle of an abseil rope put it in the delft platter in the beak of the stork for when he comes our son for when he returns speedwell and snapdragon here under my meandering fingertips rustles a needlework basket cold lining of jewelcase thumb and forefinger have become detached from the fiddling world and free of god's odds and ends a woman's things rings shards reels that slip now and roll over the planks there was a time when I could sew could hem could fix could cast on stitches make buttonholes and knit could punch holes stitch a seam could pin on pin up hook could pump the singer's pedal reconcile the world with itself close its flaps weave its threads sew on its sequins and fill mattresses with its coir and look upon it and find it was good underneath down here there are even shirt-patterns dress patterns trouser-patterns take

them by all means do with them as you see fit from now on I'm an
unadorned woman my ravels and my rags nobody can assemble there
is no map or direction with which to navigate me.

*

Saturday 11 March 1972 four o'clock

A. vanished into thin air I suppose not odd that she's unhappy. She was
looking forward so much to Jakkie's being here this weekend from Heidelberg but he brought along a friend & they left immediately with Jak
for an air show in Cape Town. Will only be back tomorrow afternoon
late. A. had cooked & baked but they took along only a little bit of
her biltong and dried-fruit sweets for the road. You can give him & his
pal each a nice food parcel to take back to the hostel I say but the face
remains set on sulk. Must go & look for hr.

11 March six o'clock

Have just been to cast an eye over the milking so there was Julies flirt-
ing with A. Hey there he says my griddle-cake how about it supposedly
to the cow but I can hear it's actually for A. He doesn't look at her he
talks straight into the udder that he's milking. For what does she walk
around sniff-sniff in the hills all day just like a wildcat? is she perhaps
ruttish redcat tigercat? ggggh does she hiss at me? They say all she sticks
in & pulls out is a needle & a rag stick stick snip snip she doesn't look
left or right pity about those titties about that bottom that dried-out
sweet potato. A. pretends not to hear shirrrr-shirrrr she strains the first
milk of one cow after the other.

Thought to myself Julies you'd better keep your trap shut my boy but I
didn't want to interfere & I wanted to see what would happen & made
myself small behind the tank. It's certainly not the first time but she just
remains silent & he carries on.

No, he says, his foot is skew since the axle hit him head-over-heels
but he knows Gaat was there Gaat wasn't she his little nurse that day.
Didn't he feel it how she squeezed shut his veins so he didn't bleed
empty how she doctored him that he didn't kick the bucket didn't he see
how she cut white bands with her little shiny scissors snip snip snip how
she bandaged his head nicely pinned all the loose ends together nicely
with hr safety pins. But this foot of his just won't get fixed the toes keep
dragging sideways in the sand just like a hub-less wheel he'll never get

to the moon all cripple like this but who wants to see the moon if he can gravy sweet potato? He thought by himself perhaps old shuffle-shoe could have a chance to snitch a snatch with the little laundry-mangle between them they have three good legs & three arms & that's enough for getting up on the lucerne-rick. Shipps-shipps he carries on uncouthly with the teats. Just take off he says beforehand for Djeesus-sake that cap with the point & that snow-white apron otherwise he schemes he's riding in the redcross police van peeeeeep paaaaaaawp. He gives hr a flowery headscarf he gives hr a red flowery dress with a sash around the middle then what does she say about that? Shorrr-shorrr he milks rudely with his head pressed into the cow's stomach & A. pretends not to see any of it.

Do I wish she had a heart? Do I fear it? The heart or the absence of one?

1 May 1973
A. not herself since Jakkie has been at boarding school in Heidelberg. Works herself to a standstill before he comes home every weekend sweeps the garden paths scrubs the stoep washes curtains & polishes door-knobs & all the copper & silver & bakes the cakes & tarts & pies that he likes. Knits him beautiful cable-pattern jerseys with wool that she buys with her own money when we go to town. He's not the king I say he's just a child don't wear yourself to a rag he doesn't even notice but she just carries on.

What can I do about it? I do try every time when Jakkie comes home to arrange something that's at least an outing for A. as well. Picnic or to the ferry or the Bontebok Park or last year to the wildflower show or to the sea. Otherwise she doesn't go anywhere & sees nothing apart from the farm & the town. But it's difficult now that she's no longer a nanny. Jakkie jests get a wheelchair he says then he can pretend to have cerebral palsy then A. can go along everywhere as his nurse then he's hr licence. He says every time he sees her the point of her cap is longer. Haven't noticed it myself now I see all the caps are indeed higher on top & more pointed & completely filled with embroidery complicated patterns overlocked at top with little holes & scallops. Jakkie says she looks like the Pope.

A. crochets her own pullovers makes all her own house-dresses & aprons. Told J. we owe her a knitting machine for what she saves us in store-bought clothes or then at least my old Singer. He says that's going too far give them the little finger & they take the whole hand & A.'s already got hold of all of us up to the armpits. A. is not 'them', I say. J. says she's not 'us' either & a sewing machine won't solve the problem it's just like a chamber in parliament before you know it they want to pass laws. J. says if he catches Jakkie again teaching A. to dance in the outside room then he'll send him to the Paul Roos Gymnasium in Stellenbosch from Standard Eight, & then we'll only see him during holidays. He says he'll place him further & further away if things don't 'normalise'. What is normal? I ask. Nothing on Gdrift is normal, he says. It's a hospital full of female experiments if at least it had served a good purpose or had a practical application but he thinks we're way past the point of no return & we must just note that he's not the one who laid the tracks here he's been a mere passenger for a long time now he asks himself why he doesn't jump off the train it would be better than to ride to perdition knowingly with a little gang of saboteurs on board.

Would I mind if he left me? I have Jakkie. And Agaat.

5 April 1974
Decided to increase Agaat's salary but not directly with money with animals. She's had a cow & a few sheep from the start. Had them & their progeny branded over the years & she kept tally. By now 30 Jersey & 120 merinos & a few goats. The arrangement is she can sell as she sees fit not that she has anything to spend the money on but I tell hr save it build up a nest-egg for yourself you never know what may happen one day. For the time being it's between hr & me. J. would never approve it if I consulted him about it in advance but if he asks I'll say see it as A.'s pension she'll also be old one day.

I leave her free to decide for hrself when she wants to have the animals serviced or dipped & sheared & so forth so that she can feel she has a bit of independence here what else does she have? She takes very good care. See hr often inspecting hr animals. Hr cows yield more milk than mine & her sheep's wool is better. See she makes extra hay & even with hr last profit ordered hrself a few drums of molasses from the co-op & she regularly drives hr merinos next to the drift & she stands behind them hrself so that they can eat as much as they like of the long grass there. Only hr bunch of goats is a nuisance half domesticated the creatures & sometimes escape from their pen & eat my plants in the garden.

12 July 1974
Drove out today with A. for hr birthday 26 she is. How time flies! Went & had a picnic next to the Huis River. Had a good view of their working at the new pass. Nice strong stone walls packed there. If there'd been this fast road when you had to give birth to Jakkie, Même, she says out of the blue then we wouldn't even have had to stop. It's been a long time since she's called me Même.

Jakkie sent hr a parcel that she opened there at the picnic a blood-red apron with a card that I'm not allowed to see & that left her completely silent for the rest of the picnic & all the way home. Ai, she does miss him so. He says he sings in the school choir there in Heidelberg but all that the music teacher knows is Whispering Hope.

14 September 1974
Jakkie home for the spring holiday. Busy time on the farm. A. busy all day & Jakkie at a bit of a loose end. Come let me help you with your German I say but he doesn't want me to. Then I said let's sing it's the best way of learning a language but in fact I wanted to get some idea of how the voice had broken. So I taught him Der Musensohn: Und nach dem Takte reget/Und nach dem Mass beweget. A delicate tenor as I'd suspected & still the perfect pitch & the fine sensitivity, ag it would be a sin if he didn't develop it. The most important thing is that I made some contact with him again.

Saturday 15 February 1975 half past six
Terrible day! It's just me here in the house, feels as if I'm going mad. What must I do to escape this hell? Seems as if everything I undertake is doomed.

By four o'clock this afternoon back already from long weekend at Witsand. Do miss Jakkie so much now that he's at school in Stellenbosch & it's generally more relaxed in the beach house. Thought it might be nice if we ate out for a change as a family in the hotel there at the end of the weekend but what a fiasco! Jakkie (full of enlightened ideas these days) says he doesn't want to go if Agaat can't go along. There you have it, said J., A. is the government of Gdrift but out there she's a domestic & look what I've brought up in my wisdom & now Jakkie also has wrong ideas in his head.

Surely there'll be facilities for the kitchen staff I thought a little table somewhere where she can sit & eat. So A. goes along in her best cap very reluctant but for Jakkie's sake. When we arrive there she doesn't want to know anything about the hotel kitchen & she won't budge & she stays sitting in the car & next thing Jakkie gets up suddenly without apology or explanation & takes his plate of food with him to go & give it to A. & apparently she then scolded him so fiercely that he threw the plate on the ground. This Jak then found out because when Jakkie didn't return to the table he went to see what was happening outside & when they eventually returned to the dining room Jakkie's face was blood-red & he had a white ring round his mouth. Heard later that Jak had thrashed Jakkie with his belt right there in front of A. How could J. do such a thing? The child is fifteen already & very over-sensitive. Terrible atmosphere because then we still had to pack everything at the beach house & Jak shouts at everybody & goes like a bat out of hell back within two hours. When we got here he made Jakkie pack immediately & ordered Dawid to take him back to Stellenbosch in the bakkie.

A. has disappeared it's almost dark & she's not back yet what's going to happen to us here? J. is out of his mind charged out of here in his running-clothes. How can they just leave me all on my own like this after all that?

15

For supper there's spinach. For dessert there'll be stewed prunes.

Green food and black food. 12 December. Already noted on the calendar, entered in the log book.

Puree.

In the Braun.

Zimmmm-zoommm.

And after that strained three times through a sieve.

Fine but fibre-rich.

Agaat came and stood in the doorway with her little hand folded in her big hand to tell me all this. She couldn't control the timbre of her voice. Couldn't spare me the details of pulping. She tried. But she couldn't. Triumphantly. Clipped. A real elocution lesson. Lips tensed around the p's. Breath expelled robustly as if she'd rather be singing. If only I could prompt her to perform something. A libretto for the great purgation scene. Prima donna on her Procrustean bed.

Or something of the kind.

In her present mood she'd rather call the thing by name outright.

Sometimes I wonder whether, if I were suddenly to recover my speech, we could in these last days find a language to understand each other.

In which to make last jokes.

Or first jokes.

First smile.

First word.

But perhaps a lot of jabbering would have prevented us from getting to where we are now. Where that is I don't know. I just have to guess. And she has to guess. Our positions in this studio, who is in the chair of the drawing-master, who the model on the podium. Both beginners rather, I tend to feel, with a stick of charcoal in the hand, dumbfounded before each other's nakedness, without anybody to instruct us in the fashioning of a faithful representation.

Perhaps I'm reading too much into everything she does and says. Perhaps I'm imaging her evil. Or her goodness. Perhaps I've been delirious all this time because of a lack of oxygen.

Perhaps I'm more clear-minded than I've ever been. And perhaps she's trying at all costs to make me keep my wits about me. By providing me with material, pricks to kick against.

I know how Agaat's mind operates. She has no respect for a helpless human being. Possibly still pity. But not for long, then she wants to see signs of independence. She knows she'll have to generate it in me herself if she wants to see it, reaction, resistance. Because only when she's brought me to that will she have something to subjugate.

Spinach and prunes, thus.

Her chin has made that clear.

She will no longer be a passive spectator of my constipation.

She is now taking control of my bowels.

If she gets nothing else out of me, that she will get out of me.

Shit I shall shit, says her attitude. For her I shall address myself to the pan with abandon. Even if it is the last time. That's one thing of which I shall not deprive her. I may be struck dumb in the mouth, and too cowardly to face her for one moment longer than is necessary, and too ungrateful to appreciate it, the spectacle that she's contrived here in the room. But my stomach, my stomach and its overflow are hers. My last honourable mechanism. She'll work it for me. Work it and make it work. For the night is coming.

And if her ministrations don't have the desired effect, then she'll push a pipe up me and pump me full of lukewarm saline water. Would I rather have that? The glug-glug in my ears while I'm filled up from below like a gallon canister of Caltex? The bed tilted head-down at fifty degrees? Shaken by the feet to get rid of air bubbles?

Has she forgotten that she embraced my feet? Or is she pretending she meant nothing by that? Can she really have forgotten that she bowed her head over my shins, crumpled up her untouchable cap against my shins?

That was yesterday. Today, apparently, the Cape is Dutch again. Without a crease in the gable is her cap. Perhaps she embroidered herself a cap especially for the occasion. An allegory. Millions of tubes running through the stars. Stuck into the Black Hole, to mock the Evil One in her pit until she gives a sign of life?

Come and bend down here close to me, Agaat, so that I can check whether that's your latest needlepoint strategy. Give me a dream from the point of your needle. How many angels are there dancing there? And will you accompany me to heaven as embroiderer of deathbed stories? How would you design your deathbed accompanist if you were to be given the chance?

For supper there is spinach. For dessert there'll be stewed prunes.

With quite a little air of importance she said it. In the chest register of the mezzo-domestico, the one who has to keep her pose under all circumstances, an air hostess on a doomed flight, a waitress in *Towering Inferno*.

As if she's singing of duck's tongues in port-wine sauce, or of pumpkin flowers in batter.

From its earliest incipience this morning the meal has been prepared with an amplitude of gesture. The first you-don't-know-what's-in-store-for-you-madam look I got just after breakfast, while I was still sprawling unproductively on the bedpan. With the dish full of springy, curling spinach-beet leaves she marched down the passage past my room to go and rinse them in the bath. Fresh from her vegetable garden of which she's so proud. Left right, left right, all she lacked was fife and drum. On better days she holds the sunripe strawberries under my nose before she mashes them with a fork. But today it's green. Colour of the dragon. The pennants are fluttering for the last battle of The Spout.

Three thorough rinses I heard, a stirring and a shaking and a splashing in the bath. This afternoon I got the smell, mercifully braised in butter with onion, a shred of bacon if I can still trust my nose. An hour ago the Braun started singing in the kitchen, at the high pitch of the puree setting. Zimmm-zoommm. Six, seven eight batches. I could hear the wet spinach slapping up in the jug, could see the slurry ooze down on the inside. Who does she think is supposed to eat it all? She'll get three teaspoons into me, maybe four. And she won't eat any of it herself.

Now she has enough for a constipated army. Perhaps she wishes she had a whole hospital of casualties to care for. So that she could repeat her ministrations from bed to bed. So that a Revolution of the Shitting Classes could erupt. Which she could suppress with a counter-offensive. Bored to death she must be. Three years long the same routines, over and over, the washing, the feeding, the pans.

In fact I know what she wants to achieve with her noisy preparations. She wants to attract attention. She wants to build up tension. She wants me to know that she's advancing. With a ruffle of drums. Tralalee tralaley!

Is it for my sake or for hers? Perhaps by this time she can't believe that she's held out so long with me so ill. Three years' dying. A lifetime's diaries. Perhaps she herself feels like a ghost by this time. Perhaps I'm sustaining her with my dependence.

The one old ghost had a very hard time and the other old ghost did its bit. Long live the two! Tralalee tralaley! Tralalee tralaley!

Who then thought up this pretty little song?

Two geese brought it over the sea.

Mach Toten lebendig.

Macht Kranken gesund.

The Farted Bride. The Three-cornered Pan.

What would Agaat be without her overtures?

The prunes have been stewing since early morning. I heard her take the packets out of the grocery cupboard, one, two, three. I heard her plop them in the water to soak before she put them on, heard her squeeze out the pips, plinks, plinks, into an enamel bowl.

Here they come, Mrs De Wet. Thou shalt behold thine prunes. More nourishing than sour grapes.

Perhaps she will relent. Perhaps she'll make a souffle. Just for the beauty of it. Would that be the reason for the march-tempo that I hear approaching down the passage? A risen light-green puff of a spinach souffle in a white dish?

No. She's selecting a tape. Thwick thwock, she pushes it into the player. Volume. Balance. Not a souffle. *The Slave Chorus. The Grand March. Va pensiero.*

I know this, this out-of-the-blue music-making. Accompaniment to the meal if she doesn't feel like talking to me.

Camouflage, the music is at times. When there are visitors. To chase them away she deliberately chooses the chickle-chockle on little drums and tin guitars that interests Jakkie so much. So that I shouldn't hear what she's discussing with them in the sitting room. But what's this all of a sudden that I'm not supposed to hear when all day I'm allowed to hear spinach pureeing and prunes plopping? I prick up my ears. Tchick, I hear under the music.

And another tchick. Open with the sideboard and shut.

What could it be? Whatever it is, it proceeds at a leisurely pace, to the beat of the music, down the passage.

I mustn't hope for it. Fantastic timing it would be.

What do I see?

Yes I see. My eyes are open. I must believe them. With the rolls of maps held out in front of her on her arms she marches into the room solemnly. An offering. She stops just inside the door for me to take good note. She drags up a chair with one arm. Her face absolutely straight. She gets onto the chair. One by one she takes the rolls, hangs them by the loops from the picture rail. Doesn't open them. Everyone rolled up and still secured with little bows.

Right, Agaat, Mrs de Wet here understands the trade-off!

An evacuation for an exposition! Fair enough!

A poop for a peep!

A panful for a panorama of Grootmoedersdrift!

Who else could think up that anagnorisis should coincide with catharsis?

Yes, Agaat, right enough, what is Mrs de Wet going to see? Mrs de Wet is going to see her arse. I know how your mind works. First Jak and now I. Calculated in such a way that we have only ourselves to thank.

Now she wants me to applaud. Now that I'm tired and worn out with everything that she's been pushing under my nose. Now that I've become so feeble and so heavy of breath. Now that I must shit for old times' sake. Without any pressure of my own. A mere sewer.

And here my spinach is now. Steaming in a saucer on the bridge. A bit of bicarbonate of soda to make it green.

But first there is another manoeuvre.

A shake manoeuvre. Little brown bottle. Shiny teaspoon.

First the Pink Lady, says Agaat, then the spinach.

The Lady is pink as the gums of dentures are pink. She is deposited on the seam of my tongue. She tastes of chalk and chewing gum. Three times she enters me. Agaat pleats her mouth.

Yuck, she says, I don't know how you get it down.

Never mind, Agaat, I know.

Just a spoonful of spinach makes the medicine go down, Agaat sings.

Three sips of chlorophyll.

With every teaspoon her excitement increases. She can't hide it. Could never. From the beginning her area of expertise. Ever since I've been unable to get onto the toilet seat myself, clean myself, she started formulating her rules and regulations, more and more complicated as my paralysis increased. Clean and unblocked she wanted to keep me all through my sickbed.

As if the second coming itself would take place along that passage.

Three sips of sweet black cellulose.

Tasty, the little prunes, says Agaat.

My dosing is a hurried business tonight. Who wouldn't start becoming impatient for a denouement? Agaat has switched off the music.

Doesn't want to miss anything. Especially not my crapulent opening chords.

It's explosive, I know, the mixture of pink and green and black gunge. A rainbow preceding the deluge. An old Grootmoedersdrift recipe.

My stomach starts churning. Ghorrr! it goes. Ghorrr! and gharrr! and gu! and blub! And in between the little singing sounds, zimmm-zoommm.

Agaat's merry-go-round. Music to her ears.

Strike up, she says with a straight face.

She pulls the sheets from me. No nonsense tonight. We're going to make doubly sure. She puts on latex gloves. She pops a suppository from its silver container. Translucent it is. Glycerine. For the laxation of the sensitive system. It has the shape of a bomb.

Not even time to turn me on my side tonight. A short cut will do as well. She pushes a hand in between my legs from the front. She runs a finger through the split of my buttocks to find the right entrance. She pushes in a finger to relax the sphincter.

Nothing wrong with the arse, she mutters. Old nag's arse. Wouldn't say it's been cut open. Mommy's mattress button.

The point of the pill is hard. She pushes it in without ceremony.

Take it, she says, take, swallow it. Otherwise I'm taking the horse's pill-gun.

Listening is all very well, but who has ever argued with a sphincter?

She pushes it in still deeper.

I feel the muscle slip shut, contract the pill into my anus. Immediately I feel the effect.

Plop, plop, Agaat discards the gloves into the bin. She doesn't cover me again with the sheet.

Hold on, she says to me, I'm just returning the tray.

As casually as if-you-please.

Hold on.

Am I Atlas? The myth is the wrong way round. The earth like heaven is not above us, but inside us. For us to retain in our cavities and to surrender through our orifices.

What do I hear Agaat sing as she marches down the corridor? Not Italian, no.

Tho' there's one motor gone we will still carry on, We're coming in on a wing and a prayer.

There the pan perches covered with its clean white cloth. There hang the maps rolled up against the wall. There's a merry rattling in the kitchen. Small arms. Beyond the ridge the regiment is mustering. What do I hear, is Agaat singing there? Singing so that I can hear where she is?

The Braun is being packed away in its box in the pantry.

Are you still holding on? the call comes, I'm just putting the spinach in the fridge quickly!

As if I could call back.

It cramps. A cloudburst somewhere higher up. A burgeoning mass. Completely fluid. Definitely a risk trying to pass wind.

Just don't, Agaat calls through the clatter of dishes, just don't go and squitter all over your bed, I put on clean sheets this morning.

I start to sweat.

The prune saucepan is scraped out. Slap, goes the lid of the rubbish bin. Heavy artillery!

Tralalee tralaley! Tralalee tralaley!

I feel as if I'm going to faint. I close my eyes. I concentrate on a point above my nose. The crepe-sole shoes approach down the passage.

I must, I must march all the way to death.

Aitsa, says Agaat, look at the old mare sweating. Now we've really got you going, seems to me.

A hand lands lightly on my shin. Sweet as a dove.

I open my eyes. Thunder and lightning. Bring the pan!

Yes, I'm bringing it, don't rush me now, you make me wait for hours every morning.

Bringthepanthepan!

So, Ounooi, have you seen yet what I brought you this evening? A surprise. All this time I've been thinking there's something that you want to see but I kept missing it. And so it was this all the time? Am I right? All the time? The maps? Yes or no?

Panpanpanpan!

The maps please, from out there in the sideboard, right under your nose. That's what you've been asking all this time? Am I right, yes or no, Ounooi? There I go carrying in just about the whole yard in here and it's just down the passage in the sitting room where all this time I've forgotten to look.

Butter couldn't melt. Lying without turning a hair. There she stands with the pan in the air, the white cloth over the arm.

Yes, Agaat, you're right. So put the ridges under my arse instead of your holy of holiest pan. From Bot River to Heidelberg, the municipalities, the districts, the regions. Unroll it under me, keep the edges together, and watch me make a sewerage farm out of them. And if the local is too lowly for you, bring the seven continents so that I can shit them into oblivion for you one by one. What does it matter in any case?

Fold the water map into a little boat, set the contour map for a sail. Caulk the holds with pulp from Grootmoedersdrift. Then I sail away on my last voyage in it.

Up to my chin in shit.

Once and for ever put in my place.

Would that satisfy you?

Hey hey hey! Convulsion-kick! The animal's just about had it but it's the kick that hurts most!

Keep your damned pan then. Stick it up your own arse. Rather give me the Republic and its provinces, the whole South, then I'll darken for you the Light of the Word that the Dutch supposedly brought here on the Dromedaris. You're excellent proof of what a bad idea it was. Your name may be holy, but your soul, Agaat, is at times as black as the hearth out of which you crawled. Don't you have any mercy? Have you now decided it's time for me to paddle-paddle through shit to the underworld? Time for those who came to play God the Creator over you? Have you now decided there's no remedying this confusion and this gibberish? Well, be comforted. The last trump is being sounded.

Here it comes. Here I lie, I can do no other. Covered whiter than snow or not.

Don't carry on so, Ounooi. You're not a child, good heavens!

Just in time. The enamel is cold under my buttocks.

She pinches her nose with one hand, pulls over the sheet with the other. Oh say can you hear, she says on a bated breath, the thunder almighty?

She picks at the little pink bows. Zirrts, the maps roll open. All along the picture rail, two full walls.

Zirrts, zirrts, zirrts, she says, as she unties them. Prrts, prrts, prrts, she mimics the sounds emanating from me. O'er the veld it comes wafting wide, she says.

She gestures with wide-open arms at the exhibition. Everything is there, even the house plans and the schemes for the landscaping of the garden. Graphs, tables, indexes.

Right, says Agaat, how shall we go about it?

Leave me in peace! Get out! Out!

No, come on now, come, come, since when can you do only one thing at a time? The way you're carrying on, you'll need a second pan at any moment in any case, I'm not getting out of here now. But I'm also not going to stand around here wasting my time, of that you can be sure.

Agaat turns on her heel swiftly. Right turn. Tchi! goes her sole on the wooden floor. With quick brisk steps she stalks out. Parade ground. She yanks open the broom cupboard in the passage. It sounds as if every-thing inside is falling out. The broomsticks roll over the floorboards. They are kicked aside. Salute and halt on the big cymbals! She returns with the feather duster. Parade baton.

And this is Japie, she says. She turns it around, a grey shock of feath-ers. I smell house dust.

With swift strokes she presses the point of the stick on the maps. They're the regional maps.

My stomach loosens in spasms and cramps. Over the rim of the pan. I can feel it. I can smell myself. I close my eyes.

Come now, what's this nonsense? Open your eyes and look where I'm pointing. If you knew how many sleepless nights I had because I couldn't figure out what on God's earth you could want from me!

I open my eyes. Please, I ask.

What's this please all about now? Enough of please, thank you! Blink your eyes when I press on the right place, I suspect somewhere on these maps is a spot, a weak spot or a soft spot that you want to visit again.

Hooikraal? Tygerhoek? Boschjesmansrug? Adderskop? Holgat? Van Rheenenshoogte? Lindeshof? Wolvelaagte? Varslug? Blydskap? Riet-poel? Jongensklip? Infanta? Ockertseinde?

All the battle sites. Farms, stations, towns. Beach hamlets. Wheat storages. Settlements. Train junctions. Kraals, corners, ridges, heads, holes, heights, bowers, plains, named after hay, after tigers, after bush-men and adders, long-forgotten van Rheenens and Lindes, after wolves, after fresh air and joy, after stones and pools, after distant princesses, after the end of some unfortunate Ockert. Of some of them I've never heard. She's inventing half the names. I can't see all the way to where she's pointing. I don't trust it. My own stink is in my nostrils. Acrid, grassy. Green manuring.

Come now, Ounooi, do your bit, it's not for nothing I struggled and exhausted myself guessing and slaved away trying to satisfy you. Per-haps you'd like to inform me as well what we're looking for here on these maps? So far from your bed? You can rest assured I won't give up. I don't give up and you don't give up. That's our problem, the two of us!

She settles the cap more firmly on her head, as if she's heading into a wind. She changes hands, takes the stick in the crumpled paw, grabs a blue booklet with her strong hand, fans it before her face.

Got, but what a stink you can crap!

She strips the sleeve of her bad arm up all the way to the elbow. As if she's preparing to grab a snake behind the neck. She looks straight at me.

All the better to show you, my child. She shakes the little arm at me. The handle of a mincing machine.

It's the first time that Agaat has ever pushed up her right sleeve for me like that. It's the first time that she's sworn in front of me, with her mouth at any rate, and at me. She watches me watching the arm. The same thickness all the way, a thin rod with a wrong-way-round elbow.

Vadersgaven? Vinkelrug? Blink one eye if I'm getting warm, right? Blink both eyes quickly if I'm cold, do you understand me?

What does she want me to understand? The names, of fathers and fennel, mean nothing to me. I signal, no, heavens, have done, are you mad? I close my eyes.

Open your eyes, Ounooi, or I'll fit you out with matchsticks, I'll stick your four lids up and down with plasters before you can blink an eye. Look here, here, here. Have you been here? have I? What would we have wanted there? We know our place, don't we? Where'er we walk.

Remhoogte? Bobbejaankrans? Perdekop? Slangrivier? Rotterdam? Bromberg? Heights, rock faces, hills, rivers, dams, mountains, commemorating baboons, horses, snakes; a topographical and zoological gibberish.

You know what, Ounooi, now that you're shitting yourself so gloriously over there, I suddenly feel like a little glass of sherry. The one of which you always pour me a bit when we make trifle. What do you say, would you mind? It's almost Christmas in any case. O come all ye faithful! Unto us a child is given! And apart from that, we have something to drink to, it seems to me. Here in our small corner!

Agaat's back is straight. She walks briskly. I hear the lid of the liquor cabinet slam. Bang! And then Tchi! Left about-turn!

She returns with the Old Brown sherry and a little glass. She unscrews the cap, prepares to pour, looks at me.

Shame, dry-mouth, she says, but it wouldn't agree with you, I'm afraid. She presses the open bottle in front of my nose.

Your health, she says, have you finished shitting now?

She looks at me with hard eyes. She doesn't want to read my gaze.

It feels as if my foundation is falling out. The cramps come at intervals. Writhe. I could writhe with pain, clamp my arms around my stomach, could groan, take a deep breath and exhale. I could. Fold double.

Why are you looking at me like that, are you dumb? she asks but she doesn't wait for a reply. She knocks back the sherry in one gulp. Looks at the glass, smacks her lips.

Right, she says, that gives cheer, where were we? She grabs the duster, pushes her glasses back on her nose. She reads the names in four-square march-time, taps the duster on the map like a metronome.

Uitvlugt, Niekerksbog, Avontuur.

Skeiding, Omkyk, Eigenaardigheid.

Lekkerwater. Laaste Liefde.

Vryheid.

Vermaaklikheid.

The grandfather clock strikes in between the names, a litany of longings, aspirations, achievements, losses. Agaat leaves space for the quarter. Cease-fire. Eleven o'clock. Another glass of sherry. Fantastic performance. She advances her positions.

Napky and Dipka and Kinkoe.

Caledon, Stanford, Napier.

Hermanus, Bredasdorp, Riviersonderend.

It's released from her like a flood, the names of the towns. We stayed over here (she on sacks with the smelly servant in the hovel), visited there (tea and cake for her in the shade of a great old bluegum what more could one wish for), we went to fetch this (three bolts of tweed from a ship that had run aground), or buy that (genuine Dutch tulip bulbs that flowered yellow that year), and sold something else for a song (an out-of-tune piano on which I'd still played her Farewell ye halls of marble, farewell ye hills and dales). Here was a farmer's day (a greybeard in a white coat directed parking), there a sale in execution (even the spades and pitchforks), a horse race (which big-mouth fell off his horse?), a meeting of paunches with bums sagging in khaki pants (like pigs with measles). Here was a sheep on the spit (for her the shin-bone that I kept in a white napkin), there a circus (peeped through a chink), a show, a dance, a day of prayer for rain.

All along the old battle positions.

Everything that you forgot and never even noted in your little books, says Agaat.

I was asking for this. Now there is no remedy. Now I get what I asked for and more. My bowels may be empty but now it's Agaat's turn to flush her system. She rattles off the farm names. Ting-ting on the brass band's triangle, a horseshoe on which she beats time with the tip of her duster. Such heights and flats, vleis here, kraals there, dams, spruits, drifts, fountains where she had to sit outside and hold the fort and got sheep's lung to eat.

Granted here and Begun there.

Welgelegen, Nietverdiend, Goedgevonden, Laatgevonden, well-situated, undeserved, found well or late.

A neck, a head, a ridge, a corner.

A kloof, a bush, a well.

From map to map, hoped, rejoiced, expected.

Sonderkos and Grootbaklei, Droëbek and Natteschoot. Out of Food but Full of Fight, Dry of Mouth and Wet of Loin: Agaat's inventions.

Spanned out, turned back, rested, trekked, stayed.

Dankbaar.

Nooitgedacht.

Pious assertions of gratitude, feigned surprise at such good fortune.

Môrester to Avondrood, from star of morning to gloaming of evening.

Mumbling she follows her own routes, index finger on the lines. Helter-skelter amongst the various maps. She jiggles the sleeve back over the little hand. She look-looks at me. What's the matter, Agaat?

Omkyk, she says.

Openmaak.

Soebattersvlakte.

Look round, open up, the plain of pleading. I plead with my eyes, come and clean me, I have finished now, I surrender, the white flag, you have overcome, please, then we can sleep.

That will be the day! says Agaat.

She is looking at the layout of the yard of Grootmoedersdrift, the house and garden plans. She aims up and down, forward and back. Here comes an outstretched arm, here comes a finger pointing, at me, at the plan. Here comes a stamping of feet. What is this coming here? Here comes something else. A salute.

She presses with her finger, presses, press, press, press so that it bends back, the forefinger of the strong hand, presses on all the places.

Load, powder in the pan, ramrod in the barrel, take aim, the old muzzle-loader, I feel myself coming into the line of fire. Perhaps it's a signal-cannon instead. Who's going to hear it all along the kloofs over the mountain to the Castle, Agaat?

Back room! Green door! Agaat thunders.

Huptebup, huptebup, huptebup. Here we have a goosestep with tuba thrusts, out of the sherry bottle, the legs lifted high, the toes pointed, the Third Reich come to Grootmoedersdrift, the head with the jaw surmounted by the cap turned sharp right and then left as she marches past to and fro at the foot of my bed, the duster a bayonet over one shoulder.

Mailslot! Lowroof! Candle-end!

Lockupchild! Without pot!

Shatinthecorner!

Shatupon!

Dusterstick on Agaatsarse.
Au-Au-Au!
Ai-Ai-Ai!
Neversaysorry!
Sevenyearschild.
And then?
Can-you-believe-it?
Backyard!
Skivvy-room!
Highbed!
Brownsuitcase!
Whitecap! Heartburied!
Nevertold! Unlamented!
Good-my-Arse!
Now-my-Arse! Now's-the-Time!

*

How did the fire start?

Who made the rain fall out of the wrong wind?

What did Jakkie hear of what Jak said to you that morning in the garden?

And Agaat, what did she hear?

The school holidays had started and Jakkie would be coming home from Stellenbosch. You fretted about it as always. Agaat bustling about on the trot. Jak to and fro on the stoep, ready to launch another assault on some mountain or other. He wanted to leave with Jakkie that very Friday evening.

The tug-of-war over Jakkie. You could see on the child's face how insecure it made him feel. Insecure and at the same time arrogant because he was everybody's favourite and could twist everybody's arm.

You went out onto the stoep.

He'll just want to arrive in peace and enjoy eating what Agaat's prepared for him, you said to Jak. You can go to the mountains after the weekend, can't you, otherwise what do I see of him? And, after all, Agaat would want to talk to him a bit, she's missed him so.

Jak said nothing, just tug-tugged at the mountaineering ropes that he was rolling up.

You always give the child hell when he comes home, you said, you'll be presented with the bill one day!

Jak's head was shaved as always before going on a mountaineering trip. It made his features look sharp. He looked at you wordlessly.

Things were deteriorating badly between you. After that first mountaineering trail with Jakkie in the Tradouw you had broken down. You'd never seen two such battered people. They were both of them exhausted to the point of death, full of dried blood from cuts and scratches. Fell upon their food like wolves and crawled into bed immediately. Neither of them would tell what had happened on the mountain. At last you started screaming.

You grabbed Jak by the shoulders.

Are you trying to kill him? Will you be satisfied then? If you could let his flesh rot off and pick his bones and join them together again with hinges and make yourself a boy-machine with greased gears and tinkling bells that you can throw off cliffs to your heart's content and hoist up with ropes and hooks?

All Jak wanted to do was gather his wits but you wouldn't let him be, you hammered on his chest with your fists there where he was lying against the pillows in the stoep room. He was too tired to do anything to you. But you saw how hard his eyes were, how thin his lips.

From then on, from 1971 on, he tried to take the child out of your hands, out of Agaat's hands. First he had to go to boarding school in Heidelberg. And then one fine day you woke up to find that everything had been arranged for Jakkie to go to Paul Roos from Standard Seven. Science and maths he had to study, languages and music didn't pay the rent, and he didn't want his son to squander his life on a farm one day as he, Jak, had done.

That fire, was it in 1976? Jakkie in Standard Eight? He'd be getting a lift home for the Easter break. The rains stayed away. Warm autumn weather, gusty south-easter, everything crackling with drought, the river just about empty. Perfect conditions for a veld fire.

You were concerned about water for the sheep, about the lambs on the dry stubble-fields. About the sheep-oats that had germinated too late on account of the unusual drought in December. You were preparing to cart dry feed to the mangers. You didn't want to drive the sheep into the cattle's grass pasture because that was also rather meagre for the season. The river was too low for much irrigation. You wanted all hands on the farm to help with the lamb birthing. The ewes were weaker than previous years, one of the herds not yet altogether in condition after the acidosis poisoning the previous November. Ate too many loose grains of wheat on the harvested field.

And guess who had driven them in there?

Guess who first saw that they had all lain down?

Guess who then had to doctor them?

It was beginning to seem as if events were unfolding according to a design on Grootmoedersdrift.

In whose plan were you all?

What was being made clear to you?

You were all blind. You were blind. Your mouth was dry from tranquillisers. You stared at these things, and at the faces around you, at your own face in the mirror, but nothing would surrender their secrets. You knew one part of the reasons, the people around you another part. And everybody tried to solve the riddle for himself in his solitude.

That Easter, it was a critical time. You would have preferred Jakkie and Jak to stay on the farm and help look after it. After all, it was in the interests of all of you, you felt. Why did you always have to ask for support, plead for help?

Was it because of the nature of mixed farming that there was always too much to do, and would you really have to change it all if you wanted things to run more smoothly? Was Jak right about that?

How would you have to dismantle such a complex concern and reassemble it differently, with fewer components and fewer troublesome details to attend to? Who would help you to think up and plan such an upheaval?

And what would the farm look like then? Like green wheatfields? A monotonous summer? A monoculture with a general impoverishment?

That afternoon before Jakkie's arrival. Agaat in the kitchen preparing food. Jak on the stoep with the mountaineering equipment. You in your room with your diary. That's right, it was the Easter break 1976, you had just started a new booklet.

Writing had in any case increasingly become your way of waiting to see what would happen next. Through writing you wanted to get a grip on your times and days on Grootmoedersdrift, to scrunch up and make palpable the hours, the fleeting grain of things in your hastily scribbled sentences, connecting cause and effect in the stream of events. At least then you could later turn the pages of the diaries, forward and back, and see: This happened before that, and this and that were the first signs of a catastrophe that you wrote up only much later, and this and that were simultaneously requiring attention and not without connection, even though the connection was evident only later.

That afternoon when Jakkie was due to arrive, you were sitting and writing about your farming worries. And about how you were all waiting, each in his or her own way, for this son whom you all wanted to possess and who escaped you all, not in the first place because he was by then already becoming his own person, on the contrary, but because he was afraid, in different ways, afraid and guilty and taunting each of you, because he didn't know how to please you all at the same time.

You wrote that you could hear Agaat rolling out flaky pastry, thud, thud, with the wooden roller on the kitchen table, for Jakkie's chicken pie. You went to investigate and her chin was pushed out all the way. She knew that Jak wanted to take Jakkie away to the mountains as soon as he arrived that afternoon. She knew that he wouldn't be granted a break to eat, she knew that Jak wouldn't allow any tasty food to be packed for the trip. And yet she was continuing, her lips pressed firmly together, with her preparations.

Were you imagining things, or had you heard her talk on the telephone every now and again the previous week, in the stealthy hours just after lunch while you were lying down?

Was she conniving with Jakkie again?

You didn't want to ask.

Whatever it was that Agaat had up her sleeve, you knew that her plan would always suit you better than anything that Jak could contrive. You were counting on her by this time. To make things happen in your family, or not happen. Or to stop things from happening. Or to predict things. Rain, wind, floods. She could read your mood like a sky, predict Jak's movements long before he himself knew what he was going to do.

The twilight was setting in already. You were starting to worry, Jak had gone for a drive in the bakkie earlier to see whether he didn't meet them on the road. Then the phone rang. It was Jakkie. To say that he'd torn a ligament in rugby and would only be able to get a lift home the following morning and he didn't think he'd be able to be very active, the doctor said the leg needs rest.

Was it all Jakkie's scheme? Thought up on his own?

Jak had just recently acquired television on the farm. Perhaps Jakkie wanted to stay at home watching sport rather than go mountaineering, or just wanted to relax at home? Perhaps Agaat wanted to watch television? Perhaps she wanted to get Jak away from there, because he'd forbidden her to watch television, didn't want her to see too much of the school riots in the north.

You give them the best that you have and just see what you get in return, he said, and glared at you as if it had been you who had stuffed Afrikaans down the gullets of the people.

Jak said nothing when he heard that Jakkie was no longer arriving that evening, and that he couldn't go mountaineering. He tightened his headlamp around his head, filled his water bottle in the kitchen and shouldered his rucksack.

Agaat went and fetched his ropes on the front stoep and came and put them in his hands.

Oh yes, of course, I almost forgot, what would I do without you, Agaat, Jak said.

His voice was odd. He looked her straight in the eyes. He tugged at the roll of ropes in his hands.

Without any greeting he walked away from the yard in the dusk. You and Agaat watched the little light until it disappeared up into Luipaardskloof.

Perhaps it's all to the good, said Agaat, her face expressionless.

She went and fetched her best bottle of preserved quinces from the pantry shelf and said she thought she'd make some custard quickly, to be ready when Jakkie arrived the following day.

Nine o'clock that evening Jakkie phoned from Swellendam and said he'd decided after all to come that night and would you and Agaat come to fetch him please, his lift wasn't going any further. His knee was bandaged and he had a bad limp. He and Agaat greeted each other with poker faces and he said there'd better be chicken pie and quinces and custard and she said but how else.

They didn't give you an opportunity to get a word in edgewise.

You three were together that evening as if Jak didn't exist. Jakkie tucked into the chicken pie. He wanted to watch the news on television, because of the so-called situation in the country. He was in the debating society of Paul Roos he said, and he had to take part in a debate on the advantages and disadvantages of Afrikaans as medium of instruction in black schools.

He was now really getting beyond her in his education, Agaat said, but what would he say to a game of Scrabble?

The two of you helped Agaat wash the dishes and then waited for her to have her meal in the kitchen and then you sat playing the word game around the dining room table till after half past one that night.

Why can't it always be like this? you thought. Such peace, such harmony? But every now and again you intercepted a glance between Jakkie and Agaat and knew the peace would be short-lived.

'Quick' Jakkie built. '-grass' you added for 'quickgrass'. 'Karooquick-grasses' Agaat made of this, by using a blank and spending her last 's' to make 'tricks' of 'trick' that was already in place vertically on the board. All seven letters and on a red block as well and Agaat won. But only after she'd had to show Jakkie the kind of quickgrass in the old

Handbook for Farmers because it wasn't in Chambers. He maintained Agaat was fabricating it, there was no such type of grass. Then there was a whole argument about whether a word was valid if it wasn't in Chambers and you had to decide the matter. There's more to a language than is written in a dictionary, you said, and there would have been mighty little happening on Grootmoedersdrift if you'd had to farm only with the words in Chambers.

That was how you decided. Agaat was the winner, out and out.

Agaat always wins, Jakkie said. He winked at his packed rucksack that was standing ready on the sitting room floor. You pretended not to see anything, not to see at bedtime how Agaat double-locked all the doors and windows, not to see her signalling to Jakkie with her little hand to lock the kitchen door from the inside. Pretended not to see Jakkie walking, suddenly without a limp, across the kitchen floor to lock the door with a loud grinding noise.

But Jak's onslaught did not come at night.

You had just returned the following morning from the first round of taking out feed, busy in the garden putting in plants for winter when suddenly he was standing behind you. Dishevelled. Red in the face, a white ring around his mouth, spit accumulated in the corners of his mouth.

It was twelve o'clock and the sun was shining viciously.

Jak's mountaineering clothes were torn. It looked as if he'd wrestled in the dust with some wild creature.

You carried on with your work, thought you would keep it light, would pretend not to have noticed that he was in a state.

Home is the hunter, home from the hill, you said. You moved to the flowerbed behind the plume bushes to be out of sight of the workers on the yard or of somebody coming out onto the front stoep.

Jak hauled you upright, grabbed you by the front of your dress.

Nobody would believe me, he hissed in your face, nobody, everybody would think I'm mad if I had to tell them about you, but I know I'm right! About how you really are!

You tried to keep your voice light and removed his hand and bent down next to your flowerbed where, with the little hand-trowel, you were putting in seedlings for the winter garden. Calendula, a few sowing trays of purple pansies.

A voice crying in the wilderness? you said, you must be careful, next thing the baboons will be barking at you!

Yes, said Jak, you're right, I see it in the wilderness, I see it when I'm hanging from my ropes between heaven and earth, then I understand it, dumb retarded bastard that I am, I see it only after I've run myself to a frazzle for miles, or when I'm clambering up sheer rock faces. Then I see it, then I see what's happening here!

Good heavens, Jak, what about the glories of nature? you asked. When last did you see a march rose, hmm? Or the great emperor butterfly of Grootmoedersdrift? You frequent such privileged vantage points, you should put it all to better use!

Jak kicked the trowel out of your hand and pushed you over off your haunches so that you landed flat on your behind in the flowerbed.

Why would any self-respecting woman put up with it? he shouted. Why? Why?

Why would she allow herself to be shoved around without phoning the dominee? Without telling a single mortal? Why? Why does she stay? Why does she have a child by such a man? Why does nothing of the fuck-up at home ever show to other people? Always only excuses! Her homestead, her farm, her birthright, her child, her reputation in the farming community? All just to be able to stay with this Jak de Wet, the poor bloody bugger who has to hear every day that he won't do, he's trash.

His eyes were staring wildly in his head, veins bulging on his forehead. With every question he prodded you with his foot, against your knees, against your ribs.

Jak, you'll have a heart attack, you said, calm down.

Bitch! As if you cared! Shall I tell you why you stay with me? You need me to mistreat you. Do you know why? That's how your mother taught you. And her mother before her taught her, all the way to Eve, to the tree in paradise.

Jak tore off his shirt so that the buttons popped. You were shocked at his body, so lean and so hard.

Don't look at me, Milla, that's what's bloody-well left of me and at least I know it. A wife-batterer with self-knowledge. What about you? Do you know what I see, Milla?

A cattle farmer, a connoisseur of sheep, a wheat and soil expert, a gardener. You keep things running smoothly on this godcursed little farm. But what do you look like? Like something out of your mother's old books. Genoveva of Suurbraak. And why? Because you feel inferior. Because you want to feel inferior.

Look at me, Milla! Look, here is your accomplice. I help you with it. Do you think it's possible to become like me all on one's own? And you can't tell anyone about it, can you? Where on earth would you have to begin? More difficult than a magazine story, I can tell you. There it's the hero who has the insight and the heroine who swallows it all whole.

I the precious, I the victim. How would you ever get something like that past your lips at your sanctified tea-drinking at a church bazaar? No, oh no, there you also have a substitute, there you prefer to worship your b'loved Jesus nailed to his cross. A pity the pictures always show him with his bloody little feet already neatly nailed together. Otherwise you could dream with your mouth full of bazaar cake that Pilate was poking a stick up his holy hole. Which would make him more worthy of your worship!

Jak, you'll burn in hell, stop it!

No, Milla. I've been there for a long time! You're the one pretending to be in heaven. Never a word in public, no, your mess is for the nest, for the inner chamber. Selected me by the balls, didn't you? Raised me to your hand! Bedtime story! Little woman whines for attention until she gets the kind that she most appreciates. Thud, bang, blood in the nostril, from ballroom to slapstick in two winks.

Backbone of the nation, bah! Thanks to you and your kind the Afrikaner deserves an early demise. You're a pestilential species!

See what you look like! You like it. Tell me: How do you rape somebody who wants to be raped?

You just wanted not to be seen by anybody. To and fro you stepped as he shoved you, just to remain behind the plume bush. The sharp leaves cut your hands every time you fell against the bush.

Fall, come fall once more, then I'll have earned some points. Then you'll notice me! An Oscar for Jack the Ripper!

He slapped your garden hat off your head with one hand and caught you on the cheek with the other hand, and as you ducked away, again on the other cheek. Left, right, left. The slaps burnt on your skin.

A healthy flush! A few good slaps! That's all you can tolerate from me isn't it? Otherwise you don't trust how much I love you.

Papa's little princess! So scared of the wolf in the dark! Au, stubbed her little toe! That's where it comes from. That's the beginning of it all. That's what you did with Jakkie when he was small. What will you say when your heir turns out a bloody faggot one day? When I was his age, I'd long since lain with girls, but where does he lie? In the outside room, I bet. What's to come of it?

Jak, you don't know what you're saying, I can't listen to this any longer.

You sat amongst the leaves of the plume bush and pulled up your knees and lowered your head. He bent open your arms, squatted by you, spoke into your face, you could smell him, his unwashed body, his bitter breath.

Sis, you said, sis, you stink, get away from me.

With all the shoving and wriggling the seeds of the plume had come loose, white itchy feathery tips that descended around your heads, clung to your arms.

What's a bit of sweat, Milla, compared with the smell that hovers here over Grootmoedersdrift?

Look at Agaat! What must she think of you when she hears you allow yourself to be shouted at and beaten up? Every day at her post. Starched and ironed. A masterly maid! She plays you much better than I do, doesn't twitch a muscle when you find fault. And she learns from it, Milla, I'm telling you today, and don't forget it, all the time she's learning from us.

You tried to get to your feet, shouted against his tirade. Then why don't you go away? Why do you stay with me if I'm so dreadful?

You grabbed at him, thought he would come to his senses if he felt a touch. But he took your hands and threw them from him.

I can't go away, Milla, even if I wanted to. I'm stuck here! You batten on me! But I'm almost done, do you hear me, almost. Then you can advance again. You've provided a reserve, after all. In the hanslam camp. Agaat Lourier. Pre-raped. Yes, don't look at me like that, it's the truth! As no man can rape a woman. She's ready for you! To the bitter end! Because that much I can tell you now, I'm not going to make it all the way with you, Milla, that I know in my bones!

Jak kicked over the seed trays, trampled the new seedlings.

Pansies! he shouted.

The two of you think you can stop me from getting to Jakkie. You think you can scheme behind my back. You think you can make him soft, you and your skivvy. With your caterwauling and your carryings-on and your nods and winks. What is to become of him? What am I to tell him about his mother if he asks me? Have you thought of that? He knows more than you think in any case. And do you know how? Your skivvy tells him! Blow by blow!

Jak, you're out of your mind, you must get help, you said, as calmly and as firmly as you could.

Then he shoved you out from behind the plume bush almost into Jakkie standing there with his white bandage around his leg and a basket of dried pears that he'd fetched from the drying-trays. Jak didn't see him at first. You signalled at him with your hands behind you to be quiet, but his final sentences sounded out loud in the open. And then you saw Agaat running up the stoep steps and she was pressing her hands to her ears.

Help! What help! I'm not the one who was sick here first, Jak shouted after you, it's you, you're the one who's sick here. I'll get well, I'll get myself away from here, even if I have to do away with myself!

Jak looked into Jakkie's face for a single moment and half brushed over his eyes. Then he walked away in the opposite direction, towards the sheds, his bare upper body white in the sun.

Jakkie walked in front of you to the house. Hobbling.

Walk properly dammit, I know you're putting it on! you wanted to shout at him.

But how could you? You pressed both your hands to your glowing cheeks. A healthy flush. You looked at the palms of your hands, your forearms, criss-crossed with tiny itchy cuts all the way to the crook of your arm.

Agaat kept the announcement for dessert. Concentration-camp pudding. You could tell from its appearance that it hadn't been a good day in the kitchen. Baked in too much of a hurry, so that the sauce bubbled out at the sides, burnt black on the edge of the white enamel dish. All the food was burnt. She'd just disappeared in her usual manner in the afternoon and put in an appearance only after five to cook. And then she stood by while you were eating. It was a silence broken only by the rubbing of the creeper against the window frames, and now and again the chittering of a loose gutter in a gust of wind. You had a fire-red rash on your hands and arms and you were full of white streaks where the Lacto Calamine Lotion had dried on you.

You look as if you've been in the wars, Ma, said Jakkie.

Jak put his knife down hard.

Agaat carelessly slid the pudding-dish from her oven gloves onto the table.

With the back of his spoon Jakkie tapped the hard crust of the pudding.

Oops, little accident, he said.

Such little accidents will happen from time to time, you said. Why don't you rather tell us how exactly you hurt your leg? Did somebody tackle you badly, or what?

Then Agaat rammed the serving-spoon into the centre of the pudding and it stayed upright.

Just above Koggelmanklip, she said, to the left of the upper reservoir next to the kloof, there in the dry stubble and all along the protea bushes.

What about that? Jak asked.

There the foothill is burning.

I could swear I've been smelling something, Jakkie exclaimed and got to his feet before he remembered about his leg. Agaat darted him a sharp look.

Au! he exclaimed and fell back in his chair.

So why don't you speak up if you can smell it? she asked, her eyes fixed on Jakkie's face.

You ran out onto the front stoep. If that was where the fire had started, it had jumped in the meantime. There were several patches on fire all along the flank of the first foothill in front of the house. The flames were leaping up high and moving forward fast in the gusty wind. You could hear the crackling all the way from the yard. The strip of proteas and fynbos stretching from under the reservoir almost all the way to the wattles, was one seething mass of flames. You could hear from the loud cracks how the brittle wood of the wattles and the rooi-krans caught fire.

What I've always predicted will happen, has happened, you said.

Of course you've always predicted it and of course you've been say-ing for a long time we should eradicate the alien invaders because they burn too easily, because of course you're a nature conservationist but nobody ever listens to you until it's too late, Jak said without looking at you.

It was clear that there was nothing to be done about the fire. The labourers were arriving in batches on the yard. Dawid hooked the water cart to the tractor. There was a shouting for sacks and spades. But they remained standing there dazed in a little group, pressing their hats to their heads. Now and again looked at you on the stoep. Mak-ing a firebreak wasn't an option with the wind. That everyone knew, extinguishing even less.

Look! Look! Jakkie called. It was a klipspringer that had come over the river. The first one, with bewildered zig-zag leaps. As you stood there, more and more small game scattered over the yard. Hares, buck, skunks, even a jackal or two. You sent two farmboys to the river to res-cue the tortoises. You knew how they could run from fire.

My goats, Agaat said suddenly. Her hands flew to her cap. She pulled it deeper over her forehead, My goats, my goats, she mumbled. Jakkie gazed after her anxiously but she didn't return his look. Agaat's goats were tethered on the other side of the river in a patch of lucerne that she had sown there for her herd. Every year her cows calved and her hand-ful of slaughter-lambs she could sell well to the butcher in Swellendam. The goats were the latest addition, bought from the Okkenels.

The poor things are perishing of neglect down there at the huts, she'd said, the workers can rather buy cheap healthy goat's meat from me than have them suffer from mange and blowfly and get slaughtered before they're properly dead.

Gone she was with her quirt to go and untether her goats and drive them out.

Jak had the roofs of the sheds watered and the vehicles moved out. You had wet newspaper packed on the hay in the shed. You felt as if you were drifting a few centimetres above the ground. In a stupor you packed a few cases and put in food so that you could get out if need be. The yard was dry, there were bales of hay, dry lucerne in the shed. One spark on the thatched roof of the homestead could spell the end. All the stubble-fields further to the back, all the newborn lambs. But you couldn't feel anything more that day. A paralysis had come over you, a bafflement as you stood there on the stoep next to Jakkie. Nailed to one spot he was through his own lying, too proud, or too scared, to give in.

You watched him closely. What kind of man is this, this child of yours, who can in a crisis like this put up a front, who can persist so in his own deceit? How scared must he not be that his father will find out that he's been lying about his leg? How scared must he not be to leave Agaat in the lurch? How many such conspiracies had there been in the past of which you didn't even know?

Ma, I smell rain!

That was Jakkie's voice next to you. Little tongues of flame were licking through the oaks next to the drift. You pointed with your finger, more to silence him than anything else. You didn't want him to talk. There was something pleading in his tone, as if he wanted to console you, apologise to you. His gaze was anxious, he couldn't even start confessing.

The rain splashed out of the gusty south-easter. Fat plopping drops. A stray cloud, an evaporated day, scooped up by a rogue wind on the open sea and left exactly there where a fire was raging inland, a freak, something that didn't even happen in books because it didn't conform to any pattern of probability.

The three of you stood there on the stoep and watched the fire being rained into oblivion in front of your eyes.

A wet black soot covered the whole yard the next morning. The foothill in front of the house was burnt down from Luiperdskloof all the way to the slopes on The Glen side. From far away, there where you saw her standing at the crossing-place by the river, Agaat showed up against the blackened tree trunks. She was doing her rounds, making a survey of the damage. You turned around and went inside. You didn't want her to see you. But you noticed when she came in by the kitchen door, that her whole apron all the way to her cap was covered in fine black specks. You stretched out a hand. She jerked away her head.

Don't wipe, she said, it streaks.

Dawid came and told you an hour later in the backyard that one of Agaat's kids was lying with a broken neck there by the river and he didn't understand it, it wasn't tethered any more, and its mother had been driven to safety in the hanslam camp behind the house that night.

It's sopping wet and full of mud, Nooi. Dawid hesitated, cleared his throat.

Seems to me it stayed behind there, it seems somebody got at him quite badly, drowned it on purpose or something. There are skid marks there in the mud on the little bank. It was dragged in there, seems to me.

Agaat appeared in the doorway of the outside room with a black-and-white bundle of freshly laundered clothing in her arms.

Take it for yourselves, Dawid, clean it well before you slaughter, you have to make the best of such accidents. I suppose it lost its bearings in the fire.

She pressed past you. You could hear the clothes pegs rattling in her apron pocket.

Only later that day did you pick up the flat piece of river mud on the sitting room floor. Jakkie was sitting on the green sofa with Agaat on her knees in front of him. She was rubbing in his sore leg with Deep Heat.

Now what mud is this lying here? you wanted to ask but their faces forbade you.

The piece of trampled mud was grooved with the pattern of Agaat's school shoe. You said nothing. You went and threw it into the drain in the backyard. You stood there for a long time contemplating her washing, strange so on a Sunday, on the line. White and black it billowed and slapped there in the gusty south-easter. Two aprons, two pairs of socks, two caps, two black dresses. You went and took them down before they could blow full of soot again. You were surprised at the weight of the wind-dry material in your arms. Lighter than one would think, you thought at first, but when you hung it over the lower door of the outside room, it suddenly felt heavier, as if immediately drenched with the smell of the outside room: Red soap, Jik, Omo, Reckitt's Blue, starch, mothballs, borax, linoleum, body, bed, hair, Mum, calamine, rooibos tea, wool, thread, cloth.

You stood there for a long time in front of the dark hole of the door before you could turn away.

*

all at last cleared up the dominee the doctor the attorney attest now my last will and testament my farm on leasehold and also the homestead go to agaat until when she reaches eighty she has to hand it over to my son who must make further provision for her up to her death here is her funeral scheme their share as earlier to sow reverts to the okkenels they are henceforth answerable to agaat and she to them as mutually agreed the money from furniture cattle and yard sales and savings of the last seven years she may farm with on a modest scale to meet all her needs and requirements and to fall back on there is her pension reinforced herewith by hundred thousand rand plus extensively enlarged personal-nursing fee

my life I give into her hands for as long as she can carry me no hospital no pumps tubes wires except if I should want to determine differently later only for pain and inconvenience to relieve me of them I ask as I always have my drops agaat must dose me I am her sick merino sheep her exhausted soil her fallow land full of white stones her blown-up cow and acre of lodged grain her rusty wheat her drift from now on in flood she must have my hole dug and have the ring wall neatly whitewashed carve the meaning of everything on my headstone in her mouth I place my last word and in her eye over my departed body the last curse or blessing

because she knows what it is to be a farmer woman: windmill siphon corner post gate-latch and keystone the index of everything how do you convince her of her end how does one clear her up for death how does one get her switched off?

ask agaat that's how it's done

when her testament is at last written and her codicils when her estate has been wound up her herds diminished her yard tidied up and her cupboards and drawers cleaned out her giveaways sorted her workers given notice the whole rest of her personal detritus lipsticks powderboxes nail polish empty tissue-boxes burnt her funeral planned to the last detail her hole dug her coffin in the attic lined with satin

then ask agaat nicely

as edification she will hang the final index before the nose of her near-dead nooi:

Symptoms	Medicine	Therapy
Tiredness	Pyridostigmine	Energy conservation Mechanical aids Work modification
Spasticity Joint pains	Baclofen Tizanadine Sodium dantroline	Movement spectrum exercises
Cramps	Quinine sulphate	Massage
Fasciculation	Carbamazephine	Reassurance
Sialorrhea	Anticholinergic medicines	Salivary gland radiation Mechanical aspiration aids
Thick phlegm	Beta blocker	Consumption of liquids
Pseudo-bulbar laughing and crying	Tri-cyclic anti-depressant Lithium	None
Pulmonary secretions and expectoration	Dextrometorphane	Rehydration, humid air, aspiration aids
Choking	Sisapride	Change in food consistency
Depression	Anti-depressants	Counselling and psychiatric counselling Support
Insomnia	Opiates	Hospital bed
Pulmonary embolus	Bronchial dilators Morphine	Non-invasive or permanent ventilation Ventilator
Constipation	Bisacodyl	Liquids
Stasis of the colon	Lactulose	Energetic exercise

*

14 November 1978

So then Jakkie brought a little girlfriend home for the first time after the matric exams. More to satisfy Jak than anything else I think because he doesn't seem to be wildly excited. Was quite the little gentleman but I know him his heart isn't in it. The poor little thing talks nineteen to the dozen from nervousness & Jak drinks too much & of course couldn't stand it any more after a while & goes & fetches an old poetry anthology of mine from the shelf. No she must realise the little Isabel in this house high literature is read. How well does she know her poetry he wants to know. Jakkie still tried to put a stop to it but Jak was in full declamatory flight. Oh show me the place where once we stood once when you were mine. They fled out of there the children as soon as they had a chance ai I was so embarrassed.

Apparently Jakkie wanted to take her along to Witsand but now of course she doesn't want to come any more. A. smiles about this because now she'll have Jakkie to herself. He won't fall for her type says A. she's too light for him for what type then I ask. The fynbos & cave type says Agaat or spring tide whatever that may mean but she seems quite taken with her own diagnosis.

The last few holidays he's spent long hours reading in his room with a plate of A.'s cookies except when J. orders him to varnish the woodwork or otherwise he goes for long runs on his own or goes fishing with A. & reads her stories & poems. Tanned & muscled the child. Can sometimes not believe how attractive he is. Something of a daredevil too, just like his father, thinks nothing of swimming into the sea & emerging somewhere else far away. The girls peek at him & he banters with them but that's all. He sometimes goes out when there's a party & stays out late but then I always hear afterwards he found a book to read somewhere in a room. Perhaps this year I should have a party for him at our house to celebrate his results.

They'll hear early in January he says he's not worried about it. But does he have other worries? He can be so absent. Easy-going in the daily round but reserved in a new way the last few years. He feels further & further away from me. J. says it's because he thinks he's better than us since he's been to Paul Roos he's got a swollen head in that town of snobs they say it's contagious. I say Jakkie is not as self-satisfied as his father he's looking for himself. Look what look! Jak exclaims his country is looking for him let him go & put some hair on his chest in the Defence Force the enemy is ready to take over the country. I tell Jak for somebody who can think up such outlandish theories on his own wife his political pronouncements really are extremely simple-minded.

19 November 1978
Went & made the mistake of wanting to take Jakkie along to church this morning. At first he didn't want to. Said it was too hot for a suit but J. said to him my boy you'll do as I say. Not that J. is all that religious either it's more a matter of being seen in the right place & perhaps that's what irks Jakkie.

He's been through his catechism & all along with the other boys in Stellenbosch & I see his Bible lying there on his night-table but how things are with him spiritually I wouldn't know he talks to me about nothing except trivialities. Today he really had the fidgets in the pew & sighed & sat with his forehead in his hands & bit his cheeks & vanished into thin air when we got here & he's not turning up for lunch.

Dominee preached on the spies in the land of Canaan. A wee bit over-inspired perhaps but still a striking analogy that he drew. Numbers 13. Send thou men, that they may search the land of Canaan, which I give unto the children of Israel: Of every tribe of their fathers shall ye send a man & these were their names: Of the tribe of Reuben, Shammua the son of Zaccur. Of the tribe of Simeon, Shaphat the son of Hori. Of the tribe of Judah, Caleb the son of Jephunneh etc. The application turned out to be the border war & the instruction to the Afrikaner spies just as to the children of Israel & see the land what it is; & the people that dwelleth therein, whether they be strong or weak, few or many & about Caleb who said Let us go up at once & possess it; for we are well able to overcome it. And about the nay-sayers who said it was impossible & brought up an evil report of the land which they had searched unto the children of Israel such as that the children of Anak were descended from giants & would crush the Israelites like locusts & about the people who murmured against Moses & Aaron: Wherefore hath the Lord brought us unto this land, to fall by the sword, that our wives & children should be the prey? The dominee warned from the pulpit against false prophets who speak excellent Afrikaans & cite the Bible & don't hesitate to undermine their own nation in their mother-tongue & in their church. Beyers Naude of course & that other Kotze dominee from Johannesburg. Then he followed through the analogy & concluded quite strikingly with a list of the sons of the Overberg who have been called up for the January intake: Of the Delports of Groot-bos, Erik, the son of Flip, of the Du Toits of Riviersonderend, Hugo, the son of Lieb, of the Neethlings of Lindeshof, Jurie, the son of Gaf. Then Jak said half in jest in the car: And of the de Wets of Grootmoedersdrift: Jakobus Christiaan, the son of J.C. Senior & Kamilla née Redelinghuys. Would Jakkie not go & get up on his hind legs about it something ter-rible heaven knows why it's not as if it was meant ill.

4 July 1979 Front stoep
Mountain still overcast after the snow yesterday dark blue in the south with rainbow it's cold & still perhaps another precipitation advancing. Listening to Schubert's string quintet in C major (that second move-ment, where does it spring from? from the approach of death?) some or other moth that has eaten the covers of my records ai I have so little time for myself on this farm. Feel as if I've forgotten everything I ever learnt. J. gone to drop Jakkie at Cape Town station. Didn't want to go along. A. neither. Took leave here at home for her sake she can't exactly give him a hug in her apron there amongst all the people.

Lots of talking at table again last night A. standing there with hr hands on her stomach hr face in the shadows. I know what she's thinking: He's still so young. The plan is that directly after his basic training at Valhalla & the officer's course in Waterkloof he'll join the Air Force permanently & after his flying training at Langebaan Road go to uni-versity for his engineering degree three birds with one stone says J. he won't have to interrupt his studies later for national service he earns a salary while he's studying & with every exam that he passes he gets more stripes & further promotion is guaranteed. Apparently the best & most honourable career for a young man in SA today & if he's lucky he'll get the chance on top of it all to wipe out communists.

Wonder where A. is. Disappeared into thin air when they left here. What on earth does she do to console herself?

4 July 6 o'clock
J. not back yet. A. is though a plume of smoke in the chimney. Com-fort fire. Must be cold after her escapades. Tracked hr this afternoon down next to the wild-fig avenue & further down next to the river she couldn't cross rushing water so there she stood & did hr funny

movements forward & back turn around stamping the feet the arm up the cap down. Could only half make out hr singing by standing at the water upstream & downstream. Snowstorm. Perhaps not all there in the top storey.

Quarter past 6

Just heard the door of the outside room open & and peeked behind the woodshed at her feeding the hanslammers again the singing quite gives me the shivers. Couldn't make head or tail perhaps if I try to write down what I remember of it. Child is gone/time is short/put in the oar/ shift round the rudder/put up the chock/wind up the ratchet/under the mill sits the one-armed dwarf/hear her turn/it's the meal it's the snow it's the salt it's the bone/listen to it grind/agaat agaat agaat.

Rather ominous. Typical. Always makes herself larger than she is at times of crisis.

8 July 1979

Has snowed again. Light sprinkling lower down than yesterday just like castor sugar. Can smell it clean white sheets piled up in the sky. A. always excited by weather conditions. Have to give hr extra jobs to keep her occupied. Should perhaps increase the size of her herds a bit so that she has more to see to. See the first letters to Jakkie are already written & lying ready for posting on the sideboard.

9 July 1979

Perhaps I should really try again this year to make something special of Agaat's birthday (31!) now with Jakkie gone like that & doing his own thing I get the feeling that the diary-keeping doesn't really make very much sense any more. Don't have that much to report on any more. Agaat is Agaat. I think I made the best of hr that I could. More I think than many other people could have managed. Can't complain apart from that. She's now quite a housekeeper & keeps a sharp eye on all aspects of the farming. Perhaps with Jakkie finally gone there will in any event now be less occasion for tension here in the house & she'll from now on be able just to live with us without strife.

Maybe bake a large chocolate cake? Place a nice bunch of flowers in front of hr door as a surprise & on the 12th drive with her to Witsand? She's so fond of the sea when it rains. So many shades of grey & white she always says such an almost black sea.

16

W·H·O S·T·A·R·T·E·D T. F·I·R·E O·N M·O·U·N·T·A·I·N, I ask.

I look at the alarm clock. It's taken ten minutes to spell out, even with Agaat's abbreviations of articles and conjunctions.

Do you think it was me by any chance? Agaat asks with her eyes. She looks away quickly.

Yes, I signal, according to our customary code. One blink with both eyes.

She looks at me just long enough to catch my reply.

Hottentot madonna, she says.

She pushes at the side of her cap, she grasps the stick of the duster more firmly, she lets me continue, she taps on the chart. After every tap she looks at me. A tap B tap C tap D tap.

D is right I blink with my right eye. It must be so boring for her. Then she ticks from A again. I stop her on I, I is right.

And then she has to start tapping again from the beginning, as far as D. D·I·D We again spelt 'did'.

D·I·D Y·O·U S·T·A·R·T· T·H·E F·I·R·E . . .

In the hayloft? she completes my sentence. Quite correct, that's what I wanted to ask. She places the duster upright in the corner. End of conversation.

I should have stuck to the weather, to the rainfall figures, the sheep-stealing statistics for the year of Our Lord 1996. I should have kept to pure farming matters, to how she wants to run things henceforth here on Grootmoedersdrift. I should have known that by this time.

She comes to stand by my bed. She folds her hands on her stomach. Her reply comes direct and without hesitation.

The cream separator, she says, to ensure that it works properly, place it on a solid foundation and make sure that it is dead level. If a machine separates badly, that may be because it is turned too fast or too slow. The speed can be adjusted only when the milk-supply tank is half empty. If a first-class machine does not separate properly, it is because the supply tank is out of balance and vibrates excessively, or because the centrifuge is not calibrated in the spring when the milk is poor and again in the autumn when it is richer. Watch the spout where the cream runs through. If the cream tends to cover the spout, the speed is too high for the quantity of milk passing through the supply tank, if it emerges from the spout in scallops, it is being turned too slowly. If the cream falls from the spout into the cream dish almost but not quite perpendicularly, that is in the case of the vast majority of creamers about the right consistency. In any case rinse the supply tank regularly with skimmed milk.

Farmer's Handbook. I was asking for it. Douse the fire with cream. Extremely original. What argument can I bring against that? She will recite all her texts to me rather than talk to me openly.

I flicker my eyes. Bravo! that means.

She ignores me. She bends to unhook the urine bag. She drags the chamber pot under the open tube to catch the drops. Tip, I hear it drop on the enamel, tip.

Leroux first came to fit the catheter for the urine bag and then came to make the hole for the gut bag. Home surgery with local anaesthetic. Agaat's decision. The wound was supposed to heal first before the bag could be attached, but it wouldn't. Now every time she empties the bag she has to perform a major disinfection around the stoma. She enjoys it. All my orifices interest her. The more I have the better.

I had to be moved as little as possible, was the consensus. The pan was too high for me. So lower the madam. That was what Agaat decided. Make a hole in her side. She threatens me every day with the feeding tube in my trachea as well, but I refuse. I don't want another artificial portal punched into me. I don't want to eat anything more. I want to talk. There's a lot to talk about. Now that we've found a way with the alphabet chart.

She holds up the full urine bag for me to see. Dark yellow, almost amber-coloured it is, but not clear.

Cloudy, she says, but it makes the bluest blue.

She opens the stoep door, holds the bag far away from her, walks out with small brisk steps. I watch the mirror. There she is in image now. She knows the range of the reflection, she'll see to it that she stays within it.

Douse the fire with cream, put out the flames with my last dark fluids.

I mustn't complain, I was asking for it.

The hydrangeas are deep purplish-blue, just the colour for my funeral arrangements. That's what she wants to say with the whole palaver of emptying the bag so conspicuously. She knows I can see her in the mirror. There are other hydrangeas around the corner as well where she could go and empty it out. But these are from the mother stock. Here she learnt to empty her own little chamber pot.

That's the kind of risk I run since I've been able to talk to her. Her punishments become subtler. The message is: Your influence will be felt for a long time yet, even unto the capillary roots of the plants of your garden. I'll keep up the old traditions for you.

I see her crouch down between the leaves. Only her behind sticks out.

I understand, Agaat. You turn your arse on the last conflagration that you've perpetrated here in the sickbay.

She stands back. She examines her handiwork. Beautiful voluptuous, purple orbs of flowers.

Pissy, pissy in the pot, who makes the bluest of the lot?

Am I imagining things, or is she shaking her head there?

How dare I ask her such things? Imagine, she an arsonist! Am I going out of my mind now?

Go ahead and shake your head, Agaat. I know it was you. Who else?

She puts the empty bag down on the lawn. Here come the little scissors from the top pocket of her apron. She snips one, two, three, four, five flowers. She moves out of range. She'll go round the back to the kitchen to put them in water, then go and select a vase in the sitting room. Perhaps I'll be lucky. Perhaps I'll be given flowers next to my bed today. That will teach me to keep my questions to myself.

I wonder about the timing of the sudden appearance of our new means of communication. The old alphabet chart. Would she have remembered it all of a sudden out of the blue? A technique she read about long ago in the pamphlets and conveniently forgot about? Or did she avoid it because she was too tired? Because she realised she would be empowering me in my last moments here where I no longer hesitate to speak my mind? Because she could guess what would come out, what had to come out between us?

Perhaps it will never come out, perhaps there's even less of a chance now than before. Perhaps that which has to be said has nothing to do with the truth.

And do I myself know what it is? Is the truth beyond what happened or didn't happen, what happened how and where? Beyond the facts? I'm the one who's being tested to see whether I have the words to arrive there.

Perhaps it was the maps that gave her the idea. The place names. The pointing at the dots of the towns till I nod, yes, tell me about Protem, tell me about Klipdale, what happened there, what we did there, who we saw there.

Shall I ask her? How did you come upon the idea of hanging it there, the alphabet chart, the old yellowed, varnished cardboard sheet with the fold down the middle, with the ornate capitals and the Bible pictures and the scenes from the history of salvation, stiff prophets and visions amongst grapevines and sheaves of corn?

I could ask, now that I can pose questions.

Why did you keep it till now? After all, you've known all along that I'm itching to talk, you could surely have guessed that I'm lying here brooding over all my life?

I could confront her with it. Perhaps she'd only wave a little blue book in front of my nose. Because she did find it after all then, the third parcel. About her first life on Grootmoedersdrift. Barely alive and I her source of life.

Now it's the other way round.

Me dying and she to accompany me.

Who's going to give in first? On the facts of the past? Or does our assignment lie here in this present?

Here I'm cutting my own throat now, she said when she hung up the alphabet.

Did I hear aright? She whispered it on the inhalation.

Here I'm cutting my own throat now.

But whose throat is it really? It's my spelt-out words that she has to pronounce for me, it's my sentences that she has to complete aloud for me.

Who'd want to bluff at the end? That everything is in order? Forgive and forget and depart in peace?

Perhaps it would have been better to have kept to eye signals to the very end, without any chance of a retort on my part. Perhaps we could have brought the matter to a workable conclusion if we'd resigned ourselves to the list of questions?

Are you cold? Are you hot? Are you hungry? Are you tired? Too dark? Too light? Do you want to poo? Do you want to pee? Do you want to read? Do you want to listen to SAfm?

Yes and no.

But it's getting more complicated. Now she's added to the alphabet auxiliary lists on slips of paper, opening phrases and conjunctions. She's stuck them up there close to hand around the chart, short cuts by which we can arrive more quickly at the point. They stir and rustle with every draught or current here in the room, they flutter up and down when Agaat walks past, the loose slips, as if they were alive.

I am, I wish, I fear, I hope, I believe.

Because, but, and, nevertheless, notwithstanding, even so.

Necessary conjunction which betonkeneth concord, who wrote that again?

Milla. Jak. Agaat. Jakkie.

I'm no longer hungry, and I'm beyond tired . . .

Whom did I love in my lifetime and why?

I have, I will, I can, I want. Or not. I would be able to. I would have wanted. If I could have it over, then . . . What might have been.

There's a whole grammar developing there on the wall. Every day there's more of it. Question mark, exclamation mark, swearword, dots to mark an implication. A skeleton of language, written down in print and in script with a Koki chalk, bigger, more complicated than Agaat on her own, than I or the two of us together could think up. If it had to be fleshed out as well . . . muscles, skin, hair, nerves, glands . . .

How, when, who, why, what . . .

But my nerves are extinct and my muscles are moist cotton wool, my hair grey strands, my skin worn, my glands dry dumplings. My secretions trickle out of me through tubes. My poo and my pee are no longer my own. My sphincters no longer open and close me. I am one might say permeable.

Why would she want now of all times to invest me with language?

Up, down, under, before, behind, above, in.

Or perhaps 'invest with' is the wrong expression here.

Goad with, perhaps.

She is the one who takes up Japie. She can put him down whenever she wants. Or she can pick him up and walk out and go and dust somewhere. Or she can turn him round to point his stick at the map.

Japie mostly stays in the corner of the room. She holds him in the left hand, she always starts from the beginning again, she points, letter by letter. A is for Adam, B for Babel , C for Christ, our Redeemer and Lord. She looks at what I signal and she points and she points until there's a word, three words, half a sentence, and then she starts guessing.

Don't put words into my mouth, exclamation mark, I then have to spell out for her. Don't anticipate my meanings, don't impose the wrong stress, wrong nuances on me. Exclamation, exclamation, exclamation!

My protest is not of much use. She gets impatient when it takes too long. She wants to make my sentences flow for me. She wants me to sing. She's looking for a rhythm. A march from the FAK.

Onward, onward, ever onward, by forest and by foam, ever shall we wander, ever shall we roam.

I can see it in her face. Shift-boss habits. She taps the beat on the railing of the bed. Then the words come.

Don't shirk! There's a nation to lead, there's a war-cry to heed, there's work! There's no glory or fame, there's no compromise tame, there's but following the hot bright flame. Come on!

If I have managed to produce something, an exposition, complete with nevertheless and notwithstanding, it's my turn to exert pressure. Then she must reply. It's only common decency, her responding, I spelt out for her. But she often remains quiet. Or she says, next sentence please. Or she shrugs her shoulders, which means, you answer it yourself. Or she puts down the duster and walks out. Or she looks at me until I shut my eyes.

Put in a bookmark, she says then, then we can remember where we were, this is one of your long stories again, and I can't see how it's to end.

I was alone, I felt useless, I wanted to do something for my fellow humans.

She goes to stand by the stoep door and looks out. Or she takes up after a while where we left off, and leaves me talking to myself.

I did not realise what a big responsibility it would be, I did not think far enough.

Just go ahead and forget that I'm here, her face says, I just spell out everything for you and say it out loud so that you can hear what you sound like.

Jak was always against it and I resisted him, for years I resisted him but the pressure was too great and then I gave in.

She can't always keep her voice neutral. She charges my sentences with her own resonances. Disbelief, emphasis, mockery. She adds on and improvises. To my own ears I sound like running commentary rather than original intention.

Do something for your fellow humans? Or do something with your fellow humans or to your fellow humans? Fellow human or in- or super-human? Or half human? Less human than yourself?

Sometimes when we've completed a sentence, she doesn't repeat it at all, so that I lose my thread amongst stray words.

Sorry. Powerless. Guilty. I am. I shall be. But. How am I to. Die. Question mark.

Then she changes the subject. Or she says, for heaven's sake get to the point, Ounooi, you're much too long-winded again today.

As if there were endless days extending before me. As if tomorrow could be much different for me from today.

It takes so much time, this business. Clarity is not guaranteed. It causes misunderstandings instead, that we then laboriously have to clear up again. The tapping and winking and spelling is harder on my eyes than the splint ever was heavy on my hand. Her prefabricated phrases block me rather than help me, my language feels like a brutal instrument with which I'm torturing myself. How long will I still be able to blink my eyes? The left wants to droop shut, the right opens wider than I'm used to. If my eyelids freeze, that's the end.

The chance, I'm getting a last chance. Perhaps I should rather associate freely than try to explain point by point, let her see who I've become in the meantime, here speechless on my bed, delirious, yearning, a poet of losses, a teller of legends.

The task weighs more heavily on my mind than the writing of my last words when I could still write. It's more momentous than the making of my inventories for the clearing-out, my will, my self-determination codicil.

It's more difficult than any last wish. It causes complications at a stage when she, and I, had hoped that things would become easier. Now the close will be more difficult than either of us could ever have predicted.

I can understand very well that she wants to keep the talking within limits, has established a fixed structure for it. She keeps us to it strictly. One hour in the morning, one hour in the evening.

Before she goes to bed, I'm granted another few sentences, if she feels the need herself, when she's done reading from the blue booklets, the last parcel from the sideboard, the first lot that I filled with my writing, without abbreviations, full particulars with the explicitness of the beginner.

She took a long time to remove the string with which it was still bound. The first few days that it was lying here, she fiddled with the knot a few times, but then let it be again. At length she snipped it off with her scissors and started reading in a whispered intake of breath, as if she wanted to vacuum the words.

When she's had enough, then she gets up, then she takes the duster. Then I know it helps her to talk to me, but mostly about trivialities. Harmless.

It helps her to believe that I'm harmless. She even wants to believe in my goodness, it seems to me. But then I have to be potent as well, because what would virtue be for Agaat without power?

That's something she can't tolerate.

If on the other hand, as happens on some days, she makes me out to be entirely bad, then she feels that she's bad herself. And that she doesn't want to be. That she can't be. Her name is Good.

Would it be good to forgive me? It would be too easy. And it would solve nothing.

Would it be good to take revenge? It's been a long time since that satisfied her, avenging yourself on a helpless victim is not interesting.

How can I help her?

Too many sentences to spell out. I must keep my text simple. I can't tell her story on her behalf, and if she's too tongue-tied and has too little pride to do it herself, then it's not my fault.

How many Jerseys do you now have in your herd? That I'm allowed to ask. How many heifers are you going to sell in autumn? What's your price? What does the market look like? She supplies the figures.

If you carry on like this, you're going to be a rich farmer one day, I'm allowed to say.

What good is it going to do me? her face asks then. When she sees that I've caught her out in self-pity, she backtracks quickly. As with the tirade yesterday.

Yes, I just have to give, give, give nowadays to keep the labourers happy. The creatures of late seem to want to guzzle and guts, even steal the dogs' food out of their bowls around the back. Before you fell ill they were still happy with flour and coffee and now and again their smoked pork and their sack of beans and onions and pumpkins. But no, now it's a sheep a month on top of it, and then I have to provide for the women and children as well, if the one isn't suffering from this, then the other complains of that. They eat you out of house and home and they're too lazy to work, they just want to lie in their hovels. I told Dawid a long time ago the whole lot must go, I want casual labourers, or better still, I get in a team of Transkei kaffirs every now and again, they're happy anyway with mealie-meal porridge and sour milk.

I said nothing in reply. And she knew why.

In the silence that followed, she took up her embroidery and sat working wordlessly for two hours. That's the way it often goes since we've been able to talk, as if she's trying to gather strength for the next conversation.

She's sitting just too far away for me to see what's she's doing there on her cloth.

She'll show me when she's done, she says.

Apparently it contains all the stitches in the book.

Diagonal ripple-stitch, odd wave-stitch, step-stitch, honeycomb-stitch, blanket-stitch, hemstitch, paving-stitch, wreath-stitch.

There's still a lot to fill in, she says, filling-in patterns for drawn-fabric work, sheaves, ears of corn, stars, eyelets, flowers, diamonds, wheels, shadow-blocks.

Some parts she has to unpick and redo, though much smaller, otherwise not everything fits in so well. It takes much longer than she thought to get everything in place, she says.

Everything? Every what thing? Rather say it's a pastime till I'm in my place six feet under.

Sometimes when I can no longer bear it, the two of us together like this, trapped in the room, without any escape, I plead without disguise. I flicker through my tears. One eye flutters more rapidly than the other.

Please, talk to me, I want to talk, I want to explain things.

Sometimes she consents, but venture one sentence into the maze, and she stops.

Look for the butterfly, Agaat! You've seen it before! Show it to me!

But mainly she ignores it when I'm like that. Mouth set in a sulk. Chin out. Her eyes flash. The message is clear.

Your soul! Me having to look for your soul! Bugger your soul!

I can guess what she's feeling, what sentences she's addressing to me in her heart. Once I spelt it out for her word by word.

It's too late for tears now, tears just make you choke. So choose. Choke or talk about things you can afford to talk about.

She pretended not to understand whose words these were.

I never cry, she said, you're the one who cries.

Just so, I said.

She just gave me a look and walked out.

I'm not made of glass, she said later, while she was soaping my arms.

She was washing me very gently. I don't think I'd ever felt her touch me so gently, as if she were afraid I'd break.

I'm not made of glass.

She knows she's transparent to me, she knows I can read her thoughts and express them too. It's no longer all that safe for her in this sickbay. She's decided to restore my voice to me. And she wants to honour her decision. She knows she's caught in her own snare.

Gently she soaped me. Once more on an inhalation she said: Not of glass!

She was washing my arm with her strong hand. The washcloth disappeared a long time ago. My skin is too thin. When she saw the dampness in my eyes, she stopped immediately.

No, not again, she said, and rubbed me dry with a rough towel.

That was yesterday.

This morning I woke up again with the headache. Through the haze in my head I wanted to understand it, the dynamic between us. I can't understand it. It's too difficult for me. I wanted to explain it when the talking-hour struck.

Then something entirely different to what I'd planned came out of me. Because I feel so powerless, so needy, then I attacked her, then I started casting aspersions upon her.

You and the fires of Grootmoedersdrift, Agaat. The fire on the mountain, the fire in the hayloft, was that you?

Accusations have always set her off. And complaints. And criticism. If I can't mollify her, that's the only alternative. I can anger her. And if I can anger her, I can get angry myself. That would be better than nothing.

Who's the arsonist here on the farm? Who's the great setter of fires amongst us?

That hit the mark. All that she could do, was to draw off my pee and get out and turn her backside on me to pick hydrangeas, the ones far down, those that are a bit tousled already with sun and water. The prettiest ones, the strongest, those she's saving. It's a matter of timing.

Blue-purple hydrangeas for my funeral, with the white dahlias and the white Joseph's lilies, nicely rounded off with a little ribbon of crape, I can just see it.

The quarter-hour strikes in the front room. Here comes the preview. In the grey vase. The vase that was not on the clearing-out list. Could still be used at my funeral, I thought to myself. Scenes from coming attractions, as Jak would have said. Not yet quite the demure style of the funeral arrangement. Pretty, lively, informally arranged are the voluptuous blue heads with the yellow privet branches and the bronze-coloured foliage of the prunus nigra, sprays of abelia, orange Cape honeysuckle, a few orange roses. And to round it off, under the base, how else? a few large exuberant bronze leaves of coleus, the plant we call fire-on-the-mountain.

Just look at the hydrangeas, says Agaat, they're flowering as if it's Christmas, I must take cuttings.

She clears a space on the night-table next to me. Her neck is stiff.

Just picture it, is written all over her face, what it will look like on the half-moon table at the front door, there where the guests will be entering. Sincerest condolences, Agaat, it must be a great loss for you. Will that be good enough for you? Or do you think the orange and all the branches are a bit too wild?

If I could I would like to tap the stick of the feather duster on her face. Alphabet of the underworld. Percussion band.

Hands on hips she stands and surveys her handiwork. Well then, Ounooi? Looks as if you want to have a bit of a chat, we have half an hour left.

She takes the duster by the head.

We'll gather lilacs, she sings on an inhaled breath.

A B C D E F G H

I blink H and A and G and swearword on the auxiliary list that's supposed to indicate feeling.

Wow now, says Agaat, which one now?

Y·O·U, exclamation mark, I spell, N·O·O·N·D·A·Y W·I·T·C·H.

Well I never, says Agaat, how's that for a parting shot. What else?

S·A·R·C·A·S·T·I·C, I spell, Y·O·U K·N·O·W W·H·A·T I M·E·A·N.

No, I don't know, says Agaat, you'll just have to spell it out.

F·I·R·E O·N T. M·O·U·N·T·A·I·N, I spell. I roll my eyes at the flower arrangement.

Yes, doesn't it look pretty with the blue, says Agaat.

If I'm trying to be difficult here on my deathbed, is the message, she'll pretend to think I'm senile.

Can there be a doubler barrel? How do I deal with it?

B·R·O·W·N S·U·I·T·C·A·S·E, I spell.

Where, when, why, question mark, Agaat taps for me on her scraps of paper. They flutter like leaves. I blink Y·E·S Y·E·S exclamation mark.

She puts down the stick. She reformulates my question for me in my own strain, with all my modulations of indignation. And with her own increment of pepper.

What, I ask you for the how-manieth time, happened to your brown suitcase that I put on the half-shelf of the washstand in the outside room, on the day of your birthday, twelfth July in the year of our Lord nineteen sixty, when you moved in there? What happened to all your possessions from the back room? To the pretty dresses that I hung up there for you on the railing behind the curtain, a red and a blue and a yellow one, specially made for you with my highly pregnant body and all? To your first shoes that I had bronzed?

Absolutely right, I blink. How excellently you can guess at the senile thoughts of an old woman. What is your reply to this?

Agaat stands back a little, hands on her stomach. She looks me straight in the eye. The cutting-up of an ox is her reply. Fluently she recites.

Sirloin, cut into flat slices and fried in a pan.

Wing rib, suitable for pot-roasting, bones may also be removed and meat rolled.

Flat rib, suitable for pot-roasting, may be rolled.

Prime rib, suitable for pot-roasting, may be rolled.

Mid-rib, suitable for pot-roasting, may be rolled.

Silverside and topside, suitable for corned beef, pot-roasting, biltong. Shank, may be roasted, but more suitable for salting and boiling.

Thick flank, may be salted and boiled or stewed.

Cheek, can be stewed.

Neck, for soup or stewing.

Collarbone, for soup.

Brisket, best suited to pickling and boiling.

Bones, are generally sold to kaffirs.

Tail, soup and stew.

Hoof and shin, brawn.

Pauper's rib, for soup and stew.

Do you want to hear about the cuts of the birthday hanslam as well? Agaat asks, the nice fresh braai chops for the nice fresh kitchen-skivvy? The two of them, skivvy and lamb, both cut up much better than an old tough cow, let me tell you that!

She falls in with her stick. Oh Japie is my darling she sings, so early in the morning.

Next? she asks.

V·E·R·Y F·U·N·N·Y, I spell.

She waits for the follow-up. Doesn't bat an eyelid. Lets me spill my guts. Fills me in. Tops me up.

W·H·A·T W·E·R·E Y·O·U D·O·I·N·G F·I·R·S·T N·I·G·H·T O·N M·O·U·N·T·A·I·N I·N Y·O·U·R U·N·I·F·O·R·M, question mark. S·A·W Y·O·U W·I·T·H B·I·N·O·C·S, full stop. F·U·N·N·Y S·T·E·P·S + L·A·T·E·R W·I·T·S·A·N·D E·A·R·L·Y M·O·R·N·I·N·G I·N Y·O·U·R C·L·O·T·H·E·S I·N W·A·V·E·S, full stop. S·A·T·A·N·I·C R·I·T·E·S, exclamation mark. M·A·I·D·S S·A·Y Y·O·U A·R·E P·O·S·S·E·S·S·E·D W·A·N·D·E·R A·R·O·U·N·D A·T N·I·G·H·T + L·E·A·V·E M·E H·E·R·E A·L·O·N·E, full stop. N·O·T T·A·K·E·N I·N B·Y Y·O·U·R I·N·N·O·C·E·N·C·E, comma, W·I·T·C·H, exclamation mark. = M·Y D·E·A·T·H N·O·T E·N·O·U·G·H F·O·R Y·O·U, question mark. O·N W·H·A·T C·L·I·M·A·X A·R·E Y·O·U S·E·T, question mark, swearword.

Agaat stands back from the chart, the wall full of fluttering bits of paper. She presses against her cap. She places the duster in the corner.

This time her answer is taken from the embroidery book.

Shadow-work, she says, is a form of white embroidery that is within the reach of all because the technique is very simple. It is suitable for table linen, bedspreads, pillow covers for babies, bridal veils, blouses, christening robes, children's clothes. Shadow-work is done on transparent cloth and from Italy we get special fine linen for the purpose. It can however also be done on silk organza or a good-quality Swiss organdie. Artificial fibres are not recommended.

M·O·C·K, I spell.

Mock turtle, says Agaat.

D·I·D Y·O·U D·R·O·W·N T. K·I·D T·H·A·T E·V·E·N·I·N·G O·F T. F·I·R·E, question mark. + W·H·Y, question mark. B·E·H·I·N·D M·E S·A·T·A·N, exclamation mark.

You're really jumping around this morning, says Agaat, I can't keep up.

She pulls her cap lower on her head, she stands alert for my next instalment.

W·H·Y D·I·D Y·O·U D·I·G U·P T. L·A·M·B E·A·R F·R·O·M T·H·E B·I·N, comma, W·I·T·H W·H·A·T S·U·P·E·R·S·T·I·T·I·O·N·S D·I·D Y·O·U I·N·F·E·C·T J·A·K·K·I·E, question mark.

It was my own hanslam, says Agaat, her voice uninflected. She looks out of the glass door.

What hanslam? Agaat always had nurslings, lambs, pigs, meerkat, every kind of nursling.

Sweetflour, says Agaat with her back to me.

Sweetflour? I remember Sweetflour. Discarded. One of a triplet. Full-milk Agaat fed her with extra cream and a teaspoon of clean slaked lime, from the bottle, eighteen times a day, at blood heat as her book says, reduced to six times a day, until she started eating oats and lucerne by herself. She was five months old and she came when Agaat called her. The one we slaughtered that day was a nursling wether with a fat belly.

Agaat turns back from the door. Her eyebrows on question marks. I blink at the board, show I want to spell something. She takes her stick.

Y·O·U L·I·E, exclamation mark, I spell.

I would surely never have made her slaughter her own hanslam? I would have checked up first. But did I? That ear wasn't marked. That I remember, and Dawid had called I should come and have a look when he'd caught the lamb, but I didn't go, I wanted to keep an eye, Agaat was busy ironing her first double sheet on her own that morning, I showed her how one folds it along its length on the ironing board, how one sprinkles water on it.

And, says Agaat, on top of that it was my birthday, twelfth July, you'd very kindly taught me that that was the day on which the Lord gave myself to me as a present. So then you forgot it in your hurry to get me out of the house. Then you pretended the outside room was heaven.

Agaat stuffs the knuckle of her small hand into her mouth as if she wanted to push in a stopper so that nothing more can come out of there. She regards me over the hand, for a long time. I see the entreaty in her eyes: Please, Ounooi, don't force me to get angry, I've long since given up being angry, I don't want to be angry, you provoke me, what is it you want from me? Tell me and I'll give it to you, whatever you ask, if it's within my power.

She stands ready with the stick.

H·Y·P·O·C·R·I·T·E, exclamation mark. D·O·N·T M·A·K·E T·H·O·S·E S·O·P·P·Y E·Y·E·S A·T M·E, exclamation mark. H·O·W M·A·N·Y T·I·M·E·S M·O·R·E A·R·E Y·O·U G·O·I·N·G T·O C·O·N·F·R·O·N·T M·E W·I·T·H I·T, question mark exclamation mark.

It's going too slowly. I think too fast. I only get the odd word out.

W·H·Y A·R·E Y·O·U O·N T. S·C·E·N·E S·O S·O·O·N A·T E·V·E·R·Y D·I·S·A·S·T·E·R W·O·N·D·E·R A·B·O·U·T Y·O·U·R T·R·U·E C·O·L·O·U·R·S S·I·C·K C·O·M·F·O·R·T·E·R F·I·R·E E·X·T·I·N·G·U·I·S·H·E·R S·L·I·M·E·K·N·O·C·K·E·R D·I·S·T·R·U·S·T D·E·V·I·L.

Agaat composes her own sentences from the words. I compose mine. They're quite different, the versions that emerge.

That's enough now, Ounooi, you're just upsetting yourself. I can't understand you. She puts down the stick.

I insist.

She picks it up again.

Y·O·U D·O·N·T W·A·N·T T·O U·N·D·E·R·S·T·A·N·D M·E, exclamation mark. Y·O·U P·L·A·Y D·I·R·T·Y, exclamation mark. D·O Y·O·U T·H·I·N·K Y·O·U A·R·E G·O·D W·I·T·H Y·O·U·R S·T·I·C·K, question mark exclamation mark.

By nature utterly indisposed, disabled and made opposite to all good, and wholly inclined to all evil, says Agaat.

H·O·W D·I·D Y·O·U G·E·T T·O T. D·A·M S·O Q·U·I·C·K·L·Y T·O P·U·T T. P·A·R·C·E·L W·I·T·H T. C·H·R·I·S·T·E·N·I·N·G R·O·B·E T·H·E·R·E, question mark. W·H·Y S·O D·E·V·I·O·U·S, question mark. Y·O·U K·N·O·W I C·O·U·L·D·N·T D·O A·N·Y·T·H·I·N·G A·B·O·U·T T·H·E W·H·O·L·E M·A·T·T·E·R, exclamation mark.

Agaat puts down the stick. Now I've got her. I know how angry she was about that.

Trailing-stitch, she says, morning glories, pomegranate pips, ai where are the days. Conceived in sin, I'd say. You too, you always imagined your hands were tied, with everything. But the work of my hands you were strong enough to pick up and throw into the dam! Tsk, I'd rather not think about it!

She lifts up my sheet. For a moment I think she's going to pull it over my head. She folds it back neatly, pulls it up under my chin.

You think you can wrap me up here, I flicker. You think you can tidy up and finish off this whole story as you do with everything, but you can't, it's not in your sovereign power, you need me for it!

Whiter than snow, says Agaat, she strokes my hair.

I roll my eyes to the open books with the folded-back pages on the chair. She follows my eyes.

And she takes my eyes and she reads me direct, she no longer spells with the stick.

She bends her head, I feel the hard cloth of her cap against my temple. Softly she interprets my thoughts for me. She whispers in my ear with her sweet rooibos breath, I smell the borax in the starch.

I listen to myself. Would that be what I would say if I were suddenly to have my tongue restored to me? Can I believe my ears?

What do you think you're going to achieve by rubbing my nose in what I've written in the diaries? the voice asks in my ear, a perfect imitation of how I talk.

It's your story, it's for your sake, so that you may have something in your old age to remember how you were rescued from destitution. How I made a human being out of you. You were nothing, you'd have stayed nothing, if I hadn't taken a chance with you. I'm not saying I did everything right, I constantly made mistakes, I hurt you, I humiliated you, but by what example was I to measure myself? You know what it was like in those days. Your case was highly exceptional. But I tried, under the circumstances and by the light that was available to me, I tried. Now you're making a circus of it.

A C·I·R·C·U·S! Agaat's voice sounds the letters. There's a pause before she recommences. I see the trailing-stitch on her cap, white on white violence.

It wasn't easy. Nothing was easy about your whole story, let me tell you, it ruined my marriage. And look what I have to show for it now! A C·I·R·C·U·S, A C·O·U·R·T O·F L·A·W!

Agaat straightens up, she stands back, my ear feels cold without her warm breath. What will she reply to her own ventriloquism?

Didn't know you were so interested in the little old books, Ounooi, but not now, I'll read to you again tonight. Useful bits and pieces of all kinds.

She tidies up the blue booklets on the pile. For the first time I see the embroidery book and the Handbook and the orange FAK on the dressing table. Exhibits. Chapter and verse.

The lid of the bouillon pot, sings Agaat, must be removed overnight otherwise the bouillon will go off.

A recitative from the Farmer's Handbook? What's that supposed to mean?

She looks at me.

It doesn't have the desired effect on me. I flicker at her: Go ahead and pronounce it now, Agaat! Stop your unfathomable parables. Go ahead and pronounce it all for me so that you can come to your senses, perhaps it will help if you can hear yourself say out loud what you think I think! What you think I ought to think! Mind rape, that's what it is!

Again she bends by my bed, this time on the other side. Must my ears take turns in this devilish business?

Why do you torture me on my deathbed?

Is Agaat whispering that? In my ear? Am I hearing aright? Her voice is emphatic.

Why do you let me be ravaged by itching, push and pull my limbs, screw open my mouth, taunt me, threaten me with enemas and suppositories, dig in my ears as if you think I have ear-mite, have holes punched into me, shove tubes into me, cut my hair so that I look like a prisoner of war? Why?

She stands back. She answers from her own corner, a smile as if she's ascending unto heaven. She opens her mouth wide.

When meat is cooked for the kitchen-maid or kaffir, she sings, or even for the house, it's good to boil it in the bouillon pot for the first hour or so, to extract as much nutrition as possible into the water.

Again her lips are at my ear, I feel the moistness of her mouth.

Then why do you still leave me hanging? she whispers. Why do you come and stand by my bedside in the dark? Do you want me dead? What prevents you?

Sulphured fruit must not be eaten raw, comes her reply, a floating contralto, but first boiled again to drive off the sulphur.

How many voices has Agaat?

Calm down, Ounooi, she says, close your eyes now. Think of other things. You're wandering again. But it's not serious, just relax, I'm here, I'm staying with you, I'm not going away, here I am, right here.

She moves in behind the bed, above my head I hear the words that well up in me, lisping they drip from Agaat's tongue.

And the slops you feed me! I'll choke. And that will be too soon for you. You still want your pound of flesh from me, remember! Living flesh. What satisfaction would a dead liver give you? A dead heart? You want to pluck me out of the hole with a wire. Like a mole. Well, keep your wire! Soon I'll be in a hole where even you won't be able to get at me. Except if you dig me up to chew my bones. Bone hunger!

Agaat appears next to my bed. She looks at me.

How are we doing? she asks. She goes and writes something.

Who marks the day high up there on the calendar? The thirteenth of December, I recall and I remember. Could I have imagined it all? Am I dreaming?

She looks at me, smiles, writes something again.

Abracadabra, she says, twirls a little circle next to her head with her index finger.

Could she mean that I've lost my wits? I'm raving? It's not me, witch! You're the one who's raving, you're the one who's trying to rave my rave for me! Not a word past my lips for three years now. The mute cannot rave! But they can hear!

There, there, Ounooi, don't be scared, she says, it's just the little light, it's going on and off now. In your head.

That's a good one! Interprets me to the brink of Babel, to the threshold of death. But there are limits! Back! Stand back! You're too close! My death is of me! And my bed! There are boundaries!

Agaat goes to stand by the door. She clasps her hands round her body, the knuckle of the small hand in her mouth.

Take the stick, take the stick, I signal.

She comes nearer, takes the stick.

T·H·E·R·E A·R·E B·O·U·N·D·A·R·I·E·S, I spell, B·O·N·E M·A·G·G·O·T.

Agaat taps seven exclamation marks of her own. She puts down the stick. She bends her head over me, regards me, presses shut her eyes with the thumb and index finger of her left hand. And with the fingers of her small hand, mine. Her fingers are cold on my eyelids.

Rest, she says, it won't be long now, we're almost there.

The first letter that you intercepted was addressed to Jakkie at Langebaan, his official numbers and codes written in stiff black block letters on the envelope. You wanted to know what Agaat had been writing to him, sitting there in her room for hours on end.

The first letter, no it couldn't have been the first. There were many. When you unfolded it the change in form of address struck you. No longer Dear Boetie as when he was at school or Dear Private when he was doing his basic training. Dear Airman Captain de Wet it was now. Your heart contracted inside you, sitting there reading next to the road, pulled off into a gate entrance on the way to town.

You'd told Agaat that Jakkie was now in a high-security position and that her correspondence wasn't private. Jakkie had warned you and Jak. No searching questions about his movements, his further specialised studies, would be answered, and your private declarations and revelations might just end up under eyes they were not intended for. And here was Agaat's camouflage now. All that she thought she could hide, was how close she was to him.

The words with which she concluded that letter, were even more poignant. No longer: Your loving Nêne. Respectfully yours, she now wrote. And no longer just Gaat. Now it was her full name: Agaat Lourier.

But as your eyes wandered over the densely packed lines, it was mainly the loving that you discerned, that was undiminished. It was in her descriptions. The jackal so delicately sniffing at the twig, its wide green eye in the night, as it approaches the yard with plans of its own. It was in the specific selection of things that she named. The three pink eggs of the little nightjar on the footpath to the old orchard. The way in which she wrote up the tiniest impressions, struck you. A love letter compared to yours. What would the Defence Force censorship make of it, you wondered. Like encrypted writing it would surely seem to them, like some code or other.

Your own letter was in your handbag. On the slender side. What you had to report was really rather meagre against Agaat's epistle.

She held forth on everything that happened on the farm or didn't happen. A chronicle. With wetted finger you counted, thirty pages, all in the precise upright handwriting she'd taught herself. You were amazed at the grasp she had of everything, from piss-ups amongst the farm workers to the service schedule of farm vehicles and the number of bales of wool, the variation in the quality of the milk and the cream in the spring and the fall, the treatment of the wheat seed against fungus. A record keeper's statistics. She predicted the rains for Jakkie—a fine grey mizzle in the early morning just enough to make the eels stick out their noses—and guessed the wind for the following week for him and estimated the surge in the mountain streams and rivers for him with the naked eye and compared it with the average of the seasons. As if the farm belonged to him and to her.

What could you shore up against that? Against the number of cows covered, the report on the first signs of nasal bot among the sheep? What she left out, were the dreadful daily quarrels between you and Jak and the swearing and the tears. To judge by Agaat's letter the Grootmoedersdrift homestead was a model of peace and harmony.

Why did it infuriate you so immoderately that day next to the road? The prettification to which every paragraph bore witness, was in the best possible taste. You couldn't have done it better yourself.

You read the whole thing. At the end, for a whole paragraph, she asked questions, intimate questions from the nêne of old. What do they give you to eat there in the mess? Do you see meat in those army stews? Do you sleep warm enough? Is your pillow filled properly? Are your superiors well disposed towards you? Are you healthy? Are you safe? Do your subordinates listen to your commands? Are you getting used yet to taking off, to the blow to the heart and the horse rearing up? (rein it in) Do your ears still close up when you come down? (chew a dried peach) When are you coming home again?

The disquiet that was also in your and Jak's hearts, she formulated as: *I pray for your blessed and kept return from the distant skies.*

It was herself she was comforting with the quince-mousse dessert she was thinking up for him, the roast of hare in pomegranate sauce that she would place steaming before him.

You wanted to read the letter again, you put it back into your handbag. Agaat's blue Croxley envelopes you usually licked, and pressed closed again as best you might, asked at the post office for a bit of sticky tape. Your transgressions you trusted would be covered by the far more visible and sanctioned incursions of the military security that according to Jakkie opened and stamped everything. But this letter you didn't want to let go, there was a tenderness and an obsession to these formulations after which you hungered.

Jak had his own formulae in which to clothe this new situation for himself.

How is Pa's soldier? he'd ask on the phone when Jakkie phoned.

You listened in on the second phone. Jakkie could give him answers pertaining to his number of logged flying hours, the sensation of breaking through the sound barrier, the training with the ejector seat in the simulator.

He was a body of potentials for his father, a model of endurance, of physical discipline, of drilled limbs and sharpened reflexes.

And you? What could you ask this child about whom you felt your knowledge was of the second order, of the third, after Jak with whom he had had his baptism of fire in the mountains, after Agaat on whose bosom he'd grown up?

She was the one to whom he handed his laundry bag every time he came home, and who packed his suitcase for him when he left again.

What could you respond, what add, to the smile, the poker faces exchanged with the handing over of the bag, the handing back of the suitcase?

You knew of the little surprises with which from childhood they'd spoilt each other. Quartz pebbles, mouse skulls, tanned moleskins, under a pillow, in a shoe. Later, Agaat's jerseys and pullovers for Jakkie, a bow tie and a new shirt that she went to buy him in town with her own money, cellophane packets of fudge and taffy and fennel cookies that she hid amongst his clothes.

And Jakkie's gifts to her, boxes of fine chocolate, sachets of saffron and cardamom from the spice stores of the Boland, story books, Croxley writing-pads and envelopes, magazines, headscarves and fragrances.

Not that she ever used the perfume. The little bottles stood untouched, like an exhibition of trophies, on the shelf above her washing-table. The scarves she used as wall decorations for her room. She scrutinised them for new designs that she could embroider.

Your attention and interest you felt passed Jakkie by, unheeded. Was it for your sake that he joined the Air Force choir? He sent you their record. Side one, *The Lord is My Shepherd*. Side two, *Oh for a gun in my strong right hand*. He was more attuned to his father's ideals, to Agaat's favour than to your concern. From the sidelines you watched things develop.

As a member of the Permanent Force's elite corps of highly trained personnel Jakkie made rapid progress, just as Jak had predicted. He could study and earn a salary at the same time. He obtained a degree in aeronautical engineering. In case he won't be able to fly all his life, he said, then he can design machinery for the Air Force.

Like what? Jak wanted to know.

The plans are there, but it's classified information, Jakkie sent word. All that you got to know in that time, was that the Bureau of Mechanical Engineering at Stellenbosch was a kind of front for Armscor. You had some misgivings about this, but Jak said why could the Afrikaner's cultural headquarters not also be his arms factory, it goes without saying, that's how all honourable nations consolidate themselves.

You both knew that Jakkie wasn't really interested in politics, all he wanted to do was fly the Air Force's modern fighter planes. That was Jak's great dream. At supper table he read you and Agaat extracts and showed you pictures of aeroplanes from *Paratus* and *Jane's Defence Weekly*, to which he subscribed.

You knew that Jakkie was flying Impalas and Mirages. You and Jak knew that it wasn't child's play in South West. You knew that it was the supreme game of heroes, that those who took part in the war against the Cubans in Angola were awarded the highest honours. You had the right to be proud, he was the child of all three of you.

But what was it that you felt there at the supper table when Agaat received a thick letter from him, thicker than that to his parents, and you and Jak asked her to read it aloud? It wasn't pride, it was loss that united the two of you there under the lamplight. As united as you could ever be. Because you and Jak were suspicious of Agaat whose eyes sometimes glided rapidly over the lines, over the bits she left out. Jakkie's letters to her you didn't dare open or intercept.

You were dependent upon each other's fictions about Jakkie. You were his family, but he belonged to the war, to secret operations. Later when it leaked out in the press, Jak bloodthirstily speculated about Jakkie's part in the preservation of country and nation.

Oh please just shut up! you shouted at Jak when it became too much for you.

You locked yourself in your room, went to lie down on your bed, crying. You couldn't figure out with whom you were most angry. With Jakkie who wasn't open about his activities, with the Defence Force that employed him for its own purposes, or with the government that maintained a dour silence.

But it was the scene there in the dining room that really irked you, the scene with Jak and Agaat, she standing opposite him on the other side of the table, her hands on the back of the chair, half of her face in shadow. Jak telling tales of bombed-out enemy positions, of smoking Migs exploding in fireballs. Was she flattered to serve as audience to the fantasies of the baas?

It sickened you. You tried to keep yourself going with hard work, but then there was always the apprehension, the suspicion in those years, the late seventies, early eighties.

You went to see the doctor. He prescribed a stronger tranquilliser, better sleeping draughts. That helped, but it made you feel as if you were only half alive. Agaat checked your consumption closely. She was particularly interested in your faints, in the weakness that sometimes overcame you in the middle of wool-classing or during the stamping of the wool bales. Exaggeratedly solicitous she'd be then. Irony, no, sarcasm was in the crook of the elbow of the strong arm she offered to accompany you to your room.

After such an episode, after she'd attended to you in your room, she could go missing for hours. Stay with me, Agaat, you asked, but she closed the curtains. Stay with me, I feel scared, you said, but she remained standing there for just a moment, in the twilit room, with her hands folded under her breasts, her white cap, her white apron like nurse's clothing, before walking out tchi-tchi on her thick-soled school shoes.

Was it one late afternoon that you woke up after such a collapse, after a dream that she had run off, that you went out? You had to look very closely, with the binoculars. She was walking with her head held high. From far away you could make that out. Unimpeachable in her solid body with her even tread she approached, unswervingly, as if she were in a play. This time she wasn't on the koppie in front of the house where she always, in full silhouette, looked larger than she really was. She was approaching along the footpath in the dryland through the twilit wheatfields, her white cap like a prow above the stalks of wheat.

After half an hour she came in by the back door. All innocence, a castaway lamb under her arm, a story about a hare that had ended up in the jackal trap, a basket of lay-away eggs. That's the way it always was.

A report of a gate lying wide open, of an empty drinking trough, of a windmill that doesn't cast, of another kerbstone washed away from the bridge over the drift, of a plume of smoke in the poplar forest. But you knew that there was much more than met the eye to her walks. That evening again, when she'd brought in the food for you, she waited, emphatically and intransigently, for you to tell Jak what she'd found, noticed, suspected. And then she listened, expressionlessly, because the actual information you couldn't communicate. You didn't know what it was.

You shut your ears to your own voice pronouncing the deceitful words. You screamed at Agaat.

Stop staring at me as if I'm false! What have I done to you? What do you want me to say?

You slammed your fists on the table. Your glass broke. You put your hand in your mouth, you wanted to pluck out your tongue.

Jak looked at you askance.

My toastmistress, he said, lifted his glass, and carried on eating.

Agaat picked up the shards and took you to your room. She made you take your medicine and covered you with blankets, switched on the night-light by your bed. You listened to her serving Jak's dessert and coffee, clearing up, closing the windows of the living room for the night.

Those sounds, that silence in which Agaat at length ate her evening meal behind a closed kitchen door, the back door that she pulled shut and locked behind her, the slamming of the screen door, the scuffing of the door of the outside room, all those black sounds to which you were listening in your room lying on your back, they were the opposite of music, they were the sounds of damnation.

Is that what's become of my paradise here this side of the Tradouw? you thought.

Is that why you wanted to create the garden? Was that your response to the war stories with which Jak entertained Agaat evening after evening? A spell, a safeguard against the distant war and its hurt? Or to gain Agaat for yourself? To win back something of your dream?

You steeled yourself, went in to Jak at night, lay down next to him on his divan in his stoep room, satisfied him while he was half asleep.

What is all this, the stories of keening engines and missiles and explosions and blood and smoke and disembodied limbs and blackened ruins? you asked him after he had come, softly, persuasively, as one would talk to an upset child, so that he would answer you half in a daze, so that you could get the truth out of him.

I know you're scared, just like me, you said, I know you're worried. Who do you want to punish with such premonitions? What do you want to achieve by it? After all, you love him, he's our son, why do you make him out to be one who sows destruction and death? With whom are you angry? Of whom are you afraid?

For a long time you listened by his mouth, to what he would say.

Our minerals, the white man's future, he mumbled, the terrorists, we must prepare ourselves spiritually against the enemy, there are sacrifices to be made . . .

Jak, that's not what I'm asking, you said, that I can hear on the television any day that I have a mind to. Jakkie's your child, he's the future. For the sake of what exactly do you want to sacrifice him?

He defends the borders, Jak said, that's what we whites should have done from the start in this country. He's obeying orders, and fortunately it's no longer your and your handmaiden's orders.

You're fighting against me, you said, you won the child over to your side and now you're inciting Agaat against me as well with your bloodthirsty talk.

If the people at home weaken, it's bad for the morale of the men on the border, Milla, you can support him by showing a bit more fighting spirit instead of taking to your room on any pretext. Why don't you join the Southern Cross and do something useful for the war?

A paradise, you whispered, your head on his chest, that's what you promised me, do you remember? Long ago. A flower garden without equal. Let's make a garden for Jakkie, he won't always want to fly jet fighters. He'll come home one day, and then we can show it to him, a sign of . . . a sign . . .

You couldn't say it, of what it was supposed to be a sign.

Go ahead, he mumbled, make your garden, you do just what you want to in any case.

You went out onto the stoep. The sweet clove smell of carnations was in the air, the intoxication of the hedge full of white moonflowers. There had always been a garden on Grootmoedersdrift, in summer always a show of hydrangeas and agapanthus, but you wanted more than a higgledy-piggledy farm garden, you wanted to create a bower of beauty, on a few hectares, a park in which you could lose yourself, with arcades of rambling roses and round ponds with fountains, garden rooms such as you'd seen in the magazines, with laid-out paths and boxwood hedges and vantage points, with mixed beds throbbing with larkspur and poppies, striking accent plants, conifers and flaxes, and flowering trees and shrubs in all seasons. Formal of design you wanted the garden to be, but informally planted. Like a story you wanted it, a fragrant visitable book full of details forming part of a pattern so subtle that one would be able to trace it only after a while. That's how you wanted your garden to be, a composition, a sonata with theme and developments and repetitions in varying keys, something that would form the jewel in the crown of Grootmoedersdrift farm.

Jak grumbled about money when he saw you were in earnest.

You brandished in front of his face the quotation for a de-wrinkling operation that Agaat had found in one of his pockets.

Thousands of rands! It's your vanity that will ruin us, you said. Why don't you ever want to help me with anything?

He grabbed your wrists. Keep your nose out of my affairs, to look at you, you're actually the one who could do with a bit of plastic surgery. Reconstruction for Kamilla!

He pushed his fingers into the corners of your mouth. You tried to resist, to take his fingers out of your mouth.

Just look at you, this misery who calls herself Mrs de Wet. Permanently down in the mouth!

Agaat came upon you. Jak threw your hands from him and wiped his thumb and forefinger, which he'd had in your mouth, on his pants.

What do you want here? he asked.

Agaat's voice was hard, her businesslike housekeeping voice with which she often broke up your quarrels.

I beg your pardon, Mr de Wet, she said, I just wanted to return the ash pan to the fireplace.

You kept your hands in front of your face, ashamed of her coming upon you like that.

Sometimes, Agaat said, and what she said did not accord with her tone, sometimes I wish I could . . .

You looked round. There she stood, the iron poker in her strong hand. It was superficially evident that she was referring to Jak, to something that she wanted to do to him. But her gaze was fixed on you.

Get out of here, you managed to say, it's none of your business.

It is, she said, and flung the poker into the copper tray, it is most certainly my business.

Did she say that? Had you heard correctly?

Get out of here, immediately, Jak said.

Without looking at you, she walked out with rapid little steps and her head high. If she didn't say it, her crooked drawn-up shoulder said it: It's the only business I have, you and your husband and your child and your buggering around.

You kept wondering about Jak in that time when Jakkie went to the border. From his first breakdown on the night of his great nursery rhyme—how old was Jakkie then? eleven, twelve?—you felt that he was working at and building and adjusting his theory of you, of who you were, and what you had done to him. It hurt more than any shove or slap.

So if you don't want to help me with the garden, you said, please do go ahead and write it up some time, all the stories that you've been accumulating against me for years, everything that you sit and think up about me, so that I can read it, because I don't get the whole picture, only the tirades and the obscure parables.

Go ahead and write yourself, it's no use your trying to pretend all of a sudden that you're interested in what I think, I've been thinking it for a long time and I've been saying it for a long time, from the very start. Your problem is that that you don't notice a thing, Milla. And now all of a sudden you want me to be your gardener, get knotted, I say.

You were sorry for him. His face and still-fit body were at last starting to show their age. It wasn't only yourself, you realised, you wanted to console him as well with the garden, you wanted to soothe him as well.

You woke up one Sunday morning towards six o'clock with the garden layout practically complete in your mind.

Jak was away, the house was quiet. On Sunday mornings Agaat was off duty. You walked to the kitchen to make yourself some coffee. On an impulse you walked out into the backyard in your nightdress and knocked on the upper door of the outside room. It was wide open.

Come, I'm making us some nice coffee and rusks, I have a wonderful idea, Agaat, you must help me.

You started talking before you'd seen her. Your words dried up when you looked into her eyes.

The curtains were open. The room was bright with light. Agaat was sitting and embroidering in the deep chair in front of the window, her bare feet on a little mat of sewn-together moleskins. She was without her cap. Her hair radiated in combed-out peaks from her head. It was the first time in twenty years that you'd seen her without her cap. You felt as if you'd caught her naked, but you stood there and kept gazing.

The unkempt hair mass made her look feral. You wanted to look away, but you couldn't. The hair filled the otherwise tidy room like a conspiracy against everything in league with daylight and subordination. From the enormity of hair your eyes strayed to the grisly cement-work around the fireplace. To and fro you looked, at her head and at the clusters of shells and skulls and quartz pebbles and marbles and little slivers of iron, rivets. It was as if Agaat had recreated her unkempt self there in low relief.

Her embroidery basket was standing by her feet, with the tight balls of thread and needles stuck into their proper places in the pockets and loops. The high white bed was immaculately made, with all her large embroidered pillows neatly arranged against the bedpost. On her clothes-rail the black dresses and the white aprons hung neatly serried. On the shelf above, fitted into one another three-by-three, the starched white caps, densely embroidered like mitres. But all of that, plus the zinc bath in its place under the washbasin, the table scrubbed white, the kettle shiny with scouring, the hearth-opening clean, the buffed noses of three pairs of black school shoes peeping out from under the curtain in front of the apple-crate cupboard, the Singer's black body neatly folded back into the stowaway cavity, was not enough to reassure you. The clumps of steel wool on her head, the manner in which she looked at you in her ungroomed state, there where you stood in the door, yourself with sleep-fuzzed hair and an unwashed face, with your thin shins and white knees sticking out from under your pink flannel bed-jacket, that unnerved you. You clutched the front of your nightdress, even though it was buttoned. You felt as if she were assessing you naked.

I'm coming, she said, and stuck out her chin to manifest her displeasure, but the effect of it, without the cap, was one of vulnerability.

With an odd, reprimanded feeling you went and flung on a dress and dragged a comb through your hair so that when you went to sit down at the kitchen table you would at least not compare unfavourably with her. You knew how snow-white-starched she would report for duty.

She declined the rusk and drank her coffee with tight little sips. Her chin was stuck out and she listened to your plan with her eyes fixed to the wall, her cap a rampart before her head.

You had to control yourself not just to gather again all the papers and the coloured pencils and the gardening books that you'd set out and say to her she may leave now, thank you. Why should you suddenly become an apologist for your idea? A sort of sycophantish subordinate?

But you didn't want to give up, you wouldn't let yourself be quenched, and you changed your tack, excitedly you explained, elbows on the table, as lightly and merrily as you could.

Was she upset because you'd seen her embroidery-work? Nobody was ever allowed to see Agaat's creations before they were quite complete, the cloth neatly washed and ironed and spread out for inspection. And this one was a huge cloth that she must have started that very morning, only the edges had been seamed. Were there sleeves attached? A neck-hole? You didn't want to look too hard. Those unruly wads bowed over the fine white cloth, the hand working rapidly and accurately with the needle. It was the sight of that that suddenly made you feel terribly guilty about the letter. The one that you'd read over and over again. How long had it been in your handbag before you'd eventually posted it? Had you ever posted it?

Without looking up you filled one page after the other with your drawings and slid them in front of Agaat. One to explain the structure of the terraces, wider and narrower for variation, with stone walls and connecting steps that were supposed to lead the eye to the front door of the homestead. One to explain the scheme of arches and arcades and trellises that would grant the visitor access to prettily framed pictures of the garden. Another one to chart the location of the fountain and the fish ponds and the watercourses connecting them with one another, and one to indicate the irrigation pipes. The last one was to illustrate the colour scheme, blue and purple and white and green would predominate, with here and there an accent of bronze and copper and ochre. And then on the west side there had to be a formal herb garden with everything fragrant and tasty, with a sundial in the centre and paths of fine gravel as you'd seen in the books.

You took your time over every map, coloured in the levels unhurriedly, and kept talking softly all the time as if to yourself before presenting the end result at higher volume.

Coax, you thought, soft-soap, even it if takes hours. At length you got up to fetch a jar of green-fig preserve, Agaat's favourite, from the pantry shelf. It was eleven o'clock and perhaps she could be won over with something to eat. Bread and butter and green figs. Anything to get her to open her mouth.

How about something special for the two old sweet-tooths on a sunny Sunday morning, you called airily from the pantry, and added even more airily.

So what do you say, Agaat? Do you feel up to it?

With a scraping sound you dragged the stepladder across the pantry floor and mounted its creaking rungs. You had to gain a bit of time to consider what your next move would be, perhaps a suggestion to go outside, to view the area under consideration, to asses the old garden as it was? That might bring some relief to the atmosphere, a displacement away from the square table-top where you were trapped together, something to break through the tension of the presentation and approval.

But the tension was even more palpable there where you were standing four shelves high on a rickety stepladder facing several seasons' jars of preserved fruit, chutneys, jams, syrups and pickles.

Suddenly the thought occurred to you to fall off the ladder. That would be an instant solution. All balances would be restored in the wink of an eye. You would be paralysed with shock and pain and Agaat would jump to help and attend to you, and then you'd be able to exploit the situation of badly sprained employer to get her where you wanted her.

Where exactly you wanted Agaat, was what you asked yourself while you read the labels.

Albertas (old orchard) thick syrup 1970, Clingstone (old orchard) in brandy syrup 1971, Quince jelly 1973, Prickly-pear syrup 1975, Fine apricot 1980, Whole-fruit apricot and peach pickle (curried) 1981, Peach pickle (chilli) 1981.

Every preserving-jar in front of you on the shelf Agaat had handled, the picking, the peeling, the slicing, the boiling, the bottling, the labels were all in her upright handwriting.

Wholefruit kumquat jam (front orchard) 1972, Lemon marmalade 1972, Bitter orange marmalade, Wild watermelon (Gdrift, dryland),

Sourfig cinnamon-sugar syrup (Witsand dunes), Green-fig (Pink fig tree) 10 October 1980.

You felt dizzy. For a moment the fall was a definite possibility. You supported yourself against the shelf.

Then you saw Agaat beneath you, head buried in one of the garden books that you'd set out on the table, the strong hand firmly clamped around one leg of the ladder.

Are you managing here? she asked. I see here they also talk of colour schemes.

The tone was sticky with sanctimoniousness. You were recalled from the faint to sudden fury. You could sweep off the whole shelf of bottles with your arm onto her head. She wouldn't even know what hit her. A cluster bomb of preserves.

Jakkie phoned yesterday, she began, her voice low.

He says they called him on the carpet to ask who this Agaat-person is and why her letters arrived sometimes open, sometimes gummed shut. They're scared of sabotage, he says, but he doesn't understand it, because it's mainly the other side's people who are sent letter-bombs, he's scared his superiors will think he's turned wrong or something and it's the secret police who want to eliminate him. He says he's had it with war. He says he has nightmares.

That's how your garden began.

After her deposition Agaat took the garden books to the outside room and made her own study of them. You kept thinking of the letter. Would she have seen it, you wondered? Would she have looked in your bag? When she went to take out the new pills from the chemist? You tried to remember when you'd eventually gone to post it, tried in vain to recollect licking and resealing it.

In the evenings after supper when Jak had gone to the stoep, Agaat would come and sit with you at the dining room table and make recommendations and see to it that you planned it all in the finest detail until your eyes were ready to fall shut. Then she made strong coffee which in turn kept you from sleep.

Take an extra Valium she'd say if you complained.

She persuaded Dawid to help you with the big things.

Jak stood on the sidelines, now and again when you weren't looking, lent a hand when Dawid asked him.

You had a strong pump installed at the dam and on Agaat's recommendation had a reservoir built for the summer on the rise behind the house. She saw a small bulldozer and scraper at Barlows in town and you hired it to construct the terraces.

Of compost material there was enough. You had big heaps made up from manure and straw from the stables. Agaat pushed a length of steel wire into each one and went and felt it every morning. It mustn't be too hot, otherwise it kills the microbes, she learnt from her book.

She reckoned that the farm hotnots, as she called them, were too idle and too few for the garden work and at her insistence you got a team of convicts from town to dig trenches, stack stone walls and dig out the flowerbeds three feet deep to improve the soil texture with additions of compost.

Agaat cooked great pots of rice and pork for the convicts and kept them lively with jugs of sweet Frisco every three hours. With a short quirt she walked to and fro behind the lines with the guard to see that there was no idling.

When it's spring again, she taught them, and the second and third voices of the refrain, day in, day out.

She had more or less burnt herself out by the time you were ready to go to Starke Ayres in Grabouw to buy seed and bulbs and trees and shrubs.

Those were your best times together, those excursions, those long hours in fragrant nurseries with your reference books and looking at the exotic flowering-habits and feeling the leaves of all the unfamiliar plants. And the names of the roses that you translated for Agaat, crepuscule, evening twilight, and explained, Mary Stuart, queen of the Scots with her long jaw, and wine-red Mario Lanza that she knew from your record with the songs from *The Student Prince*. Overhead the moon is bee-a-ming, you hummed together there in the nursery avenues. For the first time you had picnics again alone together, in the rose gardens of Elgin, in parks, on a bench under the huge wild fig tree with thirteen trunks, Ficus craterostoma in the botanical gardens of Kirstenbosch.

Cold sausage, sandwiches with thick butter and apricot jam and coffee with condensed milk from the thermos flask, Agaat's favourite picnic fare. Together you sat on the old green travelling-rug in the Gardens, after you'd shown her the statue of Jan van Riebeeck and the Castle and the fountains in Adderley Street and the flower market where the Malay women tried to speak to Agaat in their Cape tongue and she didn't really understand them.

People stared at you, the formally clad servant and the older white woman, as if you were a psychiatric patient, they looked at you, let out in the custody of your housekeeper.

See, I told you I'd show you Cape Town one day, you wanted to say, but you thought better of it.

She read your mind.

Well, would you believe, here I am actually seeing Table Mountain, she said and swallowed the rest of the sentence.

Let's go for a drive, you said, then you can see it from the back as well.

With the map on her lap Agaat followed as you drove across Kloof Nek and read the names out loud of the corners and the bays and the heads. Lion's Head, Kommetjie, Kalk Bay.

Beyond Simon's Town you stopped at a little nature reserve next to the sea and went to show her the penguins.

Agaat's face at the sight of the waddling nestling colony, to see her face as she gazed at the great world passing her by, the tanker on the horizon, the streets, the buildings, the shifting peninsula with its two horizons. On the way home she didn't say a word.

After the structures of stone and wood had arisen in Grootmoedersdrift's new garden, you did most of the work yourselves, sowed the seeds and planted the seedlings and thinned them and transplanted them from the seed trays and made cuttings and tied up the tendrils and scattered the snail poison and sprayed the roses. And now and then transplanted a thing that wasn't in the right position, or grafted a little struggling tree onto a stronger trunk.

Without Agaat you couldn't have managed it, you said in your little speech at the first spring celebration the following year. At Agaat's suggestion you presented a garden festival and fund-raising drive for the border soldiers. You invited the local branches of the WAU and the Women's Mission Union and the Southern Cross and the tea-drinking was opened by the dominee's wife with scripture and prayer and closed with a hymn.

You peeped at Agaat where she was standing behind the cake table with her hand held in front of her stomach. Her eyes weren't shut during the prayer. And with the closing hymn she stared straight into the blue sky and swayed lightly on her heels as she sang along, her black-and-white clothes sharply etched against the purple irises in the bed behind her, her fine descant floating above the hymn there in the open.

O goodness God's ne'er praised enow, who would it not profoundly move.

*

who unpacks the boxes from bockmann independent living aids? see the fat green letters on the brown cardboard it's fall 1994 land of hope and glory who cuts open the brown packing-tape? who pulls off blocks

*of foamalite and plastic packaging? it's metal tubes chrome rods sup-
port surfaces who reads the instructions? who click-clacks the pieces
into one another there they stand my externalised skeletons my walking frames one with legs one with wheels*

tarantula or fortuna
choose!

*who grabs the spider by the head? who shows the way? this is how
you do it you lean forward on the crossbar who says it's like walking
with a little table but without the top? don't look at your feet your feet
are of no importance you drag them after your legs you keep straight
you make a rigid knee the other one is like walking with the tea-trolley
but without the tea you roll ahead you drag behind the wheels are
braked you can adjust them if they turn too easily you fall*

*who shall tell the walker from the frame? and the wheel from the
revolution? the imitator from the imitated?*

*who walks demonstration laps on the red polished stoep? who turns
round at the furthest point with retracted chin with pursed lips? who
cries soundlessly without tears?*

*I see she makes a rigid knee she flattens her feet she drops the arches
drops her shoulders they bulge under apron bands her knuckles show
white on the chrome*

we'll take both she says

*the frame for the morning the wheels for the evening we support
your last steps so god willing twofold*

*

*Wednesday 16 December 1953 quarter past three (day one Day
of the Covenant!)*
The great clean-up has begun. She's still groggy with the valerian. I
thought I'd grasp my opportunity. Cut off the hair and washed with tar
medicine and then with shampoo and applied ointment. Bad ringworm.
Fiddled out the gouts of ear wax with matches and cotton wool and cut
the nails. Big struggle to get the teeth brushed. Gums inflamed, lots of
rotten teeth. Milk teeth fortunately, must be extracted, the whole lot
while we're about it. Disinfected the mouth with extract of cloves. The
whole body first rubbed with oils and then soaked in a hot bath for half
an hour, afterwards scrubbed down with hard sponge and nailbrush
and soap. Scabs, raw patches everywhere. Half limp, the little body.
Eyes keep falling shut. Look at me, Asgat, I say, everything will turn out
all right. Must think up another name.

Dried well and the whole body rubbed with oil again, all the nicks and cuts disinfected and covered with plasters. Full of little black moles. Must have them looked at, some of them don't seem right to me. Privates extremely tender and inflamed. God knows what happened to the creature, discarded, forgotten. Tomorrow to the doctor so that he can have a look at her. Who knows she may have all kinds of diseases. Must get inoculated.

Pox. Diphtheria. Polio. Can't have an infection erupting here on the farm.

Made her bed in the back room. No window, door can be locked. Immediately fast asleep. In old pyjama jacket of Jak's. Quite lost in it. Gave her another double dose of tranquillisers so that she can sleep for a long time. Suffering from shock it seems. Suppose to be expected.

Still 16 December half past eight

It's dead quiet but a different kind of quiet to the usual. As if the house has acquired an ominous charge. Went to see, she's out like a light.

Have brought something huge upon myself here. Feel exhausted/weepy/angry with myself or something.

Jak goes about grinding his teeth chronically. Selfish, he mumbles, what about me? I wait for the explosion. I'm trying to think of a name that will suit her, that she will take as her own, something not too far from what she's used to. Agnes, Aggenys, Anna. Perhaps then Aspatat provisionally, it's better than nothing and it's better than Asgat, ash-pit, ash arse, good Lord above!

18 December ten o'clock

I must force her to eat, clamp her between my knees, force open the jaws with one hand, push spoon between the teeth, tip, quickly press the mouth shut. With the other hand rub the throat to make her swallow. Only thin milky porridge, lots of sugar. Won't chew anything. Put down a bottle with teat next to her, she doesn't even look at it.

I'm scared she'll take to her heels again, I keep her locked up in the back when I can't be with her. I feel bad about it but what else can I do? A lead? Perhaps not a bad idea for the first while. Dog lead with harness? Perhaps she doesn't even want to run off.

When I put her up straight, she won't stiffen her legs. Falls over, plays dead when I get close. What wild animals do, insects, when they feel danger threatening. Fall over. Protective colouring. Try not to be seen. Instinct.

Today she's sitting in the corner in a little heap with her knuckle in her mouth. A sign of progress already, I suppose, that at least she's sitting up. Yesterday she crawled in under the bed. I had to drag her out of there three times. Clung to the bed-leg with the good hand. Surprisingly tough, the little monkey, that hand I just about had to prise open to get her to let go. The third time I gave her a sharp slap over the buttocks. She must learn, my goodness. She can't come and play her tricks on me. Showed her Japie. A good old-fashioned duster with a solid wooden handle.

How old could she be? Four? Five? Could be anything, she looks badly undernourished and underdeveloped to me.

I must first get her into condition a bit before I take her to the doctor. Don't really want to hear what all he'll have to say. Mother says I'm off my rocker. Who put it in my way? I ask. You, Mother, as you put everything in my way.

Jak paces up and down scolding. Do you think you're a saint? he asks. Who are you going to wear yourself to a rag for now? Whose victim are you going to make yourself now? All I need to concern myself with is becoming a real mother, he says. Better that he insults me than that he says nothing.

19 December ten o'clock morning

Must simply go and sit and write down how it came about, the whole story, right from the beginning. The dam, the whirligigs round and round, the door creaking open. But it feels too long, too much. Where does something like that really begin? I must make time, before the details of it fade. I must supply the background, put into words the commission. Perhaps that will help me to look beyond the trees and see the forest.

19 December half past two afternoon

Dense as a stone. Not a peep. Close, black, dense, light, like coal. Won't talk. Won't eat. Clenches her hands in fists, one knuckle in the mouth, it's all pink and raw already.

She refuses absolutely to look at me. Her eyes just scamper furtively past my legs. Shrinks away when I come closer, turns the head away as if expecting a blow.

I try everything. Today pulled her in an apple box cart (OuKarel's handiwork with a strap around the legs and across the chest so that she can't escape) to the dam. Sat by the water's edge. Won't look, won't see. Showed her the whirligigs again, ducklings, everything that she should be able to recognise, but she shows no reaction. Pulled her to the drift, showed her the little boat, one day we'll row in it, I say, but the neck stays between the shoulders.

Dug up a cap because the head looks bad, all bare like that and full of sores. She doesn't like things on her head it seems, she pulls it off when I'm not looking, at least it's a sign of life.

Gave her worm medicine. Soiled her panties something dreadful. Scolded and gave a good hiding with the duster handle, what's the use? She's very far behind her age I think. Could see the worms, flat pieces of tapeworm, round dog-worms.

Ordered nappies from the chemist, waterproof drawers. Wet her bed three nights running. Mattress ruined. Had fourth bath, still tightly-rolled into a bundle. Pitch would sooner soak out of a ship than the stiffness in this child's limbs. Can't reach anywhere with the washcloth. She keeps her head pulled in, arms rigid against the body, knees clenched together.

21 December

Aspatat has a cold! Coughing and snottering. Must be from the first washing there in the dam on Goedbegin. Fancy a bit more co-operation with the eating, maybe because the nose is blocked, so she has to open her mouth to breathe. At least she's swallowing better. Jaws more relaxed. Must start with proteins. Today fish oil and vitamin C. Hellish battle. Gave malt syrup and lecithin on porridge. Sweet things do the trick, it seems. Will have to start using it as reward.

Sawed a hole in the door of the back room. Had Dawid install an old copper post-box flap over the slit. I must be able to see what she does when she's alone. Suspect she's sly, suspect she's pretending to be stupid. Remembered the hessian sack Lys gave along, put it in the room with her. She looks at it for hours. Doesn't move.

Head-sores healing nicely.

Went and dug up my old children's books in the cellar. Read rhymes to her. Who'd have thought that! I remember them bit-by-bit as I come across them.

> Old mumblemould
> I have a cold
> I have it now
> I give it to you
> I tie it up here
> And I'm in the clear.

Jak says I'm wasting my time and why am I spoiling our Christmas? I ask where is your faith, where is your heart? I possess neither the one nor the other, I do it exclusively for myself, for nobody else, he says. I don't dare use other people for my own purposes like that, he says. I'll see what comes of it, apparently.

He's just jealous, feels neglected. I devote all my free time to her.

Must succeed in this, I must make it work, make it worthwhile.

It feels as if the whole world is against me. First Mother, now Jak.

Must go and see the dominee about this, the child can't stay so nameless.

22 December

Now I have a cold! Must have got it from her. Jak says it's but the beginning. He doesn't want to go anywhere near her. She gives him the creeps, he says, the idea gives him the creeps. He says I'm sick. He taps against his head when I peer through the slot at what she's doing. What a whopper of a Christmas present I've got, he says. Unto us a child is born, unto us a woolly's given, out loud down the passage, I say, Jak bethink yourself, what if she can hear and understand you?

Perhaps after all better get to the doctor if he can still see me before Christmas. Her poo is completely yellow from all the runny food she's eating.

Made red jelly and custard, showed it to her dished up in a bowl and said if she was good and allowed me to wash her nicely in the bath, she could have it. She's still not looking at me, but it does seem as if she hears me. (Must have ears tested. Deaf and dumb perhaps? I remember the funny high squeaking sounds. Retarded perhaps? You never know with these people. Generations of in-breeding, violence, disease, alcohol. Children of Ham.)

Fifth bath, still no relaxation in the limbs. It's almost as if she's holding her breath. Teeth do seem to part more easily, I fancy. She bites the spoon. Let go, I say, let go then you get more. I have to pull at it and wiggle it, then she lets go after a while.

Just like a dog. Reward works. Got down a fair amount of jelly.

She can have it every day if she's good, I say. If she learns nicely to sit on the pot for me, learns nicely to look me in the eye, eats her other food nicely and takes her medicine. Learns to sit nice and upright and to walk smartly. If she's a good girl. Only then.

Practise every day with her on pot at regular times. Hour after breakfast, hour after supper. Sit, I say. Pee. Poo. Push. I make little moaning sounds to encourage her. Pour water out of a glass into a jug for the pee. She is closed, shut as a vault. She presses her head into her lap. Then I walk out and lock the door and watch her through the slit. She hasn't noticed it yet because she's always looking down at the ground. She crawls off the pot as soon as I'm out, slither-crawls into the corner of the room as if she's trying to squeeze herself into the wall. Then I relent and put on the nappy. The privates look better but they're stretched and loose. Shudder to think what happened there. Wanted to put in my finger to feel, but she locks closed her legs. Doctor will have to look.

She has to get moving, then the poo will also get going. I tell her she mustn't be so timid. She could run like a hare that day at Mother's. I tap out the rhyme of the rabbit for her on the table-top.

> There goes a bunny
> says Sarah Honey
> Shoot her with an arrow
> shouts Mrs Farrow
> It's too short
> says Mr Port
> It's over the hill

say Jack and Jill
Overshot the mark
says Jenny Dark
Right through the tail
says Dominee Heyl
It's hit the spot
says Auntie Dot
Put her in the pot
says John the Scot
Add a bit of mustard
says coy Miss Custard
Now to carve a fillet
says old Doctor Willet
Tastes very good
says wicked Willy Wood
You're a killer
says little Miss Milla.

27 December half past eleven morning

Both of us recovered fortunately. Christmas day rather quiet. Ma came but she didn't even go to look in the back room. I put the radio in the room with Aspatat while we were eating so that she could listen to the Christmas carols. It can get hot there in the back room with the door shut like that, but I can't really let her wander around at will.

Definite progress in the eating department. Little by little, but we're getting there. This morning mealie-meal porridge with a little lump of butter and syrup, this afternoon mashed potatoes, meat sauce, sweet pumpkin puree. Cinnamon porridge this evening. And red jelly and custard. A bit more lively, I think. Jak's gone to friends in town, but I can't yet leave her here alone.

Half past seven evening

Great breakthrough! Got the bright idea just now, after reading her a bedtime story. Put three pink Star sweets in her hessian sack, left it at the foot of the bed.

I wonder what's in here, I said. Do you still remember? They're your own little things that you know! Do you remember Lys? Lys packed it for you to play with when you came here. Don't you just want to have a look? Perhaps there's something good inside that I put in there for you.

Go on, you like sweet things, don't you? Then I went out and peeped through the spy-hole to see what she would do.

The room was in twilight. I switched off the light in the passage to see better. Dead-still she lay under the covers for a long time. Then she sat up straight, there's a hand creeping out! First the strong one, then the little paw like a flat-iron. Then she sat up even straighter. First stared fixedly at the sack. Then her eyes moved. The first time in just this way, I could see the whites showing. Forward inclination in the body, the head rigid on the neck. My heart beat very fast. I could feel myself straining my own body forward, as if it was I that had to get to the sack. My knuckles I see are raw where I bit them from the tension, didn't even notice.

Fist in the mouth, fist out of the mouth she sits there, sits weighing and wondering, an eternity it felt like. Hand creeping cautiously to the lip of the sack. Gauging with the fingertips the hessian fringe, then the ravels of the sack between thumb and forefinger. Then she pulled in her breath sharply. Open is the hand, in slips the hand, mole wriggling in the sack! Deeper and deeper up to the elbow. Further still up to the armpit. Then the other hand, the weak one, like an outrider. Feel feel feel. There! Got it! Then both hands are working. Wrapping off. Teeth apart. Quickly she slips it into the mouth-hole. Lump in the cheek. Sucks. Smoothes flat the bit of paper, folds it, can you believe it! with quick precise little fingers, and puts the paper back into the bag!

I trembled. I couldn't believe it. But that wasn't all.

Then she took the moleskin and the little wheel and the stick out of the sack. Mole in the neck, stick in the wheel. Head at an angle. Fur against the cheek. Point against the rim. One, two, three, small revolutions she makes with the little wheel on the cover. Everything together again, from the beginning, breathe in and once more. Mole in the neck, stick in the wheel, roll! Bull's-eye! Her own game! I told Jack when he came home.

Fantastic! he shouted, bravo! He clapped hands loudly. His face was ugly. Now you've broken her in. Clay in your hands. A blank page. Now you can impress anything upon her. Just see to it that you know your story, Milla. It'd better be a good one. The one that you fobbed off on me didn't work so well.

Lord, he can be so terrible.

So phoned Mother instead. She just listened. Right at the end she said what I suppose I could have expected: You're making yourself a bed, Milla, but it's your life, you must do as you see fit. She did though ask whether I'd taken her to a doctor. Suppose I must do something about it.

4 January 1954

Took her today for a once-over. Don't know if it was a good thing. She's terrified all over again. Ai, it breaks my heart, after all my trouble the last few days to tame her. While I was about it I had all the milk-teeth drawn at the out-patient's clinic for the coloureds there next to old Kriek's rooms. Set up a commotion, certainly not mute. They don't give anaesthetic there. Blood on the new frock in front. Had to apologise to the next doctor because I didn't want to drive back all the way to the farm then to go and get clean clothes on her. Ramrod-rigid and wild and convulsive she was all the time, threw her little hat as far as she could. It took two sisters to hold her down on the trolley bed. The internal examination showed exactly what I'd suspected. Multiple penetration, says the little chap, Leroux's holiday partner. He's too young, looks pretty inexperienced to me, but on top of that he was arrogant as well. He doesn't know if she'll ever be able to have children. All the better, we both of us thought. Apart from that there's nothing wrong. The flat black moles are not malignant, be can burn off the one on her cheek, he says, but he thinks it gives her face a bit of character—I think he's making fun of me. There are, though, signs of malnutrition. Weak right hand and arm probably an ante-natal injury. Eyes, ears, throat, nose, pooper, examined all the holes. Tonsils will have to go. She was fairly upset by all the shiny instruments. The squeaking noise again. Inoculations high up on the little deformed arm. Took blood samples. Pale gums and rim of eye suggest anaemia, but that can be put right. She has to be fed lots of liver and spinach. Doctor can't say if she's mentally in order. Looks to him like a state of shock. I must bring her again when she can talk, then he'll be able to form an opinion. He stares at me with such blunt eyes, the little doctor. How do I get her to talk? I ask. I must decide how much I want to spend, he says. Remediation is nowadays possible for all kinds of handicaps. It depends on what your ultimate goal is with someone like that, he says. Half provoking, as if he suspects me of something. Got annoyed with the man, as if I had to account for myself to him. I'll work on her myself until she's caught up, I said. I'll look after her, she has nobody else on the face of the earth. There are few people who are prepared to do so much for the underprivileged, Mrs de Wet. Drily. Felt humiliated when I walked out of there. What kind of attitude is that to somebody who wants to do something that everyone is forever preaching and praying about? Love thy neighbour as thyself? Then they should by rights rather be asking: What can we do to help you with the poor child on whom you've taken pity? Hypocrites! The old wall-eyed nurse Schippers and so-called highly educated Sister Goedhals with their po faces in their white uniforms, tchi, tchi, on the crêpe-soled shoes, they stared me out of the door of the consulting room, as if I were trespassing on their territory, as if I'd polluted it. That's the last time that I'll take them Christmas prunes! How is the world supposed to become a better place if that's how the medical profession feels about the under-privileged?

Bought a cup of ice-cream for A. and myself afterwards from the café. Needed it. Went and sat in a quiet spot next to the river with her. Couldn't get the ice-cream into her. Knuckle in the mouth. Quite closed up all over again. On the way back bought a celluloid windmill on a stick and showed her how it works. Sang her an old song, The Magic Mill, from my childhood and was moved to tears by it myself.

> Turn the mill in the mountain's fall
> turn the mill in the sea
> turn the mill in the time of joy
> nobody ever content can be.

She didn't want to take it from me. I held it out of the car window with one hand so that it could spin.

> Turn fine the good white salt
> turn soft the falling snow
> grind small the grains of wheat
> nothing's too hard for the mill of God.

Watched her in the mirror. Sits there with large eyes fixed in her face. It looks as if she's crying without tears.

Nothing to cry about, Aspatat, I say, we're getting you ready for life, that's all. Just the tiniest flickering when I mention her name. But it's not your real name, I say. Your name you still have to be given.

Still 4 January after supper
Had a terrible storm of crying, couldn't stop. Too many emotions for

one day I suppose. Jak says I'm putting it on. He says it's New Year's disease.

She would take in absolutely nothing. No tea. No jelly. So took her to the room early. I can't any more. Feel as if I have to start all over. Have just been to peer through the slot at what she's doing. Sits in the corner all hunched up with rigid eyes and looks at the door. She's cottoned on to the spy-slot. I put all the drawn teeth into her shoes so that the mouse can bring money.

Can still not stop crying. Don't know what about.

Jak mocks me by repeating the rhymes that I say to her.
> Oh bat oh bat
> butter and bread
> you come in here
> you're good as dead!

He says I mustn't blubber now, I must now chew what I've bitten off, he says I must go and cry somewhere else, he wants to sleep. So now I'm sitting here in the living room. The house is heavy and still. It feels as if a disaster has struck. Is it of my doing?

6 January 1954
Jelly for breakfast, afternoon and evening. That's all she'll eat. I can see the mouth is still sore from the drawing of the teeth. Sit with her in the garden in the morning. Sing everything that comes into my head, talk non-stop everything I can think of, all the names of the flowers. Clack my teeth, smack my lips, click my tongue, show all the speaking mouth parts. Imitate all sounds, brrr goes the tractor, bzzz goes the bee, clippety-clop gallops the horse, moo says the cow, baa-baa says the sheep.

Tried to explain her surname, Lourier, to her with the twigs of the laurel tree. Aspatat Lourier, down at the weir, Aspatat Lourier feels no fear. She slowly started to thaw a bit today. Watches me surreptitiously when I'm not looking. Still won't take anything from me. Sweets, yes, but only when I'm not looking. I don't want to teach her underhand ways. I close my eyes with the sweets open in my hand, she doesn't take them, she's more wary than a tame meerkat.

Have a sore throat from all the singing and talking. How long still before she's going to become human? I feel I must prove something. To myself, to Jak, to my mother, to the community. Why do I always give myself the most difficult missions? The most difficult farm, the most difficult husband, and now this damaged child without a name?

I've exceeded the limits of my abilities with her. As if I'm trying to come to terms with something in myself. What exactly is it that's driving me? With something like this most normal people would give up before they've even started on it. Perhaps those nurses were right after all, the little sceptical doctor? Perhaps I'm just wasting everybody's time here? And then without any guarantee of success either, without support from the community. But is it fair? People here are quite prepared to clap hands if you've accomplished anything unusual, are only too fond of bragging of an achievement from among their own ranks, as long as it never cost them any extra money or effort. If it had been another country, would it have been better? But every country has its share of pettiness, I suppose.

10 January

I have nightmares about the child. Dream I pull out her tongue like an aerial, one section, two, three, longer and longer I pull it out, my hands slip as I try to get a grip on it, there's no end to it, she laughs from the back of her throat, thousands upon thousands of red tonsils wave like seaweed, her tongue shudders in my hands, like a fishing rod, there's something heavy biting and tugging at the line, pulling me off my feet, drawing me in, into her mouth, then I wake up screaming. Jak shakes me by the shoulders and slaps my face. He says he's not giving it much longer. He says the day will come when I'll open my eyes and she'll be gone for ever. He'll see to it, he says, and nobody'll breathe a word. I, I say, I'll breathe a word.

16 January

Breakthrough! This morning in the garden, all of a sudden, her gaze perks up. She raises her little eyebrows, the mole on her cheek moves up and down. She looks past my shoulder, looks at something behind me. Then she looks straight in my eyes for the very first time, and then back again over my shoulder, as if she wants to say: Look behind you! Look! Beware! Look! I play back with my eyes, raise my eyebrows: What do you see? Behind you! she signals with her eyes. What can it be? I make my eyes ask to and fro. She looks more and more urgently, she holds my gaze, she directs my eyes, I'm almost overcome with feeling her own will stirring, the very first time!!!

So then it turned out it was Jak all the time who'd stood there making faces at her behind my back. He gets more out of her than I. He laughs, says it's easy, all it is, she knows who's actually the baas here on Grootmoedersdrift, just maybe she'll succeed one day in bringing it home to his wife as well.

17 January

I use Jak's code now. It works well. I look past her. Look, I say with my eyes, look behind you. What? asks her gaze. Look, look, beware behind you, there's something. Then I step back, pretend I'm trying to get away from the 'something'. It's the only way to get her to move in my direction, a kind of scampering crawl, then she stops, on all fours, just before she reaches me. I don't want to scare her, but it's the only way. When at last she dares to look round, I show her, ag, it's only a cloud, it's the sun, it's a tree, it's a bird. Nothing to be scared of!

Now we play it all the time. She's starting to bluff back with her gaze. She understands quite well how it works, the eye game. Now I can at least spare my voice a bit, I was getting quite hoarse. Now there definitely is communication, I'm certainly not imagining it. I set my eyes in every possible way, I look in surprise at a spot right behind her, then she jumps round, or I stare soulfully at a place far behind her, she gazes into my eyes for a long time before turning round to see what it is.

20 January

She's in thrall to my eyes now. She looks everywhere that I look. Ever more complicated bluffing games we play, surprise games, guessing games. I could never have dreamed you can achieve so much with your eyes.

For instance I look past her but she doesn't look. You'd better see what's going on there, I signal with my eyes, but she doesn't look, she holds out. It's very very pretty! I signal, or, it's really ugly, or, it's terribly creepy, or, it's very nice, or, it's going to catch you!

At last she looks, mostly there's nothing in particular and when she looks back I evade her glance, all innocence. Then she comes and stands against me until I look at her. Then I shut my eyes to indicate: Close your eyes. Then I put down a cookie or a sweet somewhere. Then I signal again, look there, behind you is something nice. But then I have to look away until she's eaten it. I must just take care that she doesn't react to reward exclusively. There won't always be a reward. She must simply learn to speak now. You can't live by looking alone. I take out the duster. She's going to get Japie, I say, on her backside, if she won't talk.

21 January 1954

I always have a struggle with her in the mornings, she lies all huddled up and doesn't want to budge. Just like a little cold animal that has to warm up first. Now I've thought up a warming-up exercise. 'The Greeting to the Sun' I call it. I demonstrate it to her, first nice and high on the toes, then stretch with one arm, then stretch with the other (the little weak arm I still have to operate for her, but I'm sure it'll catch up), one big step forward, one big step backward, dip at the knees, down with the head, up with the head, good morning, o mighty king sun!

If she doesn't want to, I rap her with the stick of the feather duster, that usually does the trick. I simply have to apply discipline here. We're going to do it every morning, I say, until you jump out of bed in the mornings and do it of your own accord.

22 January

She must guess what I'm looking at, we play, she must point to what I'm looking at. At first the hand was close to the body, just a little protruding finger pointing, this or that, now she's pointing with the whole arm, has even been running these last two days to the tree or its shadow, or the red-hot pokers, or the row of agapanthus, or the tap, or the fish pond or the stoep steps and then I call the name of the thing: Flower! Stone! Water! then she touches it quickly, as if she's afraid it'll bite. Perhaps she learns more from my saying a few words than from my talking non-stop.

27 January

I no longer have to lock her up all the time during the day. She follows me everywhere. Are you my tail, I ask? She only looks for my eyes. I show her in my picture book: Horse's tail, pig's tail, sheep's tail, dog's tail. There is a little finger pointing now, with its own will and purpose. Horse's eye, pig's eye, sheep's eye, dog's eye, she shows. I leave the books with her in the room. She pages for herself when I don't look, but with such cautious fingers as if the pages are scorching her.

30 January
First day without nappy and without accident. This morning there was pee in the pot, so she must have got up by herself in the night, or early this morning. Saar says she poos in the garden when we're not looking.

Don't poo in the garden, Aspatat, I say, you'll get worms again, poo in your pot otherwise you're not getting any jelly.

1 February
Jelly threat works well. For two days didn't get any jelly. Comes into the kitchen today to show me with the eyes: Come and see! Come and see! until I follow her down the passage. Look! the eyes signal. Look! the protruding finger points. A fine turd in the pot it was!

Oh sis! I say, one doesn't show people one's poo, it's impolite, you say nicely: Excuse me, I'm going to the bathroom, and you do your number two nicely and wipe your tail nicely and then you get jelly. Now you've pooed in the pot nicely, but don't think it's that easy, jelly you'll get when you've learnt to speak nice full sentences.

Then it looked at the ground and jutted out the chin! First sulk! First clear facial expression to play on my feelings! It excited me very much, but I can't show it. Tidy up your face, then you'll have jelly, I say. Then she rearranged the face and looked me straight in the eye, ever so sanctimonious. I had to look away. Couldn't help wanting to laugh. Just like a little puppy that begs even though she knows she's not allowed to.

5 February
Is eating well now, every day. Chicken and vegetables, with the hands when I'm not looking. First little slice of brown bread as well. Just has to be hungry enough. Doesn't want to handle cutlery herself yet. Just as if she doesn't want the insides of her hands to be seen. A few times already I've forced open the hands, pressed in the palms, felt through all knucklebones, couldn't feel anything wrong, except that the small hand is colder and limper. Perhaps also it's just become lazy, from being hidden all the time and never being used, the little arm though is clearly deformed.

You could fold the pink sweet's wrapper, I say, don't think I didn't see it. You can do everything with those little hands of yours. She just stares at me with big eyes.

6 February

I open the little weak hand and put the hand-bell in it, I shake it with my hand folded around hers, but when I let go, she drops the bell.

7 February

Devised a little game, call-each-other-with-bells. I take the bronze bell and she has the silver one with her in the room. If she answers my ring-ing with her ringing, I'll unlock the door of her room, I say. I ring it in the kitchen and creep closer and peep through the slot. What would make her so scared of picking up something, I wonder? She sits and just looks at the bell, does though hold it now for a few seconds if I put it in her deformed hand. We're going to make it strong, I say, we're going to make it clever just like your other hand, we're going to exercise it and give it nice things to do every day.

8 February

Went to see Ds van der Lught in town this morning. Quite patient and fatherly. It's a very big responsibility, he says, but the Lord put it in your way to teach you patience and humility.

Only over tea could I bring myself to touch on the matter of the name. The nicknames with which she grew up in her own home, he just shook his head, was immediately very helpful, took thick reference books off his shelf. 'Agaat' he suggested then. Odd name, don't know it at all, but then he explained, it's Dutch for Agatha, it's close to the sound of Asgat with the guttural 'g', it's a semi-precious stone, I say, quite, he says, you only see the value of it if it's correctly polished, but that's not all, look with me in the book here, it's from the Greek 'agathos' which means 'good'. And if your name is good, he says, it's a self-fulfilling prophecy. Like a holy brand it will be, like an immanent destiny, the name on the brow, to do good, to want to be good, goodness itself. We'll have her baptised accordingly when she's a bit bigger, when she can understand what's happening to her, he says. Then we knelt and he prayed for me and for Agaat and the commission I'd accepted and he thanked the Lord for another heathen soul added to the flock by the good works of a devoted child of God, a stalk gathered into the sheaf.

I must write the commission as Dominee helped me to clarify it today. My task and vocation with this. Now I no longer feel so alone with it. And I must write up the beginning, the beginning of everything, before I forget the feeling, of how I found her and knew she was mine.

17

P·R·A·Y I make Agaat spell. P tap R tap A tap Y tap, that's right,
P·R·A·Y.

I do it with the left eye. It's the only one that can still blink. The other
one, the right, has started staring, overnight. Or a few nights ago? How
long have I slept?

I no longer know. I drift off without knowing, I dream I come to and
it's another day's evening or two afternoons later. All that I know is that
the winking-reflex is gone in my right eye, all that I feel is a faint spasm
now and again round the eyeball, but the eyelids no longer move.

Now Agaat comes and with the fingers of her small hand she presses
the lower lid up to keep the eye moist. But I know what she thinks
would be preferable. I can see it in her face, that jaw. She'll stick down
the staring eye with a wad of cotton wool and a plaster.

Nobody can want to wink someone else's eye for her.

Enough is enough.

How to make peace with one eye, an unfathomable interpreter and
the alphabet? If peace it can be called.

Can I make it with her?

We could make a flower garden. She dug up a photo here that Dawid
still took of us, when the trellising for the rambling roses was put up.
Our faces, Agaat's and mine, elated with working and planning. We're
standing there amongst the holes and the trenches and the heaps of soil,
but we look as if we can already see everything in flower.

Could one hope for more, after all?

I smell the gillyflowers, the wild pinks through the open door.

Would that have to be peace enough for us? The paradisiacal garden?

Next to me is the large hydrangea arrangement. How long have I been
sleeping? Two days? Three? Four? This morning she gave the flowers a

look that I know but too well. Past their prime. One day more. Then they have to get out of here. Onto the compost heap. Ready to be dug in.

Pray, she repeats my first word of the talking-hour. A light touch of disbelief I discern there.

She steps back from the board, places the duster in the corner. There's a red streak of dust on her sock. Her cap is skew. Where was she again in the night? She turns to the mirror. Arms by the sides. Then she lifts her hands. But they don't go to her head. It's not to pin her cap straight. She regards herself with her hands in the air. Outnumbered, it says. Surrender.

P·R·A·Y, I asked. It's the only opening I can devise to initiate what I want to plead for. Don't throw them out. Our blue-purple hydrangeas. Don't throw yourself out, and me neither. Hold us for a while yet. There is beauty also in flowers that fade. Their last hour provides stuff for contemplation. Contemplate it for me. For whom do you in any case want to refresh the vase? It's our last flower arrangement with a history in this room. Remember, you salvaged the vase. And stuck it together. And it never leaked.

She reads to me from the Bible every evening. Lamentations. How is the gold become dim! How is the most fine gold changed! The stones of the sanctuary are poured out in the top of every street. And then she prays. The *Our Father*. The safest prayer under the circumstances. Forgive us our trespasses.

Now it's morning. The curtains are open. I've been washed, she's dripped three drops of tea with a dropper at the back of my tongue, wiped out the inside of my mouth with a sponge, cursorily. The tea was cold. She'd forgotten to add sugar. The sponge was rough, bitterish. Aloe. Wormwood. The peppermint's run out, and why buy a new tube at this stage?

Last night, was it last night? Or the night before last? The squabble about Jakkie? I could still blink with both eyes.

She spelt out everything I wanted to say. Not a word in reply. Stepped forward and back with the stick, kept on her glasses so that I couldn't see her eyes. Looked at what I was blinking, tapped short and sharp with the duster handle, let me have my say as fast as she could, her voice neutral in repeating my questions for me, said nothing in reply. It was worse like that than when she imitates my intonation. That's been her style the last few days. Cool and casual. But there's a rumbling somewhere inside her.

I feel the tea trickle out of me. Would it be warmer now than when it went into me? Sweeter? Or salty? Or sad? I feel devastated by my outburst and spelt out like that I don't even have the excuse that I lost my temper spontaneously, I wanted to get at her.

D·I·D Y·O·U R·E·A·L·L·Y H·A·V·E M·I·L·K W·H·E·N Y·O·U L·E·T J·A·K·K·I·E D·R·I·N·K F·R·O·M Y·O·U, question mark. W·H·Y D·I·D Y·O·U N·E·V·E·R T·E·L·L M·E T·H·A·T Y·O·U H·A·D S·E·E·N T. B·L·U·E E·M·P·E·R·O·R B·U·T·T·E·R·F·L·Y I·N T. F·O·R·E·S·T, question mark. I W·A·S T·H·E·R·E B·E·H·I·N·D T. R·O·C·K F·I·G I S·P·I·E·D O·N Y·O·U I S·A·W E·V·E·R·Y·T·H·I·N·G, exclamation mark. S·T·O·L·E H·I·M F·R·O·M M·E, exclamation mark. T·O·O·K H·I·M O·U·T O·F M·E F·U·L·L O·F B·L·O·O·D + S·L·I·M·E + W·R·A·P·P·E·D H·I·M + T·O·O·K H·I·M + N·E·V·E·R R·E·T·U·R·N·E·D H·I·M B·U·T Y·O·U S·A·W W·H·A·T C·A·M·E O·F I·T, colon. H·E W·H·O B·E·N·D·S T·O H·I·M·S·E·L·F A J·O·Y D·O·T·H T·H·E W·I·N·G·E·D L·I·F·E D·E·S·T·R·O·Y, full stop. S·L·E·E·P·I·N·G P·I·L·L·S I·N H·I·S W·I·N·E Y·O·U C·O·U·L·D H·A·V·E K·I·L·L·E·D H·I·M T·H·A·T F·I·R·S·T L·E·T·T·E·R O·F H·I·S T·H·A·T S·U·P·P·O·S·E·D·L·Y A·R·R·I·V·E·D A M·O·N·T·H A·F·T·E·R H·E L·E·F·T, comma, S·L·A·N·T·E·D L·E·T·T·E·R·S F·O·R·W·A·R·D + B·A·C·K T·O C·A·M·O·U·F·L·A·G·E Y·O·U·R H·A·N·D·W·R·I·T·I·N·G question mark. H·E K·N·E·W N·O·T·H·I·N·G O·F I·T H·E W·O·U·L·D N·O·T H·A·V·E U·S·E·D P·O·S·T O·F·F·I·C·E T·H·E·N + H·I·S C·O·N·C·E·R·N·E·D L·I·T·T·L·E C·A·L·L·S N·O·W·A·D·A·Y·S, question mark. D·O Y·O·U I·N·V·E·N·T A·L·L T·H·A·T A·S W·E·L·L A·S Y·O·U A·L·W·A·Y·S D·I·D, question mark. I·T·S Y·O·U·R F·A·U·L·T T·H·A·T H·E L·E·F·T L·I·K·E T·H·A·T, exclamation mark. W·H·A·T A·L·L D·I·D Y·O·U T·E·L·L H·I·M I·N T·H·A·T P·L·A·N·E T·H·A·T N·I·G·H·T O·F H·I·S B·I·R·T·H·D·A·Y, question mark. I·T·S Y·O·U·R F·A·U·L·T T·H·A·T J·A·K C·A·M·E T·O G·R·I·E·F N·O·T T·H·A·T I M·I·S·S H·I·M, accent mark, N·O·T I·N T. L·E·A·S·T, exclamation mark. B·U·T T·H·E·R·E = A·F·T·E·R A·L·L S·U·C·H A T·H·I·N·G A·S G·R·A·T·I·T·U·D·E, exclamation, D·I·S·G·R·A·C·E, exclamation. S·E·A·R·C·H·E·D W·H·O·L·E H·O·U·S·E C·R·O·S·S E·X·A·M·I·N·A·T·I·O·N·S + Y·O·U B·E·H·I·N·D T. K·I·T·C·H·E·N D·O·O·R L·I·S·T·E·N·I·N·G H·O·W Y·O·U·R P·L·O·T·S D·I·S·T·I·L, exclamation exclamation exclamation, M·Y O·N·L·Y C·H·I·L·D, exclamation D·O·E·S H·E K·N·O·W I A·M D·Y·I·N·G H·E·R·E, question mark. W·H·Y D·O Y·O·U K·E·E·P M·E I·N T·H·E D·A·R·K, swearword, A·B·O·U·T H·I·S P·L·A·N·S, exclamation question mark.

When I'd done, she came and stood by the foot of the bed, untied her apron, unbuttoned her dress in front, bared her small crooked shoulder in front of me and folded her hands in front of her. At first she talked, but the words had a cadence, a kind of songspeech it was, full of archaic expressions.

In the life of the sheep
weaning-time is the most critical time.
You who are the farmers of the future,
must make every effort to see
that the little lambs do not suffer over-much.
That their first growth is good is essential
because once marred in their development,
they never mend again.

I closed the eye that could close. I couldn't look upon the crooked shoulder any longer, the expression on Agaat's face, her mouth twisting as if she were weeping the words.

What did she want me to make of it?

Therefore, before you banish the ewes,
the lambs must walk for a while with their mothers
together in the best grazing
to acquaint them with their new place.
Although mourning can never be forestalled,
they will then have to suffer much less sorrow.

I could close one eye, that's right, now I remember, that was the moment, that was when it happened for the first time, the other eye remained staring. And still I had to endure it, the incantation, on the pattern, so it sounded to me, of the aboriginal lamentations on Jakkie's tape.

After separation the ewes must never
walk in the neighbouring camp,
but far enough on vlei and hill,
and best below the wind
for their bleating not to be heard by their lambs.
A child as is well-known,
can tell her mother's voice from a thousand others,
and from as far away as four full miles.
And furthermore, as lambs are really stupid,
and huddle together against the fence,
and stampede themselves into a heap in one corner of the camp,
you must let a few old-ewes walk with them.

I tried to turn my eye up, downwards, sideways, but for the first time it was stuck, totally unyielding in its socket and I had to keep looking at her. I relaxed my focus, tried to haze out the image. But under the white cap the brown smudge of Agaat's face kept looming, distorted, rippling, like an underwater statue singing.

The motherly full-mouthed sheep
will disinterestedly
calm the little weanlings,
and lure them to the grazing and to water
so that they do not lose condition.
Carefully to milk out the bereaved ewe,
is on the other hand your duty,
the more so if you have been blessed
with an abundant season.

When the song was done, she wrenched back her arm into its sleeve and went and sat in the Redman Chief, strapped herself in, clicked shut the buckle and started reading from a blue booklet. Only her lips moved. When she saw I was looking at her, she pressed the knob, grabbed the steering column and turned the chair, a soughing right-about turn. Only the high black back I could see, the chrome grips on either side, the deeply treaded black rubber of the back wheels. Only a whispering I heard from time to time from behind the backrest, moaning sounds, as if the chair had a life of its own.

Could I have dreamed it all? The snuffling, the forward and backward manoeuvring of the chair, the leisurely turnabouts, first this way round and the other way round? The fluttering of pages, the tearing sounds, the groaning, the sighing? The backward recline setting, the forward incline setting, the automatic rocking function, at a small angle, just lightly to and fro, to go to sleep? To relieve the bodily aches of the seated?

Did I think it all up? Such a bare shoulder you could surely not dream up? Such a chair? There it looms in the middle of the room, a throne of black leather and chrome, the embroidery heaped up on the seat. Like a burnished throne.

I'm not dreaming now, I'm wide awake. It's morning, I smell the garden, I see the hydrangea arrangement. I remember. Over there in the corner stands the duster where Agaat has just put it down.

P·R·A·Y, I spelled.

Pray, she repeated, with the trace of a question in it. She's waiting for me to speak more. How can I explain why I want a prayer to be said? A way in it is, a snare. How else am I to find out what she's turning over in her mind? Where she went to in the night?

411

Three times I was aware of her standing next to my bed in the dark. After the last time I heard her go out at the back. But I didn't hear the outside room's door open. It was the door of the storeroom. I heard something fall, a clattering of spades and tools, a muffled exclamation. And then nothing, only the wind, and floating on it a rumour, an image, an intimation of discord, of lamentation, of a beating of the breast, the white cross straining across shoulders, screams in the night, against the red stones, in the red dust of summer, a shaking of the firmament, a star shower, a dark glow from the mountain, a weal across the eye, across the cheek, a burning grey bloom, but not my own tears. Old as the bloom on black-ripe Christmas plums it was, soft and powerful. I heard the dogs bark, in the distance, high up, from across the river, from the direction of the mountain. Boela's bark, Koffie's bark, upset, deranged, a barking after whatever possesses human beings.

Pray for me, Agaat, pray for whatever possesses human beings. Pray for the last plum season that I shall live to see.

You can't prescribe people's prayers.

Forgive us our trespasses as we forgive those that trespass against us.

Lead us not into temptation. And forgive us our trespasses.

How simple that sounds, but who leads whom and who trespasses against whom here?

Why create a temptable human being?

Forty days in the wilderness! Here it is, marked down for me in the calendar. 6 November to 16 December. The calendar is clamped fast to the reading stand, over the commission, over the symptoms and their futile bygone treatment.

Forty days. All the kingdoms of the world, if thou therefore wilt worship me, all shall be thine. That she read from the Bible. When? Yesterday afternoon?

If thou therefore wilt worship me, shall be thine? What's that supposed to mean? Does she think she's Beelzebub?

I have two days left to make a full forty. How many quarter-hours is that? I can't count any more, the dark and the light hours, the ray of sun on the altar. Sixteen December is circled. The Day of the Covenant, the Day of Reconciliation.

An affirmative calendar! Can anybody be so deliberate! So pathetic! So literal! Or is it pure coincidence? Is everything that's happened here pure coincidence? Is it only I who dreamed up the causes and the effects, the reasons and the grounds? And she who rearranged them? Because without that one cannot live and cannot die?

Pray for me, Agaat, wipe the grey bloom from my cheek, from your cheek. There is a possibility of lustre. The black-ripe fruit. The sweet moisture. Wipe the bloom on your sleeve. Let there be radiance.

What are you doing there in front of the mirror?

Are you verily rolling up your sleeve in front of me again?

Why the exposure all the time? What am I supposed to see that I haven't seen yet? I know it, don't I. Your deformed arm. I brought you up, didn't I?

Your right sleeve, up, further up, over that shrunken hand of yours. Over that thin straight little forearm, bare as a crowbar? The round elbow a length of bent copper tubing? A brazen snake in the desert? Are you raising it above me? Your black sleeve, rolled up as far as your armpit, for a clean blow, for a straight strike? At which part of me are you going to aim? Are you going to penetrate me with it? Through the heart? With the same arm that made me pity you in the first instance?

One shouldn't pity deformities! Every deformity is a weapon, a lever, the seat of power and devastation.

Is that what you're trying to get across to me?

She holds the arm athwart her face. She turns it, moves it down. A fencing foil. One pace back she takes, one pace forward. Dip at the knees! Up jerks the shoulder!

Before the railings of my bed.

As on the moonlit night of the burial of the heart.

As in the Tradouw with the umbilical cord that jerks, the rope from which the child is suspended.

As before the sick bull in the holding pen.

As before the foaming waves of Witsand in the black bathing costume.

Low she keeps.

High she aims.

Does she want to charge?

Does she want to kneel?

Does she want to be assumed in glory?

What convulsion of self-exposure, what furious salutation is this?

No, she puts her knuckle in her mouth.

She takes her knuckle out of her mouth. She has broken the skin. Blood flows from it.

On this fragrant morning before my unbalanced gaze she prays.

Lord God in heaven, comes her voice.

Hear me!

Foot-rot!

Stinking smut!

She dips her head, the white cap casts a splash against the mirror.

Pip!

Roup!

Glanders!

Greasy heel!

Contagious abortion!

Waterpepper knotweed!

Who do I have other than you? Don't go away from me! Don't leave me! What would I ever do without you, with my words?

I'm looking for the suitcase!

Have mercy on me!

For thy Name's sake.

Amen.

*

January '84. You and Jak got a special invitation to attend the medal parade at Ysterplaat. The Air Force crest was thickly embossed on the card. The instruction was that the guests of honour should be formally dressed. *Ladies requested to wear head-covering and gloves.* After the ceremony a lunch with choral song in a hall and in the afternoon a military air show. Jakkie would sing and form part of a formation-flight squadron. He'd already informed you himself of the event just after returning from Operation Askari where they'd bombed the shit and toe-nails out of the Cubans, as Jak put it.

Jak came to press the card into your hand in the garden where you and Agaat were giving the roses a summer pruning.

First order, gold, Cross of Honour for outstanding service, leadership and bravery in specialised high-risk warfare, he read.

You passed the card to Agaat. Her mouth was set in a line, a flickering of eyelids. She said nothing.

You'd noticed, by then for more than a year, that Jakkie was no longer replying so regularly to her letters. You read her objections to this, she knew that her letters were now destined for your eyes as well. She taunted you in every intercepted letter.

I understand if you're too busy to write back, Captain, in that case just send a card to say that you're still alive, or make the phone ring three times to say you're thinking of me, your mother and I will know it's you.

To that there was in fact a reply, over Christmas, 1983 it was.

It was quite a thick letter delivered by hand by a fellow-pilot of Jakkie's passing through on leave. On the front it said only *Gaat*.

It had a blob of red sealing wax on the back. For Mr and Mrs J.C. de Wet there was an envelope with four photos with writing on the back, swift hard scribbles with a ballpoint pen. Over and over you switched the photos and read, over and over Agaat took them from you and read. What were the two of you supposed to do with it? Fierce was the writing: *Rambo de Wet next to his Impala after he'd bombed FAPLA positions at Mulondo on 23 December '83. Could see f-all of the cumulonimbus almost came a cropper. Sh-tting myself with the SAM's left and right round my head, one Impala shot in the tail but landed safely at Ondongwa, your own little Rambo also hit by a SAM-7, had to land at Ongiva, fortunately they'd fixed the landing strip there a few weeks earlier otherwise he'd definitely have seen his arse.*

On the second photo the pen had started to slip.

Schwarzenegger of the Overberg with infected eardrum (left, note the plug) with his Mirage F-I after the photo-recce of Cuvelai. Had to fly under the radar, just about heard the thorn bushes scraping his belly.

Photo three was damaged, so hard had he pressed on the pen. What could it mean, the references to himself in the third person? That's not how you knew him.

de Wet after his sufficiently hard-arsed command of two Alouettes through ack-ack to cover the troops on the ground at Cuvelai. It's the only position that really saw its arse. The FAPLA is as cosily as ever entrenched at Cahama, Mulondo and Caiundo. The SADF top brass are making a glorious b-lls-up. They think we're bats with radar in our heads. Overhead the moon is beaming, ha!

Photo four was a group photo of pilots in front of their sleeping quarters, clearly reluctant to pose.

We now hear here that the Caiundo attack had never even been properly approved at Ops HQ. Hence the sulks. Military & national strategy are non-existent we scheme. Regional conflict my arse, it's a full-on international f-ck-up! It could have been prevented. Pik & Magnus are sitting on their brains down there in Pretoria. Sorry, Pa, but that's my story and I'm sticking to it! Hope to see you at the survival parade in February!

You showed Jak the photos only at supper.

He took them away from you quickly.

You didn't see them, he said, you don't know anything about this. What else? was there a letter? I want to see it, now on the spot!

He held out his hand to Agaat.

Ash, in my fireplace, she said.

You went to buy yourself a new blue dress and a matching hat with a turn-up brim and a new handbag at De Jagers in town. The dress was too short and Agaat let out the hem for you.

It could be a long day, you said to Jak, I'm taking Gaat along for company.

Over my dead body, said Jak, in that Agatha Christie outfit of hers, it's a gala occasion and we're guests of honour of the Air Force, she won't be allowed, we're going to eat with the VIPs in the mess, what do you want to do with her then? There aren't any amenities.

I'll eat, Jak, and then I'll excuse myself, it'll have been a whole morning's to-do and then I'll want to rest, then I won't want to look at a lot of aeroplanes.

You said it casually, so as not to upset him.

We can look for a shady tree, you said to Agaat, also as if it were the most ordinary thing on earth. Then we'll be out of the crush, we can read magazines, you can pack a picnic for yourself, take the cool bag, I take my knitting, you pack your embroidery-basket, then at least we can make the afternoon worth our while for ourselves in our own way, I have no desire to get a crick in my neck from staring up into the air all the time.

Will I see him? Agaat asked.

You'll see him in the air, you've always wanted to see what it looks like.

She glared at you.

You waited until Jak had pulled out the car, before you gave the signal. Agaat was ready, the house was locked. You opened the front and back doors simultaneously. You got in at the same time, Agaat with her baskets and tins, you with your cream-coloured handbag and the new shoes for which you'd had to stick plasters to your heels.

Jak was furious, he swore at everything ahead of him and overtook on double white lines up blind rises. In Swellendam he stopped with squealing tyres in front of the off-sales and bought a six-pack of beer, started drinking it immediately.

You didn't even dare look back. You felt Agaat's jaw jutting into your neck. Of all the summers of my life, you thought, this one is the ugliest. The hills were dry and dreadful, False Bay's water flashed like steel when you crossed Sir Lowry's Pass.

A curtain-raiser of lighter planes and gliders was in progress when you arrived. From far away you could already see the cars flashing in the sun, whole fields of them.

Can we please just try to find a little shade, you asked.

There was a separate entrance a long way further, a sandy road amongst the rooikrans bushes, the only greenery as far as the eye could see. You saw coloured people capering and dancing with bottles in the air when low-flying planes came by. You heard them holler, salacious comments for the helicopters that came and hovered on the spot in the air and double-decker Tiger Moths flying upside down. They were draped all over one another.

That'll be the day that I'll park my car for you amongst a crowd of drunken hotnots, Jak said, but we can drop her here so long, here amidst her family of the flats, then she can learn to speak a bit of Cape, will do her good, her sounding like the *Farmer's Weekly* in an apron. Do you think one afternoon is enough for rehabilitation? If you could teach her, Milla, just imagine how quickly they'll get on top of her.

That's enough, you warned, but you knew it was in vain. This was Jak's four-beer bravado.

Agaat is nice and grown up, isn't she, he persisted, I thought that was why she came along today specially, and it's high time, stands drying up in the stable like an unserviced mare.

Hey chickelay chickelee, Jak sang, and swayed his body behind the steering wheel, come sit by me, chickelay chickelee!

You didn't know how he'd come upon the little song all of a sudden. With such an expression too, as he looked around at Agaat. Even when you were young, he'd never looked at you with such an expression, not even as a joke. And this was no joke. You were ashamed, in three directions.

Come on, Agaat, he taunted, while he drove slowly through the clusters of coloured people, gave them a fright and made them scatter by accelerating unexpectedly, what do you say? Have you seen anything that interests you yet? I'll pay him for you, you know, so you can crutch him, a real city goffel with long heels and a gap between his front teeth and a shiny shirt! You're stuck out there on Grootmoedersdrift without any company, if you're satisfied, we'll buy him for you. You've got the whole day to try him out. On appro.

Jak took his hands off the steering wheel and twisted and rubbed his palms in the air in front of him.

Ride the woolly, hip-hip hay, hip-hip hay! he sang.

The people yelled across the shiny BMW in the sand there, they pushed their tongues through their front teeth at Agaat, swore at Jak, hammered their hands on the roof.

It was a mistake, you realised. Not one of you should have come along. Jak was ashamed to drive with the coloured woman in the back of his car, he was ashamed of you sitting next to him in your big blue hat.

Amongst the vast wastes of motor cars he at last found a parking place.

Sorry! you signalled with your eyes at Agaat as you got out. You took ten rand out of your purse and placed it on the seat.

Cooldrink, you spelt with your eyes.

Agaat gave you the dead eye. She had a long white envelope in her hands.

Give it to him, she said, don't fold it.

You put it in your handbag. Between your gloved fingertips you thought you felt a slight thickening in the envelope, a texture.

It was terribly hot on the parade ground. The air above the tar shimmered. All the women in your block of seats were wearing hats. Only in the first row where the wives of the ministers and the brigadiers and the generals were sitting, sunshades had been put up.

The chaplain opened the parade with scripture reading. He prayed that the angels would guard over the brave soldiers who had to drive away the Philistines from our borders.

The Prime Minster made a speech. He pointed with his finger. He wiped his brow with a white handkerchief.

The Minister of Defence spoke. South Africa has the best defence force in Africa, he said. He read the weapons off a list. They're all here to be seen today he said, but they're worth nothing without the well-trained youths manning them. We care for the injured. Our hearts go out to the friends and family of those who fell in the service of their fatherland, he said, it was the highest sacrifice that was asked, that was brought. Another list. The dead.

Then a salute was fired, the last post was sounded, the band played, the national anthem was sung.

After that the medals and the honourable mentions.

There was a stamping of feet, a waving of flags, a saluting. Jak cursed the heat. You were sitting at the back of the block. There were too many hats and umbrellas in front of you for you to see much. When it was Jakkie's turn, you got to your feet. He looked just like all the others, small, there on the barren surface and under the wide white-blue sky. His medal was pinned on, he stepped back, saluted, you sat down. The applause in the open air sounded like twigs snapping.

Afterwards Jakkie came to greet you. You'd last seen him almost nine months earlier. He was a different man. Clean-shaven, creaseless, a guardedness in his eyes, something around his mouth that you couldn't place.

Agaat, you wanted to say, but your mouth was numb. You wanted to take out the envelope. Your gloved fingers slip-slided over the smooth chrome clip of your handbag,

Jak flick-flicked his finger against Jakkie's chest where his medal was dangling.

Eighteen carats, he said.

Agaat, you wanted to say, but other people joined you to congratulate Jakkie. A corporal with a guest list herded you into the brick building where the lunch was to take place. The air inside was muggy with food smells and an undertone of hot metal. The ceiling was high and the hall was dusky but it wasn't cool. There were fans against the ceiling churning the warm air. You were conducted to your seats. The choir sang three little songs. *From the welter of the ages*, and then a medley with *Daisy, daisy, give me your answer do* and other songs, and, while the seafood cocktail was being served, a canon, *Come Lord Jesus, be our guest, let these thy gifts to us be blessed.* The conductor signalled to the people in the hall when to join in and sing along. You couldn't identify Jakkie's voice amongst the tenors. You couldn't even recognise him there on the rostrum, they all looked alike. There were two other pairs of parents at your table. Jak had the wine opened, poured, asked for another bottle and started chatting to the men. You looked at the other women. What was in their eyes? Nothing. Made up with eye shadow and mascara. Just like yours.

Jakkie and two other captains came to join you at your table. They exchanged glances without talking.

Next was the buffet. You noticed too late that the other women had left their hats and handbags at the tables. Again and again men's shoulders bumped and brushed against the rim of your hat. Your nose was sweating but you had the tray in your hands already. Your heels were burning in your shoes.

Give me your handbag and gloves, Ma, said Jakkie.

Was there impatience in his voice? He cast one look around and a junior materialised to take charge of them.

Your hat, madam? the little chap asked.

Jakkie gave him a look and he stepped back smartly and marched away with one arm pumping up and down and the bag and gloves on his flat hand in front of him like a cake on a tray.

Jak gave you a look. It was a hall full of furious eyes, you felt.

From the stainless steel trays you had pumpkin served for you, potatoes, cauliflower in white sauce, peas. You thought of Agaat in the hot car in the parking lot. In a flash you imagined a separate table, all seated with servants in black-and-white uniforms. Perhaps you'd have another chance at the table to give Jakkie her envelope.

Madam? the carver asked, pork, lamb, beef, or a bit of everything?

Come, Milla, said Jak, pushing his tray into your back, the queue is long.

Lamb, you said, just a small portion.

Jakkie ate nothing. I can't fly on a full stomach, he said. He and the other two kept glancing at their watches. He was far from you. Why didn't you get up and walk around the table and give him the envelope? You looked at his uniform. It didn't have a pocket into which it would fit without a corner showing. You can't have a piece of white paper sticking out of the neat blue uniform, can you?

Jak was in his element. He'd loosened his tie and taken off his jacket. He was showing off his knowledge of fighter planes. A third bottle of wine arrived. The other women didn't drink and you were too shy to hold out your glass again. It would have helped, a bit more alcohol, you thought. How can I get out of here? you wondered.

You tried to grasp your opportunity when Jakkie excused himself.

I suppose I won't see you again, he said. He shook Jak's hand, squeezed your shoulder. You tried to get up. Are you coming home for your birthday? you wanted to ask, but you couldn't. This wasn't the place for it. He'd gone before you could pick up your handbag from the floor. You had an image of the white envelope there in the gloom of your bag. What could it contain?

Sit down, Milla, there's dessert and coffee to come, said Jak. The smell of the coffee under the hot ceiling turned your stomach. You stirred striations of chocolate sauce through the ice cream.

He can see like an eagle, that boy of mine, Jak was bragging.

You could vaguely, above the hubbub in the hall, make out the sound of the jets warming up.

He can balance on a three-strand steel wire one foot before the other, not an ounce of fear in him. I taught him from early on, in the mountains, in the kloofs, in the waterfalls, hand over hand on a slack chain with a rucksack on his back. He could keep his head in a butter-churn, that lad.

Then you were outside again in the white heat. You saw the women putting on their hats again, this time to protect their faces against the sun. But Jak stopped you.

For heaven's sake take that thing off, you know you can't see a damn thing from under that brim!

The first rending din was upon you, seven Impalas squirting orange, white and blue plumes of smoke from their tails. A self-important voice on the public address system asked for applause. How silly, you thought, it's not as if they can hear up there in their capsules? That's the way things have been all day, you thought. The occasion wasn't for the soldiers. But for whom was it? The women trailed after the men over the tarmac, stood around where they congregated in little groups around the elephant tanks, the rooikat helicopters, the bush pigs, the bushbuck. Armoured game reserve, you thought.

Jak said, tidy up your face, it's in the national interest.

Up and down on the hot tarmac of the showgrounds Jak walked telling and retelling his little band of new-found friends, or rank strangers, or just anybody who would listen, that it was his son up there against the blue, ascending straight up to the sun. You could see that he'd drunk too much, that he was still furious. You screwed up your eyes trying to see, the flakes of steel, how they tumbled spinning downward in formation, the tiny shards on the horizon that sped closer in silent ranks, and passed in silence, the ear-splitting noise lagging them at a distance.

Whenever there was a moment's silence amongst the shrieking of engines and the commentary over the loudspeaker supplying the velocities and details of supersonic and subsonic engine capacities, Jak resumed his account to the bystanders. He gesticulated with his hands, bellowed into his audience's ears to be heard above the noise.

You caught scraps of it.

. . . then I test his reaction time . . . stabiliser muscles . . . reflexes, eye-to-hand coordination . . . exceptionally fit . . . they whisk a man in those flight simulators so that for days he thinks he's custard.

With an excuse of headache you got out of there and returned to the parking lot. You couldn't remember where the car was parked. You started searching amongst the rows and rows of cars. Your shoes were hurting you but you couldn't take them off on the hot tar. The hard roofs of the cars and their glass and their chrome and their side-view mirrors reflected into your eyes so that you couldn't distinguish colours. You became aware of walking in circles, you couldn't remember in which row you'd been and which not. After a while you became confused about the colour of your car. It was a silver-blue BMW but there were many silverish cars that at a distance looked like BMWs. Silver-grey, silver-green, silver-khaki. Then you went and stood on the top step of an electricity substation and tried to read the number plates as far as you could see. CBY, CEY, CA, CAT but no CCK. Still later you just peered through the windows of cars, through the windows of three, four cars at a time to see if you could spot somebody sitting. Sometimes you thought you saw Agaat's cap. Then you went closer but it would turn out to be a hat, or one of those dogs with red lolling tongues that sway when you drive.

Nowhere was there any shade. As you brushed past the cars, the metal burnt you through your clothes so that time after time you started back, all the time the heat-glow from the car bodies radiated down on you, at short intervals there was the thunderous whistle of the grey needle-nosed fighter planes that sheared low over the roofs out of nowhere, and set the whole parking lot glittering and echoing before swooping away again into the blue, tilting their wings in precisely measured quarter turns, belly up, back up, perilously on the side-fins through the high masts of the loudspeakers and the wires and the towers.

Anti-aircraft avoidance nosedives below radar range for espionage photography of enemy positions, the commentary went, deafening from the loudspeaker trumpets.

This is what hell is like, you thought, this is the temperature, this is the sound of hell. Just so do you search there for someone you've lost.

Gaat! you wanted to scream, there in the deserted parking lot.

Gaat! to make her white cap suddenly materialise above the expanse of motor cars.

Here, Gaat, here! you'd call and wave your hands so that she'd come and fetch you. She'd see that you were in need but pretend that it was nothing.

That's how you were used to doing one to the other.

You couldn't find the car. You found the ablution block and felt heartened but not for long. It wasn't the same one that you'd run into quickly that morning when you arrived. That had been a red-polished cement floor, not grey. Poor Agaat, you thought, where would she have found a place to pee?

Under the flat tin roof of the ablution it was oppressively hot. It smelt strongly of Jeyes Fluid, but at least it was in the shade. You could still hear the announcements on the loudspeakers, but they were muffled now.

In the gloom you rinsed your face and wrists again and again at the basin. The water was warm. You took off your shoes and stockings. The plasters on your heels were scrunched up. You dripped water onto your chafed feet and dried them with toilet paper. You wet your handkerchief and wiped your armpits and back under your dress, and underneath your bra, from above and below.

You lowered yourself against the wall until you could sit on the cement, your legs paralysed all of a sudden. You remembered the envelope. You opened it. It was a delicately embroidered bookmark.

For your Bible, Jakkie, the accompanying card said, put it in with Psalm 23. Remember, the Lord is your Shepherd in all the dangers that you have to face. Love, Agaat.

You rested your head on your knees and wept.

Later the noise of the jet fighters abated. You started hearing other sounds, softer snoring sounds as of toy aeroplanes. It was comforting after the violence of the fighters. You felt sleepy, drifted off. Until somebody came in later and asked you if you were feeling ill and you said no, just hot. Then you got up and washed your face again, applied make-up, powdered your nose. You went into a toilet cubicle and put on your stockings again, folded bits of toilet paper and pushed them into the backs of your shoes.

Outside, hundreds of people were making their way to their cars. There were only a few of the little traffic helicopters in the air and the voice of the announcer, much softer now, interspersed with march music. You searched for the gate through which you'd entered the parking lot from the showgrounds, but you were forced back by the streams of people moving in the opposite direction. To and fro next to the chicken wire you walked trying to perhaps spot Jak or one of the table companions to attract their attention. You were panicky. What if you didn't find Jak? What if he just decided to leave without you? What if then for good measure he chucked Agaat out of the car as well? Would she have the common sense to just remain sitting dead-still in one spot until there were just the two of you left there in the empty parking lot?

You could do nothing but wait in the crush. You remained standing against the chicken wire with your handbag and your hat in your hands. Later you put on the hat in order to be more visible. People smiled at you.

How did you eventually reach the car, reach home?

There are shreds that you remember. Jak charging, swearing, past the slow line of cars on the left shoulder of the service road, Agaat tumbling around on the back seat rigid as a totem pole. You clinging with both hands to the door handle on your side. The abuse that you had to listen to as far as you travelled, the terrifying speed.

You and this golliwog of yours, I'm never taking you anywhere again! Never, do you hear? I'm not going to have my name dragged through the mud in front of the whole goddamned world. That was how Jak began. Spit showered the car as he spoke.

It's a great day in my son's life and from beginning to end you cause nothing but embarrassment! There I had to drop everybody just like that to tag along looking for you and your pet woolly-lamb, I was still thinking after the heat of the day let's take a few people and Jakkie out for a drink somewhere in a nice restaurant overlooking the sea, but no, Milla gets lost so that I have to get the whole of Ysterplaat on red alert! Where were you in any case that you didn't hear it on the loudspeakers? Mrs Milla de Wet, would Mrs Milla de Wet please go to Gate B, her husband Mr Jak de Wet is waiting for her there. Mrs de Wet! Mrs de Wet! Everybody's laughing at me, the man who can't look after his wife, there I am for hours standing at Gate B and then on top of it all I have to explain what a wog's doing in the whites-only toilet. How do you think one explains something like that? And that after I warned you. From the start! But you won't listen! It's Agaat here and Agaat there and Agaat everywhere! Jesusgodjerusalemalmighty, I have so had enough! Do you hear me? Of you and the scum you brought into my house! Enough! Enough! Enough!

Jak didn't speak again. He switched on the radio and turned the knob of the shortwave band, to and fro through the crackling whistling stations until he found what he was looking for. The news and weather forecast. He turned up the volume all the way. There'd been more riots on the Rand and reports of subversive activities. And the forecast for the winter-rainfall area from the Hottentots Holland mountains to Cape Agulhas was a strong south-easter, temperatures of more than thirty degrees and a warning of a fire hazard.

It was deep dusk by the time you got home. That hour of the Overberg summer that always filled you with apprehension. The deceptive light, the smell of sunbaked dust, the wind fraying out the bluegums.

Agaat opened the gate and didn't get back into the car. Not that Jak waited, he pulled off in a cloud of dust and charged in violently over the gravel. You caught a glimpse of Agaat in the side mirror. The dogs were jumping up against her. She bumped them aside with her hips.

Later, after you'd had your bath, after Jak had withdrawn himself, you switched on the table lamps and drew the curtains in the house, fed the dogs and fetched the cream in the little room where the separator stood. In the backyard everything was dark and still. The bolt on the door of the outside room was still drawn. The bottles for the house milk had not been sterilised and set out on the table in the kitchen as usual. The tray that Agaat always put out on the work surface with cups for supper, was standing up straight behind the kettle on the shelf. You looked in the food tins that you'd brought out of the car. The sausage sweaty, the sandwiches soggy, untouched.

You got the torch and put on a pair of tackies to go and look for Agaat. At first you were angry. Why should I have to fret myself? you thought. Everybody flaunts their feelings, but does anybody ever ask me what I'm feeling?

But you were hungry and you felt alone. Agaat would be hungry. You wanted to sit at the kitchen table having tea while she made tomato eggs.

At the dam you ordered the dogs, look for Agaat, look!

Itchy goose-down blew up against you. The quacking and gabbling of ducks and geese and smaller waterfowl clamoured as far as the dogs ran and there was a barking and a splashing and a fluttering of wings and a rustling in the reeds before everything became still again. After a while they were back, came and sat by you with gaping mouths.

You switched off the torch. The dogs' racing breaths made it impossible to listen properly.

Go home, you showed them, get home you two.

What did you want to listen for? A sighing over the water? A weeping in the grass?

Those weren't Agaat's sounds.

The brisk untying of apron bands, yes. The intake of breath when she picked up something with the weak hand, the squelching of her rubber soles. But those were all indoor sounds, caught and reflected by floors and walls and ceilings, the sounds of the bright domestic hours. Now the house against the rise with its table lamps behind the curtains looked to you like a glowing coal in the night.

You'd have to listen for a low humming, you thought, or a crackling. Conditions were favourable.

There were still two places where you could go and look, in the poplar grove by the little vlei on the other side of the dam, and on the koppie in front of the house where she often walked.

You didn't switch on the torch again and on the level ground under the dam wall you found your way to the vlei. There was almost no water in it. You sniffed the air for the smell of fire, but there was only the stench of duckweed and something else, dead cat.

Further along next to the poplar grove the smell got stronger. When you entered the grove, you switched on the torch again and flashed up against the white trunks of the poplars. You tried to imagine, Agaat, swinging from her apron bands, the head with the white cap tilted forward. But it wasn't an honest image, you thought. You could more realistically expect a blunt object to the head.

What were you thinking? That she'd allow herself to be found by you? To be comforted? What were you really looking for there in the dark? Your whole body was in turmoil. There was a metallic taste in your mouth.

You didn't see the ditch in time. The torch shot from your hand as you tumbled down the side. You screamed as you tried to find a hand-hold against the side, but the soil was mushy and muddy and broke up into lumps under your hands. Then you were at the bottom, there was something under your feet, it gave way with a smacking sound, you sank into it up to your ankles. Something crawled against your legs. You screamed again, with long steps tried to get out of the muck. The stench was unbearable. Then you saw the torch lying faintly gleaming.

And it was shining on something that crawled. It took a while for you to make out what it was. The head of a cow, half rotten, with white maggots writhing in the eye sockets and the ears and in the bloated-open mouth and muzzle in which nothing was visible of the gentle expression of the Jersey.

How did you get home? You wanted to escape from your own skin. You ran, a flare of stench.

You got your shoes off, rinsed yourself as well as you could under the jet of the garden hose. There was light in the backyard. You remained standing in the door of the kitchen. You didn't want to go into the house in your dirty dress.

Agaat didn't want to see you. She was pouring the milk from the cans neatly into the bottles. She was wearing a clean apron and a new uniform, a fresh stiffly starched cap on her head. The tea cups were set out, you could hear the kettle boiling. She extracted a bottle from the steaming bowl of water by the mouth with forceps and inverted it to drip dry. One, two, three drops in the bowl. Shake, shake, shake.

She looked up. Wooden eye.

Sis, what's that stink, she said, I'm working with milk here. She looked down and tsk-ed at the bail of the can that kept on falling over her hand as she poured out the milk.

Bring a towel, you said, and my slippers and an old dressing-gown.

The towels, Agaat said with her head in the steam, are in the linen cupboard in the passage, your old dressing-gown is behind the bathroom door, your slippers are in front of your bed.

That was the first time. There had been other times, but never accompanied by words.

You charged at her, you wanted to shake her, you wanted to slap her right there where she was standing with the open bottle of boiling water held out in front of her.

Please, she said to you with a straight voice, her eyes on your cheeks, bring my stuff, please, Agaat.

Put it down, put that bottle down, now this minute, I'm not letting myself be threatened, not by you!

That was what you screamed, wanted to scream, but it sounded like a plea, like please, it's not my fault.

Then Jak was there in his pyjamas, at the inside door. Agaat carefully placed the bottle on the table. She stood aside, her right hand clenched in the left hand in front of her.

Bravo! Jak exclaimed, bravo! Have we really still not had enough concert for one day? The madam, the maid and the milk. How-manieth act?

He walked to the fridge and poured a glass of milk, tasted and spat it out in the sink.

Sour milk on Grootmoedersdrift, he said, I wish you'd mark the bottles.

She, you said and pointed with your finger.

Jak went and sat at the kitchen table.

So tell the baas what's the problem here, Agaat? he said.

Agaat remained standing, swayed forward and back on her rubber soles.

She, you said again.

No, Milla, not she, you, you stink something dreadful, look at your dress, where have you been?

The cow, the cow in the ditch in the poplar grove, you cried.

Yes, the stupid cow, walked where she shouldn't have walked, fell and broke her leg. I had to shoot her.

Agaat moved closer and gathered the full bottles together.

Wait, said Jak, put down, I also want to recite my last lines of the day.

For a moment you thought Agaat was smirking.

My only advice, Gaat, is, don't let yourself be misled, butter-fingers, a falling fashion, gets lost in the parking lot, gets lost on her own farm, it's all put on. Mrs Helpless de Wet with the querulous bleat is a costume. Trying to attract attention, that's all.

Because, and I'm sure you know this, but I'm just reminding you, actually she's perfectly sure-footed, Queen of the Night, immortal, and she rules the world around here. But you wouldn't think it, would you, because she always needs something and it's never enough. Now too hot, now too cold, now too sweet, now too sour. Impossible to please.

Are we heartless, are we cruel, you and I? Then that's only because that's the way she wants us. She, my dear little fuzzy foundling, made us, took us apart and reassembled us. Meccano a la Milla. We are power food for her, our fury is pure vitamin. She thrives on it.

So you go ahead and inspect her well for maggots, you're your nooi's governess after all, and you know all about maggots don't you, you know they enter by the soft spots, under the skin and devour you from the inside until one fine day you simply disintegrate and then everybody says, hey, that's funny, she was never even sick.

*

from the easy chair to the wheelchair in three months it's like walking with a tea trolley but without the tea instead of the teapot now Mrs de Wet poked up propped up patched up strapped up in her wheelchair she's jingling less all the time a dream in a peel a ripple on a pool she is now herself a walking frame on wheels for her nurse her independent living-aid the good old sort she hoists ounooi into it when she has to make the bed and pushes her where she wants her doll by the window doll by the wall doll gazing limply at the floor in the hall sometimes she's rolled up to where there's sweeping to be done or peeling it's better than just having to lie there on her back from wheelchair to wheelchair in less than a year the first chair that she remembers was a spyder from pride mobility products she could propel the high wheels with her own hands the second chair was electrical by redman power chairs with five gears and a joystick hopeful as a courting-candle the third an omega trac full of springs and suspension on which she could drive like an armoured tank over a dam wall the fourth was by permobil an ibot 30-2 a throne on gyroscopes that could climb stoep steps apart from electronics inspired by the purposes of a phantom the last is by froglegs an absolutely ordinary chair because even if she wanted to she could no longer go forward on her own and weaned at last of her hands and her feet and her little wheels she rolls every day like a wash of the sluice with her dreams through the frames and lintels and passages of her house

*

17 February 1954

Agaat reacts to her new name! I say her bedtime prayer: Gentle Jesus my name's Agaat make clean and pure my heart. She doesn't close her eyes, keeps gazing at me wide-eyed. Agaat is good, Agaat is sweet, Agaat's a child of the Lord and He keeps watch over her while she sleeps. Good as gold, as rain, as salt, good as the blaze in the heart of the wood. I don't know if my words achieve anything, I feel the child must learn to associate herself with beautiful and good things, shame still so small and already so damaged by life. I sing to her: Sleep my child, sleep tight, with roses bedight and Sleep baby sleep, Your daddy tends the sheep. Perhaps I should change the words, the child instead of my child and something I don't know what instead of 'your daddy', I wouldn't want her to get wrong ideas now, but I don't suppose it can do any harm, she's so small still.

20 February 1954

Agaat's brought me something for the first time, and taken something from me. Truly a big mile-stone!

This morning still half-asleep I had this bright idea. Just suddenly knew it would work given that the hand-bell won't, something with a greater effect, a more dramatic function it should have, and I thought and I thought and suddenly I knew just the thing! Dug up my father's old tinderbox, demonstrated how you strike the flintstone till you get a spark. Made a little fire on a piece of corrugated iron in the backyard with wisps of grass and pine cones. Great interest! All eyes! On the haunches tight against me. Go and fetch another pine cone, I say. Would you believe it she actually goes and fetches another pine cone! Actually knows where to find a pine cone! And comes and gives it in my hand!

Do you want it? I ask then, do you want the tinderbox? The little hand appears, and takes it out of my hand, careful not to touch me, but tightly the little hand clasps and tightly the little hand holds and she fiddles with it and smells it, the tinder smell.

In front of me! While I'm there! Praise the Lord!

Taught her one doesn't play with fire, only when I'm there is she allowed to strike the flintstone or light a match. It may help to exercise the lazy hand because you can't operate the tinderbox with just one hand. Taught her you say thank you when you're given a present. And if you can't say it with your mouth, then you say it with your eyes. Slow blink with the eyes, once and a small bow of the head means 'thank you' I teach her. Thank you for jelly, thank you for food and clothes and a house, thank you for a tinderbox. Solemnly went and squirreled it away in her hessian sack.

Phoned home. Could have known what the reaction would be. Watch out, says my mother, everything you put in there, will come back to you.

25 February 1954

Made a fire again! This time with a magnifying glass from Jak's office. Will have to get him another one, he looks at the maps with it. White-hot outside. I got burnt blood-red on my neck from sitting still in the sun with the lens. A newspaper fire. Go and fetch grass, I say, go on, go and fetch twigs. Gone and back in a flash she was. Knows about making a fire, it seems. Then believe it or not she holds out her hand for the lens. How does one ask? Please, you say. Otherwise you look straight in the eye of the one who must give and you blink twice quickly with the eyelids. We practised till I was satisfied. Big please. Pretty please. Then again thank you, thank you very, very much with the eyes, close the eyelids slowly and nod forward with the head. She put the lens also in the sack with her other things. Must get her another bag, or a little suitcase, the sack stinks.

27 February 1954

A third fire! Agaat thinks I can do magic. With a flat bit of softwood, half mouldy with wood-mite, and a straight stick. Next to the river in the shade. It took hours, later the sweat was pouring off me, you can't let go, otherwise you have to start all over again. Twirl, twirl, twirl in the little hole. Up and down, my hands burning after a while. First you smell it, the first little curl of smoke appears, up from the base of the stick. Agaat on her knees, looks as if she wants to stare it on fire. Blinks the eyes, looks at me, blinks the eyes, blinks at the turn-stick, blinks at the flat piece of wood. Please! Please! Fire fire in my hand, I say, who sees the first spark in the land? When the smoke was curling properly, I took out the stick, here comes the little hand with the smallest, finest threads of dry straw. As if she's done it often before, as if she knows exactly how, she sprinkles a few shreds into the hole, blows with pursed lips, could hardly believe it, anther shred she adds, blows with the gentlest breath, until the little flame leaps up. Wherever did you see it, Agaat? How do you know so well to start a fire? Who taught you?

Then she looks over my left shoulder, I look round, see nothing, then she looks over my right shoulder, I look round, still nothing, then she looks on the ground, then in the air, then in the palm of her strong hand! And I fold it open nicely and make a show of looking and see nothing. All prim and proper she looks at me!

I think that's the first joke, the first tale that she's told me.

Who taught you about fire?

The Nowherewoman, the woman without name, who is everywhere but who can't be seen, she taught me about starting a fire.

Then I continued the tale: Once upon a time there was a little girl who wanted to learn how to start a fire, and I watched her closely to see if she'd give an indication, hot or cold, but she doesn't let herself be read.

Perhaps there were concrete and specific circumstances when she was still very small, many more, far worse than one could dream up in a fairy tale.

4 March 1954

Agaat is a closed book. Sometimes I think she's wiser than she is. Sometimes I think she's retarded. When you have to communicate through the eyes, live by inferences, misunderstandings are easy. I must remember she's only a child. Seriously damaged. I mustn't want to read too much into things. I mustn't expect too much. Can't help thinking it's the most challenging and also the most promising task I've ever set myself, that the Lord entrusted to me to enrich and fortify me in my spiritual life, to feed my capacity to love my neighbour, to sharpen my insight into my fellow man. I must write down the commission. I must write how I found her otherwise I'll forget how it was, but it seems too much, I'm scared to commit it to writing. Would I find the right words?

6 March

I encourage her to touch things and tug at them, open her hands, to give, receive. Go and fetch my little book, I say, so that I can write down how you are. She knows exactly what I'm talking about, brings it and opens it for me on a blank page. It's going better by the day now. Must silence her because she grabs the silver hand-bell in the dining room and then J. comes to eat and the food isn't nearly ready. It's just the talking that must still be sorted out, everything else will follow quickly once we've got that on track.

11 March

I play shadow puppets for her against the wall. Rabbit, snake, camel, dove. She opens her hands now, the strong hand more readily than the weak, the sly hand, the monkey paw, as I call it. I take the little hand in mine, I open and close it, open and close so that it can become human, I say, but she doesn't like it, she always keeps it half out of play, the weak arm always half out of the way, as if it's private property. I count to five on the fingers of the good hand, I give them names. Pinkie, Golddinky, Laureltree, Eyewasher, Bugsquasher. At night I leave a candle-end with her. I peep through the slot to see what she's doing. She lies and stares at the flame for hours. Plays shadows against the wall with her hands. Weak hand makes the snout, ears, tail. Strong hand the neck of the buck, the head of the horse. Earlier this evening I thought I heard a whispering on a long in-breath like somebody counting sheep and not wanting to lose tally, I suppose I mustn't expect miracles. She doesn't sleep before the candle is burnt down. Every evening before bedtime she brings the candlestick so that I can fit a new candle-end, she carries it to her room as if it's a great treasure.

14 March, seven o'clock

Agaat can talk! So I wasn't wrong about the whispering! She talks to herself in bed but I can't make out what. The whispering is on the in-breath. I see the little chest swell as she takes the breath. Have just gone to press my ear against the slot, a rustling of little sentences, almost voiced, repetition of the same word or phrases, but I only now and again catch something. The rhymes I say to her all the time? Fragments of the stories that I tell? Granny, why are Granny's ears so big, Granny, why are Granny's teeth so long. I know she understands. When I'm telling a story, she looks at me wide-eyed. Sometimes I get the impression she's on the point of asking me something about the stories. But it's as if she's assessing me, as if she's scared that I'm going to take something from her if she opens her mouth.

Quarter past seven

I could spoil everything if I exert pressure now. Have been to listen at the door of the back room again, this time it was unmistakable. What do I hear there?

In the road is a hole, in the hole is a stone, in the stone is a sound. In one sustained in-breath she said the riddle!

Her finger was on the tip of her tongue, as I always have it when I'm saying the riddle to entice her to talk, as if language is something one can taste.

I went to sit on the side of her bed. I won't look, I whispered, I look elsewhere, then you tell me what you lie here and say to yourself, won't you?

I swung my legs onto the bed so that I could lean against the bedpost, tried to relax, so that she could relax as well. Wanted her half to forget that I was there and just carry on with her bedtime stories. Sat there for probably an hour without saying anything. She said nothing further but that's the best that I've yet felt with her. Peaceful. Secure. A kind of motherhood even.

Half past eight
Sat on the stoep for a long time, tried to think of everything that happened there in Agaat's little back room tonight. It's as if I'm too scared to write it down. As if writing would efface the fragile event, as if words would spoil everything.

It smelt sweet there with her in the little bed. Agaat's breath, her little body smell sweet nowadays. All the sores and ringworms have healed, the bad teeth have been pulled, she eats well and sleeps well, has regular bowel movements, has a bath every evening. Not at all as hunched up and bewildered as at first. Sweet, like a little rabbit. And then there was also the twig of fennel that she'd picked this afternoon that I'd put in a little jar next to her bed. I picked a leaf and crushed it between my fingers and smelt it and made her smell it too. Dreamy the little eyes were in mine, they half closed from the aroma. If she were to say something, I thought to myself, it would be because she was almost asleep.

I wanted to press her to me. But that's against the rules.

Twenty to nine
And then!
My hand trembles to write it.
Then I bent down and whispered in her ear.
What did I say to her?

Ten to nine
I'm so hungry, I'm so thirsty, I said, because you don't want to talk to me and I know you can talk, because I hear you, through the hole in the door, how you talk to yourself in bed and I see your lips move and I wonder what you're saying.

I knelt by the bedside.

Perhaps you can say your new name for me?

I blinked with my eyes to ask, big please!

Twenty past nine

Why is it taking me so long to write it up? I'd rather just think about it again and again. It's too precious! It's too fine! Words spoil it. Who could understand?

I held my ear right next to her mouth, a good ten minutes long I breathed in her little fennel breath.

I imagined the tip of her will as the rolled-up tip of a fern. Did I say it out loud? That she should also imagine it? A tender green ringlet with little folded-in fingers?

I bent it open with my attention.

Then it came into my ear, like the rushing of my own blood, against the deep end of the roof of her mouth, a gentle guttural-fricative, the sound of a shell against my ear, the g-g-g of Agaat.

I felt faint, lowered my head on her chest.

Fast asleep she was when I lifted my head. I must have slumbered off myself. Had I dreamt it all?

When I got up, she opened her eyes.
I opened my mouth to say her name.

Then she also opened her mouth.

Then we said her name at the same time. Sweet, full in my mouth, like a mouthful of something heavenly. Lord my God, the child You have given me.

Ten o'clock

Still I have the feeling of satiety. Now still as I'm writing here, hour upon hour, I feel it, a tingling fulfilled feeling through my whole body, as I imagine it must feel to suckle a child. Can it be that you feed someone else and feel replete yourself with it?

Perhaps it's the mere fact that she could go to sleep with me so close to her that makes me feel like this.

It's the first time in my life that I understand it like this, the impersonal unity of all living things. It doesn't matter who is who. The speaker and the listener. The shell and the sea, the mother cat and the human hand that stirs her blind litter, the wind and the soughing pine, the dry drift and the flood. It's one energy. We are one, Agaat and I, I feel it stir in my navel.

17 March 1954

Agaat spoke to me again! Admittedly through a closed door, but still! First we played the knock-knock rhyme, on either side of the door, I say the words and she knocks the rhythm.

> She looks for her man
> and she looks for her child
> her patience is thin
> and her eyes are wild
> she knock-knocks!
> she knock-knocks!
> knock-knock!
> knock-knock!

By the second verse I hear another voice beneath mine.

> She knocks with her body
> To know if she can
> Who has eaten
> Her child and her man?
> Knock-knock, knock-knock.

Then I remained quiet and Agaat actually started the third verse on her own, rapidly on the in-breath.

> Her hunger is great
> and her blood is thin
> she keeps her heart
> on a drawing pin.

Who's speaking? I ask behind the door.
Me.
Who's me?
I am me and you are she.

What's her name?
Agaat.
Agaat who?
Agaat Lourier.
Who is she?
Crawled out of the flea-blanket!
Where does she come from?
Oupa rode a pig!

18 March 1954

Back room door open on a chink. We sit on either side of it on the floor. We sing, we talk, rhymes, songs. Not real sentences yet, but better than nothing. She's evidently taken in everything, literally every word that I've taught her up to now, she can't be retarded! Everything but. Just Jak that's nasty. Coon kindergarten, he calls out when he hears us.

20 March 1954

If she doesn't want to talk to me properly face to face, she doesn't get food and she stays in her room. That's the rule. Two days now.

21 March 1954

Back in the corner with the knuckle in the mouth. Ashen-faced, her moles look black. I simply lock her up. She must be taught to obey me. I send Saar to empty the pot. I say at the door what there is to eat. But she must ask properly in a full sentence what I must dish up for her. I've run out of patience.

22 March 1954

After three days without food it came at last: 'May I please have jelly with custard.'

Word for word, said after me, on the in-breath, whispered, eye cast down.

Jelly is for independent people, not parrots, I said. And you look into my eyes when you talk to me, otherwise I don't hear you.

Gave her a crust of dry bread. Mouth a sour slit, chin out, hungry enough, ate the bread to the last crumb. Obstinate little blighter!

23 March '54

Caught Saar smuggling food to the back room this afternoon. Keeping key in my bra now. Won't allow my discipline to be subverted here.

24 March '54

Breakthrough! At last! Lift the clapper of the slot, up she jumps, dances on one leg, claps hands, sings along gulp-gulp.

> Little turkey jumps over the ditch
> Little turkey runs from the witch

Then I left the door open, so wouldn't the little saucebox follow me to the kitchen with the tin plate from the bread. Sits down on the chair, says Thank you for the world so sweet, thank you for the food we eat, words swallowed. Couldn't help laughing. Ate a big plate of food. Let go the spoon when I wasn't looking, stuffed it in with the hands. Let her be for the time being. Jelly and custard afterwards. What do you say when you've eaten food? Blinks slowly with the eyes, head to the front, thank you very much, softly on an in-breath, as if she's scared I'll steal her breath. In any case sounds more like imitation than sincerely meant. How does one teach somebody sincerity? What comes first? Sincerity or words of sincerity? But that's in the future, such distinctions. First just win her confidence to breathe fearlessly in the presence of her benefactor, blink in and out with the eyes, open and closed!

25 March '54

I stand behind her and pull her ears, do you see the Cape? and I pull harder, do you see the Cape yet? I pull until she makes a sound. The kitchen maids look at me as if I'm mad. Ai, nooi, they say, mind your own business, I say.

28 March '54

She must learn to speak on the out-breath. I blow on her eyelids until she opens her eyes in the morning. She keeps them shut tight, I blow and blow. Look into my eyes, Agaat! Blow out the breath of night! Sing: Early to bed and early to rise, makes a man healthy, wealthy and wise, sing: Higgledy, piggledy, pop, the dog has eaten the mop. You can only sing on an out-breath, on plenty of out-breath, sing Praise the Lord rise up rejoicing, oh my soul what rich reward. She looks at me with the heavens-what's-up-with-you-look. I press my finger on the mole on her cheek. Here, I say, is your exclamation mark. I count the moles in her neck. Here are your nine stars.

29 March '54

First smile!! An unseasonal little shower of rain fell here, and a lot of butterflies drowned, so we put them in the sun and they came back to life, and flew up and then Agaat SMILED!

2 April '54

Lessons in the prodigality of breath. The wind blows s-s-s-s-s, the cow blows mooo, the sheep blows baaa, the donkey brays hee-haw, the flower blows out its scent, the direction of a gaze is a blowing wind. North-west! South-east! All living things take a draught of air and blow it out with a sound in a direction, the hands before the mouth form a trumpet, for lack of a snout or a lowing muzzle. Call! I'm calling you! Hear! But she doesn't call back. Agaat has no faith in her own store of breath. As if she might jeopardise her life by talking.

8 April '54 tea-time morning

Breakthrough! And this time in my own slow wits! Agaat teaches me but I don't grasp the lessons fast enough! Only today did I put two and two together: She has of course exhaled once, blew with the making of the fire, her lips puckered and all! So I have to play with fire to get her going! She looks at me with an 'I-can-see-you've-got-a-plan' look. I'll put it into action this moment, I'll wager my life that it'll work! Must just prepare the way slowly and cautiously, it's not an opportunity I want to waste.

8 April twelve o'clock

Looks as if it's going to work! Went and dug up the old bellows from the cellar, still from Pa's farm smithy. Very neglected, the old thing, peep, goes the dry hinge between the outer covers. First I sat with her in the backyard in the sun, rubbed the leather surfaces with lots of red polish, left it to absorb nicely in the sun, buffed it, all willingly she helps me, we got down to all the concertina folds of the book, the copper mounting as well, cleaned the hinges and rivets, polished everything to a shine with Brasso, sanded down the wooden handles, applied varnish. It's a beautiful antique, I must say. Agaat makes me remember things, opens my eyes, to things that get lost, things that I've neglected.

Her little hands flutter all over the body of the thing. Very excited she is about this thing, it's almost as if she can guess what it is, as if she knows it already!

After lunch

Hold your palm in front of the spout, I say, I pull open the handles, I
close the handles, peep, goes the neck, feel the wind, I say, just so the
human lungs work, left and right, put your hands on both sides of my
ribs, feel the river swelling, swell and go down, in and out, the sun
comes up, the sun goes down, peep, says Agaat with held-back breath.
Come let's oil the hinge, if you can get the fire going with the wind of
your words, then the bellows are yours to keep, an extra lung to breathe
along with yours, a fire-fiddle, a puffing book with hundreds of pages.

12 April '54

Beatrice phoned the river's in flood from the unseasonal showers that
have been falling all the time. I ran down to the drift with Agaat, without telling her what was going to happen. Let's call the water! I said.

Open your ears, I say. Listen! Agaat all eyes. We look up in the drift
with binocular fists. Hand cupped behind the ear. I make a trumpet for
our mouths.

> River come, river come!
> From the mountain's store of water!
> From the fern-fringed waterfalls!
> From the rainman's dripping sleeve!

And then it came! She thinks I can do magic! I show, I say, I blow, I
patter off the names of all the things that are washed down there by
the river.

Twigs and leaves and skeletons of small game, fallen nests and root-
clusters, the whole battleground of a dry riverbed gathered in a roiling,
rustling mass of words, in a fume of dust at the foot of the water, the
solid wall bulking in behind, the wattle branches blowing up before
the advance, the wind in the wake of the first wave, the smells of wild
bush: buchu, rooikat piss, khaki bush, torn away from the catchment
area. Listen, I say, I have the river in my mouth, it's the beginning of all
things. Is that blasphemy?

I want Agaat to understand that if you call things by their names, you
have power over them. But never mind words, she's becoming quite her
own little person, scratched out a mole there with a stick, just in time.
Roll around, roll around, little pink claws scrabbling before the flood,
its little coat all teeming with colour. We sat together and watched it

drying, how the snout first came to life, how it dug itself in, blindly in under a damp dark mound. Agaat scratches it open, puts her finger into the hole, looks at me, with little 'I-want-to-go-in' eyes.

You're not a mole, I say, you're an above-ground creature, you walk in the light.

18 April '54
Jak no longer wants to eat in Agaat's presence in the evenings. She gives him the creeps, he says. So now I bathe her and feed her in the kitchen in the early evening and put her to bed so that he doesn't have to have any dealings with her.

You'll see yet what she's going to mean for us, I say.

He says I mustn't make him complicit in my latest project. He's already complicit enough in my farm, in my house, in my everything. Don't know what I must do with Jak. He takes offence if I ask him the slightest little thing.

19 April '54
We practise facial expressions. I try to develop the mobility of the face beyond just the eyes, around the mouth, in the carriage of the body. Look friendly, look sad, look excited. Look like a full moon, a field mouse, a blossom tree, a dead wall, fresh fire. The 'dead wall' she does very well! I play notes on the piano for her and then I press on spots of her face and give a sound value to every spot. She's my little brown piano I say, I'll play her full of notes until she sounds like a concert.

21 April '54
At last! First rhyme on the out-breath, first own independent words! The Lord is my witness, I'm thoroughly exhausted with trying to breathe life into the child. Did then make the promised big bellows-fire here in the back next to the slaughter-bluegum. Assorted woods for the best effect, wattle, bluegum, oily pine cones. A lesson in sound for two. First we lay blowing on either side of the woodpile. As the wood started ticking, snapping, popping, crackling, we imitated sounds, we stoked a blend of sounds, kips, phuit, shffiit, gh-gh-gh-gh, ts-s-s-s-k, ph-ph-ph-ut, b-hub.

Your mouth is a spark, the roof of your mouth is fire, the shaft of the flame is your tongue!

Then we danced the fire! Two flames! Agaat quite inspired. Jumps up and down, whirling the little legs, quaking with the arms. Altogether wild. I blow with the bellows under her dress. You're the fire! I egg her on. Just had to stop her from coming too close.

> Hip-up and Hop-down, I sing to her:
> Climb the stairs
> Hip-up falls down
> And hip-down goes up
> What is it?

And there it came at last, after more than three months' trouble: A fire and its ashes and smoke! she yells and swings her arms, of her own accord she yells it, with a breath coming straight out! She grabs the bellows, all you can see are sparks flying, so hard does she work it, she presses the lower handle against her body with the weak hand and pumps it with the strong.

We extinguished it with a pail of water. She wanted to catch the white, hot, hissing whirls of steam with her hands.

Let them be, I said, they turn into clouds that bring rain again.

Clouds can't burn, she says. She blows the bellows under them. Phirrrt, phorrrt, up in the air.

Burn, cloud, burn! she calls.

My ears were ringing with it. My blood felt too much for my veins. Now she'd made the bellows her own, I said, to keep for ever as a souvenir of how she came to talk in the world.

I hope she can calm down, perhaps just a little bit of valerian tonight at bed-time.

14 May '54

Agaat is starting to grow. I weigh and measure her regularly. She's catching up nicely now. Had her at the doctor's again, easier this time, he says she's perfectly normal except for the mechanical defect of the little arm. I make her stand against the door frame of the back room and make pencil marks every month. I write her weight on the calendar in her room. She eats everything and I no longer have to keep track of it, only spinach she refuses flatly. I poo green, she says.

24 May 1954

I now always use fire for special lessons. She learns faster like that. It binds her attention. Reacts more spontaneously. More open to me. In the evening in front of the fire in the sitting room I read from my old Children's Bible everything from front to back. Then she has to tell it back to me. The blood on the door frames, the red sea, the column of fire in the desert. We've now almost reached the gospels. In good full sentences and nice and straight of back, shoulders nicely pulled back, her hands clasped in front of her she has to repeat the stories. Sometimes she clams shut, then I make her pump the bellows and talk along with the bellows, then it goes better again. She now sleeps with the bellows in her bed. When she opens her eyes in the morning, she starts pumping the book.

18

What time could it be? Why is everything so quiet? When is Agaat coming?

I wish I could have one last bath.

How distant they seem, the days when I could make my way to the bathroom on my own with my walking sticks.

Agaat has abandoned the great ablutions. She still appears with a tub full of steaming hot water, but it's only a gesture.

I hear six strokes. Is it evening? Or morning?

She'll be here any moment now with her fragrant waters. She'll dip the cloth in it. She'll wring it quite dry, she'll leave it over my face to steam. Then she'll dip her small hand in the water and dab me with it till my whole body is full of cool wet patches.

Often I wake up only when she's already doing it. Touching me with water. She gets to every part of me but I'm no longer invaded or besieged.

It feels as if she's embalming me.

Small baptism she calls it.

She doesn't say it out loud. I read it in her eyes. She makes sure that I can see, she uncovers my patched eye when she's working on my body, so that I can see what's happening, so that I shouldn't get a fright. She keeps me going with our eye game. One-eye game it is now, because the other one has fallen shut. She sees to it that my mind stays active, all the time I must interpret, she knows when it's too difficult, then she gives me audible clues.

Listen to the knocking, children, she sings when she auscultates me lightly, more to keep me alive than to get rid of the phlegm, it feels.

Perhaps I may yet get to see Jakkie.

Have we bought him a Christmas present?

443

I can't remember.

And what will Agaat think up for me for Christmas? Would she think of asking me? She'll press her finger on her help list. Tattered, worn it hangs there on the wall. I hope, I fear, I wish . . .

I wish I could bath.

Would I get it spelt out still? B·A·T·H? Request an immersion?

It's easier than P·R·A·Y.

The caress of hot water, the tingling. How I long for it! In the contracting circle of delight it was a last small treat. The sensation of weightlessness, of being immersed.

I could imagine that I was lying motionless in the bath just as always, before I got sick. With foam or oils or bath salts. Or mustard after a hard day's work.

Agaat always gave me a full hour for that invalid's bath, just came and added hot water every now and again. Saw to it that I didn't slide down, pulled the little rubber mat under me back a bit, put a bathing cap on my head so that my hair shouldn't get wet.

Usually the bath included a hairwash. I could lie back completely and almost float, with her strong arm under me, and the small mouse-paw with the fused fingers tilting my head back in the water to massage my scalp.

So pleasurable, the floating feeling, with my neck free of the chafing neckbrace.

It made me smile.

I could still smile then.

That's what it would be like, I thought then of death, a floating away on a lukewarm pond amongst bulrushes.

Once I looked up at her and saw we were thinking the same thought.

Or I thought it was the same.

I wanted to say something about it. I wanted to whisper, it is good. That we think it, that we dream it.

I could produce only a groan.

Don't fret, Ounooi, Agaat said, don't be scared, I'm holding you.

Had she misunderstood me?

Not that she always wanted to help me.

She often looked on passively at my struggle to get to the bathroom. It was the last of my exertions. I could exert myself.

Perhaps she thought it was good exercise.

If I wanted to bath at seven o'clock it took me ten minutes to the bathroom with the Viking Strider. With the four-prong stick, six months later, it already took much longer. The walking frame in the end meant half an hour of wrestling. When I started preparing myself and the first stumbling sounded on the floorboards, Agaat started singing *Onward Christian soldiers*.

She didn't always feel like bathing me. She hoped that I'd give up halfway and hobble back to my room. The points of the walking sticks, the stilts and castors of the walking frame all kept snagging on everything. It exhausted me, the bumping and the getting stuck, the manoeuvring around corners.

The bathroom door was the last door that she'd unscrewed, as if there she'd wanted to retain a barricade to the very last.

Against my nakedness, I thought.

How did she think she was going to avert it all?

Keep nicely to the middle, or watch out for the telephone stool, Agaat called from the kitchen. And a while later, as if she didn't know exactly how I was getting on: Where have you got to now, Ounooi? Passage cupboard? Spare room? Growth rate?

As if I could shout a reply.

The 'growth rate', the pencil marks just before the bathroom next to the door frame of the children's room. There where Agaat made Jakkie stand every August and with a pencil marked above his head how tall he was. Would it still be there? Or would she have scrubbed it off in the great scrub-lust that took hold of her when we'd cleared up the house? Scrub-lust and paint-lust. Sanitised for my sake.

Two rows of marks. The other was past the bathroom over the passage threshold, where the ceiling became lower, at the end of the passage, there where the light cast only a dim glow.

You could see it properly only when the light of the back room itself was on.

But nobody ever switched on a light there any more.

The door was shut.

No need to unscrew it either.

Nobody ever ventured there any more.

At one stage I used the closed door at the end of the passage as a lever. To help me negotiate the turn to the right at the bathroom door.

Then I focused on the copper letter-slot in the door.

Exactly at eye level.

It worked on me like a ray of fire.

It motivated my lame body. Eventually I had to turn my head away, and then my body, with a great lifting of one side of the walking frame, more than I had to lift it simply to move forward one pace with my dangling feet. I had to swing the frame through the air, at least a quarter of a turn, to position myself to enter by the bathroom door.

With the neckbrace I could no longer look back, but I knew that Agaat was leaning backwards on the kitchen table to look down the passage.

That's what she always did when I moved anywhere during that time.

I could feel what she was thinking.

When I'd almost made my way through the bathroom door, she came down the passage to the tune of *Oh ye'll tak' the high road and I'll tak' the low road*. And brushed past me through the doorway to run the water. And then past me again to fetch the towels.

When the water was running, I had to see to it that I got myself into the bathroom in time because I had to ring the bell around my neck to signal that the bath was full. The bell that she'd hung there with the words: Give the cow a bell to keep her out of the ditch.

I had to lift one arm from the walking frame, or detach it from the elbow support, to ring the bell. One, two tinkles I could manage.

If the copper letter-slot caught my eye, if I stood there for too long facing the dead door before I could manage the great about-turn, Agaat marched past behind me, furious, on her heels, and opened the bath taps all the way and went out by the back door with a slamming of the screen door and stayed away as long as was necessary to create a situation.

A few times the bathtub overflowed, all over the bathroom floor and down the passage, and when at last I could turn away, the feet of the walking frame splashed in the water so that I lost my balance.

Twice I fell.

To the ringing of bells.

Both times she scolded me terribly.

Now see how everything's flooded here! You'll break a hip and then what are we going to do? It's because you stand there like a lizard staring at the sun, what for? There's nothing to be seen there. It's the end of the road.

On such evenings she brought the wheelchair and pushed me shh-hirrr, through the water back to my room and left me right there while she mopped up the passage.

The bath I could write off.

The most difficult in the end was getting me into the tub itself.

With the new automatic wheelchair IBot, July 1995 I got it, the trip from my room to the bathroom took less than two minutes, but eventually it became impossible for Agaat to get me out of the chair onto the side of the bath. My back was too limp, I could no longer be of any use with the holding or supporting. Only in one arm did I still have a little bit of grip.

Well, then I'll just have to piggy-back you, Agaat said, and crouched in front of the wheelchair.

I remember the evening, I was naked already on the leather seat, she'd taken off my white nightgown over my head, she'd removed my neckbrace so that my head lolled on my chest. Surrounded by the shiny black levers and control knobs and gear sticks I looked to myself like a rag doll, the chair like a rampant animal.

Willy-nilly I had to gaze at my own lap, at the meagre little tuft of hair there. I couldn't lift my head to avert my eyes.

Come on, press the forward tilt button and then you let yourself slide down onto my back. Hook that one little-bit-of-an-arm around my neck, I'm waiting!

Her voice sounded as if she were saying: Come, come, switch off the winch-axle, hook on the shallow-tooth harrow, or, get the mowing-snaffle into her mouth.

Farming as usual.

I groaned to signify, perhaps we should just give it up. In front of me the big white cross looked like a traffic sign.

Quarantine.

Beware.

Cripples crossing.

To the pool of healing? No, a fantasy of flight.

Agaat's arms were extended backwards to catch hold of me, the thin one and the thick in the black sleeves of the housedress, the cuffs white wing-tips. Her head was held high, the back of the cap peaked in the air, a crane taking off.

Press on the knob! Agaat called. Who dares, wins!

What next then once I'm on your back? I groaned, are you going to chuck me off with a hup from one shoulder like a sack into the water?

I wouldn't have groaned if I'd thought I could utter intelligible words, but an emotion I could then still express with my sounds.

I looked at the tub full of water. I saw it suddenly, in a flash, Agaat, the moment that she feels my full weight on her, jerking up her shoulder sideways and throwing me, against the wall, so that I fall down into the bath, a red veil in the water, bubbles.

Domestic help and nurse of years' standing maintains it was an accident.

What are you hanging there betwixt heaven and earth for, Ounooi? Are you seeing ghosts again? she said. Come now, I can't spend the rest of my life squatting here on my haunches. Giddy up! I have a horse and a shiny dappled horse!

A fantasy of horse-riding.

Elevated Forward Slow Tilt. One finger can still find the little icon on the control panel. The IBot zoomed and reared up and whooshed. Agaat lifted her hindquarters to get to the right height to catch hold of me. The apron's bow around her middle a sharp white lily on a pool.

And I'm coming to fetch you yet, she sang.

My buttocks were sticking to the leather seat. She got hold of me by my thighs on both sides and pulled me off onto her back. Hup! she shook me up onto her back. My arms a slack harness on both sides of her head. Hup! over her hips, astride.

Oh, I have a horse!

Tighten your arms around my neck!

My head fell forward on her shoulder. Her hair against my cheek. Always softer than I thought. Her neck. The nine-star. The sinews as she strained. Lifebuoy. Mum. Whaleback. White crest on the forehead.

And then she came upright. Her strong hand under my buttocks so that I couldn't slide off her. Her clothes against my stomach and breast hard and coarse before I could feel the warmth of her body.

On my horse my shiny dappled ho-o-o-rse, with a brand-new saddle 'n bit! How now, she asked softly on the in-breath.

Had she cursed?

There was something by which I could feel the decision.

A ridge that gathered in the cloth of her dress.

And then something beyond the ridge, a boundary, a step, right through herself.

Then she got into the bath with me.

Shoes and all.

Squats with me lower and lower, arranges my legs on either side of her until we both can sit, with a plash, a splash, her dress a bladder of air around her, a black rampart against my stomach, the black blacker yet as far as the water is sucked up her back, the white bow wilted.

I could still hear the tap, plink-plink, in the water, could hear the bluegums siffling through the chink of the bathroom window, a plover flying up, the dog nosing its dish over the cement of the backyard.

How long did we sit like that? I felt her breath against me, a support under mine. Deep breaths with intervals between.

I must have fallen asleep like that with my head against her back.

I woke up when she opened the tap to add hot water. She stirred it with her hands on both sides to distribute it, closed the tap, still remained sitting like that. The grandfather clock chimed. Quarter past eight. My time expired.

Then she straightened her legs and pushed back so that I could lean against the back of the tub. And she got up, with the dress clinging to her lower body. She pulled it away from her legs but the heavy cloth clung again, her thighs like two tree trunks.

Dripping out of the bath.

Sit just like that and don't go to sleep again I'm coming now, she signalled with her eyes. Without twitching a muscle. As if she got into the bath with me fully-clothed every day.

Schlup-thud, schlup-thump, slowly down the passage in the wet shoes.

Never have I heard her walk so slowly. Never so heavily, a horse under a coat marching two legs to a side through a drift, hearse and drummer following.

But that was my mother's funeral, her theatrical directions.

What will mine be like?

It's in Agaat's hands.

Does one wash a body before laying it out? With soap? With carbolic?

Agaat will wash me, I'm sure, pure I shall meet my Maker, whiter than snow before she crosses my hands for me.

Will she be able to resist straightening my fingers?

Perhaps she'll splint my hands.

Perhaps she'll break my fingers.

What will it be like when the funeral eaters have left?

I see her standing at the gate when the last guests have left, when Jakkie's gone back to Canada. The gate will hold her, its silver inner cross, the tensed wires and the pipes of which it's constructed.

She won't be able to turn back immediately.

She'll feel the hasp with the fingertips of the little hand, even though she knows it's in place, feel the black iron ring, the double wire hook over which it slides. Her other hand, the strong one, will enclose the upper pipe, let go and grasp again so that the knuckles show white.

It won't be the first time. So she stood every day when Jakkie went to school by bus, and every time after that when he went away after weekends or holidays. Then I had to go and fetch her there, or call her back from the stoep.

Come, Agaat, we must go and pull potatoes! Come, we must go and plait onions, come, the hanslammers are bleating for their bottles!

Come, little Agaat, we have to slaughter your last hanslam and the ear you may keep this time.

She'll stand there and nobody will call her.

The dogs will sniff at her hems. They'll press their wet muzzles into the backs of her legs. Jump up against her so that she'd be thrown slightly off balance.

Come, Agaat, whatever are you standing like that for.

The gate of Grootmoedersdrift. Yard gate.

Gate of Agaat's world.

She'll lift the black iron ring of the hook and then let it drop back.

The gate is closed, the road is white, the way is back and forward. And even further back to its undiscoverable beginning.

When she lets go of the iron ring, she'll bring both hands to her head. She'll press her cap closer to her head.

I'll be there, Agaat. For a moment there'll be a smell of fennel. I'll touch the white embroidered edge of your cap with new fingertips. Just so that you'll wonder, along the rippling of your gills: What Christmas breeze now?

And I tell you: To notice a breeze there where you're standing will be a new beginning, a fern-tip of courage, a thimbleful.

But what will I be able to do about the motherless dust, about the empty road beyond the gate, the barren summered world around Groot-moedersdrift, the white heat, the ashen fallow-fields, the sheep with their snouts on the scale, their lips scavenging for the dry pods of vetch? What would I be able to do about the dry little pit-dams, the black shadows of bluegums, what about the white eviscerate boulders on the Heidelberg plain, the black rocks in the Korenland River?

It will feel too large and lonely for you. You will step back from the gate. You will turn round. The yard, the house, will feel too small. Small and deserted and inexorable. You will want to shut your eyes. You will open them again. You will want to crawl into your hearth. You will crawl out again. You won't know what you're about. You'll go round the back, past the sheds to the backyard. Your feet won't feel as if they belong to you, your steps will feel too long, your legs too loose. The milk-can there next to the screen door will seem to you like a thing you've never known. You will lift its lid by the chain and let go of it again. You will push open the door of the little creamery. The smell will drain you of your strength. With the front end of your cap against the separator's cool shiny chrome you will stand for a while. Blindly you'll feel for the handle and start turning till the high keening sound is released and you feel the vibration against your forehead.

Oh, my little Agaat, my child that I pushed away from me, my child that I forsook after I'd appropriated her, that I caught without capturing her, that I locked up before I'd unlocked her!

Why did I not keep you as I found you? What made me abduct you over the pass? What made me steal you from beyond the rugged mountains? Why can I only now be with you like this, in a fantasy of my own death?

Why only now love you with this inexpressible regret?

And how must I let you know this?

See, in the twilight I lead a cow before you, a gentle Jersey cow, the colour of caramel, the colour of burnt sugar, she smells of straw and a cud of lucerne. I place your hands on her nose, your palm on her lips. You are the eye-reader. There it is, bucketfuls of mercy in those defenceless pupils. I bring you in the vlei to the whitest arum lily rolled up. Take it by its ragged edge and whistle. It will open as the poet says with starlight in its throat. Here a bokmakierie hiccoughs in the wild mallow, all love contained therein, too much to endure. Just smell the buchu, and imagine the soft wet winter that will once more penetrate the soil. Let yourself be consoled, Agaat, now that language has forsaken me and one eye has fallen shut and the other stares unblinkingly, now I find this longing in my heart to console you, in anticipation, for the hereafter.

Am I vain in thinking you will miss me? That you will long to look after me, to wash me and doctor me and dress me in my bed, your last doll with whom you had to play for four years? Who is consoled by the thought that you will long for me as I was at the very end? Which me, which one of my voices will you want to commemorate? Look well, listen well, you will know when I depart. If you are sleeping, you will be woken up by it.

Who is it that clasps the irons of the gate for one last time, that lifts the ring to go out? Who hesitates there by the bars of the cattle grid, who inclines the neck slowly there where the noonday sun falls between the rails? What hoofs are these that cautiously start stepping over the obstacle? Is it a fluttering of any significance?

Are you going to hand me your starched cap to hold for a moment before you take it back again, you who remain behind?

*

They shut your mouth for you, Jak and Agaat. From that night that you fell into the ditch onto the rotten cow. And by the autumn of the following year they'd started collaborating on planning Jakkie's birthday feast. A farewell birthday.

You gathered that he'd had his fill of the Defence Force, he was considering a career as a civilian pilot, but first he had to serve out his contract. Agaat knew more, you could see it on her face.

You wrote to Jakkie asking him who all you should invite. Somewhat abruptly he replied: Invite who you want to.

You were affronted. Don't be so ungrateful, Jakkie, you told him on the telephone, all we're trying to do is arrange something pleasant for you.

Then he sent a list: Gaf's Jurie, Lieb's Hugo, Flip's Erik.

Jak took out his disappointment on you. He threatened Jakkie with his inheritance to make him stay on in the Air Force. That you picked up a few times when he was talking to him on the telephone.

In the evenings after supper Jak recalled Agaat from the kitchen. She had to present her planning for the feast to him. Ostentatiously spiteful pleasure Agaat derived from this. She ignored you. And Jak ignored you. Mockingly they imitated your style of entertaining to the last detail.

The flower garden must look its best, Jak said, as if he'd ever felt anything for the garden.

With red felt-tipped markers they ticked off on their lists every task completed, a mimicry of your method of doing.

You lost your appetite during this time, mostly stayed in your room, listened to Agaat regulating the movements on the yard and in the house. Your house was filled with a clattering and a shifting and a bumping, creaking floorboards, the chirring of newspaper on the window panes, incessant footsteps, sweeping and scrubbing, the clipping of sheep-shears in the garden. You plugged your ears with cotton wool and Vaseline.

In the evening you took your place at the table when Agaat rang the bell. She avoided your eyes, carried her perfect meals to the table, filled your plates and remained standing mutely behind your chairs. You scrabbled around in the food with your fork. Little Miss Muffet is stuffed, Jak would say, stuffed with her pills and her tears. As a reprimand he would hold out his plate with a large gesture for a second helping.

Agaat was imperturbable, you can still see her, how she places herself before the table to dish up for him, her hands in the air, her face in the shadow of the lampshade. You were hypnotised by the wrists in the starched white cuffs, the strong hand carving with the knife, the weak hand, deep in its sleeve, supporting the meat platter, nudging closer the gravy boat. You couldn't look away from Agaat's hands, the doing-hand and the helping-hand, the white and the black and the brown of Agaat's arms and hands under the bright light on the spotless damask. She never put a finger wrong.

Jak drank a lot at supper. A renewed kind of garrulousness was generated by this. No longer furious, no longer passionate, but bitter, and cynical, and despairing.

The baas of Grootmoedersdrift, he would say, with his glass in the air, drinks to Agaat.

Later you came to know his refrain.

All hail the skivvy! The baas prefers the tyranny at one remove!

Keep my glass filled, Agaat, he said, but keep your madam sober, it's her fate not to be allowed to carouse with her subjects.

And for Agaat our most total of teetotallers, Jak often said, her I shall keep topping up with words until one day she erupts in eloquence, pissed with wisdom. That's what always happens to those who know and don't say!

Agaat smirked when he talked like that.

What was to happen to you all? Something inexorable was hanging over you. The law and the prophets was the phrase haunting your mind all the time. But by that stage you'd long since given up reading the Bible.

Even for that Agaat made up. Her latest was that in the evenings she commandeered all the labourers, no, everybody in the huts, big and small, to the backyard for scripture and prayers. A kind of revivalist sermon she delivered there to them every evening, on the pattern of the broadcast services on the radio, filled with invocations of the fatherland and exorcisms of the enemy. A plot it was, you knew, she wasn't really a believer, she just knew how it worked. She wanted their co-operation for the preparation for the feast. After the sermon there was of course vetkoek, soup, cinnamon porridge. She nagged at Jak to pour the tots with a heavier hand at knocking-off time so that they should be warmly receptive to the gospel by the time they gathered in the backyard.

During the day she drove them, along with the extra labourers, men and women that Jak had allocated to her and paid to beautify the garden for the feast.

Single-handedly he transported everything she needed by lorry: soil, bark and straw for the rose gardens, fertiliser and new trees and shrubs. He went to Cape Town and bought dozens of garden torches and lanterns. He ordered a marquee tent with smart wrought-iron tables and chairs from a hiring-supply company and had wood chopped and dry-piled and had new spits welded and new braai areas built.

For the guests who'd be staying over, he hired luxury sleeping-tents with mosquito netting and bathrooms, even built a sauna down by the dam.

Jak helped Agaat like a diligent labourer. He cast himself as her foreman. His irony was bitter and full of loathing, his obedience a grotesque display directed at you. You saw the labourers laugh when Jak trotted off to execute Agaat's instructions.

She accompanied Jak to the lands to select and brand the slaughter-animals and he went and assembled extra slaughter-staff and kitchen help for the feast according to her specifications. They had the outbuildings painted and the yard tidied up.

Jak had a landing strip graded. He would rent a two-seater plane so that Jakkie could treat his friends to pleasure flips during the festivities.

He made a feint of reporting the progress with the preparations to you in the evenings, while Agaat stood by taciturn. The drunker he got, the more he wanted Agaat to play along.

Didn't he realise that Agaat was playing her own game with you?

She said not a word.

If then at length he lost his temper, he inveighed against both of you.

Ag, how stupid of me to think that the slave-girl could ever really take the master's part! After all, the slave-girl is in thrall to the mistress. They're you might say each other's extension cord. Closed circuit.

Did Jak himself understand that much about everything? At times you got that impression, as on the evening when he filled three glasses with wine and took sips from all three, kept decanting wine from one to the other.

Come Milla, he said, don't you think it's time for a little poem? What's that one that you were always so fond of quoting to me? Love is the empty glass. And then? Bitter? Dark? That holds the hollow heart? Is that how it goes?

But then, you're Siamese twins, aren't you, you two, can't the two of you recite it for me? Isn't that how your joint unholy history started? With your nonsense-rhymes, not so? There was a woolly, wonderfully, with a paw, like a claw.

Jak knocked over the gravy boat.

Agaat cleaned up without twitching a muscle, as if these were gestures and a text that she knew. As if Jak were an actor whose words she was rehearsing with him to check that he was word-perfect.

How does the rest of it go, Agaat? Don't you remember it any more, your good Afrikaner education? Jak asked. Agaat just looked at him, the cloth with which she was mopping up the gravy in her hand.

Yes, Gaat, what are you staring at me like that for? Or are you perhaps drinking in my every word? But your mouth is zipped up of course! Talking is the baas's responsibility high and dry here on his little box. You and your miesies, you can put on the nappy and cook the pumpkin and cut the roup from a chicken's tongue, but when it's a matter of judgement and interpretation then you're mute, the two of you. Not that you ever shut up, oh, no, it's an eternal chattering. Ad nauseam. About what? About nothing I'm telling you. Tra-lee tra-la. But if the shit hits the fan, he who's the baas gets to clean the fan. He must start up the whole shit-story here and explain the parable. You can lay nothing but wind-eggs, you and Madame Butterfly here.

Jak peered at you, his gaze unsteady with alcohol. Or what am I talking? Milla my pilla oh so silla? Are you also saying nothing tonight?

You didn't look up. Jak got up unsteadily from his chair and struck his breast.

It's my tragedy this, Agaat. You're standing there with your lip latched to your chin because you know, don't you, that your history has already been written up for you, day and date. Who would ever think of one day telling my tale? It wouldn't be for the mass market.

You two, you are the trashy novel, ladies' fiction for the airport.

The women of Grootmoedersdrift!

Agaat Lourier and Milla Redelinghuys, a tale that will rend the heart of every mother! Deep, I tell you! The stone and the bat! The silenced minority, the last domestic trench, the aborted revolution, now on the shelves for the first time! Mother Smother and Maid Overpaid!

That evening late you went to sit in the garden. You wanted to think, you couldn't understand what point it was that Jak was trying to make, whether he had a point. It must have been very late when you got up from the garden bench, a clear night, Orion had shifted across to the west already. The plovers called out in overflight, a broken scale, two notes, three notes, four. It was Easter and you could hear the new lambs bleating on the hills beyond the drift.

You wanted to go to your room through the stoep door. Jak's light was on. You heard movement, a sound, you went back down the stairs and went and stood on a terrace further on and higher up from where you could see into his office. Just the central rod, the upper halves of the weights, as he lifted them, were visible for a moment, then they disappeared, jerkily, dangerously fast.

You climbed onto the stump of the cut-down fig tree under his window. His face was upside down. At this angle it looked like a mask. He was naked except for a truss of synthetic material around his waist. His chest was heaving, the sinews in his neck thin with straining, the muscles in his upper arms quivering. The weights were clearly too heavy. Between the grunts you heard other sounds. Only then could you make out the expression on his face. Tears down his cheeks. Bubbles of mucus under his nose.

You wanted to go in to him. I am part of this pain, you wanted to say to him, but you couldn't. You leant your head against the window sill and listened till the sobs died down.

When it was still, you looked again. He was curled up there on the carpet. Around him the shiny rods and the round iron disks were scattered. His arms were around his head. There was a moth around the light, large loose shadows flapped in the room. From the gleam of the red midriff support you could see his breathing. He wasn't sleeping. His jaws were moving as he muttered.

Jak's tale.

Agaat's tale.

Selvage and face.

You had eavesdropped on them both. The tales that were clenched back behind jawbones, those that were roared into the wind, into the reeds, into the blowing bluegum tatters, those that were broadcast through the chimneys, those that were distilled from the depths of the bottle, those that were declaimed on the dust roads of the dryland, those that were muttered into mouthpieces.

Was there somebody on the other side that day when you heard Agaat talking on the phone? Or had it been designed specially for your ears? How could you know? You had been her teacher.

You were standing behind the door in the kitchen where you knew she often stood listening when you were talking on the phone.

Yes, Jakkie, Agaat was saying, that's not news to me, you know, I know, everybody knows your mother and your father, they're not easy people, but we all have our faults. And they'll always be your mother and your father.

No, I'm not defending them, I'm just saying.

Stop it, what do you want me to say? They've always been nothing but good to me.

What do you mean? I have food, I have clothes, I have a house . . . and everything . . .

No, you can't say that, no you can't.

Jakkie, stop it, your father would never say anything like that. You're making it up because you're very angry with him.

No, Jakkie, they look after me and they're my people.

No, I'm not hiding it, why would I now stand here and lie to you?

Your mother has a hard time with him, he's difficult, but she's also difficult.

No, Jakkie, it's not that bad either.

No, I don't know what he said to you and I don't want to know, if he has a complaint, he can tell me about it himself.

No, I don't interfere.

No, that's their business.

No, I'm not playing dumb. And I'm not playing innocent.

That's not true. I know everything and see everything.

No, I say nothing to nobody. Why should I? They don't do me any harm.

No, you don't know what you're saying.

Never mind. Never you mind now, Boetie, why are you so obstreperous this morning?

Of course I want you to stay!

Of course! You're my brother. You're the only little brother I have.

No, you needn't worry about me, I can look after myself.

I'll miss you, yes, more even than I miss you already.

Of course I'll write. I'll write even more.

I will, every week.

About the clover.

About the rain too.

About the drift, everything.

I will.

About the wind.

About the smell of my fennel, they say it's sprung up all the way to Mossel Bay!

I'll give you seeds to take along.

Of course I love you, terribly much, you don't know how much.

No, you don't know, you can't know. You're my child too, you know that, don't you? But first come to have your birthday with Gaat. I'm making everything that you like. For one last time. Your sheep's neck and sweet pumpkin, your lovely chicken pie.

No, you can't possibly want to pull out now.

No, it's all been arranged, Jakkie!

No, it would break my heart, listen to me!

No, go on, come now. Your mother and I are gardening for you for August.

Sowed yes. Namaqualand daisies. Bokbaai vygies. Your father's even rented an aeroplane for you.

Never! Oh no! Just forget it!

No, I'd be far too scared.

No, I'll never. Not a damn. Over the Kapokberg? Oh heavens no, Jakkie.

Over the plain? To the rivermouth?

No! Not why not, just not.

The y of the why and the double-u of the trouble-you.

Yes, Boetie.

The tip of the fern.

Never mind now, I know it's hard.

Yes, I know you must. You must talk, yes. I want to hear it all.

No, I won't shut my ears to it, I'm not stupid, I know what I know. I read the papers, yes, I hear what they say.

Yes, Jakkie, don't cry, come, hush, hush, don't cry any more, I know it's hard, I understand, you're angry.

No, I won't and I don't want to.

It's not my place, that's why.

No, that's not true, I do have a place.

No, Jakkie, don't carry on like that. So what do you want me to do then?

I'll never leave her alone. She needs me. I have an obligation.

Are you starting that again? You came along and found me here when you came to your senses and that's that.

No, I don't want to.

Where would I have to go? Who would want me . . . as . . . as I am?

No, Boetie, you know that's not what I'm talking about.

No, Boetie, not yet now, perhaps one day. When I'm old one day, when I'm grey.

I will, I promise. Everything I'll tell you, one day.

No, Jakkie, that's right, you must do as your heart tells you to.

I'll take care, whatever happens. You know I will.

Well, they take care of me too. I'd honestly not be suited to any other place. I don't have a choice.

Then that's the way it is.

So then they have only me. It's better than nothing. And so then I only have them. That's also better than nothing.

Yes, you will be happy, of course you will.

Don't say never, Jakkie, that girl was just not your sort, that's all.

No, I know, the young fellows too, unpolished as your mother would say, whoever would want to eat sheep's head and drink vaaljapie with them?

No, you'll find someone, you're such a handsome chap, and so learned, a chip off the old block.

Yes I will. I always think of you. I pray for you.

No, Jakkie, you mustn't talk like that.

No, go and read your Bible like a good boy. To every thing there's a season, a time to stay and a time to go. In Ecclesiastes, you go and read it, it will comfort you.

Do you still have your bookmark?

The one I sent with your mother when you got your medal? In a white envelope?

Oh well, then I don't know, I'll just have to make you another.

If I was there? No, but they told me it was a very swanky affair, only your mother's new shoes hurt her.

No, I'll ask her about the bookmark. You must bring along your cross of honour so that I can see it, your father says it's eighteen carat gold.

Then you could stand it no longer. You emerged from behind the door.

Agaat held the receiver away from her ear, glared at you.

You wanted to take the receiver from her hand. Without a goodbye she got up off the stool and smoothed her apron. You grabbed at the telephone in her hand. Agaat let go, the receiver swung against the wall. When you got hold of it at last, there was only a dialling tone.

You followed her to the kitchen, grabbed her by the front of her dress and shook her back and forth.

Who are you? How many thousands of devils are you? For what do you pretend to be a holy angel of light? Dear, good Agaat of Groot-moedersdrift who doesn't grumble and doesn't grouse no matter what! Who'll take care, who knows her place, who doesn't interfere! Who's only too grateful! Who's so very religious! Who are you trying to bamboozle? You're a Satan! It's my child! Mine! Mine! Do you hear me! So why don't you just tell him what's happening here? Or do you want to entice him away further and further? With your milksop of mealy-mouthed flattery? Is that your plan? He knows you're lying! He knows! He knows! You think up a different story for each of us here according to your convenience. Witch! You're a witch and you're witching us here! If I'd only known, if I could only have known what I was doing that day when I took you in here. A curse you are. I hate you.

You struck her through the face. You remember your hands plucking at the collar of the uniform, a button popping, your fists hammering, on her breast, on her shoulders.

She stood stock-still absorbing the blows without moving a muscle, without retreating by a single step, without any retort.

Until you lowered your hands and averted your face.

You sank into a chair, with your head on your hands on the kitchen table. A whimpering came from you. You couldn't stop moaning. Vaguely you were aware of movements, a kettle being filled, cups rattling, water starting to boil.

There was only the sound of rubber soles on the linoleum, then the smell of tea before your nose. You lifted your head. Agaat's strong hand was adding sugar to the cup. One, two, and a little bit more. With great assurance. Sweeter than you ever took it. She stirred it. There was something specific about the stirring. It wasn't impatient and it wasn't fast. It was businesslike. It was reassuring. Did that signify peace? The teaspoon was back in the saucer.

Then, from the fingertips of the small hand, two disprins.

And then she was out by the back door.

There was a rumbling in the yard of the lorry delivering the marquee tent and the clanking of poles and ropes and pegs being unloaded.

And amongst the male voices, Agaat's voice issuing orders:

Put it here! Here! Put it up, there!

Her voice warning. Not through my flowerbeds! Careful with the little trees, their tips! It's their growth points! If you injure one of them!

Her voice threatening: That one, he'll get the horsewhip!

You were shaky for days after the falling-out. Migraine, a pressure on the chest, a muscle twitching in your eye.

Agaat carried peppermint extracts to your darkened bedroom, cloths with mustard for your headache, eucalyptus extract for steaming over a bowl of boiling water.

For days after the incident she herself looked a shade greyer of face. Her cap was wilted as if she'd lost her knack with the starching and the ironing.

It would be fatal not to seek reconciliation. And you were the one most deeply in the wrong, you had most to be forgiven for.

She had you exactly where she wanted you.

She desired more than just a functional settlement, she wanted you just right for the feast. Cheerful, gentle. For Jakkie's sake she wanted it. For the neighbours and the community. She wanted to keep her household together, and you had to help her with it.

And she wanted it, in spite of years of training in dissembling, and for the sake of a good farewell, all candid and sincere as well. For that not one of you was equipped.

She knew it very well, even though all her preparations proceeded according to plan. A grimace of chill chagrin was around her mouth, her crooked shoulder was skewer and sharper as she bustled about.

You couldn't help her. How were the two of you to break through it? Table settings, words of welcome, pluming fountains, the prescribed dishes carried in steaming at the prescribed hour. That was the order of Grootmoedersdrift, the tradition, an annual institution, the swank party for Jakkie, the only child, the heir, the eternal to-do about him.

You took no initiative. You surrendered yourself to Agaat's ministrations, also to her attempts at reconciliation if that was what one could call them: The passing of an object marginally closer than was necessary, the less formal tone, the stray remarks on the weather that she slipped in, the rose in the vase on the dining table in the evenings, the extra trouble she took with your and Jak's food and clothes.

Give me your party dresses, Ounooi, Agaat would say after lunch, let me go through them a bit for you, there won't be time at the last minute. Her tone was strict, but in her eyes there was something pleading.

Two days later all the dresses with seams and hems taken in or let out as necessary and buttons and zippers sewn on, washed and ironed and fragrantly arrayed in your wardrobe. And all you could say was: Thank you, Gaat, I never seem to get round to it myself.

To win Jak's favour Agaat unpacked his whole shoe cupboard and waxed and polished everything, even his riding saddles and leggings.

These she then left in a line in front of the cupboard for a day or two so that he could inspect them before she packed them away.

And Jak, too, could say nothing but: Thank you, Gaat, what is a farmer without well-maintained footwear.

With such little sentences you all defused the tension between you, that which you would conspire to withhold from Jakkie.

Are there ashtrays in the marquee, Gaat? you'd ask, when in fact what you really wanted to ask was: Is there a chance, do you think, that we could persuade him to stay on for a few days after the guests have left?

Will you make two green and two red pennants for the landing strip, Gaat? Jak asked and Agaat would set her mouth in a tight line and go and execute the task conscientiously and Jak would follow her with his eyes, you could see, with his real question congealed on his lips: Do you know how long his pass is this time? Do you know where he's planning to go when his contract expires?

Shall we order ice in town, Ounooi? Then they'll deliver it on Friday at seven, half we can keep in the little slaughterhouse's cool-room for the Saturday? Agaat asked while you could tell from her tone that she really wanted to say: I'd never chuck hot water on you, surely you know that!

It was as if you'd all thrown in the towel.

Yes, Gaat, Jak would often say of an evening just before Jakkie's arrival, a glass of wine nonchalantly in his hand, whatever would we have done without you? Here we are stuck on Grootmoedersdrift, worn down in body and spirit, and you place liver patties and tomato salad before us and set the pace every day. Don't you ever get tired of it, then?

You looked at her where, without any sign of even having heard, she was dishing up food. Solid under the lamplight her bib, her chest solid, like a wall, invisibly inscribed, from the moment you took her in, with your and Jak's pronouncements, your prescriptions and prohibitions. A wall, a heart of stone that the two of you had implanted in her. And that was all that she could give back to you.

You watched her, her gestures, her phrases, her gaze. She was a whole compilation of you, she contained you within her, she was the arena in which the two of you wrestled with yourselves.

That was all that she could be, from the beginning.

Your archive.

Without her you and Jak would have known nothing of yourselves. She was your parliament, your hall of mirrors.

What must it feel like to be Agaat? How could you ever find that out? Would you be able to figure out what she was saying if she could explain it?

She would have to explicate it in a language other than the tongue you had taught her.

How would you understand her then? Who would interpret for her?

Privately you thought if the new heaven and the new earth were to be an empty, light place without discord or misunderstanding, then you would in spite of everything prefer life on Grootmoedersdrift with Agaat to beatitude, and surrounding you, instead of the heavenly void, the mountains and rivers and humped hills of the Overberg. And you would between yourselves devise an adequate language with rugged musical words in which you could argue and find each other. The language of reed and rushes. For, you thought, what would be the joy of finding each other without having been lost to each other?

Only when Agaat was present, in those last weeks before the feast, could you talk and could Jak talk, could you speak normal sentences to each other.

Was it in this time that Jak without any explanation came to sleep in your bed a few nights? Daddy-like in his pyjamas, complete with his glasses and book?

It was in spite of himself, you thought. And because he knew that it was too late. To seek consolation against the knowledge. That's why he came, towards bedtime, with his pillows and his glass of water.

Neither of you made any overtures to the other. Each occupied a side of the bed. He slept quietly, you could hardly feel his heat and his weight. Like a husk you thought, a dry membrane. In the morning when you woke up, he was gone.

When Agaat wasn't present, when you were alone together, you endured each other wordlessly. When in the evenings she drew the kitchen door shut, after she'd rinsed your teacups, and you heard her talking to the dogs, heard her enter the outside room, then it was a consolation for the two of you, where you were left behind under the shaded light of the table lamps in the sitting room, to know that she would be at her post the following morning, and that she would be there when Jakkie arrived and that she would help mediate his departure.

His departure! You didn't want to consider it.

Where did he want to go? You could see that it upset Jak terribly.

You couldn't talk to each other about it. Together you brushed your teeth and had your baths in the bathroom, until at last one turned the back on the other.

Jakkie's mother and father, Agaat's household, you thought, what are we more than that? And what have we made of them? But it was Agaat who was more urgent in your stocktaking.

What would Agaat do before going to bed, you lay there wondering wide-eyed in the dark next to Jak.

How would she get round to unbuttoning her uniform in front, and pulling out the pins of her cap and putting it down? Would she close her eyes first before looking at herself in the mirror without the white peak? And would she then stick her hands into the combed-flat mat of hair and massage her scalp? Would she work loose her hair until it stood in tag-locks around her head and would that then make her feel different? Look at herself in the mirror and smile? Fling her head back and laugh and stretch her arms above her head and roll her head on her shoulders so that the shadows of her hairdo slid over the linoleum like tumbleweed in a high wind?

Would something like that be possible in that outside room? Such a secret other self, such a concealed feral energy?

It was a fantasy you couldn't sustain for long, so mendacious, so banal was it. It was what one read in bad novels. In such a book Agaat would then have had a band of supporters, a claque of hand-clappers and whistlers, a villain with a feather in his hat who could egg her on.

No, it couldn't be like that. She would creak and rustle as she stepped out of her stays and, square in her full-length petticoat, hand on her side, glared at the cap, at the apron, glared at the black dress, lying in a heap there on the floor. She would drape herself in her nightgown like a toga and betake herself to her bed in grim and magisterial dudgeon.

You wanted to soothe yourself with these images. You knew none of it really fitted. There was no sportiveness and there was no self-importance either.

You knew how it would really be, as if you yourself knew the steps.

It would be quiet there. The linoleum on the cement would scrunch sandily under her feet. It would smell of soap and starch, of freshly ironed laundry. The bare light bulb would cast its shadow on the floor, in the hollowed-out seat of the collapsed easy chair. The embroidered cloths would radiate starkly from the walls, Moses in the burning bramble-bush, Elijah in his chariot of fire.

Perhaps she would switch off the light and first sit still for a while in a chair to think over the day?

Perhaps she would light a little fire to ponder by?

But you knew that even that was your own wishful thinking.

There was not then, at that stage, any space between Agaat and Agaat.

She was in preparation for Jakkie's arrival and Jakkie's departure.

She was living outside herself, leaner, sharper, like somebody the day before she leaves on a journey, the suitcases all packed, the usual routine scaled down and intense.

In that room.

There everything would be tidy and bare and rustling.

Rapidly she would wash, rapidly dry herself, thoroughly as in an institution, without dawdling, without a single gesture of self-cherishing. Everything would be in its place, as if for inspection. No tarrying, no reflection.

She would switch off the light at the door and wait in the dark for a moment until she could see again. Barefoot she would walk to the bed, hitch up her nightdress, get onto the bed with one knee first, worm in under the tensed sheets, without burrowing them loose, find a hollow for her head.

Would she lie open-eyed in the dark, first with her face to the window onto the yard? Would she lie looking at the glow of the moon through the curtains? Through a chink? At a star?

No, she would turn round on the other side, with her face to the wall.

And then with a sigh, a sigh you'd want to allow her, she'd close her eyes to sleep.

You thought all these things. All the time in that period before Jakkie's birthday you thought about Agaat.

How did it come about then that that July of all Julys you once again forgot her birthday? For the third time?

*

waterchair coalblack hoisting sound at high C soap-resistant insulated rustfree synthetically upholstered so as not to scratch the bathtub weight limit 200 kilos for stouter fatter cripples but a thin one a lightweight to hoist her a joke to let down a doddle to bathe her child's play on a double-decker bench minus armrests screwed to the water's edge lower than the wheelchair so that she can slip effortlessly into it aquasitz by julius bach as one would expect from germans seatbelt neckring hydraulically we row along row along press the button then she rises up derricked over the edge and then again lowered to the bottom a light shock adjust the backrest lie back relax unlike the inner tube on which she gyrates on the whirlpool what is that she hears? a demonstration lesson? doctor unpacking bench again agent of bach in africa? but he left a long time ago! what does she hear in the dead of night? over and over the hoisting sound up and across and down seventy times seven times? she takes to her ibot mute medium cruise down the passage who's there all alone in her bath? neck clamped in hoops straps tightened asleep in the waterchair? she sounds alarm with her chicken-claw waltzing mathilda jesu joy of man's desiring blue danube jeepers creepers where'd ya get them peepers strangers in the night what a wonderful world who thinks it all up for the mutes? the walkers the waltzers the yearners? Your call will be answered her rescuer is out of reach in the dry bathtub hands folded on the chest the little one enfolded in the larger legs out straight ankles next to each other black and white and brown how rich her colour how soft her skin in the stark white cradle a capsule chair a space flight get up bathmaster! wake up gatekeeper! it's not time yet for the last voyage sing to me if you knew susie as I know susie beyond the robot notes sing loud and clear a human song sing! a vulgar caterwauling against this drawn-out decrepitude

7 June 1954

Quite shaky now, ai good heavens! I had to dose Agaat with a tranquilliser and take some drops myself. So there we had a whole drama this evening coming back from the dance in town, just as well we didn't stay too late.

I no longer lock her door, except when Jak and I go out, then I feel it's safer like that. I always put her to sleep in any case before we leave. But as soon as I put my foot inside the door tonight, I knew something was wrong.

There she was huddled in the corner, eyes staring in the head, lucky I went to look immediately! With the funnel of the bellows in her mouth. Blood everywhere on the bedding, from her hands, nails torn to pieces to the quick. Won't talk, shock or something. Thought at first she'd been assaulted, but the door was locked and I had the key in my handbag. Just now when I went to check, saw the scratch marks on the door, pure splinters! Some panic or other? I can't understand it! Had to bandage her little hands, what a struggle to straighten the arms, her whole body convulsed again.

8 June 1954

Mystery cleared up! Only this morning discovered the poo and pee in the corner of the room, under the old telephone directory that I'd given her to play with! Saar, good Lord the woman! forgot yesterday to replace the little chamber pot in the back room after she'd cleaned it! That such a little oversight could cause such a setback, breaks my heart! Probably thought she was going to be given a hiding again because she'd soiled. So she tried to break down the door.

Now I have to start all over again.

It's not your fault, you had no choice, I've been trying to explain for a whole day, you don't get punished if you couldn't do anything to prevent a bad thing. You don't get punished just because you're a human with natural needs. It was an accident! It's not so bad! It's just an old telephone book! Where else were you supposed to? If you have to go, you have to go. It's Saar's fault. I've scolded Saar.

It looks as if she doesn't understand me. Has a wild look in her eyes.

9 June
Constipated! Understandable, shame. Doesn't want to eat.

10 June
Still hasn't pooed since the fright of the other evening. Small hand got hurt badly from digging away at the door.

11 June
Ai good Lord, gave Brooklax to get her tummy going, so then she soiled her pants and ran away I can't find her! Just hope I haven't caused a whole problem here.

15 June
Made a huge fire for her and danced and blew with the bellows and pretended we were witches, who's afraid of a big bad poo. Going better!

17 June 1954
Every day great progress now, I feel. She's speaking fluently now. She gets a hiding with the duster-stick if she speaks on the in-breath and if she stuffs her knuckle into her mouth and if she doesn't look into my eyes nicely when she talks. That's the minimum, I say, you talk properly with a straight-out breath, you breathe between every sentence and you look at people full-face, otherwise people will think you're devious.

11 July 1954
Suppose A. must have a birthday some time or other. Phoned Ma to have enquiries made about her date of birth at the hovels on Goedbegin.

She says they don't know exactly. It was before the winter, they think end May '47 or '48. So she must have been four or five when I found her. But May has passed, I don't suppose it matters that much.

And Lys sends greetings, apparently. I'm going to bake a chocolate cake tonight with six candles on it. Tomorrow is the day! Agaat's birthday. I feel I must celebrate it so that she can start becoming human here on Gdrift. Explained to her nicely: we commemorate the day that the Lord gave you as gift to yourself and to me.

12 July half past eight
Perhaps not such a bright idea to let Agaat have a birthday. Didn't

occur to me that you need other people for such a birthday. In the end had Saar's children come in their Sunday best. Handed out cake and cooldrinks at a little table in the backyard. Had to keep an eye all the time. As soon as I turn my back, the taunting starts. Donkey-jaw, dassie-paw. I make eye signals at Agaat. Never mind, they don't know any better. Later just sent the children home and phoned Beatrice to come over. Made Agaat recite rhymes and tell us tales in the sitting room and clapped hands every time when she'd finished. Everything from jack be nimble jack be quick to let us shine for Jesus.

Beatrice can't believe it, good heavens, she says, but her praise doesn't sound genuine, she thinks I'm batty to put so much into the child, she says I'm neglecting my social life, she asks what Jak says about it all and then I'm very cautious what I say. Beatrice is at heart a head-girl. She'll never do anything that deviates, take a risk or put herself at hazard for something or somebody else. Never take sides. I understand more clearly all the time that I'll have to believe in this on my own, even though it's literally what everybody is always preaching and professing. Perhaps their problem is exactly that I'm taking the Word so literally.

16 August 1954

Today we gardened all day, first plaited a garland from tulip stems and sorrel flowers and then sowed herb seeds in the backyard, I make her chew the seeds to teach her the taste of everything: coriander, dill, poppy-seed, she likes dill best. What does it taste like? I ask. Like drop, she says with a clever face, liquorice. You get drop from me when you're good, soethout, I teach her the Afrikaans word, sweetwood because it's sweet, Agaat because she's good. Drop is drop, she says. So what's a dropper? Perhaps she's very intelligent, she must have heard us talking at fencing-time. A hanging picket, I teach her, because it's not anchored, it just hangs in the fence.

13 September 1954

Now that the soul is awakening in her and she's outgrown the terrors of her origins, at least in body (weight and height normal for the first time now), it's time for Agaat to be baptised. As long as it's a private ceremony, says Dominee, it can take place in the white church. He'll arrange for witnesses. He agrees that it's time for her to have the faith of her guardian beatified in her so that she can grown up in the mercy of the covenant.

14 September
Difficult to explain to A. about the baptism. Now that she's nice and
grown up and can sing and speak, I said, and is obedient and can wash
and dress herself and can fasten her buttons and buckles and knows the
Bible stories and says her prayers every evening, she must be branded
on the forehead as a child of the Lord with water from the font.

Must I sit in a chair with my mouth wide open? she asks. Didn't understand at first, only after a while remembered about the tooth-pulling.
Must have made a big impression.

I took out the album with my own christening-photos to explain. She
was fascinated by the christening-dress, went and dug it up out of
the linen cupboard to show her. Moths had got into it, full of holes,
will have to get rid of it, will in any case probably never be used on
Grootmoedersdrift. Over and over she touched the pleats and frills and
double collars of the outfit. Old-fashioned full of frills the old thing, still
from Ma's family. Why a dress like that? she asks.

Christening-dress, confirmation dress, wedding dress, shroud, the four
dresses in a woman's life in Christ, I explained. Showed her my wedding
dress with the sewn-on voile sleeves. And there I started crying on the
pages. Little brown finger smoothes away the wetness. Then I felt the
little hand in mine, the first time so of her own accord.

Nothing to about cry, I hear.

First had to go to the bathroom to regain control of myself. Too much
intimacy not a good thing now. She must learn to know her place here.

20 September
Finished smocking Agaat's white christening-dress. Looks ever so smart
in it. Made her try it on tonight before bedtime to pin up the hem.

Must I lie with my legs open before the font? she asks. Still the day of
the doctors haunting her.

Tried to explain, it's not her legs that she needs to open but her heart,
it's not her body but her soul that we're talking about, as her body was
healed by the doctor, the Dominee will now mend her soul so that one
day she can get into heaven with the angels. She doesn't understand.

Are there going to be cold shiny things that they push into me? No, I say, only the service, and she must just answer yes to all the questions, so that her name that she's been given can be written in the Great Book of Life. Otherwise what? she asks. Otherwise Agaat Lourier will blow around without any purpose, a floating seed in the wind and will never fall to the ground and perish and bear good fruit, I say. She regards me with big eyes.

21 September

Nightmares and bedwetting last night. Agaat says she doesn't want to be baptised. I say she must, otherwise she'll burn in the devil's fiery hell. She asks who's the devil, does he have bellows, she says she knows fires, she'd rather burn, she's not scared. I say if she's good we can make a fire the evening of the christening and dance. I'll bake an orange cake. She says she wants to take her bellows along to the christening. It must absolutely be polished for the occasion.

23 September ten o'clock

Christening thank God all over late this afternoon! A whole business before the time. Should have expected it, I suppose. Agaat ran away when she had to get dressed. Had to run after her and catch her, Saar and I. Cornered her down in the poplar grove against the bank. Rigid with ferocity again. Had to give her a few good strokes on the buttocks. Didn't want to dress herself. Had to be stuffed into her new clothes piece by piece, white socks up to the knees and shiny shoes, head drawn into the shoulder because the gauze of the bonnet supposedly scratched her in the neck. Your head must be covered in the house of the Lord, I said. Didn't want to let go of the bellows when we had to leave. More than quarter of an hour late. You're disgracing me with your devils on this great day, I said. A Child of the Lord doesn't behave like this. Remember your name means Good, I said, and today you're being given that name by the dominee, he's the servant of the Lord. Does the dominee wear a coat like the doctor's? she asks.

Ds van der Lught fortunately patience itself. Let be, he said when I wanted to take away the bellows and settle the bonnet. He'd commandeered the verger and the organist and oubaas Groenewald who looks after the gardens for the occasion. And apart from that it was just the principal elder and myself. Jak would have nothing to do with it. Ma neither.

Yellow light through the wrinkled glass of the church window, Agaat's skin whiter than it is. Cold there in the bare benches, such a thin little tune on one note on the organ from high up in the dark gallery. Agaat all goose pimples when I took her to the front to stand for the service. Bellows drag along. Dominee peers sternly from under his eyebrows as if Agaat and I were guilty of much more than just original sin. We sing:

> Jesus, Lord, our hope so true,
> we're here to do as you ordain:
> Our children we all bring to you—
> their share in you for good to claim.
> In the name of God the Father,
> Son and Holy Ghost for ever,
> Lord, we ask that this child may
> serve thee as long as she may live
> and also find in every way
> You are good and will forgive.
> Oh we praise thee, faithful Father!
> Guide us with our children further.

Then the organist came down and the dominee said: We and our children, and our foundlings, those whom we protect and take pity on, the heathens whom we save from damnation, are conceived and born in sin, the sprinkling with water shows the impurity of our souls. We must distrust ourselves and seek salvation outside ourselves.

The late-afternoon sun through the yellow glass catches the shiny edge of the font, it looks as if there's no water in it, I hold Agaat's hand tightly, feel her strain backwards as Dominee's voice becomes progressively deeper and heavier. Thought he might have kept it a bit shorter, it's only Agaat after all. But perhaps I was the one who had to hear it all one more time. Old Groenewald stands there with his hands crossed over his crotch, nods his head, twirls his thumbs over each other. Real old actor.

We must crucify our old selves and live in fear of God. If sometimes through weakness we stumble into sin, we must not doubt the mercy of God or remain wallowing in sin.

Then first a prayer. Close your eyes, I whisper to Agaat, I peep at the elder who's rocking forward and back and gulping back the sleepiness. Therefore we pray thee to show mercy also to this thine adopted child and to initiate her through the Holy Ghost into Jesus Christ thine son so that through the baptism she may be buried with Him in death and may be resurrected with Him in the new life. Grant that she will shoulder her cross cheerfully in the service of her guardians and her masters, follow Christ daily and adhere to Him in sincere faith, firm hope and ardent love, until eventually she will meekly leave this life that inevitably issues in death for your sake and so that she may on the last day appear fearlessly before the judgement seat of Christ thine Son.

Open your eyes, now you must answer yes to all the questions, I whisper to Agaat. So Dominee peers at Agaat from under his eyebrows. Do you believe in the only true God who created heaven and earth and everything in it out of nothing? Do you believe that nothing in heaven or on the earth happens without His Divine Will? Do you acknowledge that by nature you are wholly incapable of any good and inclined to all evil? Do you profess that through faith you receive forgiveness of your sins in His blood?

Agaat utters just one little peep on an in-breath. I squeeze her in the neck so that she should say yes nicely. But no! She takes the handle of the bellows, she squeezes out a little bit of wind, pffft, hey you! I have to nudge her. The organist catches my eye, suppresses a smile. Then I have to prod her in the back to make her step forward. Come, the Dominee beckons, pushing up his gown a little over his right hand, Agaat pulls back, I take her by both her shoulders and steer her to the front, because by now I can feel she's preparing to run away, I prod her until she's standing properly. A cloud moves over the sun, the church goes dark, I feel superstitious, as if the mark of Ham is falling on me as well, hold your head forward, I say, I pull the bonnet backwards, I pinch her in the neck so that she can keep her head up straight, because she keeps on pulling it in as if she's scared she'll be slapped.

Agaat Lourier, I baptise you in the name of the Father and of the Son and of the Holy Ghost. He sprinkles water on Agaat's forehead three times. I can feel her stiffen in my grasp, strain back with her head, eyes tightly shut as if it the water were corrosive.

Then another prayer with Dominee's hand on Agaat's head. I grip her by the neck so that she can't pull away. Feel her veins pulsing under my thumbs. Grant that she will live in all justice under our only Teacher, King and High Priest and courageously do battle against and vanquish sin, the devil and all his cohorts and that she will honour and praise the only true God, Father, Son and Holy Ghost for ever and ever. Amen.

Then the organist goes up into gallery again, we few sing for Agaat.
> Jesus takes our little children
> To himself with a heart of love;
> No one ever shall us hinder
> That we freely to him move.
> Jesus hears our weakest prayer
> Wherever on earth we roam.
> Day or night, we know he's there
> And we'll never walk alone.
> Jesus Lord so far above us
> Leads us on, his willing band,
> And we know that he will love us:
> He himself has ta'en our hand.
> Praise the Lord, in all etern'ty!
> Hallelujah! Amen!

The organist had to play loud chords to make up for our meagre sound. A. looks up with staring eyes at the organist up there in the organ cage in front of the mirror amongst the bundle of pipes thick and thin. They're flutes, I whisper in her ear, they sound like harps and trumpets. Listen well, it's the voice of the angels of the Lord, they're calling you to his flock.

Go in peace, says the dominee, and lifts his arms for the blessing. Agaat starts back from the wide black sleeves of the gown.

Then there was only the baptism register to be signed. The stamp already stuck to the certificate. The light had to be switched on in the stuffy side-room because it was already thick twilight. Agaat stands chin on the chest and goes pfft-pfft with the bellows. You see, I say, it didn't hurt at all. She can now be put through her catechism later in the mission church and become a full member there, says Dominee. Old Groenewald solemnly rummages in his trouser pocket, produces a toffee for A. The elder gives her five rand. For your piggy bank, he says. There's a whole cake waiting at home, I say, if anybody would like to come over tonight. Thank heavens nobody accepted the invitation. We'd had drama enough for one day, really not in the mood for every-body's comments and Jak's attitude.

The organist left the church with us. In the old days, she says to Agaat, they had to produce wind for the organ to play, with a bellows like yours, only a big one. She fiddles around in her bosom, emerges with a lace handkerchief, holds it in front of Agaat's nose. Smell, it's got a nice smell, it's for you so that you can remember your christening. What does one say? I had to prod again. Agaat just moves her lips slightly. I can't hear, I say, you're acting really sheepish today. You look a bit pale around the gills, says the verger, eat your toffee so that you can liven up. Never mind, says the organist, it's over now, must be mighty strange for such a poor little hotnot, where did you find her?

I was bitterly relieved to drive away from there at last.

She didn't want to eat her evening meal. Had to make the fire that I'd promised her, in the fireplace, she remained sitting there while we ate. Heard her every now and again blowing with the bellows. Went to sleep right there in a little heap. When I picked her up to put her to bed, she opened her eyes. Out of the blue. Straight-out breath, own wind, loud and clear, full sentence: Where is the cross I have to shoulder? Jak heard it. Just you wait, it won't be long now, he sneered. What in God's name can he mean by that? Nowadays he looks at me with such an expression of revulsion.

Took her a slice of orange cake and tea to her room. She looks at me with wide eyes while she's eating it. Full of questions. I'm quite surprised at how much of it she's remembered. What's the judgement seat? Why the blood? It's a fine time to get your voice back, I say, you disgraced me very nicely there in front of the people. Am I bad? she asks, no I say, your name is Good, but you're inclined to evil like all of us. Why? Because we're sinful creatures. Is Même also sinful? she asks, so what does Même's name mean then?

Milla, Kamilla, I've never yet wondered about it myself.

It's the name of a white flower my mother gave to me, I said for want of a better answer. She looks at me as if she doesn't believe me. Little children like you shouldn't be bothering their heads with such difficult questions, I say, but I can see she's not satisfied.

My neck is sore, she complains when I blow out her candle. That's from pulling your neck in between your shoulders in front of the pulpit, just like a donkey that doesn't want to be yoked, I say, and I thought I'd seize the opportunity, see, that's what I mean by sinful, you were very jibbing there in front of the pulpit. That Uncle Tokoloshe's hand was heavy on my head, she says, and Même's hand was pushing into my neck. Lord, the child, she's very precocious.

2 October 1954

Drove to Malgas today with Agaat. Wanted to cross the Breede River by punt, but she refused. Punt, she says over and over, she does it with every new word that she learns. Punt, shunt, cunt, I had to put a stop to it, she's getting far too forward, but I taught her to rhyme myself and there I have it now! I'll scrub down your tongue with Sunlight soap, I warn. Really not a good tendency these word games at any time, suitable or not. In the end just shut my eyes and sat with the screaming child in the car till they'd hauled us across. Then went through to Witsand. Rainy there. Picked up shells, pebbles. Taught her all the colours of the sea and the beach. Mother-of-pearl lustre, slate-grey, silver-grey, gull-white, mussel-black, stone-grey. Agaat holds everything against her skin and then against mine. White looks whiter against my skin and grey greyer, she announces solemnly. Just like that. The river mouth lagoon was stormy with waves. Later went to sit by the fire in the hotel to dry out. Fortunately no people in the middle of the week, otherwise she would have had to stay in the car. Can see trouble ahead in public places, but she's still a child. They brought her hot milk in a tin mug.

5 October

I'm getting Agaat used to her role in the house. Put an apple box in front of the sink so that she can reach. Now washes the coffee cups every morning for me. Already quite adroit with the weak hand, inborn carefulness it seems. I indulge her by letting her wash Jak's socks and handkerchiefs and underpants in the tub in the backyard. She doesn't want one to look when she's working with both hands. Sleeve of weak hand always dirty and wet, she doesn't want me to roll up that side.

9 October 1954

First reading and writing lesson. Using the Biblical ABC, two birds with one stone, went to unearth old alphabet chart in cellar with which Ma still taught me.

A is for Adam, every animal gets a name.
Then Eve his companion to Paradise came.
B is for Babel, a tower they built.

Confusion of tongues the wages of guilt.
C is for Christ, our Redeemer and Lord:
To Him we must listen, His favour afford.

She holds the pencil in the left hand just like the knife. Still shy of the weak hand, keeps it out of the way, hides it more if one looks. I say, Agaat, the Lord made you like that, you needn't be ashamed.

10 October

Why do my pebbles and shells go grey? asks Agaat, my tongue is tired with licking them. We put them in a glass bottle next to her bed to look pretty again. Water is to shells what love is to the soul of people, I say. Without love the soul turns grey as ash, and dry and cold. I'm brown as mud and my mouth is full of spit, says Agaat. She licks her forearm and shows me. She tucks her hands under her armpits. Loaves in the oven, she says, warm as warm, feel. Becoming really sharp, the little child.

Phoned Ma to tell her how well we're getting on, full of insinuations as always: Pleased you have something to warm yourself with, my child.

13 October

To the forest with Agaat. Quite high up in the indigenous bush. Told her about the giant emperor butterfly that's black on the outside and inside blue like an eye when it spreads its wings. The jewel of the forest. Apatura iris. The eye that guards the secret of the soul. Only good people get to see it. Has Même seen it yet? asks Agaat. She looks at me like that, I can't lie. I hope to see it in my lifetime, I say. We can come every day, she says, how many days are a lifetime? If we find it, then we catch it and put it in a bottle and then it can't escape, she says. Cruel little grin. Where does it come from? I mustn't forget that this child led a different life before I found her. No, I tell her, a butterfly is like the soul of a person, it dries out in captivity. Where do the bats live? she asks.

14 October 1954

We now read and write every day. She's making remarkably quick progress. We count sums on our fingers and toes. Agaat leaves her weak hand out of the count. I give my hand in its place, I turn the page and rub out her wrong-way-round threes and fives when she's struggling, she keeps one hand under the table.

Together we make up a whole person with two strong hands, I say. Am I your child? asks Agaat. You're my little monkey, I say. We learn the wind directions and the names of the months and the seasons of the year and its festivals and what they stand for. In this way I feed her a bit of (religious) history. Good Friday, Easter Monday, Van Riebeeck Day, Day of the Covenant. I found you on the Day of the Covenant, do you remember? I ask. That shows that it's all in the Lord's plan. She just looks at me wide-eyed.

15 October
Our herbs that we planted are growing lush and beautiful. Agaat picks slips of everything and tastes everything, chews the seeds. Knows all the names, parsley, celery. Fennel still her favourite. Fennel and coriander, I say, the one is like the other. Isn't, she says, the one is for liquorice, the other is for dried sausage. She's very perceptive, has an amazing memory, not to be wondered at I suppose, she gets so much attention, I repeat everything until it's penetrated, a child must be drilled, is what I've always believed.

16 October
Gave Saar such a dressing-down this morning. Agaat busy in the backyard washing Jak's underpants and handkerchiefs and socks in the zinc tub. I hear Saar mocking: You must rub, little girl, you must rub! His snot's thick and his feet stink and his snake spits such big gobs. The kitchen maids are jealous of Agaat. They're full of gibes. Won't allow them to come and spoil all my hard work here.

18 October
Had to intervene today. Saar's children taunting Agaat in the backyard. Whose child are you can I have one too! So then they grab all the washing she's done already, throw it into the dust. She does nothing, just juts out the chin. Funny, Agaat doesn't cry, have never seen her cry no matter what happens. Don't take any notice of them, I say, they're not your sort.

This evening at bedtime she says: They say I come from a drunkcunt on the other side of the mountain. Sis, that's ugly, I say. Clearly old enough to start asking questions now. She looks at me with big eyes. What would she be thinking in that coconut of hers? How much would she remember? I dosed her so heavily to get her here. And then she slept for days from the valerian. Don't quite know what story to tell her. Perhaps just the simple truth, but I feel now is not the time yet.

I must in any case first write it down myself before I forget it, what it felt like, how it came about. The commission, the task, spelt out in black and white, for her sake, so that she can read it one day (though I wonder anew every day what exactly I'm trying to bring about here and why I'm doing it as I'm doing it, and what's going to come of it, Heaven forfend!).

Then, tonight as I was getting up off the bed (must have slumbered in for a while there with her), she woke up. Out of the blue she says: Lys is my sister, she showed me how to catch a mole. How do you catch a mole? You look for the hills, you see which one is fresh and then you squat one mole-day away and you pee on the ground. You wait and you wait and you pee and you pee all the time on the same spot. And then? You have your wire and your stick. And then? Then you wait and you keep your eyes open and you say all the time mole, mole, here's the hole! And then? Then he pushes a hole in that spot because the soil is soft from your pee. Then he pushes, then he pushes, then you wait until he's pushed hand-high, then you hook the wire quickly into his hole and you jab with the stick, one blow and pluck, then you get him by the hind leg, he can't see, but he can bite like anything. And then? Then you flatten his head with a stone, then you skin him. Why do you want the skin? It's soft. How do you get it soft? You stick your wire through, you wind it with your wire, Lys holds the one point, or you hook it to a thorn bush, then you wring the skin every day until it's soft.

Dear Lord above! Would rather not think what else lurks in that past!

20 October

Took A. to town with me today, had hair appointment, she kept on wanting to take my hand, walk next to me nicely, I said, you don't hold hands in town, you're nice and grown-up now. A. very fascinated with the hairdresser, takes the little broom from the servant there and starts sweeping up my hair into the dustpan, where does hair come from? she asks. Otherwise very good all the time while I was doing shopping.

Then I bumped into Beatrice in Kriel and Co. and she says we must go and have a cooldrink at the Good Hope Café. What about Agaat? I ask. Buy her an ice-cream and tell her she must wait outside, says B. Ai, she can be so unfeeling! The child is so small still. No, I say, I'll speak to Georgie. Hmph, sea kaffir, says Beatrice, he won't mind, but he should know who's really his clientele. Then I asked for a table at the back half behind the screen in front of the kitchen door and then the waitress in her white apron and cap, thud, flap, through the swing doors, brings A. a huge cream soda float with a long-stemmed teaspoon and a straw so that her eyes widen like saucers. Then other waitresses come out as well to look at A. Go away, I say, it's just a child. And then A. eats the whole thing, I should have known it was too much, but B. had ordered it, from spite or something. Her whole face said, so you want to don't you, now you'd better eat your way through what's in front of you and see what comes of it. A. sucks and sucks at the milky green stuff in the long glass, her eyes fixed fast on Tretchikoff's Dying Swan hanging there against the wall. When we got outside, she puked something terrible on the pavement and I held her head over the gutter and B. marched click, clack, on her high heels away from us as if she didn't know us. Really, some people.

23 October

I show all the pictures of vehicles. Strange response. Ship? I'll never get into that! Aeroplane? No never, I'll run away! Train? See it steam, salt-and-pepper-now-I-go-better, I press the two-tone of the train whistle for her on the piano. No, alla, I'll jump off! I'd rather walk! But you ride down to the lands in the bakkie with me? Yes, but it's Même who drives it!

27 October 1954

A. was very naughty today. Stole kindling out of the Aga and set fire in the backyard to an unread newspaper and a lot of brand-new brown-paper bags that I use for storing herb seed, the little blighter! Got to her good and well with the duster. Don't know what I'm going to tell Jak, he has such a thing about his newspaper. Gave her a good fright, pretended to be phoning the police, made as if I was telling the constable on the phone how naughty she was, asked that they should come and take her away and lock her up in a cell with bars behind a great iron door without food and without pee-pot. Now I really scared the blue heebie-jeebies out of her! That's right, she should rather be scared than get all forward here. Now she's good and terrified of the telephone. She listens around the corner every time I speak. I make full use of every opportunity. I ring off when I've talked to someone, but I keep the receiver to my ear, and pretend I'm telling the dominee and the police and the magistrate all her tricks and transgressions. This is really a very good way I've discovered of keeping her in her place.

4 November 1954

Almost the end of the year again. The first year of Agaat's life with me. How quickly the time has passed! How different to other years!

I want to write up the beginning of the story but it's so hot and I'm sitting here on the stoep and I'm feeling exhausted. I try to think back to that day, when exactly the idea got hold of me, why I did it. Because some days I really don't know any more. We make excellent progress three, four days a week and then there's some or other setback again. And then she has this way of looking at me that drives me wild. As if I'd destroyed her whole life when for once I have to chastise her! How else must she learn what is good and what is bad?

The Lord is my witness, I don't know if I'm up to this! I sometimes no longer know myself with this child in the house. How is it possible that the small, deformed, pig-headed, mute child in the back room can make me feel like this? It's she who's nothing. And all I wanted to do, was to make a human being of her, to give her something to live for, a house, opportunities, love.

I'm frustrated and impatient and I can't help it, sometimes she nauseates me (yes, I'm ashamed of myself, but it's true!). The long jaw, the bulbous eyes that can glare so coercively, the untameable woolly mop, the little crank-handle of an arm, the sly manner at times, the cruelty that sometimes breaks through. How does one make a good heart in a creature that's so damaged? How will I ever put enough flesh on the puny little body? How do I get all her senses and her mind operative? (Not to mention her conscience!). And a will (but obedient!) and a soul? She resists me, she's a long way from being tamed.

Sometimes I feel as if the child is a dark little storage cubicle into which I stuff everything that occurs to me and just hope for the best and that one day when I open the door, she'll walk out of there, fine and straight, all her limbs sound and strong, grateful and ready to serve, a solid person who will make all my tears and misery worthwhile. So that I can show all the world: See, I told you! You didn't want to believe me, did you?

15 November 1954 morning

Saar came to call me just now from the garden in the back, come and see, Mies, what Agaat is playing. On tiptoe through the kitchen door and peep at her from behind the door. Wouldn't there be an inquisition of the rag doll on the telephone stool! She deliberately places the doll filled with river sand in such a position that she has to fall off. Then she falls off, then she gets a slap, then she falls off, then she gets a finger in the eye!

Sit, doll, sit! If you can't sit up straight nicely and look at me, and answer me when I speak to you, then I'm phoning the police!

Next thing she clambers onto the telephone stool, takes the receiver off its cradle. Hello, hello police? Come and fetch her, lock her up! She's full of stuffing! She looks at me cheekily! She plays dumb! She does her business in her panties!

No lack of imagination, whatever else may be wanting!

19

The sharpening of the knives.

How many hours ago? I was still asleep, if you can call it sleep, the drowsy delirium in which I drift.

Sudden swishing sounds in the dark by the bed's head.

Mighty striking-up. Last movement. Metal on metal. Con brio.

From the movement of air against my face I could infer her position. To and fro the rhythm firmed, a rocking to the tempo of the sleeper. She was whetting without varying the angle of the whetting-rod to my bed, a duller sound close to her body, a high sibilant hiss at the furthest point of the rod. The point of the rod was on the railing at the head of the bed, a whetting-wind over my forehead.

Oh, Agaat, what else will you still think up for me? Sharpening knives over the tip of my comatose nose.

It was the big knife, to judge by the sound, the one with the three silver studs on the handle. And it was the longest whetting-rod, the heavy one with the cast-iron handle, the one that's stored in the long bottom drawer next to the old Aga because it doesn't fit anywhere else.

It was a culinary demonstration. How old was she? Not old enough yet to handle sharp objects.

See, you support the rod against your waist and the point you rest on the edge of the table.

But that was long ago. The point of the rod now on the top railing of my bed, close to my head. The point of support the midriff of Agaat.

Dangerous game! If the rod were to slip! If the knife were to skip! If the blade were to snap! The meaning of danger! Life-threatening!

Yes, that's how you do it! Remind me that I still exist! No lack of imagination! Whatever else may be wanting!

How many hours ago? Perhaps she too can no longer count down

482

my hours cleanly. Perhaps she tallies them now by the sharpening of
knives, by blades of grass, by the blooms of the bougainvillea dropping
with the lightest of rustlings on the stoep.

My honed, grass-light hours.

The apron bands creaked as she sharpened.

Where are you rowing me to, Agaat, to what coast, to what river mouth?

Seven knives I counted by ear, they're all there, down to the very thin
worn-down little one with the crooked blade for scraping carrots and
cucumbers in the kitchen of Grootmoedersdrift. Through my chinks I
could see them flashing.

Wings of herons, a stormy sky.

Where are you flying to with blades, Agaat, to which high Langeberg
horizon?

The bed sang.

In my closeness she found hollows of marrow for me. What more
could I want?

Come and stand here in front of me, you're big enough to learn to
handle sharp objects.

I take her hands in mine, the small hand in my right hand. I press the
whetting-rod against her body, the strong hand holds the knife, I show
her the stroke, it must sing, I say, come let's make the knives sing!

Why, she asks, do my hands feel as if they're asleep for hours after
I've been sharpening?

That shows you're doing it right, it means the knowledge is going
into you, into your flesh and into your bones so that you won't forget
the lesson: You shall know a good kitchen by the edges of its knives, a
farm by the sharpness of its shares and its scythes.

Did I imagine that I heard our whetting-song? On the in-breath?

Hey ho, hitch up the wagon.

Yes, Agaat, the wheat stands white in the fields. The front-cutter
mows a swathe through the blades of wheat. Over the contours the
wagon rocks with its load of golden sheaves. My bed with shiny railings, filled with Kleintrou and filled with Daeraad.

Can I still believe my ears?

Yes, I heard it, the rustling of newspaper, peels falling on a tin surface. The big enamel bowl from Ma's time, the one with the three red
roses in the base, the white one with the black riffled edge around the
top, and the spreading black patches where the enamel has gone. No
longer suitable for milk, but good enough for blood, for peels. I could
discern it through my fissures, the great white stain catching and reflecting the light, a cloud drifting through the room.

Shall I come to rain? Shall I be brought to fruition? Sweet? A sweeter ending than one would have expected after this? How?

A lengthy peeling it was. Hours on end. A slicing, a grating. At long intervals the chunks plashed into bowls of water.

Why is she whetting and peeling here in my room? Why do I see her shadow low down there on the floor? A shadow on her knees? A cloud dripping onto a cloud?

The smell was green and sweet and raw, traces of beans, lazy housewife, of peas, sugarsnow, of cabbage, of carrots, of turnips and radishes, of freshly-pulled fennel bulbs, the whole vegetable garden below the drift, the irrigation water, the loam darkened with barrow-loads of compost.

With the thud of the boer pumpkin on the floorboards I started to understand.

I was supposed to be able to hear the kitchen. In full concert. Pull out all the stops.

Toccata and fugue.

I had to hear and smell what it would be like when I'm gone. The onset of the funeral meal, with how much conviction it would be undertaken. The preparation for the guests, with concentration, with dedication, with virtuoso fingering.

It was supposed to console me. It was supposed to reassure me. I was in the knives, I was in the peels, in the drawers, in the enamel bowls, I was the rich black compost, I was the soil, and nothing would ever grow without me. Nothing, to the end of time, without my having farmed here, and none of the people remaining here and living off the land.

My last meal. That was what she was preparing for me. For the abstemious guest of honour.

Eight o'clock. Will she come and eat it on my behalf?

The table is set. Damask, flowers, wine, candles, silver, crystal, porcelain. Four courses at the foot of my bed.

She removed the plaster from my staring eye, she splinted open the collapsed one, she put drops in both so that I could behold it all.

Here come the dishes now. Here they come one by one. The white porcelain. Here, gliding past, is the large oval platter with the leg of lamb, complete with the knuckle-bone. Garnished with rosemary, blue blooms and all. Fatty rind crisp and brown.

She'd been grazed on bushy scrub for extra taste and flavour, earmarked early on, cleansed with milk and bran, stalked from behind where she was a-dreaming in the clover, and before she knew it, before fear could bane her . . .

Ag Agaat, you would have lent a hand there with your butcher's sleeve! You would have done it clean and fast, with respect for the wool, respect for the membranes.

She flourishes open the napkin in a single sweep, tucks it into the front of her apron, gardenia on her bib.

Forty-three years together on earth.

Her cap tilts forward. For the sake of the invisible congregation.

We're laughing at them the merest bit, I see, Agaat.

Come Lord Jesus, be our guest, let these thy gifts to us be blessed.

Why do people want to eat when somebody's died?

When have I seen her eating seated at a table?

In the dining room of old, at the far end of the table, Abba, Father bless this food for our everlasting good, the little silver shovel in the little hand, the little blunt silver fork in the other.

At the kitchen table, early evenings with me, an extra spoon in my hand: Come, another bite. Stories and rhymes to make it go down.

> And when the clock struck twelve,
> her dish was of enamel made,
> her mug of tin,
> her knife her fork her spoon
> hidden under the kitchen sink.
> Here, your things, in case of need,
> They have their place as you do now,
> You are of another breed.

With nail polish I painted a capital A on the underside of the plate, on the underside of the mug, so that they couldn't get mixed up with those of the other servants.

She always packed it, her cutlery, even for a picnic, a church bazaar, for the holiday at Witsand, wrapped in a white cloth.

She eats her picnic behind a tree, her bazaar food behind the verger's garden wall. Behind a closed kitchen door she eats when the house has fallen silent. The trunk of the tree says *forbidden*, the door says *no trespassers*. How high the wall is there under the seringas.

I went and peeped through the kitchen window one evening. Her place set with enamel, the long-pronged fork, the old bone-handled knife, the tin mug of water. The blue plate from the warming oven, the pulling-out of the chair, the sitting-down as if to boiled human flesh, the hands to the cap, if it's settled squarely, the hands to the apron bands, if they're running at right angles across the shoulders, the measured forkfuls, the steady pace, the spot at the furthest edge of the table where her eyes are fixed when she chews, her mouth shut tight, with scarcely visible movement of the jaws, straight back, straight head, without a sign of gulping, except for the small sip of water afterwards, as if it's salt water, or bitter water, or blood.

She knew there was somebody, warned me, set down the knife and fork in the plate, folded her hands in her lap, and gazed in front of her, and waited. I was slow to understand, slow to get away from the window, the dogs were jumping up against me. She got up, came and drew the curtain in my face, little tugs, unhurried, as if I weren't there, as if the only face she had seen was her own reflection in the pane. And later it was Jakkie's riddle, the solitary dining of his nêne.

Why can't I look when you're eating, Gaat?

Because my teeth are so big, Boetie!

Why can't I see when you're drinking, Gaat?

Because I milk the kitchen snake into my mug, my child!

Why do you always sit alone?

Because I'm the one in alone!

Why do you draw the curtains?

So that my fork shouldn't hook the lightning!

Why do you close the door?

So that my knife shouldn't run away through the door!

What do you eat then, Agaat?

Steamed frog, baked lizard and soup made of the tears of stones!

Stop it, the child has nightmares!

Carry on, because your même must die!

Is it a song? Why does is sound so familiar?

The table is singing at the end of my bed.

The starched sheets are singing.

Death's divinities.

The lids are removed, the steam arises.

My eye that can't blink becomes all-seeing. No moth or rust can destroy such a sight.

Agaat carves for herself.

Agaat dishes a plateful. White and green and yellow and red.

My mouth that cannot speak, now epicurean.

Eat me a psalm of pumpkin and sweet potato, the orange and the ochre, dig a pyramid over me, an underground silo, pierce peep-holes for the stars, mill the angles of the moonbeams in the grooves.

Is the right oar in the rowlock, and the left, is it there, is it greased? What about the meat with the shiny fatty rind, has it been wrapped for me in the white muslin? Who gets the knuckle bone? Who delivers the dumplings? Where in heaven's name to go with the cabbage rissoles? What to do with the baked bat?

The cave wall suppurates.

Pick the umbrella membranes off the wing-spokes with your teeth!

Because she must become other and roast through all the way to the pips and dispose of her whole self and selfishness must become her own master no longer hunger after otherman's heart or liver no longer thirst after otherchild's tears full-steam ahead to the whiter of the twin lights beware of the black and red roofs of damnation thus is it written in the Book of Death. Where did I read it?

I get between her teeth. My body, my blood. She traces the four quarters of the wind on her bib, with her fork she sounds a gong of crystal.

She gets up from the table.

Look, it is finished, she says. She unfolds it. She holds the big cloth before me. The one at which she's been labouring all this time.

It will just have to be finished now, she says, I can't do more than this. But before I wash and starch it, I must first put it on and go and lie in your grave with it. This very night is the trial.

My ear that can't hear, what was that?

She holds the smock above her head like a tent. Over the white apron and over the black sleeves drapes the densely embroidered cloth. Her cap goes under, her cap comes up through the neck-hole.

Oh where did you get that frock, where did you get that shroud?

I spy with my single eye, I spy.

I spy on the frock the sea at Infanta, I spy the land at Skeiding.

In laidwork and blackwork and braiding and cross-stitch and canvas.

It's the fire, it's the flood, it's the feast.

The shearing, the calving, the way of the women, a heron against the sky, a blue emperor in the forest, everything from here to the Hottentots Holland, all the scenes of Grootmoedersdrift.

They swirl before me, they twirl before me, the last merry-go-round. Ritornello.

And here my herald, who tries it on for me and displays it. The fourth dress of woman.

Out onto the gangplank she strides. The ship lies ready, the whistles blow.

Oh, my old piano, I don't know her, her face a sorrowing ruin.

Is it good enough to be buried in? she asks with her eyes.

With her mouth she says: It's the best I could do. Do you remember the cloth? The Glenshee linen? For one day when I'm a master, you said. First the history of South Africa you said, and then heaven.

She tightens the drawstrings around her neck.

She smiles a substitute smile. Oh, my most macabre Agaat! I see it in her eyes, only I can see it, I who fattened those eyes! The eye of the master, to the brink of the grave!

Breastwork against the worms, says Agaat's gaze. Joke! And the hem I'll sew shut once you're in, then they can't get in at the bottom either, at any rate not while your hair is growing that last little bit!

But for the time being the nether regions must remain unstitched.

For the scout goes by foot.

Two black noses of school shoes peer out. Steam rises from the cap. Diabolus in musica! She genuflects, she departs for that white-walled place. Tchi, thci, tchi, go her soles on the track.

*

The beginning of the end. That's what you felt all the time during that last feast, that last visit of Jakkie's. The end that is always a repetition of the beginning. A charging-around in vehicles, a sightseeing tour, a dead sheep, a live sheep, a remembered sheep, a shepherd with staff, birds' eggs in a bowl, an aeroplane, a fire, the blue birthday-mountains, the white arum lilies in the vlei, the mother, the father, the son, the dishes overflowing, the people, the coming and the going.

And Agaat.

This time it was Jakkie who tried to get at her.

You felt the eyes of the guest scrutinising him, scrutinising the commissions and omissions of all of you.

The food nauseated you.

You felt as if you were floating above the ground all the time. Your tongue felt too big for your mouth, your jaw was numb. You tried to pronounce the proper phrases as well as possible.

Such a run-up, such momentum, so much hope, so much effort, such a wager. To catch the butterfly. And then when it's in your hand, it's a fluttering against your palm, the gold dust disperses on your thumb, the rainbow fades, the antennae falter against your wrist.

Paradise is lost when its boundaries come into sight.

Compose your face, Jak said, don't be such a drama queen.

But his own face was white. And Jakkie was pale under his three-days' stubble.

It was the first time that he'd arrived home unshaven, in a wrinkled shirt, in a borrowed car full of mud splashes. His own was broken-down in the garage in Saldanha, he said.

You were used to his arriving as if out of a bandbox. To impress all of you, you used to think.

He always brought his case full of blue and white shirts and pants and caps and tunics. For Agaat's sake, you thought, so that she could marvel at the epaulettes and the buttons and the military-style turn-ups of the trouser legs and the sleeves, so that she could revel in the neat piles of ironing that she created out of them, every pleat ironed to a knife's edge, all spots and stains soaked out and bleached, the buttons and pins and stripes and belts buffed to a new gloss.

That weekend he had a suitcase with him that you didn't know, full of ordinary clothes that seemed too big for him.

Never mind, he said to Agaat when she wanted to take it, it's all clean. And many happy returns again for the birthday that's passed, I have something for you, but I must wrap it first. And then he asked to be excused, he had to make a quick phone call about something or other, and he took out his diary to look up a number.

Was that when you remembered?

You fetched a sheet of gift-wrap from the cupboard in the passage and slid it under his door while he was changing. You thought: I'll say nothing, later when Jakkie has left, I'll tell her I'm sorry.

Did you ever? Was there time to worry about Agaat's forgotten birthday after everything that followed on Jakkie's visit?

You looked at them leaving, Jakkie dour, introverted, Agaat with the basket of biscuits and the flask of coffee that you'd packed as of old for their walking-tour of the farm. You went to inspect his room that she'd prepared for him.

There were flowers on the table as Jakkie liked it, as Agaat had taught him to like it, as you'd taught Agaat. Reeds and grasses and foliage and yellow seedheads of fennel squashed in amongst arum lilies. On his night-table there was a midnight-blue earthenware bowl with birds' eggs, from the collection they'd built up when Jakkie was a lad. You couldn't think how Agaat had kept the eggs unbroken all those years. But there they were, whole and sound, a brown-flecked plover's egg, three white dove's eggs, blue finch eggs, the stonechat's green egg with russet specks around the big end. And the great prize, two salmon-coloured eggs, marbled with dark-pink and purple. The nightjar's eggs. The one squatting in the dirt road calling: Oh-lord-oh-lord-deliver-us.

At the foot of the bed was the brown foot-rug that Agaat had knitted and that Jakkie had grown up with. His pillows were covered in pillow slips on which she'd long ago embroidered white on white, The Good Shepherd, The Wise Virgin. As a child he'd always wanted everything in his room to be the same as in hers.

You went and sat on the bed, stroked your hands over the pillows, over the foot-rug to feel the textures. You remembered, Jakkie's warm little body as you handed him to each other, wrapped in Agaat's foot-rug when he went to sleep in front of the fire with her in the outside room. You remembered how you'd laid him down on his pillows that Agaat had embroidered for him so that he shouldn't miss her too much at night, Jakkie's little fingers as he felt over the pillows, over the rounded backs of sheep, over the shepherd's staff, beside the flame of the replenished lamp.

How Agaat rubbed his head.

Sleep softly now, Gaat's little one.

You got up and opened the windows. One of Agaat's aprons was draped over the half-door of the outside room, she'd put on a clean one for the walk.

Jakkie's jacket was over the chair. His diary, would it be in his inside pocket? But you didn't look. You stood there and thought of Agaat's letters to him that you'd intercepted. His case lying open. A book on top of the clothes. Polish poems translated into English. Zbiegnew Herbert. The poet was unknown to you, your son's taste in literature an enigma to you.

You went looking for them in the old orchard, took along a cloth pocket for late oranges as alibi.

You entered by the furthest point of the orchard. The smell of rotten citrus in the sun was stupefying. It made you feel dizzy. Row after row you walked the orchard without seeing them. Near the quince avenue you felt their presence, but everything was dead still. You went closer, along the other side of the avenue, your footsteps camouflaged by the rushing water. They were sitting in the shade against the bank of the irrigation furrow with their feet in the water. Jakkie upended the flask in the cap, shook out the last drops, and drank. Agaat was looking in front of her. You could tell from her back that she was dejected and defeated. Jakkie screwed the cap back on.

So that's the story, he said. There's no turning back any more and I don't know what lies ahead.

He looked in front of him.

They sat like that for a long time.

The sun was scorching your shoulders where you had lain down flat behind the bank. In front of you their backs were like closed doors. Perhaps they were talking softly without looking at each other but you couldn't hear anything any more. Then Jakkie leant forward far over the furrow and turned his face at an angle to Agaat. Then you could read his lips.

What does the water sound like when the sluice opens in the irrigation furrow?

He answered his own question.

G-g-g-g-g-a-a-a-t.

He drew the a's out, scraped the g's gently against his palate.

Do you remember, Gaat? The sound of the sea in a shell? The sound of the wind in the wheat? Do you remember how you made me listen? And everything sounded like your name. Ggggg-aaat, says the black pine tree in the rain, the spurwinged goose when it flies up says gaat-agaatagaat, the drift when it's in flood from far away, do you remember?

Ai, you were still very small.

I always wanted to know where you came from, what your name means.

Yes, you were an inquisitive one, you.

I still am. You said you'd tell.

One day, not yet.

One day when? I'm leaving, remember.

One day when the time is ripe.

It's time, the oranges are rotten!

Jakkie turned on his side and leant against the bank. He selected an orange from the basket, took a penknife out of his pocket.

Do you remember the knife?

Do you still have it?

I never throw away anything you've given me. Do you remember when you gave it to me?

Yes, it was when you turned nine, on your birthday. I had to ask nicely. Your father said you'd just get up to no good with it.

He said if I wanted a knife I had to be a man and a man can dock a tail. He forced me. You too, Ma too. My own hanslam you selected for it, would you believe.

Jakkie was speaking more loudly, vehemently, you could hear that he was upset.

I'm no longer scared of him, Gaat, for that I've almost seen my arse too many times in the service of his pathetic National Party. Fucking Mirages that fuck out, fucking missiles around my ears. Killed hundreds of people, more than I'll ever know. Jesus, what a disgrace! How must I live with it for the rest of my life? I'm ashamed of it, that it happened to me, that I didn't see it sooner. Always just: You'll do what I tell you, chappie, salute, general! I puke of it, of this pathetic lot who tell themselves they've been placed here on the southernmost tip with a purpose and they represent something grandiose in the procession of nations. O wide and sorrowful land blah blah blah with flag and Word and trumpet. It's sick! Sick! It's better that I go away before I do something rash. He's pathetic, my father. My mother too, she's pathetic. They keep each other pathetic, the two of them, with all their wealth and wisdom. The whole community here intoning their anthem, pee-ep, squeak the little wives, bu-urp croak the husbands, they with their stud farms breeding bulls for the abattoir and babies for the army, they with their church steeples and iron fists towering towards heaven. Who do they think they are? Blind and deaf against the whole world? How long must it still carry on? And their God, he's one of them, half-a-head elevated above the bald pate of the local dominee, God Almighty, the Auditor of the Land Bank.

The orchard has ears.

That's what Agaat said. You knew it was meant for you. You wormed away backwards and came to your feet carefully and walked back. You picked up a few oranges at random to have something in the pocket, a proof.

Pathetic, you thought, my child thinks I'm pathetic.

You went and changed into another dress. Nobody need know that you'd crawled on your stomach. On your back where the August sun had beaten down, it felt hot for a long time after, itchy all over the shoulders.

All the time that afternoon while Jak was taking Jakkie around on the farm to see his latest activities, you felt as if another tape was spooling in your head with commentary.

The bokbaai vygies a feverish rash, the Namaqualand daisies a knee-high blaze. The whole garden an indictment, wide and sorrowful.

Jakkie stood gazing at it.

Gaat's work, you said.

Gaat's and mine, Jak said. Your mother, don't you know, had fainting fits for months on end. She went and fell into the ditch that evening after your medal parade. Agaat must have told you. On top of a rotten cow. Got such a fright she was all aquiver.

Jak held open the door of the new abattoir for Jakkie. He'd always been squeamish, he said, about the slaughtering on the block, the old axes and the knives at the draining-gutter under the bluegums, where the dogs lick, where the gauze cage sways in the wind.

An abattoir was an asset on Grootmoedersdrift, he said, solidly built, complete with shiny steel surfaces, neon lights, completely automated bearing-surfaces, industrial refrigeration plants. Jak tapped against the wall, stroked the shiny surfaces with the back of his hand.

Pale in the light of the cooler, in deep marinading dishes, lay the sheep and the suckling pigs with their legs tied together. Agaat had already threaded them along the spine on the central braai rods for the spit-braai the following day.

You stood back out of the cool-room. The dull light over the rumps, the ribs and legs, the headlessness, the disgrace.

You'd stood next to Agaat the day when the installers came to demonstrate the machinery. You couldn't watch, the fear of the animals between the railings of the isolation pen, the swinging up onto the moving hook of the living animal, the blood in the drainage chutes, the screaming saw-blade.

See, now somebody with one hand can slaughter all on her own, Jak had shouted at her above the noise.

Jak took a sheep's head out of the cooler, held it up by the ears before Jakkie. The head from the slaughter, belonging to Dawid and company, that they'd not collected yet. He slotted the blade into the grooves with a click and took hold of the head on either side by the ears. Slowly he guided it over the steel surface to the blade.

Now watch closely, he shouted above the din to Jakkie, no mess, no splinters, no force, as quick as breaking your neck.

It was a little year-old merino ewe, earmarked for the knife, a well-filled round fringe of wool on the forehead, the ears velvety, pinkish, the wrinkled nose of her race, the mouth already slightly crooked and shrunken under the nipple-coloured snout.

Jak pressed the head down on the neck, pushed it against the blade with his hands on either side on the cheeks. There was a jolt as the teeth of the saw seized the wool and then it was bone, a scream rising higher and higher as the fleece got thicker along the forehead.

Jak came away from the blade with the two open halves to show you. It looked like a cross-section model in a biology laboratory, the soft grey hemispheres of the brain, the white sinus chambers, the brown furrows of the nasal passages, the mouth cavity with the long halves of purplish tongue, thinner than you'd expect, from which a trickle of blood was welling, the jaw with the two front teeth sawn apart.

Easy, see, said Jak and clapped the two halves closed like a book. He turned the head at a right angle and starting from the snout he cut it up into cubes with rapid strokes, so that the outsides fell open onto the sawing surface like the pieces of a jigsaw. He switched off the machine, removed the blade and put it in the sink, and swept the blocks into the off-cuts pail with the back of his hand.

Child's play, he said, and with his foot he pushed the pail in by the door of the cool-room.

What could have been going through Jak's head? The logic of his sightseeing tour escaped you.

Next was Jak's new merino stud rams. Under the direction of the stock-breeding expert of the Tygerhoek experimental farm he'd done experiments to determine the influence of the various feeds and feed supplements on the fertility of the sheep. You listened to him explaining all this to Jakkie. You could have sworn he was a stud farmer.

There were four rams, a dozen or so ewes, each in a separate pen with a number and a steel post-box in which the records of their feeding schedule were kept.

What you see here is worth tens of thousands of rand, said Jak, all the champions of Katbosch and Zoetendals Valley and Van Rheenen's Heights.

They're all very close already to the Super Utility Merino. That's the objective.

Jakkie wasn't listening. As if he were on the look-out, his eyes kept wandering in the direction of the road which one could see from the pens.

What he was looking for, said Jak, was one hundred per cent prepotency, a lambing rate of a hundred and fifty per cent, early weaning time and the greatest possible uniformity and regularity of build, plus then super-wool qualities.

You all had to examine the one ram with him.

Hannibal, it said on the tin name-tag.

If you consider, Jak said, that there were only fat-tailed Hottentot sheep with knock-knees and Cape sheep covered in tatters in this country when the white man arrived here, then we've come a long way.

The ram retreated slightly on its delicate little feet as you approached.

Down on your haunches, said Jak, otherwise he'll get a fright.

He clicked his tongue and murmured reassuringly.

Finer of fleece than the Rambouillet and even than the Vermont, hardier than the Saxony, more compact than the Australian, such a South African merino. Perfectly adapted to our conditions.

Jak folded open the fleece on the back so that you could see the wool.

Four inches, very soft, not a cross-thread in sight, just see how wide is the staple, he said. Feel. Top spinning quality. Look at the deep crimp.

Jak isolated one tuft.

He took Jakkie's hand and put his fingers on the tuft. See how it stands up, nice cauliflower tip as well. Just feel the character. Deep character.

He opened the fleece in two other places.

Just see, everywhere the same, even to the belly, and well-oiled throughout.

Jakkie was more interested in his father's tone than in the information, that you could deduce from the way in which he started leading him on.

Just look at that head! Jakkie said. Only you heard the mockery.

Yes, now isn't that spiff, Hannibal, Jak said, and turned to the sheep, we're talking about your head.

Jak was on one knee next to the ram and took its jaw in his hands.

Big, strong, open face, alert and masculine.

He pulled open the mouth a bit so that one could see the gums and the teeth.

Broad mouth, free of blemishes. And just feel that silky-soft skin on the nose.

Jakkie rubbed over the nose with cautious fingers.

He'd never realised, he said, that a sheep had such a long nose.

As it should be, Jak said, long and finely-curved, and just see how wide a curve the horns make around the head and how big the ears are, lively soft ears for his baas.

Here and there and everywhere Jak touched the ram, as if he were sculpting something.

Broad in the shoulders, broad in the chest, deep ribcage. Sturdy flanks. See how spacious the leap of the ribs, how straight the topline from the neck to the tail, square across the rump, well-filled buttocks, enough place for the balls.

He squeezed the soft downy scrotum lightly.

The ram picked up its back foot and step-stepped when Jak touched its nuts. Jak caught the paw and steadied the ram by the horn with his other hand.

Wait, Hannibal, he said, we're inspecting your feet. Straight and strong from the heel to the knee, he won't stumble or twist, this sheep. Just look at that hoof, nice and amber in colour.

Jak got up and closed up the wool where he'd opened it.

Jeez, Pa, Jakkie said, you should become a praise-singer for sheep, that was quite a text for the prodigal son.

You weren't surprised that evening at table when Jak got going.

So what do you say about the political situation these days? he asked Jakkie.

Really, is it necessary, you tried to intervene, we're enjoying our meal so much.

For Agaat's sake you said that, to console her where she was standing with a guarded expression over her dishes. Because we weren't enjoying our meal. There was a silence around the table.

Agaat's hand. It was impressive what she'd brought about there. Extra special just for the family, on top of all the preparations for the great feast the following day. All the old favourites, the choice dishes that Jakkie had grown up with, were on the table. A steamed river eel on spinach to start. Chicken pie, ox tongue, roast hare with field mushrooms that she'd dried the previous autumn, stewed dried peaches and roast potatoes, green beans with onion and shiny sweet-potatoes and cauliflower with mustard cheese sauce and pumpkin fritters, and a salad of baby beetroot in a vinegar reduction, and baby onions in a sweet-and-sour sauce. Everything dished up in the best porcelain and garnished with fresh parsley and chives and rosemary and mint.

She hadn't as usual first asked permission to use the best table linen and the crystal glasses and the silver. There were two candelabra with candles and a flat table arrangement of cinerarias and creeper shoots. Around Jakkie's plate she'd made a birthday garland of the first blue wine-cup babiana that she'd gone to gather in the fynbos-kloof.

What made you think that it was for herself as well? You tried to remember why you'd forgotten her birthday. Twelfth of July. The thought made the food congeal in your mouth. The day of the tele-phone conversation? Had that been the birthday?

You could find out if you wanted to. You'd be able to get Jakkie on his own, could ask him if she'd really been talking to him that day. Whether it was on the twelfth of July. But you said nothing then, you remained silent. You felt it welling up around you, the tide of things that had to be said. Your arms felt numb. You felt hot. Your whole body was itching.

I'm asking, what do my son's politics look like these days? Jak insisted. Jak had drunk too much. You placed your hand on his, but he shook it off, gesticulated with his fork in the air.

He's in the Air Force after all, surely he must know more than the man in the street.

Jakkie twirled his glass in his hand. You caught his eye, signalled: Be quiet, just ignore. You beckoned to Agaat to clear the table.

Jak threw his hands in the air.

Are you all going to ignore me now? Have you swallowed your tongue, Jakkie? Then answer me when I'm speaking to you, chappie. Agaat, put down the dishes, you'll just have to hear as well what your pet says to us. Kleinbaas Jakkie here, it seems he wants away, a little bird told me, away from his beloved nursemaid with whom he speaks in secret on the telephone.

Then Jakkie let go of his glass and it tilted out of his hand, and the wine splashed a long red stain on the white tablecloth.

Pa, he managed, and then Agaat was in between with cloths and water and salt, you could see her touching Jakkie, how she was trying to calm him with her body, now this side of him, now that, now over one shoulder and then over the other. She brought a clean glass from the kitchen and poured it full of wine for him and topped up Jak's glass. A whole bustle she organised there around the glasses, as if she were trying to distract their attention by sleight of hand.

Our beloved Gaat, Jak continued, our baker and butler, just like a hen trying to keep her chickens together. Look at this dabchick, Gaat, he gets quite out of kilter when his father wants to catechise him.

Jakkie got up, threw down his napkin. Jak leant over the table and pushed him back into his chair.

No, have a seat first so that I can tell you something, man, he said, as if he were at a congenial gathering of farmers.

He started in a roundabout way, with Elsa Joubert's book about which people were writing letters in the press at the time. The one your mother bought and never finished, he said, ostensibly because it was too sad, as if your mother's ever had problems with any sadness. His eyes played mockingly over you, but you weren't the one in his sights. Jakkie must explain to him what structural violence is, he said.

Jakkie looked up and looked away, his body was quaking with the trembling of his legs under the table. Agaat tried to sidle away towards the kitchen.

Then Jak got up and pulled out the chair at the far end of the table, tap-tapped his hand on the backrest.

Come, Gaat, come and sit down for a while, this was always your place, wasn't it, he said. You must listen very carefully now, your klein-baas, Captain de Wet here, is going to give us an exposition. I don't see any structural violence or any other violence against you except that little half-way arm of yours. Fucked crooked or kicked crooked, doesn't matter. No long journeys for you, only a nice servant's room with a fireplace, settled for life here on Grootmoedersdrift. Structural advantages, I'd say. White people's food, white people's language, a white apron, white sheets and here's your little white pet who shares his little secrets with you that his own mother and father aren't allowed to hear. They hear only the little white lies. Come on, Jakkie, tell us, what is structural violence?

Jak walked around the table and gestured to Agaat to sit down on the chair. For a moment you thought he was going to take her by the thin arm, but he didn't, he just gestured with his head. Agaat shut off her regard. Very upright, very rigidly she sat down on the edge of the chair.

White tablecloths, white candles, fragrant white flowers, Jak said and gestured with open arms, so white is she that she plays back all the little white things as she knows we like them. Exactly what old Poppie Whatsername also did, recounted her miseries as she knew the writer wanted to hear them, a story that could be sold, it's being translated into all kinds of languages nowadays, they say. Even shares in the profits, the kaffir-girl. Remarkable business, Afrikaners making a name for themselves with coon stories that they pick up in the backyard and spread far and wide as gospel truth.

Jak took a large gulp from his glass.

Should your father tell you what he thinks, Jakkie? He thinks the world finds us whites in this country interesting only for what we're supposed to have done to the hotnots and the kaffirs. And then they're going to hold it against us all over again because we dare write down on behalf of the so-called victims what we did to them. No, we should rather kindly teach the poor devils to write their own stories and package it for them. First-class export produce. Whether we'll then see anything of the profits is another matter!

Jak's tongue was dragging. His gestures were emphatic.

At least he's not violent, you thought. You tried to catch Agaat's eye in case he should become violent. She feigned blindness to you, her eyes were on Jakkie who was taking substantial gulps from his new glass of wine.

How about it, Agaat? Jak prodded, you're the exception here after all. Your nooi has already taught you nicely how to write, hasn't she. Dear sir, yours respectfully, if I may make so bold. More Afrikaans than the whole lot of newspaper journalists can dream of. You after all write long letters to dear gracious Captain de Wet here. He can surely not have thrown them away. Perhaps he should collect them and post them to dear Mrs Joubert so that she can brush up your Dutch a bit so that everyone can understand it. Then you'll have a new life. Then they'll come and interview you. That Poppie didn't know whether she was coming or going, so, apparently, they thronged around her to make TV movies. Over and over the same story of her long journey she had to tell, she must have got bored to death, wouldn't surprise me if in the end she started adding on a journey here and a journey there, to at least keep the matter interesting for herself.

Jakkie shook his head, covered his face with his hands.

Jak, that's enough, you said.

Jak kept talking over your interjection. How about it, Agaat? You wouldn't have to add on anything if they asked you. Your story is better than the back page of the *Rapport*.

Bring pen and paper, then I'll give you the long and short of it, he said to Agaat.

She didn't move, remained looking in front of her. Jak walked up and down dictating.

White woman childless steals baby woolly with one arm stop one-armed woolly catches baby boy on mountain pass stop toy aeroplane explodes stop woolly saves stop woolly gives tit/shit/bread/head.

Perhaps you'd prefer a little song, Jak said. Your mother here after all always taught you little songs. That's what you understand.

Jak didn't sing. Here beyond the hill on our farm, he said, the sheep get bluetongue, the wheat gets rust, wifey blubbers, hubby batters, you name it, every disaster in the book.

And then? The son grows up, he squashes his father flat on the rocks of the Huis River, he becomes a soldier, a fighter pilot, for three years he bombs every FAPLA, SWAPO, MPLA and Cuban from an Impala in the moonlight in South West.

And look at him now! Strikes a funk at twenty-five in the year of our Lord nineteen eighty-five in our beleaguered South Africa, with bugger-all to say for himself. Just when we need him most.

And the woolly just writes on.

Jak first saluted Agaat, and then Jakkie.

I'm sure you are aware, dear Captain, that Mrs de Wet, your esteemed mother, opens all her servant's letters to her son here . . .

Jakkie glared at you for a moment, and then at Agaat. He blinked his eyes slowly, and put his head on his arms on the table.

So, Agaat, Jak said, that's the story. Can you think us up a conclusion? After all, you're used to embroidering!

How long did it last? Half an hour, an hour? Jak looked as if he was going to start crying. He slammed his fist on the table, but there was no strength in the blow.

Don't you people have anything to say? he shouted.

He rocked drunkenly on his feet.

Don't you have anything to say then! What does one have to do to make you wake up? Spineless! That's why things will end badly for us! That's why the enemy is sharpening its teeth on our borders! The Afri-kaner women, they who should be carrying the torch, they're useless, the Afrikaner youth, characterless, without ideals, even the Afrikaner skivvies are struck dumb! Is this what our ancestors tamed this land for with their muzzle-loaders, with the clothes on their bodies and their wagons against the barbarian hordes? Come, Agaat, where are the days when your kind cut the throats of their masters in their sleep?

Then you'll have something to write about, instead of the sentimental chirry-chirping of yours, one two buckle my shoe, onky-bonky here's my donkey, pat-a-cake, as if you're in a children's book, not exactly top secrets that you're sharing with your kleinbaas the traitor!

Jak sank unsteadily into an armchair, mumbled something now and again, more and more slowly, like a piece of clockwork running down.

Jakkie remained slumped with his head on his arms. After a while he no longer looked up.

You looked at the head, the shape of it exactly like Jak's, the unshaven cheek of the strange young man, your son, amongst the dishes of food and the dirty plates, his lips muttering in the salt through which the spilt wine was starting to seep pinkly. You looked at Agaat whose eyes rolled slowly from side to side like those of a chameleon without her turning her head an inch left or right. A fly settled on the cauliflower. Agaat flapped it away.

You remained sitting there, you and Agaat, long after the talking had ceased. There was only the ticking of the grandfather clock, the quarter strokes of two quarters, the bothersome fly around your heads. Then Agaat got up. She avoided your eyes, touched her cap to feel if it was properly settled.

Let's take them to their rooms, she said.

As if it were the most ordinary thing on earth.

You put your arms around them, under the arms, between you, down the passage, first one, then the other, got them to their beds, took off their shoes.

Was it later that night, or the following night, or only after the weekend that you tried to check, emptied out the tablets on your bedspread, tried to count them, the drops, the powders? But you couldn't remember how many of everything there was supposed to be. And in those weeks before the feast you were in any case taking more of everything. Agaat counted out your pills for you in the morning and put them out on your dressing table because you could sometimes not remember whether you'd taken them, so dosed yourself double in the evenings and then was too drained the next day to do anything.

Would she have gone so far as to doctor Jak and Jakkie's drinks? You didn't dare ask her. You were scared she'd say something about the letters. You went and checked in your handbag, in the carrier bags in your wardrobe, to see whether there was perhaps one that you'd forgotten to post. The one, the ode on Grootmoedersdrift, you looked for that again, but you couldn't find it. You found nothing. You were scared. Suddenly it was important to be able to remember the smallest detail exactly. But you couldn't remember. Things had slipped in your memory. Had you let slip something, to Jak, to Jakkie, was it from that that Jak could make out that you'd read Agaat's letters? Or had Agaat brought it to their attention?

You remembered the diaries. After Jakkie joined the Defence Force you'd stopped keeping a diary. You collected the booklets in the top cupboard of the spare room where you'd pushed them in amongst the eiderdowns. You paged through a few. Could you perhaps have hidden some of Agaat's letters that you'd forgotten to post in them? Your eye fell here and there on what you'd written. What of any importance could anybody read into them?

That's what you thought but you weren't sure. Your handwriting struck you as strange, more upright, harder than you thought of yourself as writing. You tied the booklets up in piles with kitchen string. Your hands were trembling. You locked them in the sideboard with the other documents.

There you stood in the sitting room, shaky, after you'd locked up the books. The sideboard gleaming, darker than usual. The dining-table, cleared, glossy, with a vase of flowers on top. No sign of the meal earlier or of the discord. But the dining room felt ominous. Every familiar thing was, under its surface, at its core, as if charged with dynamite.

You felt somebody was looking at you, there where you were standing with the key of the sideboard in your hand, but the curtains were drawn, the back door was closed, there was nobody. Here it is now, you thought, the last link that's chafing through. Everything you lived for, everything that you built up, all the facades that you maintained, the whole lie that you lived. The last link.

The key was sweating in your hand.

At last you slapped it down on the table for all the world to see.

You went and sat on a chair in your room in the dark, a woman over an abyss, the coming of morning a ghastliness, the first thrush a deathly herald. Agaat bringing your coffee and saying nothing about your just sitting there in the previous night's clothes, just raising her eyebrows over the pills that she'd put out for you and that you'd not taken.

You were scared of her. More scared of her when she was right under your eyes than behind your back. You cringed away from the brisk pace at which she kept doing her work. It was as if she'd been beating you with sticks, with irons, since the previous evening, and still now, the day of the feast. You couldn't believe it, the calm cheerful face she put on.

Till late that night she kept it up.

Till the flying in the aeroplane.

Only then could you breathe in an odd sort of way.

Then it was her turn to be beaten.

Was it the abominations of your own family that opened your eyes to the power or impotence branded on the faces, the whitewashed disgraces of the guests who started arriving in groups or pairs the following day? Was it the lack of sleep? The pills you hadn't taken? So that you, for the first time in how many years, were soberly and austerely aware of what was happening around you?

12 August 1985. You are cordially invited.

You suddenly saw everything so clearly through Jakkie's eyes, pe-eep squeak the wives, bu-urp croak the husbands, the high-pitched little-girl voices in which the women twittered, the coarse bravado of the men, the children insolent or timorous, the childminders, feigning docil-ity, but already casting long glances towards leftovers in the kitchen, bread, fat, candles and cloths and soap and matches. A pillage it would be again, as always.

You saw yourself standing in the garden mirrors, in your red dress. You heard your voice warbling. You shook the hands, pressed your cheek against the powdery cheeks of the women, kissed the slobbery mouths of the men.

My mother is pathetic, they keep each other pathetic, the whole community. Jakkie's words of the previous day. Your child. Blood of your blood. Not impossible, surely, that his message had taken effect on you immediately. Brainwashing, another voice in you protested, that's how subversion and brainwashing operate.

Welcome, welcome to Grootmoedersdrift! you said again and again.

Clearly I'm stuck between two cycles of brainwashing, and me without my pills as well.

You looked at Jak and Jakkie, emboldened in their display by a need to make up for the previous evening. Both ashamed of their lack of memory, they tried to tell each other what a load of crap they'd talked. Agaat rubbed it in. The Alka Seltzer and the vitamins, the big can of orange juice and the pot of strong coffee that stood ready by their breakfast plates that morning.

And then there was the moment, after breakfast, when Agaat over-played her hand, when Jakkie had to promise her solemnly that he wouldn't drink any more on his birthday, and that he would make a nice speech. That's as far as you could hear, before Agaat went into her room.

He stood talking over the half-door.

On my own birthday, Gaat?! he exclaimed. He averted his face from the door of the outside room. You were looking out of the kitchen door, saw the expression come over his face, the one you'd so often seen in Jak, the desire to inflict hurt.

You saw Agaat appear in the doorway. You saw her catching Jakkie's glance.

The next sentence you could only partially make out.

Then you can explain it! was what it sounded like, and: No, I'm not going to write anything, next thing it will find its way into the wrong hands. So you go ahead and write something! Think up something!

Was that what you heard? His face was half inside Agaat's door. Then he pulled back his head and the sun fell on his brown curls, long, you thought, for an officer who'd only just been granted a pass.

Well, he said, his hands on the half-door, if I'm not even allowed to drink on my own birthday, and if I have to pronounce according to your precepts, you heard him say, then you, my dear Agaat, will get into the plane this evening so that I can show you what Grootmoedersdrift looks like from up there! A full moon has been requisitioned especially for you! Wonderland by Night!

Jak was coming from the direction of the sitting room, walked past you in the kitchen, out into the backyard. He heard what Jakkie was saying. They laughed together at the prospect of loading Agaat into the aeroplane. They were on their way to inspect the fuel supply and the landing strip.

Those were the movements of that morning, the voices, the sentences, the faces in doorways, the backs, the fronts, the standing still, the turning away, the walking past.

You waited as the feast continued into evening, the torches and the fires lit, the silhouettes of skewered animals rotating on spits. Grotesque it looked to you. And smelt too, the air dense with roasted flesh. Witches' Sabbath. But who were the witches? Surely not these cordial effusive people who'd come from far and wide for your son's birthday? Perhaps I'm psychotic, you thought, perhaps I've been dependent on my medication for so long that I degenerate into an enemy of the people if I skip a day. That's what Jak always said: Take your pills, Milla, so that you can shut up while the men make war.

You tried in vain to vanquish the thoughts. But you kept looking out for the first stirrings of mischief as the great bowls of salad and the baskets of bread were carried in under Agaat's command. You tried to keep a clear line of sight as you helped to serve the people, all the old acquaintances, and their children who were gathered there like replicas unto the third and the fourth generation. You couldn't snap out of it. All the convivial noises sounded so false to you. Even Beatrice and Thys, your oldest friends, aroused your distrust. They were the dominee's confidants. They would carry report of every guffaw that was too loud and every note that was false and every drop that was drunk in excess. To the nearest hundred rand they'd be able to estimate the cost of the whole thing. They'd be able to calculate the tithe that would be proportionate to the cost and submit it to the representative of God in the Swellendam district and he would in his own time and season come and claim it for the swelling of the church coffers. You could talk to them, to protect Agaat, to speak to Jak. You could try to talk to Dominee himself.

But what would they be able to do about it? About your presentiment that a slow explosion was blowing all of Grootmoedersdrift into hundreds of shards and chunks? You were alone with the sensation. You tried to shake it off, had coffee brought to you to bring you to your senses. Lack of sleep, you thought.

There were the sallow Dieners of Vreugdevol with their smooth blue-black hair, pure Malay, you realised for the first time. Pass for white, whatever that might mean here on the other side of Sir Lowry's Pass. The heads were bowed low over the plates, the gills shone as they peered at each other around the white wrought-iron table, as if they were engaged in an eating contest. You went across to them to try to rid yourself of the odd perspective, but they were so engrossed in stuffing themselves, they hardly greeted you.

So then for want of something more constructive to do you took a jug of ice to the Froneman table. For there wife and children with woebegone eyes were sucking away at lukewarm glasses of cooldrink under the stern gaze of their teetotal father.

Ice, you said, try a bit of ice, it makes everything taste better.

Like somebody from the Salvation Army you sounded to your own ears. They smirked at you half-heartedly.

To one side at their own table were the Killjoys of Loch Maguire. This evening, you thought, their melancholy was extra evident. Pol Knoblauch, the bluebeard with the stiff neck, people said he fiddled with the farm labourers' little boys, and his wife the soprano of the church gallery. Every week at the gynaecologist's for indeterminate complaints, it was said.

And the rich Meyers family of Konstandhof, the seven brothers, all with the fine features and the little high-pitched voices, all of them with the glad eye and the one undescended ball as the rumour ran. And their Meyers sisters and female cousins with the mad streak, the whole lot of them, either worked up or down with pills.

Do I also look like that? you wondered. In the faint light of the marquee your red dress appeared black when you looked down. The sleeves felt too heavy on your arms. It felt as if you were moving ever more slowly.

Suddenly Gawie Tredoux was next to you. Just standing there, without a word. His voice when he spoke was tired.

Are you thinking what I'm thinking, Milla? At the best of times our people are fodder for low-brow soap operas, at the worst for old men with grand plans. And all the young ones want to do nowadays is surf and smoke dagga and play guitar.

You looked at him. He'd aged. Got dumped by his wife. His son a member of some rock group or other that toured all over the country with protest songs.

Look after yourself well, Milla, he said, you know I'm always there if you need me. He squeezed your shoulder.

Thank you for your trouble, tell Agaat as well, everything tip-top as usual, but I'll be on my way now, not in the mood for a party this evening, you neither, it seems to me, but that's life, old girl, just grin and bear it, tomorrow's another day.

So as not to subside into tears, you betook yourself to the hand-picked wives of the Meyers brothers, a harem of shared resentment under the command of their mother-in-law, the painted-up old matriarch of whom it was rumoured that she'd been a photo model in her youth. In spite of her advanced age it was very clear in the candlelight where her sons' high cheekbones had sprung from. Half maliciously, half gloatingly, her daughters-in-law sat by her and complimented you on the feast, on your son, on your husband. They were sisters under duress. Heir mares. Assessed on the hind-quarters and bought in for the purpose. Fertiliser Princesses. Co-op Queens. Style, Overberg Barbie, as Jak would say. You could easily spot the sons, the precocious lordliness with which they were appraising the girls.

And there was Jakkie amid it all, amiability itself. He'd kept to his word, it seemed to you. He greeted, served, endured. He replied to Jak's speech, albeit not with great warmth, correctly and with the proper number of tame jokes. He expressed his thanks. My dear mother, my mainstay of a father. The only sign of a more alert, more intelligent creature under all the formalities were the special words full of double meanings to Agaat whom he had called to the front next to him during his speech.

He thanked her for the food and the garden and the planning of the whole feast. She is someone who reaches great heights, she is someone who spreads her wings wide, she showed him as a child how the blue crane becomes airborne, white-throat crows go from here to great Tradouw, she showed him what a tailwind does to the flight of a weaver, and a headwind to a gull, she named the clouds for him and taught him to read the currents in the air and told how the devil constructed whirlwinds from the dust of the hills.

And: It will be an honour and a privilege for him to take her as his first passenger on a special birthday flight.

There was loud applause. 'Smear that mouth with jam!' one shouted. 'Real smooth talker De Wet!'

Jakkie handed the parcel, wrapped in your gift wrap, to Agaat. It was also her birthday recently, he said, and it's something she'll need for her first flight.

'Open it! Open it!' people shouted.

Agaat struggled with the paper, embarrassed with the little hand that didn't want to grip properly in front of an audience. Jakkie took it out of her hand and stripped off the sticky-tape and gave it back to her.

Take it out, he gestured with his head.

It was a shimmering, shiny raw silk headscarf, plain red. It slithered and shone in the lamplight as Agaat shook out the folds.

You saw Agaat's eyes flashing. How could she say: Blow in my face so that I can smell whether you've been drinking? Could she tell from his words that he was too eloquent? How far is it permitted for a servant to investigate the breath of her kleinbaas?

You thought of the scene of Jakkie five years old blowing into Agaat's face where she was standing before him on her knees.

Stole chocolates!

Chewed fennel seeds!

Ate apricot jam on your bread! she could guess with shut eyes.

Why hadn't you tried to talk Jakkie out of the idea of flying?

You took him by the shoulder. Hard he is, you thought, far removed from me. Even without the stiff blue serge of his captain's uniform his body felt unyielding.

You want to make a spectacle of her. That's all you said.

He removed your hand from his body and put it aside as if it were a marmot. You were close enough, you could smell the liquor on his breath. He had a contrary look in his eyes.

Ma, he said, what happens now, is between me and Agaat. My bit I've done . . .

He looked away before he carried on talking.

She'll get into that Cessna with me and feel how it feels to be as free as a bird. Because that's what she's scared of. That's what you're all scared of. You're more scared of freedom than you are of the communists. Even if it fell into your laps you wouldn't recognise it or know what to do with it.

So I'm not permitted to say what I want to say. Agaat's orders, she actually thinks she can prevent the whole assembled Overberg's evening being spoilt for them here. Then she has to pay for it. I'm not the one who's making a spectacle of her, she's making a spectacle of herself. It was on her behalf amongst others that I wanted to speak. So if I may not do it, and she can not do it, better then that we go up into the air together.

Jakkie glared at you.

Perhaps she'll be able to tell me at last up there in the clouds where she came from and how she ended up here on Grootmoedersdrift, in her stupid cap and school shoes, there in the back in the outside room, so faithful, so prematurely aged and so set in her ways, with her embroidery and her writing pads, a tyrant over others here on the farm.

They hate her, they mock her. It's you who made her like that, Ma, you and Pa. She's more screwed up than Frankenstein's monster.

You sound like your father, you wanted to say, it's a different story, but it's the same arrogance.

But you didn't. You were ashamed that he could say one thing and do the opposite and not notice it.

You went in the jeep to the landing strip, at speed over the drift and slip-slide round the bend on the other side of the bridge, because it had been flooded till recently. Jakkie was driving, a whole line of cars following with guests who didn't want to miss it.

You're not going to fly with me in that apron and with that white cap on your head, Jakkie said to Agaat.

I am, said Agaat.

You are not your apron and your cap, Agaat, Jakkie said, and turned round to her.

I am, Agaat said.

Well, then tonight you're going to feel what it's like for a change not being yourself, because that's what you wanted from me and I did as you said. Where's the scarf?

I'm not wearing the scarf, she said.

Take off that bishop's cap of yours and tie on the scarf, Gaat. And off with that apron, this moment!

Then look in front of you, said Agaat.

Aitsa, Jak said, now the current's flowing!

They laughed, your husband and your son.

You saw sparks, a rustling of the static electricity in the scarf as Agaat pulled it out of her apron pocket. You got out, following Jak and Jakkie.

Around the runway there was a bustle of men setting up the two rows of tractor headlights for the take-off. A few women had come along and were standing to one side chatting. Children were swarming around the plane. You turned away. There was a full moon, a clear night with the chill of the recent winter still in the air. You turned back again. The little white plane at the far end of the runway looked as if it had been glued together from planks, a splash of white paint against the black outlines of the hills.

Jakkie climbed in. Against the light you could see him checking the controls. The headlight came on, a harsh beam over the stony ground of the fallow field, and then the red and green lights on the tips of the wings. The engine putt-putted and took and when it was at full strength, the propeller started turning slowly, faster and faster till it was only a grey haze in front of the nose. A cloud of dust was slowly being churned up around the body. In the fumes you could see the tailfin waggling, first to the right and then to the left.

Then the passenger door opened, a hand beckoned. The back door of the jeep opened, the red scarf was tied round Agaat's head, nurse-style, with a peak in front and a triangular flap at the back. How did she figure it out so soon? you wondered. Would she have practised in her room in the evenings with all the scarves that Jakkie had brought home over the years?

The children yelled. In between the men called out with hands cupped in front of their mouths.

Strap yourself in, Gaat!

Say your prayers, Gaat!

Hee, now you're going to see a flying goffel!

God, but she'll shit herself, the creature!

Piss in her pants!

If she's wearing pants!

Jakkie, do you have a pee-pot in that fly-machine?

She's going to puke!

Fly her till she pukes on the Catholics' roof!

On the apostolics!

On the kaffir location!

Agaat looked neither left nor right. Up against the stepladder she climbed, the tip of the scarf was fluttering wildly in the slipstream. With the little hand she held it behind her head. It was half an Agaat up there on the running-board, her hips narrow without the waist-band of the apron, her shoulder crooked without the white cross-bands. She hoisted herself into the door-opening with the strong hand. The little door slammed shut. Through the window you could see her staring straight ahead, her chin to the fore, her lips a thin line.

And then they were away with a jolt and a bump, faster and faster until the head lifted at the far end of the runway. For a moment they were invisible behind the plateau. You could hear the engine labour for height. Then they arced back. Once, twice, three times the headlight dipped and the wings waggled to one side. The children waved and shouted at the salute.

A few times the plane circled over the yard, higher and still higher before striking a course in a straight line in the direction of the town.

As if he wanted Agaat to experience what it felt like to go away, you thought.

You didn't want to drive back with Jak. You wanted to be alone to watch the tail-lights get smaller and smaller, the one white flank in the moonlight fainter and fainter. You wanted to think of Agaat in that cabin and the landscape unrecognisable from that height. You wanted to think and you didn't want to think. You started walking back on your own along the road to the house. Some distance further down the yard was glowing and flickering with fires and torches and lit-up tents and the reflection of coloured lanterns in the dam. That's what it would look like from the aeroplane. If you didn't know what you knew, you could imagine that it was a fairy tale.

Your shoes, should you rather have taken them off? you wondered when you crossed the drift to the house. You had to step carefully there, so deeply rutted was the drift with car tracks. Halfway through you slipped badly and lost your balance, and stood still to recover your equilibrium, and to look and to listen. Grootmoedersdrift, you thought, how much must this crossing have seen. There were the shiny circle-tracks of insects on the water, the croaking of frogs, the distant sounds of the feast in the yard, coarse laughter at the dam. The black trunks of the wattles and the black stream in the light of the torches, the fluttering of moths around the light. If only I could read all these together, you thought, all these signs, if the meaning of everything could only be revealed to me here, a pointer for the future. The damp was starting to seep through your soles. You looked down, the polish of your shoes flickered eerily in the dark, as if your feet were packed in fire. Jak had had the torches planted there for the guests, Agaat's orders, so that they would see the hitch in the bridge when they came around the corner. Not that that was the greatest problem. You should have had the silt hoed away there, the kerb was almost covered in it. You took off your shoes and scraped off the sticky black mud with a twig.

How long was Agaat in the air? Half an hour? Somebody charged into the garden in the jeep and deposited her at the mouth of the reception tent. A clutch of children jumped in to grab the next flip. You couldn't see who was driving. The jeep left black soil-tracks on the lawn in pulling off. Agaat was in her white cap and her apron. The red scarf's point was hanging out of her apron pocket. With rapid steps she walked along the yard to the house. A bunch of children clustered behind her.

What did you see Agaat? Did you nip, Agaat?

You trotted to catch up with her.

Tell, Gaat, what did you see? the children prodded.

Nothing, you heard her say, it's night.

Baas, Agaat, you heard a male voice prompting, nothing, baas, it's night, baas.

It was the white foreman who played chauffeur for one of the Meyers brothers.

D'you think because you were up there in the air you can now forget all about manners? I'm sure you saw something. Now tell us nicely what you saw.

The church tower, baas.

How do you know it was the church tower?

It's got lights.

Baas.

Yes, baas.

Yes, baas, what?

The church tower has lights, baas.

Mr Lotriet, you addressed the man, your people want to leave, they're looking for you there in the tent. And there's strong coffee, looks as if you could do with some before you risk it on the road.

The man slunk off with a mumbled yes, Mrs de Wet, fine, Mrs de Wet.

Where are your manners? you scolded the children.

Come, Agaat, pleased to see you're in one piece. I'm walking with you.

I'm walking alone, Agaat said to you.

You followed her. The sound of the aeroplane drowned out your voice. Low over the tops of the bluegums and the roofs of the outbuildings it sheared in the direction of the dam. You heard screams and saw the lanterns bobbing on the raft as the people fell flat to get out of the way.

A line of hired waiters with big trays full of dishes of dessert brushed past you on the garden path. The smell of baked chocolate pudding and date pudding and brandy tarts and liqueur sponges in your nose, Agaat's puddings for Jakkie's birthday, Jakkie who was yawing to and fro over the yard in the plane so that it sounded as if all hell had broken loose.

Twice you heard something spoken next to you before you could quite catch what was being said.

Agaat can't come and dish now, Mies, she's gotten behind with her work in the kitchen. It was Saar. The hesitation in her voice made you press on.

Is she fit to work?

She's sitting there in her room in the dark, she says her head is sore.

It helped, that you had something to do. You wanted to put an end to the evening. Your actions felt sluggish, your voice muted. It was getting too late for your liking. You sent somebody to chase people off the raft, issued orders that the garden lanterns should be blown out so long and the torches extinguished. You blew out the lanterns in the marquee yourself and started emptying the ashtrays and picking up the butts from the floor. You found yourself standing behind a pudding table, faced with a horde of children of whom the bigger ones had been drinking furtively. Rudely they pointed at what they wanted you to dish up, prodded their fingers into the bowls, a feral look in their eyes.

Hey you! Back! Lietja snarled at one whose sleeve was trailing in the bowl and pushed him away with the back of a spoon against the chest. The plates of the others she heaped up with a grin, everything mixed up.

It was never like that when Agaat stood behind the tables. She preserved the order of the distribution point, gauged the local level of manners. She would have said: Adults first! and like the crack of a whip that would have made the children stand back. She would have made everybody first look at the offering, she would have told them what everything was, all the wonderful names, and then she would have dished bit-by-bit and said come back for more, there's plenty more.

Over the chaos of the pudding table you looked into the tent.

Around the drinks table across the way the men were huddling together. It was the younger ones who, wet with perspiration from the dancing, were coming to quench their thirst. Raucously they shouted their orders at the waiters. Heads flung back they drank from beer bottles, belched, and then again heads together talked and laughed.

Early evening already you'd seen the hay barn's door ajar and once or twice had seen a couple go in and out. Now it was evident from the men's attitudes that they were bragging to one another about their conquests. Two of the childminders sat at one table removing straw from their hair. The women and some of the older and more restrained couples gazed at them expressionlessly.

Every now and again the aeroplane flew low over the roof of the tent, fluttering the candle flames on the tables. Everybody looked up as if they expected to see the wings gash through the tarpaulin.

You crossed the yard to the barn. A clashing of metal was audible, against the grain of the music. It was the ploughshare under the wild fig in front of the door of the barn. It was Corrie Meyers on only one high-heeled shoe. She was hammering on the ploughshare with the crowbar that Jak had hung there to summon the labourers for falling-in time. The crowbar was too heavy for her. Every time she lifted it, her wrists with the silver bangles buckled. Every time she delivered a blow she lost her balance, so that she had to clutch at the swinging share to steady herself.

Corrie's lipstick was smudged and her mascara was running down her cheeks.

I cannot look at it, I cannot look at it for one minute longer. Hound! Fucking low hound!

Surabaya Johnny. You pretended not to see her.

The barn was murky. Somebody had unscrewed most of the yellow bulbs that Jak had had fitted round the walls. The place smelt of sweat and liquor and stale perfume. On the bales of hay couples were sitting and smooching. Most of those standing on the sidelines were young girls on the prowl and married women making use of the evening to feel some other body under their hands. The dancers were moving in a track along the sides of the barn. The music was too fast, there was something frenetic about the movements of those who could keep up, while the less fleet of foot fell about, bumping into one another and stepping on one another's toes.

You heard swearing, fuck out of our way here, look where you're damn-well stepping, man.

At the back of the barn the band blared on. In the dim light the musicians plucked and slapped their guitars. The drummer bullied the other instruments.

You noticed Riekert Meyers amongst the dancers. He was giving his own performance in the middle of the floor with a young blonde woman whom you didn't know. Riekert spun the girl from his fingertips, first this side round then the other and he pulled her close into him and danced up behind her, with his hands low over her stomach and his hips against her buttocks. You could see on the woman's face what was happening. The sly sulk, the spite, the satiated vanity that the Meyers brothers induced in all their concubines. He had a sweet little smile on his heart-shaped face. The band was playing for him. A hot little number, as it was known.

You were the first to hear what Corrie Meyers was screaming. She barged smilingly into the dancers and screamed into their faces.

As if it were their foreheads that were on fire.

As if the flames were in her own mouth.

You were outside in an instant. The hay barn was a mass of flame. Smoke and flames were pouring out of ventilation holes and the open door. Through the chink you could catch a glimpse of the inferno inside. It was August and the new lucerne hay was gassy, there were wheat-straw bales with which the stables were kept dry. Behind you the dancers were starting to cluster together with the sluggish reactions of people who have drunk too much. The people came out of the tent and pointed. Nobody did a thing.

The plane was circling about the yard. Will that be enough to satisfy Jakkie now? you thought.

Was that when Agaat appeared? In her black-and-white there in the clearing before the blazing barn? The one to whom all looked, the one who turned round, lifted her good hand for silence, and started issuing orders left and right: You and you and you do this that and the other!

The woodshed and the onion store and the petrol tanks and diesel storage first! she called. Wet the ground all around!

The ordinary garden hoses wouldn't reach far enough, you knew.

She was the one who remembered the water cart in which water was transported for the cattle in summer, which ever since the last fire you'd always kept filled with water.

Get out the tractor, hitch the water cart, wet the ground first around the fuel tanks, she commanded. She had a bale of wheat-sacks dragged out of the barn.

Untie them! Wet them! Bring them! Jump! she bellowed.

Where's Jak? you called. Somebody shouted that he was still over at the landing strip.

Agaat sent for the long ladders under the lean-to. She had the young men clamber up, she had the wet sacks draped over the tanks. The men responded to her commands as if she were a general.

Dawid was blundering about and looking wildly around him. Him she sent to the pump-house at the dam to switch on the pump. The pump served the garden irrigation, if it was switched on, at least the house would be safe.

But she thought up something else. She knew where the irrigation pipes ran in shallow trenches in the garden, and she knew where the pipes ran above-ground. She gathered a team of the hired waiters and the kitchen maids and showed them where they had to dig up the pipes. In line they dragged up onto the yard length upon length of black irrigation pipe with spray-heads and laid them around the outbuildings. Here and there a connection had to be made.

Agaat took the orange connectors and the knives and the clamps and the screwdrivers out of her apron pockets. Everybody stood staring amazed at the plan. Then she went and against the side wall of the house she turned the handle across to open the valve.

Lift the pipe! Hold the heads! Lift them, hold them, aim for the roofs! All together, one, two, three! Agaat shouted.

Arms akimbo, she watched her plan being put into effect. Every water-point was manned by somebody holding the hammer of the spray-head so that the jet could shoot up thick and high. In an instant the gutters of all the buildings were gushing with water. Gradually the soil of the yard grew dark and slippery.

The corrugated-iron sheeting of the roof of the hay barn started popping off from the heat with the cold water on top. There were loud reports and blows as the plates shot out and fell to the ground. Long tongues of fire licked out and a rain of sparks mizzled on everything.

The men were instructed to get the implements out of the big barn and to park them at a safe distance. Tractors and combines and valuable pieces of smaller machinery and supplies of paraffin and oil. Wet sacks were thrown over everything. Everywhere people were running around with buckets of water as commanded by Agaat. The spray-heads were directed at the gaping holes in the roof of the hay barn and you could hear the hissing as the water hit the flames. Thick clouds of steam billowed out of the roof.

You saw Agaat talking to Jakkie.

A fine time to get here! Don't you hide yourself now! Fill with water, five empty molasses drums, you, she told him. Screw off the caps and roll them in through the door of the hay barn so that we can get right in under the fire with the water.

It was over as abruptly as it had started. Within an hour the hay barn was a black smoking shell. The people were standing around the yard in little groups, shocked sober, their clothes stained with mud and soot.

Where were Jak and Jakkie? You looked around, but you couldn't see them among the assembled. Agaat struck the ploughshare. When everybody had assembled under the wild almond, she looked at you.

You thanked the people for their assistance and their presence at the feast.

I am sorry, you said, that it had to end like this.

Some of the older people came to look for Agaat with you to shake her hand, but she'd disappeared. She didn't sleep in her room that night.

The next morning Jakkie was gone.

You heard doors slam in the night, were aware of car headlights sweeping over the yard, voices, but you were too heavy with your medication to get up. You thought you were dreaming. Did you hear the sideboard opening, tchick? closing, tchick? When you woke up, at ten o'clock the next morning, black scraps of burnt paper were swirling past the glazed stoep-door in front of your room.

You went to the kitchen. Jak was standing in front of Agaat. You pushed past him. She was holding one hand in the other. You went to Jakkie's room. His suitcase was gone. His bed hadn't been slept in.

First came the military police and then the security branch.

They questioned you and Jak about your political views. About what you knew of Jakkie's attitude to politics, his feelings about the Angolan war and about his movements the last few months.

You both said that he'd always been only positive and correct and enthusiastic about his career in the Air Force.

They wouldn't answer any of your questions.

They searched the house.

They found nothing.

When they'd finished, Agaat brought in tea. Not that you wanted to serve these people tea. It was she who wanted to see their faces. You knew she was standing in the kitchen eavesdropping on everything.

Whether you could provide the names of Jakkie's confidants, they asked again and again.

You treated Agaat as if she'd been hired the day before. She behaved like a servant who came in once a week.

It's in the national interest, said the officer, that you should immediately report every attempt on Jakkie's part to make contact to the nearest police station, and that your failure to do so will make you accomplices.

To what? asked Jak.

It's not possible to say at this stage, the chap replied, it could hinder the investigation.

The letter arrived a month later. Dawid had gone to collect the post in town and went to give the letter to Agaat in the backyard. You went to wait in the sitting room. It took half an hour. Then Agaat was standing in the doorway of the sitting room holding out the letter to you and saying: Read.

You read the first sentence.

Dear Gaat, by the time you get this letter I'll have left the country, I asked somebody to post it for me in town once I'd gone, I hope it doesn't get intercepted.

The handwriting looked different from Jakkie's usual hand. Letters leaning forward and back at random, it must have been scribbled down in great haste.

Then Jak came in and grabbed it from your hands.

The two of you watched him reading it, his eyes racing over the lines. Jak turned white and then red and then he stuffed the letter into his pants pocket and stormed out.

You listened to him driving the car out of the carriage, hard in reverse, you saw him stopping in the mud-puddle at the gate, flinging open the gate and charging over the cattle grid so that the iron bars leapt up behind the wheels, the dogs barking in pursuit.

Agaat sat down. It was the first time, since her childhood, that she'd sat down like that with you in an easy chair in the sitting room.

But she didn't sit back, she sat on the edge of the chair.

What does he write? I asked.

She didn't answer you. Her hands went to her cap but she dropped them before she'd touched it. She looked as if she was listening, as if she wanted nothing near her ears in order to hear better, it looked as if she was counting.

Please, you said, how long must I still be kept in the dark?

You must have sat there for half an hour. There was a bright silence in the yard, birdsong in the September garden, the colours of crowfoot and anemones rioting in the mirror above the half-moon table, a trace of fennel.

Then you heard the crash.

Agaat remained sitting, her hands in her lap, looking straight ahead. Then she got up as if summoned to an everyday task. You remember the image, Agaat at the front door, etched against the bright frame of the spring day as she turned round to face you.

It's down by the drift, she said, call Dawid, bring the bakkie, hurry.

You looked after her trotting down the road, one hand to the cap.

You went and struck the gong.

They were all there when you arrived on the scene. Dawid and Agaat and a whole lot of children and women from the labourers' cottages. The Alfa's back section was sticking up out of the water. One back wheel was still spinning. The top was down.

Jak was hanging over the water a bit further along.

A broken wattle branch had penetrated his chest in front and emerged from his back.

Agaat didn't look at you.

Take him down there, she ordered Dawid and Julies, but in the end they had to saw off the branch. With branch and all they carried him out onto the bank. His face wore an expression of surprise. His jaw was dislocated. Agaat closed his eyes. Both of you put a foot on his chest on either side and pull with four hands, Agaat said.

One two three, she counted.

The branch came out with a glugging sound.

Sit down, Agaat said, and supported you under the elbow. You couldn't stay upright.

So there you were lying in the green grass. You and Jak. And Jak's branch.

The blood seeped away in the muddy water of the drift. The colour of the blood clashed violently with the red of the Alfa.

Agaat sent the women and the children home. Dawid and the other labourers had to go and fetch the tractor and a tow-rope and the stretcher. Saar and Lietja had to phone the doctor and fetch smelling salts from the medicine chest.

When everybody had gone, she bent and pulled the letter out of Jak's trouser pocket, still as crumpled as when he'd stuffed it in there. It was covered in blood. The writing was smudged.

He wanted to go and hand it in to the police, Agaat said. And then he couldn't get it past his conscience. And then he charged back, and then he couldn't make the bend.

She separated the sheets of paper and smoothed them, carefully, and put them away in her apron pocket.

Let's just revive you, then I'll read it to you, then I'll burn it, then we won't know anything more about it.

Then she bent down and with a quick tug-and-push movement she reset Jak's jaw.

Useful, you thought, she learnt to do it early with sheep emerging skew-jawed from the dipping-trough.

517

She came and held the bottle of smelling salts under your nose.

Just see how he skidded, Agaat pointed out.

You looked, the muddy track with the kink, the missing kerbstone from the shallow bridge.

When they put Jak down in the backyard, you heard it for the first time, under the keening from the kitchen, the formulation which they would snigger over unto the third and the fourth generation of labourers on the farm.

The baas of Grootmoedersdrift!

Aheu!

And so he saw his arse!

In the drift of Grootmoedersdrift!

*

they have not heard from me for so long they may well think I am dead it leaves me cold really I cannot deny I have let the world slip by my hand sometimes I still have the urge to call to scream to get up the need walks in waves but congeals an ocean of glassy gel noiseless salty white coast a dream but I am not sleeping am not dead am awake between me and me all hollows are silted shut a mountain without caves storeys without stairwell trapped in a lift the lift is myself no space to lift an arm sound the alarm the alarm is myself no space between me and me I fill myself fully my filling tissue-tension in a stalk would I burst? a pomegranate fall from a tree? messy but disposable? who will sweep up the pips in a scoop, who will scrape the sole of a shoe over the stain on the stone? or shall I leak from myself wind from an inner tube? carried out over an arm to the place of all inner tubes? images no longer offer solace my filling seed soil wind I am who I am impermeable no turn up or down or round possible the sight of a dead wall could relieve me but I am myself the wall am name am flour am history have occurred my damage is dense is black my tongue silts my mouth full of water oh my soul in me there is no room for you to mortify yourself

*

27 May 1955

Jak says we must make A. move in with Dawid and them and accustom her to her own people. The sooner the better he says, the child will grow up messed-up, she has no playmates. As if he cared one scrap about that. But he is right when he says the white children who come here don't know any better, they think she's farm stock & then they snub her.

I protest! She's an exceptional somebody & she's developed from the grimmest misery out of just about nothing. Every day I have reason to believe that all my trouble and dedication were not in vain & that the faith I had in the matter and every drop of sweat and tears that I put into her has now started bearing fruit. Everything has a purpose, I say to Jak, she's been given to me to learn something about myself. To learn what it is that really matters in this life. Jak says I sound like a Jehovah's Witness on Eau de Cologne. He says he thought I'd achieved total illumination some time ago and it's not a matter of A. because all I can talk about is myself & and I can really spare him my sickly sentimental stories they give him a pain because all he sees in front of him is the worst case of megalomania & control freakery south of the Sahara.

That's not true! I play with her & I teach her to sing & dance. If he were only to give her a bit of attention & to take the time to get closer to her he'd see that she's an extremely interesting little person (perhaps that's not the right word, rather wilful, intense, complicated, imaginative—too much so—rather a live wire than a flat tyre as Pa always used to say).

28 May 1955

Bought A. 24 new crayons & 10 jars of poster paints. This evening learnt to write & draw sheep hen donkey rooster. Good perception especially the shape & position of ears mouth etc. I teach her to mix the colours & to cover the whole page not just in the one corner. She's managing well already but I can still see the backlog.

This evening I thought she was sleeping already, she came & showed me a picture of the farm with GROTMODERSDRUF solemnly written at the top. You have wings because you are my angel she says. I had to help with the practising of the wings on a separate sheet. Only Lucifer the rebellious angel has such spindly black wings I say. Jak has a thatch of black hair on his head & thick black eyebrows & two red spots for cheeks, is sitting on the bonnet of a red car with black wheels. She couldn't quite get the little man into the car I had to show her & so there I was X2 with my red dress & patched-up wings & Jak X2 first on top of & then inside his car in front of the Grootmoedersdrift homestead complete with chimney & gables & green trees & blue mountains & a flower garden full of birds & lambs & butterflies.

There are two of me now & two of Jak & one of every living thing but where are you then? I ask. She's inside she says. You're looking for me I'm hiding from you in the fireplace. Shame the poor child can she be altogether happy? I wonder.

30 May
This morning A. jumps up & down on hr bed & suddenly manages to produce a whistle. Now she can't stop jumping & the whistle comes more & more regularly great excitement!

4 June '55
New habit of A.'s. She presses her head against me, you always smell so nice she says. Pushes hr head into my jersey drawer when I'm getting dressed & then just now she disappeared into thin air & I search & I search there I find her in my room, half crawled into the bottom shelf & gone to sleep there with hr head on my jerseys. Now I understand why the cupboard is always so untidy. Always find the little red jersey on top & warm from her sleeping on it. What are you doing in my wardrobe? I scold, sorry she says & my heart grows soft, I press her to me. Your body is sweet she whispers in my ear can I also smell like that one day?

4 June '55
Our best thing nowadays is to walk in the veld & learn the names of things. Insects, birds, small reptiles, small mammals, grass varieties, wild flowers, stones. I take Pa's old reference books along in a rucksack & a notebook & a pair of binoculars & her magnifying glass & then we identify things & collect examples. I learn remarkable things myself. A. has a good eye, remembers all marks, sees things that I don't notice, white speckled breast of a lesser kestrel in a tree, pupae in the grass & cocoons hanging from twigs, webs spun between blades of grass, lizard skeletons, droppings of hare & dassie & antelope. The hangings of the fiscal shrike interest her. That's why its name is Johnny Hangman I explain but then of course I had to explain the death penalty & its reasons as well.

Showed her a while ago a fossil that Pa picked up way back in the mountains & now she's got a thing about it, is forever picking up rocks & says break it open there's something in it & then upon my word she's been right three or four times! How do you know? I ask. Some stones are warmer than others she says. Can it be that the child has second sight? Arrived here the other day with a little frog, didn't even know such a thing existed tiny as a match-head, micro-frog according to the amphibians book & today again the loveliest little ivory frog. First had to explain ivory & then how an elephant's tooth made its way to the name of a frog.

Mole snake, fruit bat, horse-shoe, tapeworm, finch-grass, drift-sand, smother-crop, cannibal spider, emperor butterfly. Soon discovered compounds don't always work in the same way, sometimes had to think up something to satisfy her.

So then I had this bright idea, a fortunate inspiration it was, or not even that, a premonition & I looked under Agate in Pa's old minerals book & there it was! Remarkable! Cloud agate Plume agate Fire agate Eye agate Iris agate Snakeskin agate Moss agate Rainbow agate! Look, I say, all the world is in your name. The things of the world are tied to one another at all points with words I say & we know one thing through the name of another thing & we join the names together. It's a chain & if you move one link then they all move the possibilities are endless.

She wants to go & catch that blue butterfly, she says, for hr collection. I say you don't catch it it's holy. She's not scared of butterflies she says they don't bite what is holy. I said I'd think. Full of that kind of question nowadays. Where is heaven, why do people die, where is one's soul attached, why is a thing the thing that it is & not another thing. Heaven is a stone she says out of the blue. Yes I say precious stone walls of jasper & streets of gold. No she says that's not what she means & she shows me the stone with the fossilised fern leaf. That's the soul she says trapped in heaven, I ask you!

In the evenings she unpacks all our finds & arranges them by kind. Can't keep up with dishes & bottles boxes bands & scrapbooks & felt squares, pins, thumb tacks, paper clips for all the specimens she wants to display. Remarkably precise & persistent the child, it's exceptional I think. I give her a free hand even though it smells like a witchdoctor's shop there in her little room. Saar & Lietja say she was born with the caul. What an adventure!

7 June '55

This afternoon after lunch A. disappeared into thin air & returned very dirty. Had actually walked to the forest on hr own! I gave hr a good hiding. The tokoloshe will catch you, I said it's no place for little children remember your name is Good. Good, she says crying, one good two goods, goods is loose goods she says crying & and goods are a lot of things that don't have a name & goods are your goods that you have in your suitcase, stolen goods. Not at a loss for words. I tell hr look out you don't talk back at me do you want another hiding? Good is true good is beautiful good is noble.

8 June '55

What all are you writing in your little book? asks Agaat. A story, I say, about a little girl who can whistle already! Can I too? she asks. Here she is now taking the red crayon!

I Rite in my meme's boke.
I Lov hir veRRy mutch.
My one hand is big and the utheR is smal,
She Lovs me veRRy mutch to.

Let's spell properly:
wRite
book
Love
heR
veRy
much
otheR
smaLL
too

She's speaking good Afrikaans now. Only the infinitive of the verb in combination with preposition creates problems at times. To about laugh, she says, to about cry.

10 June 1955

I put up all the pictures she draws on the walls of her room, two eagle owls on a branch, a red princess with a crown on her head, a bristling black cat on yellow paper. The child amazes me. Looks at me the other day when we were having a picnic under the big old rock fig: Why can a tree only be a tree? Because it's holy I say. What is holy? she asks again. I say everything that's wild everything that's free, everything that we didn't make ourselves, everything that we can't cling to & tie down. Your soul is holy. Wouldn't she gaze at me: But you caught me & tamed me. So I pressed hr close to me, shame.

12 July 1955
Baked a pretty birthday cake with seven candles collected a whole box-ful of little reading books from everybody who no longer uses them nicely wrapped in shiny paper & a ribbon but then there was another incident ai, one of the children I invited apparently mocked A. so she locked him in the outside toilet & he bawled the place down. Gave her a terrific hiding more because she refuses to tell me what he's supposed to have said to her that made her lock him up. You tell me everything, you don't have secrets from me I tell her, only good secrets you're allowed that the Lord knows about.

16 September 1955
Just saw something that breaks my heart. Heard just now back there in the kitchen the red-chested cuckoo in the front garden but it carries on & on & and I go & look here on the front stoep to see where they're nesting & all the time it was A. standing on the stoep all concentration. Every time he calls she whistles back wheet-wheet-wooee & then she waits until he replies, the little face sheer wonder, she can't believe what's happening. Just left again quietly because I could see it was a very private moment & thus far she hasn't breathed a word of it to me. She goes around with I-have-a-secret written all over her face.

17 April 1956
All the drilling every day has not been in vain, A. really coming along so nicely in reading & writing. Saw her today sitting there & spelling out the stories in the Children's Bible, asks me a big word every now & again: Righteousness, compassion, hallucination, ire, damnation, grace. I write them all down, nicely split up in syllables & put them up in her room next to her other lists so that she can absorb them. Have done memorising & summarising exercises and comprehension tests with her a few times. She's not stupid at all, I tend to keep it to the Farmer's Weekly & to farming matters that she knows. Hmmm, says Jak, teach the young idea how to shoot. Sarcastic as always.

3 May 1956
A. has the habit of just disappearing. Give her a hiding regularly but she carries on doing it. Had to scold like anything again yesterday. What do

you do when you run off, what kind of mischief do you get up to? I dig she says. I look at the nails, I see the soil. What do you dig! I ask. Little furrows she says. What kind of little furrows? For seed, she says. Then a great light dawned for me about the fennel that's shooting up every-where in the garden & in the yard & next to the irrigation furrow & the orchard all the way to beyond the dirt road in the dryland I noticed the yellow heads of fennel in flower. You're infesting the place! I say, you're making work for yourself, you'll pull up every last bush! I won't she says they're my plants. Impossible at times the child, wonder how long she's been at it. Yes says Jak, Minister of Fennel one day.

28 June 1956

Last night a squabble with Jak again because apparently I'm spending too much time & money on A. Should never have shown him the cloth I bought. Red for a party dress for hr birthday in two weeks' time. He says he doesn't want a cake-gobbling here again it always just leads to unpleasantness & he's tired of answering people's questions about it. He says people ask him if Agaat addresses him as baas or pa or uncle. So now I teach her I'm nooi Milla & Jak is Mr de Wet. But she forgets, she still calls me Même when she's glad or excited, & Jak of course will have nothing but baas.

10 November 1956

She remains self-conscious about the little arm. It's too hot in summer for long sleeves but she won't wear short-sleeved dresses & you can't really have the child walk around with just one long sleeve.

15 November 1956

Found a solution at last. From fine crochet-cotton crocheted a pretty little jersey to wear over hr dresses, the right-hand sleeve is longer & with a cuff that covers half the little hand. Looks as if she'll wear it like that. White ribbons in the hair as well. I make hr stand in front of the mirror. Now you look just like a snowflake I say.

18 November 1956

Crawled into bed with A. again last night & slept till the morning Jak leaves me just like that when he's done & he's not satisfied till I scream he's hurting me as if that will do any good. Woke up in the early morn-ing with A. crept up completely into me when I got up she woke up half-asleep still: I can whistle like the birds do you know? kokkewiet & johnny hangman & dikkop all of them.

22 November 1956
Got a bright idea from an old book for A.'s hair. I usually keep it cut short but can't manage the woolly head all that well. So then we sat for hours in the backyard in the shade against the wall & I plaited her hair in little strings flat against the scalp but I couldn't get it regular & in straight lines as in the picture. Must take a lot of practice like basket-weaving. So then the kitchen-girls laughed at the result: Now mies has just got Agaat white & then she tries to turn her into a Transkei kaffir-girl & then A. heard it & ran away when she saw herself in the mirror the fat was really in the fire & I had to undo it all & it took much longer than the plaiting itself because by now everything was properly knotted & it pulled & Agaat screamed like a banshee. A whole palaver. I suppose it's better just to wash it every day with Johnson's baby shampoo at least one knows it's clean.

10 February 1957
Went to collect old arithmetic books from the school day before yesterday to work through. She multiplies & divides like anything & recites her tables to 6, not all that far behind the standard twos in town. Have started teaching hr notes & simple scales just for the one hand. The other one's fingers can still not open all that well. We play simple tunes together I play the right hand. Must say I enjoy it tremendously. Jak says teach an ape to play chopsticks today & tomorrow he plays chop-chop with your head.

24 February 1957
Took A. up into Luipaardskloof to the bat cave she's very fascinated by a mouse that can fly creepy & smelly the place & the swarms wheeling about our heads A. just wants to stay to look & asks how do they hang how do they sleep why do they squeak like that. Managed with great difficulty to get hold of one. Could show hr nicely the membrane between the spokes & the big ear for receiving the bounced-back squeaking sounds & the pig-like little snout-beak.

23 March 1957
Unpacked my old music books & started practising again after all these years, little Bach partitas & the old evergreens that aren't too difficult to play. Liebestraum, Song Without Words, Largo. Gives me quite a new lease on life.

A. can't get enough of music. Play hr Pa's old records on the wind-up gramophone. She likes the lieder best, once I've told her the story

& the words she wants to listen again & again, mad about the folk tunes of Mahler, St Anthony preaching to the fish & Wo die schönen Trompetten blasen. I play it until we can sing along little bits. She blows the trumpet notes through a rolled-up sheet of paper, beats the drums of ghost soldiers on saucepan lids & marches all over the house. We powder hr face white & draw a skull with charcoal on hr face & then she enters completely into it all. Kill myself laughing at all the actions. Just have to be careful always that Jak doesn't come across it because he's full of mockery as if he's ashamed of playing & gentleness & laughter.

Let hr listen to the radio to the classical music programmes & teach hr the names of the pieces, the tempo indications, tell her the stories of the operas. She already knows many of the FAK songs & quite a few psalms & hymns. We sing them together in the morning when I wake hr & in the evenings when she goes to bed & when we're working in the kitchen or driving to the sheep. Teach her the second voice. Oh moon you drift so slow & Let me wander through the heather are hr best. Can carry a tune quite well the little child. As pants the hart for cooling streams she whistles there in hr room when she's pinning her rose beetles to the felt. A whistling woman & a crowing hen is neither good for God nor men I say. What's a hart she asks. Found a photo of a hart in the old Encyclopaedia Britannica, absorbs knowledge like a sponge. Sits there & pages in the old books in the sitting room whenever she has a chance. Reads on hr own now every day three new words & three new things as I drilled her & write it down & sticks it up in hr room. Zither, lute, tambourine. Even copies it from the drawings.

Shame, how much the wiser is she for all of it? Should I send hr to school? I don't know what I thought would come of it. Will just have to see how things develop. She's now varnishing all the bugs with hard shells to try to preserve them but they just dissolve all the more quickly from it. Will have to phone nature conservation to ask them how one does it.

15 April 1957

A. has now thought up a whole dance of hr own on the model of the Greeting to the Sun which she still does every morning. Decided to keep it up every day from the start because I still see sometimes the stiffness & the withdrawal into herself as soon as she's tired or tense. The Greeting works well as light exercise for the crooked shoulder. Now there's no stopping her now she's even teaching me. Again this morning we had the so-called dance of the emperor butterfly that first sits dead still with its wings tightly folded, half-frozen in the morning twilight with dew on its nose & the outside of the wings pitch-black with white stars & its antennae still filmed with night & then it unfolds its wings with the dawning so she tells & she invents the dance as she goes along. Once, twice, three times slowly the wings open as soon as he catches the first rays of the sun & then he feels one wing is different & he turns his head & looks over his shoulder & he sees hey, but this wing is a heavenly blue on the inside & it tickles & it trills & it shimmers & he gets the urge to fly, quite intoxicated with his own colour in the sun that's rising higher & higher & shining brighter & brighter & he doesn't know if he wants the blue rather on the one or rather on the other wing he tries to have it on both.

Heaven knows where she fetches it all from. She's never seen the Apatura iris itself it's just what I've told hr about it.

A whole extended dance of the two of us it turned into this morning. First in hr room where she explained the dance & then into my room & out of my room by the door of the side stoep & round the front again & down the stoep steps & down the garden path & through the last gillyflowers & around the great oak in the middle of the garden. Even the little thin arm flutters & flaps along in the long crocheted sleeve. Then I chase hr & then she chases me & it tripples & it leaps with extended legs over the flowerbeds. Point your toes Gaat! I call & demonstrate the ballet position with the hands & she teaches me the quick flashing-open of the wings & the tilt & the sheer ascent & the tumbling & the drop of the great forest butterfly then we both roll in the grass, she half on top of me, our limbs intertwined. Caught! she shouts. Then she puts hr arms around my neck & says: Close your eyes open your eyes my Même you're my only mother. Now I'm crying too much to carry on writing here.

2 August 1958
Quarrel with J. about A.: What do I want to do with hr when she's big? he asks, after all she can't stay in the house with us for ever. I'd better make a plan, he says, it's either she or him.

25 August 1958
All hell loose here. Went out to B. to deliver down for her eiderdowns this afternoon. When I got back A. was sitting in the corner in hr room

& it's chaos. Apparently J. got the idea into his head that A.'s stuff in her collections is infesting the house with beetles & wood-borer & mites & undesirable fungi & heaven knows what else & then he chucked out the whole lot in a heap in the backyard. Ordered A. to get rid of the rest. Apparently doesn't want a single object or picture or list of words or feather or horn or packet of fennel seed in hr room except what belongs in a bedroom.

Helped her to rescue what could be rescued & consoled I'll help to start all over again with the collection but she's inconsolable over hr birds' eggs & hr mounted insects & dried wild flowers. Even the leopard skull smashed there in the backyard. Good Lord it's all the child possesses such innocent little playthings. Fortunately the fossil stones are unharmed.

Very sad about all the pictures that J. tore up. Thought I'd keep a few for hr from when she was small so that one day when she's grown up she can marvel at them.

26 August 1958
A. sulking. What does she want me to do? I can't exactly fling J. over my lap & give him a hiding for what he's done? I know better than to scold him. Best is to stay out of his way & not to confront him. She refuses to eat sits there at table & glares at me as if I'm the one who broke her stuff.

28 August 1958
Took A. to the circus tonight to console her & then that also turned out a fiasco because we bought three tickets but then they wouldn't let her go in with us on the white side. The man was in fact quite rude. What could I do? So then we went to the non-white entrance & then the white ticket wasn't right & if she wouldn't make me buy a coloured ticket & all & then she didn't want to go in on her own but by then Jak & I already had our tickets & of course by this time he was already irritated with all the trouble with his now-do-you-see expression on his face. So I suggested that he should go in & Agaat & I would stroll around outside amongst the cages & the caravans outside & look at the animals & the artistes because it was still dusk. A whole to-do there at the entrance to the approach tent: The elephant & the ponies with plumed crests & the horse-lifter with his tiger-skin suit & the clowns starting to practise to be funny. We would then go & wait for him in

the car. But that was then of course not good enough either & he grabs me by the arm there amongst all the people & he hisses in my ear: You will go in with me woman & then I had to leave the poor A. right there. Had just enough time to give her money for an ice-cream. Terrible sitting there in the tent. Could enjoy nothing so upset was I & I could think of nothing but A. who's really not used to strange places & so many people. When we came out she was sitting in the dust next to the car in the parking lot because of course it was locked all the time. Fortunately it wasn't cold but now she's angry with me all over again & all I was trying to do was make it up to her.

J. has just been here glaring at me: Write! Write! with those little claw-paws of yours what good is it going to do you? There's a life here to be lived & decisions to be taken & work to be done & next thing I see you're sitting & churning away at your silly little books & I'm waiting for you in the room don't forget I'm your husband & I also have my needs. When he's like that there's nothing to be done about it. Will just have to go so that he can have done & cool off.

29 August 1958
Crawled in behind A's back in tears again last night. J. particularly rough after the whole circus episode & swears & scolds & abuses me to my very soul. Another dress with a broken zip. I suppose I shouldn't turn to the poor child for refuge. In the end she was the one who comforted me. Never mind she says I don't have to feel bad she looked through a slit in the tent & saw the ringmaster's high hat & the antics of Tickey & the trapeze artists on the highest rung their red velvet slippers with the shiny stuff & then she stood back when the drums started ruffling to say here it comes they're going to jump & then she could see from the shadows on the tent wall & the spotlights how they swung & let go & turned somersaults in the air & caught each other by the arms at the last minute & then she went closer again & saw the trumpets shining as they were lifted to blow. So then of course I cried more than ever & the more I cried the more tightly she locked her arms around me. Nothing to about cry she whispers in my ear, must I go & make Même a glass of warm milk? Father in heaven how am I going to resolve this matter?

23 February 1959
A. very responsible helps only too diligently with everything around the place: Stacks pumpkins pulls potatoes plucks the geese. She shines in the kitchen, can make a good white sauce already & a quite presentable

stew & hr flapjacks & scones are excellent. She's managing very well with needle & thread. Gave hr a needlework basket for hr little things. Teach hr something new every day, buttonhole flat-seam blanket-stitch. I praise hr often & she reacts excellently to praise & encouragement & tries only to excel & improve herself. She's even been to pick blackberries & made blackberry jam according to the recipe in the book without one sticky patch in the kitchen. For the rest very perceptive came & reported that the chickens were sneezing & we could prevent an outbreak of roup. Lost only about four day-old chickens & all the others including turkeys & ducks treated preventatively. J. has this idea that he can build poultry-runs in a draught so that's what he has for it. He says the chickens got it from me & A. we infect everything we touch & what will I do if he gets chicken flu?

11 March 1959

A. solemnly came to sing to me this morning for my birthday. Best wishes dear Même on this your birthday, That the Lord you will keep we earnestly pray. She'd baked an orange cake first thing this morning all on her own & written 33 on it with icing sugar in higgledy-piggledy letters. Then she gave me wrapped in a scrap of green velvet stitched with blanket-stitch & tied with a red ribbon hr prettiest fossil. Was with her the day she picked it up on the mountain. Haven't yet been able to make out what it is. Some or other floating seed with membranous wing or otherwise a membrane-winged insect. A parasitic wasp perhaps. Looks exactly like a little galleon & the stone-ripples look like waves. A remarkable likeness. Can't really believe she wants to give it to me. It's our ship, just the two of us where are we sailing to? she asks me. What could be happening in the child's head?

10 October 1959

Can't abide J.'s aggression towards A. any longer. An unbearable atmosphere in the house. She's an early bloomer he says she ogles him. What nonsense but perhaps I'm missing something. Hear the maids teasing in the kitchen: But you're pushing tits Aspatat. She's been moody of late. I suppose the start of the trouble.

13 October 1959

A. reads all the time went & fetched a lot of Ma's books out of the cellar last year. Genoveva, Alone in the World, Prisoner of Zenda, Scarlet Pimpernel, In the Footsteps of the Master by HV Morton & In the Steps of St Paul by HV Morton & Late Harvest. A. knows them all by heart

& asks for more books. J. doesn't approve of hr reading adult books. What's the difference I ask after all she reads the Farmer's Weekly.

27 October 1959

Lay awake all night about A. She's always been inclined to disappear but now it's getting too bad. Saar & Lietja say they find her roaming with her reading-book down there by the labourers' cottages but she runs away when they call hr. Must be looking for company shame. I suppose I must tackle the facts of life. Shouldn't be difficult she knows about covering & lambing & calving & all creatures great & small birds & bees. Came to tell me the other day she'd uncoupled the terrier single-handedly when one of the labourers' dogs got stuck in her again.

3 November 1959

Really rather put out by conversation with Beatrice this morning. Suspect she drove over on purpose to come & bring me the news. Apparently people are gossiping about A.'s situation & it seems the dominee's wife has plenty to say on the subject. No it would appear we're involved in 'subtly undermining community values' & defeating the ends of the political policy of the authorities & what would happen if everybody did what I'm doing with A.

A good question I suppose.

B. just carries on & on: Yes it will jeopardise Jak's position in the church & the farmers' associations & the regional branch of the party here if we don't set our house in order & heaven knows what else.

I say Jak's church is skin-deep anyway & the child means so much to me & even though Jak & I differ on the subject I still feel as though I'm a better wife to Jak because I have more love in my heart & can care for an independent creature. B. looks at me askance but I carry on. Through hr I see the world through fresh eyes I say & I ask: Does she Beatrice have any idea what it is to be childless?

B. sits there with a sceptical slant to hr face & drinks hr tea with her little finger aloft. That's all very good & pretty & noble she says but I should really think very well about the long-term consequences not only for us but for the broader community & also for A. herself. At this her mouth contracts into a nasty little slit. (J. always says it's the can't-get-the-knot-through-the-hole mouth & he doesn't want to know what she looks like down south.)

Must say it's an aspect of B. that I haven't been so aware of before but I'm noticing it more & more frequently of late. I know old Thys belongs to the Broederbond & he's now proposed Jak but Jak feels little for the idea. I know why: They read too many books there. Beatrice says old Thys pores over the dictionary every evening it's way beyond him.

I say I'm not sure about such secret organisations & I vote Nationalist but I'm not ashamed to object in public to such skulduggery. B. says it's top secret & who am I now to think I can turn against the leaders & intellectuals of my people I'll cut my own throat & Jak's as well if that's my attitude & I'd better realise on which side my bread is buttered & 'they' can make things very difficult for people who are not well disposed to the national cause & we'll never reach the top rung if 'they' know Jak de Wet's wife swims upstream however learned & refined she may be. So I went off to make tea to keep my temper within bounds & when I came in again she carried on exactly where she'd left off.

Yes, she says, A. can't do a thing with the education that I'm giving her & what use does one in any case have for an over-educated servant on a farm. She's not a servant I say & then B. said well she hasn't noticed other people's children of the same age sweeping stoeps & feeding chickens & serving tea to guests & calling their mothers Nooi. I say A. & I understand each other it's play names & play work it's a special relationship. B. says what's the use the two of us thinking it's a game & it's special & everybody else in the country thinks it's abnormal & a sin before God.

Will have to go & talk to the dominee myself. Can't altogether believe what B. tells me about the judgement of the pastorie. After all Van der Lught himself named her & baptised her? How can he turn like that? Could swear it's that wife of his that's the real poison pusher.

16 December 1959

Period two weeks late if my sums are right. Has happened before. Perhaps the ado about A. that's telling on my system she's so tuned in to my moods she sees immediately when I'm depressed & always asks if it's she who's done something wrong. This morning I found by my bed a bunch of hydrangeas made up with red leaves of fire-on-the-mountain in the grey vase they won't last long she says it's too hot but it's to cheer me up asks me if I'm feeling ill.

23 December '59

Had blood drawn today. Dr had left on holiday already & only his partner there & he can't tell me when the results will be available. He says with somebody who's been trying for such a long time as I they want to be absolutely sure & it has to go to Cape Town for analysis.

26 December '59

Walking up & down & waiting for the phone to ring or not to ring don't know which one in case it's bad news. Ate nothing yesterday. Almost don't want to think it. Dear God! After all that! A. circles around me like a bothersome bee if it's not coffee then it's tea that she brings get off with you I say. She knows something is going on you can't hide anything from hr.

30 December '59

Fancy I'm nauseous all the time. Have phoned but there's no reply. A. tries to comfort me, puts flowers in the grey vase every day. Lord they really can't keep me in the dark like this. Festive season. Everybody gone. Was sitting there just now with my head between my knees with nausea then I felt A.'s little hand putting something in mine. Chew she says in my ear it helps for when you're feeling sick. Fennel seed. What is Même's wish for the new year? she asks.

1 January 1960

Too trembly to write. Too superstitious to write it down here in black & white in case it disappears! Dr happened to be in his consulting rooms & there was the result from the laboratory! Positive! I'm walking around with it like a pearl under my heart. Haven't told J. yet. Must wait for the right moment. Tonight we're going out to Frambooskop— big party. One of the Scott brothers is coming back to take over the berry farming the old man can apparently not keep it up. Perhaps if J. is in a good mood tonight when we get back I'll tell him.

A. asks what are you thinking? What's eating you? I say I'm thinking curiosity killed the cat. Why are your cheeks so red? To look prettier my child I say in front of the mirror. Couldn't stop looking at myself today so then I caught hr eye in the mirror looking at me oddly then I clicked it was because I'd said 'my child'. Oh gracious heavens how unthinking of me. Now I'm going to have my own child. What will she make of that?

Perhaps it's the Lord's will that it should happen just now perhaps it will make things clearer & decisions easier. What are you going to wear tonight? A. asks. Take out my black dress with the wide sleeves that I last wore on my honeymoon when we went dancing. Aitsa, says A. queen of the night & she whistles the tune of the great aria from The Magic Flute all down the passage all melancholy it sounds. Ai she always whistles when she's feeling happy & busy & to tease me because she knows she's not supposed to whistle.

2 January 1960

Went & crawled in with A. after the scrap again last night. Was ever so miserable. Perhaps B. is right perhaps one should just keep one's mouth shut about everything. Perhaps I angered that crowd of men with my talking about fertiliser & the soil. What on earth got into me? A. pretended to be asleep when I slipped into her bed. Had she eavesdropped & heard me telling J. about the child? Perhaps she heard what he said then? She's downcast today she must have gone to unearth the shards of the vase J. broke last night out of the rubbish bin because I found it this afternoon all neatly stuck together. Don't know if it will hold water but won't throw it away for the time being to spare A.'s feelings. She looks as if she wants to cry all the time. I feel as sick as a dog.

7 July 1960

Can't find the right book heavens things go so fast nowadays & it's so difficult to keep one's wits about one through it all. Would rather not page back too much here. A.'s childhood & growing up. Feels like a lifetime since I last wrote in this one. Changed into a different person in the span of six months. Lord be thanked no longer nauseous. Just swollen ankles & heartburn in the mornings.

Had a situation again with Ma this weekend. First it was J. & his dog-kicking & then Ma presumed to preach to me about men. No she says I must send the story of J.'s battering into the world via the housemaids & especially A. I ask you the child my messenger to somebody like B.! Why must I listen to a single word she says? After she kept poor Pa under her thumb all his life with hr prescriptions. The worst is that that I'd left the outside room that I'd prepared for A. open by accident after I'd shown Ma all my preparations there & that Saar of course

took the gap when she came in in the late afternoon for the milk &
went in there. Clearly inspected everything to the last detail & then she
was prancing around the kitchen with a spiteful expression & provoking A. with a so-called 'secret' & that after all the trouble I'd taken to
work there only at night when everybody was asleep. Had succeeded
so well in hiding it from A. till now. So I took Saar aside & tried to talk
to her about it. Wouldn't she just interrupt me & answer me all cheekily: Never ever I won't tell her anything about it Mies & if she notices
anything I'll say it's my room. I'll say I've done now with my hotnot hut
down there next to the drift & its leaking roof & the mosquitoes that
eat me alive at night. It's me who's going to stay in the back here a nice
soft bed & a mirror & a stove & tea & rusks & a white cap & a white
apron just like the maids in the Royal Hotel.

Lord what kind of trouble we can expect from this again. If you think
you do right by one then the same thing is a wrong to somebody else.

20

Agaat's footsteps, they're different from when she wants to open the curtains, wants to open the stoep door. They're always different when she's setting her mind on opening my eyes. The tread of somebody who has a book in hand and is too burdened by the contents to read it to its conclusion, and yet feels obliged, compelled. Even though the ending is predictable and has been foreseen for too long.

That's what it felt like the last few times when she opened my eyes. She couldn't look at me.

But today it feels different. Have I at last been brought back to normal proportions? I've always felt too big and always too much in this bed, her expectations of me far too high. I've allowed myself to be influenced by that. Made my life, her life, more difficult than was necessary.

But today it is different.

Whom did I become for her overnight?

Suddenly she's no longer measuring herself by me.

I wait for her to open my eyes for me. What can I give her to study? My blue irises, my motionless eyeballs, the white of my sclera, the black of my pupils? Not much more than that. That is what has remained.

When she left here in the night, last night? she closed both my eyes, the sleeping eye that she distended before the meal and the stare-eye that I can no longer blink or shut, caulked my limbs as if I were a ship, smeared pitch between my planks before she set sail in the embroidered garment.

Did I dream it? The white cap, the white gown at the black wrought-iron gate, the white ring-wall? The taking-off of the shoes?

Did I see it? The gliding passage between the headstones, the feet in the heap of black soil, the sinking away up to the ankles?

A ritardando on loamy clods, lento, lento sostenuto, then the looking

536

down and the hesitation, the lowering into the hole, for a moment only the cap, a mainsail above the waves.

Did I invent it?

And when at length she was lying flat on her back in my grave there in the old family cemetery, was the night then a star-filled rectangle, the Bear and the Scorpion, the Goat and the Ram, the whole ream and the seasons stippled on the great hourglass of the firmaments?

And the Southern Cross, was it visible to her as it always lies above Grootmoedersdrift in the last half of December? Tilted on the rib, a cast anchor?

Was there a trilling? Did I feel the chill under my back? Was there an unevenness under my shoulders? Were my wings properly folded under me? Were the four corners of the Milky Way squared? And the sides, were they dug down plumb?

And the song? Did I hear it then? The song of which the ending is like the beginning? Arising muffled from a dark place?

A tree grows in the earth
And blooms in beauty—
O tree!

For hours it went on, sometimes at long intervals. I sang along, in my dream I could sing, a second voice.

And on the tree grows a branch,
a comely branch,
a lovely branch!

Later the words submerged in the depths soared up and from the heights floated over the yard, a great coloratura voice out of the mountain, words that tied the long rope of cause and effect together in a noose.

Then the child laughed,
a comely laugh, a lovely laugh!
Then the child laughed with the woman,
the woman sits on the bed,
the bed comes forth from the feather,
the feather comes forth from the dove,
the dove hatches from the egg,
the egg lies in the nest,
the nest is on the branch,
the branch grows on the tree,
the tree grows in the earth,
and blooms in beauty—
o tree!

In my end is my beginning. Now it's morning.

A new sound!

The new footfall of Agaat, as if she's lost weight overnight.

What do I hear? The locks of a suitcase being opened, old-fashioned sprung clips that click as if they've been oiled? When is she going to approach and open my eyes so that I can see what's happening?

Her shadow falls on my bed, on my skin. Out of the coolness materialises a hand. How light her hand is on my forehead! And now on my cheeks, how different are her palms!

They are poised now for the final chord. For the last kneading. As good as it gets, they say. No more we can do for you. A bread is a bread mixed like that and risen like that and at some point it has to be baked. And music isn't music if it carries on for ever. There's an introit and an amen. That's the minimum for a mass. Even the fantasy for solo harp has to conform to the requirement of closure. Once touched, once sounded, even the last note must eventually die away.

Here we have now the taking-off of my eyepatches, the pulling-off of my plasters, the casting-off of the cotton wool. Shaft by shaft the light opens up. Pale red is the dawn behind my lids. The pitch is soaked off with cool wet swabs. And here are her finger-tips now on my eyelashes. To pull them apart. To risk it. As I taught her.

She arose out of that grave of mine last night.

She went up into the mountain. Now it's my turn, now she's coming to fetch me from the water. I strain to keep up, to get where she is, to do my bit.

Ag, that I could speak now! I would want to ask her if she remembers. The butterflies we picked out of pools. After the showers that fell so unseasonably that first year after I got her. Too heavy to fly, trapped by the rain. We took them out of the mud, blew on the stuck-together wingtips until we found fingerholds, carefully, carefully like wet scraps of tissue paper we pulled the wings apart so that one shouldn't come off on the other.

Slowly we did it with much tsk-ing and ai-ing from me, because she herself wasn't yet speaking then. For hours on end we kept at it there with the dripping of the last drops and the calling of the frogs in our ears. We placed the butterflies in the sun, dozens of them, as we opened them up, on the earth wall of the irrigation furrow. Then we sat down on the other side with our chins on our drawn-up knees and waited.

Who's the first to see something move, I played with her. We stared fixedly. As if dead the little creatures lay.

I wasn't sure. I was taking a chance. I remembered vaguely from my childhood that it could work. I saw her looking at the half-dead little things in the puddles, with a sullen face, her chin far out, her lips pursed, as if she'd prefer to step on them.

It took half an hour.

First the colour returned. Some were orange and white and black, others yellow and black and blue. Then one stirred, then another, then two, three, till the whole wall seemed to be breathing with wings opening and shutting.

See, I signalled to her with my eyes, you didn't want to believe me!

Then she smiled.

I remember the day. She must also be able to remember it, she read it out, quite recently, from my diary. February, 28 February 1954. Would she still be able to remember it? Her fingertips on the lashes of my upper lid?

That was the first time I saw her smile. With the chin drawn in and an inward pinching of the little lips, a reluctant smile, but it was a smile. I looked away not to embarrass her further. But I remember thinking it was a miracle. I saw more colours than there in fact were because everything was swimming before my eyes. First one butterfly flew up, then two, three, then all together in a cloud shimmering over our heads before they eddied up next to the quince avenue, and then in amongst the trees of the old orchard.

Now it's my turn. My upper lash is pulled up, fingertips pull down the lower lid. My eye is lost, I can't find the seeing-slit.

Up, Agaat whispers, look up!

She presses on my eyeball, light rolling movements upwards.

Come, eye, come!

There it is!

I see you!

And I see you!

In the staring eye she puts some drops. The lids of the other one she sticks open, above and below, with strips of plaster. At first her eyes are only on her hands where she's working. She takes her time. I wait for her to look at me again. Both my eyes feel stretched open slightly too wide.

I must look to her like an extremely surprised person.

That brown case full of my things, remember? It was as if I'd buried it there yesterday. As if it'd been sulphured.

I can't close my eyes to listen better. I must look at her, her face is right above mine. She looks at me as one would look at a dam full of water. She doesn't prick through my cornea. She doesn't penetrate me with a blunt object. She doesn't fish in vain for the end of the rainbow.

She's accepted that it's beyond her, me and my dying.

She smiles at me.

I see my reflection in her eyes.

Everything is still there, she says, exactly as you packed it. Clothes, boots, ribbons. And shells and eggs and stones and bones, my lists, my story books, everything. Only the insects have disintegrated, and the pressed flowers are a bit ragged. And look here, even my sack with which I arrived here on Grootmoedersdrift. Do you remember? In the beginning you hid sweets inside for me.

To get me going.

I was terribly timid, wasn't I?

And just see what else is inside!

Agaat places something against my cheek before I can see what it is.

Feel, she says, there's nothing as soft as a moleskin.

She nestles it in my neck.

Even my wheel and my stick, she says.

She pushes the point of the stick into the rim of the wheel, rolls it over the covers over the incline of my body. I can feel it tracking over the skin of my belly.

Down the road to open the gate for me so long, with her white ribbons fluttering and her white bobby socks and her green dress. And her wheel and her stick.

My eyes can't stay open like this for too long. You must be able to blink. And the mountains freeze in that moment. It's life that passes in the blinking of an eye. While dying itself can last for an eternity.

Poor Jak. Never had time to pose. Flew through the air. Shrike-spiked on a branch. Never looked back. Stayed stuck in the drift.

Would I have preferred it like that? Instantaneous? Without deferment?

And Agaat, how would she prefer it if she could choose? On impact rather than this clearing-up and fitting-in, this emptying-out and filling-in, this never-ending improvisation? Hip-up hop-down in slow motion? With the bellows-book opened wide to blow out one long sustained blast of air, to keep the ember alive for as long as may be necessary?

What have we left of all that? Of all the twirling of the stick in the hole?

A fireplace, this bed, a stealthy little smoke arising.

A frock in which to bury me.

Sulphured conservation cloth.

Tried on and tried out.

A rat is what I smell!

I see it's now been hung here next to my bed on top of the maps. Washed and ironed and starched. The white embroidery is luminous. If one were to turn it over, all the threads on the other side would be sewn back and tied down and worked away. Otherwise it wouldn't be Agaat's work.

I would like to ask, ag, if I could speak I would now like to ask: Do you remember how Jakkie used to sit by you when he was small? He just couldn't believe that a picture could emerge from under the needle.

How do you do it, Gaat?

Do you remember how he persisted?

You couldn't really answer his question.

You fetch it and stretch it and tie it together, you said, you prod it and prick it, you slip it and snip it, you slide it in cotton-thread frames, you hold it and fold it, you pleat it and ply it, you bleach it and dye it and unravel again, you stitch on the stipple, you struggle with pattern, you deck it and speck it in rows and in ranks, in steps and in stripes and arches and bridges, and crosses and jambs of doors and of dams, you trace it and track it and fill it and span it and just see what's come of the cloth, a story, a rhyme, a picture for the pillow, for the spread on the bed, for the band round the cuff, for the cloth on the table, for the fourth dress of woman.

Will Jakkie still see me in it, Agaat? Will he remember me in it one day? Laid out and dressed in the Glenshee?

I think I recognise the weft. So it's true what she said? My great present to her for her first embroidery lesson? For one day when she will have mastered the art?

My eyes are drying out. Will she add drops once more so that I can try and make out everything she's embroidered there? So many tiny details, in places it looks like musical notation. A piece of sheet music? What could it be? If Agaat could compose? A symphonic tone poem?

Or programme music, like *Carnival of the Animals*? An aria for two female voices and farm noises?

But no, it's not as pretty as that. Here around the central portion it looks like a page from a manual, a guide to dying, a do-it-yourself book with illustrations, all the information in captions around the body embroidered there in the coffin position, the hands already folded on the chest. A woman in a frock in a woman in a frock I'd be.

Ounooi, says Agaat, your people have come to say goodbye to you. In one hand she has something, I can't see what it is. The Bible? With the other hand she beckons down the corridor. I hear the clicking of dogs' toenails on the floorboards.

What must I see? To whom is she beckoning there at the other end of the passage? Come! Come! The dogs? Boela and little Koffie? Who? There at the door? Who's there? Dawid, Julies with the drag-foot, Saar, Lietja, Kadys, a few well-grown young ones, a few little ones. All in Sunday best, a smell of cheap soap in the room, satin ribbons in the little girls' hair, their mothers in floral scarves, the men with their hats in their hands.

So these are all the ones I'll be farming on with here on Grootmoedersdrift, Ounooi, says Agaat.

Her voice is factual. As if she's leading evidence. She's showing them, I've been alive all this time, three years long in this bed. She shows I'm now moving on. She shows the reins, at the moment of changing hands.

Good morning, um, says Dawid. His cool light-green gaze rests in mine for a moment. He doesn't know which one of my eyes to peer into. He rotates his hat in his hand.

Oumies, says Saar, we'll look well.

Oumies was good to us, says Lietja. We will, we will . . . stay here under Agaat.

The message is clear. I see how they look at each other, how they assess it, the new order. We'll have to see. We'll just have to make the best.

I see the hands of the adults resting on the shoulders of the children.

Look children, look, that's what it looks like.

The children are standing dead still, the little girls in their still new unbleached dresses, the unironed shirt collars of the boys, white against the brown skins. Their eyes are big. One of them is holding Boela by the scruff of the neck. The little dog is making whimpering noises under the bed.

Agaat takes up position at the foot of the bed. She looks at me.

It's good, Agaat, it will go well, I wish you good cheer, and as much peace as is possible.

The ounooi says, Agaat interprets, she says thank you that you've come to greet her. You are all good people, she says. She wishes you all peace and prosperity, also for the coming Christmas and a blessed new year. She says that from now one you must be given two sheep every Christmas and a whole tolly as well and a vat of vaaljapie as always. She says she knows you'll work well with me. Just as well as I've worked with her all my life here on Grootmoedersdrift.

Amen, says Kadys in a professional mourner's voice. Amen, the others mumble under their breaths. Dawid squashes his hat on his head.

A suppressed giggle? I see one child nudging another in the ribs. The group is starting to disintegrate.

Agaat opens the book where she's been holding her finger. The cover is worn, dark blue. She announces:

From the section Soil and factors that can influence plant growth, from the chapter An unchecked danger, from the paragraph, The erosion process. Page three hundred and fifty-five.

It is written there:

Many of us will still remember that not so many years ago there were in certain districts very beautiful large and famous vleis covered in wild clover, vlei grass, and other useful plant species; in which there were also to be found pools and pans filled all year round with clean clear water. Surrounding these pans were bulrushes (*Prionium serratum*), sedge (*Cyperus textilis*) and other beautiful plants. Where are the vleis today? They have altogether disappeared and in their stead you find only a nest of hideous ditches, and where of old wild clover displayed its pretty flowers, there is now just here and there a hideous little bitter-berry (*Chrysocoma tenuifolia*). There is no drop of water to be found because the network of ditches forms such a perfect conduit that, as soon as the rainwater touches the earth, it is flushed away to other and bigger ditches that can take it away further until it ends up in the sea. This whole vlei area that once upon a time could carry and fatten more cattle than any other part of the veld, of the same size on the farm, can nowadays hardly feed a mountain tortiss.

She closes the book. She smiles at me.

Tortiss.

She takes her little scissors out of the top pocket of her apron, cuts a strip of plaster, sticks down the stare-eye. She pulls off the tuft of Vaseline-soaked cotton wool holding the other eye open. I feel the upper lid descending slowly. Firmly she starts singing. I feel her breath on my face. I feel the dogs bumping against the bed. A wet snout burrows in under my hand.

> Abide with Me; fast falls the eventide;
> The darkness deepens; Lord with me abide.
> When other helpers fail and comforts flee,
> Help of the helpless, O abide with me.

Behind Agaat they fall in, drawn-out, they drag the notes, through bone and marrow, the women just about weeping.

> Swift to its close ebbs out life's little day;
> Earth's joys grow dim; its glories pass away;
> Change and decay in all around I see;

O Thou who changest not, abide with me!

Now everyone is transported by the power of the hymn. High rises Agaat's descant for the last verse.

Heaven's morning breaks, and earth's vain shadows flee;
In life, in death, O Lord, abide with me.
Where is death's sting? Where, grave, thy victory?
I triumph still, if Thou abide with me!

*

The beginning you never recorded. You couldn't bring yourself to it. It would take too long, you told yourself. A piece of explanation while everything was already in motion. Your marriage, farming with all its ramifications. There was in any case something cryptic about the beginning. You always told yourself, one day. When you're not so busy. When you'll be able to focus. When you'll be able to sit down at your leisure and try to piece together everything as it happened. The whirligigs, circling on the dam, you still wanted to look up the scientific name. As if that would help. *Gyrinus natans*. Excuses, all of it.

Now you understand the actual reason. Or one of them.

It wasn't meant for the diary.

Nothing about it was meant for a diary.

It would have to be taken up into the family saga direct: Grootmoedersdrift, farm, house, man, wife, child.

First child.

From the beginning. It was never a story on its own.

Especially not the early beginnings.

You thought you could make of the whole Agaat a separate chapter. You thought you could quarantine it in this way. As if it were a thing you could tend in an isolation-pen so that nobody need experience your failures and your mistakes at first hand.

With her you never discussed any of your considerations and sentiments around her adoption. You forbade her ever to ask anything about it. You told yourself that it was best that way for her own sake, that when the time was ripe you'd rather give her the whole record so that she could read through it herself.

But you forgot about it.

There were incidents that reminded you again of your resolution. But by then it was too difficult. Once you wrote the commission in the front of the first booklet, when things were going well, just after Jakkie's birth. Another time, a few other times, you tried to conclude it, made a last entry, till it dried up of its own accord. One day you had all the volumes in your hand, arranged them in parcels, bound them with string and stowed them away and suppressed the thought that you'd ever had such a plan, such an intention, to hand it to the one whom it most concerned. You missed your chance. Again and again you missed it. In the end you simply wanted to get the whole lot out of the way. And because you could no longer move on your own, you told her to go and burn it.

And then your deathbed became the fireplace. Crackling with ripeness the time that accrued to her. Wind-dry the material. Your eyes and your ears the hearths into which she could cram the Quink-inscribed pages of Croxley Exercise Books. In a sequence determined by her. With so many omissions and additions that nobody, not even you, would ever be able to ascertain the true facts.

You couldn't easily improve on her timing. Nor its presentation. Parcel after parcel she fetched the diaries from the sideboard, keeping the best for last.

Timing. That should have been the second name of the Lord. Instead of Providence. Instead of Mercy.

Timing. Chance. Coincidence. From the beginning it had flowed strongly though the whole history.

That week in 1953, mid-December, Day of the Covenant. The harvest was in, there was breathing space on Grootmoedersdrift. You wanted to get away from Jak. He'd caused one delay after the other again through his negligence with the combine. You wanted to get away from the squabbles and the slaps. You wanted to go to your mother. A week you spent with her and then you were ready to leave. You'd brought out your suitcases already.

Then she started talking, out of the blue, with the good God of Timing whispering in her ear, about the labourers, families you'd known since childhood, and who'd lived on Goedbegin for generations, the Septembers, the Louriers.

Maria Lourier is still there, she said, your nanny, do you remember? Piet's dead, from TB they say. He just suddenly went into a decline and then he died off. She's taken another husband now, one Joppies as they call him, but his real name is Damon, Damon Steefert, a man from Worcester with a long jaw but for the rest from the dregs, swears and drinks and batters and the Lord only knows what else, and there's been a child come from it all, the wretched Maria, I warned her, she's well into her forties. Things aren't at all well down there in the cottages, perhaps you should go and say something, they do bad things with the child, all of them, a little girl, something wrong with her apparently, deformed or something, won't talk, sits inside the fireplace all day they say.

Your mother's feigned chatter. Did she know what she was doing? Did it dawn on her while she was bringing it up? You fancied that she was talking more slowly, as if she could feel something stirring, an idea, a plan.

You could have started saying something. You could at least have opened your mouth. But you were enthralled by the tale. A bad mother, a discarded child.

That was the story she dangled in front of your nose.

Was that how she sought to avenge herself on you? To ensure that you wouldn't escape your portion of pain in life?

You remember the day well, when you set off under your mother's watchful eye by the back door to the labourers' cottages.

Be careful, it's a holiday! she called after you.

There were cicadas chirring louder and louder the further you walked, devil's thorns sticking to your sandals at every step, prickle-grass on your hem, the white-hot sun of the noonday hour, no shadows.

It was quiet around the cottages, the hangover silence of the Day of the Covenant, a stink of excrement hanging over everything. Skinny dogs lying around with flies in their eyes.

Maria was sitting at the back against the house under the fig-tree in a tattered dress, a warp around the mouth that you didn't know. The two sons were there, Dakkie and Hekkie, your erstwhile playmates, with scars across their cheeks that hadn't been there when you played with them as a child. They replied to your questions sullenly. Only once did Maria come half erect, only when you were about to leave, only when you asked so where is your new husband, and I hear you've had another child. Almost as if she wanted to prevent you from asking it, wanted to prevent its being discussed, she got to her feet and gestured vaguely and then sank back on the bench against the wall, chin on the chest.

The back door was ajar but you walked round the front to go in, you knocked and waited and then turned the knob and pushed open the door, took in your breath and held it when the smother hit you, of rotten piss, of vomit, of old sweet liquor, of unwashed human bodies, of cold cinders and half-burnt bluegum wood. At first you could see nothing, so dark was it in the front room, then through a half-open door in another room, a mattress on the floor and a coil of dirty bedding in which you could make out a man's lower body.

Only when you pushed open a shutter did you notice the child, crouched in the corner of the blackened hearth with the knuckles of one hand crammed into her mouth.

You went on your knees in front of the hearth. The child was bitterly thin, the little legs full of scratches and bruises, her bony body visible in patches through the rags in which she was dressed. One foot was turned in and one little arm she kept pushed in behind her back. You found the child's eyes, but only for a moment before she jerked away her head and screwed her eyes shut as if expecting a blow.

Never mind, I won't do anything to you, you said.

The child started trembling.

I really won't do anything to you, you tried again and extended a hand but the child pressed her head between her knees, and pulled the hidden arm from behind her back and clamped it around her head.

It was a deformed arm, thin and undeveloped, the hand bent down from the wrist, the fingers half squashed together, the thumb folded in so that it looked like a shell, like the hand that your father taught you to make by candlelight when you wanted to imitate the flat head of a snake.

You got to your feet and leant forward in the hearth-opening towards the child.

What's your name? you whispered softly, tell the kleinnooi what your name is, won't you? For a long time there was silence, only the child's breath coming faster.

What do they call you? Tell me, then you come to me, then I'll stop them hurting you, the oumies says they do bad things to you.

In the silence you heard the man groan and turn over in his sleep. Must I ask your father, hmmm?

Then you heard it, from the cavern of the child's body where she'd stowed her head, a guttural sound.

Say again, I couldn't hear so well, say?

You went still closer. Of iron she smelt, of blood, of soot and grass and through the holes of her clothes you could see the skin moving over her ribs. You saw the small spasm of the diaphragm as the child said her name.

Again all you could make out was a scraping sound.

Ggggg-what? you asked, that's not a name, say it again for the kleinnooi so that I can hear nicely, come. Gogga? Grieta? Gesiena? Genys?

You turned your head with you ear against the child's face and imitated the ggggg-sound. You could feel her breath on your face. This time you heard the ggggg clearly, like a sigh it sounded, like a rill in the fynbos, very soft, and distant, like the sound you hear before you've even realised what you're hearing.

That was the beginning. That sound. You felt empty and full at the same time from it, felt sorrow and pity surging in your throat. Ggggg at the back of the throat, as if it were a sound that belonged to yourself.

You stood back and clasped your arms around your body. Something convulsed in your lower belly. You put your hands to your face as if you wanted to trace with your fingers the expression that you felt there to make sure.

You didn't want to go home right away, wanted to hold it fast a while longer. In such a mood you could only arouse suspicion in your mother's house. And you wanted to gather it, fold it away inside yourself in a place from which you could safely retrieve it, at night in your bed, in the half-hour of privacy while you were having your bath, on your evening walk.

You walked to the old dam, to the willow trees, the ruin of the little pump house on the water's edge behind which you would be invisible. There you found a place to sit down, on a tree-root with your feet in the water, and tried to fathom the feeling, the vague sweetness and sorrow. The heat of the summer's afternoon overwhelmed it, the dizzying sound of the cicadas, the call of the kingfisher on the dry branch in the middle of the dam.

From their grazing on the shallow side of the dam the ducks came swimming towards you. You closed your eyes, tried to melt yourself into the cloudy dark-red that one sees inside one's eyelids when the sun shines on them.

Ggggg, you said over and over, as softly as you could, under the tone of the cicadas. Under the low chattering of the ducks, under the trail of the willow's foliage on the bank.

When you opened your eyes the world was bright and strange. You held your breath. You were waiting for something, you looked down at the water in front of you. There was nothing except fine circles on the surface, the water insect and its little twin shadow, the hooked scribble-claws, broader around the ankles as if wearing boots, with also their reflections, and between the two sets of claws, between above and below, a single ripple inscribing the surface of the water with rapidly successive perfect circles, overlapping, circling against one another, fading away, starting anew, a weltering writing on water. A fugue it reminded you of. You could hardly imagine that it was the work of a single creature.

When you got home hours later, your mother was predictably upset.

Where have you been wandering on this blazing Sunday? Something could have happened to you!

Something did, you wanted to say. I myself happened, my almost forgotten self. But you said nothing and went to the pantry and hand on hip inspected the contents of the shelves while trying to steel yourself against the tone of her voice.

Milla, are you going to tell me what's happening? Just look at your face! You mustn't come and try your nonsense here with me. No wonder Jak can't get along with you. What are you blubbering about now?

Your voice sounded heavy and shaky.

I'm blubbering about whirligigs, Mother, about the beauty of their existence, however insignificant, wrinkles on water, circles that vanish without ever having been anything, except that I've seen them.

What are you talking about in God's name, Milla?

I'm talking about the fact that down there in the cottages there's a child suffering in the most appalling manner, and because you know it and don't do anything about it!

Oh, good Lord, I should have known! she said, all I meant was that you must tell Maria to get a grip on herself and tell her to get her house in order. Don't interfere in the affairs of the workers, Milla! All you do is incur trouble and misery. Listen to what I'm telling you today. What are you looking for here in the pantry, anyway?

You'd opened the bread-tin already and had started cutting thick slices of bread.

What do you think you're doing, Milla? That's this morning's freshly-baked bread, there's day-before-yesterday's bread in the chickens' feed-bag.

You ignored her, took butter out of the fridge and started spreading it on the slices with apricot jam. You took the leftover leg of lamb from lunch-time out of the fridge and started carving slices from it.

You're just creating trouble here, Milla. Tomorrow we'll have a string of children in front of my door saying they want bread and they want meat. Where is it to end? The people know their place on this farm and I'm not going to allow your rashness to foul up my affairs here!

You brought the whole leg of lamb to your mouth, thought you wanted to bite into it and spit it out in her face. But you just lifted the joint in both hands and let go of it so that it fell on the floor by her feet.

Keep your meat then, Ma, keep it and guzzle it on your own while the children around you are perishing of hunger!

You were out of there with a basket in which you'd thrown the slices of bread, roughly stuck together, and a few pieces of fruit that you'd grabbed from the fruit platter in the front room.

Around the workers' cottages everything was quiet. You went in by the front room and found the child there in same position. You placed the basket by her feet.

Here, just look what I brought you! It's just for you, you hear? Eat it quickly before they take if from you. I'll tell your mother not to bother you.

Maria? a man's voice called harshly from the bedroom. You went out quickly and walked round the back where a bickering conversation fell silent as you came round the corner.

You kept your voice even and commanding.

Maria, I've brought food for the little one, see to it that she eats it. I want to see you at the house, tomorrow morning, nine o'clock, and you bring her along, d'you hear. We must have a little talk, you and I.

The woman gazed at you.

Have you understood me well, Maria, nine o'clock, not a minute later. And remember to bring back the basket.

I sound like my mother, you thought. You wanted to cry. You turned round quickly and walked home, straight in by the front door to the telephone, and booked a trunk call home through the farm exchange. You wanted to act in terms of the insight of the afternoon, in the spirit of the whirligig, you wouldn't allow yourself to be put off your resolve, and you didn't want time to pass over it, because you knew that the power of the everyday, the perspective of those with the whip-hand, could in the blink of an eye make the mere idea seem like the sheerest folly.

Come and fetch me, Jak, I want to come back. And I'm bringing someone with me, somebody who needs care, you announced later that evening when the call came through.

Just not your mother, Jak started.

My mother can care for herself, Jak, it's the youngest child of Maria of Piet who was, she's being terribly neglected here in the hovels, she'll perish if somebody doesn't intervene.

What nonsense, Milla! If the people want to perish, then they perish, why must I take responsibility for it?

You needn't do anything, Jak, it's my child and I'll raise her.

Between you there was the usual barrage of clicks and beeps of the fellow-listeners on the party line.

When Jak spoke again, his voice was dry.

We'll talk later, Milla, you obviously have no idea . . .

Never you mind, Jak, all shall be well . . .

I'll be there at twelve tomorrow, and then I'll want to leave at once, tell your mother I won't be eating.

He put down the phone in your ear. You stood there clutching the receiver to your chest. Images rose before you, of you hand-in-hand with the child turning your back on Jak and walking away, of you glaring at him until he lowered his head and stood aside to allow you to pass.

Your mother came out into the passage. Without a word you walked past her and went to your room and started packing your things.

One by one you held your clothes up in front of you in the unsteady light of the generator: Floral smock, sleeveless summer blouse, full-length petticoat hemmed with lace, before you folded them and packed them in the case. The generator switched off. Through the window you caught a glimpse of a torch moving away from the house in the direction of the cottages. You thought of the child there, in the dark, amongst the people you'd seen that afternoon.

Open-eyed you lay in the dark amongst the cases on the bed and thought about what you'd say, to the frowning elders, to the little deacon of the farm collection in his black frock-coat, to the hatted-and-handbagged older women at the ward prayer-meeting, to George the Greek of the Good Hope Café, to sanctimonious Beatrice, to MooiJak de Wet arranging his cravat in front of the mirror before going out on a Saturday evening.

Your neat speech wouldn't stand up, no matter how often you rehearsed it in your head: Here I stand, I can do no other.

The argument faded before your excitement. Your heart started beating so hard that you had to get up to drink water from the ewer, to light the candle and snuff it again, to stand by the open window look-ing out over the yard. Your heart. You placed your hand against your neck to feel the pulse.

Here we go round the mulberry bush, went through your head, one two buckle my shoe, blind man's buff, you're it, you must hide, you must seek, you're out, ring-a-ring-a'roses, pocket full of posies, a-tishoo! a-tishoo! we all fall down, pat-a-cake, pat-a-cake, baker's man, bake me a cake as fast as you can, four stand in the road four hang in the road, two gore you in the groin and one flicks away flies, what is it? Look at the clouds, do you see the cayman with its pointy tail and do you see the centipede, do you see the Magicman? And the swift-spit snake? Let's count the horses stamping their hoofs behind the moon and the stars of the Southern Cross and of the Scorpion and the thirty-three fleeces of the thistle till we get sleepy, till we sleep. Out-side walks a sheep. Iron on the hoof, pumpkin on the roof, down in the stable all the calves are fast asleep. Do you hear the rainman shuf-fle-shambling along the Langeberg? Do you see his grey sleeve trailing along the slopes? And the wind in the black pines, and the wind in the ears of wheat hissing over the hills, as far as the ear can hear, the hills of Rietpoel and the hills of Protem, the round-backed hills of Klipdale and Riviersonderend, the dale of rocks and the river without end, swishing and sweeping, one rustling billowing blanket of sweet quivering stalks to where the lands end against the slopes of the mountain of which this side is Over. Overberg. And on the other side the Table Mountain that I'll go and show you one day when you're grown up.

The next day you were waiting for them at the back door. You saw the bickering party approaching from afar, hurrying to the yard. Maria with the basket in one hand and the refractory child in the other. And Lys, the eldest daughter by Maria's first husband. Hessian bag in one hand, gesticulating with the other. According to your mother the only member of the family who was worth anything. She worked in the house. She was the one who tattled the tales of the cast-off child.

Behind you in the kitchen your mother cleared her throat.

Think before you act, Milla, you're not the only one who's going to be affected by this, she said. Hard-heeled she stalked into the house.

Sheepishly the little group came to a halt before you. Maria mumbled a greeting, her head hanging. Lys stepped forward, performed an arm gesture, a sweep of the elbow, signifying that she could be trusted as the representative of her family's interests.

Morning Kleinnooi, I've heard Kleinnooi wants to see my mother and the child, so I came along to hear what the kleinnooi has in her heart, if the kleinnooi doesn't mind.

The little girl didn't make a sound, just wriggled with all her might to escape.

Maria yanked the child closer.

This picture didn't accord at all with your fantasies. In Lys's gaze there was something you couldn't fathom. As if she had a suspicion of what was coming. She met your eye insolently. You had to look away.

What would you have thought if you'd been she? So, you in your floral dress, with your armpits smelling of lavender, bite it off, and chew it as we've been chewing it for a long time, and then you swallow it gobbet by gobbet with your whitey spit. Take! Guzzle it! It's our crippledness here that's been born to us!

Is that what Lys thought? Improbable. Absolutely practical considerations rather, you realised. Her voice was full of calculation when she started speaking, her eyes much more impertinent than her voice.

Kleinnooi, excuse, but is Kleinnooi perhaps feeling out of sorts?

Not out of sorts, out of place, you felt out of your depth, caught out. There were, except in your head, no histrionic thoughts, only a scene that must have played hundreds of times in the past, on farms everywhere in the region.

No what, Lys, I'm fine, let's just get out of the sun, come in, I have cooldrink for us.

You walked ahead of them into the kitchen to where you'd set out the glasses and the Oros and opened the fridge to take out the cold water. Behind you you felt how Lys, as an initiate in the whiteman's home, accepted the unusual invitation on behalf of the others and hustled them in at the back door.

So tell me a bit about the child, you started while you poured the cooldrinks into the glasses.

How did she get so deformed?

Lys had her story ready, she delivered it in between smacking gulps of Oros.

No, Kleinnooi, she was just born like that, she started, her arms folded, regarding the child.

Very small and red, with the little hanging arm, at first we thought it was a bit of gut hanging out. Dakkie said sis, Hekkie said take away.

And you, Lys? you wanted to ask, but you swallowed your words.

Ma here was quite odd from looking at it. Didn't want to give the child tit.

Lys waited behind her glass for a reaction.

We said to Ma, Ma take her, give her tit, she's going to kick the bucket.

That's enough, Lys, you wanted to say, but the woman was playing for the benefit of Ma in the gallery.

Pa Joppies said give here, let me go and get rid of that, it's not my child, my arms are straight as poles, both, my hands are as good as shovels, look, nothing's the matter with me. Yes, Pa Joppies, I thought to myself, your two feet with which you kicked Ma good and proper in the belly when she was carrying, they're straight too.

You gathered the empty glasses.

So this child got her kicks in the other place already, Kleinnooi.

Lys scraped her chair across the floor as she turned it round to the sink to get your attention.

And then later when they started kicking her so, they just waited for her to start walking, to get the foot in under nicely, Hekkie and Dakkie both, then I said, if you wanted her dead, you should've kicked and have done when she came out, then she didn't know of anything. Now she's a person. Now you must have respects. The Lord made her like that. She also has a right.

You waited for the Lord's appurtenances, the devil, the angels, three crows of the cock.

But they won't listen and I get the kicks if I try to get in between and our ma she turns her back on it and says nothing, she's scared of them. Those two, they've become like savages under their new pa. Looks to me they want to be like him, kick harder and hit harder and curse harder . . .

Lys worked herself up for the climax.

As if they want to go Satan one better with fire, with blows coming down so that you smell sulphur and hear a screaming like pigs down in the poplars, and more I'd rather not say, the Lord is my witness . . . So it will be a deliverance, it will be a mercy, that's what I'm saying, if the kleinnooi . . . if . . .

If the kleinnooi what, Lys?

Actually you wanted to scream at the woman and throw her out of the kitchen by the scruff of her neck.

Lys had a firm grip on the child's thin arm, but she was a bit calmer now and stood there, one foot over the other, the glass of cooldrink untouched in front of her on the kitchen table. She started trembling and once, twice, looked anxiously from face to face.

You caught her eye and tried a smile, sent her a wordless message: Come, we must be brave now you and I, now we have to help each other here!

The child's look just grazed me, she started squirming ferociously. Her glass of cooldrink fell from the table, shattered on the floor, a chair capsized.

Never mind, you said, it doesn't matter.

Your mother appeared in the doorway, small and old there in the door.

Sorry, Ounooi, excuse, Ounooi, Lys said, on her knees with the scoop and the broom and the floor-cloth, very subservient, but with a venomous set of the mouth. I'll clean everything nicely, Ounooi.

You put an arm around your mother's shoulder and accompanied her some way down the passage.

Sorry about the ruckus, you said.

Ai Milla, my dear child . . .

My dear child, you thought, must I figure in a Greek tragedy before you can call me your 'dear child'?

She turned away and opened the linen cupboard in the passage.

You'd better clean up that little one before you load her into the car.

She fished out a little worn towel from the cupboard and with a sharp yank tore it in two and pressed the two halves into your hands.

One for washing, she said, and one for drying.

When you got back to the backyard you found them standing outside next to the water tank.

You talked past Lys who was waiting arms akimbo.

Maria, I'm taking the child to Grootmoedersdrift and I, my husband and I, we'll look after her. What's her name?

You felt Lys's eyes sliding over your face. You didn't want to look at her, but she was the one who replied.

She doesn't really have a name, we call her Gat, Asgat, because she sits with her arse in the ash in the fireplace all the time. She won't wear a panty.

She won't want for anything, you said. Either you give her over into my care or your days are numbered here on Goedbegin. There's quite enough reason to fire the whole lot of you. You squat on the ounooi's back and mess with one another and don't pull your weight. You go home now and leave her here, the ounooi and I will manage from here on and the kleinbaas will be here just now. I'll phone the police and report that Joppie beats his wife so that they can be prepared if there's trouble again. The ounooi knows what's going on and she now knows what to do if he or Dakkie or Hekkie misbehaves any more. Is that clear?

It's right like that, Kleinnooi, we're only too grateful.

With your hand you signalled to Lys to be quiet.

Maria, have you understood me well here?

Maria stood there with her chin on her chest.

I want to hear a clear yes out of you, Maria, look at me.

Lys smirked.

A dull sound came from the older woman. Her lips stuck out, but she said nothing more. She didn't look up.

We brought her things, said Lys, picked up the little hessian bag from the ground and held it out to you.

That's good, Lys, just put it down, I'll have a look.

She can talk too if she wants. She eats porridge with sugar.

That's good, Lys, I'll see to that.

You put your hand on the child.

Kleinnooi must watch out, she's wild, she'll pull free and run away, here, take the bad arm, it's the rein.

That's enough, Lys, you can go home now, all of you.

You took the child's good hand.

Maria's hand came up feebly next to her body, her head was hanging.

Bye bye, Asgat, Lys said, behave yourself, you hear. Tonight you'll have meat and bread and sweets, you'll see, and a snow-white bed to sleep in, all to yourself. I put your wheel in the bag and your stick and your moleskin.

You left the dirty bag full of bumps and lumps on the ground.

Cool down, you thought, cool down first. Both of us.

Let's walk to the dam, then we look at the ducklings, there where I'm taking you there's also a dam like that with ducks, just prettier, with green heads, and you can swim in our dam, can you swim? I'll teach you to swim, first with a little tube around you, till you feel you can do it yourself and then I'll hold my hands under you so that you can feel you're floating, and then I'll show you how one does like a little dog, round and round in a circle while I'm holding you, and then little bits on your own till you're nice and strong and then one day we'll swim to the middle or we'll go rowing on the drift with a picnic in the boat just for you and me and a coloured blanket to sit on and then we'll spread it in the shade and then we'll eat, nice fresh bread spread with thick butter and apricot jam, just like the sandwiches that I brought you yesterday, you remember, they were nice weren't they? And red cooldrink. And a sausage and cheese and hard-boiled eggs, and blood-red slices of watermelon. Do you know watermelon? And when we're finished, then I'll sing you a song.

You looked at your shadows in the footpath, a woman in a hurry with a jibbing child. You sang.

The bottom of the bottle, the bottom of the bottle
the bottom of the bottle fell out.

Open your mouth open your mouth
open your mouth nice and wide,
so the syrup can flow inside.

You were walking much too fast, dragging the child behind you. She strained back, pulled to one side, looking for an escape route.

I'm walking a bit too fast for you? And I'm talking so much! Let's walk a bit slower, it's not far now.

The dam wouldn't get any closer and the house seemed too far away to turn back. It was very hot. You felt shaky. It hadn't been a good idea just to set off like that without a plan. Time was short. You looked on your watch. Quarter past ten. In an hour's time Jak would be there. He was always punctual when he had to come and fetch you from your mother's.

Your knees started knocking. Nausea welled up in you. You gulped to swallow it down. Once you looked back. The front door was closed and the shutters fastened against the heat of the day.

Come let me carry you the last little bit.

You bent down and lifted the child onto your hip. You felt the pelvic bones against your waist, the wiry body straining away from you. And then. A twist, a slip, a duck, under your arm, a sinewy thing slithering down your side. She left you standing, swiftly, swerving, between the bushes and the tussocks aiming for the cottages to the left of the dam.

You were off balance when you started running. You crashed down. Coming to your feet you were missing a sandal. Over bush and tussock you leapt, within a few paces you were right behind her. But you felt clumsy, you couldn't anticipate the child's sidesteps. Your one bare foot crippled you.

I must pass her, in a straight line, you thought, I must get ahead and cut her off, before she's seen, before Joppies sees her. Because they wouldn't have told him, or perhaps they would. Both possibilities could spell the end.

The end of what? it flashed through you. You did think that then. A grey streak of lateral considerations that streamed past you along with the tussocks and the ant-heaps and the bushes.

Nothing has really begun, you thought, I can let her go, I can go home, I can go back to the farm and just carry on where I left off. I needn't put myself out. Not if the child herself doesn't want to. Not if nobody else, not even my own mother, cares, if not even my husband is going to support me. Not if it seems that I'll have to fight for something that's the self-evident duty of civilised people.

You thought it all, as you ran and jumped and grabbed after the child.

Stand still! you screamed, watch out! as you cut in in front of her and grabbed her by the waist and fell down hard with her. The child tried to scrabble away on all fours. You dived after her full-length, grabbed her by one foot. Hand over hand you hauled her in. Ankle, calf, thigh, rump, arms, shoulders, till you were sprawling half on top of her. The dust billowed around you.

You coughed and scolded. You had to wrestle against the wriggling that persisted under you. With arms and legs you had to stop her, on both sides, from worming her way out from under you.

You're not getting away! you managed to say. I have to look after you. You're mine now. And now you open your ears and you listen to me well, I'll thrash your backside blood-red for you if you don't behave yourself now. If you're good, I won't do anything to you. If you carry on being naughty and running away I'll tell the kleinbaas and he'll take off his belt and flog you till your backside comes out in red welts and then we'll tie a rope around your neck and tie you to a pole like a baboon, the whole day long until you're tame.

The child's breath juddered. A squeaking sound emerged.

You realised what you'd said. You pressed your head against the child's collar-bone.

No, that's not true, I don't mean it, I'm stupid, stupid, stupid, forgive me, I promise you never ever again, never will anybody hurt you again. And you're not naughty, you're just scared. Because you have to go away and because you don't know what's going to happen. Don't be scared, just don't be scared. Nobody will beat you, not I and also not the kleinbaas. Everything will be fine, I promise, your stick is there and the wheel, Lys packed them. And your moleskin. Tonight when we've got to the farm over the mountain you can have them and play with them before you go to bed and all day tomorrow.

You wished the child would cry. Then you'd be able to comfort her. Then you could soothe her and coax her and make promises and give assurances and hold her and offer her something to drink, something to eat. But you were the one who cried. The child went limp. You picked her up and walked on towards the dam with her. She was light. Your tears dripped on her.

Never mind, you said over and over again, never mind, there's nothing to cry about.

Your dress was torn out of its seam at the waist in two places and your knee was bleeding. The child was grey with dust and full of scratches.

I must use this limp terror to get her cleaned up, you thought.

At the dam you drew the child's rags over her head. You tucked your own dress into the elastic of your panty. You stopped talking. There was another feeling. Pretty words, you thought, are not what's going to put matters straight between us, not now and perhaps for a whole long time yet. You I'll have to rule with a firm hand.

You put her down and went and stood in front of her and pulled her off the dam wall. On the first contact with the water there was another squeaking sound, but softer and feebler this time. The child pulled up her knees, but soon lowered them again. You clamped her with one arm around the chest and started washing her with the other hand. The water left dark lines on the dusty skin. On the wet skin there were still other darker stains, here and there reddish ones that looked like burn marks, spots of scabies, ringworm, and older inflamed scars. You kept on splashing water till everything was dark and then got out the handkerchief that you had in the front of your bra and started washing her, first wiped the face, behind the ears and then the neck, that was badly encrusted. You shuddered at the thickly-caked frizzy hair that had certainly never been combed or plaited or even washed. But that would have to wait. You started to wash the child's front with the handkerchief. Under your hand you felt the bump of a carelessly tied-back umbilical cord, a tension in the body when you wiped across the lower body. You didn't go any further, just splashed a bit of water up between the little legs and at the back in the cleft of the buttocks.

There, you said, more to yourself than to the child, now at least one of us is more or less respectable.

Jak was there already with the bakkie. It was parked at an angle with one wheel across the wall of the irrigation furrow, you recognised the sign. You took a detour around the back and dressed the child in a clean bleached dress that you got from the hessian bag. Then you locked her in the outhouse. You peered through the slit to see what she was doing. She scrambled onto the plank and pressed herself up against one corner, fist in the mouth, staring fixedly into the sitting-hole. There wasn't a lid. A smell of Jeyes Fluid hovered in the air. The outside toilet was no longer in house use. Only the maids went there.

Don't fall into the hole, there are bats down there, I'll be back just now, you whispered before you turned the catch and hooked in the latch. An image flitted past your eyes, of the child trying to crawl to the light ahead through an encrusted pipe poppling with human turds. You rubbed your eyes to get rid of the image. The pit didn't have an open sewer to the outside.

You had to keep your head and act, as fast as you could.

You knew Jak would be in the living room with your mother.

Be there in a minute! you called as lightly as you could and ran down the passage to the bathroom where you had a lightning-quick bath and disinfected the cut on your knee. You went through the bathroom cabinets and found ointment and plasters. You rifled through your mother's medicine bottles. You slipped three sleeping pills and a bottle of valerian drops into the pocket of your dressing-gown. Rubbing your wet hair with a towel you stepped into the silence of the living room and through the towel planted a kiss on Jak's cheek. He just stared straight ahead. You babbled through it all.

Heavens, Jak, you must have driven like the wind and then almost into the irrigation furrow, did you see where your front wheel is?

Milla, he said.

Where is . . .? your mother asked.

She's waiting in the back, you called over your shoulder, we're just about ready.

You crammed your suitcases and put them out in the passage. You threw on a dress and drew a comb through your hair, a touch of lipstick, a splash of perfume and ran down the passage to the backyard.

And now, now I'm dosing you for the road before there's more trouble than there is already.

That's what you said even before you'd got the toilet door open.

You held the dropper of valerian at the ready and on entering grabbed the child, clamped fast her head, forced open her mouth. You felt something snapping in you over the way you were treating her. The only remedy, you told yourself. You pinched shut her nose so that she had to swallow the sleeping pill as well. You rubbed her gullet hard. You could feel the little rings of cartilage under your fingers.

Swallow, you hissed, swallow so that you can calm down, swallow, I'm not taking any more nonsense from you.

*

forehead of flame eyes of soot mouth from which glowing coals crumble roaring of flames lamenting and wailing cast me in a hearth of ice press my front in the snow roll me into a snowball one side of me the other side of me my cold and my hot my wet and my dry who can reconcile my moieties? neither glue nor thongs nor balm nor coalescence nor grafting nor oculation nor welding through my head runs a crack no sentence is completed no wisdom gained nothing more to swallow my teeth are loose my tongue abscised with exhaustion an apple of glass falls from my mouth oh last lip and jaw of woe oh last dream in mistletoe before the pitch may enfold me

is there then a last scream coming from me?

whose are the hands here around my belly squeezing my breath in and out? whose warm weight supporting me from behind and from below? gathering me from the front? rescuing me from the moieties dreamt? who collects my parts? who splints my neck in a straight line and lifts my chin so that my gullet should not become entangled in itself? who gently parts my shoulders like wings? who places a knee between my knees so that I should not cleave to my own flesh? who is a buoy beneath me so that I should not sink from my own weight not perish? in what body am I sustained as in a crib? tilted as in a cradle? who breathes beneath me as if I'm lying on a living bedstead my pulse ignited with another pulse my breath to the rhythm of another my insight capsulated in sturdy scaffolds my sentences erected on other sentences like walls built on a rock? Who?

where are you agaat?

here I am
a voice speaking for me a riddle where there is rest
a candle being lit for me in a mirror
my rod and my staff my whirling wheel
a mouth that with mine mists the glass in the valley of the shadow
of death
where you go there I shall go
your house is my house
your land is my land
the land that the Lord thy God giveth you
is this the beginning now this lightness? can I venture it on my own?
am I at last membrane between a willow and its reflection? A meniscus
that transmits an image? Am I the crown of leaves in the air like the
crown of leaves in the water? Yes without lamentation without sighing
a permeable world world without end this rustling region culm inclin-
ing to culm the stone on the bank like the stone in the dam carried
from cloud to cloud on the south-easter where the clover does not
know of the humus and the stalk of the wheat does not deny the ear
its fullness and the blue crane rises clamouring above the ripples of her
beating wings framed by the reflected cloud and the reflected tree on
the wash of the still river whose call returns to her for a last time from
the valley in carillons in canon-thunder where to the smallest circling
water-creature zealously writing everything reflects so with open eyes
into the white light so whispering to my soul to go
in my overberg
over the bent world brooding
in my hand the hand of the small agaat

EPILOGUE

The turbulence is less now, the plane has been humming evenly for a few hours. Can still not sleep. The last few days on the farm remain with me, the dust on the Suurbraak road, the dried-up drift, stones, cattle grids, flower arrangements, legs of pork, professions of grief. And just look at him now. His bag of samples knocking at his knees.

Not puzzled things out for myself by a long shot, but I'm making fair progress, especially after this lot. God help us. Gaat making people by the graveside sing the third verse of *Die Stem*: . . . When the wedding bells are chiming, Or when those we love depart.

And then all eyes on me for: . . . Thou dost know us for thy children . . .We are thine, and we shall stand, Be it life or death to answer Thy call, beloved land!

Wake up and smell the red-bait, as Pa would have said. Poor Pa with his ill-judged exclamations. Did at least make a note for my article on nationalism and music. Thys's body language! The shoulders thrust back militaristically, the eyes cast up grimly, old Beatrice peering at the horizon. The labourers, men and women, sang it like a hymn, eyes rolled back in the head. Word-perfect beginning to end.

Trust Agaat. She would have no truck with the new anthem. Only Dawid didn't open his mouth. Totem pole. He watched me closely, whether I was singing along. And then also: *As pants the hart for cooling streams*, all the verses according to Ma's directions, a whole programme there before the coffin could be lowered.

It's a Boeing 747, this time. A light vibration, now and again a few faint shocks, but not as bad as on take-off. The bag by my feet is starting to get in my way.

Inconvenient stuff to cart along. These fragments. Apart from the blue Delft birth-plate and the parcel of fennel seed, the horn and the bellows. Extra hand luggage that couldn't go in the hold. Wild aromas of Africa, dry protein. Will have to be declared on arrival. Will in all probability be sniffed out by the customs dogs. Be confiscated.

Agaat insisted.

Blow me a note on it every now and again, she said, looked away.

I'll hear it, she said. Thought that's what she said, only her lips moved. Then her voice was clear again.

And make yourself a nice fire in your fireplace. Do you have a fireplace? It's covered in snow almost all year round there where you are, isn't it?

Still ten hours of flying to the snow. The cabin in semi-darkness. Here and there the yellow shaft of a cabin light over the book of a late reader, a hostess in the aisle with glasses of orange juice, with extra blankets, with milk bottles for a baby. A few rugby players still up and down. Without exception younger than twenty, raucous all through the meal. Now and again sang a snatch, *Make her say no make her say oh*, to the tune of Macarena. Will have to write something about it. Wine, women and balls. Now also at last to rest.

Sleep that knits up the ravelled sleeve of care.

A nightmare it was. Had still considered a tour of the Overberg, a few tape recordings in the townships, all the old places once more, the farms and little towns with the odd names of which I try to tell people in Toronto. Entertainment for Vermaaklikheid, Le Fleuve Eternel for Riviersonderend. Rather just let be.

I do admire our Good Lord for his aesthetic flair in creating a world that is at one and the same time both heaven and hell. Who wrote that? Konrad? *The Garden Party*. Ma's funeral obsequies, posies wherever you look, the garden in full flower, around it the summer drought.

Discrepancy, a gritty feeling ever since I set foot on land. The trip from the airport, the light glaring white, the blaze that blinds one. Arid red lands next to the road, black shadows of bluegums, pit dams with yellow condensation-rings, a last slimy dreg at the bottom. It's always been like that. When and where did my romantic yearnings originate? Deserted farmyards, neglected buildings, rusty bits of machinery.

My standards have shifted, of civilisation, of human dignity. Drove for a long time behind an open lorry, full of labourers being carted to town for their Saturday shopping. Crush in the main street. Stayed in my car, stared out of my eyes. Boundary-maintaining body language if ever. Drunkenness in the streets of Swellendam. Your mother's cunt! the coloureds yell at one another, unmistakable the inflection. Hurrying through them the whites with quick little steps and stolid faces.

As if from behind three-inch glass, suddenly it was there, the old realisation. I don't belong here.

Have been away for too long.

More than a decade.

Perhaps too short.

Gaat didn't twitch a muscle. Her cap was higher, more densely embroidered than I remembered it, spectacles on her nose. For the rest she was as always, perhaps a bit stouter, her chin pushed far out, her steps energetic, her soles squelching on the wooden floor. Apartheid Cyborg. Assembled from loose components plus audiotape.

The funeral food made me sick, the quantities, and then after that a whole week's recycling till Gaat had it put out in enamel dishes for the workers. The children falling upon it before the adults could even get to it. Agaat letting fly with a cane among them.

Can't stop thinking about it. An abundance that never suffices, as always on Grootmoedersdrift. And everything sweet. Sweet sweet-potatoes, sweet pumpkin, sweet stewed fruit, sweet yellow rice, sweet peas, banana salad in yellow condensed-milk mayonnaise.

The undertaker, pudgy little fingers, chatty, his theme the embroidered shroud: Genesis and Grootmoedersdrift in one, a true work of art, must have taken a lifetime, every stitch in its place.

Relieved after all that I was too late. Couldn't have stomached it. Agaat herself sewing Ma up in the fully embroidered gown, Agaat lifting Ma into the coffin, placing the hand-splint that she wrote with in the last years in the coffin as well and screwing down the lid. Nobody else was allowed to touch her, according to the undertaker.

And then also the diaries, perhaps that's what's bloating my stomach. Like sheep dip. Takes a while to be excreted into the bloodstream. Was asking for it. Perhaps I should be grateful. Perhaps its effect is more like inoculation against smallpox.

Two days after the funeral. The yard still after the midday meal. Me naked on my bed in the spare room, the heat pressing on my chest.

Gaat's white apron hanging from the hook behind the kitchen door. The big apron pocket, Agaat's marsupium in which she stows her keys. Stuck my hand in there, goose pimples all over, a scoundrel, naked in his deceased mother's house.

The key to the only room in the house that was locked, the only room in all the house that had a door. New hinges but no explanations.

The silence with that key in my hand, heavy as before the offering up of prayer, before the laying on of hands, before the sprinkling of the forehead, like those silences of my childhood, the town church, the re-echoing coughs in the pews. The roof ticked with the heat, the floorboards in the passage creaked under my feet. My heart beating. The same feeling I had as a child when I slipped away in the afternoons to the outside room. To be with Agaat, with her soft body in the night-dress where she was taking forty winks, her smell of starch and Mum.

Dark it was in the room. Locked the door and stood still to accustom my eyes.

Ma's room. For a moment it was just like always. Drawn curtains, an atmosphere of aches and pains, an aroma of grievance, of anxiety. Meine Ruh ist hin, mein Herz ist schwer. Soft radio music. Midday concert. But this time it was quiet.

And there before me: A high bed piled with pillows, a dark stain on the top one, objects dangling from the ceiling. Chrome railings, benches, chairs, steel frames. Cramped it felt, the walls covered in stuff. Installation for percussion. Shadows shifting behind the curtains.

That's the way it was. As always. More questions than answers.

Her voice! Muted, from somewhere. Some things don't have reasons, Jakkie, some things just are the way they are. And you don't have to believe everything you're told. There's a lot of ill will. There are old wives' tales.

Walked through the room with long strides, plucked open curtains, unlocked and threw open stoep doors. There were too many smells, of cloth and upholstery, and dry grass and vanilla, medicine, disinfectant, soap, breath, a sweetish miasma of mortality.

Turned round, surveyed the room. The afternoon light on the floor, points of light on chrome and glass. Trumped. Ali Baba's cave. Not quite an accurate simile. The murky realm of mothers, rather. Monstrous specimens everywhere. Samples of some weird mnemonic.

Dresses and hats, mirrors, watches, maps, photos, yellowed diagrams, pieces of paper scribbled over with lists of phrases: I wish, I fear, I hope, I dream. Question marks, exclamation marks, a chart with the letters of the alphabet: V *is Canaan's vine bearing bunches so black, the explorer returns with a bunch on his back.*

Ran my hands over everything, over the feathers, the seeds, ears of wheat in an old ginger-beer jar, scraps of paper pinned to the curtains.

One by one I picked up the objects and put them down again, the skull of a buck, of a baboon, a lizard's skeleton, a ram's horn, a trocar and cannula.

Cranked once the meat-mincer screwed down to the end of a table. The empty metallic sound on wood. The mills of God.

There were my varnished birds' eggs in a bowl, the old binoculars in their leather case with the red lining, Oupa's old telescope with which Ma taught me and Gaat about the stars.

The moon and the stars, that's about all that was missing from that room.

There were butterflies pinned to green felt, a copper pestle, the blue Delft birth-plate, now in my suitcase, a spade, a tarred rope, a combine

blade, a dried-up sheep's ear, a horseshoe, three droppers, a wire spanner, a bag of compost, jars of soil samples, a wire clipper, a Coopers
dosing-can for sheep medicine, a rusty sickle.

Not quite pictures in a gallery.

Also a worn brown suitcase, lichen around the locks, set up on the
arm rests of a straight-backed chair right next to the bed, full of mouldering bits of cloth and paper and bone, a few marbles. Musty. Corpus
delicti. Lifted it off and sat down in the chair, dizzy.

It was Gaat's handiwork, unmistakable. Miss Havisham in the death
chamber.

What would I myself have selected to commemorate my mother? So
vaguely present in my life, compared with Gaat.

Definitely more than commemoration had happened there. To judge
by the placing of the chairs, a kangaroo court rather. And me there
naked amongst the deceased props a nude figure in a Kienholz environment. He would be jealous of it. Homunculus in the skull nursery.

At last I could get up. Simply had to go and see what the dark object
on the pillow was. A little pelt, soft-brayed, of a mole, of a bat. Suspended by threads from the ceiling, the rim of a little wheel. And a stick.
Analyse that.

Only after a while noticed the Croxley booklets lying everywhere in
little piles. Pages from these torn out and pinned to the curtain, filled
with Ma's handwriting. Diaries. From before my birth. Everything that
Milla de Wet saw fit to bequeath her readers. In the hope that somebody would discover it. And I wasn't the first reader. She must have
reread the diary herself, several times, there were corrections in her
handwriting with dates, days and even months, years later than the
original entry. As if she'd had trouble rendering the whole truth in just
one version.

I was nervous of being caught, but got enough read to form an
idea, especially the parts underlined in red with dates in the margin
in Gaat's hand and ticked off as 'read', the first, the second and the
third time. Some parts were read every day of the last months. Read
from the wheelchair, inside the walking frame, in the hip-bath, as Gaat
had noted on each page. Sung, recited, copied in block letters with a
different line division on the counter-page, biblical texts, curses, indict-
ments. All the words written out in full, the sentences provided with
punctuation. As if she couldn't tolerate the abbreviations and untidi-
ness.

Two of the copied-out sheets were still clamped to the reading-frame.
14 September 1960, a month after my birth:

As directed by the Almighty God, Ruler of our joint Destinies and Keeper of the Book of Life, I Kamilla de Wet (neé Redelinghuys) dedicate this journal to the history of Agaat Lourier, daughter of Maria Lourier of Barrydale and Damon (Joppies) Steefert of Worcester so that there may be a record one day of her being chosen and of the precious opportunities granted to her on the farm Grootmoedersdrift of a Christian education and of all the privileges of a good Afrikaner home. So that in reading this one day she may ponder the unfathomable ways of Providence, who worked through me, His obedient servant and woman of His people, to deliver her from the bitter deprivation in which she certainly would have perished as an outcast amongst her own people. I pray for mercy to fulfil this great task of education that I have undertaken to the glory of God to the best of my ability.

Let His will be done.
His kingdom come.
For His is the power and the glory,
For ever and ever.
Amen.

Could she really have written that? My sentimental, hypochondriac mother with her head full of romantic German melodies? So force-fed with the insanity of this country? Sounded more like Pa's language. Toastmaster bravado. But without a trace of irony.

I loved her, in my way. But that I shouldn't have read.

Also not the epitaph. In the barn in the back Agaat went to show it to me, the headstone, neatly engraved.

Kamilla Redelinghuys. 11/3/1926–16/12/1996
Passed away peacefully.
And then God saw that it was Good.

How people can get it into their heads.

Cold I am all of a sudden. Could I be the only person awake in this plane? Moonlight on the cloud canopy. The curtain of the service galley has been drawn.

How can Grootmoedersdrift determine my idea of myself? Unavoidable. And yet, the meaning of my existence is elsewhere, always and in principle elsewhere, even if I were to stay here, in a realm of thought where the thoughts assess themselves, the region where you always listen at a distance.

Is listening enough? For how long? Before I'm forced to do something?

At least my will has been lodged with the attorneys in Swellendam, the farm made over to Agaat. She can bequeath it one day to whomever she wants. Is man enough, will battle through the rest. With hand-plough and mules, with churn and sickle and harness-cask and threshing-floor if need be, like the first farmers on the land. She's part of the place, from the beginning. Calloused, salted, brayed, the lessons of the masters engraved in her like the law on the tablets of stone, deeper and clearer than I could ever preserve it. She knows the soil. She knows the language. She knows her place. She'll look after herself. And maintain her shrine inviolate. Going every day to beat her forehead in its white cap against the bedstead like a Jew by the Wailing Wall. With this difference: The promised land is hers already, her creator is keeping remote control. Six feet under.

It's not a country for me to live in. To study, yes. *The Fat-Anna Schotisse. The Stormberg Vastrap.* Nobody has yet written up how exactly this music functioned in the identity-formation of the Afrikaner. Only ever *Heimwee* by S. le Roux Marais. Couldn't with the best will in the world call that a fado.

Yesterday's newspaper I left at the airport. Remarkable journalism. Rugby players on the front page and the back page and the centre pages, lawlessness and corruption, child rape, political denial of AIDS, middle-class sex scandals, letters from indignant creationists.

How in God's name is it to carry on from here?

In the first place: For the execution of useful research the impulse to go and work for the Red Cross must be suppressed. That's what I tell myself.

I just want to cauterise it all neatly now. A dry white scar, une cicatrice. Perhaps still slightly sensitive during changes of season in the northern hemisphere. Mourning is a life-long occupation, says my therapist. That is what I must do then. Must learn to do. Mourn my mother, my mothers, the white one and the brown one. Mourn my country. Pa who understood better than Ma how things worked between them, but who couldn't help himself.

They had to lug the branch out of him, I've since heard, with the letter that Gaat wrote on my behalf, covered in blood in his pants pocket. Fancy the detail. Just after it happened, she wrote to me that he'd had an accident with his car in the drift, full stop.

So it was 'my' letter, then, that caused it. My poor father.

My poor mother.

What remains? Grieving. Grieving till I've mastered the hat-trick.

The difficult triple sanity: Wafer, stone, and flower in turn. de Wet individuated.

Do I hear something under the engine noise, through the air conditioning? A melody? A rhythm?

Why that? Of all things? Gaat's story, the last story that she always had to tell me before I'd go to sleep, the one she never wanted Ma to hear. Her voice close to me, her forehead bent over me, the embroidery on her cap very close, white sheep, white flowers, white, mountains and trees . . .

Images behind my eyelids. High up in my nose a prickling, sooty, smoky, the ember-fire in Gaat's room. Every word. If she left out one, I knew. If she told anything differently, I protested. Or I said, start all over, you're not telling it right. Emphases, rhythms, repetitions, questions. Agaat's strong arm around my shoulders, her small hand on my chest. Her voice, incantatory.

Once upon a time, long, long ago, there was a woman who was terribly unhappy. She lived with her husband on a farm at the foot of a big blue mountain next to a river. Her house stood close to a drift amongst high trees in a garden filled with flowers. It had two white gables and a stoep and many rooms inside. At night when the noises of day died down, and she heard the river flowing, the wind in the trees, the sound of the sleeping mountain, g-g-g-g-g-g-g-g-g-g-g, like the soughing of a shell against your ear, then she was very sad and then she cried in her bed, softly so that her husband shouldn't wake up. He was a good-looking man with shiny black hair, but his heart was cold. In a loud voice he bragged about nothing at all, his hand was cruel and his head was filled with flippancies. He couldn't comfort her.

The man was one reason for her unhappiness. But there was another greater reason. Can you guess what it was?

Was she as ugly as sin?

No, she was pretty enough.

Was she poor?

No, she was rich.

Was she without friends?

No, she knew lots of people.

Had her mother cast her off?

No, her mother was fond enough of her, even though she was strict and a bit stingy.

Then I don't know. Why then was she so unhappy?

She was childless, the woman, and she couldn't fall pregnant and she'd been married for seven years. That was the reason for her sadness.

But then one day she went to visit her mother's farm beyond the big blue mountain. And when twelve o'clock struck, her mother said to her:

Go and see there in the labourers' cottages, there's a little girl who's been cast off, perhaps you can help her.

And the woman reached the houses of the workers, small brown houses on dry brown soil, and she thought, what am I doing here? Here there are only feather-legged chickens and dogs lying long-tongue in the sun.

But the door to one of the little houses was ajar. And the woman went to stand at the opening and called and knocked, but nobody came out.

So then she pushed open the door.

G-g-g-g-creaked the hinge.

It was pitch-dark inside. At first she could make out nothing, but when her eyes got accustomed, she saw a pitch-black hole. It was the fireplace, full of ash and soot and burnt-out logs. And in the corner of the hearth sat a pitch-black something.

And she went closer and she saw the thing had legs.

And the thing had arms.

And the thing's head was hidden deep in her clothes.

And the clothes had holes.

And through the holes she counted ribs.

And the elbows were chapped.

And the knees were grazed.

And the hair full of lice.

And the ears were stopped with wax.

And around the neck was a necklace of dirt.

And the feet were full of mud.

And the woman looked even closer and saw that the thing had one arm thinner than the other and one crooked shoulder and one hand with fingers clawed together, it looked like the head of a snake.

And the woman knelt before the thing in the fireplace and she asked:

What is your name?

And she pricked up her ears to hear but there was no reply.

What is your name? she asked again, are you perhaps the child that's been cast off?

And she listened even more closely and still she heard nothing.

Look at me, she said, tell me, what do they call you?

And she put her hand on the crooked shoulder and the creature shrank into itself and then she heard something.

G-g-g-g-g-g-g-g-g-g-g-g.

And the thing looked even blacker than before, and she felt as cold under the woman's hand as a burnt-out coal.

And then the woman got very angry.

Little rapscallion, she said, and she grabbed the thing by the neck and plucked it out of the hearth-hole and she dragged it out, out by the door, into the bright sunshine.

Stand up straight, she said, so that I can see what kind of an animal you are!

And then she saw that it was a little girl. And the child took one look at her, and she jerked loose, and took off from there, the chickens scattered and the dogs made way and the woman ran after.

Little tin-arse, she screamed, you I'm catching today!

Over the ditches the little girl jumped, barefoot over the stones, through the thorns, this way round a bush, other way round a tree, over an ant-hill, faster than the white-foot hare with the woman right behind her. And they ran and they ran, far over the veld, far over the fallow land, and down the dust-road all the way to the top of the dam wall, and the woman grabbed her round the body, and she fell on top of the child flat on the ground.

And the child kicked, and the child bit, and she wriggled, and she coughed and she blew and she g-g-g-g-g-ed and she squeaked, but the woman held on with all her might and she said:

You I'm washing white as snow today!

And she dragged her to the dam and she dunked her in and she started washing her with a white handkerchief, but the handkerchief turned black and the water turned black and the child stayed black.

You I'm taking home today, said the woman, you I'm taming, you I'm turning white!

And she packed her in a little box, as small as a watch, as black as a cricket and she took her along over the mountain to the house with the two white gables by the river.

What is that, asked the husband?

It's a child, said the woman.

It's a stone, said the husband, it's a piece of coal.

And the woman said, just you wait, you'll see, her I'll cut down to size, her I'll wash till she's clean.

And the woman she scours and the woman she spits and the woman she blows and the woman she buffs and the woman she rubs and the woman she scrubs, and the child doesn't turn white, but she does come out clean and she's turned out brown.

What's your name? Is your tongue gone, then, little ash-potato, asks the woman, open your mouth.

But the child wouldn't talk and the child wouldn't eat and child she stayed as shut as a stone.

And the woman she pinches and the woman she slaps and the woman she threatens and the woman she pleads and the woman she swears and the woman she screams and jumps up and down and later she's worn out with struggling and she locks up the child in the back room of the house and she sits down in a little heap with her head on her knees and she weeps.

Dumbstupid woman! the farmer scolded. *Look, now you're even unhappier than you were before. It's a bad child you've brought into our house, it's a dung beetle.*

And the woman said: *Just you wait, you'll see, I know she's good, she'll bring us lots of happiness yet.*

And the woman made a slot in the door and she whistled through it at the child, and all day she sang and she played the piano and she rang the bells and she struck on sticks and she made her dresses and shadow-animals and verses and the sweetest foods. But the child stayed small and hard and stiff and she said not a word and she slid away under her bed and she rolled herself into a ball in the corner of her room.

And then one day the woman had a bright idea and she said:

I found you in the cold pitch-black fireplace. Perhaps what you need is a real live fire!

And when the woman said 'fire' then the child's eyes shone like two morning stars, and she leapt up there, can you believe it, and she became as lively as an ant and she searched for dry grasses and a ball of paper and she gathered the twigs and the sticks and she carried three pine cones and five old mealie cobs and piled everything in a heap and the woman dragged up three big logs and she took an ember from the stove and she placed it under the heap and she said to the child:

Now blow, my child, for all you're worth, and do get some life!

And the child she bulged her cheeks and she blew and she blew with all her might, and before long a little spiral of smoke arose and a little flame leapt up and the heap caught fire. And it crackled and sputtered and the sparks they flew and the fire it flared up and the flames they beckoned with hot red hands and they said:

Come, little child, come! And dance and sing because we are the place you come from! You come from the hearth, you come from the wind, from the glow of the wood, from the soot-black chimney that sucks up sparks and that speckles the lily with ash, you come from the smoke that turns the sun red as copper and the moon as yellow as gold.

And from that day the little girl was good and sweet and a child like every other child and she was baptised with the name Good.

And the woman taught her to bake and cook and wash and iron and sweep and polish and knit and sew with needle and thread. And she taught her to read and to write. And she tied a ribbon in her hair and showed her a mirror and she said:

See, now you are a human being.

And she took her to the forest and the sea and the fields. And she taught Good the names of the plants and the fishes and the animals and the bugs and the flowers, the months and the days and the time for sowing and the time for reaping and the lambing-time and the shearing-time and the psalms and the hymns of thankfulness. And Good wore a red dress and learnt hard and was in everything she did as good as her name. And Good wore a green dress and she grew up and got strong and had good manners and said her prayers and ate at table with the farmer and his wife and slept in her room at the end of the passage. And every evening the woman told her the story of how she had rescued her from the pitch-black hearth and made of her a child in the house and a human being in the mirror. And the woman's breath was sweet and her hands were soft on Good's head. And sometimes when the woman's husband beat her, she crawled into Good's bed at night for comfort and slept by her till morning.

And then one day after seven years something happened that changed everything.

The woman was expecting her own baby.

Out she said to Good. Out of my house, from now on you live in a little room outside in the backyard.

Take your things!

Here's a suitcase!

And off with the red dress and off with the green! Here is your apron and here is your cap keep it white and here is your dress it is black and here is your bed next to the dogs' kennel and here is your plate and your mug of tin and from now on you'll eat alone.

And here's your book to learn how to farm and the Bible, see to it that you look after your soul and here's a big white cloth learn to embroider nicely to decorate your room.

From now on you're my slave. You'll work for a wage.

And Good's heart was very very sore. But not for long and then it grew as hard as a stone and black as soot and cold as a burnt-out coal.

And she took the suitcase filled with the dresses and shoes and things of the child she'd been and went and buried it deep in a hole on the high blue mountain across the river. And piled black stones on top of it. And trampled it with her new black shoes and cocked her crooked shoulder and pointed with her snake's-head hand and said:

Now, Good, you are dead.

Nobody noticed anything of Good's mourning because she cried without tears. Every day she kept doing her work faithfully. Fed the dogs, scrubbed the kitchen floor, cleaned the fireplace, polished the silver and buffed the table to a shine and rubbed the sheets in the soapy water till they were staring-white and ironed them in knife-sharp folds and stacked them in neat piles in the linen cupboard. She plaited onions and packed pumpkins and slaughtered sheep and plucked geese and cut lucerne with the sickle and brought flowers from the garden and arranged them in vases, the roses, the lilies, the grass.

And the woman said: My good slave, your work is good.

But Good looked at the woman's hands folded around her stomach that grew bigger and bigger with the child she was expecting. And her mouth was bitter as aloe and her insides were filled with bile.

And after eight months and two weeks in the middle of the morning the woman got birth pains and she said to Good:

Come with me, I'm going to my mother over the mountain. But pack everything that I need, a knife and scissors and forceps and cloths and towels and water and fire, because this child may well want out before noon.

And when they were halfway there, then the woman screamed: The child wants to come!

And there beneath the high sun next to the road where the waterfall foams, Good made a bed of snow-white cloths, and she poured water into a snow-white bowl and she whispered between the woman's snow-white legs:

Come, little buttermilk, come come little bluegum-flower, come out, snow-white lamb of my même, come!

And the woman she blows and the woman she strains and the woman she farts. And Good she runs and Good she pulls and Good she spits and Good she pushes, and she calls and she curses and she prays and she pleads but the child is stuck like a key in a lock.

Help me! the woman cries, grey are the cliffs and black is the river, Good, I'm going to die, help me!

And Good takes a knife and she takes forceps and scissors and she takes a deep breath and she cuts open the woman's stomach from top to bottom. And when noon struck in the church towers on both sides of the mountain, then she took the child out of the blood and the slime and she cut the string and she cleaned him and she covered him in cloth and she gave him a name that only she knew about.

You-are-mine she called him.

And he grew up on her breast and she washed him when he was dirty and gave him milk when he was thirsty and rubbed his tummy when he had winds and cooled his forehead when he had fever, and cradled him and comforted him when he cried and sang to him and dressed him and undressed him and put him to sleep every evening in her room in the backyard before she took him into the house. Taught him to walk, taught him to talk and swim and dance and fly and blow on the curved horn of the ram.

I am a slave but You-are-mine, she always whispered in his ear before she handed him over to his mother.

And his mother looked on at Good teaching the child to walk and talk, teaching him to swim and dance and fly.

And she listened to them calling each other by blowing on the horn, the child and his minder far over vlei and hill.

And every evening Good told him how she had rescued him from the grey cliffs and from the black river and chanted rhymes and asked him riddles and hummed songs on blades of grass between her lips by the fire in the outside room and with her little laundry-mangle hand made him shadow-pictures on the wall.

And the woman eavesdropped at the door. She could see through the chink and she could hear through the keyhole and she was jealous, but what could she say and what could she do?

And Good caught the little boy silver fish in the sea, and copper frogs in the dam and showed him the blue butterfly in the forest, and made him trousers of red velvet and a shirt of green cotton and embroidered the Good Shepherd and the Wise Virgin in white on his pillow slips.

See, you are a human being, she showed him in the mirror, and You-are-mine.

And he laughed in her eyes and played at her feet and skipped at her hand under the high trees around the house with the two white gables on the river next to the blue mountain and her heart was lightened and her insides were warmed. And her bile subsided because he was the light of her life.

Tell me more Dolores. Grimm meets Goth in the Overberg.

There's another story here.

The world is large.

'Suddener than we fancy it, more spiteful and gay than one supposes, incorrigibly plural.'

Where do I get that from?

'Soundlessly collateral and incompatible.'

That I would change. Not 'soundlessly'. Full-sounding, rather, full-soundingly collateral and incompatible.

I'll keep the ram's-horn on the window sill.

Des Knaben Wunderhorn.

And the bellows by the firedog next to the JetEagle.

Blaes blaest—blaes blidt—i blinde,
blaes friskhed til min hyttes baenk
med myge, vege vinde
og regn I sagte staenk.
Blaes blaest—blaes op—fanfarer,
til natten åbenbarer . . .

North and south, a frozen interval, a butterfly on felt.

On the flight-information screen the blue dart of the Boeing approaches the great green body of Canada. Plectrum and harp.

I close my eyes to sleep.

GLOSSARY OF AFRIKAANS AND SOUTH AFRICAN ENGLISH WORDS

OED = *Oxford English Dictionary*, Second Edition
ODSAE = *Oxford Dictionary of South African English* (1996)

aitsa: hey! How now!

askoek: a dough-cake baked in embers (ODSAE)

baas: employer, owner, manager, now offensive to many (ODSAE)

bakkie: a light truck, a pick-up (ODSAE)

bloedsap: An Afrikaner supporting a predominantly English-speaking political party and not the National Party (ODSAE)

boetie: little brother, an affectionate or sometimes condescending form of address

bokmakierie: a species of shrike

Boland: an area of the Western Cape lying to the west of the Hex River Mountains (ODSAE)

braai, braaivleis: barbecue

Broederbond: An exclusive (originally secret) organisation promoting the economic and political interests of Afrikaners (ODSAE)

daeraad: a strain of wheat (literally dawning)

dagga: marijuana

Die Stem: *Die Stem van Suid-Afrika (The Call of South Africa)* formerly the only, now joint national anthem

dikkop: stone curlew

dominee: title of and form of address for a minister of the Dutch Reformed Churches

donga: a channel or gully formed by the action of water (OED)

drift: a passage of a river; a ford (OED)

eland: the largest member of the antelope tribe . . . much valued for its flesh (OED)

FAK: Federation of Afrikaans Cultural Associations; the song anthology produced by the Federation

frikkadel: a ball of minced meat, fried or baked (OED)

fynbos: Cape macchia, a vegetation type of small, often heath-like trees and shrubs with fine, hard leaves, characteristic particularly of the Western Cape (ODSAE)

galjoen: a sea-fish, *Coracinus capensis* (OED)

goffel: an insulting term for a 'coloured' person (ODSAE)

grootbos: forest, contrasted with fynbos (q.v.)

hanslam (pl. hanslammers): an orphanes or rejected lamb which is reared by hand (ODSAE)

hotnot: an insulting term of address or reference to a 'coloured' person. Also attrib. (ODSAE)

klaaslouw bush: Athenasia

kleinbaas: young or small 'baas' (q.v.), junior

kleinnooi: young or small 'nooi' (q.v.)

kleintrou: strain of wheat (literally little faith)

klipspringer: small mountain antelope (literally rock-leaper) (ODSAE)

kloof: a deep narrow valley; a ravine or gorge between mountains (OED)

koelie: an offensive term for an Indian person

kokkewiet: the bou-bou shrike

koppie: a small hill, hillock

krantz: a sheer rock face, a precipice (ODSAE)

même: vernacular affectionate term for mother

mies: a term of address to a (white) woman, especially an employer (ODSAE)

oubaas: literally old master, the elderly male owner of a home, farm or business, the employer of the servants and labourers who work there (ODSAE)

oumies: old 'mies' (q.v.)

ounooi: old 'nooi' (q.v)

oupa: grandfather

nooi: a term of address to a (white) woman

pastorie: the dwelling of a pastor of the Dutch Reformed Church (OED)

riempie: a thin strip of worked leather, used esp. for thonging the backs and seats of chairs, settles, and other furniture (ODSAE)

rooibos: any of several shrubs of the genus Asphalathus, cultivated for their leaves (ODSAE); the tea made from these leaves

rooikrans: invasive yellow-flowered tree, *Acacia cyclops* (ODSAE)

sis: yuck! expression of disgust

sluit: a ditch

spanspek: sweet-melon

stoep: a verandah or porch, whether open, covered, or enclosed (ODSAE)

tackies: sports shoes or running shoes

tollie: a young ox, a young bull-calf (ODSAE)

tokoloshe: in African folklore, a mischievous and lascivious water-sprite or goblin (ODSAE)

vaaljapie: any rough new wine . . . produced privately on farms; any inferior wine (ODSAE)

vastrap: a fast dance similar to the quickstep (ODSAE)

velskoen: an outdoor shoe made of hide

vetkoek: a small unsweetened cake of deep-fried dough (ODSAE)

vlei: a piece of low-lying ground covered with water during the rainy season (OED)

vygie: noon-flower, *mesembryanthemum*, fig-marigold

WAU: Women's Agricultural Union

ACKNOWLEDGEMENTS

The author and the translator acknowledge the direct and indirect use in the voices of the characters—sometimes with acknowledgment, sometimes not—of textual material from Afrikaans and other (farm) novels as well as poems, in translation, of amongst others Elisabeth Eybers and Wilna Stockenström. In the Prologue and Epilogue there are amongst others quotations from poems by Philip Larkin: 'Cut Grass', 'Arrivals, Departures', 'Having grown up in shade of Church and State', 'Many famous feet have trod' and 'As a war in years of peace'(*Collected Poems*, 1988, The Marvell Press, Faber and Faber, London), and from a poem by Louis Macneice titled 'Snow'. In the body of the novel there are phrases from Thomas Elyot, Shakespeare, John Donne and Gerard Manley Hopkins. The Danish poem at the end, 'Natteregn', is by Nis Petersen (1897–1943), set to music in 1971 by Jørgen Jersild as part of the song cycle 'Tre romantiske korsange'.

MARLENE VAN NIEKERK is an award-winning poet, novelist, and short story writer. Her novel *Triomf* (translated by Leon de Kock) was a *New York Times* Notable Book, 2004, and won the Central News Agency Literary Award, the M-Net Prize in South Africa, and the prestigious Noma Award, the first Afrikaans novel to do so. *Agaat* received the *Sunday Times* Fiction Prize and the Hertzog Prize. Van Niekerk is currently an associate professor in Afrikaans and Dutch literature and creative writing at Stellenbosch University in South Africa.

MICHIEL HEYNS's novels include *The Children's Day*, *The Reluctant Passenger*, and *The Typewriter's Tale*. He has translated two works by Marlene van Niekerk, *Memorandum* and *Agaat*, for which he received the English Academy's Sol Plaatje Award for Translation. He also translated *Equatoria* by Tom Dreyer (Aflame Books UK, 2008). His latest novel, *Bodies Politic*, was recently published by Jonathan Ball.